WALKING BETWEEN WORLDS

A NOVEL OF AN AMERICAN IN MEXICO

[based on a true story]

written by
Robert Alquzok
© 1998-2001

Neimas dream excerpt from *EXODUS: the Dolph/in Saga*, ISBN 1-928798-35-7

Copyright © 1990-1999 by Martin A. Enticknap

obtained with permission from its author: Martin A. Enticknap

Historical excerpts about the Tlaxcaltecans and The Lord of Tlaxcala translated to English from booklet:

El Señor de Tlaxcala de Bustamante, N.L., Mex. (Noticia Histórica y Novena)

por: Monseñor Aureliano Tapia Méndez (Cronista de la Arquidiócesis de Monterrey)

Producciones al Voleo el Troquel, S.A., Monterrey, N.L., México, 1994

cover art work done by: Brian Matthews

Jobsoft Design and Development

Murfreesboro, Tennessee

Library of Congress Control Number: 2001129080

ISBN: 1-928798-02-0

Armstrong Valley Publishing Company

P.O. Box 1275

Murfreesboro, TN 37133-1275

Phone: 615-895-5445

Fax: 615-893-2688

printed in the United States of America

Table of Contents

Excerpt

January 5, 1998

Roland was talking to the head law enforcement agents at the police station. They weren't believing his story, even though Roland had photos to defend his case. Needless to say, Roland was quite worried for his safety, and he certainly didn't want to go to jail for something he knew he wasn't guilty of. He was innocent.

For someone who had been a good friend for so long, he just could not believe that his "friend" had accused him of stealing, and for the accusations to have reached him third party last week made matters even worse. Neither the friend nor spouse wanted anything to do with him now. It had come as an absolute shock to him two weeks ago when he had approached them, because he intuitively sensed that they were being sullen with him, and was suddenly told, "I don't want to talk to you!" He had no idea why they had mysteriously rejected him, until a week later, which was now one week ago, when he heard through the grapevine from other people in the town that his "friends" were spreading gossip that he had stolen from them!

Yesterday, he had written them a letter to appeal their shrewd tactics and accusations and to explain to them and assure them that he did not steal from them. Instead of their receiving the letter properly, reading it, and coming to Roland to discuss the problem to make amends, which people in their right mind would have done, they tore the letter up without reading it, went to the police station, and reported Roland for following them, bothering them, and for stealing!

The chief police officer kept interrogating Roland with questions, and he was also believing that Roland was a drug trafficker, which he certainly was not. He sat there across from the officer, still explaining his story, and the officer continued to respond by looking at Roland in a manner of disbelief. Roland was silently praying for reason to prevail. He was in serious danger!

At the same time, he thought of a good way to get revenge on his two "friends." He no longer had any mercy for them. The friendship was definitely ruined for their having reported him and for putting him in this type of danger. He swore that if he made it through this, he was definitely going to proceed with action and serve them what they now deserved. Roland didn't normally believe in "an eye for an eye" tactics, but for what his "friends" had just done, he would make an exception.

He just hoped more than anything that the police officers would soon release him.

*   *   *

Preface Pages

Roland Jocelyn was born and raised on a farm northwest of Shelbyville in middle Tennessee. He was born in August 1965, and in those days, life was very rural. Farming was the major way of life. Shelbyville was a small town with barely more than 5,000 inhabitants. His parents had recently moved into the farmhouse and were getting used to rural life after having lived for a year in North Carolina. His father was a doctor and had recently secured a farm loan and had purchased the property from an aunt who lived in Dallas, Texas. She was the last living sibling of his mother, who had died several months before Roland was born. Roland had a sister who was two years younger.

The Jocelyn family lived on a rural road near the small town of Longview, which was several miles north of a community called Unionville. They lived between two highways: US 41-A, several miles to the south, and State Route 99 to the north. Both highways intersected in a small town called Eagleville. Highway 99 was a two-lane country road that ran from Eagleville to Murfreesboro. The highway was narrow and had plenty of humps and dips. Care had to be taken when crossing some of its narrow bridges, some of which were situated right on curves. Middle Tennessee had a rural life in those days.

Roland attended a small country school for elementary and middle school. However, for grades 9 through 12, he attended a comprehensive school called Longview High School, which took in the whole region west of Shelbyville. Nearly 2,000 students attended that school each year. After graduating from high school, Roland went on to study and obtain a degree in Electrical Engineering at Tennessee Technological University in Cookeville.

Roland, ever since early childhood, had a strong desire to learn Spanish. He didn't exactly know why, except that he thought he might put it to good use during future trips to Mexico or South America. He therefore took two years of Spanish in high school, studied it well, and learned to speak it. At the time, Spanish speaking people were next to none in middle Tennessee. Little did Roland know, that was going to change.

By the 1980's, the whole region was changing. Progress and growth was getting out of hand. Federal Interstates had been built nationwide. Lots of construction was being done. Farms were now being sold for subdivisions throughout nearly the whole county. Plus, people were moving in.

When Roland was born, there were only two races of people, blacks and whites, (African Americans and European Americans) living in middle Tennessee. In 1980, numerous Laotian refugees came and took up permanent residence. Ten years later in 1990, Mexicans began to move up to Tennessee and settle, bringing the number of races up to four. Their numbers increased dramatically, and by 1998, Roland had made friends with numerous Mexicans and spoke Spanish with them as fluently as if he were speaking English.

It's possible that a part of Roland knew why he would need Spanish. As time went on and Shelbyville grew, Mexicans became integrated in the culture. They were becoming a staple in the American workforce and economy. Other people in Tennessee were making friends with Mexicans, and some were even getting married to them. It was in 1996 that Roland started making more regular trips to northern Mexico. Most of his friendships from high school and college had dried up by that time. While he still made some new friends in Tennessee, he also went to Mexico in search of more friends.

For his adventures there, his real life counterpart has written this novel.

1

September 2, 1980

It was Roland Jocelyn's first day at Longview High School. He was in 5th period Spanish 1 class, and it was his first time to meet his new teacher, Isalia Ives. She was originally from Eagle Pass, Texas, and Roland was glad to have a teacher who spoke Spanish with the correct accent. She first taught them the Spanish words for *again* (otra vez), which literally meant another time. Then she had them all practice the most important part of Spanish pronunciation, how to roll the r's.

"Okay, take out your cars and act like you're playing with them in the sandbox," she directed. Next, she made the tutter sound, fluttering her tongue while touching the roof of her mouth. "RRRRRRR RRRRRRR RRRRRRR"

It was a very effective way of teaching the class, and Roland understood immediately.

Over the next two weeks, she began to teach them the words of the Spanish language, starting with the verbs: *hablar*, *comer*, and *vivir*.

Meanwhile, Roland was enjoying his friends who were in that class, and he was content with his scheduling. As an extra added bonus, he had 2nd period PE class with Mrs. Jenkins, and his best friends were in that same class with him. They used to play sports together.

Suddenly, around the 10th of September, Roland and four others were notified of a schedule change that made him swap 2nd and 5th periods. Isalia needed 5 more people in her 2nd period Spanish class, and though Roland appealed, it was to no avail. He was pulled away from his best friends in that PE class, and he was placed in a 5th period PE class where he knew absolutely no one. He adjusted and made new friends the best he could, and while he was mostly successful, it just wasn't the same goodness that he had previously enjoyed during his first week in high school.

Roland had a very clear mind, and he whizzed through Spanish, making A+'s. He was learning Spanish with ease, and he really appreciated that the teacher had the correct accent. Isalia noticed Roland's intelligence, and during the first session of parent conferences, she gave his parents a great report, which to her was like eating dessert.

February 1981

It was a normal day in the winter of 1981, and Roland Jocelyn was in Spanish 1 class, taught by Isalia Ives. His desk was right across from her desk, and as he sat there one day, he suddenly noticed a subtle subduing force that was seemingly somehow being placed on him. He had no idea what it was, except that he immediately knew that he could no longer think so clearly as he had done up to this day. As time would move on, he would realize that for several years to come, ten to be exact, his excellent memory for details would not be quite so sharp.

Though he didn't know at the time what the mysterious force was, he did note it in his memory and would never forget when and where it happened to him. He would also not realize for numerous years to come what other implications and curses the subconsciously programmed force placed on him would cause, and it all began when he was sitting right across from his Spanish teacher, Isalia Ives, a woman he and his family would know and become good friends with for the next 17 years.

It was several weeks later that she had her class do a recitation. Each person stood in front of the class and recited a paragraph in Spanish. This one was titled: *Mi Mejor Amigo* (My Best Friend). Roland couldn't decide who his best friend was, and he didn't like the idea of singling out any one person above all the others. To him it didn't seem fair. He decided to choose a childhood friend who was no longer in the same school with him. Roland would always remember what the last phrase in the recitation said.

"A mí me gusta muchísimo mi mejor amigo." (To me, my best friend pleases me very much.)

It would be years later when he would finally make some close friends in Mexico that he would realize what other more subtle implications that phrase meant and carried with it.

As he looked back on it years later, he wished he had made somebody up or even better, chosen someone who he would later be good friends with . . . much later . . . a Mexican. He wished he had known the future.

He would have taken great delight in surprising his teacher by starting his recitation:

"Mi mejor amigo se llama . . .   (My best friend is . . .
Todavía no nace . . ."   He is still not born . . .)

That would have thrown his teacher for a loop and made her think a little bit! It certainly would have been a unique way of doing the *My Best Friend* recitation.

September 1981

It was the fall of the next year, and Roland Jocelyn was now a sophomore at Longview High School. He had done very well his freshman year, having made all A's in all subjects. A week of school had gone by, and Roland was in Isalia's Spanish II class, and he was looking forward to learning a good bit more Spanish. He enjoyed Spanish class. Isalia each Friday would show them slides from her and her husband's various summer trips to Mexico. Among them were slides of the town of Bustamante, Nuevo León, and she used to tell them about the Lion's Head Mountain, about her cousins living in that town, other residents and sights, as well. Roland was looking forward to seeing more slides this year.

One day in class, strangely enough, Roland was feeling sleepy. It was at a time in class when the students were translating dialogue passages in their textbooks. Suddenly, Isalia cried out a gesture as if in pain! She nearly fainted. Roland, who was sitting across the desk from her, noticed and asked her if she was all right. Other members in the class followed by asking her the same. She delayed a few seconds and came around to answer, ". . . I . . . I don't know *what* that was that just came over me! Excuse me. I'll be . . . right back, in just a few minutes. Continue with your dialogue exercises." She got up and left the room, returning five minutes later.

The next day, Mrs. Summar, a substitute was there in Isalia's place. Isalia wasn't feeling well, and she was at home recovering, Roland and his classmates found out. In fact yesterday, right after Roland's Spanish class, which was 3rd period, Isalia had signed out and gone home for the rest of the day.

*   *   *

3

July 11, 1986

It was a cold, wet summer day, and Roland Jocelyn, who was nearly 21 at the time, was backpacking on the Pacific Crest Trail in Washington's Alpine Lakes Wilderness. He had been hiking for four days. The first three days had been warm and sunny, but yesterday had been wet and rainy.

On the second day of his hike, he had met two young fellows named Jeff and Tim from Seattle, and the three of them visited and chatted with each other at Spectacle Lake where they camped together. Jeff had hiked the Pacific Crest Trail through Alpine Lakes Wilderness with his father last year, and he recommended that Roland camp at Tuck Lake on the way to Stevens Pass. The next morning, Jeff, Tim, and Roland hiked a few miles along the trail, and then they parted ways, never to see each other again.

For the next two days, Roland hiked alone, and he missed his new friends he had just met. Roland kept thinking of a certain song that he had heard on the radio during the past year. It was titled: "A Good Heart" by the group, *Feargal Sharkey*. Over and over again, he could hear it playing in his mind as he walked the trail further north.

"A good heart these days is hard to find . . . True love, the lasting kind.
A good heart these days is hard to find . . . All about love, and what it can do to you . . ."

He took Jeff's suggestion and had camped last night at Tuck Lake which was up on a mountain east of the trail. This morning, he came down the trail and saw two fellows on their way up to the same lake. They stopped and talked a few minutes. One of them told Roland that earlier this morning, they had seen another fellow who looked somewhat like him. They wished each other well, and Roland made his way down the steep trail, rejoining the Pacific Crest Trail at a place called Deception Pass.

There, he turned right and began walking north. He knew he had 21 miles left to reach the next major road crossing, U.S. Highway 2 at Stevens Pass, Washington. He had walked probably only 150 yards when he came across a most curious thing . . . a bag of flowers hanging from a Fir tree. There were daisy-like flowers, Tiger Lily blooms, thistle blooms, Glacier Lilies, and other types of native flowers in the small bouquet. Also attached to the bouquet was a note from a forest ranger saying how awful it was to pick native flowers and hang them from a tree. Roland stood and looked at the flowers for a minute and wondered why they were put there.

He looked at his watch. It was 9:20 AM Pacific Standard Time. He knew he had miles to cover, 20.9 to be exact, so he proceeded. It was the only time he would ever see flowers purposefully placed on a tree on any of his walks and travels.

*   *   *

CHAPTER 1

THE PREVIOUS TRIPS

It was late December 1990, and Roland decided to travel to Bustamante, Nuevo León in Mexico. His former high school Spanish teacher, Isalia Ives, was sending him to visit the Quevalo family who were her cousins, and he was looking forward to meeting and knowing them.

Seven years earlier, she had sent Roland to Monterrey, Nuevo León to stay for several weeks with a former high school exchange student friend, Guillermo Velazco and his mother, Esalina, and family. Roland had wanted to stay with them again over Christmas vacation of 1990, but they were going to be busy, and things were complicated. Roland would find out much later that there were other underlying reasons why they didn't want to receive him into their home.

It was at that time that Isalia came forth and told Roland all about her cousins, the Quevalos, in Bustamante, Nuevo León, a small town with around 3,000 residents. In some ways, the whole town was like a large family. Most of the residents were lifetime natives, and they were related and connected to each other in various ways.

There were no banks, no law offices, no fast-food restaurants, no convenience stores, and no traffic lights. However, there was a small police station near the plaza in the center of town, and their patrol vehicles were old pickup trucks. Bustamante did not even have a fuel station. The nearest one was a Pemex station ten kilometers away in the neighboring town of Villaldama.

It would be another seven years before a bank called Banorte would be installed in the town's plaza on July 13, 1998, and it would be the turn of the millennium before Pemex would finally install a fuel station in May 2000 at the entrance to the town.

On numerous street corners throughout the town, there were small places of business, which could best be compared to the old country stores of America's past.

The main street through the town was called Calle Gral. Mier. (Gral. is the Spanish abbreviation for *General*.) Numerous streets intersected and crossed the main street. Nearly every house came right up to the sidewalk, and most of the streets were quite narrow. In some places it was difficult for two vehicles to pass by each other.

Many of the houses were made of adobe and of concrete blocks. Some of the old adobe houses, especially in the town's central plaza, dated back hundreds of years, to the 1600's when the town used to be called San Miguel de Aguayo. All of them had ancient wooden doors, and the windows had traditional wrought iron grill work to keep out thieves.

Isalia told Roland how great her cousins the Quevalos were, saying that they were the "salt of the earth," that they were down to earth people with a genuine sense of hospitality and friendliness.

The Quevalo family had a decent residence situated within a grove of large Pecan trees (locally called Nogal) and Avocado trees (locally called Aguacate). In fact, most of Bustamante sat in the middle of an oasis, and there were Pecan trees throughout the town, except for the upper reaches nearer to the mountains. The center of the town sat five kilometers from the foot of the towering mountain range, and its main feature was the Lion's Head Mountain, elevation 1,860 meters (6,100 feet), locally called *La Cabeza de León*, because its outlines did indeed have the appearance of a lion resting and facing south.

Isalia was born and raised in Eagle Pass, Texas in 1934, and she was of a hardy and tenacious family of decent moral values. She had somewhat strict parents, and she took into herself her father's intense and commanding characteristics, which were useful to her for what she would become, a Spanish teacher. Her mother had extra senses and could see people's auras, and as a result, Isalia became interested in the arts and sciences along those lines. Isalia got married early in life to a kind military man named Clayton Ives. They had moved to Tennessee in the mid 1950's. Her mother was born and raised in Bustamante, and her mother's niece was Sarita Quevalo, the mother of the Quevalo family.

She told Roland how her cousins would have time to spend with him and show him around the area. She phoned them prior to sending Roland to them, and they told her they would receive him with open arms. She told him there were seven children in all, told him their names, and what each one of them did. She said the youngest of the seven was a son, Pancho, age 25, the same age as Roland and that Roland would be able to talk and practice Spanish with him to his heart's content.

To Roland, the Quevalos sounded like a great family, and he sincerely looked forward to visiting them. He really appreciated Isalia's telling him about her cousins and recommending him to them. As a token of appreciation he did something to help Isalia out. He had noticed that Isalia and Clayton's driveway was rough and in poor condition with large potholes. He took three pickup truck loads of gravel in his family's pickup truck to her residence from the nearest quarry, and he filled up the potholes appropriately. All of this was a gift to her. She was very appreciating and happy to receive the gravel, and she told Roland he was one of the nicest people that she knew.

Right after Christmas, 1990, Roland drove his 1970 Ford Fairlane station wagon to Mexico. He made the trip in two days, spending the night with cousins in Dallas. It was the first time Roland had ever driven his car into that country. He had wanted to drive his car there in previous years, but Isalia had warned him against driving to Mexico. She said the federal inspection stations were dangerous, and that they were known to machine gun down people travelling in their vehicles. While there may have been one or two incidents of that having occurred, Roland didn't look upon that risk as serious danger. After all, many people used the highway, and it was a major thoroughfare. He was determined to drive to Mexico this time. No more scare tactics from Isalia.

He crossed the border at Laredo-Nuevo Laredo, and the officials issued Roland a permit and tourist card. There was no inspection, and he proceeded down the 2-lane national highway, Hwy 85, to Sabinas Hidalgo, passing the second inspection along the way. In places to the left, the government was building a new 4-lane highway, an Autopista. Mexico was beginning to install Autopistas nationwide. They were to be toll roads with limited access.

Two hours later, Roland reached Sabinas Hidalgo. He looked for the turnoff to Villaldama and Bustamante, but he couldn't find it. There were no signs indicating it, and he asked someone where it was. It was difficult for Roland to communicate in Spanish, but he managed to understand the fellow, and he turned right, according to his directions. It was another three kilometers across town, and he used his instincts to guess a left and a right turn to put him on the narrow, 18-foot-wide highway to Villaldama.

The highway wound its way among some hills, repeatedly crossing a river on low-water concrete bridges that had no guard rails. Then the curves somewhat straightened as he left the hills and crossed the valley to Villaldama. Once through Villaldama, he arrived at State Highway Nuevo León 1, the alternate Monterrey-Laredo highway, which went through Anahuac. He turned right and a few kilometers later made a left turn on the road that went into Bustamante. There was a railroad track that ran parallel to State Highway 1. Freight trains used it regularly. Bustamante had a small, disused railway station next to the crossing. Roland crossed the track and drove the five kilometers into town, arriving at the Quevalos in the late afternoon. It was December 28, 1990.

The family graciously received him and began to know him. They took Roland to their son's place around the corner and set him up with a room and bed to sleep in. In this house lived Lorenzo Quevalo and his new wife Glenda. Roland did indeed feel graciously received, and he was glad that he had come.

Roland had brought several gifts with him including a black rotary dial wall phone, which he installed for them. There were also some gifts that Isalia had sent with him. He remembered very well the sincere thanks from the 8-year-old son of one of the daughters. His name was Eliud, (pronounced Elly-ood), and he came across to Roland as a sweet, genuine child.

Isalia had previously explained to Roland the custom of offering $10 per night to your hosts. It was a custom she practiced wherever she stayed, and she would usually leave the money at the time of leaving. With that done, the people always wanted her, and they welcomed her graciously into their home. She had explained that taking gifts to your hosts was a good idea, as well. Plus, it was fair, she thought.

In those days, Roland's Spanish was not very good, and he had practiced very little Spanish since staying with the Velazco family in 1983. Needless to say, it was a *struggle* for Roland to communicate with the members of the Quevalo family. Over a period of a few days, much of the Spanish that he had forgotten came back to him. Though he didn't realize it at the time, he would still have a long ways to go before becoming fluent in that language.

The Quevalos lived in an old and original adobe house which was right up to the street, separated only by the sidewalk, as was the style for nearly all of the houses in Bustamante. They did part of their living outside with a small separate kitchen that was in the backyard. Chickens entered and left the "facility" on a regular basis, and members of the Quevalo family frequently shewed them away to run them off. Most of the cooking was done over a fireplace, and the kitchen sink was not even in the kitchen. It was adjacent to the kitchen, outdoors, and under a Myrtle shrub. This is how they lived, from building to building, and to go from one room to the next, they had to step outside.

One of their daughters was India. She was Eliud's mother, and she had a small concrete block house at the edge of their property, fifteen meters from the main house. On the footpath between their houses, there was a junk car, an old Renault 12, annoyingly in the way and partially blocking the path. Roland asked them why they didn't move the car into the backyard, and they answered that a Pecan tree limb could fall on it back there. Where the car was parked, there were no trees overhead.

Chickens lived in the backyard, along with ducks, turkeys, and geese. Roland used to go back there and throw them his fruit cores and watch them race to it and fight over it. The winner would get the piece down its throat as quickly as possible, and whole. It used to make him laugh to watch them compete with each other.

The Quevalo family ran a bakery, and each day, they baked various types of bread and cookies. He used to go into the separate building and watch the Quevalo sisters knead large amounts of dough, which they would divide into around 100 units, after which they would bake it on many flat metal sheets in an igloo-shaped adobe stove (orno) outside behind the building.

They had a vending area by the street, and they had a large sign in front of their house identifying their place of business. There were several display tables where they sold their various types of bread. In addition to their baked goods, they also sold local crafts, ceramic statues, cookware, and even some rocking chairs. Each morning when they opened, one of the Quevalo daughters would hand throw water onto the street from a bucket, a sacred daily ritual that all business owners did, to bring good luck and more sales.

Roland stayed for nine days with the Quevalo family. They did indeed have time to spend with him. Six out of the seven children were still living on Quevalo property in Bustamante. The youngest daughter, Lorena, lived in Monterrey, and she would soon be getting married.

One day, several of them, including Lorenzo, took him to the Ojo del Agua, a spring and pond up in the canyon several kilometers out of town. From Bustamante, a rough, one-lane gravel road wound its way along the creek through the canyon, passing by the Ojo del Agua and continuing to various ranches in the desert valley on the other side of the mountains. It was a beautiful area with mountains on both sides, and the spring was situated in a grove of Anaqua, Ash, Mesquite, Sycamore, and Willow trees.

While they were at the Ojo del Agua, they had a picnic. Lorenzo told him some of Bustamante's history. In the old days, it was called San Miguel de Aguayo. Before that, the region was called Boca de Leones.

Throughout the thousands of years of Bustamante's prehistory, there was a race of native humans called the Alazapa Indians. They were very brave warriors who repeatedly came and attacked the more peaceful race of Tlaxcaltecan Indians, who settled in the 1600's. With the help of the Spanish settlers, the last of the Alazapa were wiped out by the mid 1800's.

The main church of Bustamante, called Templo Parroquial de San Miguel Arcángel, was situated on the west side of the central plaza. It was a Roman Catholic church, and inside it, there was a bloody statue of Jesus hanging on the cross above the pulpit at the front end of the aisleway. Off to the side in a small room, there was a glass encased mannequin of Jesus. There was a story behind it, that it came from the Tlaxcaltecan Indians in the late 1600's, and in those days they used to call the town and region *Boca de Leones*, (Mouth of the Lions). The town then came to be called San Miguel de Aguayo in honor of Marqués de Aguayo. It was much later that the name Bustamante came about, having been named after one of Mexico's presidents, Gral. Anastasio Bustamante, of the early 1800's.

Lorenzo explained that every early August, they have a carnival in Bustamante, and on August 6, they have a big celebration where they have a devout marching procession and carry the church's statue of Jesus hanging on the cross throughout the streets of the town. It is such an important event, that each year all of the residents are notified ahead of time so that they will know what streets are used, and they hang decorations on the front of their houses in honor of Jesus.

Roland looked at the scenery around the Ojo del Agua. The mountains stood very high and graceful on both sides of the canyon. Lorenzo told Roland that the canyon now looked a lot different than it used to. Tall trees of Anaqua, Ash, and Willow used to flourish throughout the canyon, and it was a lot more beautiful prior to September 1988. Hurricane Gilberto came at that time. Lots of wind blew, and though it hardly rained in Bustamante, it rained in torrents in the desert valley to the west. Walls of water barreled down the canyon, destroying nearly everything in its path, and Bustamante was flooded right up to the church and plaza! Adobe homes nearer the river were tumbled down. Some people and all their belongings were washed away. Destruction was severe, and Villaldama and Sabinas Hidalgo received their share, minutes later. Recovery was slow, and people fled for their lives to stay with friends and relatives who lived on higher ground. As the weeks went by, people began to clean up and rebuild. For years, people would refer to Hurricane Gilberto and the destruction it wrought.

During his stay, Roland took some of the Quevalo sisters to Monterrey in his station wagon. On the way there, they stopped for gasoline in Villaldama, since Bustamante didn't have its own station. The attendant came to fill up the tank with what was called Gasolina Nova, which was leaded gas and the only one available at this Pemex station. It carried a blue label. There was no self service anywhere in Mexico, and the only petroleum company which sold gasoline in Mexico was Pemex. The prices of their different grades were all regulated, that is, the same price throughout the whole country. In larger cities, they had recently begun selling unleaded fuel. It was called Magna Sin, and it carried a green label.

Roland paid the attendant and drove to Monterrey. A few kilometers down the road, the engine began pinging, and Roland pulled over. The Quevalo sisters asked Roland what the problem was, and he explained that the engine was pinging due to low octane gas, which Nova was! He set back the timing a little bit on the distributor, and he added some octane boost which he happened to bring with him. There! That solved that problem. He got back on the highway and drove them the rest of the way to Monterrey.

They stayed at Lorena's house, which was in Monterrey's northern suburb of San Nicolas. Lorena and her boyfriend Ricardo accompanied Roland, and they saw different sites in Monterrey that day. They also briefly stopped by and visited with the Velazco family. Guillermo had to rush off to work only one minute after their arrival. However, Esalina was glad to see Roland, and she visited with him and the Quevalos for nearly an hour. She was very complimentary of Roland and told the Quevalos many good things about him and about his family in Tennessee, as she had visited Tennessee in 1984.

Up in the mountains above Bustamante, there was a very large cave. It was simply named Grutas de Bustamante, and it was perched on the eastern mountain slopes at an elevation several hundred meters above the town. A gravel road led out of town and gently climbed the valley floor to the foot of the mountains where the road came to an end. There was a small white building there called *El Cono*. That was where a cave guide, whose name was Rogelio, usually waited for tourists who wanted to see the caves.

The cono got its name from the conical shaped building that stood there previously. It had a Palm leaf thatched roof, and it was replaced some ten years ago by the present white concrete block building, which was intended to be a hotel for cave tourists.

One day, some of the Quevalos took Roland to the cono, where they found Rogelio, and he took them up there.

From the upper parts of Bustamante to the cono, the land was dominated by mostly Mesquite shrubs and Nopal Cactus, among other plants. To Mexicans, this type of terrain was known as the *Monte*.

At the cono, they were around 200 meters above the elevation of Bustamante and were on the upper edge of the valley floor. From the cono, the route was by footpath, and the slopes of the mountains began only 100 meters beyond the cono. To their right was a large, dry riverbed with a major dropoff to reach it.

They began the 45-minute walk up the footpath to the cave. Rogelio made this climb at least five days a week, sometimes more than once in a day when there were lots of tourists. They talked with each other about the cave and also about the amount of tourism. Rogelio said there were actually only a few tourists on most days.

They ascended rather steeply in places, and they passed through various large shrubs of Mesquite and other local plants. The names of some of them were: Anacahuita, Barreta, Buajillo, Cenizo, Chapote, Colorín, Coyotillo, Frijolillo, Granjeno, and Palo Blanco. Also there were Fan Palms.

In places along the first section of the trail, there were huge Agave plants, locally called Maguey (*Agave havardiana*). They sometimes sent up tall stalks of blooms up to ten meters in height, and they could also be seen growing throughout the desert valley and in Bustamante itself.

There were plenty of other plants, as well. There were Desert Spoons, locally called Zotól (*Dasylirion Wheeleri*). There were plenty of Lechuguilla plants, Pita de Zabandoque, Zoyate, Espadín, and Huapilla.

In addition to that, there were plenty of varieties of Cactus plants, such as the large Prickly Pear Cactus, locally called Nopal (*Opuntia lindheimeri*). Other types were called Biznaga, Candelilla, Coyonoxtle, Ocotiyo, Peyote, Tazajillo, and Tesajo.

As they continued ascending, they began to see a few Oak trees. Around 15 minutes up the trail, they took a rest and sat under a fairly large Oak tree situated next to a rock face. Then they ascended the steepest and most treacherous section of the trail. Under their feet was fairly loose rock and scree, and they had to watch their step as they proceeded. After another hundred meters, they were through it, and the rest of the climb was more moderate with switchbacks.

The climb had taken 45 minutes. They were now at an elevation of 1,000 meters, 500 meters above the elevation of Bustamante. As they crested a rise, an open area came into view, and the cave's entrance was tucked into two rock faces on either side, almost like a crevice. The entrance to the cave was guarded by a heavy iron gate to keep vandals out.

Rogelio unlocked the gate, and he took Roland and the Quevalos on a tour of the cave. They made a fairly long descent on the footpath to the floor of the first room. There were electric lights inside, as they had run electricity all the way from Bustamante some years ago. Roland was impressed by the huge formations of calcified stalagmites and stalactites. Rogelio explained that the formations were entirely protected now, and for that reason, the iron gate had been installed at the entrance. All of the rock inside the cave was limestone. In fact, the whole mountain range was of limestone. It was Roland's first time inside the cave, and he was really amazed at its size. The first room was huge, and there were more large rooms further in!

The caves of Bustamante are some of the largest in the world. They were discovered by chance in 1906 by one of the natives of Bustamante, when he was up in the mountains manning his goats. His name was Juan Gomez Cázares. Not long after discovering the caves, Juan led a group of 12 men, and they ventured for 15 days deeper and deeper into the cave. They would have gone further, but they came to a room which was self illuminated, and they discovered a bright white light at the other end, a strangely clear and brilliant light of a type they had never seen before! Thinking it was something from another world or reality, they immediately turned around and fled in fear! It took them 9 more days to return to the entrance. Since that time, there have been major expeditions to search for the end of the caves, and to this day, the end has never been found. The caves are a mystery indeed.

Roland also went hiking in the mountains up above the caves, and he really enjoyed it. The scenery was spectacular. There was a deep and treacherous gully which was forested with Ash, Cherry, Elm, Hickory, Maple, and Oak trees, and higher up along the ridge, Roland came to a continuous forest of Hickories and Oaks.

He walked on through the highland forest for nearly half an hour, following what seemed to be bear paths, and he reached a beautiful grassy saddle. The views were excellent in all directions. Bustamante could be seen down in the valley to the right. Roland turned left and walked through the grassy meadow laden with Lechuguilla and Maguey plants, some of which had tall bloom stalks from when they had bloomed the previous summer. There were also the green blades of Mexican Rain Lilies (*Zephyranthes drummondii*) and Onion (*Allium*) plants.

Soon Roland came to an immense cliff that sharply dropped off to the desert valley to the west. It was a massive dropoff, and it must have been 300 meters to the chasm directly below him. He was awe inspired, and he didn't get too close. Various mountain ranges could be seen in the distance. He enjoyed the views, explored the area some more, and then hiked back down the mountain, arriving back in Bustamante by evening.

All in all, Roland enjoyed his stay with the Quevalos. He had a lot of laughs with them, and they came to accept Roland as one of the family, calling him a primo (cousin). Toward the end of his stay, the two sons: Lorenzo and Pancho talked to Roland about the possibility of buying a Ford truck and bringing it to them. They described the options they preferred, and Roland told them he would see what he could do. On the morning that Roland left, every member of the Quevalo family saw him off and said goodbye. Roland felt sad to leave. He returned to Tennessee in time to begin his last semester at Tennessee Technological University in Cookeville, Tennessee, January 1991.

His Spanish teacher, Isalia Ives, was overjoyed that Roland had been so well received by her cousins, the Quevalos. She explained to Roland that they loved him.

*   *   *

Isalia Ives, since the fall of 1980, had become good friends with Roland and his parents. Though Roland initially considered Isalia to be a little bit on the different side and somewhat intense at times, he was glad that she had taken to him and his parents so well. He remembered at their first parent conference with Isalia that she had been very complimentary of him. Also, at the school's fall festival a month later, Roland's parents and Isalia had a great visit. From then on, Isalia's friendship with them was in full force.

For some reason, Roland had, since age 11, had a strong desire to learn Spanish. Something told him he would need it, with his hopes and plans of travelling in the future to Mexico and other Spanish speaking countries further south. As a result, he excelled in Spanish for the two years he took it in high school.

He would have taken a third and fourth year, but Longview High School only offered two years, and no more. During Roland's junior year in high school, Isalia petitioned for a Spanish III class, and the class made with 18 people who signed up. After all that effort, the principal cancelled it because he assigned her to teach a general English I class during that same period the next year. That displeased Roland at the time, but in the long run, it was probably for the best.

Several times, Isalia and her husband Clayton had invited Roland and his parents over to her house, and they had come out to the Jocelyn's farm also. Sometimes, she would have her sister Roma visiting from Texas, and she would bring her out to the farm to visit, as well.

In fact, there were several of Roland's male classmates that Isalia had become good friends with. One of them was a childhood friend who Roland had known in scouts. His name was Danny. Isalia had signed photographs of several of her special student friends hanging on a wall in her house, among them Hugh, and Jack. It always puzzled Roland how Clayton didn't have any objection to that, but then, such is life.

It was in the early part of 1991 that Clayton suffered from a heart attack, and he was hospitalized for several days. Isalia notified Roland's family very soon after it happened, and they gave her their best wishes. She was worried about him and then realized that it might not be much longer before he might die. However, as fate would have it, he lived for another six years.

It was in the summer of 1991 that Isalia came out with her sister to visit the Jocelyns, so she could discuss plans for getting her cousins a truck, trailer, and even a tractor. She also related the whole story of Clayton's heart attack and what he and she went through. She finished off her story by saying:

". . . and I've done all my grieving. I'm prepared for him to die whenever that day comes."

Though they never told her, Roland and his parents thought that was *most strange*, that a person would take care of her grieving and have it all wrapped up and finished, as it would later turn out, six years ahead of time! Granted, Isalia did have a tendency to handle things in a one-track manner, but what was normal in society was for a person to grieve a spouse's death *after* he/she dies, *not* before. What was Isalia afraid of, or what was she avoiding? Needless to say, Roland and his parents began to realize that she was indeed different, and that she, for some reason, did not want to properly deal with grief at the proper time. Nevertheless, they saw Isalia as a nice woman, and they appreciated her friendship with them.

*   *   *

During the course of the semester in the early part of 1991, Roland was on the lookout for a 6-cylinder manual Ford truck of the early 1980's. Finally, in the fall of 1991, he found one listed in the newspaper, and with Isalia supplying the money, he went with a friend of his and bought it for $2,000. It was a 1981 model. It was colored blue, and it had a standard shift.

The Quevalos also communicated to Isalia that they wanted a 16-foot flatbed trailer. So, with Isalia's money, Roland went to a farm equipment supply store and bought one of them for $700.

Roland had been looking for an engineering job after having graduated in May 1991 with a degree in Electrical Engineering, and he had been unsuccessful, as the job market was very tight during that whole period and would remain so until 1993. As a result, he didn't have a full-time job, and he had time to devote to the truck and trailer project for the Quevalos.

Off and on for the next several weeks, Roland had to make repairs to the truck, replacing all the brakes and front end linkage. It ended up costing around $1,000 in parts. Roland donated the labor for his appreciation for the Quevalo family.

As it turned out, Isalia ended up loaning nearly $4,000 to her cousins for the purchase of the truck and trailer and for the repairs. She and her cousins had evidently made arrangements on how they would later pay her back. Through her friend, Esalina Velazco, the Quevalos would gradually pay Isalia back, and Esalina's son would invest the money in stock, there in Mexico. Isalia's plan was to use the money for her future stays in Mexico. However, it was not such a wise decision because the stock, as it turned out, devalued to 25% of its original amount, a terrible loss! In addition to that, the Mexican peso devalued also.

Around two months before Roland and Isalia departed to Mexico, they talked over some plans. She mentioned that a friend of Clayton's named Luke Wiggins, who was a university agricultural professor in east Tennessee, expressed interest in going to Mexico to also stay with the Quevalos. He would also stay in Lorenzo's house with Roland and teach the people of the town some more ways of agriculture. He wanted to stay several months. As Isalia talked it over with Roland, he sounded agreeable enough to it.

Nearer the time of leaving, Isalia informed Roland with the sudden news that Luke Wiggins was no longer going to go . . . because he had suddenly gotten married! Now that was surprising, and it did not please Isalia at all. She felt like she had the rug pulled out from under her. She said she could kill him for his having backed out, in addition to the more surprising news of his having suddenly married! He had backed out only a week before they departed.

It was toward the end of November 1991 when Roland took Isalia to Mexico in the Ford truck, towing the trailer behind them. The truck was loaded with his baggage and his bicycle and gifts from Roland and Isalia both. In addition to that, Roland had loaded his largest Redwood tree to give to the Quevalos, and he would later plant it in their backyard before he would return to Tennessee.

As they left, Roland drove them through the usual backroad to access State Highway 99, but he found that road surprisingly closed because the state highway department had recently begun the widening of the highway, as it was a narrow, two-lane winding highway with narrow bridges. He had to go several miles out of the way to go around the annoying road block, and he finally accessed the highway further southwest. With that hurdle behind them, they were now freely on their way to Eagleville . . . and beyond.

It took them three days to get to Mexico, and they talked and told stories during the long drive. She told Roland how she and Clayton met, when they moved to middle Tennessee, and she told Roland about how she became a Spanish teacher. For several years after they arrived, she was the accountant for class registration records at one of Nashville's universities, and in those days, registration was done manually. It was a very busy job for her, and after several years of hard work, she threw up her hands and started training to be a teacher instead. With her knowledge of Spanish, being her first language, she was a natural for being a good Spanish teacher. Meanwhile, the registration office was having a blue fit! They had to hire *three* people to replace Isalia and do all the work she, alone, had done for several years.

Roland expressed his amazement that it took three people to replace her, and she explained to Roland that she used to have a very sharp mind and an excellent memory, but something had happened, and now that she was pushing 60, she couldn't remember things as well. Of course, Roland knew that a lot of people became dull in the mind as they grew older, but for the way she had told Roland, he decided to ask her what it was that had happened. She hesitated, not wanting to answer, and Roland kindly insisted by asking again. She then answered that when her son Laurence left home and moved away, she hadn't wanted him to leave, and she suffered such grieving spells that she lost her sharpness of memory from that day forward. Something about her severe grieving had partially fractured her mind, she explained. That was in 1972, and she was never quite the same as before . . . with her memory.

Though Isalia didn't mention it, she had also been suffering from a recurring dream for quite some years.

Isalia also told several stories about Bustamante from the old days. One of them was about how the government came in around 1910. Pancho Villa's army was rounding up men to fight in his war. A lot of people fled town and ran for their lives. They took refuge and stayed hidden in the nearby mountains. Many took refuge in the newly discovered cave.

Isalia told Roland a hair-raising story about a time when she was having her hair done down in Taxco, and while the beautician was tending to Isalia's hair, she tapped her twice on the head. Suddenly, Isalia felt a force enter her body from head to foot and wash over her. Then it took a stronghold and attempted to strangle her, not physically, but it was snuffing the very life out of her! Isalia struggled, and as she became alarmed, she prayed very hard, and the force finally left her. She said she had never been so afraid in all her life! She didn't know what that force had been! Roland listened to her story with awe, and he also wondered what it had been.

Isalia also told another hair-raising story about a time when she and her husband Clayton were leaving Taxco in their car. It was the summer of 1980. A few kilometers outside of Taxco, some people, armed with machine guns suddenly motioned them to stop on the highway. Clayton did just that, and they wanted to see what they had in the trunk of the car. Isalia clammed up and said nothing, and before they had come to a complete stop, she had directed Clayton to say nothing more than, "No hablo español," to tell them that he doesn't speak Spanish. Isalia and Clayton were both scared. Their good friends in Taxco had just given Clayton an old rifle, a collector's item. They certainly interrogated him about that one! Clayton repeated several times the phrase that Isalia had directed him to say. They continued inspecting the contents in the trunk and finally told Clayton to close the lid and that he and Isalia were free to go. Roland asked Isalia if the people were in uniform, and she said they were not. Because of that, she had been very afraid for their safety and was silently praying for them to make it through that. They made it. The south of Mexico was generally known to be more dangerous than northern Mexico.

Isalia was very complimentary and appreciating of Roland on the way down there. She explained to him how this was all chosen and planned out ahead of time from higher up, that their project was a mission for the poor, and was according to destiny. She was in good spirits. Roland was doing a grand favor for her cousins, and she knew it and appreciated it. Isalia also explained that she had adopted her cousins as recipients of help and gifts and that she would do all she could to help them because they deserved it.

Meanwhile, back at Isalia's home, she had her nice granddaughter Missy, age 15, living with her, and she told Roland about her boyfriend, Mitchell, who was living in Chattanooga. Isalia was crazy about her granddaughter, loved her, and said that she would be satisfied with having her live with her for always. She could also get married to her boyfriend, Mitchell, and the two of them would be welcome to live with her. That was kind of Isalia to be that hospitable to her granddaughter.

They talked about philosophy and beliefs, more weird experiences, and the rest of it. Isalia told Roland that she believed that each person's spirit, before being born on Earth, chooses who its parents and family will be, and appropriately enters the world at an exact moment of conception and place of choosing.

She also told Roland the story of how she got to know one of her special student friends, Danny. Of course, Roland also knew Danny, having been a childhood friend of his in scouts. For the connection to scouts, Roland's parents and Danny's parents became very good friends, friends for life. Isalia said that Danny took a special liking to her. He expressed interest in being a sincere friend, and the friendship went into full force right then and there. The next year, Danny and his family moved to Georgia, and Isalia and Clayton went down there to visit him and his family. Esalina's son, Guillermo Velazco was an exchange student that year, and since he was living with Isalia and Clayton, they took him down there, as well. Coincidentally as it turned out, Danny's father and Clayton already knew each other from several years earlier, with their common interest in wood shop, and they had a great weekend visit.

Isalia appreciated her student friends like Danny, Hugh, Jack, and also Roland.

When they arrived to Laredo, they detached the trailer at a friend of the Quevalo's who lived there, and they crossed the border at Nuevo Laredo. Customs allowed them to cross without any trouble and without any inspection. 25 kilometers into the country, they passed through the second inspection. Roland pressed the button and got the green light . . . no inspection. They made it in with all their stuff, including Roland's Redwood tree. Isalia said she had prayed hard that they would make it through so easily.

Roland's plans were to stay with the Quevalos for the winter and become fluent in Spanish. Isalia was only to stay with them for a couple of days and then go stay with her friend, Esalina, in Monterrey for a few more days, after which she would fly home to Tennessee. Esalina was one of Isalia's best friends, and they loved each other like sisters. During the three day trip from Tennessee, Isalia had told Roland some things about them, as well. Guillermo had done very well with his business of being a stock broker, and he made a lot of money. His mother, Esalina, had struggled to make ends meet in the past, but now she would never have to lift her finger again to work. Guillermo had fixed that. Roland remembered how headstrong and aggressive Guillermo was, and he knew he had enough drive to achieve the goal of becoming rich. Isalia also told Roland about Guillermo's dressing room, how everything was in its place and so perfect. *Whatever suits his fancy, including his suits!* Roland thought. Roland never liked dressing up, anyway.

The Quevalo family graciously received Isalia and Roland. They were very glad to receive the Redwood tree. They made it their Christmas tree and placed the Christ nativity scene underneath it. Roland and the Quevalos made an on-the-spot verbal agreement that he would plant the tree in their backyard before he would return to Tennessee.

Isalia talked with her cousins about Roland, telling them that he had spent many hours repairing the truck and that he wasn't charging any labor. However, in return for that, he wanted to stay with them without paying any rent. They happily consented, and Roland happily stayed.

Two days later, Isalia boarded a ZuaZua bus to go to Monterrey to stay with Esalina.

Roland had brought among his gifts a rectangular shaped Cedar box to give to someone in Bustamante, and Isalia had told him that when he meets the girl of his dreams, he could give it to her. Evidently, she must have thought that he had a future wife waiting for him in Bustamante, and that he was sure to find her during his stay this upcoming winter. While there may indeed have been one waiting for him, she certainly wasn't to be found so soon as Isalia had thought.

Roland had been wondering for some years why it was one of Isalia's obsessions that Roland find a girlfriend and get married. Roland hadn't given much thought to girlfriends and marriage, and it was literally one of the last things on his mind. His desires were to travel, enjoy making friends, and to go running around with them.

*　　*　　*

He remembered nearly three years earlier in January 1989 that he had gone to her house to pick up a Royal 440 manual typewriter that she was giving him. It was the typewriter that she had used for many years in her Spanish classes. She told Roland that she thought he deserved it. He was glad to receive it, and he would use it from time to time.

Roland remembered a sign he had seen on several occasions in Isalia's house. It was a ceramic decoration tablet hanging on the wall by the kitchen table. He looked at it and read it. It said:

Love is a friend who never once removes his hand.

While on that visit, she told him that she had placed an order for him for a wife, and in her mind, she was sure that a girlfriend would come his way soon. After all, she had also placed an order for a wife for one of her student friends, Danny, and he had recently gotten married to a nice young woman who he had fallen madly in love with. Despite Isalia's claims, Roland knew he would not be ready for anything like a wife for at least some number of years yet.

He also remembered five years before that, the spring of 1984, when he had taken a young Mexican girl, Beatriz, to the senior prom. She was an exchange student, and she was living with Isalia and Clayton. Unfortunately, no other family had taken her in for the year. Roland drove his car to her residence to collect her. He wore no tuxedo nor a tie. Those two things were against his beliefs.

Though he took it with a grain of salt, he couldn't help but think how strange it was the way Isalia gave Roland explicit instructions on exactly what do with Beatriz on the prom date. She told Roland to open and close the door for her whenever Beatriz would step in or out of the car and also in or out of any buildings. She told him to kiss her at the appropriate times, and she also made sure and told him what those appropriate times would be. She told Roland exactly how to hold her while dancing with her, and she even went on to tell him exactly how to eat properly with his mouth closed (as if he didn't already know that) at the place he would take her out to eat, and which hand to hold the fork, knife, and spoon with, and to pay for her meal, as well. With all of that said, Isalia released Beatriz to Roland's care, and she also told him to bring her back *very late*.

It was rather embarrassing to Roland for Isalia to give him instructions as if he had no common sense nor knew how to take a girl on a date. Further, she had given the instructions right there in front of Beatriz! Even though it was true that he had done very little dating, he wasn't *that* naive! Beatriz didn't need to hear all of that, but then Roland sensed that Isalia had already given her a complete and thorough run-down about his mannerisms ahead of time.

Beatriz stepped into Roland's car, and they went on their date. Roland did not *kiss her* nor *hold her hand*. He treated her like a friend, like a normal human being, and in a normal manner, and after the prom dance, he took her home by 11:30 PM. The only thing he hadn't liked about the date was that Beatriz had, when they were eating supper, repeatedly told Roland the exact proper etiquette of dining. Things like that just didn't matter to Roland. His philosophy was to get the food in his mouth in a decent reasonable manner, and chew with his mouth closed when possible.

As a result, Roland felt very depressed the next day, and he took a bicycle ride for 25 miles in hopes of making himself feel better. He stopped at the closed Versailles Grocery and rested on the porch, wondering about the meaning of life, hoping he would soon feel better. Roland had been suffering from a little bit of depression during the past few months as it was, and knowing that a good friend of his was contemplating suicide didn't help matters either.

His name was Eric, and Roland had met him out at Isalia's house during the welcoming party for Beatriz the day she had arrived from Mexico. Roland's friend was presently in Isalia's Spanish class, and he was in conflict with himself, suffering from adolescence and growing pains. Eric's best friend Jim, who was also in Isalia's class, had shot and killed himself a few months ago, and Eric was quite sad about it. Depression had set in. Roland befriended Eric as much as he could, having him come visit out at his farm, doing other activities, and even taking him on a weekend trip to Atlanta's Six Flags. They had some good times, and it helped Eric get his mind off his sadness.

Roland really wanted to help his friend Eric see the beauty of life and to see reason for continuing to live, but he just could not conceive of the correct choice of words to explain it to him. He was suffering from that mysterious force that had somehow gently descended onto and washed over him in February 1981, which had occurred in Isalia's class, and since that time, thinking had just not been as easy for him.

*   *   *

February 1981

It was a whispy wintery day in the world of the spirits on the other side. Two spirit guides: Sarlo and Malluck had been talking over a deal with another spiritual being from a different level of existence from a faraway and different part of the galaxy. The alien spirit's name was Messofilo.

"Look here," Messofilo urged them. "I need to latch onto someone for at least ten years and have a look at planet Earth through his eyes, and the one you guide and protect is an excellent choice."

"It's against spirit world rules," Sarlo explained, speaking both for himself and Malluck.

"What's he ever going to know?" Messofilo argued. "He won't detect my presence, and besides, he doesn't believe in spirits, anyway."

"We've been looking after him for the past 15½ years since he was born," Malluck now explained, "and he's had enough trouble growing up as it is, adjusting to the ways and lives of the human species on Earth."

"Malluck and I were assigned to him at the time of his birth," Sarlo added, "and our duty is to protect and guide him through his lifetime."

"Your entering would interfere with his energies," Malluck added.

"I realize that," Messofilo told them, "but if you'll just let me latch on, I'll put in a good word for you to your spiritual superiors. Besides, I'll be in a different dimensional frequency."

"Look, it's like I just told you . . ." Sarlo began.

"More than that," Messofilo went on, "I'll grant the two of you spiritual access to my realm in my region of the galaxy . . . along with some *pleasure*." Messofilo showed them an irresistible smile. Both Sarlo and Malluck were telepathically presented with exquisite scenery of the world where Messofilo came from, in addition to a few moments of the most pleasurable feelings of ecstasy they had ever experienced. Messofilo's offer and transmissions were entirely false, but then he kept that detail to himself.

"Okay, okay, you've got the deal," Sarlo consented. "Just do what you need to do, and then exit from his presence."

"That I will do, indeed," Messofilo agreed.

"Let me tell you," Malluck explained. "Our protectee has a phenomenal memory for details such as dates and numbers. He's been thought to be autistic, but he's of a different sort, his spirit having come from a different part of the galaxy. This is his first lifetime experience on planet Earth, and . . ."

Sarlo and Malluck continued briefing Messofilo about their protectee's 15-year history. They finalized the plans, and then Messofilo departed.

Though he made no mention of it, Messofilo subcontracted two beings to do his work for him. They were from a place called Wimbisenho. Their names were Sasjurech and Sojornbloc. They also carried some secret programs with them which they would install into Roland's subconscious mind at the time they would latch on. These programs were designed to cause certain others to take a dislike to Roland . . . all to make the "10-year attachment" more *interesting* to Sasjurech and Sojornbloc so that they could experience the feelings of rejection that would come with it.

They waited until the right opportunity to descend and make the attachment. It was when Roland was in class one day, sitting right across from his Spanish teacher. Under Messofilo's direction and guidance, Sasjurech and Sojornbloc would use her subconscious mind as well, as a means of establishing a lasting mental connection with Roland. The day came, and in a matter of seconds, the attachment was made.

*   *   *

When Roland had returned to school the next Monday after the prom date, he had happened to see Isalia. She took him to one side and lectured several minutes to him on how to prepare for having a serious girlfriend and a wife, which as far as she was concerned, he would *have*! This sent Roland reeling in his mind and his feelings. He felt most uncomfortable, and he didn't need her lectures on how she thought his life needed to be!. . . especially pertaining to dating and marriage!!

*   *   *

Seven years had gone by since that date with Beatriz. He had not dated again. After all, he had not been rewarded with good feelings, and even though he was aware there were other much more compatible women out there, he had just not bothered. Besides, he had plenty of other things of interest to do instead . . . namely travelling.

Roland began his stay in late November 1991 with the Quevalo family. He had brought his mountain bike with him, and he rode it around town and also into the canyon.

One day, Roland and Pancho and Pancho's brother-in-law drove to Laredo and San Antonio with the intention of Pancho's buying a tractor to bring back to Mexico. Pancho was very determined to accomplish this task, but he did not succeed in finding what he wanted, in addition to new Mexican rules and import duties that would be charged. Further, Roland had difficulty passing the truck and trailer over the border into Mexico because of registration difficulties arising from the recently purchased truck and trailer. The rules in December 1991 were more strict and different than they had been the previous month, when Roland and Isalia had brought the truck in without a problem.

Roland had a friend from Tennessee whose name was Darren, and he was going to fly to Monterrey and take a bus to Bustamante to visit Roland. Darren, like Roland, spoke Spanish. The Quevalo family had already told Roland they would happily receive Darren since he was a friend of his. Darren arrived to Monterrey and first looked up another friend of his whose name was Manuel. Since Darren was on a tight schedule, he was unable to catch an appropriate bus to Bustamante and ended up spending all his time with Manuel. He never came to Bustamante at all, and Roland was disappointed. He had looked forward to introducing his friend, Darren, to his friends the Quevalos and showing him around the town he had become acquainted with.

It was becoming the story of Roland's life that in one way or another, he was always somehow second choice, and it was becoming annoying to him. He recalled that six months earlier, he had been invited by a college friend to stay with him and his parents at the beach in South Carolina. His friend's parents said that their son needed a "playmate at the beach." Roland happily accepted the invitation and drove his car there. When Roland arrived, they were already there. While it was still okay with him, he noticed and was somewhat surprised that his friend had also brought along his best friend from high school, thereby putting Roland in second position. Still he enjoyed his stay. No more than Roland was taking note in his own mind of these occurrences that had taken place.

Roland was enjoying his stay in Bustamante. He used to bicycle around town and explore. One day he bicycled into the canyon to see the Ojo del Agua.

Eliud had a friend of his come over and play at times. His name was Moises. He was a cheerful and friendly child who talked to Roland. Moises already knew a decent amount about cars, and he had plans of being a mechanic in the future. Roland was impressed, and he was glad to know that there were children as intelligent as Eliud and Moises.

Roland ran around with Pancho some of the time, and he helped the Quevalos with their chores. At times he would go with Pancho to the ranch north of town, where he attended to and fed some animals. Sometimes, they attended to their crops, plowing by means of an ox-

19

drawn plow, and they cut grass off of other fields using a sickle.

Since it didn't always rain enough, Bustamante had an elaborate irrigation scheme controlled by locks, gates, and canals. There were several canals in town, through which the water flowed, passing under streets and even under houses. All of the water that flowed through those channels had its source from the Ojo del Agua up in the canyon. There was a two week cycle and a schedule that was adhered to. On those certain days, every two weeks, several of the Quevalos went to their ranch, and using picks and hoes, they would manually create the irrigation ditches appropriate to water their crops.

Roland used to chat with Lorenzo and Pancho about various things, and he became good friends with both of them. They told Roland about how they built fences there in Mexico. They used small fence stakes, as compared to the big fence posts up in Tennessee. Then they would string 5 or 6 strands of barbed wire. They would cut the fence stakes or poles from a tree called Barreta, which had yellowish colored wood that was very hard. However, in order that the wood last, it was very important to cut it during a full moon, because if it was cut at other times during the moon cycle, the wood would soon become infested with ground insects and rot. Roland looked at Pancho and Lorenzo in disbelief, and he asked them if that was a superstition. No, they insisted it was true . . . not a superstition. They explained that the genetic code of the Barreta tree had a certain cycle synchronized with the moon cycle in such a way that the wood had its most durable properties and characteristics at every full moon! Therefore, if the trees were cut at a full moon, the poles would last.

Speaking of superstitions or reality, Lorenzo and Pancho related a story from several years ago when there was a solar eclipse. For weeks following the eclipse, there was a lot of sickness all over town. They weren't really sure why, but it was very strange. Who knows? Perhaps the belief systems of the people thought the sicknesses into reality, because there had been an eclipse!

One day, Lorenzo and a friend of his, Daniel Mata, took Roland up in the mountains to cut Palm leaves for use in weaving chair bottoms and backs. A couple of times, Pancho took Roland to the canyon to cut fallen Ash trees for making chairs.

In addition to the ranch work, Pancho was also starting a carpentry business where he made and sold chairs for a living. His business was situated under a large pole barn in the Quevalo's backyard. He had various rocking chairs and upright chairs, and all of them were made to look rustic according to the older and traditional styles of the past. All of the chair bottoms were woven with an ever continuous strand of twisted Fan Palm leaves. Some of the chair backs were also woven with Fan Palm leaves while others had wooden backs. He kindly showed Roland how to make them, and Roland started making two chairs to later take back home with him. Pancho had a homemade table saw of an impressive design. Years later, Roland would also make one for himself in Tennessee.

One afternoon, Roland saw a big flatbed truck going up and down the streets of town. It was loaded with chair and table dining sets, and vendors were walking beside the truck, carrying chairs and calling out to each house they passed. As Roland would find out, it was a common practice for vendors to travel all over Mexico, selling furniture items, necessities, and even paintings throughout the small towns. It was a lucrative business for them because small town residents needed furniture, and they didn't have vehicles to drive to Sabinas Hidalgo or Monterrey to visit the stores. Other trucks would arrive regularly with fruits and vegetables and even small shrubs and trees for sale.

The same general practice was done with selling LP gas or butane. Trucks from Sabinas Hidalgo arrived every week day, honking their horns as they passed by, and residents who needed their LP gas tank filled would emerge from their houses, their tank beside them, and flag them down. All residents had gas stoves, and many of them had gas boilers for their hot water. No one, absolutely no one, had electric stoves.

Roland enjoyed going hiking in the mountains on some of the days when it was sunny. However, in December 1991, it was mostly wet and cloudy, and it drizzled a lot. He also caught the gripa (flu) and was in bed a couple of days with that.

Roland got word from his parents by telephone that his grandmother had terminal cancer and was dying. On Christmas morning, he boarded a bus to go home to Tennessee to attend the funeral. It was a sad time for his family, and a lot of decisions had to be made. On December 27, 1991, while in Crossville where his grandmother had lived, he noticed a brown 1980 Ford F-100 truck for sale for $2,000 firm. It appeared to be in good condition, and he took it for a test drive. He told the owner that he would see if he could take out a loan for the money and would call him soon with an answer.

When he got back home, he called Isalia on the phone and asked her if she could loan him $2,000 so he could buy the truck. She said she didn't have the money but that she would be glad to take out a loan for him. That was kind of her, and she went on to tell Roland that she was sorry to hear about his grandmother.

Roland went over to her house, and they wrote out an agreement that when he would return from Mexico, he would begin to pay her back for the loan. She kept quiet about it and told Roland that she didn't want her husband to know about it. Roland understood and thanked her very much for the loan. He went to the bank and cashed her $2,000 check, and he and a friend of his went to Crossville where he bought the truck.

He stayed home for ten days and decided to drive his newly purchased truck to Mexico and finish his stay with the Quevalos. Thoughtful as Roland was, he kindly bought them some items they might need, like a couple of bow saws and a Royal manual typewriter. Of course, he was under the assumption that the Quevalos would gladly receive the items and reimburse him for them. Further, he had loaded his truck with Walnut and Cedar logs to give to them. He was sure Pancho would be overjoyed to receive them.

*   *   *

Wimbisenho, January 1992

A group of spirits gathered for a meeting down at Wimbisenho, which was an exquisite cavern some 500 meters under the beautiful rolling hillsides of the South Island of New Zealand.

Arfifra was talking to her friends. She was a female spirit of egotistically gorgeous appearance, so beautifully symmetrical she was . . . even palindromic in some respects. She spoke with a sense of elegance.

"The day has come that we move on to a new place, to experience shall we say . . . new culture."

"Where are we going to move to?" Sasjurech wanted to know.

"What if it doesn't work out?" Sojornbloc added.

"I like it here in Wimbisenho," Draaktra added.

"I know you do," Arfifra told him, "but the time has come, and we must move on to bigger and better things. Besides, Roland has taken a special liking to Mexico, thanks to my protectee Isalia. Plus, we've been invited by one of my favorite friends Torxtalo. The forces have moved together, and there will be plenty of rich and rewarding experiences for us there. You'll see."

"Where is the new place?" Sojornbloc wanted to know.

"Torxtalo and I have scouted out the countryside in northern Mexico, and we have found a most exquisite cavern, even prettier than this one, in the rolling hills west of Sabinas Hidalgo. I have decided to call it Nuevo Wimbisenho. Plus, I have . . ."

* * *

On January 10, 1992, Roland re-entered Mexico and had considerable difficulty in being allowed to take his truck over the border. Mexico required at least six months of ample insurance on the vehicle, and that created a real problem since U.S. policies were only six months long. Roland had to make several phone calls to Tennessee to his then obliging insurance agents and had a copy of his policy faxed to him. Well, Mexican Customs would not allow him in with the policy because the six month policy only lasted two more months. He spent the night in Laredo, and the next day he went to a different bridge, the new Colombia Solidarity Bridge and succeeded in passing the truck over the border since he had carefully changed the 3 to a 9 for the month of expiration on the policy copy. Mexican Customs looked at the policy and commented, "Ah, sí. Este es bueno," saying that it was good. Roland didn't like having to falsify documents, but then it was the only way, if he was going to bring his truck in with him. Besides, he had a truckload of Walnut and Cedar logs that he didn't want to forfeit!

From the Colombia Bridge, he took a narrow, 18-foot-wide highway, which had some ugly potholes, to access Nuevo León Highway 1, the Laredo-Anahuac-Monterrey highway. This highway was a little bit wider (20 feet), and it ran through the towns of Anahuac, Lampazos, and Villaldama to reach Monterrey further south.

This highway was also suffering from chronic pothole disease in certain sections. Mexico's highways were notorious for bad potholes, and one had to be on the constant lookout for them, negotiating around them and dodging them. Some sections were so awful that everyone had to slow down and carefully creep through them, because they were much worse than speed bumps! Plus, Nuevo León's government was notorious for building narrow highways. Less pavement was required, and by that tactic they could efficiently trim costs.

A few kilometers before Villaldama, Roland reached the right hand turnoff for Bustamante and drove into town. Roland stayed until January 31. Things didn't go so well this time. He didn't get along with the Quevalos quite so well, and little things caused resentment to build up. The Quevalos had expenses to make and taxes to pay, and much of their savings was eaten up, in addition to the cost of their having to painstakingly register the truck and trailer. Not only that, they had recently purchased some property in the lower end of town, where they had plans of building a second shop. The Quevalos expressed resentment at Roland for his kind expectations that they would happily receive the typewriter and bow saws. They reimbursed Roland for them, but not without the oldest sister, Lola, angrily declaring to Pancho to charge Roland for the Palm leaves that he used for making his two chairs.

Pancho explained his philosophy about giving, that it was great to give, but charging was another matter altogether. Pancho explained that when you loan (*prestar*) money to someone, that is the same as giving, and he told Roland the money Isalia loaned for the truck and trailer was a gift. Roland thought differently. He knew Isalia expected to be paid the $4,000 that she had loaned them.

One morning, Roland shaved in the kitchen sink, which was the only sink in the entire house. Lorenzo's wife asked Roland not to do that anymore. Then she walked into the next room where Lorenzo was, and she was ranting and raving about it. Evidently, she was quite angry about that!

Later that day, Roland found a bookcase slid across the doorway between the room where he slept and the rest of Lorenzo's house. That blocked Roland from entering the rest of the house. He knew why and he rightfully went to the rest of the Quevalos, including Lorenzo, and complained that he felt unwelcome. It caused a considerable disagreement among the Quevalo sisters, and Lorenzo, under the circumstances, slid the bookcase back into the corner of the room, and he assured Roland that he was indeed welcome. Roland appreciated Lorenzo's understandingness in the situation.

The big disagreement arrived when Roland, at the end of January, stated that he wanted to plant the Redwood tree. He was then informed of the Mexican custom that one does not take down the tree and nativity scene until February 2. Nevertheless, Roland insisted that he wanted to plant it, as that was the verbal agreement he and the Quevalos had made. Sarita, the mother in the family, angrily consented, saying, "¡Quítalo! Este no tiene abuela." Lorenzo took it down, and Roland took the tree to the backyard and planted it. Though Roland didn't realize it, he had unknowing committed a sin worthy of being cursed a thousand times . . . in the view of the Quevalo family! According to the Catholic religion, it was of utmost importance that the tree and nativity scene remain in place until February 2 of each year, to be taken down that night with a sincere religious blessing ceremony.

Later that day, Sarita told Roland that he was no longer welcome to stay with them, that he would stay in a hotel the next time he would come to Bustamante! She also stated that they didn't want his type. Two of the daughters were always scowling at him. Pancho, the youngest son, wouldn't even talk to Roland, and he carried an angry look on his face for the rest of Roland's stay. That really upset Roland because he thought Pancho had become a true friend. Further, he was wondering why in the world Pancho showed no appreciation for the Walnut and Cedar logs he had *given* to him . . . yes, *given* to him!

Even India, who had always been friendly with Roland, was scowling at him each time she walked by him. Roland had taken her to Sabinas Hidalgo, and yes things had gone well, but that evening, he decided to buy some of her *dulces* (candy) to take back to his family in Tennessee. He asked her if she would give him a special price since he had taken her to Sabinas Hidalgo. Well, little did Roland realize it until later, India was quite offended, and he later found out that she accused him of *charging* her for the trip to Sabinas Hidalgo! Since when was it so bad to ask for a special price?

Later that afternoon, Lola brought Roland's load of wet laundry to him and dumped the lot on top of him in an angry manner. Roland angrily responded by telling her to be nice!

Roland really felt hurt by the Quevalo's rejection. All he had done was plant the Redwood tree he had given them. What was so bad about that? It really made Roland angry.

That night, he went and talked to some friends of his, Chely and Vico, who sympathized with Roland. He explained to them how the Quevalos had turned against him, after all the help he had given them. It was then that Chely proceeded to tell Roland some interesting but hair-raising tales about the Quevalos, with the request that he not tell the Quevalos what he would now know, because they would get angry at Chely and Vico. Chely told Roland that when Lorena announced to her family that she was going to get engaged to her boyfriend Ricardo of Monterrey, her parents and siblings got very angry. They did not approve of an outsider, a boyfriend from another area. Pancho and India cornered their sister into a room, wouldn't let her leave, and they knocked her around, yelled at her, abused her, and beat her up! Then they ran her off! Roland was absolutely shocked at such barbaric behavior, and for them to do that to one of their own family, how terrible! They had no reason because Ricardo was a decent man. The problem was, he was not from Bustamante. Roland asked Chely where Lorena went after that, and Chely said that Lorena went to stay with other friends in town. It was then that Chely said she and Vico are Lorena's friends, and they only know the Quevalos because of their friendship with Lorena.

With that being told to Roland, he was in shock. He knew he would never think the same of Pancho and India again. How in the world did Lorena forgive her family and reunite with them? Roland now saw Pancho as he actually was, an angry *enojón* (hothead). Having seen Pancho's and India's recent scowls was now adding up and making sense.

The next day, Roland went up into one of the mountain canyons to cool off. He composed and wrote them quite a letter, expressing his disapproval of their ungratefulness after all the help he had given them. He also reminded them of how he had helped them, and he listed all of the details. The letter was five pages long, and he knew they deserved that letter. He didn't normally believe in shoving in somebody's face, but in this case, he felt like it was justified.

Upon returning to town, he happened to see Moises sitting on a sidewalk. He had a friendly smile on his face. Roland was glad to see him, and they talked a few minutes. During their conversation, Moises mentioned that his family had come over to Mexico three generations ago from the country of Lebanon. So, not all Mexicans came from Spanish origin. Of course, most Mexicans were a mixture of native Indians (native Mexicans) and Spanish ancestors, but there were also some from places like Arabia. Plus, some of the Spaniards that came over had Arabian names, for example Arámbula, because the Arabians had control or dominion over Spain for several centuries in the early part of the millennium.

Roland enjoyed talking to Moises, and he realized that children in Mexico are not as shy as American children. Bustamante did have a lot of good to offer, and seeing Moises represented, as far as Roland knew, a good sign. He hoped they would know each other and become good friends in the future.

The next morning, Roland loaded his things on his truck. He said goodbye to the Quevalos, told them he wished to go on being friends with them, handed them the letter, and drove out of town. He remembered seeing the oldest daughter, Lola, sweeping the street in front of their house, and she had a scowl on her face.

Roland returned home to Tennessee with his brown Ford truck. He went over to Isalia's house and told her everything, and he showed her a copy of the letter he had written them. She read all of it and then told him he had done the right thing, and that if he wasn't welcome, then she herself didn't feel welcome either. She told Roland that for the bad the Quevalos had done to him, it would come back on them ten fold. Roland felt a lot better that Isalia would talk to them and set things straight. He thanked her.

Roland also told her what Pancho had said.

"What do you mean Pancho said the truck and trailer was the same as a *gift*?!" Isalia reacted with alarm on her face.

"I don't know. That's what Pancho said. I just thought I'd let you know about it."

"Well I'm glad you did. I can't give them that $4,000. They've got to pay me back!"

"Well, of course they do. You might want to clarify that with them, Isalia."

"I sure will, when I call them tonight!" she declared.

Roland and Isalia talked a while longer. Isalia assured him he had done well and that the Quevalos were at fault. Roland felt a lot better, more at peace, and he went home.

Well, two days later, Roland went back over to Isalia's house. Yes, she had talked to the Quevalos, but she had completely changed. She now thought the Quevalos were right and that Roland was entirely wrong! She ranted and raved and waved her arms up in the air as she complained that he had dared to plant that Redwood tree before February 2. She informed Roland that the Quevalos were very upset with the letter he wrote them. In fact, they were furious! Further, she brought it to Roland's attention that it was very bad to have shaved in the kitchen sink, (even though that was the only sink in the entire house!).

Isalia also scolded Roland for being stubborn. Roland defended himself by stating that by being stubborn, he accomplished many of his goals, which he wouldn't have been able to accomplish without being persistent and sticking with whatever project was at hand until it was finished.

There was a whole load of complaints the Quevalos had about Roland. They had also asked Isalia if Roland lived in a cave. The whole situation just made Roland more irritated.

She also revealed to him that she knew about the incident when Roland had walked in his underwear from the shower to the bedroom in the Velazco's house during his stay with them in 1983, and for that reason, Guillermo never wanted to know Roland again. She told him, "They don't want you, Roland!!" To Roland, it had been entirely unintentional, and it had never crossed his mind that it was bad, until Guillermo had thrown a fit and gotten really angry at him for his having walked like that. Never did Roland think that it would be cause for not being welcome again in their home and to cause Guillermo to have such long lasting grudges for 15¼ more years!

Roland went home from Isalia's house, angry at the whole situation, and he was realizing that he had not succeeded in making any close friends at all in Mexico. He knew he did not deserve the rejection he had just received from the Quevalos, and he was also displeased at Isalia for not having defended him to the Quevalos. After all, Roland was a decent, kind, honest person who had sincerely helped the Quevalos out. Isalia insisted to Roland that he forgive the Quevalo family and bless them, and over time, Roland did his best to bring himself to forgive them.

Around two weeks later, Roland got a letter from Isalia stating that he needed to get on with it and begin to pay her back the $2,000 she had loaned him. She suggested that he either come up with the money or sell the truck to pay her. She went on to state that she had made an insurance payment and with the $2,000 being absent from the account, the payment had been very difficult to make. Roland then realized that she had not actually taken out a loan for him. She had borrowed the money from her husband's bank account. Now he realized why she didn't want her husband to know about it in the first place.

Roland called her on the phone as soon as the letter arrived, and he said to her, "Isalia, I'll have you paid as quick as I can."

She answered, "Don't worry. There's no rush."

Wonder why she said that? The letter sounded urgent.

Roland's parents decided to step in and help. They loaned him the $2,000, as there was a storage building project they were about to begin, and they said for him to go pay Isalia. He called her right back, and he said he would come over that evening with the cash. She said that was wonderful. That night, he arrived at her house, and without Clayton knowing about it, she quietly accepted the money, plus $47 interest for the month and a half it had been loaned out.

Next, she put the bundle of money to her mouth and kissed it! Roland certainly noticed her actions, and while he realized it was very important to her that she be paid back, he also observed that she had more of a love of money than he realized. Granted Roland liked having money because money was nearly always required to travel and enjoy, and to purchase items of necessity. However, he was not in love with money, and he certainly never kissed it.

*   *   *

Roland's parents needed a storage building built on their farm, and that spring, he and a friend of his spent some two months building it. It measured 24 x 40 feet in size and was made of board and batten. Things were going just fine until Roland woke up one morning with a mysteriously inflamed left knee. There was just no explanation as to how it got that way because the night before, it was fine. That left Roland very puzzled, and the problem wasn't easily overcome. He continued his work, but with a limp for the next several weeks, until he finally got better.

In July 1992, Isalia called Roland's parents and asked if she could bring her sister, Roma, and come out to visit them. She sat on the front porch and really told some entertaining stories. Roland and his parents listened with interest as she related to them the reason she had left Longview High School two years earlier. She had been at Longview since its opening in 1972. Roland and his parents wondered why she had been transferred.

She was now at a high school east of there and said she felt like she had died and gone to heaven in comparison to how she had felt at Longview. According to her story, Longview's principal, Howard Wallace, had been overbearing and too controlling over her. She said the workload at Longview seemed like 25 times what it was now, at her new location. She told stories of how Mr. Wallace would enter the classroom unannounced, whisper comments in her ear, and leave. She told other stories about him as well, and she went on to mention that Mr. Wallace would soon meet his match.

Roland and his parents wondered how much of this was really true. After all, they were friends with Longview High School's principal. They knew him to be a stern and serious man with an imposing stature, which was necessary to keep law and order in a high school where there were bound to be rebellious teenage students, but in truth he was a genuine and friendly man who certainly had a good reputation throughout the county. He cared about his school and about the students.

The Previous Trips

Since Isalia was no longer compatible with Longview High School's principal, she had been transferred to another high school where, as it turned out, her good friend was principal. His name was Cason Butler, and back in the late 1970's, he had been unjustly fired from his position as Longview High School's principal over some insignificant accusations. Isalia related the whole story about how Longview's janitor, who had testified against him, had died soon after the firing, and how another high official of the county schools had literally died in pieces soon after the firing. He had to have a leg amputated, then another, and in months he was dead. The school superintendent who had pushed the firing soon suffered some bad luck, as well.

Natural law had certainly worked very well for Mr. Butler. He got elected county school superintendent several years later, was offered compensation and back pay, and those who had earlier caused his removal as Longview High School's principal were severely punished by either dying or suffering very bad luck. As it turned out, the former school superintendent became a principle in the same county, which meant that Cason Butler was now his boss. They had literally swapped places. The irony of it was amazing!

All of this Isalia related in a fervent and most interesting manner, waving her arms up and down as she spoke, and she added emphasis to certain words to make her stories sound more interesting and unusual.

*   *   *

Roland continued looking for the *real* job, a position with an electrical engineering firm. No opportunities came forth, and in January 1993 he started his own business of self employment, doing carpentry, building and repairs, and also painting for other people so he could earn money. He saved money so he could drive out West in August and September.

Roland used to draw for fun during his childhood and adolescence, but he had set it aside in more recent years. However, he always had a good eye for art, and in the back of his mind, he was thinking about becoming an artist, to do paintings of a unique type. He had always had an interest about life on other planets and other star systems. He used to wonder a lot about it. More ideas were now coming to him. Specifically, Roland wanted to do paintings of some scenes from alien worlds, artwork with a unique theme, something different to impress the people at gallery shows, something to make them *think* and *wonder.*

In April 1993, *Roland had a special dream of being with several good friends of his who he didn't know in real life. They were human beings identical to humans here on Earth, but they lived in another star system, perhaps Vega. They transported themselves utilizing a certain thought process that brought on a special energy which made them disappear and then seconds later reappear in the place to where they thought themselves.* It was one of the most interesting dreams Roland ever had. He was quite amazed by it all, and for several weeks, he really missed those friends he had known in that one dream.

Though Roland never knew it, at that same moment in time, there was a very special universal appointment taking place at a location called *Green Central*, which was on one of the planets around the star Vega in the Lyran constellation. The meeting was a very special one in that it included people from various galaxies, and their main reason for meeting was in concern for the trees and the ecological balance of several planets, especially that of planet Earth. That special gathering was known as *The Meeting of the Alquzokans.*

*   *   *

April 1990 (three years earlier)

Roland was sleeping in the cabin in the corner of the yard of his parents' farm. It was something like 5 AM, and it was already beginning to be daylight outside. He was awakened by the sound of two men who were standing at the foot of the bed, and they were speaking a very foreign language, a language he knew he had *never* heard before.

"Waira com pura opicanana . . . copley cupi nanaak Alquzok," Selím said to Igor, saying that Roland was asleep at the moment, that it was important that he be protected, that he was an *Alquzok*.

Though Roland made efforts to move and turn around to see who the two men were, he was unable to move at all. He had been telepathically immobilized by them because they thought Roland wouldn't understand and might freak out. All Roland wanted to do was be more straightforward with them, meet them, and talk with them.

He went back to sleep, and an hour later, he woke up with the thoughts that he had only dreamed it. His thoughts had been purposefully transformed by Selím and Igor so that he would think he just dreamed it, but he knew that what he had heard was too real for that, and perhaps they didn't realize how much Roland remembered, with his phenomenal memory.

What was actually taking place was a changing of Roland's guardian angels from Selím to Igor. Igor was being assigned to Roland to protect his life for the next ten years' dangerous experiences he was destined to have.

Roland had been in Australia and New Zealand earlier that year, and he had been home for approximately three weeks. While he had been hiking in the mountains of Australia's Tasmania, 15 guardian angels were having a reunion on one of the mountain tops, Mt. Oakleigh to be precise. They had taken notice of Roland and for his special characteristics, especially his interest in trees and plants, they decided to assign him new a protector . . . Igor.

*　　*　　*

Months before Roland took his trip out West, he invited several friends and cousins to take the trip with him and to accompany him while hiking the John Muir Trail. No one took him up on it. It really puzzled Roland how, despite the fact that he invited people who loved to travel and go hiking, not a one of them could spare even three weeks of time to go with him. One of them, Chris, lived in England, and he wrote back saying, "I would love to!!" Roland and Chris had met each other while hiking in Australia's Tasmania. Some of the people he invited were still in college, and since the trip would be in the summer, surely one of them would have the time. But nothing of the kind happened. It was just seemingly too much to expect and must have been beyond reason! That was what people must have thought. Of course, Roland wasn't in agreement with that, but what more could he do? He took the entire trip by himself, and he walked the entire John Muir Trail in three weeks . . . by himself. The scenery was absolutely spectacular, and he took several pictures. When he got home, he made a collage of the 12 best pictures from his hike, and he mailed color copies to each of the people he had invited, so they could see what they missed. Chris wrote back and commented, "I am sooooo envious!" Chris really had wanted to come over and hike the John Muir Trail with Roland, but his bank account just happened to be drained at the exact time, plus he happened to land a job with an engineering firm in London.

Finally, in January 1994, Roland was hired by an engineering firm, a company with 70 employees in Nashville. Things went well for a couple of months. One day, the executive of the company told Roland he expected him "to wear a shirt and tie from now on," and Roland didn't like that at all. Wearing a tie felt like a hangman's noose around his neck, and there was just no way he could bring himself to put one on. The shirt and pants, yes, but not the tie. For a while, he thought that no one really minded since there were numerous other employees there without ties.

One day, exactly three months into the job, he had a major wreck while driving down narrow two-lane State Highway 96, the highway to Franklin. He suddenly saw a car stopped to turn left in front of him, and on the rain slick road, there was no way he could stop, and he rear-ended her car at a speed of what must have been 45 mph. No one was injured, but her rear-ended car was totalled, and his white 1980 Ford LTD station wagon was badly damaged in the front.

He managed to drive the car home, called the office and said that he would not be able to come to work. Immediately, he went to a salvage yard and bought $250 worth of car parts: a fender, a hood, grill parts, and a radiator. When he got back home, he called his friend Roger Schultz, and he came and helped Roland repair his car. By 2 AM, they had it all fixed. They had even spray painted the replaced hood and fender white.

When Roland went to work the next day with his already fixed car, his boss must have thought that Roland lied about the wreck in the first place, and the next day, they let him go. The 90-day probationary period was up, anyway, and while they never said anything about the wreck having been the reason, Roland instinctively sensed that was the underlying cause.

After all, in the three months that he had worked there, he had noticed that several of the employees had upgraded their car status. One employee had replaced his 9-year-old Honda CRX with a new black Nissan 300 ZX with $1,200 tires. Another one had replaced his Pontiac Bonneville with a brand new sleek, shiny, blue coupe, a Lincoln Continental Mark VIII. Another employee who carried a cowboy image replaced his vehicle with a new, sleek, black stepside Chevrolet pickup truck. The executive of the company must not have been satisfied with his new black, luxurious Toyota Lexus, so he bought another new black, luxurious Toyota Lexus, this time with *gold trim*. Roland used to watch from the upper office window as the executive would drive away to meetings in his new car. He would unconsciously touch his tie on his neck to check and make sure it was properly tight and fitted. Though the executive didn't realize it, he only had three more years to live, before a heart attack would suddenly get him.

With the above upgrading of the employees' cars, and with Roland's car being an old station wagon needing a paint job, how could the company have tolerated having Roland on their work force any longer? They just could not have the appearance of that old car in their parking lot!

He thought he had made some friends at work during those three months. He used to walk around the place on breaks and talk to the other employees. One of the fellows near his age took a liking to him right away, and he realized in a positive way that Roland was not like the others. He had a wife and kids, and he used to give Roland pointers on how to fit in better. Well, after Roland left, he never ever heard from any of those employees again, not even the one who he thought had become his friend.

Throughout Roland's life, it was almost always a case of his having to look up his friends to keep up with any of them at all. Very rarely did he hear from a friend of his out of the clear blue. He came to learn that in general, friends just don't make a practice of keeping up with each other. In fact, many of them don't even answer, that is, respond.

Roland was at first not pleased to have been let go. He had feelings of rejection, but then he was overjoyed at having been given three entire months of severance pay, the amount being $4,400. He already knew what he was going to do: take a trip to England and Scotland with his bicycle and backpack. He would travel around there for the summer and then return to Tennessee to begin another engineering job.

After all, his friend Chris was living in England, and he had repeatedly invited him over. Roland was really looking forward to it. He immediately bought a plane ticket from British Airways, and he flew over there the next month.

Roland enjoyed his trip to Great Britain and Ireland. While he was there, he hiked for 6 days on the West Highland Way from Glasgow to Ft. William, Scotland, hiked to the top of Ben Nevis, the highest point in Britain at 4,406 feet, and hiked for another 6 days on the northern section of the Pennine Way in northern England and Scotland.

He remembered and thought about his three-month engineering job, and he was now realizing how much he had disliked it. Never was he able to pass a day at work without hearing numerous employees uttering foul language! Roland had detested foul language since he was age 12. It was absolutely *appalling* to Roland how the other employees used foul language so freely that it would certainly have offended just about anyone! Roland knew that was very unprofessional behavior, and since they were indeed professionals at an engineering firm, they should have acted like professionals!

He remembered the last day at work. It was pouring rain so hard that after he was dismissed, he couldn't leave the building to run to his car. He had to wait for an hour! In fact, it had been very wet the whole season, and Roland had lost count on how many times it had flooded! A month earlier, it had rained 12 inches in 24 hours, and the police had to close Highway 96 for three days for high water! He was so tired of the rain. At least here in Great Britain it was mostly dry and sunny.

He also remembered receiving his severance paycheck from the accountant on the last day. The chief executive happened to be in the room, and Roland was going to say goodbye to him and thank him for having hired him. Well, the executive must have known Roland was standing there because he quickly walked out of the room, immediately turned the other way, and left! Roland was somewhat taken aback that he had not had the decency to wish him well on his last day at work. As a result, Roland never spoke to him. However, he did thank the accountant for the check. He wished Roland well and for him to have a great trip.

While walking through the town of Bellingham on the Pennine Way, Roland bought a postcard of the Lake District with a beautiful small lake lined by trees along its shore with mountains seen in the distance. He wrote that chief executive an anonymous short note, which he thoroughly enjoyed writing. The note said, "Glad I'm here, not there!" He laughed as he mailed it and wondered what the other employees would think of that one!

Also while walking the northern section of the Pennine Way, Roland walked into a remote mountain refuge hut and met a person who would have an influence on him which would steer him down a different road of life, likely a better one in the long run. After all, Roland didn't perfectly fit in, like most of society did, and he was realizing that being an employee for a company was just not for him.

The fellow he met was named Ivanhoe. He was an artist and a unique one, to say the least. He told Roland he had done numerous drawings and paintings of scenes from alien worlds! Wow! Roland mentioned that was a major interest of his also, and he immediately expressed interest in seeing his artwork. Ivanhoe also told Roland that he had amazingly clear dreams, and he related several strange experiences of his life. He had an excellent photographic memory, and he could accurately draw the images of what he saw in his mind. They had a very interesting discussion, and Roland definitely told him about his April 1993 dream. Ivanhoe found that amazing indeed. So, he related to Roland a fantastic dream from an alien world that he had experienced last year. Roland realized that Ivanhoe was very adept at astral travel, and they talked for two hours. Then they parted ways. They would see each other again two years later. They would also remain in contact by mail and by telephone.

Roland spent the night by himself in that remote mountain refuge hut. Ivanhoe went to camp several miles south of there. Roland felt somewhat stunned that he had just met and had a very unique conversation with a person like Ivanhoe about subjects, such as other levels of reality. Roland had been hoping he would meet someone like that along the time line, and now he had.

* * *

June 5, 1994

Martoncíon and his son, Selím were observing through a holographic window from their higher level in the world of the spirits. Igor was with them, as well.

"Success! Success indeed!" Selím told Igor. They shook hands in truimph.

"We got them to meet each other," said Selím.

"That will be very beneficial to both of them in the years to come," Igor commented.

"Yes, their paths have crossed," Martoncíon stated with happiness, "and my protectee Ivanhoe is aware of it in his own way."

"We can be very proud of this important meeting between Roland and Ivanhoe," said Selím. "This is a great day for all of us."

"Right you are, Selím," Igor agreed.

"Chris was an important link for us," Martoncíon pointed out. "I'm glad that . . ."

* * *

Roland had been lured into travelling over to England by his friend Chris, who was living in London. Chris had been writing him letters inviting him to come over so that they could go travelling and hiking together. However, shortly before Roland arrived, Chris had gotten a serious girlfriend, and the situation was a different kettle of fish, altogether. Apart from a tour from tree to tree in London's Kew Gardens, Chris wanted to spend all of his time with his new girlfriend who he was totally in love with, and each of the three times that Roland stopped by to visit, Chris seemingly had to rush off to see his girlfriend shortly after Roland arrived. Needless to say, Roland felt in second position.

In addition to that, Chris had angrily refused to take Roland to the airport on the grounds that Roland's £10 offer wasn't good enough. Chris had also complained to him for expecting him to take him to the airport. Roland was wondering if Chris was a true friend after all, and he later got his answer. Despite several letters that Roland wrote Chris afterwards, he never ever heard from him again. However, he did receive an angry letter from Chris' former female landlord who had intercepted and opened his mail! That was a hard situation for

Roland to swallow. He really thought he had made a true friend in Chris, especially with their common interest in trees and travelling. It just didn't make any sense. Roland was coming to realize that most people do not have it in them to forgive one another and that friendships are easily broken over seemingly small disagreements. Roland also suspected that Chris had been jealous of Roland for having been paid three months of severance pay and for having therefore had the freedom to travel to Great Britain.

Despite the obvious rejection by Chris, the lure did serve a major purpose. Roland was at the right place at the right time to meet Ivanhoe. In fact, Ivanhoe had told Roland shortly after they had met in that remote mountain refuge hut that they were meant to meet. Had Chris not been seemingly caused to write those letters of invitation, Roland likely would not have visited Great Britain in 1994. After all, Chris had not been genuine with his invitations. He just thought he had.

Though Roland never knew it, Chris had been scared off by a strange dream he had had about Roland.

Chris was hiking along a trail with a group of friends, including Roland. Chris was the only one among them with an orange in his backpack. Suddenly, Roland disappeared in a flash of white light, and they saw it! Chris and his friends then rummaged Roland's backpack, which had stayed behind, and they found a bunch of occult books, drugs, and other satanic materials. They threw it all away and continued hiking up the trail. Then they were really given a scare when Roland made a mysterious appearance several miles up the trail. As they approached Roland, he walked over to a tree and stood by it. Roland's backpack was beside him, and in a sneering manner, he was bouncing Chris' orange up and down in his hand!

Chris woke up in sheer fright! He was screaming, and his girlfriend, who was in bed with him, did what she could to eventually calm him down.

Even though Roland never did drugs nor occult satanic rituals in real life, for Chris' general paranoia of occult sciences, and his inability to be straightforward, he erroneously believed that Roland did. That was the real reason for Chris' rejection of Roland. Plus while Roland was sight-seeing in London, Chris took the liberty of disrespectfully rummaging through Roland's backpack, dumping the contents on the bed to search for the above said materials, none of which he found. When Roland returned, he found his backpack all topsy turvy and shoved into the corner of the room! He was not best pleased. The mistake that had been made was that while Roland was visiting, he casually told Chris about his interesting April 1993 dream, which resulted in Chris having his nightmare. That loss of friendship with Chris really made Roland sad.

When Roland returned home from his trip to Great Britain, he decided not to go back to work for a company. He didn't like the atmosphere of the company he worked for, anyway.

One day he went over to visit his Spanish teacher, Isalia. She and her husband Clayton lived on a fine expanse of wooded acreage. They had a nice long driveway that led back to the most quaint cabin one could imagine. There was a beautiful Spruce tree that grew next to the corner of the house. The yard, or meadow, was nicely kept and plenty of trees, most of them Elms, grew throughout. There were other outbuildings, the main one being Clayton's immaculate and well kept woodshop. Behind the house, the land dropped sharply to reach the banks of Hurricane Creek, one of the northern tributaries of the wild and scenic Duck River.

Isalia had just retired, and she was now taking up flower gardening as a wonderful hobby. In fact, she enjoyed it so much that she felt like a bird let out of its cage. From time to time, Roland would come and do work for her and Clayton.

"So, what are you going to do now?" Isalia asked Roland. "You've been let go from your job."

"I believe I'm going to go back to carpentry and painting. It gives me more freedom to travel instead of only having one or two weeks off per year. Plus, I've got some ideas going, and I want to do some artwork."

"Well, you know that wreck happened for a reason," Isalia pointed out.

"I have to admit that wreck was strange the way it happened. It was so sudden."

"I know. You see, life has a destiny to it, and you were steered off that course and put on the right road."

"I . . . well, I do feel like I was barking up the wrong tree."

"That's right," Isalia agreed. "It wasn't your destiny."

Roland and Isalia talked for some time. She gave Roland some spiritual guidance, and she recommended a book called *A Course in Miracles* for him to read.

During that summer and fall, Roland worked several days over at Isalia and Clayton's place. There were numerous flower bulbs and shrubs to plant, and Roland helped with landscaping, building rock walls and flower beds. Isalia was so impressed that she told Roland that, in a past life, he must have been in on the design of the great pyramids of Egypt. Clayton was so impressed with Roland's rock work that he hired him to repair the top of his chimney. Both of them were very complimentary, and they very much appreciated Roland.

Sometimes, Isalia worked alongside Roland, and they had conversations. Roland told her stories and told her about his relationships with other people he had known. He told her about Ivanhoe, about Chris, and also about several women he had known in past years. Isalia mentioned to Roland again that she had placed an order with those "upstairs" for a wife for him. They enjoyed their conversations, and Roland looked upon Isalia as a guiding light, in some ways. He confided in her and told her personal stories.

Roland had been reading various books pertaining to philosophy and religions, and he talked to her some more about the concept of how it's possible for a spirit to choose where and in what family it's going to be born. Isalia explained to Roland about the concept, how it works, and that it is the belief of the Mormon religion.

Isalia kept Roland updated on how her cousins, the Quevalos, were doing. She told him about Esalina and her son, Guillermo, and she said that Guillermo had recently gotten a serious girlfriend and was possibly heading toward marriage. Roland missed Mexico, and he wanted to return there and make amends with the Quevalos.

Isalia also told Roland about Danny and his family. He was happily married to a wonderful wife. Their careers were going very well, and they had two children.

She also told Roland about how well Hugh was doing with his news and reporting career. Recently, Hugh was asked during an interview who had been the most influential along the lines of spirituality during his life, and he had replied that it was his Spanish teacher, Isalia. A comment of honor that was indeed.

In January 1995, Roland became inspired to make a calendar of unique scenes from alien worlds. Several scenes came from that special April 1993 dream. In fact Roland would paint enough drawings for several calendars, which he would later compile into a book. Plus, he was communicating with Ivanhoe to see if he wanted to send over some copies of his paintings. Perhaps Roland could compile a calendar for him, as well.

By this time, Roland had decided not to return to a company for work. He would return to working for himself with his carpentry and painting business and doing artwork in his spare time. Plus, he would have more time to travel, while if he were working for a company, he would only get two weeks off per year, if he was lucky. With Roland's strong desire to travel, he knew that working for a company was not an option.

In June 1995, Ivanhoe finally sent Roland some copies of his excellent paintings and artwork. Impressive was an understatement. They were fabulous! In fact, Ivanhoe had just obtained a computer paint program and had generated some fantastic scenes from that, as well. Some of the scenes looked like they were from clear the other side of the galaxy! Roland looked at the scenes over and over, admiring Ivanhoe's accuracy and precision. Roland called him immediately, thanked him for sharing them with him, and he recommended that he definitely do a calendar. He said he would think about it seriously.

Roland went to visit friends in Nashville that afternoon, and he took the copies of Ivanhoe's artwork with him. His friends were awe inspired, to say the least! While in Nashville, Roland went to an office supply store, and he made some color copies of the artwork, which he would store in a different building on his parents' farm. Roland was that way with a lot of documents, keeping archival copies in another building.

While Roland was there making the copies, he kept noticing one of the fellow workers. He came across as very familiar. *Who is that person?* Roland thought to himself. *Why does he look so familiar?* Roland continued making the copies as he thought about it.

Also that summer, Isalia suddenly called Roland with *great news* for him. Her son Laurence had made a deal with a computer software business where he lived out West. He needed an associate in the business, and he came to Tennessee for a visit. Roland drove over to Isalia and Clayton's house to talk over the business plans with Laurence. They got in Isalia's car, and she drove them to several stores while Laurence explained the great business plan to Roland and how there was quite a promise of decent income from selling the valuable software to different businesses. They also visited one of the computer supply stores to see what was available as a used computer for Roland, as he still didn't have one of his own.

As they walked into the store, Isalia told both Roland and Laurence, "I think of any people in the world, both of you deserve happiness." That was a very nice comment from Isalia.

Laurence's plan was for Roland to attend a three day training session in Salt Lake City, Utah later in the summer. That actually worked out well for Roland, as he was planning to drive out there and visit a ranch in Montana for a month, where he would work, and *also* have a place to concentrate and do paintings for another calendar. He drove out there in mid July, and in late August, he drove to Jackson, Wyoming, and to the High Uintas mountains in northeast Utah to hike and camp a few days.

After that, he drove over to Pleasant Grove, Utah and visited with one of his friends from school. His name was Elton, and he received Roland to stay in his house with his wife and family.

Roland attended the training session, and he realized how disorganized the company was, and months later, as he would find out, they never finished designing the software sufficiently, and they went out of business.

Well, as it turned out, Elton's wife wasn't best pleased by Roland's visit, even though he was friendly to everyone. She was just that way, not wanting to serve Roland meals until everyone else was served first. When Roland left Elton's house after the training session, he asked Elton if he could stay in the future. Elton skirted the answer, and after Roland persisted in asking three times, Elton answered yes, but for Roland to call first. Roland realized that something had cooled down in Elton and his family, not that he had done anything wrong, but he just noticed. What had happened? It concerned Roland. Elton and his family had always been very friendly and receiving in the past when Roland had visited them on previous trips out West.

He left and drove over to Mt. Timpanogos, and he hiked to the top of it. The views were spectacular. Over the next few days, Roland drove back home to Tennessee.

*   *   *

CHAPTER 2

THE RETURN OF ROLAND

In January 1996, Roland returned to Bustamante to visit the Quevalos again, in hopes of restoring the lost friendship with them. It had been nearly four years since he had been there. Roland had talked to Isalia and said that he missed Bustamante and the Quevalos, even though things had gone sour. She advised him to write the Quevalos a letter asking them to forgive him. Of course, he knew the Quevalos were the ones who were much more at fault, but nevertheless, he agreed that was a good idea, and he typed out a one-page letter in Spanish. Isalia proofread it, and then he mailed it to them. That had been two months ago. Isalia had also phoned the Quevalos and asked them to forgive Roland, and they did because Isalia had told them to.

Roland drove his white 1980 Ford LTD station wagon with a 6 cylinder manual which he had, with considerable difficulty, installed in the car. He stayed overnight with cousins in Dallas, and he arrived in Bustamante on the afternoon of the second day, January 2, 1996. He first stopped by Lorenzo's house. They happily greeted each other. Roland had forgotten a considerable part of his Spanish, but over the course of the next two weeks, he would recall it again.

Lorenzo took Roland over to his family's house and place of business, and all of the Quevalos were glad to see him. He expressed his regrets about writing that letter to them four years ago. Lorena responded by saying that what had happened four years ago was the past and that this was a new year. She was always the nicest of the Quevalo sisters, and that was a nice forgiving comment indeed. Roland gave them some gifts, including some items that Isalia had sent with him. Roland asked them if they had received his letter, and they said they hadn't. That wasn't surprising. The mail system in Mexico was just that way, and it was a common occurrence that some mail . . . just didn't arrive.

They invited him into the kitchen to eat lunch with them, and they caught each other up on the latest events. Roland also met their maid whose name was Lavinia. She seemed a friendly enough woman. Little did Roland know how well he would get to know her and her whole family in the years that would come.

Chely and Vico came over by chance, and Chely offered her father's vacant house as a place for Roland to stay. Several of the Quevalos went with Roland to the location which was one kilometer from the Quevalo's residence. They mopped the dusty floor and loaned Roland a cot to sleep on. He was feeling truly welcomed back to Bustamante.

Each day, Roland would walk or drive to the Quevalos for the day, and he visited with Lorenzo and Pancho. Sometimes, he visited with the Quevalo sisters. They took Roland over to their new shop in the lower end of town. It was across from the soccer field, a good location indeed. Every weekend, they sold concessions and baked goods to the players and spectators, and the business was thriving.

Roland enjoyed his time with the Quevalos, and they told stories. One night, Mr. Quevalo, age 89, told him stories of giants (extraterrestrials) that visited the region many thousands of years ago.

He made several trips to Sabinas Hidalgo, and he looked up some friends of his who he had known in 1992. Their names were Ricardo and Alicia Velazco, and they were glad to see Roland. They ran an electric repair shop which was called Taller Electrico.

One day, Roland took Lorenzo to Monterrey, and they did several errands. They also dropped by Esalina Velazco's house. She was standing on the street in front of her house, as she was waiting for a taxi. She was glad to see Roland and they briefly visited until the taxi arrived.

Roland also went hiking in the mountains, and one of the times, he was taken up there by Daniel Mata, who made regular trips to the mountains to collect plants, herbs, and Fan Palm leaves. As they passed by the cave, Daniel told Roland that his son-in-law, Ramiro Gomez was now the cave guide. Rogelio had stepped down from that position last year.

A few days later, Roland went up in the mountains by himself, and he climbed the west ridge of the Lion's Head Mountain, turned left, and followed the main ridge to the section of the mountains above the caves, and began his descent. He must have lost his way, because he came to an impassable dropoff, had to turn around and head back uphill, turn right, and descend through the creek gorge to the bottom of the mountain.

It was a rough descent, and never had he been in a more dangerous situation in his whole life! Darkness was less than an hour away, and he came to frightening dropoffs in the creek. Roland maneuvered himself down each dropoff, except the last one where he had to purposefully let himself drop 3 meters! He hung onto the cliff edge, having let himself down as far as he could, let go, and hoped for the best. It was a miracle, and he got up without broken bones.

He still had one more descent to make where he had to let himself slide down a 60° angle slick rocky surface for some 30 meters and right into a pool of water at the bottom of the slide! He got up from that, soaking wet, and he walked down the rest of the creek and back into town. He was a little banged up, but he would be all right in a few days.

When he arrived in town, he found Daniel Mata, and he told him of his precarious descent. Daniel was very surprised that Roland had made it out of there alive and walking! He repeatedly told him, "La unica salida es caer," saying that the only way down that gorge is to fall. He informed Roland that he was the only one who had ever descended that route without breaking any bones and still walking, and it was indeed a miracle.

Roland also visited Lorenzo and told him what happened.

That night, as Roland lay in bed, he couldn't sleep very well. He shuddered from feelings of panic, realizing how close he came to being literally stuck in the mountains and possibly dying. Miraculously, he had lived through it, and he was glad to be safely back in Bustamante.

Roland decided he would rectify the situation and clear a trail up the mountains above the cave. There was already a trail there, but it was severely overgrown, and had it been more visible, he would have located it when descending the creek gorge and would have saved himself the harrowing, treacherous descent he had to take!

On January 14, on a Sunday morning, Roland set out shortly after the crack of dawn with his daypack and a machete. He was walking on the gravel road leaving Bustamante for the foot of the mountains.

A young fellow pulled up in his blue 1973 Chrysler Dart and said to Roland, "¿Vas para arriba?" asking if he was going up in the mountains.

"Sí," Roland answered, saying yes.

"Vámonos," said the fellow in a friendly manner, immediately inviting him to come with him.

Roland walked around the front of the car and got in. Immediately, he felt a strong sense of familiarity, only the third or fourth time he had experienced this in his life. His name was Leonardo. He was age 22, and he lived in Villaldama, the next town over. Roland felt like he had known him before, and he felt the strong connection of immediate friendship. Leonardo placed the column shift lever in first gear, engaged the clutch, and proceeded to drive him to the cono at the top end of the road. They hiked up to the cave and talked about various things along the way. The two of them enjoyed their time together and were pleased to meet each other, as Leonardo had been totally unsuccessful in bringing other friends with him for this excursion. They sat near the cave entrance while they waited for Ramiro, the cave guide. After chatting a while longer, Roland decided to head further up the mountain to clear a section of the overgrown trail for future use. They swapped addresses, wished each other well, and then they parted. Roland felt somewhat stunned, realizing that he had just made a good friend.

Also, while Roland was in Bustamante those two weeks, the Quevalo family and Chely had asked him to do a favor for the church. They had several pages of literature about the Señor de Tlaxcala, a 300-year-old mannequin of Jesus that was in the main church in Bustamante. It was also about the Tlaxcaltecan Indians who had settled Bustamante several hundred years ago, and it included a brief history of Bustamante, as well. They needed it to be translated to English. Roland went to work and spent hours translating the difficult Spanish which was absolutely full of run-ons. He ended up taking the work home to Tennessee with him, letting Isalia check it and proofread it. A week later, he faxed the finished typed pages to Bustamante.

*   *   *

THE TLAXCALTECANS IN BOCA DE LEONES OF THE NUEVO REINO DE LEON

The venerated statue of the crucified Christ called "Señor de Tlaxcala" (Lord of Tlaxcala) has a well documented history intertwined with the history of the Tlaxcaltecan Indians. Those indigenous ones presented themselves as docile to the conquerors and were used as allies by Hernán Cortés. In 1591, a written document was sent from King Felipe II, and it gave to the Tlaxcaltecan Indians numerous royal priviledges so that they could accompany the Spaniards in their expeditions.

By order of Virrey Luis de Velazco, 400 families left Tlaxcala with the protection of the Spanish crown, and they advanced to the Norte de la Nueva España (North of the New Spain) and founded villages that served as peaceful settlements for the Chichimecas tribes.

In 1591, some Indians left the Tlaxcaltecan settlement, which was called Pueblo de San Esteban de Nueva Tlaxcala and was near Saltillo. They arrived at the region known as the Boca de Leones in the Nuevo Reino de León. After learning that there was water, they applied for a license to settle in that region on June 8, 1686. They applied to the governor, Augustín de Echéverz y Savízar, marquis of San Miguel de Aguayo. Already in the government of Francisco Cuervo y Valdes, on September 16, 1687, they were given legal possession, "by the captain Deigo de Villarreal. Serving as witness was the titled José Guajardo, beneficiary priest of the said kingdom," and the population came to be called San Miguel de Aguayo (today Bustamante, Nuevo León) in honor of Marqués de Aguayo. The Tlaxcaltecans who received the possession were Melchor Cáseres, José Felipe, Santiago and Silvestre Salvador.

Three months after the founding of the Boca de Leones, the Tlaxcaltecans invited the Franciscan fathers Francisco Esteves and Francisco Hidalgo, of the College of Santa Cruz of Querétaro to found a mission there. They had not been welcome in Santiago de la Monclova.

The patent for the mission of the Boca de Leones with the title of Nuestra Señora de los Dolores was signed in Querétaro on August 18, 1689 by the Father Fontcubera, president of the capitol. On the following September 15, the bishop of Guadalajara, don Santiago de León Garavito, authorized jurisdiction of the mission.

The diverse names of the Tlaxcalteca foundation have been: village of San Miguel de Aguayo, mission of Nuestra Señora de los Dolores de la Nueva Tlaxcala, San Miguel de Nuestra Señora de los Dolores, and today Bustamante, Nuevo León.

At some ten leagues from Los Dolores, the captain Juan Villarreal and his companions Francisco Barvarigo and Antonio González discovered the first mines in the Boca de Leones. In the Barvarigo terrains, they founded that year the Real y Minas de San Pedro de Boca de Leones, today known as Villaldama, N.L. In that village, the monks of the College of Zacatecas later founded the Franciscan mission.

The historical clergyman Antonio Portillo Valadez, points out that "in the territory called 'Boca de Leones' the Tlaxcaltecan village was the first to be established and be known as the Boca de Leones (today Bustamante, N.L.), and it's where the first mission of the College of Querétaro was founded, meanwhile the Real y Minas de San Pedro de Boca de Leones (today Villaldama, N.L.) was two leagues from the above by the old road, and it's where the mission of the College of Zacatecas was founded."

THE LORD OF TLAXCALA

Published in front of a "History and Novena dedicated to the Lord of Tlaxcala" by José Antonio Portillo Valadez, when he was a priest in Bustamante, we have the documents of the history of the venerable statue of the Christ, that until now, we knew of it only in a short phrase that preceded the novena composed by Francisco Antonio González de Paredes, and published in 1800.

The first document is the one of a gift of a statue of the crucified Christ that was in very poor condition. It was donated on April 26, 1688 by the priest Nicolás de Saldívar in Real de Ramos Salinas (San Luis Potosí), in behalf of Bernabé García, native and neighbor of the area, and also in behalf of his sons and heirs. It had the following conditions: "That within six months the statue shall be repaired; that on every Palm Saturday the statue shall be taken to the parish of Real de Ramos; and on every Holy Thursday it shall be taken out in a procession and that twelve candles shall accompany the statue with each candle weighing at least half a pound. The said gift was presented as firm and valid in Real de Ramos on April 26, 1688."

The historical news that precedes the novena, written by González de Paredes, says that the Indian finished restoring the statue, and that "after some time, Bernabé García decided to move from the village of Ramos al Real de Santiago de las Sabinas, near the parish of San Pedro de Boca de Leones del Nuevo Reino de León. He obtained first from the priest don Nicolás de Saldívar license and permission to carry the sacred statue with him and his wife to the said Real de las Sabinas. After several years, Bernabé died, leaving his wife the treasure of the sacred statue."

After Bernabé died, his widow Ana María, taking advantage of the visit of the bishop of Guadalajara, Fray Felipe Galindo, asked him to give her a document of the statue of the Christ as a protection "so that no one under any pretext could take away the statue that don Nicholás de Saldívar made as a donation." On December 31, 1700 in Real de las Sabinas, the bishop signed the document and sent it to Ana María "so that it serves to her as a security so that no one can take away the afore mentioned from her nor her said heirs. Anyone wishing to take it away would be severely penalized as it was her right to do so."

The widow, Ana María, being "up in her years, being in need of food, and not having anyone to look after her," made a pact with the Tlaxcaltecan Indians to donate the statue to them forever, with the understanding that they would help her in her sustenance by supplying her with 621 kilograms of corn each year during the rest of her life, and thus they made a verbal contract.

By 1715, being in San Miguel de Aguayo the titled don Francisco de Barbadillo Victoria, who would be governor of Nuevo Reino de León 4 years later, was notified of the donation made by the Indian, Ana María, of the statue of the crucified Christ to the village of San Miguel de Aguayo, and the Tlaxcaltecan authorities asked Barbadillo to authorize the remake of previous documents and that they write on their sheet of paper: "We appear before you to let you know that the afore mentioned gave to us the statue that don Nicolás de Saldívar made on behalf of her late husband. The document and statue that don Fray Felipe Galindo, bishop of Guadalajara, gave to her were in bad condition due to the passage of time. She is getting old and might lose her memory. Therefore, while she can testify of the veracity of the above, we ask that the clerk take her testimony and documents and rewrite them for our protection."

The original papers made by the priest Saldívar were filed along with the documents given to Ana María by the Bishop Galindo. The new document was also filed stating the donation given to the Tlaxcaltecan Indians of San Miguel de Aguayo, under the direction of the lawyer Francisco de Barbadillo Victoria. The property was declared nontransferable so that the statue would be forever guarded and worshipped as they had promised by word of mouth. The notarized document "gave validity to the transfer and rights so that the Tlaxcaltecans would never alienate themselves from it, said document to be precise and irrevocable. The placing was in the church of this village and in no other place." The following people signed the solemn deed: the governor of the village, Diego Bautista; the mayor Augustín de la Cruz; the councilmen, Juan Antonio de la Cruz and Francisco Clemente; the elder judge, Francisco González; and the clerk of the village, Felipe de Santiago. With the authority and in the presence of the lawyer Barbadillo, the clerk of his majesty and receiver Manuel de la Torre, signed that solemn deed on December 19, 1718.

Since then, the old Misión de San Miguel in the parish of Boca de Leones, started to call the statue of the crucified Jesus, our Lord of Tlaxcala.

The devotion to the venerated statue extends to the whole district and to the distant places where the old inhabitants of Bustamante live. Within the conditions of modern life, it solemnizes itself with popular and religious celebrations that are celebrated with a novena beginning July 28 with pilgrimages, Tlaxcaltecan dances with matachines, prayers and songs of worship, to terminate on the day of the fiesta of August 6 with a devout procession in which the statue of the Lord of Tlaxcala is carried through the streets of the village.

The archaic celebration is still kept today, as stated in penances, tribulations, and perils, "Worthy be the Lord of Tlaxcala!"

*   *   *

On the evening of the day Roland had met Leonardo, he asked Lola if he could make a call to Monterrey so he could talk to Leonardo and find out how things went for him during the excursion of the cave. Lola told him no, that the call would be very expensive. Roland felt taken aback at the turn of hospitality, and he realized that there was probably some residual resentment from four years earlier now coming back to life.

The Return of Roland

The next morning, Roland went to Lorenzo and complained that Lola had not let him use the phone. With that said, he took Roland over to his parents' house, took him to the phone, and personally let him use it. Roland gave Lorenzo some money and succeeded in phoning Leonardo from the Quevalo's residence. Leonardo said he enjoyed the tour of the cave. He asked Roland to be sure and look him up the next time he comes to Mexico which would be a year later. Roland assured him he would, and they wished each other well.

Before Roland could leave, Lorenzo's sister Olana made her appearance in the room where the phone was, and she firmly told Lorenzo to tell Roland to be sure and pay for the phone call because Lola had said so. Lorenzo was so annoyed by his sister's inhospitality that he chased her away, angrily telling her that Roland had already paid!

Before Roland left Bustamante he bought some Fan Palm leaves for future use in weaving chair bottoms and backs. The next day, he left Bustamante to go back home to Tennessee.

When he crossed the Colombia-Solidarity Bridge, the U.S. Customs officials were rather sarcastic with him as they gave him a thorough inspection, complete with running a sniffing dog through the whole car. Matters were made worse when a tall slender negroe agriculture inspector with an *attitude* came over and told Roland he would not be able to bring in the 2 sacks of Fan Palm leaves. They might be contaminated. Roland contested and told the man that he had brought leaves in four years earlier without a problem, and that these leaves had been boiled in salt water for 30 minutes. They were *sterile*.

The man didn't like Roland's defending his case, and he rudely told Roland, "No, it's *two* hours at 120 degrees, and *you* don't have a permit!"

Roland explained that he needed the leaves to weave chair bottoms, and the officer said he couldn't help him there. So, Roland insisted on seeing the regulations in writing, and the officer got irritated. Roland still insisted, and the officer eventually obliged, but only let Roland glance at the documents, and he refused to give Roland a Xerox copy of it! The Ag officer was a brick wall, and Roland had to leave the Palm leaves there, to be destroyed. When he got home, he complained to the U.S. Dept. of Agriculture and learned that it was indeed permissible to bring in dried Fan Palm leaves. A written permit was *not* required. Roland was right, and while they apologized, he never got his leaves back. The next year, he would bring in a total of 5 feed sackfuls of the leaves to make up for the past, and he would carry documentation and copies of the department letters to prove his point.

He picked some Fan Palmetto leaves from a forest in Louisiana on the way home, and he stopped by his cousins' house in Mandeville overnight.

Roland was so glad to have restored his friendship with the Quevalo family. However, he was having a few second thoughts because of the way Lola and Olana had been inhospitable about the use of the phone. He decided to let that slide and not count that against them.

More than anything, Roland was really glad to have his new friendship with Leonardo. He felt like that was an extra added bonus and reward for his having done the translation for the church. Two weeks after returning home, Roland received a nice letter from Leonardo, telling him how his tour of the caves went and for Roland to call him when he returns next year. Roland felt really content with the whole situation, and he *told Isalia all about it*. She was happy for him.

*   *   *

During 1996, Roland undertook several projects. By now, he had enough drawings done in his spare time to do several calendars, and he managed to get some of them published. A calendar company in Nashville happily took on the project. They were very impressed with the scenes, and they decided to make *three* calendars and compile and publish a book, as well. Roland was very pleased, and over the next several months, he worked with them as they carried the project through to completion.

He continued with his carpentry and painting business, as well. One of the first major projects he did for several weeks after arriving home from Mexico in mid January was to help Isalia and her husband, Clayton, build a large deck up above the banks of Hurricane Creek bordering their property. It was a major project, as it turned out, and Isalia named it the "big white elephant." Roland had started it in December, and he finished it with them when he returned from Mexico. It dragged out over a period of two months, and it was more costly than Isalia anticipated, partly because she had expanded the original proposed size, in addition to Clayton's detailed and precise technical drawings of the deck plans, which he spent several weeks preparing.

Roland was realizing how much of a perfectionist Clayton was, but even still, he didn't show an obsession with it. He did his perfection so smoothly and with the greatest of ease and skill. Roland appreciated him and his immaculate, well organized machine shop, and he knew that Clayton had great talent. He had been a high school woodshop teacher, and he was also a fine wood sculptor. Clayton spent a lot of time in his woodshop, even living there, and he enjoyed his hobbies. He had a den in the back of the shop where he would relax at times and watch TV. There was a wood burning stove and a couch and even a bed. It was a nice get-away place for him.

While in Mexico, Roland had bought a ceramic statue of an Indian, known as Geronimo. It stood around three feet tall. He brought it home, and one morning he took it over to Isalia and Clayton's house and gave it to Clayton. He was so pleasantly surprised to receive that statue that he commented, "This is my pride and *joy*!" Clayton continued to admire it, and he took it to his woodshop and placed it in his favorite and most honored spot. Roland worked with them on the deck that day, and at the end of the day when Roland got in his truck to go home, he found a small box of wood chisels on his seat. Each chisel had a wooden handle with the initial R stamped on it. Roland asked Clayton about them, and he kindly told Roland, "Happy Birthday." That was very kind of Clayton. He was sincerely grateful for that Geronimo statue.

With Clayton's precise plans drawn out, he and Roland, and even Isalia over the next several weeks made serious progress on that deck. They built and built, placing pillars in precise concrete forms, and they built the floor. As they were nailing down the floor, they ran out of the 16-foot deck floor boards. Isalia gave Roland a look of total blame, and though Roland thought he had calculated correctly, they were considerably lacking on the required deck lumber to finish the floor. Clayton saw no problem with it, realizing that's just what went along with big projects like this, but Isalia wasn't pleased at all, and she went on and on, scolding Roland for having miscalculated. Roland did his best to explain, but that wasn't good enough for her. Though she was displeased for days, she ordered the extra lumber, costing them an extra $330. She finally got over it and was pleased with the deck after all.

Two days later, when the extra lumber was delivered by Lowe's, Roland went to the pile to start taking the pieces to the deck. He noticed that they looked short, and when he measured them, they were 14 feet instead of 16 feet. He told Clayton and Isalia. Clayton was not pleased with Lowe's mistake, but Isalia freaked out and cussed repeatedly. That upset Roland, as hearing foul language was *never* pleasurable to him. He was surprised at Isalia, the way she ranted and raved with no sense of control. Clayton calmed her down, went to the phone, and called Lowe's. In an hour, they arrived with the correct lumber, delivered it, and recollected the mistaken lumber.

Later that day, as fate would have it, Roland accidently bruised his finger. He lost his temper and threw the skillsaw onto the deck floor. Isalia saw Roland's reaction. She asked Roland if he was all right, and he answered that he didn't know yet. At the end of that day, Isalia told Roland as a friend that it was unprofessional for him to have thrown his tantrum. Roland pointed out that she needed to put herself in his place and see how she would have reacted. As she went on to scold Roland more, he quickly pointed out that it had very much displeased him how she had also been unprofessional and lost her temper this morning at the wrong length lumber and had cussed repeatedly! They finished correcting each other, and Roland went home for the day.

Another day, Isalia was agitated with the form and shape of the deck steps, and as Roland was in the process of figuring out how to build them under Clayton's suggestions, which were good ones, she suddenly snapped to her husband, "Forget it! Just build them straight!"

He reacted angrily to her and said, "Don't get so *angry* about it, Isalia!"

Clayton didn't like the impatient nature of his wife. In more recent years, they didn't get along very well, and as a result, Clayton spent more time in his woodshop than he did in the main house with his wife. In past years they used to travel together to Mexico every summer. However, for the last ten years, they had taken nearly all their trips separately.

Also, there were several days that Roland had wanted to come over and finish the deck, but Isalia was going to be away on a trip and would therefore not be at home. Roland said that he and Clayton could finish the deck without her, but she objected to that and then said that she must be present for them to finish the deck, because of Clayton's delicate character. Roland thought that was most strange, and he detected a sense of mistrust, but he had no choice but to accept it and wait until Isalia would return.

Several weeks later, Roland finished the deck project with them. They were all pleased. Roland and Isalia put any differences behind them, forgave each other, and remained friends.

Roland and Ivanhoe kept in contact with each other by mail and by phone. In March, Ivanhoe took a most terrible case of the flu, which went into pneumonia. He was gravely ill for several weeks, and when Roland found out about it, he decided he would try something. He called up Isalia one night and asked her if she would say a prayer for Ivanhoe, and Roland requested that she ask that a healer be sent to Ivanhoe.

Isalia said she would be glad to, and she said a sincere prayer that night.

Around a week later, a surprise letter arrived from Ivanhoe. He told Roland that overnight, he had been cured. Some beings had come to visit him, and they made repairs to his body. When he woke up in the morning, he was fine. The grave illness was completely *gone*.

Wow! How great! Roland called up Isalia and told her the miraculous news, and he let her know that Ivanhoe had been cured, coincidentally, the same night she had said her prayer!

Isalia was very glad to know that, and she told Roland that Clayton was always amazed at how she could pray for something, and it would almost always come true.

She told Roland that Clayton was not feeling so well himself. Roland was aware of that. He had noticed that Clayton didn't look as much alive as in past years.

"Why don't you say a prayer for him, too?" Roland asked Isalia.

"He doesn't want to continue to live."

"How do you know? Say one anyway," Roland advised her. "I never believed that saying a prayer could change an outcome, but I do now."

"Oh, they do," Isalia verified. "Saying prayers do change things."

"Then why don't you say one for Clayton?" Roland again suggested.

"Some people *need* their sicknesses. It's their destiny. Ivanhoe is still young, but Clayton doesn't want to live."

"Well, okay," said Roland.

"I hope you understand what I mean," said Isalia.

"Yeah, okay. Whatever, but I really am *amazed* that Ivanhoe was cured that same night you said your prayer. Thank you, Isalia."

"You're welcome, Roland. I was glad to do it. Keep reading that book: *A Course in Miracles.*"

*   *   *

In May 1996, Roland had an autograph party for his calendars and book compilation. It was a good clean party with no drinking nor smoking, just the way Roland liked it. Several of his friends and relatives and even some of his teachers came and bought the "calendars" and "books". The publisher had promised to have them off the press by May 9, but something mysterious happened, and the printer couldn't be found. They were delayed, and it would be several months before they would finally be printed. Despite the setback, Roland went through with the "autographing" and he collected checks and wrote receipts to each person who bought from him. He thanked them and said he would deliver the calendars and books as soon as they would be off the press.

Isalia was one of the people who came to the party, and she bragged to others about Roland and how he and she made "an awesome team" with all the work he had done out at her place, from landscaping work to the deck project, "the big white elephant." Roland was rather surprised at her enthusiastically positive comments, having remembered her disgust at the time. However, he was very glad to see that she had come around and so much appreciated his work after all.

A few nights later, Roland suddenly woke up with mysterious pain in his lower left abdomen! It didn't go away, and it persisted off and on for the next year! He bought some colon cleanser, which helped some, but still it was bothersome at times.

In May and June of 1996, Roland decided to go over to Great Britain and Spain to visit friends, including Ivanhoe, and another friend in northern Spain. He had done several carpentry jobs and had saved his money.

He visited Ivanhoe for several days, and he enjoyed his stay. They visited several of the ancient archaeological sites in the area, and Roland soon realized that Scotland had a lot of history behind it. They talked about numerous subjects. Roland again offered to publish a calendar for Ivanhoe, but he was still undecided at the time.

Unfortunately, they had a little disagreement which originated from certain areas of dissatisfaction about lack of appreciation on favors having been done. Roland wrote a letter after having stayed there, and he received a reply letter declaring that the friendship was terminated indefinitely with no wish from Ivanhoe to have any future contact at all! Roland just felt devastated, and it made him angry. He was realizing that for nearly every good friend which he had made during this decade, the friendship would sooner or later be sabotaged, or seemingly self destruct. He wondered why his good friendships were becoming seemingly impossible to keep!

He went to northern Spain to visit a friend there, and he enjoyed his stay with him and his family (parents and brother). Everything went all right, except that his friend was agitated nearly all the time because he was studying for final exams at the exact time Roland was there. Roland was unable to go at a later time because his plane flight back home from London, England was scheduled only a week later, and he had to be back in England in time to catch that flight.

Next, he went to the Pyrenees Mountains to hike and camp for several days. While he was camping among the European Beech trees, he had a dream about the Tulip Poplars, the *Liriodendrons*. He was looking at a special Poplar leaf that had a whole array of Poplar leaflets. It was from another variety of Poplar known as the Poplar Reale, a variety that doesn't exist on Earth's surface. When Roland woke up, he put two and two together and realized a revelation, from which he would do several more unique paintings. At least that realization was some compensation for him.

Later, back home in Tennessee, Roland was introduced to Chip Collins, age 24, by his long time friend Roger Schultz at the end of July 1996. Roland recognized Chip right away. He was the familiar fellow Roland had seen the year before at the office supply store, where he had copied Ivanhoe's excellent artwork. Roland was glad to meet a new friend, and he welcomed the opportunity. He was quite surprised to find out that Chip was Roger's next door neighbor! He was easy to relate to and was an energetic person with plenty of spark and enthusiasm. His name Chip was appropriate because he was indeed chipper. A week later, Roland went back over to the place of business to talk to him about a certain car part. Chip decided to take a break, went out into the parking lot and chatted with Roland for twenty minutes. He still came across as very familiar, and Roland didn't know why. No matter what, he knew he had made a new friend, and he had genuinely good feelings about it.

Finally in August, Roland's calendars and book compilation came off the press in Nashville. Nearly 10,000 copies were printed altogether. They were very impressive. He went to the printer and collected several boxes, and he appropriately delivered the calendars and books to those who had already ordered copies. He felt really content with himself, having published his artwork in such a fine format.

One of the first people to receive copies of Roland's book and calendars was Isalia. He went over to her house and proudly autographed them to her. She was thrilled, and she took him down to the deck by the creek. They placed Roland's finished products on the deck floor between them, joined hands, and she said a sincere prayer, asking for doors to open and for marketing success for both Roland and his published artwork. She said the prayer three times in English and once in Spanish. That was very kind of her, and Roland appreciated it.

"Thank you very much, Isalia," Roland told her.

"You're welcome. I wish you the best of success with it, and when you're famous one day, I'm going to proudly stand up and announce, 'I know him. He was my Spanish student.'"

*   *   *

Nuevo Wimbisenho

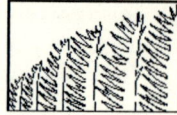

"What a grand intention of Isalia," Arfifra declared.

"Lovely indeed," Sojornbloc agreed.

"Looks like there will be some wonderful opportunities for us in this one," said Sasjurech.

"Indeed there will be," Arfifra verified.

"I'll see who I can contact," said Sasjurech.

"Let's see if we can achieve . . ."

*　　*　　*

In September, Roland drove out West for several weeks to go hiking and camping in the mountains of Oregon and California. While he was there, he realized numerous coincidences associated with Chip, including his phone number matching a number he had dialled in a dream over a year earlier, their age difference nearly matching that same number, and finally, Chip's phone number also having significance when compared to certain underlying numerical statistics in Ivanhoe's paintings from aliens worlds! Roland wondered what it was all leading up to.

While Roland was out West, he also visited his cousin who had three teenagers. He was glad to see Roland and was very impressed with his calendars and artwork, and they visited that evening. While they were talking, and with Roland's full intent of having a good visit with them, things quickly went sour when his cousin proceeded to rant and rave over a matter of state wilderness areas not charging admission fees to out of staters. Things "struck a chord" with his cousin, and he began scaring Roland. It made no sense until he caught the smell of alcohol on his cousin's breath. Roland took his things out of the house and slept in his car for the night, and he made a conviction right then and there that he would associate most closely *only* with people who don't drink. They would be his better friends. Roland talked to his cousin's teenage sons, and he told them that he would not be back. He had come for a friendly visit, not a ranting and raving spell! One of his sons gave Roland a friendly touch on the shoulder. The next morning, Roland's cousin was kind enough to offer an apology, which Roland accepted.

*　　*　　*

Roland thought back several years. From 1983 forward, he had been virtually unsuccessful in finding a travelling companion.

He studied hard in school, and he was the *Salutatorian* of his high school graduating class in 1984. He went on to study a degree in Electrical Engineering at Cookeville's Tennessee Technological University, graduating from there in 1991. He would have graduated sooner, but he had a strong desire to travel, and he took two separate years off and worked and travelled, going to Australia and New Zealand to backpack and bicycle. Besides, he needed a break from the rigorous school curriculum. Both of those trips he took by himself.

While he made friends at Tennessee Tech, he had quite a bit of difficulty finding a travelling companion to accompany him on summer trips to the western United States.

46

The Return of Roland

Despite posting advertisements at several universities, he had no takers. He was surprised that there weren't more people interested, and he soon discovered that nearly everyone had to work their tails off in the summer and therefore weren't free to travel. Granted, Roland had to work and earn his money too, but he was very frugal and earned his money on weekends during the school years and therefore was more freed up in the summers. However, there was one new friend who was genuinely excited and really wanted to go, but he, like most of the students, had to work in the summers.

In the summer of 1985, Roland drove out West for the first time. He had to go alone, but still he enjoyed the trip, backpacking and hiking in the mountains of several states. He visited his cousin and three sons for several days and had a great time. For the next three summers, he travelled out West again to enjoy more.

Finally, three years later in 1988, that same friend did accompany Roland, but much to Roland's dismay, his friend's heart was not in the trip. He had somehow lost most or all of his enthusiasm. That friend of his somehow, quite by fate obviously, secured a girlfriend only weeks before their departure date. Roland speculated that maybe his friend had gotten the girlfriend to justify his taking the trip. To be able to travel with Roland, (who was a friend of the same sex), he had to have a girlfriend in check, back home in Tennessee. That was important to him for his trip with Roland, to make it implicitly clear that he was not gay . . . as if Roland were gay.

As a result, his friend was lovesick, and for their whole trip his heart was back in Tennessee with her. He would call her by telephone every two days and have long conversations with her. Roland had to sit in the car and wait on him each time. His friend was in unhappy spirits much of the time, and what really got to Roland was how his friend, on the last day driving home, complained for three hours about everything Roland did to displease him. Roland had quite an earful, and he was shocked at how displeased his friend was, if he could still be called that. After he delivered him to his home in east Tennessee, their friendship went separate ways. Basically, Roland felt and knew that he had been second choice for the entire trip.

After that experience, Roland really wished even more for some fellow friend to travel with him on at least one trip out West, someone who he would really feel compatible with and whose heart would be in the trip . . . someone who would just *not* have a girlfriend. They would enjoy the trip together, go hiking and camping in the mountains and wilderness, and then drive home, content with each other about how well the trip went. How Roland wished for that to occur, to correct the 1988 trip with his malcontent friend. Even though Roland continued to talk with and invite people to travel with him, his wish had still not come true.

(Though Roland didn't realize it, there was one fellow who would have accompanied him. He had known him in 1983. Though Roland had thought of him many times over the years, he was somehow prevented from thinking of him in the right context so that he could have realized he was the one. Mysteriously, it had never occurred to Roland to invite him to travel with him.)

Roland had made friends and enjoyed several of them through the years, but the fact remained that he had not succeeded in finding a fellow friend to travel with on long trips. As a result, he felt like some cycle or pattern of life, in other words a jinx, had been preventing him from knowing and enjoying the friends he was really meant to have. In the years to come, he would set out to identify just what that jinx was, where it was coming from, and to bring it to a halt.

Roland thought about his new friend Chip from the office supply store. Chip used to have a girlfriend, but for a bad experience with her a couple of years earlier, he no longer had one. Perhaps Chip would travel with Roland in the future, and he wouldn't have to worry about lovesickness and long phone conversations taking place with a girlfriend. Roland might actually be number one, for a change.

*   *   *

When Roland returned home from his trip, it turned out that the Schultz immediately hired him for several weeks of work to be done around their house. At around 4 PM each day, Chip would arrive home next door from his work, and Roland used to walk over there to casually chat and visit with him. Chip used to tell some tall tales about his wild experiences, and they had some good laughs. To Roland, it seemed like destiny was working in his favor. He was enjoying the opportunity, and he realized that the reason he had the several weeks of work to do at the Schultz was so that he would have the chance to become friends with Chip.

Suddenly, three months after Roland and Chip had become seemingly good friends, he brushed Roland off for no real reason. Roland made efforts to talk to him to find out why he had suddenly changed. Each time he went to talk to Chip, he made himself appear very busy like he didn't have time to talk. It was appalling to Roland how Chip had mysteriously brushed him off, and he felt frustrated and hurt by what had happened. Who knows? Perhaps Chip had a dream that scared him off. At least Roland had the satisfaction that he would do some interesting paintings incorporating some of Chip's tall tales and experiences.

He was wondering why so many coincidences had been set up between him and Chip since the friendship was only a temporary one. Again, Roland's friendship was preceded by others, and Chip already had two other friends with whom he did things regularly. Roland was feeling somewhat lonely and rejected, having had considerable trouble making friends over the past five years! Many people were having trouble understanding Roland's personality. He realized he was never better than second place in anyone's mind, and that disturbed him. No one seemed to have time to spend with Roland as far as doing activities with him and going hiking with him.

Roland had sometimes consulted with Isalia about his friendships with other people, as she was a good friend of his and also his parents. He confided in her. He sometimes brought over literature that he had written, some of the matters private, and he let her read and have copies of them. He had gained enough trust in her to do so. Isalia was impressed at Roland's memory for details. She created a file folder with Roland's name on it, and it had a collection of stories Roland had written about several friends of his through the times, the latest one being Chip.

Even though Roland was willing to overlook it and continue his friendship with Chip, there was one thing about Chip that had really concerned him. He had told Roland a story about how he was at a party some years ago, and some gay man around 40 years old was sitting by him at the time. The man reached over and touched Chip on the leg. Chip was drunk at the time, and he instantly reacted with total anger, grabbed a VCR, and crashed it over the man's head, ruining the VCR, and knocking the man out! A few days later, Roland questioned Chip about his severity for only being touched on the leg, and Chip fervently explained that the man was *making advances* at him! Chip had also told the man that if he ever saw him again, he would kill him! Roland was surprised how angry Chip was about that, and years later. Perhaps the brush off was for the best, for reasons of Chip's volatile nature, but since Roland had achieved a decent friendship with him at the start, he wanted it to continue. After all, Roland was stubborn, and he had good reason. He had lost numerous friends through the decade, and he had to make a stand to the forces that be and declare that he was going to keep his friends!

Roland asked Isalia what she thought the problem was with his friendship with Chip, and she told him, "You know what I really think it is?"

Roland gestured her to continue.

"I think you're coming on too strong. You've scared him off."

Roland somewhat agreed with her, seeing how Chip had been acting recently, but he really didn't think he had been that much out of order. Yes, he had gone to Chip several times over the past month in efforts to speak to him, but then how *else* was he supposed to do it? Still, he felt disgusted at the increasing impossibility of making and *keeping* new friends.

Even Roland's previously obliging car insurance company had brushed him off! Roland's Ford LTD wagon had stopped running one day, and he realized the engine would have to be rebuilt. As a result, Roland wanted to insure one of his other cars for a couple of days, and they told him that would be the last time they would ever do it, no exceptions, not even to take one of his cars to the emissions testing station! The insurance company had changed hands, and the kind obliging insurance agents who used to work there had either retired or moved on. Anyway, Roland personally visited the office to appeal their decision, and they were cold shouldered to him. So, he wrote them a letter, and they wouldn't answer! Well, that irritated Roland. He went *straight* over their heads and complained about them to their superiors at the head office. They appreciated Roland's concern, attended to his needs, and they assigned him a different agent at a different office with the same insurance company. The new agent allowed him to add a different vehicle for a day or two from time to time. After all, he sometimes needed to drive a car not presently insured to the emissions testing station so he could register it, and he knew he was reasonable to expect the insurance companies to cover his car for days like that. Plus, he wanted to drive one of his other cars for pleasure on occasion. For past appreciation, Roland called up the retired insurance agent, and he thanked her for her kindness and understanding, during the years she had run the company. She was glad to hear from him, and she said she was sorry the new people at that company had become cold shouldered.

One day in late 1996, Roland went over to Isalia's house to do some work for her. He was working with her in the yard, and she was planting bulbs and flowers.

Somebody Roland knew had suggested to him that he go to graduate school, that he needed it badly, even though it had been five years since he had graduated from Tennessee Tech University. Roland had already chosen his road in life, to be an artist and work for himself instead of be an engineer working for a company. Isalia said the cost of going back to school just wouldn't be worth it, in addition to the loss of income. He already had his degree from university, and he was better off, making a living. Roland didn't always agree with Isalia, but on this issue, they both agreed. Roland felt like Tennessee Tech had always tried to weed him out, right to the last final exam before he graduated. It had been a constant worry, and Roland was so glad to be out of there when he graduated in 1991. He was free of school, and he had served his time there. Life was for other matters now.

They got to talking about friendships in general, and Isalia told Roland about a friend of hers, Mrs. Tinkerton.

"Roland, I just lost a friend of 30 years last week . . . Mrs. Tinkerton."

"You mean the lady you travelled to Europe with?"

"Yes."

"What happened Isalia?"

"Well, she was telling me what color car to buy. I told her I was choosing grey, and she insisted I choose red. She went on to explain why red was the better color for me. Our whole friendship, we'd been having little disagreements like that, and I was really tired of it."

"What did you do?"

"I said to her, 'You have my permission to cancel this friendship, right now!'"

"And she said to me, 'I don't need you in my world!' and that was it, right there. We're no longer friends."

"Isalia, friends of 30 years are friends for a lifetime."

"I know, but I was tired of the bickering. It was time, and I'm *glad* it's over."

They continued working in the yard. Several months later, Isalia and Mrs. Tinkerton made amends and restored their friendship. Roland was glad to know that.

Roland for several years now had been considering bridges as symbolizing friendships. Some were big and wide. Others were very short. Others were on back roads while still others were long and narrow and situated surprisingly on major thoroughfares and highways! One of them in particular was the narrow truss bridge over the Stones River, the bridge to Lascassas on State Highway 96. It was amazing the highway department had left it in use for so long. There it stood, in use, with no scheduling to replace it, and it was only 18½ feet wide. The whole highway, except for that one bridge, had been widened nearly 20 years earlier. While Roland didn't suspect the bridge had anything to do with Isalia's friendships, he realized that somewhere out there, there were probably two old friends who had been friends for longer than anticipated, and the bridge was still standing for them . . . waiting for them. Little did Roland know, that bridge . . .

Around a week later, Roland went over to Isalia's house again. Her son, Laurence, from California was there visiting, and he and Roland talked over ideas that he had for his artwork and calendars. He had several very good suggestions about how Roland could go about promoting them, like offering restaurant coupons with each sale when going door to door, and having several university students write papers on the abstractness or underlying meanings of the artwork, for one of their writing projects in either a philosophy or English class. Isalia mentioned to Roland that it was no accident that Roland was there with them that day, talking with Isalia and her son, Laurence.

At the same time, Isalia brought up that one lady friend of hers had seen Roland's artwork and didn't like it at all. When Roland asked her who that lady was, Isalia declared that she wasn't going to tell him! Roland pointed out that it wasn't possible that everyone was going to like his artwork. However, there were some other middle aged women who did indeed like it very much. Roland had received a nice letter from a lady in England who was very intrigued by his artwork and calendars.

The Return of Roland

Roland also talked some more about Chip with Isalia and Laurence. He told Roland that those things just happen and to look ahead at the positive side of things. Roland asked him that if Chip didn't wish to continue knowing him, why didn't he just say so? Laurence answered that Chip still wanted to be polite and didn't want to make Roland feel bad. Roland admitted that was likely true. Isalia added comment by telling Roland that he didn't need Chip. Perhaps Chip wasn't sure how to come to Roland and tell him the truth that he didn't want to talk to him anymore, nor that he welcomed his coming over. Roland enjoyed the visit with Isalia and Laurence and later went home.

That night, Roland stepped outside and made a wish out loud, a wish for a fellow travelling companion to take long trips with, someone friendly and compatible, someone approximately his height and size, and someone who would be content with him and the trip on the last day returning home. Amen.

As far as Roland friendships were concerned, perhaps things would improve, and he would have better luck in Mexico.

CHAPTER 3

FRIENDSHIPS BEGIN

It was late December 1996, and Roland had decided to return to Bustamante to visit his Spanish teacher's cousins again. Roland and Leonardo had communicated by mail and by telephone, and he looked forward to doing some activities with him, including going in the mountains and camping. Roland had not forgotten that Leonardo had requested that he look him up the next time he comes to Mexico.

This time he took his Ford F-100 truck. He made the two day trip, staying with his cousins in Dallas, and he arrived at the Quevalo's residence on the evening of December 27, 1996.

India greeted him as he pulled into the driveway. She commented that he looked worried, like he might be in love with someone. Well, Roland knew he wasn't in love with anyone. However, he had given plenty of thought to the fact that he had been having such trouble making friends, and he had thought a lot about his most recent past friend, Chip Collins. Perhaps India had misinterpreted and misread Roland's appearance upon his arrival. Now that Roland was in Mexico, it no longer mattered to him so much about Chip. He knew that he and Leonardo would be able to have some adventures and do some things together.

Roland was planning to stay for the winter so he would have an opportunity to do some more paintings. He was thinking about doing another calendar, a compilation of some beautiful scenes from the mountains and forest up above Bustamante. He was looking forward to what he would paint, and he had good feelings about it.

Roland had carried a new TV to the Quevalos, a gift from Isalia, and some of the sisters called her by phone and thanked her. They called her Santa Claus. They also let Roland dial direct to his home in Tennessee so he could let his parents know he had arrived safely. That night, he also phoned Leonardo's residence in Villaldama and spoke to his brother Julian. He made arrangements to go over there and visit the next day.

Roland slept in his truck that night, as he would for the next several weeks. The Quevalos just didn't have the bed space like they used to. Around 8 AM, he got up. At that time, Pancho's three workers arrived. They were named Alejandro, Juan, and Raul. He greeted them as he stepped out of the camper top of his truck by saying, "Buenos días." They returned the same greeting.

Pancho came to them, and they helped him load some things in his old Ford pickup truck. Roland commented to Pancho how nice it must be to have working companions to keep him company while he works. Roland told Pancho how difficult it was to find help in Tennessee and that he wished he had a working companion. The others heard what Roland was telling Pancho in Spanish, and though Roland didn't know it at the time, he had just planted an idea in the mind of one of Pancho's three workers. His name was Raul Zacatón. Little did he know what all that would lead to.

Roland went to the Quevalo's separate kitchen building and had some breakfast. Sarita made and served flour tortillas with beans. Afterwards, he got ready and drove his truck over to Leonardo's house, arriving around 10 AM.

Leonardo's father greeted him and talked to him for a few minutes while Leonardo finished showering. He soon stepped out of the bathroom and greeted Roland. They ended up spending the whole day together, and Roland enjoyed it. He showed him his photo album of pictures, and they talked a while. Then they had lunch, after which Leonardo took him over to a bunch of friends on the west side of the highway.

There, Leonardo and his brother, Julian, rounded up a bunch of guys, most of them in their 20's and 30's, and several of them piled into the back of the old Dodge pickup truck that Leonardo was driving. One of the guys also brought along a second truck. Leonardo told Roland that most of them were borachos (drunks). Roland stayed in the cab with Leonardo. Next, they drove over to a Servi-Car, a store that sells cases of soda and beer on the side of the highway, and the others all bought plenty of cartons of beer!

Roland was beginning to worry that this good friend of his might be a boracho, a heavy drinker, especially since Leonardo said that he liked to drink also. So, Roland asked him if he drank a lot or a little. He answered that he drank a little. Roland would realize later that Leonardo was indeed truthful with his answer, and that was good.

Leonardo drove with the truckload of guys and beer, the other truck following, to a dirt road south of Villaldama, and for several kilometers, they followed a narrow dirt lane west to the foot of the mountains where they parked. From there, they walked up the foothills of the mountains to a beautiful spring and woods of Sycamore and Oak trees. There was a cabin up there owned by Leonardo's family, and they rested there for a while.

The other 20 or so guys were drinking and smoking all the way. While Roland enjoyed the day with Leonardo, he had to admit to himself that he was not very impressed with Leonardo's friends. As it turned out, Leonardo and Roland were the only ones who did not drink nor smoke. Leonardo probably would have had a beer or two, but he was feeling bad in the stomach. Roland watched the others repeatedly offer Leonardo beer, and he kept turning them down. No matter what Leonardo's true reasons were, Roland really appreciated him for not taking a single drink.

Near the end of the day, everyone returned to Villaldama. Many of the guys were plenty drunk, and Roland felt awkward around them. He rode with Leonardo in the cab of the Dodge pickup truck as he drove them back to town. He delivered the guys who rode in the back of the truck, and the other truck went its separate way.

That evening, Roland continued to visit with Leonardo and his family. He met Leonardo's sister, and he had supper with them. Before leaving, he gave them one of his calendars as a gesture of friendship. Since it was dark, Leonardo rode with Roland back to Bustamante, and then he rode back to Villaldama with his father who had followed them. It was Roland's first time ever to drive at night in Mexico.

Roland and Leonardo had made plans to go hiking and camping in the mountains later in the week, and they said they would see each other then. They parted ways, and he and his father returned home. A part of Roland momentarily felt strange, as if he wouldn't be seeing Leonardo again.

The next day, Roland drove over to Sabinas Hidalgo and visited with his friends, Ricardo and Alicia Velazco, at the Taller Electrico. He gave them one of his calendars, which they found intriguing. They were glad to see Roland, and they visited for several hours.

On the way back, Roland stopped at Leonardo's house in Villaldama, but only his father was there. He welcomed Roland inside, and they talked a few minutes.

He returned to Bustamante and visited with the Quevalos for the evening. India came forth and offered a piece of land across and down the street for him to park his truck and sleep in it. She also had a small shed where she let Roland store his things so he wouldn't have to carry them in his truck all the time.

The next morning, Leonardo and Roland were supposed to go camping in the mountains, and he was supposed to meet Roland at 10 AM at the Quevalos. He had not heard otherwise from him, so he assumed the plans were still on go. Five minutes till ten, India's son, Eliud, emerged from the house and came down the street to intercept Roland at his truck where he was packing his backpack.

"Dijo el muchacho que no podía. Habló por teléfono," said Eliud, telling Roland that Leonardo had just called and said that he could not go. Leonardo's uncle had just died, and that was the reason. Roland didn't want to believe what he had felt when he had parted with Leonardo the other night, but now he was having to admit it to himself.

Well, Roland did the best of a lost situation. He had brought two Cedar trees with him from Tennessee, and he decided to plant one of them in the mountains. He had given the other one to the Quevalos. Lorenzo carried Roland in his blue Ford pickup truck to the cono at the end of the road, and he explained to the attendant that Roland wished to plant the Cedar tree up in the mountains. That was fine with him, and Roland started walking. He also carried a bush ax to clear the somewhat overgrown trail, and he planted the tree in a good location of the gully well up into the mountains. It would live and do well.

In the evening, Roland talked with Lorenzo about the coincidences he had experienced, especially concerning Chip Collins and also Ivanhoe. In fact, one of Ivanhoe's previous phone numbers matched the Quevalo's phone number, short of a truncated zero. His next number missed the Quevalo's newer shop phone number by only one digit. Roland had also had a clear dream of misdialling Ivanhoe's phone number, and short of a truncated zero, that wrong number exactly matched Chip's number. Roland wrote out the coincidence data and matching phone numbers, age differences, and other data on a sheet of paper for Lorenzo to see, and Lorenzo commented to him that coincidences just happen. They are not to be taken so seriously. In fact, Lorenzo told Roland that he seemed to be a slave to the coincidence data that he had figured out, and he was obsessed with it, to some degree. While he knew Lorenzo was right to some extent, Roland knew within his own mind that there had to be one or more good reasons why there had been so many coincidences between him, Chip, and Ivanhoe.

Even though Roland had been brushed off by Chip, he still wished to continue being his friend, and prior to coming to Mexico, he had made several efforts to talk to Chip about his joining Roland in his self-employed business of carpentry and painting. As Roland talked to Lorenzo, he explained that Chip was under a lot of stress at his job of working for an office supply store, and he wanted to change jobs. Despite Roland's willingness to help Chip out, every time he went to Chip to talk to him about it, he had always been seemingly very busy and had repeatedly brushed him off. It had frustrated Roland considerably, and he decided to write Chip a postcard where he would finally get to make the partnership offer.

The next day, Roland drove over to Villaldama again to talk to Leonardo, but he didn't find him at home. His brother Julian answered the door and talked to him a while.

He returned to Bustamante where he wrote some post cards, including the one to Chip, and he also went searching for Fan Palm leaves and bought five feed sackfuls of them, a total of 360 fronds.

The next day was New Year's Day, and it was now 1997. There had been a *baile* (dance) on New Year's Eve in the town's social center, and its noise had boomed all over town. Roland had trouble sleeping, but with his ear plugs, he had successfully gotten some sleep.

That morning, Roland chatted with Pancho for a while, and then he picked up his tools, as he had a project in mind. He wanted to clear the trail all the way to the ridge top of the mountains, and he set out walking with hand clippers, lopping shears, and a bow saw.

In 45 minutes, he reached the cono at the end of the road, and he began his ascent on the trail, passing by the cave 45 minutes later. He had his three tools wrapped up in a bed sheet so that no one would question him, especially the cave guide, Ramiro.

Once beyond the cave, now in the higher reaches of the mountains, he began work, and he successfully cleared a good section of the trail. He would return several more times over the next month to clear the trail further up the mountain each time. Each day, he hid his tools at the location where he had stopped clearing. At one point, the trail passed through a steep ravine, a crevice actually. Roland hung a long rope through that section, and he tied knots every two feet along it.

He returned to the cono by the evening, and he met some young fellows from Sabinas Hidalgo. One of them was named Ramón. They were easy to talk to, and Roland enjoyed talking and laughing with them. Their family gave Roland a lift back to the town center.

The next day, Roland drove to Sabinas Hidalgo and visited with the Velazco family again. This time their son, Ramiro, age 20, was there, and he and Roland talked for a while. He also talked with Ricardo's mother, who was an energetic woman in her 80's. As it turned out, she was a palm reader. She predicted that Roland would be married twice. Well, that was just her prediction because Roland knew that wouldn't be so. He knew that if he were to marry at all, he would only marry once.

He returned to Bustamante, and he visited with Pancho and his workers who were painting ten large rocking chairs that they had just made. Pancho and the others were teasing Raul about drinking a lot. Raul laughed it off with good humor and repeatedly said that he had not been drinking. Roland looked at him and just didn't believe that Raul was the type to drink a lot, if at all, and he started talking with him. Raul was 15, and he was the same height and size as Roland. He liked Raul's personality, and he seemed to find his playful characteristics and personality familiar. As a result, Roland instinctively sensed that they would become good friends.

However, there was one factor that concerned Roland. It was the age difference. Roland was more than 16 years older at age 31. How was he going to become a close friend to someone who was just 15? He hadn't realized that Raul was so young. When he had met him the other morning, he had assumed that he was more like 20. As those thoughts ran through Roland's mind, he was regretting that they weren't closer in age to each other. He and Raul would have become very good friends . . . if only they had been closer to the same age.

The next day was January 3rd, and one of Lorenzo's friends, Mateo Balderas, and his son Fernando who was 17, offered to take Roland into the canyon to visit an old phosphorus mine where he used to work 15 to 20 years ago. They arrived in their V-6, 5-speed 1989 Chevrolet Celebrity. His son was driving, and he drove them to the canyon. There they parked, and they hiked up an abandoned road that led up to the mine, which was perched on the hillside well above the canyon floor. The cold wind blew on this somewhat moderate sunny day.

Plenty of white crystal-like rocks lined the road, and Roland and Fernando collected several specimens. Throughout the whole region, all of the mountains were made up mainly of limestone rock, and the color and texture of it was very similar to the rock in middle Tennessee. Some of the limestone had crystallized, forming the white to clear colored crystals known as Calcite. Larger sections formed rectangular parallelograms.

The mine was fairly large, and it had been abandoned some 15 years ago and declared unsafe. Mateo and Fernando took Roland in there, and Mateo told him stories of the back breaking work that he and his working companions used to do. They also found some larger white crystallized rocks, and Roland carried some of them with him.

Next, Fernando drove them to the Ojo del Agua, and Roland was absolutely amazed to see that the road had been paved all the way to the site! Even electricity had been run all the way from Bustamante. At the same time, Roland was upset to see that they had "improved" the Ojo del Agua by installing concrete swimming pools! They had also planted foreign trees like River She-Oaks (*Casuarina cunninghamiana*) from Australia. They had even gone so far as to install poles with chain links to mark boundaries and areas not to trample. It had looked so much better back in 1991 when it used to be in its more natural state.

Roland enjoyed the day with Mateo and his son. They returned to Bustamante, and they made arrangements to go hiking up one of the ridges of the Lion's Head Mountain a few days later.

Later that afternoon, Roland happened to notice one of the Teléfonos de México phone company trucks parked by the phone exchange, which was only a few blocks away from the Quevalo's residence. Roland walked over there, and the man let him enter and look at the exchange. It was a crossbar exchange, totally electro-mechanical, and it consisted of 400 lines. There were several cabinets and racks full of peanut relays. It operated by pulse. There was no touch-tone service at all. Above the building was a microwave tower. Bustamante's automatic phone exchange had been installed in the late 1980's. Before that, there was no residential phone service, just a central public telephone at the plaza that had a line from Sabinas Hidalgo.

While nearly the whole United States had been converted to digital, Mexico still had some of its small towns operating on electro-mechanical exchanges. It would be nearly the turn of the millennium before Bustamante would be upgraded to a digital exchange with touch-tone phones and service.

Roland really enjoyed the chance to see the exchange, and he thanked the man.

He also took one of the Quevalo's old chairs and replaced the Palm leaf weaving with new. It took him around four hours to reweave it. Sarita was very pleased and said that Roland was like a *máquina* (machine).

The next day, Lorenzo and Roland decided to take a look at Roland's truck because the valves were clicking. When they got the valve cover off, Lorenzo said, "Anda muy sucia," saying that the truck engine was very dirty. Roland was surprised at the amount of carbon buildup. In fact, several of the valves were lacking lubrication, and for that reason, they were clicking. They talked it over. At first, they were going to just clean the engine, but as they continued to look at it, they decided the best thing to do would be to overhaul the whole 6-cylinder 300 engine. For the while, they replaced the valve cover, and Roland continued to drive the truck until Lorenzo would have time to help him.

In the afternoon, Roland drove over to Leonardo's house in Villaldama. He wasn't there again, and his father invited him inside. Leonardo was in Monterrey, and Roland called him on the phone to see if they could make plans to go into the mountains. Leonardo explained that he was having trouble with final exams and drawings to present and said that after January 8, he would have time. Leonardo was about to graduate with a degree in architectural engineering from the University of Monterrey in the northern part of the city. His family had a second house in the northern suburb, San Nicolas de los Garza.

Roland returned to Bustamante, and when he arrived, he saw Pancho's workers just getting off work. He offered to show them his photos of Tennessee and of his family. Juan and Alejandro showed little interest and left. Raul, on the other hand, did show interest, and Roland showed him the small booklet of pictures. In fact, Raul wanted to see more pictures. So, Roland went to his truck and got his photo album of his trip to Great Britain and Spain and last year's trip to Mexico and brought it to Raul. He looked through the photos with interest.

Roland realized that he was making a real friend, and there was just no way he could let the age difference get in the way. For some reason, Raul was showing real interest in being a friend, and he showed no sense of shying away because of the age difference. Roland would later learn that in Mexico, age difference is not such a factor as it is in the United States. Mexicans look at the individual more than at the age of a person. Despite the fact that Roland was 31, he was still young and energetic, and he would later find out that Raul thought he was only 20 or 21.

Raul told Roland that he had just turned 15 the other day, December 27. That was the same day that Roland had arrived in Mexico on this trip.

The next day, Roland went into the mountains all day and cleared another section of the trail.

He returned to the Quevalos in the late afternoon, and several of the Quevalos were seated around an outdoor fire which was something they usually did in the winter evenings. Raul was also there, and Roland took a seat around the fire and visited with them.

The next day was the Día de Reyes, January 6, and in memory of him, the Quevalos would always bake a special bread called *Rosca de Reyes*. In each oval shaped loaf which was decorated with colored sweets and other things, they would implant a *mono*, which is a tiny plastic doll only 2 centimeters tall. As the pieces of the Rosca de Reyes would be served to people and eaten, the person lucky enough to find the mono would then be obligated to give a fiesta (party) to everyone the next year. So the tradition and obligation went . . . though it was seldom fulfilled. No matter what, it was a contest to see who would find the mono first, and as soon as one of them did, there would be plenty of laughs.

Roland helped Lorenzo and his friend Mateo gather lots of chairs from the town's social center where they have the dances, and using pickup trucks, they carried the chairs over to the plaza to a courtyard on the south side where they set them up.

Later that afternoon, all of the children from the town gathered, and they played a big game of *lotería* (bingo). It was a festive celebration, and Roland began to know some of the town's people, including Chilo and Mina Cantu and their family. They ran the corner store in the plaza.

The weather had been nice and sunny, but today was cooler, and it was cloudy. Another winter spell was about to set in, and Roland was about to see the coldest weather he had ever seen in Bustamante. Some nights would be below freezing.

The day after the Día de Reyes was cold indeed, and it drizzled. Roland had slept in his pickup truck again, and he had been cold. He walked over to the Quevalos and stood around the fire. He noticed that some of the Quevalo sisters resented it. They had erected a wind break made of propped up tin roofing, and many of them were cracking pecans and extracting the nuts within.

Sarita told Roland to gather some firewood and build himself a fire over where he had his truck parked and to warm himself over there. He could cook his meals over there, too. Somehow, that didn't ring right with Roland. He detected inhospitality. He said nothing and walked away.

In addition to that, Roland had asked to use the telephone to call home from time to time or to call Monterrey, and the Quevalos had told him he couldn't use it. They directed Roland to go up to the corner store and make his calls from there. Roland didn't like that. He offered to pay them for the calls he would have made, but the Quevalos would not reason with him. They thought the calls were very expensive, and they would not bother to reason out the math to figure out the rate per minute.

It was then that Pancho took Roland into their front room, and he opened a top drawer to a dresser, pulled out several Teléfonos de México phone bills, and showed them to him. While Pancho showed him the rates, Roland then noticed something that very much surprised him. It was the letter he had sent them in November 1995, more than a year ago, and it had never been opened! How strange indeed! When Roland had asked them last year if they had received that letter, they told him that they had not. Now Roland knew the truth. The Quevalos had indeed received the letter. It had arrived in Bustamante December 8, 1995, according to the Mexican postmark that had been added to the letter when it arrived at the post office in Bustamante, only two weeks after he had mailed it to them. When the letter arrived, one of them just took it and without saying anything to the others, tucked it away in the dresser with the phone bills, and they never opened it, much less, read it! Roland went to the females to talk to them about the unopened letter, and they acted like they didn't know what he was talking about. Roland didn't push the issue any further, but he was realizing how mysterious the Quevalo family was.

He had trouble keeping himself warm on this cold day. He took copies of his calendars with him and walked around town.

He visited Daniel Mata's residence where he gave them a calendar. They were impressed with the artwork. Since Daniel collected plants and herbs from the mountains, he had quite a collection of native plants and shrubs in his backyard. He and his wife had set up a beautiful rock garden with various types of Siempre Viva, Yucca, and other desert plants.

Roland also visited Vico and Chely and gave them a calendar.

Every Tuesday, the plaza would have a farmer's market set up, and Roland bought a long sleeve shirt and a sweater to put on since he was cold. With that added clothing, he felt better.

In the afternoon, he accompanied Lorenzo and his sister Lydia to the *monte* (scrubland) at the foot of the mountains. They gathered firewood, and they talked about various things.

In the evening, after Pancho's workers got off work, Raul stayed around, and he was sitting with the Quevalos around the fire. Roland joined them. The smoke from the fire kept pursuing Roland, and he kept getting up and moving to another chair around the fire. Raul decided to make light of it, and with a playful smile on his face, he took off his jacket and strategically positioned it in such a way as to make the smoke go toward Roland. This was the first time Raul was playful to Roland, and they laughed about it.

Roland asked Raul if he had thought about going to high school in the United States as an exchange student, and he explained to him the possibilities. As Raul was leaving, Roland asked him if he could come over to his house. Raul said that would be fine, and he told Roland where he lived. They made arrangements, and Roland would go by and visit on a later day.

When Roland got up the next morning, it was cold, but it was also sunny. He decided to go to Bustamante's library to look through some of their books pertaining to artwork. Plus, there was a room the size of a gymnasium across the courtyard from the library, and it had some excellent murals done by some local artists there in Nuevo León.

In the late afternoon, he walked around the streets of the town, and he looked for Raul's house. He had missed it by one block, he would later learn.

The next day, he called Leonardo's residence. He had told Roland the other day by phone that he would be returning to Villaldama today. He drove over to Villaldama and found no one at home, and he left a note saying something to the effect of, "Sorry to miss you." He also wrote that he would be leaving at the end of January to go home to Tennessee. What had happened? Each time Leonardo said he would be there, he wasn't there after all. Roland suspected that he must have stayed in Monterrey because he was busy and had to complete his presentation.

In the afternoon, Pancho got into a hurry and suddenly wanted to go to Monterrey to buy a bunch of pallets so he would later be able to extract the lumber for use in his chairs. The 1981 blue Ford truck had a leaking brake master cylinder, and Pancho went over to Lorenzo and got onto him for not having fixed the truck sooner. Lorenzo answered in an angry tone to his younger brother and firmly told him that he had not had time to fix it. Pancho, sometimes being the hasty type, hurriedly replaced the master cylinder. Roland helped him. There was a problem in making the brake lines fit the different fittings, but Roland discovered that there were proper size fittings on one of their numerous junk Ford trucks sitting around the place, and they removed the lines from that junk truck. He watched Pancho work with such haste that when he bench bled the master cylinder prior to installation, he caused the unit to spray the brake fluid all over his shirt! Finally, it was installed after more than an hour, and Roland decided to accompany Pancho to Monterrey to purchase the pallets.

On the way there, he and Pancho talked about various things. Pancho informed him that several years ago, a few months after Roland and Isalia had left the truck with the Quevalos, the Mexican federal police had pulled Pancho over while driving the blue truck, and when they discovered that the truck still carried Roland's name on the registration, they impounded the truck, tore up the paperwork, and were about to put Pancho in jail! Somehow, Pancho had gotten out of it and talked the police into registering the truck in his name after he explained to them how his family had obtained the truck from two Americans who had left it with them. Roland had not realized the trouble that Pancho had had, but within his mind, he knew that natural law had served its purpose. This was the punishment to the Quevalos for their having been so ungrateful to Roland in 1992.

They stopped by Lorena's house, and while they were there, Roland called Leonardo in Monterrey and reached him. What he suspected was right. Leonardo was busy with his presentation for graduation from university. He was very indefinite about when he would be returning to Villaldama. While Roland had Leonardo on the phone, he asked him if he could come over, and he asked him for his address. It seemed that Leonardo didn't hear him, so Roland asked him a second and even a third time before Leonardo finally told him what it was. This left Roland really wondering if he still had a friendship with the fellow at all. *What had happened?* Roland thought. *Why does Leonardo seem to be avoiding me?* These questions ran through Roland's mind. He knew he had not done anything bad to him nor out of order. Perhaps Leonardo was apprehensive about going into the mountains and camping with Roland. There might be large wild animals to disturb them in the night. Roland had had quite enough of being brushed off, and he thought, *Not Leonardo also*. On the positive side, Leonardo did indeed give his correct address instead of a false one.

On the way back to Bustamante with the truckload of pallets, Roland and Pancho talked about philosophy and human characteristics. He was realizing more and more that Pancho was a very intelligent and perceptive fellow. He explained that many people in this world have two faces and that most people are your friend when it conveniences them. Roland talked to him about Chip Collins and the job he had at an office supply store in Nashville. Pancho predicted that the store would eventually let him go and would replace him by someone who they could pay less per hour. As far as Roland could see, Pancho understood the life very well, and he understood how people operated. In addition to that, Pancho believed in extra sensory abilities of people and told Roland some stories of psychic phenomena.

He said that Chip was a person with two faces. Roland asked Pancho how many faces Raul had, and he answered that Raul had only one face, which was a compliment toward Raul. At the same time, Pancho said that Raul had a potential problem with alcohol, although right now he still didn't. Pancho thought that of Raul because Raul's father, Alejandro was indeed an alcoholic. He told Roland that Raul didn't know how to live his life. Roland hoped Pancho's predictions about Raul's drinking would not come true. If Roland could have anything to do with it, he would prevent that from happening. He would definitely talk with Raul about that. Raul deserves a better life than falling in the trap of drinking a lot.

Pancho also told Roland that he had always seen him as a person with a sad face, a person who was suffering somewhat, from the lack of friends. Roland admitted that he had been sad over various losses of friendships in the past, but he added that his spirits were very much uplifted by his new friendship with Raul. How long would this one last? Roland hoped it would be permanent.

Pancho was one of the few people in Mexico who never drank nor smoked. Roland appreciated Pancho for that, because Roland never drank nor smoked either. Roland asked Pancho what percentage of people in a town like Bustamante never drank nor smoked, and Pancho answered that for 1,000 fellows, you could find 3 who didn't . . . a very low percentage. The fact was that fun and festivities were becoming more popular, and so were the Saturday night bailes (dances). Truckloads of beer arrived for every dance, and lots of cigarettes were smoked also. At that time, very few females in Mexico were smokers, at most 10%, but that was on the uprise with modern times and cultural influences from big cities, like Monterrey.

Yes, Bustamante was a growing town with nearly 4,000 people now. There was occasional crime and theft, and the Quevalos had recently installed better fencing and protection around their property to make it more difficult for thieves to steal from them. They had even installed two scrolling metal garage doors to protect their vending area by the street at nights.

Friendships Begin

That evening, Roland, Pancho and Lorenzo talked about friendships, and Lorenzo told Roland something that Isalia told his family the first time she had called them in December 1990 to announce Roland's coming. She had told them that Roland has a hard time making friends. Roland was somewhat surprised at her insight. In those days, making friends had been easier for him since he was still in university. Was she to know something about Roland's future? He wondered why she mentioned this seemingly unnecessary detail to the Quevalos in the first place.

Roland knew it was true that he was having a hard time making friends, more so in Tennessee than in Mexico. He could make them easily enough, but making them last more than a few months seemed, *strangely enough,* to be a feat beyond capabilities. He was beginning to wonder if Leonardo was also joining the list of friends he had undeservedly lost.

Lorenzo mentioned to Roland that Pancho also has a hard time making friends. As they continued talking, Lorenzo told Roland that he needed to change his way of life, to conform and be like the rest of them, to go to the dances, listen to loud music, and date girls, among other things. Of course, Roland didn't agree with that. He had his own life. Lorenzo also went on to say that he had left the TV playing loudly at night so that Roland would accustom himself to loud noises and loud music. That didn't please Roland at all. He told Lorenzo his disapproval of his playing the TV loudly at night, but Lorenzo was determined to make him change. As a result, Roland only slept inside Lorenzo's house on the coldest nights. He had sensitive hearing, and he had to have it quiet to sleep properly, and there was no changing that. The only thing he had which helped him sleep better were his earplugs, or sleeping *outside* Lorenzo's house!

*   *   *

Roland remembered back to his childhood and teenage years.

Throughout his childhood he had had some difficulty in making friends, and there were times when he felt lonely, living a rural childhood and not having any playmates close by. He spent a lot of time going up in his family's 90-acre woods and exploring, and he also used to explore the wooded hills to the south. In addition to that, he used to ride his bicycle a lot. As a result, Roland sometimes came on a little too strong with new friends in efforts to make up for his lack of them.

Ever since the time Roland entered Kindergarten, he realized that he was different from the others. He felt very shy and didn't talk more than absolutely necessary. During the next year of school, his teacher finally coaxed him into talking. It was difficult for him to break the barrier and do so, but he succeeded. He had a strange early childhood and felt alien in some ways. It was clear that Roland had delays in social development and his interactions with other people. He was also very sensitive to even moderately loud or sharp sounds, and he despised annoying smells, including putrid perfumes and tobacco smoke. His parents wondered if he might have some autistic traits, but they weren't sure. So little research had been done on the subject. Finally, by the time he was age nine, he overcame many of his barriers and felt like he was better adjusted, but his sensitivities to loud noises, putrid gacho perfumes, and tobacco smoke continued.

Nevertheless, Roland did make some friends, and he became very good friends with one of them, Joseph Ruffner, through sixth grade. He used to come over and spend nights at Roland's house, and they would run around, play, and do things together on the farm. On some days during the summers, his mother would take them swimming at the pool in town. Other friends near his age came from out of town and visited on occasion.

As a side note, there were two other good friends who were black, and Roland had known them since second grade. They went to elementary school together and were in nearly every one of Roland's classes at that time. At the end of eighth grade, Roland was surprised and very upset when he found out that his friends would not be going to the same high school. They had actually been zoned to the other high school across the county. He had figured that since they had been in the same elementary school that they would definitely be going to the same high school. Roland inspected the zoning maps of the time and found out that they happened to live in the one block that had been zoned to the same elementary school but then to the *other* high school! The zoning line actually went well out of its way, dipped down, and surrounded the block on three sides for a block which should have been clearly zoned to Longview High School. Roland thought that was most strange, and when he asked the zoning board about it, they explained that it had been done so that the number of blacks would be divided equally between the high schools. To Roland that was not good enough. He knew that if white people had lived in that block, the zoning lines would have been normal, and they would have gone to Longview. Roland certainly never forgot it. A person's color was irrelevant, but then he knew how much some people were prejudiced against people that were of a different color. After all, he used to see his white classmates say hateful comments to the blacks. At least there would be two more races arriving to Tennessee in the coming years: Laotians and Mexicans. That would set some of those prejudiced white people in their place!

Roland also had several hobbies. He had become interested in trees at age eight, and he learned the different types of trees from a good book his parents showed him. Certain trees really intrigued him, and upon seeing photos of California's Giant Sequoias, he really wanted to go see them. His parents made a trip to San Francisco, California when he was nine, and when they brought home some Eucalyptus seeds and leaves, Roland was even more intrigued and wanted to go see the Eucalyptus trees in California. He knew they were native to Australia, and he wanted to travel there in the future, as well. Finally, five years later, he went to California with his family.

By age 16, Roland had bicycled on every backroad within a 15 to 20 mile radius of his home. His strong desire to explore had driven him to accomplish the task. A few of the bicycle rides had been 90 miles long. In addition to that, at age 15, he decided to ride his bicycle to and from his grandparents' house in Crossville, 100 miles away. He succeeded, riding there in 8 hours 25 minutes, having left home at 5:52 AM and arriving at 2:17 PM. His grandparents were sitting in the front yard at the time, and his grandmother, upon seeing him commented, "Well, I'll declare!" They were both impressed, and his grandfather complemented Roland by telling him he sure was smart to have been able to ride all that way. Roland rested there the second day and returned home on his bicycle the third day. It was quite a trip, and he remembered how his Spanish teacher had earlier told him it would not be possible, that his legs would just not handle such a long ride. He was glad to have proven her wrong on that one!

As he grew up, he did very well in school, and he did succeed in making some more friends. In university, he made even more friends. That was several years ago, and he missed some of them.

*　　*　　*

Friendships Begin

The next day, Roland went over to Mateo and Fernando's house and visited with them. They decided to go hiking up the left ridge of the Lion's Head Mountain for the afternoon, and Fernando drove them up to the cono. From there, they made their way up the treacherous ridge which was full of Lechuguilla and Zotól plants. Mateo knew the names of numerous plants, and he told Roland the names. Roland wrote the names on a piece of paper he was carrying, so he could learn and remember them.

It was a nice and sunny day, and it was much warmer than it had been the past several days. They enjoyed the views of the town and the valley below them. They made their way back down the mountain and talked about going hiking again. Though Roland didn't realize it at the time, this was the last hiking they would ever do together. Any future efforts between Roland and Fernando to go hiking never became reality because Fernando's mother usually needed him to drive her all over town in the car to do errands and visit relatives, in addition to his having to obtain his father's permission, Roland would later find out.

They returned to Bustamante, and Roland went over to where Pancho's workers were working. Raul and Eliud were visiting with each other by an outdoor fire in the work area. Roland chatted with them, and he really enjoyed it. Raul joked with Roland about several things, and they had some laughs.

While they were visiting, Roland and Raul decided to check and see which one was taller, and they got back to back and had someone else check. They were the same height. As Roland backed up to Raul, he was somewhat surprised to suddenly feel a sense of energy between them. *What was that all about?* He had never known that type of feeling before. With that, Roland realized that there was indeed a strong connection of friendship going on between the two of them.

The next day was cold and cloudy. In the morning, Roland accompanied Lorenzo and Glenda over to Villaldama in their car, and they delivered bread to various stores in the town. They also visited the farmer's market which takes place on the square every Sunday from 8 AM to 1 PM.

Lorenzo also ran Roland by Leonardo's house, but no one was there. Rumors were going around that his mother was sick with pneumonia in Monterrey, and for that reason, they didn't come to Villaldama. Roland talked with Lorenzo and Glenda about people in general, and they thought Roland was coming on too strong, that he was going over there too much and might be coming across as pushy. Well, Roland didn't think that was true. Leonardo was repeatedly not at home, and Roland had to go by there more than once to have any chance of finding him at home. Plus, he was just going about the normal maneuvers to succeed in making plans about going up in the mountains with Leonardo and camping. They also said to Roland that he was stubborn. Yes, that was true. When Roland set some goals for himself and possibly with others, he did whatever was necessary to accomplish them. To him, his maneuvers were reasonable in nature, even if others didn't agree with that.

As they were on their way back to Bustamante, Roland also recalled that Isalia had advised him not to come on too strong, and he remembered that she had sincerely told him that he had come on too strong with Chip Collins and had unknowingly scared him off. Again, Roland didn't think so. He had merely gone over there to visit and chat with him when he was working those several weeks next door at the Schultz's house.

That afternoon, Roland walked across town to Zacatón's house where Raul lived. When he arrived, Raul's sister Norma welcomed him inside. She was age 10 and was a nice looking girl, tall for her age, but not yet grown, of course. They had another sister, Irma, age 5, the youngest of them all. The parents were not there. Raul was just getting up, having slept late since it was Sunday, his day of rest each week. He called Roland over, welcoming him into the house, and they visited. His younger brother was still in bed. His name was Rigo, and he was nearly 14. Both of them had an older brother whose name was Eduardo. He was age 19 and had left home three years ago. He had crossed the river and taken up residence with some of his uncles in Salado, Texas. By now he was already married and had a family.

Raul and Rigo showed Roland a book from the Jehovah's Witness people, and they asked Roland if he believed in creation or evolution. Roland answered evolution, and Raul and Rigo agreed with him.

Roland had brought one of his calendars with him, and he gave it to Raul. He was glad to receive it, was impressed, and he offered Roland to come into the kitchen to eat some lunch with him. They talked about various things, including the subject of smoking and drinking in general. Raul told him that he drinks, but only a little bit, and that he does not smoke.

A friend of Raul's came over. His name was Angelo, and he was considerably shorter. Angelo had on boots and a thick sort of jacket. He was very quiet and appeared to be of the serious sort. He made no conversation with Roland at all.

Shortly after lunch, Roland decided to leave, seeing that Raul already had other company. As he was starting to leave, Raul gave Roland a wooden tablet with a carving of a toro and a cowboy. That was a gesture of friendship, and Raul thanked Roland for the calendar.

Another friend of Raul's arrived as Roland let himself out the door. His name was Pegaso. He was age 17 and was a little taller than Raul and Roland. He had a friendly face and appeared more talkative than Angelo. He found Roland's paintings of quite a bit of interest.

Roland walked back to the Quevalos and placed the tablet in the back of his truck. He sincerely appreciated Raul's having given it to him, and he realized he had made a real friend. He had sincere appreciation for him.

Over the course of the next week, Roland made several visits to the town's library. There were several interesting books pertaining to artwork that Roland was having a good read through. On one of those days, some of the students from the school came to the library to do research for school assignments. One of the young girls recognized Roland and called him by name. Roland recognized her as Raul's sister, Norma. Suddenly, a thought entered Roland's mind, and he thought to himself, *Could this be my future wife?* He recalled Isalia's comment from 1991 about Roland's finding the woman of his dreams here in Bustamante. Roland didn't know why, but Isalia had always thought he would find a wife here, and according to Isalia, he kept coming to Bustamante for subconscious reasons. If Norma was indeed to be the one, Roland would still have to wait for several more years. To him, that would be fine since he was in no hurry, anyway. In fact, he had told several friends prior to coming to Mexico on this trip that he would wait around ten more years before getting married, if at all.

It was a cold week for several days, and for several nights, it froze. Roland slept inside Lorenzo's house each night. Lola had not wanted Roland sleeping in there, but Lorenzo and Glenda, being of kinder heart, had insisted in Roland's favor.

During some of the afternoons, Roland would chat with Pancho and his workers. He and

Friendships Begin

Raul used to joke with each other and laugh about things.

It cleared in the middle of the week, and the weather became warmer. Roland was going to start work on his truck, but Lorenzo was not yet ready. Despite Lorenzo's delay, Sarita and her daughters were onto Roland about getting started so that he could get it fixed and be on his way back to Tennessee. Roland could sense that they were getting tired of him.

Roland went up in the mountains one of the days and cleared the trail further up the gully.

Also during the week, Roland noticed a group of fellows through the trees back of where he had his truck parked. They whistled to him and called him over. There were four of them, and their names were Alberto, Juan Angel, Roberto, and Alberto's younger brother Victor. They had a campfire going, and they were eating chicken and corn tortillas. They offered Roland some of the food and talked with him for a while. Several times over the next week, the four of them had their campfire and called Roland over to visit with them.

One evening, Raul and his younger brother Rigo were playing computer games with Eliud, and they asked Roland what the English words were for numerous Spanish words.

On the weekend, Roland went to Chely and Vico's house and made a phone call to Leonardo. He reached his father who told him that Leonardo had not returned to Villaldama since he had seen him in late December.

For the afternoon, Roland went to another section of property belonging to an aunt of the Quevalos. Raul and Eliud were gathering pecan nuts. So, Roland helped Raul and Eliud gather the nuts. Raul was playful, and while Roland was picking up pecans, he felt one lightly hit him in the back. Raul had thrown it at him. He turned around and threw one back at Raul, and they started throwing pecans back and forth to each other and laughing.

Roland also talked to Raul and Eliud about the Quevalos and how he felt unwanted by them. Raul explained in a sincere manner that they felt like he was mooching off of them, and he suggested to Roland that he go buy some food from the store and give it to the Quevalos so that they could prepare it for him. Roland realized that he had not done that. His plans were to leave some money with the Quevalos at the end of his stay. Nevertheless, later that afternoon, he took Raul's suggestion and went to the Cantu's store and bought N$60 worth of food.

When he took the food to them, they told Roland, "Gracias." Raul later came over and saw that the Quevalos felt more content. Roland would soon learn that it was only temporary.

Late that afternoon, Roland decided to drive his truck one last time before they would take the engine out of it to repair it. He wanted to drive over to Leonardo's house and see if he might be there. He invited Raul to accompany him, and as he got in the truck with Roland, he didn't want to put the seatbelt on. Roland kindly insisted, and Raul did put it on. As Roland already knew, most Mexicans just hated seatbelts, and Roland would repeatedly explain to Raul and many others the importance of wearing one for safety. They can save a person's life in a bad car crash, and it's better to have one on than not.

Raul rode with Roland over to Villaldama, and Julian was there. Leonardo, of course, was not there. Roland was just about tired of never finding Leonardo at home, and he was coming to realize that some sort of destiny or subconscious higher forces had somehow stepped in and prevented them from becoming the friends they were meant to be. Why had he gotten to know Leonardo last year, having found him so familiar at first sight? . . . unless they were really meant to be good friends. As far as Roland had been concerned, that was a good sign, and Roland had a strong feeling that he and Leonardo would become close friends. Why had something seemingly stepped in and blocked it? Perhaps their window of opportunity for becoming good friends and spending time together had already come and gone. Roland had unknowingly missed his chance, perhaps in 1991 and 1992, and then he didn't come back for four years because of bad feelings with the Quevalos. At least Roland had Raul with him, and he was beginning to feel a close friendship with him.

As Roland drove back to Bustamante, Raul told Roland that in the 15 years he had lived, he had gained quite an understanding of the life and how it worked. That made Roland feel better, especially after Pancho had commented that Raul didn't know how to live his life. The feelings Roland had were that Raul did indeed know, and that was good.

Roland also talked with Raul about the possibility of his moving over to Raul's house and leaving the Quevalos. Roland was tired of the Quevalo's sense of ill feelings and inhospitality, and he wasn't 100% pleased with having to sleep in the back of his truck each night. More than that, Lola had not wanted Roland to sleep in Lorenzo's house at all, not even on cold nights, even though he was sleeping in a room by himself and on the floor!

Raul explained that as far as he was concerned, Roland could stay with him and his family in his house, but since it was his father's house, Raul couldn't speak for him. Raul also said that when he eventually owns his own house, Roland would certainly be welcome to stay with him in his house. Roland appreciated the welcoming words from Raul, and he decided to ask his parents, Alejandro and Lavinia, if that would be all right to come over and stay.

Roland had only seen Raul's father, Alejandro Zacatón, once or twice. He had passed in front of the Quevalos on the street one day, and he was carrying his wife Lavinia in their big brown 1974 Ford Country Sedan station wagon. They did this every day to pick up their youngest daughter, Irma, from Kindergarten.

The Quevalos had rumored that Alejandro was a bad person who drank a lot and was abusive to his family. Alejandro also didn't work and was drawing government unemployment since he had fallen off a ladder several years ago where he used to work at a chicken ranch just outside of Bustamante. With those rumors in his mind, Roland wasn't sure what to think of Alejandro, and he felt apprehensive about him.

The next day was Sunday, January 19, and Roland and Lorenzo started to take the motor out of Roland's truck. They used a chain hoist to do it, and after they pulled the engine out of the truck, they lowered it onto a big wooden table. Roland had gotten Pancho's permission and had begun to hire Raul to help him with the project. Raul arrived at noon and helped them take the engine apart. He was a great help in cleaning the engine parts, and he was glad to be a part of it. It gave him a chance to learn how to do this kind of work.

Roland had given one of his business cards to Raul, and Raul opened his wallet and showed it to him. It was placed in Raul's wallet like a photo, and Raul told Roland he appreciated him. Roland felt really honored, seeing that. Raul was a friend indeed.

While they worked for the afternoon, Rigo and Eliud visited with them, and they told each other stories and had plenty of laughs. It was an enjoyable time, and Roland thoroughly enjoyed the afternoon with them. It made the work go so much better.

Raul also asked Roland about his sister, and he told Raul that she was two years younger and lived in Brooklyn in New York City. Raul expressed interest in her, and he joked that he and Roland would become brothers-in-law. Both Roland and Raul told everyone nearby,

"Vamos a ser cuñados," saying that they were going to be brothers-in-law. They laughed about it. Roland had a different idea in mind. He knew that his sister and Raul certainly would never get married to each other, but what about Raul's younger sister, Norma? Roland kept that thought to himself. For all Roland knew, in ten years, he and Raul might become brothers-in-law after all.

That night, after Raul and the others had gone home, Roland was looking for his hand cleaner which had been misplaced. He looked in his truck and all over the pole barn where they had placed some of the engine parts from the day's work. He was becoming a little frustrated because the container of hand cleaner would not turn up. Lorenzo came to Roland as he was searching for it, and he said to Roland that they would never take his things. Roland immediately assured Lorenzo that he had never thought that. The simple fact was that the hand cleaner had seemingly disappeared. The next day, Roland finally did find it, and it was hidden under some towels in the back of his truck.

Roland felt annoyed and was also surprised by Lorenzo's negative assumption that Roland thought the Quevalos would steal from him, and he went over to Lorenzo's house and had a talk with him about it. Lorenzo insisted that he really thought that and felt insulted that Roland had continually searched and searched for the hand cleaner. As far as Roland was concerned, how else was he supposed to do it? He had not said one word of blame toward anyone about possibly having taken the hand cleaner, and Lorenzo's assumption was therefore uncalled for. At the same time, Roland did realize the fact that Lorenzo had drunk 12 beers the night before. That would make anyone feel depressed and think negative for the next day or two.

For the next week, Raul would come over in the afternoons after school and help Roland clean the engine parts. Lorenzo took Roland over to Sabinas Hidalgo where they left the block, crankshaft, and head with a machine shop. Later on in the week, after they had returned to Sabinas Hidalgo to collect the parts, they started to reassemble the engine.

Roland talked with Raul about what Lorenzo had accused Roland of thinking, and he also told Raul that Lorenzo had 12 beers the night before. Raul's comment was that Lorenzo had the right to do so, and that was somewhat disturbing to Roland. 12 beers was considerably excessive, and the only reason a person would drink that much in one night would be to get drunk. Raul didn't seem to think anything bad of it. Roland began to wonder if Pancho's rumors that Raul drank a lot were true. He and Raul talked about that, and Raul said that he drinks only a little, and Roland would realize that to be the truth. Raul only drank a little and sometimes not at all. He was hoping that Raul would stay that way.

Over the course of the week, Raul and Roland become close friends. Roland went over to Raul's house more and more, and he began to know his family. Lavinia was friendly and hospitable, and she would feed Roland supper with the rest of them. Alejandro was usually never there, being away at the *cantina* (bar). On one of those evenings, Raul told Roland that this coming June, he would be graduating from the secundaria school (the equivalent of junior high school, grades 7 - 9) and could take a year off and wondered about the possibility of going to Tennessee with Roland. He told Raul that would be fine. In fact, Roland welcomed the opportunity since he had really enjoyed Raul's company over the past two weeks.

As Raul continued coming in the afternoons to help Roland with the motor, he and Raul talked about the possibilities of his going to Tennessee with him. Roland decided that they would go about obtaining a passport for Raul, and they would need the help of his parents, along with their signatures. It was a tedious process which they would begin the following week.

One of the evenings after Roland and Raul had worked on the motor, he went to Raul's house to pay him for his work so far. No one was there, and Roland went to the plaza where he easily found Raul. He noted in his mind how easily he had found him and compared it to Chip Collins and to Leonardo, who had become frustratingly difficult to locate.

Raul was chatting with Angelo, and as Roland approached them, they spoke to him. It was no time before Raul was saying things that made all of them laugh. Angelo, who had been very serious the other day when Roland had met him at Raul's house, couldn't help but laugh. From then on, Angelo nearly always showed Roland an attitude of acceptance as a friend of his . . . and for a good while.

One evening after they worked on Roland's engine, Roland gave Raul an English 741 rotary dial wall phone that he brought to Mexico to give to someone as a playtoy. He had in mind that maybe Norma and Irma could play with it. Raul accepted the phone with a smile, and he extended his hand to Roland and sincerely said, "¿Amigos?" Roland assured him that they were friends, and they shook hands the Mexican way. Raul made Roland feel really good, showing a gesture of true friendship.

They had supper at the Quevalos, and later Roland, Raul and Eliud were sitting around the outdoor fire. They were talking about Chip Collins. He had a lot of spark and enthusiasm, and he was sort of a wild party type. As they analyzed him, they derived a name for him, changing his last name and adding a second last name, which pretty much meant party animal. Roland, Raul and Eliud laughed at the name they derived, and Roland wrote it on a piece of paper. Then he tossed the paper in the fire and declared, "Chip Collins, you are no longer my preoccupation." Roland had been somewhat concerned for Chip for the past several months with wanting to be working companions with him back in Tennessee, but now with new friends, like Raul, his past friendship with Chip just didn't matter anymore.

While things were definitely on the upswing with Raul, they were not so good with the Quevalos. The previous weekend, Roland had gone over to Chely's house and had talked to her and Vico about his stay with the Quevalos. Chely and Vico were a well-to-do family, and they had a fine house in very good order. The Quevalos had an old adobe house which lacked being entirely finished. It was not as well kept, and Roland wanted to know why. Chely explained that the Quevalos work just to live, implying that they don't have extra money.

Several days later when Roland was in the Quevalo's kitchen, Sarita entered and said, "Ya no vayas a Chely, si quieres nuestra amistad," telling Roland to no longer go to Chely's house, if he still wanted the Quevalo's friendship. That didn't make Roland feel good. Evidently, Chely had visited the Quevalos and had told them what she and Roland had talked about. The Quevalos must not have liked it. Roland wanted to continue visiting Chely and Vico, and he didn't like Sarita placing conditions on their friendship.

That night, Roland had a vivid dream of talking and visiting with an older woman he knew from some meetings he had attended over the past year. She had said that she is psychic and had even been tested to be 89% accurate. She lived near Nashville, Tennessee. *In the dream, they saw each other outside under the stars. She asked him to come inside the nearby house for a reading, and the next thing he knew, they were inside, and he was lying on a couch. She asked him to make two wishes for things he wanted to come true, and he told her one of them was to meet a healer. Then she placed her hands on top of his head and asked him what he was standing on his head for. She pressed down harder and then moved her hands on either side of his head and poked him on both sides of his neck with her fingers.* Roland struggled out of the dream and woke up alarmed, and he wondered if the psychic woman had telepathically communicated with him and had warned him of something. He would talk to her about it a month later back in Tennessee. Yes, she indeed had made efforts to warn Roland of something. Two months later, she told Roland that she was searching for him and found him in Mexico. When she did, she made telepathic efforts to get that warning message to him, but Roland had interpreted it more as a nightmare through the dream level.

One day during this week, Roland went up in the mountains. As he walked by the cono, Ramiro, the cave guide was there, just ready to go up to the cave for the day. Ramiro was a kind looking Mexican and was in his early 30's. He stood around the same height as Roland. They greeted each other and then began the 45-minute walk up the footpath to the cave.

Roland noticed that Ramiro's hiking boots were worn out, and he asked him about them. Ramiro explained that he didn't have enough money to get more shoes, and they wear out so fast. Roland had an extra pair of old hiking boots that he was no longer using, and he had them with his belongings in his truck. Later that night, he would take them to Ramiro's house and give them to him.

They ascended rather steeply in places, and they passed through various large shrubs of Mesquite and other local plants. Ramiro knew a lot about the names of the plants, and once Roland found that out, he took a pen and paper out of his daypack, and as Ramiro told him the names, he wrote them down. They compared very accurately with the names Mateo had earlier given him.

Ramiro told Roland that he was his friend, and anytime he wanted to come up here to the cave, he was welcome, and he would let him enter free of charge. That was kind of Ramiro, and Roland entered with him. There was no one else who had come, and when they arrived at the cave, Ramiro unlocked the iron gate situated at the entrance. Roland went in with him, and not just into the first room where Rogelio had taken him and the Quevalos six years earlier, but *well* into the cave. Ramiro had lost his jacket the other day, and he was looking for it. Roland, meanwhile, enjoyed looking around the cave with his flashlight. It was so enormous!

An hour later, Roland and Ramiro went back up and entered the outdoors again. Ramiro returned down to the cono, and Roland continued ascending the trail and cleared another section of the trail for several hours higher up. He returned to Bustamante late that afternoon.

On the next day in the evening, Roland was at the Quevalos and was cleaning his contact lenses under the faucet of the house sink. The water was flowing at a trickle. Lydia happened to walk by and suddenly blurted out, "Apágalo, Rolando. Sale muy cara," saying for him to turn the water off, that it's expensive. At the moment, Roland had his contact lenses on his fingers and was unable to turn it off for five more seconds. Lydia angrily repeated her command with a raised voice, by which time Roland managed to reach the faucet handle, and he turned it off. That, needless to say, irritated Roland, and once he had his contacts safely put away, he walked into the next room where they were watching TV, and he confronted them! He told them he really didn't like their inhospitality. Three of the sisters got highly irritated and the mother did also.

Olana said, "No te conocimos, Rolando. Tú vienes aquí por Isalia. No más una semana y ya te vas," telling Roland that they don't know him, that he comes via Isalia, and that after a week, he must leave.

Lydia said, "De la noria, Rolando," telling him to get all of his water from the well, not from the sink.

Roland then offered to give them N$40 to pay their month's water bill.

Sarita angrily reacted by saying, "¡Ya no aquí! ¡Hasta el hotel!" telling him that he was no longer welcome there and that he can just go to the hotel.

Roland told them that he hadn't done anything out of order, and he just walked off. As he was in the backyard recollecting his thoughts, he overheard Lydia and Olana ranting and raving inside the house, talking to each other about him and how out of order he was to have used the trickle of water the way he did, how wasteful he was, et cetera, et cetera! They went on and on about it for more than half an hour!

Later, India and Roland talked, and she said that they were all tired of him. Roland made the point that he could not leave since his truck was sitting in their driveway without an engine. It would be several more days until it would be ready. India did say that she talked to Lydia, told her there was not a cause for her having gotten onto Roland so harshly, and asked her to have a little more tolerance, as Roland's time of staying with them was nearly finished. Roland agreed that Lydia had no reason to be so unreasonable.

The next morning, Lorenzo took Roland to Sabinas Hidalgo to collect the engine parts from the machine shop. He explained that the sisters and the mother get very tired each day from working, and for that reason, they cannot reason properly during the evenings. He also explained to Roland that his offer of paying the N$40 for their water bill was the same as a child making efforts to get what he wants. What warped thinking!

On the way back to Bustamante, they stopped by Leonardo's house in Villaldama, and his brother Julian said that Leonardo had just left ten minutes earlier. They had just missed him. However, Lorenzo did point out to Roland that when they pulled up, several guys had entered a house across the street and had not come back out. Leonardo was possibly one of them. Roland didn't think so. He had also seen the guys enter the house, and none of them looked like Leonardo. Nevertheless, Roland was realizing that the ways of destiny were preventing him from seeing Leonardo again. This was the same sort of thing that had happened between him and Chip Collins in November and December. For some reason, Raul was usually easy to find, and there were no obstacles in knowing him. Compared to Leonardo, the difference was very plain. Raul was meant to be Roland's true friend, and Leonardo unfortunately was not. *But why?* Roland wondered. There was just no sufficient reason for Leonardo not to be a friend, unless it was to cause Roland to realize that something might be sabotaging his friendships and that the force causing it would need to be stopped. He wondered about that and wondered if the reasons were good or bad.

The next day when Raul came to work with Roland, he told Raul how the Quevalos had been inhospitable to him. Raul felt for Roland and said for him to come stay the nights over at his place. He had gotten his father's permission. Then at the same time, Raul, with a playful smile on his face, jokingly wrote with his finger on the back window of the camper top of the truck: *Hotel Rolando*. They laughed about it. Roland really wanted to move over to Raul's house, but he was apprehensive about his father, Alejandro.

Roland and Raul had made plans to climb the Lion's Head Mountain this coming weekend.

Friendships Begin

Roland was really looking forward to it, and he was considerably worried about the possibility that Raul would stand him up like Leonardo and others had done in the past. Raul said he would accompany him for N$50 which was around $6. Otherwise, he would work for Pancho. It didn't bother Roland that Raul wanted to be paid to accompany him. After all, it was the only way that Raul could be freed up from work, and Roland felt fortunate that Raul had accepted the invitation since he felt a good friendship with him.

That evening, Roland went to Raul's house, and from there, Rigo took him to Angelo's house where Raul, Angelo and Pegaso were. They entered, and they visited in the backyard. The gathering was for Angelo's birthday. Roland wondered if they were going to be drinking. They did not, and that pleased him. This was a party that was free of drinking and free of smoking. In those days, that's the way it was for them.

As they visited with each other, it wasn't long before they were joking with each other. Even Rigo joined in on the laughing. Roland really enjoyed the evening, and he and Raul mimmicked the Quevalos and what they had said to Roland the night before. Everyone laughed so much that their sides hurt. Roland later remembered Rigo's hearty laughs with the rest of them, and he realized that a good friendship was developing between him and Rigo also. While they were standing around in the backyard laughing with each other and telling each other things that were funny, Angelo's younger brother, Hugo, was climbing trees in the backyard and spying on them. Sometimes he would playfully throw them a pecan or two to get their attention.

Shortly after 10 PM, Roland reminded Raul that it would be a good idea to go to sleep so that they would be well rested for the big day tomorrow. Raul agreed, and they all left Angelo's house to go to sleep for the night.

The next morning was Saturday, January 25, and Roland had slept in the back of his truck. He got up at 5:30 AM, well before sunrise, and had his daypack and lunch ready by nearly 7 AM. Just at that time, Raul arrived, having walked from his house. Roland was so glad to see him. He had shown up, bless his soul. Roland realized just how good and true a friend Raul was.

They walked across town and entered the foot of the mountains half an hour later on the west side of town. The climb was a long one, and the going was tough as they ascended and made their way up the narrow, rocky ridge leading up to the summit. There were plenty of Lechuguilla, Cactus, and Zotól plants to have to dodge, along with scrub Oaks and other nearly impassable shrubs. They reached the flat rocky summit at 1 PM where they had lunch and signed the log book. The weather continued to be warm and sunny.

Money could not buy the feelings of satisfaction that Roland had. Raul never backed out, bless his soul, and both he and Roland had arrived at the summit in good condition. Roland felt even more fortunate because he got to share this hike with a friend of his who he really liked. Sincere appreciation was an understatement. Roland's feelings were better than that. He was so satisfied that he told Raul that of all the friends he had ever had in Mexico that Raul was the best friend of them all. Raul responded by commenting to Roland that he was indeed his friend.

Roland had loaned Raul his older pair of tennis shoes for the hike, and since Raul didn't have any, he told him that he could keep them. Raul wasn't exactly sure how to accept such a nice gift. He was concerned that Roland might be giving too much. Nevertheless, he did accept them with thanks, and he kept them.

71

On the top, there were Siempre Viva (*Echeveria*) plants in between the limestone rocks, and there were also three or four Cypress-like shrubs. They were likely Arizona Cypress or a type of Juniper. In addition to that, there were Lechuguilla and Mountain Maguey plants. Roland and Raul collected a few Siempre Viva plants, and a few Cypress twigs, as well.

They began descending the mountain the same way they had come up this morning. It was a tricky descent, and both of them slipped and fell a couple of times. Luckily, none of the falls were serious. Roland picked up a 5-meter-long Zotól bloom spike and used it to help him make the rest of the descent more easily.

He and Raul talked about various things on the way back. Raul told Roland how he had a girlfriend in town, and that he loved to go to the dances and be with her. Raul knew that Roland didn't have a girlfriend, and he took some pleasure in boasting of his girlfriend in a friendly way.

It was around 6 PM when they finally finished the descent, reaching the small narrow canyon west of the town. The going was finally easier.

Raul also told Roland how his father, Alejandro, drank and smoked a lot. It displeased Raul that his father was that way. Roland went on to mention to Raul that he was in good physical condition to have accomplished the climb today, and that if he continued taking care of himself in the same way, he would be able to accomplish a lot in his life. It was one of Roland's ways of encouraging Raul to stay away from the habits of smoking and drinking.

As they entered town near sunset, Roland continued to carry the long pole with him. Raul told him that it looked embarrassing for him to carry it in town, and he encouraged Roland to toss it. Roland wanted to continue carrying it, and Raul told him that carrying the stick made him look like a "maricón." Roland didn't know what that word meant, and Raul explained that it meant, gay. That seemed strange to Roland that carrying a long Zotól bloom stalk would give him the appearance of being gay. He took no heed to Raul's request, continued to carry it, and they both arrived at the Quevalo's residence 20 minutes later.

As they passed by Lorenzo's house just before arriving at the main Quevalo's residence, Raul commented to Roland that Lorenzo didn't really have anything, that the house he lived in belonged to his sisters and that he was mandated by them at times. Raul explained that Lorenzo had not been successful in making enough money to buy his own place to get away from his ruling sisters. As a result, Lorenzo felt depressed and at times drank. Roland hadn't realized that detail, and Raul's intelligent explanation caused Roland to realize the truth of the situation.

As they arrived at the Quevalos, Roland handed them some of the Siempre Viva plants that he had collected on the mountain top, and the Quevalo sisters were pleased to receive them. He also gave them a Cypress twig from one of the few Arizona Cypress shrubs growing on the top. Sarita said that she knew of those shrubs and that they grow only on the very tops of the mountains in the district.

Raul told the Quevalos about the day in the mountains. Roland would later find out that many of Bustamante's residents didn't believe that Raul made it to the top, but the 25 pictures of today's adventures would later be developed and prove the nonbelievers wrong.

Raul went to the back of Roland's truck with him, so he could be paid for the day's "work." Roland told him he was so pleased that he had accompanied him that he paid him N$100, double what they had agreed on. Raul felt somewhat surprised at Roland's generosity, but he accepted the money with thanks. He would now go home and get ready for the dance, which Bustamante had every Saturday night. Raul also now told Roland the truth that he didn't really have a girlfriend, that he was just kidding with him. Roland already had suspected that Raul had been kidding earlier today, but he wasn't totally sure. Raul walked home.

Roland and Pancho talked about the day's adventures, and Pancho was impressed that Raul had made it. Roland was a little concerned that he had paid Raul too much. He asked Pancho if he had done the right thing, and Pancho said he believed that Raul had earned the money for the hard work and the extra hours. Then Pancho mentioned that Raul might take the extra money and buy a bunch of beer and get drunk. That worried Roland even more. Still, he had to reason that he had done the right thing by paying Raul double, but he wished he had waited until the next day to give him the extra N$50 bonus.

Roland got cleaned up, changed clothes, and decided to go to Raul's house. He just couldn't believe that Raul was actually going to go to the dance, after the long day of mountain climbing. When he got to Raul's house, sure enough, there he was getting dressed for the dance, and he was fixing his hair just right. He put on his black shiny boots, and his friends, Angelo and Pegaso, came over. Roland walked with all of them to the town's social center, and they entered the dance. Roland, however, didn't enter because the music was just too loud. He went back to the Quevalos and went to sleep in the back of his truck.

The next day was Sunday, January 26, and Lorenzo and Roland began to put the engine block back together. Raul said he would come over and help, to arrive at noon. Finally at 2 PM, when Raul had still not come, Roland went for him to find out why. Raul was still in bed, and he told Roland that his legs hurt. Roland had recommended to Raul that he not go to the dance, but since he had, his legs hurt even more! Raul said he was never going to go to the mountains again.

With Roland's being there, Raul managed to get out of bed, and he accompanied Roland to the Quevalos and helped him grind and seat the rest of the valves. When he arrived with Roland, Pancho's first question was, "¿Cuánto?" asking Raul how many beers he had drunk last night. Raul said that he had none. Roland was very glad and relieved to hear that, and he knew that was true because not only was Raul perfectly sober, even though he was very tired, he had no alcohol smell at all.

Mateo and his son, Fernando, came over and visited. They joked around with Roland, Raul, Pancho and Lorenzo. While they were there, Fernando threw up. He had had plenty to drink. Roland would later realize that Fernando was one who liked to get drunk at times, as many of the teenagers did in Mexico.

They finished the valve job and called it a day. Raul went home very tired, and Roland was sure that he would sleep very well.

The next morning, Roland got up at 6 AM and went to Raul's house at 7:15 AM so he could talk to Alejandro and Lavinia about buying Raul a Mexican passport. Roland arrived at the house a little early, and not wanting to wake anyone, he continued walking up the street and into the small canyon west of town. Fifteen minutes later, he returned, and Norma let him inside.

She turned on the radio, and one of David Olivarez's songs, "Me Estoy Enamorando," was playing on the radio. The morning was pleasant and warm, and the song gave a very Mexican atmosphere to the whole situation. He could feel the kind hospitality from the whole family. Lavinia soon got up and fixed breakfast for everyone. The youngest sister, Irma, had slept between her parents, and she got up with a smile on her face. Raul and Rigo got up from the double bed in the back of the room. As Raul walked by, he gave Roland a playful smile and walked on into the kitchen. They got ready for school.

Alejandro woke up, and he and Roland had their first conversation ever. Roland in a very diplomatic manner said that he had come to help Raul obtain a passport and then a VISA so that he would be able to come and work with Roland on his jobs this coming summer. Alejandro showed him the hand sign meaning lack of money, and Roland said that he would buy it for him. That pleased Alejandro, and for the next 20 minutes, they talked things over and made plans. Alejandro and Lavinia started looking for Raul's documents: birth certificate, vaccination card, ID, school grades, and they made plans to go later in the week to Sabinas Hidalgo to the passport office to apply for Raul's passport, which since he was under 18, would require the signatures of both of his parents.

Meanwhile, during the time that Roland and Alejandro talked, Raul, Rigo, and Norma walked out of the house and went to school. Lavinia brought breakfast to Roland, which he happily accepted.

Later that day, Raul came over to the Quevalos to help Roland with the motor. No more than Raul had been there five minutes than Pancho came forth and asked their help in going to his aunt's property on the other side of town to help him transplant some Pecan trees. Both Roland and Raul agreed to it, and they joined Pancho and Alejandro in Pancho's old Ford pickup truck.

Raul was feeling much better and more energetic today, and Roland enjoyed his time with them. As they carried the heavy Pecan trees to the truck, Raul said some things to make Roland laugh, and he just about dropped the Pecan tree and dirt ball he was carrying.

These trees were already sold to a client who lived in Monterrey. He had a ranch between Bustamante and Villaldama, and Pancho drove them over there to plant them. When they arrived, the client was not there. This got Pancho angry, and he took them over to Villaldama where he rounded up several law officials and the Diputado (Deputy) of Villaldama. He ran several more errands with them to several locations in Villaldama, and finally, an hour later, he took them, including the police, to the ranch and went over the written agreement with them.

Raul was playful with Roland and was making jokes, and he sometimes put bugs down his shirt. Roland put tree leaves down Raul's shirt to get him back, and that only made Raul respond more. They had some laughs, and they had the best time playing like children. After lots of playing and joking around with each other, they managed to drag the Pecan trees off the truck and plant them. Then Pancho drove them back to Bustamante.

After that, Roland and Raul cleaned more of the engine parts, and Raul told Roland, "Caíste del cielo," saying that he came down from the sky to help him. Roland was glad that Raul appreciated him, especially since he carried Roland's card in his wallet.

The next day, Alejandro drove his entire family in his big 1974 Ford Country Sedan station wagon, and Roland accompanied them. They went to Sabinas Hidalgo to see about getting Raul his passport. The car didn't run very well, and Alejandro had to recharge the battery. Also, as they were leaving town, he pulled over at a small tire shop and had his tires aired up. This was a usual practice for many Mexicans who had cars. In Villaldama, Alejandro put some gasoline in the car's tank, and they were off to Sabinas Hidalgo. The car sent out plenty of exhaust, and it was, of course, not properly sealed anymore, and some of it came inside the car. Roland rolled down the window to breathe fresh air. He remembered the manner in which Alejandro drove, slow and easy, as if he was driving a land yacht.

Alejandro's station wagon was the largest model Ford ever made. Of course, it was automatic, as all American full size cars were from 1972 forward. However, Mexico did make a few of those models with a standard shift, 3-speed on the column. Roland had actually seen one in Monterrey back in 1983, same model and same color as Alejandro's land yacht.

When they reached the passport office in Sabinas Hidalgo's central plaza, they parked and walked inside. Alejandro and Lavinia filled out the necessary paperwork. Raul had pictures made, and Roland paid the N$600 for the passport. By the next week, it would be ready. Roland would bring them back at that time.

After that, Alejandro drove them to the supermarket Centro Comercial San José, where they bought groceries. The store owned a restaurant across the street with the same name. Then Alejandro drove them to the salvage yard to look for car parts, followed by stopping by his cousin's house to visit. By late afternoon, they finally returned to Bustamante.

On the way back, Norma told Roland when she was born, July 11, 1986 at 10:20 AM. Roland thought about that date and remembered that he was hiking in the mountains in the state of Washington at that time.

Later that evening, while Roland was over at Lorenzo's house visiting, Pancho entered with a stack of Mexican money in his shirt pocket. He told Roland the police had telephoned the client in Monterrey and had made him pay Pancho for the trees, a total of US $500. He told Roland, "Este es lo que tiene que hacer cuando cobra a la gente," saying that's what one had to do when charging people for items sold. Pancho never sold any more trees. He had pushed the envelope too far.

Pancho and Lorenzo recommended that Roland take Raul and his family to Monterrey to the American Consulate to get the VISA as soon as possible, while Raul was still in school. Roland considered that a good suggestion, and he made plans accordingly.

Over the course of the following week, Raul came over in the afternoons after school and helped Roland with his truck motor. One of the afternoons, they finished assembling the motor and attached it to the chain hoist. Lorenzo was going to help, but he couldn't be found at the right time. Roland took matters into his own hands, and Raul and Eliud helped accordingly. They lowered the motor into the truck and installed it themselves. Lorenzo arrived later and was surprised to see the motor already installed.

The next morning, Roland decided to do away with something. He had written out a bunch of coincidence data and had explained it to Lorenzo, coincidences about Chip Collins, Ivanhoe, the Quevalos, and even Leonardo, all having to do with matching phone numbers and other numbers. Interesting as it was, Roland was no longer so impressed by it, and now that he had a new friend, Raul, he really didn't care about those past friends, some of whom had rejected him. He handed the pages of data to Lorenzo and told him to burn it. Lorenzo commented, "Que bueno," meaning how good it was that Roland was doing away with it.

Lorenzo tossed it into the orno fire, and a considerable amount of black smoke soon went up in the air. That surprised Roland, and Lorenzo said it was because the data was very dirty and needed to be gotten rid of. Roland was glad to get rid of it also. He released any obsessions he used to have. Even though the data was burned, Roland had backup copies at home in Tennessee. He certainly believed in documenting interesting coincidences.

That afternoon, Raul came over again, and they started the engine, which was now installed in the truck. They took the truck for a drive, and Roland let Raul drive a little bit. Some of the valves were clicking, and one of them had a worn out rocker arm and wasn't getting oil. Replacing some of those solved that problem.

That evening, Raul, Eliud, Pancho, and Roland visited for a while. Pancho expressed the desire to see Chiquihuitillos, the name of some ancient cliff paintings in the desert valley on the other side of the mountains. Roland also told Pancho that he had burned the coincidence data. Pancho and Raul said that was good. Then they explained to Roland that he was stubborn, and for that reason Chip Collins had avoided him. As Pancho demonstrated how Roland had repeatedly asked Chip questions, Raul gently poked Roland in the chest to show what being a nuisance was like. Roland saw the point. He knew that people thought he came on too strong, but he didn't really believe he was that extreme. Roland realized that Pancho and Raul understood the life pretty well, and they impressed him with their common sense on that.

A surprise came. Lola came to Roland as he was visiting with Raul, Pancho and Eliud, and she said, "Habla Leonardo," saying that Leonardo was on the phone. Leonardo was the furthest thing from Roland's mind at the moment. Roland realized that he had forgotten about him, now having new friends like Raul. He went to the phone and took the call. Leonardo had never had a chance to go into the mountains with Roland. He explained that he had decided to call since he knew Roland would be leaving tomorrow. It was then that Roland remembered that he had left a note at Leonardo's house saying that he would be leaving the end of January. While he had Leonardo on the phone, Roland made very sure to ask him why he had to ask him three times in a row for his address in Monterrey the day he had gone there with Pancho. Leonardo explained that there was a lot of noise in the house at the time Roland had called, and he couldn't hear his question. Roland left it at that, wished Leonardo well, and they finished the phone conversation.

It was now the last day of January, and Roland got up at 7:30 AM and adjusted the valves. Pancho kept coming over to help, and he was surprisingly stubborn and showed impatience. That was Pancho's intense character at times, and it was annoying to Roland. Some of Pancho's suggestions were very good, but some were too extreme, and Roland's common sense knew they were.

Raul came over in the afternoon, and they adjusted the valves again. He surprised Roland by asking him if they were going to go up in the mountains tomorrow, which was Saturday. Roland thought he never wanted to go again after his legs had been so sore last Sunday. With a look of surprise, he said to Raul, "Bueno, vamos," meaning, Sure, let's go.

They took the truck for a drive. Raul enjoyed being at the wheel. Roland could tell that Raul had not driven much, but he was quickly learning. Raul was a fast learner and had a surprising amount of dexterity and precision about how he handled things. He quickly became good at it, and he knew exactly how to engage and disengage the clutch, as well.

They took the truck to the small river on the north side of town and gave it a good washing. Raul was very friendly, and Roland was really enjoying his company. He let Raul drive some more after they washed the truck. They also circled the plaza.

At this time, feelings of a really true friendship flooded over Roland. He had never known this level of friendship before. It had been a long time for him, after all the rejection he had suffered over the past several years. He realized that he already knew Raul better than he had ever known Chip Collins. Roland had finally done it. He had made a truly good friend in Mexico. He had never realized a friendship could be as good as the one he presently had with Raul, a friend who was spending plenty of time with him because he enjoyed it. In the future, his brother Rigo would nearly equal that. Their friendship was exceptional, and it really made no difference that Raul was less than half Roland's age. They were equals in many ways, and their being the same height and size was an extra added bonus which made things even better. Roland was really enjoying Raul, and he felt like shouting with joy. Roland just sat back, enjoyed it, and let the good feelings wash over him. For the first time in ages, he felt like he was number one.

Raul drove them to his house, and they walked inside. Lavinia served them supper. Roland visited with them, and he showed them his photos of Tennessee and of Mexico.

Afterwards, they returned to the Quevalos, and Raul and Roland visited with India this evening. She enjoyed chatting with them, and she talked to them about the upcoming Día de Amor (Valentine's Day). As she explained to Roland the custom, she suddenly and casually commented:

". . . y Raul está enamorado a tí," saying that Raul was in love with Roland.

Roland did his best to squelch any embarrassment, and he went on talking as if the comment was ordinary. He really hoped Raul had not heard it. If he had, he wasn't showing any signs of it. A few minutes later, Raul wished them well, got up, and walked home. Roland went to his truck and slept for the night.

Tomorrow, they were going to go up in the mountains again.

CHAPTER 4

THE POISONOUS TONGUE

It was now a new month, the first day of February 1997.

Raul arrived on his bicycle at 8 AM, and he was ready to go. Roland was nearly ready, but he still had to run to the bathroom. Raul waited, and five minutes later, they started walking. As they walked through town, Raul complained, saying to Roland that he wasn't ready on time, that he went to the bathroom, and other things.

Roland already suspected that India's comment was bothering him, and sure enough, Raul suddenly said, "¿Por qué India dijo que estoy enamorado a tí?" Raul had indeed heard India's comment. Roland answered that he didn't know but that it bothered him, too. He assured Raul that he was his friend, and no, he was not in love in a manner as if they were gays. He also went on to tell Raul that he believed India was jealous of their friendship, and for that reason she had said the comment to give them problems with their friendship. Raul took Roland's reasoning and explanation just fine, but little did Roland realize what was yet to come because of India's poisonous comment! The comment would bother and haunt Raul for months!

Raul and Roland walked through the town and up the gravel road to the cono at the road's end. They talked again about India's comment, and Raul stopped, reached his hand out, shook hands with Roland, and said, "Mucho gusto haberte conocido, Rolando. Ya no vamos a hacer nada," saying that it was a pleasure knowing Roland and that they were no longer going to do anything together (since Roland was soon to go back to Tennessee). For a brief moment, Roland thought Raul was going to turn around and walk back to town, but he didn't. Somehow, they continued for the mountains.

When they arrived at the road's end, no one was at the cono which meant the guide, Ramiro, was more than likely at the cave entrance instead. They began the 45-minute climb to the cave and ascended rather steeply in places. Around 15 minutes up the trail, they took a rest and sat under the large Oak tree situated next to a rock face. Then they made the rest of the steep ascent to the cave entrance. As they crested the rise where the cave came into view, there were four other fellows from Monterrey who were also there. They had just arrived, having been barely ahead of Roland and Raul. All of them entered the crevice and descended steeply to entrance. The iron gate was open. As they looked inside, they could see that the lights were turned on. It never ceased to amaze Roland how absolutely enormous the size of the cave was.

They decided to enter. Ramiro was indeed there. He greeted Roland and Raul since he knew them. He he didn't charge anything to the two of them, since Roland had earlier given him some lightweight hiking boots. Then he introduced himself to the others, and they began the tour.

"Estas grutas son muy bonitas, y son unas de las más grandes en el mundo," Ramiro told them, explaining that the caves are spectacular and that they are some of the largest in the world.

They made the fairly long descent to the floor of the first room. It was Raul's first time inside the cave, and he was really amazed at its size. He was impressed by the huge formations of calcified stalagmites and stalactites.

Ramiro told them about the different formations, and the locals had even conjured up names for some of them, such as *La Ballena* and *El Bujero.*

Next, he took them deeper into the cave by leading them down a steep sloping hillside for at least 200 meters and arriving on the floor of another huge room. There were more formations, and in a couple of places there were some small ponds. As they proceeded, he turned on more lights.

They crossed the second large room, and they passed through a very narrow passageway that took them to another large room. The pathway was now treacherous and slippery, and they carefully made their way down it to the floor of that room. It was not as large as the previous two rooms but still considerably large.

Ramiro took them to the edge of that room and showed them a dropoff, telling them that cave explorers had gone on much further. This was as far as the lights went and was the limit to how far the tours were taken. He told them that cave exploration teams had come from all over the world, but still no one had ever reached the end of these caves. It remained a mystery just how far back the caves of Bustamante really went.

An hour had passed since they had entered, and Ramiro announced that it was time to return to the entrance at the top. They crossed the room, climbed the treacherous trail, passed through the narrow opening, locally called *El Bujero*, and they returned via the same route by which they had entered. Dust flew up in the air as they climbed the steep, sloping hillside to arrive at the first room. They crossed it and made the final ascent to the entrance where they walked back out into the outdoors again.

Roland and Raul thanked Ramiro, and they hiked further up the mountain. By the time they finally reached the region that Roland was working on, they only had an hour to clear the trail. They made some progress, and they hiked a little further to a highland meadow. Roland took a self timed photo of the two of them, and then they began the descent back down the mountain to Bustamante.

It had become a little cloudy, and it sprinkled on them for part of the way. They successfully descended the steepest section, including the narrow gully where Roland had installed a rope. As they were leaving the forested gully, they walked along the narrowest part of the trail which hugged the cliff on the right side and was mostly a dropoff on the left side.

This area was popular for calling out and hearing echoes. Raul called out several phrases, and he enjoyed hearing his echo. Then he surprised Roland by calling out foul language, and when Roland asked him not to say that, Raul immediately shouted out the phrase some twenty times! That really upset Roland, as he detested foul language in the first place, and he yelled, "¡Cállate!" telling him to shut up. Raul did, and Roland turned around, walked past Raul, went several hundred meters back up the trail, and retraced his steps to correct what was done, if that was possible. He was really angry, but he did his best not to lose his temper. He returned to where Raul was standing waiting for him. Though Raul explained that he didn't realize it would displease Roland so much, he knew that it would, and he had done it on purpose to get him angry. Talk about a poisonous tongue and its repercussions!

Roland knew why, and he then brought up to Raul that India's comment had really bothered him. Raul admitted that it did, and he and Roland talked some more about it the rest of the way back down the mountain. For the whole day, Roland could sense that Raul seemed bothered by something, and he knew it had to be that. Raul had been making subtle gestures of not wanting to be with Roland, and he certainly was not warm hearted like the week before when they had climbed the Lion's Head Mountain. Hopefully, Raul would soon get over it.

That night, Roland went to Raul's house to visit. He was getting ready for the Saturday night dance, as he did every Saturday night. They talked and forgave each other.

The next day, Roland decided to go right back to the mountains, this time alone! At least he would not hear any foul language, and he would walk the narrow stretch in *peace* and *quiet*! He looked forward to it. Though he wished more than anything in the world to have a good friend like Raul accompany him, he also liked his *quiet* moments and *alone*!

Roland climbed the mountain and cleared a good stretch of trail, far more than he and Raul had cleared yesterday. He was still irritated at what Raul had shouted so many times the day before, and he worked out his anger by clearing the trail with vigor! At least he had gone an entire previous month without hearing any foul language at all, the first time he had been spared for so long in his life, but then after the thousands of foul words that his recent past friend Chip had said, he reasoned that he had been given that amount of time away from hearing awful words like that, as a means of compensation.

Roland arrived at the highland forest, turned around, and descended the mountain back to Bustamante. When he passed the clearing, the views were excellent, and he could see the plains well to the east of Sabinas Hidalgo. For the next 2½ hours, he descended, arriving at the cono right at dark.

As Roland was walking on the gravel road back to Bustamante, he met a young fellow who was running. His name was Oscar, age 18, and he was studying to be a teacher. They got to talking and walked back to Bustamante together. They soon became friends, and Roland would continue to know him along with many others he would become friends with in Bustamante. Oscar invited Roland to his house to meet his family. Roland accepted, entered with him, and found them to be a nice family.

Before leaving, Roland called the Quevalos on the phone to let them know he had arrived safely from the mountains so they wouldn't send out the police to search for him. Roland then walked the two blocks over to Raul's house.

Both Raul and Rigo were there, and Lavinia gave Roland some supper, which he accepted with thanks. He was really hungry after the day of trail clearing. Raul and Rigo looked at the things in Roland's daypack, and they talked about what they had done for the day. Roland realized that everything was all right after all, and he was pleased.

He arrived at the Quevalos by 8 PM. Sarita and her daughters were indeed content and talked in a friendly manner with Roland. She asked Roland if he was actually going to move over and stay with Raul's family. Roland said that was the plan. They expressed concern that there would be danger with Raul and Rigo's father, Alejandro. The oldest daughter said that Alejandro may be friendly, but when he drinks, he may forget everything. Roland appreciated the Quevalo's concern.

Roland's parents, quite by chance, called this evening. Roland talked to them for 15 minutes, and they informed him that a terrible tornado had struck down, barely missed their house, touched down a little further east, and plowed through a populated neighborhood. It had severely damaged a house of some very good friends of theirs, and they had to move out for six months while they would have it fixed. Roland felt for them.

Roland slept in the back of his truck for the night. The next morning, he got up and fixed himself breakfast as usual. It wasn't long before Lola and Lydia Quevalo came over and said that their mother had said that he could continue to stay until the 10th of February. They had been concerned for what Alejandro might do. Roland thanked them and therefore decided to stay on.

Then Lola told Roland that Esalina Velazco had called and asked if he could go to Monterrey and pick up some things that she wanted to send to her good friend Isalia in Tennessee. Roland didn't know if he was going to go to Monterrey again during this stay, but he said he would talk to her anyway to see if he could work something out to help. Lola then told Roland he could use the phone this evening to call Esalina reverse charge (collect) and to make the call at 8 PM. Roland thanked her and made plans to call her at that time.

During the day, Roland drove his truck to Sabinas Hidalgo and did errands. He returned to Bustamante, and Raul was at the Quevalos working on chairs. They took the truck for a drive.

Roland ate supper with the Quevalos, borrowed a typewriter, and typed up a proposed letter of parental consent for Raul to go stay with Roland next year in Tennessee.

He also went to Oscar's house and arranged to go hiking with him this Wednesday. Oscar had told him about *Las Piedras Azules* (The Blue Rocks) at the foot of the mountains west of Bustamante. That sounded interesting to Roland, and he looked forward to it.

At 8 PM, Roland returned to the Quevalos and went to the phone to call Esalina. He couldn't find anyone to let them know he was going to use it, and he looked for everyone. Finally he found them in the back room on the right side of the house. They were all huddled together, saying prayers and recitations. Roland realized that they were blessing the Christmas tree and nativity scene before taking it down. So, that was indeed true about February 2nd, after all. He was glad to know that because he had thought they were lying to him back in 1992 when he had taken down the Redwood tree and planted it, and they had gotten so angry.

Out of courtesy, Roland wanted to let them know he was going to use the phone, but under the circumstances, he didn't want to interrupt them at such an *important* time to ask them if he could use the phone. For all he knew, they would be blessing the tree for hours, knowing how they had ranted and raved so, back in 1992. Besides, Lola had already given him full consent to use the phone. So, why should he have to ask again, anyway? With that reasoning, Roland went to the wall phone in the bakery, (the phone he had given them the first time he had ever come), picked up the handset, and dialled 02 for the operator. He gave her Esalina's number and called her collect.

He reached Esalina, and he told her he didn't think he would be going to Monterrey, but if he did, he could probably stop by her house and pick up the things she wanted to send to Isalia. He also asked her if she could come to Bustamante to deliver the things to the Quevalos. Esalina explained that it would be a waste of time, and if she did that, then she may as well mail the items to Isalia, but then she knew how undependable the mail system was between Mexico and the United States.

Roland hadn't been on the phone more than a minute to Esalina before Olana discovered him. Boy they got done with the blessing of their Christmas tree in a hurry! Olana had a look of shock on her face, and she angrily shouted, "¿Quién te prestó el teléfono?" (Who let you use the telephone?)

With Esalina clearly listening, and Roland made sure he did NOT cover the handset, he firmly told Olana, "No te preocupes. Llamé colectiva," telling her not to worry, that he called collect.

Olana stood there and waited while Roland finished his conversation with Esalina. Once he hung up, Olana lit into him with scolding remarks. He responded by telling Olana that Lola had given him permission this morning to come here at 8 PM and use the phone to call Esalina collect.

She didn't believe him and said, "¡No, hombre, es pura mentira!" telling him that was a lie.

Roland had really had enough of Olana and her *attitude,* and he firmly told her not to make him feel bad and that he didn't do anything wrong. Besides, it did not sit well with him that the Quevalos had not let him use the telephone to make direct dial calls from time to time, even though he had always offered to pay for the calls he would have made. With that said, he immediately walked off, went over to Lorenzo's house, and told him what happened. Lorenzo wasn't sure what to do, but he sensed that there would be some form of retaliation from the Quevalo females. Roland could sense that the daughters, especially Olana, never had forgiven him for the falling out that had occurred five years ago with the whole family, and that they also didn't trust him. Olana was very unsocial to him, and Roland had never once heard her laugh . . . at all. Actually, Olana had never liked Roland in the first place.

He told Lorenzo about Esalina's request and also that she didn't want to come to Bustamante to deliver the items. That irritated Lorenzo, and he angrily said that Esalina was very tight, that she lived in the richest colonia of Monterrey and didn't want to spend the money to come to Bustamante to deliver the items, if she really wanted to send them to Isalia!

It was the next day before Roland found out that Lola had not been a part of the blessing ceremony that evening and that she wasn't even there when Roland went to make the call.

That morning, Raul didn't go to school, and Roland took him and his parents, including Norma, to Sabinas Hidalgo to properly obtain the passport. Raul put his fingerprints on a form, and his parents signed for it, giving their permission for him to have it. The passport chosen would last for five years. They returned to Bustamante and visited a notary public to have the parental permission letter signed. Roland then found out that what he had typed was no good. The notary explained how it was supposed to be done, and he had typed out a three-page document, including the birth dates and residence address of Raul's parents. They signed the documents. Roland took Raul and his family back home and ate lunch with them.

After lunch, Roland and Raul went to the Quevalos to work on the truck for the last time, to take the valve cover off the engine to adjust the valves. Soon after arriving, Roland went into the back room out of everyone's sight, where he had gone each day to change into his old work clothes. Once he had changed, he left the room and went to a pole barn to gather his tools to begin work with Raul.

At that moment, while Roland and Raul were both standing in the pole barn, Sarita entered the back room with an angry face, and in twenty seconds, she returned to Roland with his clothes in her arms, and she firmly said, "Ya no cambies en ese cuarto. Voy a reportar tu comportamiento a Isalia, y ya no vas a regresar a México!" telling Roland never to change clothes in that room, that she was going to report his behavior to Isalia, and that as a result, he would never return to Mexico.

The Poisonous Tongue

Roland quickly answered, "Isalia no me manda," telling Sarita that Isalia doesn't mandate him. He saw Sarita's face get angrier. Roland was really put out with the bad attitudes of the Quevalos, and he really didn't care to be considerate. He blurted out to her, "¿Por qué estás enojado? Dígame. No hice nada mal. DIGAME!!" asking her why she was angry at him, that he didn't do anything wrong, and strongly insisting that she tell him!

It was at that moment that three of the daughters came to Roland. Olana spoke first, answering the question for her mother, telling him that he had used the phone without permission last night. Roland told her again that Lola had already given him permission. Then Lola told Roland that she wasn't there last night, and since he had used the phone without asking her, (as if getting her permission 12 hours earlier didn't count), that was where he had made his fault.

Roland said to them, "¡Si sienten así, ya me voy!" telling them that since they felt that way then he would leave right away.

They gave him a gesture implying, *Good Riddance.*

Roland repeated his question to Sarita about why she was so angry.

With that, Olana told Roland to shut up or they would call the police. Then Sarita picked up a garden hoe to hit Roland.

He firmly told Sarita, "¡Si me pegas con el talache, ya te llevo a la policía!" telling her that if she hits him with that garden hoe, he would carry her straight to the police!

If it was possible for them to get angrier, they did. They freaked out! Pancho arrived in his truck at that moment. Roland walked out to intercept him and told him what had just happened. Pancho accompanied him back to the females, and after they told Pancho what Roland had done, Pancho meekly said he couldn't defend him. That didn't please Roland at all, and he went on to defend himself, explaining his reasoning, but how is that possible when you're dealing with African honeybees (the Quevalo females)?!

They were going on and on about that fact that Roland hadn't asked permission the second time to use the phone and that no one had loaned it to him to use last night. The Quevalos had set Roland a trap about the phone call to Esalina. Though Lola said nothing of it, she had left on purpose right before 8 PM so that when Roland would come and make that call, he wouldn't be able to advise her, and then they could use that against him. Very clever! They had provoked the whole problem and situation so they would have a "reason" to run him off, and with this being done, he knew they were definitely not his friends.

Roland wasn't going to shove in their face, but now he did, and he reminded them, "¿Quién te **dió** el teléfono aparato?" asking them who had *given* them that phone instrument.

Lydia quickly answered, "¡Y te lo regresamos!" telling him that they would return it to him! She knew very well that Roland had given that phone to them.

Roland said he didn't want it because he already had plenty of them in his phone collection back in Tennessee. He also told them he had planned to give them some money for his having stayed with them. They told him they didn't want his money.

Roland then walked off to see how Raul was doing with the valve cover.

It was at that moment that India came to Roland absolutely hysterical, shouting at him and telling him that she was going right to the authorities to have them remove him! Roland asked her to calm down, but she wasn't about to reason, as he immediately realized. He then walked with her to the police station. He told India that he had been good. She said that they were all extremely tired of him, and anger was an understatement! She said that he lacked respect for her mother and was never supposed to yell at her. Roland told India and made it clear to her that her mother was about to hit him with the garden hoe, and he had to defend himself. He wasn't going to take that off of anybody! Age difference had nothing to do with it.

With that said, Roland ran ahead of her to make sure and arrive at the police station before her so he would have time to explain to them that he hadn't done anything wrong and that a hysterical woman was on her way to complain about him.

India arrived a minute later, and she went on and on with her complaints, including lying to the police that Roland hadn't given them anything nor bought them any food nor given them any money for his stay. Roland understood most of what she said, and he knew her statements were false. He defended himself, explaining to them what he actually did and that he had indeed given them things. The police, thanks to them and their reasoning, realized that India was hysterical, and they explained to Roland that the Quevalos didn't want Roland with them anymore and that he would have to leave their residence. They suggested he go stay with Raul since he had invited him. Roland said he would leave with pleasure, but at the moment, his truck was sitting on Quevalo property with the valves being adjusted. The police said he had the right to stay on Quevalo property long enough to put his truck back together, load it with his goods, and to leave by sunset. Roland thanked them and returned to his truck where Raul was working on it. India left the police with an angry face.

On the way back, Roland thought to collect the keys to India's building where he had his goods stored. She was keeping a key under a can on the right side of the building, and since he thought she might take the keys and deny him access to the building and his goods, he considered his action a good precautionary move. He stepped over the fence, collected the keys, and continued back to the Quevalo's main house where Raul was already working on Roland's truck.

India looked for the keys on her way back and couldn't find them as a result. She came to Roland and angrily demanded the keys! Roland said to her that he wanted his stuff out of there first. She accompanied him over there, and while she stood outside with an angry face, he took his belongings out of her building. He stacked them beside the building, to be collected upon leaving. While India was outside, Roland placed his foot on one of the dilapidated chairs and purposefully broke one of the rungs. He also purposefully dropped one of his boxes at the exact same moment to cover up the cracking sound of the breaking rung. There! That made him feel better. How dare her that she carried him to the police! Roland had done very well not to go into a rage, for all that had happened. India really did have a poisonous tongue! He knew the smartest thing he had done was to have gone to the police station ahead of her. It was important that the police also knew his side of the story because his side of the story was true . . . and not hers!

Roland returned to his truck. He was so shocked by what the Quevalos had done. He worked on his truck with Raul, and he appreciated Raul for being his friend. Raul had witnessed everything except the police visit, and they talked about it. Raul told Roland to still tell them thanks, even though they had been so ugly.

Roland went to tell Sr. Lorenzo Quevalo what had happened, that they had run him off. He declared, "¡Válgame Dios! Sí, puedes quedar," saying, Lord help me! Yes, you can stay. He was a kind man, but since he was 90, he was unable to defend Roland and make the females see reason.

The Poisonous Tongue

Two hours later, Roland and Raul had the truck loaded. He thanked the Quevalos, and the only one who wished Roland well was Lydia who said, "Que te vaya bien."

India told Roland that he lacked education for not having put the keys back in their right spot, like he was supposed to do. He never told India that he had grabbed the keys on the way back from the police station. Roland told her that her father said he could go on staying there if he wanted to. India said that with $3,000 dollars, he could. Roland knew that was ridiculous, and he gladly left the Quevalos.

The Quevalos had definitely severed any relationship with Roland now, and he really didn't care anymore. They were just not worth it. The Quevalos had created a new definition for the words: *running somebody off*. Roland was glad he was leaving. He was too flustered to drive for what had happened, so he sat in the passenger seat and let Raul drive the truck. They stopped by India's building and loaded the goods. As they drove away in the loaded truck, Roland felt true feelings of friendship and appreciation for Raul. He sincerely told him, "Gracias a tí. Eres mi amigo," telling Raul thanks and that he is his friend. How good he felt to be leaving the Quevalos. In fact, he felt like he was going away with a gold nugget and leaving the scum behind! He felt fortunate to have some friends like Raul and his family to go and stay with.

Minutes later, they pulled up in front of Alejandro and Lavinia's house, and Raul and Roland began to unload the truck. Rigo was also home, and he helped them. Roland had quite a lot of stuff, since he had collected five feed sackfuls of dried Fan Palm leaves. Rigo was glad that Roland had moved in with them, and he asked Raul and Roland what had happened. Raul proceeded to tell his brother about the incident, and he reacted with surprise.

Lavinia was home, and Norma and Irma were inside. They came outside to welcome Roland into their home. As Roland moved the last of the stuff inside the house, he sat down and ate supper with them. Lavinia talked with Raul and Roland about the horrible incident, and as Raul repeated what the Quevalo females said, Lavinia commented, "¡Que bárbaro!" meaning how barbaric, and she was right. That's just what the Quevalos were . . . barbarians!

Lavinia went on to comment that it was also barbaric how the Quevalos had made Roland sleep in his truck, and it was worse that Lola, the oldest sister, had not even wanted Roland sleeping in Lorenzo's house on the coldest nights! It had been only at Lorenzo's kindness and insistence that Roland had been allowed to sleep in that house on those particularly cold nights. Further, the meals the Quevalos served Roland were poorly done, and Roland realized that Lavinia's cooking was of much better quality.

After supper, Roland went over to Chely and Vico's house, and Chely let him use the phone to call Isalia collect. Roland did so, and Isalia accepted.

"Isalia," Roland began, "you won't believe what the Quevalos have done."

"What did they do?"

"Well, they got nasty with me, ran me off, and reported me to the police."

"Well, I can't do anything about it," Isalia told him.

What sort of comment was that? Roland thought. *Does she have no sympathy for me?*

"I know that," Roland told her, "but I would like it if you would tell them that I'm a decent person. After all, I did a lot to help them out in the past."

"I'll talk to them," said Isalia.

"Thanks, and I don't know what lies they're going to make up about me . . ." and Roland told Isalia the course of the events over several minutes.

85

"Well, I'm sorry about it," she finally said. "Just get away from them."

"Oh, I did, and with pleasure," Roland assured her. "I'm staying with a new and very good friend of mine and his family."

They wrapped up the conversation, and Roland hung up. He thanked Chely for the use of the phone, which happened to be another phone he had brought with him and given five years earlier.

Roland also went to the Alberto's house and told him what had happened. Since he was a nearby neighbor, he knew the Quevalos, and he told Roland, "Nadie las quiere, hasta la esquina," saying that no one wants them, right up the block to the corner. Roland could understand why.

Alberto also told him a story that the Quevalos were more prominent fifteen years ago, and that it had been considered by Bustamante's town council (Presidencia) to install the ZuaZua bus station on the corner right by Lorenzo's house. The Quevalos were really hoping for it, as their bakery business would therefore be right by it, and thrive. They would be able to sell their bread like it was going out of style. Well, as it turned out, the town decided to install the bus station in the central plaza, the most practical place. That rubbed the Quevalos the wrong way, and they had been resenting the Presidencia's decision and squabbling about it ever since. Roland realized that they had also been squabbling about him ever since he had planted his Redwood tree for them five years ago! He wondered why in the world he had troubled himself to forgive them the year before and become friends with them again. Furthering his friendship with them was now impossible, and Roland thought, *What a bunch of ungrateful barbarians! Good riddance!*

There was still another reason why the Quevalos were on bad relations with the Presidencia. Five years earlier, they had baked a large bread order worth over US $500 that the town had requested from them, to donate to a charity program in Monterrey to feed the hungry and poor. Well, several months went by, and the Presidencia never paid them, and Lola and Lydia had gone to them several times to charge them for the bread order. They even made a trip to the charitable organization in Monterrey to formally charge them for the order. More months went by, and no check ever arrived. The Quevalos got angry with the Presidencia, and Lydia, who was a secretary, lost her job as a result, among other things. The charity organization remained owing the $500 to the Quevalos, and after several years, they had still not paid them. The Quevalos themselves were poor, so it was a case of taking away from the poor to give to the poor.

The next day was a school holiday, and Raul went to work all day at Pancho's. Roland went to the Quevalos despite their having run him off the day before, located Pancho, and requested to talk to him. Pancho came forward, and Roland told him he still wanted to buy two chairs from him. Pancho took him in his truck to their newer shop in the lower part of town, where he had his extra chairs stored. Roland chose two Pine rocking chairs with Palm leaf woven bottoms and backs.

Roland paid him, and then they talked for an hour about the whole thing. Pancho assured Roland he was his friend, but under the circumstances, he had been unable to defend Roland because his sisters were all older than he, and they were the ones who mandated. Roland also took note and made sense of a sign that was posted by this shop. The sign said, *"Mujeres en Solidaridad,"* meaning Women in Solidarity. The Quevalo females enjoyed being in power, and they mandated like hornets! Pancho explained that his sisters were spoiled and had never suffered in their whole lives. He also said that he was soon going to build a house here on this newer property, to get away from the "hornet's nest", and he told Roland he was welcome to stay here whenever he was in town. It remained to be seen if that would ever come true. Pancho told Roland it was good that they had been able to talk about it, and Roland thanked him for his time and stated that they would go on being friends.

Roland then returned to Raul's house, and he gave one of the rocking chairs to them. The other chair, he would take home with him. They gladly received the chair, as their chairs and furniture were falling apart. Raul came home at lunch, and they talked about how things were going. Roland was so glad to be staying with the Zacatón family. He felt like he was in heaven, compared to the Quevalos.

This afternoon, Roland went to the Blue Rocks with Oscar. It was misty and cloudy with some drizzle at times. There was no visibility, but the walk was nice. Oscar showed him the large dark colored rock outcroppings, and he told him these rocks were thought to have special powers and energies. That was interesting to Roland, even though he felt nothing unusual around them. They walked from rock to rock, climbed on top of some of them, and looked at their formations. After touring the rocks, they walked back to town. Roland enjoyed the afternoon, and he found Oscar to be a friendly and peaceful fellow.

The next day, Roland and Alejandro went to the school and did other errands to get letters of recommendation from the Presidencia at the plaza, the hotel where Lavinia worked, and from the secundaria school, all in preparation for the trip to Monterrey to visit the American Consulate in hopes of obtaining a tourist VISA for Raul.

While Raul was in school that morning, Alejandro and Roland went to the Presidencia and obtained a well written letter of good standing from them. There was a fee for this of N$20. Then they went by the Hotel Ancira and secured a letter from Felipe Hernandez, after which they went to the secundaria school and spoke with the director.

Alejandro talked to him, asking him to write the letter. He said he would write it, and it would be ready the next day. It was then that Alejandro brought up that they were going to go to Monterrey tonight, to visit the American Consulate first thing in the morning. The director was considerably unobliging, and when Roland also spoke to him to explain why they needed the letter right away, he looked at Roland and smugly told him, "No conozco a usted," saying that he didn't know him. That was supposed to put Roland in his place, and he never thought much of that school director from then on.

Roland then watched and was actually impressed as Alejandro managed to alter the outcome of events. Alejandro continued talking to him, and the next thing he knew, they had come to an agreement. He watched Alejandro take N$30 out of his wallet and give it to the director. With that done, he had succeeded in persuading the director to write the letter within the hour. While Alejandro and the director had been talking, Roland had been talking to another teacher at the school who commented that the director was usually unaccommodating and was a *huevón* (lazy bum). That made Roland laugh because he already realized that there was no way the director was going to accommodate anybody . . . unless he was paid.

They returned to the house. Raul came home from school, and Lavinia served them lunch. She had their bags packed. After lunch, Alejandro and Raul loaded their goods onto Roland's truck. They made a final check to be sure they had all the paperwork in order, and they drove to Sabinas Hidalgo to pick up the passport.

Roland drove them there, and they waited at the passport office in the central plaza for two hours. The man who brought the passports every Thursday was running late. Alejandro visited his cousin around the corner, and Roland and Raul sat in front of the building and waited. They talked about Tennessee and what it was going to be like next year. Raul was not very willing to talk about it, and Roland could tell that Raul was quite worried about the upcoming events, securing the passport, going to Monterrey, and visiting the American Consulate the next morning.

Finally, the man arrived. His car had broken down, which is why he was running so late. In short order, the passports were handed out to the thirty or so people who were waiting for them. The passport looked good, with Raul's picture in it and everything.

Next, Roland took them to BanVital, a Mexican bank, where something called a Comprobante was sold for N$158, which was a piece of paper that was required by the American Consulate when applying for a VISA. Any Mexican who went to the Consulate had to have one of these in hand, or the VISA would not even be considered.

With all that done, Roland drove them to Monterrey on the Carretera Nacional, Highway 85. There were lots of tractor trailer trucks on the highway, and one would never have known there was also an Autopista, a toll freeway, if they hadn't been told. Almost no one used it because there was a hefty charge for using it, N$110, and further, Sabinas Hidalgo had no direct access to it, which made it even more useless.

Roland drove them into Monterrey at dark, and Alejandro gave directions. They first stopped by a large agriculture factory on the north side of the city, and Alejandro went inside and obtained a letter of good standing. He used to work there before he had been transferred to Bustamante in 1989. Not only did Raul need his paperwork, his father also needed his own to prove that he was financially able, for his son to obtain a VISA.

They went on to stay at some relatives of Alejandro's, and they happily received them for the night. They fed them supper, and they visited. Raul knew these cousins, and he visited with them, as well. All of them went to sleep in the back room of the house.

At 4 AM, Alejandro got Roland and Raul up, and they loaded their goods onto the truck. Roland was very tired, but he knew that leaving early had to be the way, and he drove them to the Consulate. When they arrived, it was barely after 5 AM, and there were already 150 people waiting in line. He had been told that the Consulate only let 100 or 150 people enter each morning, after which they would close the doors.

At the moment of arriving, they were greeted by a man offering to sell a position near the front of the line. Roland went ahead and paid him the requested N$150 to buy that position. That was a regular practice. The man escorted them to the head of the line, and in a very subtle manner, Alejandro, Raul and Roland got in. Then with Alejandro holding the place, Roland and Raul went over to a side building and bought a *solicitúd* (application form) for N$10 and filled it out. It was stressed by the Consulate that these forms were not for sale, but then it was impossible to get these forms ahead of time without paying for them. Roland bought an extra one to take home and keep so he would have a record of what the form looked like.

After filling it out, they returned to the line and took their positions. It would be another hour before the doors would open. They did, and they started entering. Alejandro waited outside, and Roland talked to the guard in English saying that he and Raul were friends and that Raul wanted to go to Tennessee with him this coming summer. The guard was very kind, understanding, and let them both enter.

Next, everyone was checked for weapons and then escorted into the main waiting room where they were briefed about obtaining the VISA, after which several window stations, each one with a person behind a panel of glass, were opened. In a matter of minutes, Roland and Raul were waiting in one of the lines to be attended to at one of these windows, which looked very much like bank teller windows, but with bullet proof glass added for security.

As they reached the window, they were somewhat greeted by a big tall man, (a slob), who was graying and who had plenty of scars from acne long ago. The man asked Raul for his documents, which he showed the man by passing them through the slot under the glass panel. The man began to ask questions, and as Roland began to tell him that Raul was going to go to Tennessee with him this coming summer, the man impatiently interrupted and said he wanted to see some grades. No more than Roland began to pass the grades and documents under the window than the man said that he felt strange about the whole thing. He requested to see Raul's father, and Raul told him he was waiting outside the building. Next, they escorted Roland out of the building, and brought Alejandro inside instead. Only one person was allowed to accompany the person of interest, Raul. That was standard policy at the American Consulate.

Roland waited outside for ten minutes, and finally Raul and his father came outside. Raul shook his head, No. Alejandro had a sad face. The man had not granted the VISA, and they informed Roland how unaccommodating the man was with them. No more than Alejandro got to the window than the man said he felt very strange that Raul would go with Roland to Tennessee. Next, he took the application form and scribbled through it with his ball point pen in a defiant and sneering manner, followed by ordering Raul and Alejandro to leave!! That really upset Roland. Now he understood why many Mexicans couldn't get VISAs. They were brushed off and not given proper chance to explain their reasons. The main objective of the American Consulate was to herd the Mexicans through like cattle in a period of a few hours and each applicant was only given a maximum of three minutes to present his case and hope for the miracle of a VISA, unless he was rich, in which case he/she would be given a VISA immediately!

They told Roland that the man at the window failed to return the Comprobante that Roland paid N$158 for. He now realized that it was non-refundable, whether you got the VISA or not! Furthermore, Roland had to pay a N$20 parking ticket for having parked more than two hours.

With that done, they left, and Roland drove them away to one of Alejandro's relative's houses in east Monterrey. They talked about the way the ugly man had been so unhelpful. Raul blurted out, "¡Que feo los gringos! ¡Que feo! Cochino . . . fuchila!!" Raul was really angry at the Consulate, and Roland understood with good reason.

Roland speculated that the man must have thought it most strange that a fellow of 31 would be a good friend of a 15 year old. While such a friendship may have been somewhat rare, Roland had reasoned that there was room for friendships like that to happen. It had just worked out that way, and why was that man against it? Who was he to block Raul from going to Tennessee, and why was he so suspicious? Perhaps he suspected that Roland was gay, which he was not. Roland and Raul came to call the man at the window "El Oso Feo," meaning, The Ugly Bear.

Raul mentioned that the lady who had been in the next window to the right of them likely would have given the VISA. Raul could feel that she was a kind, understanding woman, and she would have given them a decent chance. It was unfortunate that they had not been directed to her, instead. Roland was soon to learn that Raul could feel a person out ahead of time, and he was usually accurate about knowing a person's character.

They did a couple more errands in Monterrey, including driving by Esalina's house to retrieve the items to take to Isalia in Tennessee. Roland parked, and while Raul and Alejandro stayed in the truck, he went up to the fancy apartment and rang the doorbell. The maid answered and said that Esalina was unavailable. Roland explained that if Esalina wanted to send the stuff to Isalia, this was the only chance she would have, because right now is when he was here and not later. The maid went inside, and five minutes later, Guillermo came to the door with the box of goods. Boy had he gotten fat! He must have been 80 pounds overweight. He greeted Roland, shaking hands, handed him the box, and then he got in his GMC Jimmy and drove off to work.

Roland got back in his truck with Raul and Alejandro, and they drove away. He discovered an awful perfume smell, and he pulled over and had to wash his hands repeatedly to rid the smell from his hands. He even had to grab some dirt from the roadside and soil his hands with that and water and then wash them again to cut the putrid odor! Then he washed his steering wheel. Why in the world were men using perfume?! Roland had always detested the stinking stuff!

Upon leaving the city, Alejandro stepped down from the truck and stayed. He had a doctor's appointment in San Nicolas. Roland drove Raul back to Bustamante, and he let him drive for 50 kilometers along the rural highway on the way back. They arrived in the early afternoon.

Rigo was home from school, and Lavinia was also home and served them lunch. Roland and Raul informed them of the news, and they expressed their sorrow.

Raul was feeling better, and he was playful. He and Roland started playing with the corn tortillas, and Raul playfully slapped one onto Roland's forehead and started laughing. Roland knew it was all fun and games, and he returned the gesture to Raul and enjoyed the fun. They laughed and played some more. Over the course of several more days that Roland stayed in Bustamante, he really enjoyed his stay with the Zacatóns.

The next morning was Saturday, and Roland and Raul went into the mountains again, this time to explore one of the canyons on the eastern slopes. There were supposed to be Black Walnut trees growing up there, and Roland wanted to see them. They hiked up the narrow gully to an elevation of 1,000 meters (around 3,300 feet) and in addition to the Walnuts, they saw many Oak trees and Maple trees.

Roland and Raul talked about the events yesterday and how unfair and unyielding the American Consulate was. Raul told him the story about his oldest brother Eduardo, who was already married and had a family. He had crossed the Rio Grande River wetback in late 1993, when he was just 16. He was caught once and sent back to Mexico, and he only stayed for 4 days, then paid $600 to a coyote, and made the river crossing again and returned to Salado, Texas. That was nearly a year ago, and they had not heard a word from Eduardo since then. Roland asked Raul why. He answered that he didn't know, but he missed him, nevertheless.

Roland took more pictures to document the day. In one of the pictures, Roland set his self timer, and both he and Raul sat on a big Oak tree limb growing sideways. The picture came out great! If there was ever an excellent portrayal of friendship through a photograph, this was it. Both of them looked peaceful and content with one another with feelings of compatibility.

They returned to Bustamante by late afternoon, and Norma told them that the police had come by to visit. Immediately, Roland felt a sense of fear that the Quevalos were taking out some sort of revenge. Then Norma went on to tell Roland that the police said for Roland to call home, that a close family member had died! The message had come from the Quevalos via a phone call from Isalia. How strange that the Quevalos didn't go to Raul's house themselves instead of getting the police involved in it! Still, Roland felt some relief that the police were not after him. Raul had seen Roland's face of fear and had commented that Norma's comment had at first scared him. Roland confirmed that it had.

Roland and Raul went to the police station to see what the problem was. The police told Roland that a close relative had either died or was very sick, and they told him to make the call from the hotel. In Bustamante, there were no payphones as such, and Roland didn't want to call from the hotel because it was expensive. So, Roland went to the Quevalos to ask to use their phone, and of course they snubbed him and wouldn't loan it to him. He also went to Chely's house, but she wasn't home.

"Raul, vamos a ir a Villaldama a la casa de Leonardo," Roland announced to Raul, telling him that they were going to go to Villaldama to Leonardo's house to use the phone there. He drove Raul there in his truck, and Roland found Leonardo's father at home. He happily obliged, and Roland called his parents collect.

No one had died nor was there anyone very sick, Roland found out. The story had been contorted and changed, likely by both Isalia and the Quevalos, especially the latter, to make Roland worry. What had happened was the company where Roland published his book and calendars, went bankrupt and had closed! Roland was very sorry to learn that. At least they had done their part in promoting and marketing Roland's works. He would have to publish his future artwork and calendars some other way.

Roland's parents were really devastated about the incident with the Quevalos. Roland explained how they had acted like hornets and were absolutely out of order and unreasonable! His parents agreed. Roland asked them to think positive and that he would be home by Friday.

Roland let Raul drive the truck back. Raul commented on how many problems Roland had suffered, and Roland admitted that quite a number of them had occurred. He offered to pay Raul something for his having stayed with his family for the past several days. Raul said to Roland that he didn't need to pay anything, that they were glad to have him. That was very kind and hospitable of Raul to say that, and Roland thanked him.

Upon entering town, Raul passed a creeping vehicle at an intersection, and a policeman standing there blew his whistle and pulled them over. Roland explained to the cop that he was teaching Raul how to drive and asked the cop not to ticket them. Well, the cop insisted that Raul had made an infraction, and since he was less than 16, he would have to ticket him. In truth, many teenagers underage drove cars and trucks all over town, but the cop would not admit that. He directed them to the police station (comandancia) to pay the N$50 fine on the spot. Roland now drove and they followed the cop there. Upon paying, he gave Roland the piece of paper detailing the infraction, and Roland and Raul drove back home.

Raul was really angry about it, mostly angry at the cops for having ticketed him. After all, everyone drove around town without licenses, and underage. What was the big deal? At least Raul didn't have any anger at Roland, who after all, was letting Raul learn how to drive. Raul no longer drove Roland's truck, at least for this trip.

There was another American in town, an hermano of the church, and he had been staying in Bustamante for 9 months. His name was John Cranston, and he came over to Raul's house to chat with Roland. They talked about going to see the caves the next day.

Roland spent the evening at Raul's house, and Raul and Rigo went to the usual Saturday night dance. They got in at 2 AM.

The next day, John couldn't be found. Raul, Rigo, Christian, Angelo and Pegaso went with Roland to the caves. They hiked cross country through the *monte* as they called it (scrubland of Mesquites and other shrubs). It was a great day, and they took a grand tour of the cave with Ramiro, the cave guide, for some two hours. In one place Rigo became afraid to advance any further, and Roland decided to wait with him while the others went on. Raul boasted to Rigo that they were *Hombres* (Men) and would continue further in. That didn't matter to Rigo. He and Roland sat down and waited by the narrow entrance to the third, innermost section of the cave.

Afterwards, they made the walk back to Bustamante. They all had a great time playing on the way back. Raul played by taking Roland's hat off and throwing it into the bushes on the roadside. When Roland went to retrieve his hat, Raul struggled with him but unsuccessfully prevented him from reaching it.

It was a great day, and Raul, Rigo, and Roland took an afternoon nap, the three of them turned sideways on one of the double beds. Lavinia came over to them and silently observed them with her approval of having Roland in their home, and she was pleased that he was such a good friend to her sons, Raul and Rigo. To Roland, he felt like they were brothers. Roland had always wanted brothers. He didn't have any of his own. So, in a sense or subconscious way, he had been searching for a family, so he could enjoy the experience of having brothers, a relationship he had been missing all his life.

Over the next several days, the weather was cloudy and drizzly. He was preparing to leave Bustamante and return to Tennessee. His money had run out, and it was time to get home and start work again.

Rigo took Roland over to the Felipe Hernandez's carpentry business behind the Hotel Ancira. As they walked over there, Roland realized that Rigo even walked the same way as Roland. They were similar in a lot of ways, and a good friendship was well underway. Rigo had a keen sense of understanding life, a sense of maturity surprisingly advanced for a fellow of only 14. He had an intuitive sense of a person's character and situation, as well.

Rigo mentioned his birthday, which was February 26, 1983. He mentioned that he had plans of being a school teacher. He would continue with school, two years of the Prepa and four years of the Normal, and he would teach elementary school somewhere in Nuevo León.

Roland met Felipe, a kind honest man who was impressed with some of the Eastern Red Cedar wood that Roland had brought. He requested that he bring some more of it when he returns to Bustamante again. He also told Roland that he could come and use the tools and equipment to make things whenever he wished. That was kind of him. Felipe carried a good reputation throughout Bustamante, and he provided work to several young people of the town through his carpentry business where they made chairs, tables, rocking chairs, wooden plaques with designs and scenery etched into them, wooden crosses, and more. It was a thriving business, and he sold to distributors both in Mexico and the United States.

Before leaving Bustamante, Roland took one last small hike up into the mountains up one of the canyon gullies. He rested and looked up at the tall cliffs with Palm trees perched on various ledges. He really didn't want to return to Tennessee. He had made such good friends with Raul and Rigo that he already considered them to be like family. Both of them wanted Roland to stay longer, and they didn't want him to leave. Rigo had specifically requested to Roland to stay more days. Roland wanted to, but he knew it was time to go home to Tennessee. How great it felt to be wanted by them to stay longer.

They had a good last evening visiting in the house, and Raul and Rigo showed Roland pictures of their family. They also played and wrestled around with each other for a while, laughing plenty. Finally, they went to sleep at 11 PM.

Well, the day had come, and Roland was going to drive home. He was sad to leave, and he and Raul shook hands in a truly friendly manner. They both showed sadness at parting. The whole family wished Roland well, said they would miss him, and said they looked forward to his visit in June when they would go to the Consulate and apply for the VISA again.

Roland loaded his truck and drove out of town. While driving down the highway, he had tears come to his eyes, and he realized that he had made a true friend in Raul and his family, the Zacatóns. The friendship that Roland and Raul had achieved made his previous friendship with Chip Collins look like next to nothing in comparison, and Roland knew how much better a friend Raul was, and Rigo too for that matter. Though Roland didn't find out until months later, Raul was sad for days and at times, he cried. He told his mother that he wished Roland had stayed, that he missed him, and that he had wanted him for a brother. How nice it was that someone cared that much for Roland. Thank goodness India's poisonous comment had not made any lasting effects on Raul.

U.S. Customs gave Roland a much nicer inspection this time. He got to bring all 5 feed sacks of his Fan Palm leaves across the border this time. After all, he was well prepared. He had documents from the USDA, and a letter specifically stating that it was fine to pass them over the border.

The day after Roland arrived home to Tennessee, he and his parents went over to Isalia's house to have a discussion with her about the Quevalos. Roland told her everything, and he was really hoping she was going to be nicer about it than she was back in 1992. Well, she was. She did not scold Roland at all, but then his parents were with him. After all, there was no reason to scold him. Roland had done his very best, and as far as he was concerned, he proved that the Quevalos simply had distaste for him and set up traps to give them "reason" to run him off. He and his parents gave her $25 to pay for the collect phone call that Roland had placed to her the night after the Quevalos had run him off.

There was one thing Roland had done that had really bothered Isalia a lot. Roland had told Sarita, "Isalia no me manda," saying that Isalia doesn't mandate him. The Quevalos had relayed that comment to Isalia but had evidently contorted the truth and had told her that Roland had spoken badly of Isalia. Roland explained why he had told that to Sarita, and it never crossed his mind that saying that would be considered talking badly about Isalia. It seemed a little bit strange that Isalia had been so bothered by that. Roland explained to Isalia that he was totally independent and that it was true that Isalia didn't mandate him.

93

Perhaps the Quevalos thought he was under her ruling, but the truth was, he wasn't, and he had the right to go to Mexico whenever he wanted to. Further, the Quevalos shouldn't have been raising false statements!

The important thing was that Isalia said that no matter what happens, she would always love Roland and his parents, and no matter how ugly the problems had been between him and the Quevalos, it would not affect Isalia's friendship with Roland and his parents. That was good to know that Isalia was being so faithful. Roland told her and assured her that he sincerely appreciated her and that he was still glad that she had referred him to the Quevalos because without that link, no matter how bad and ugly it had become, he would never have known Raul, Rigo, nor their family.

No matter what, Roland was glad his parents had accompanied him over to Isalia's house. After all, he didn't want her scolding him the way she had back in February 1992. With his parents there, he knew she would be nicer about it, in addition to having his parents as witnesses. In truth, the Quevalos deserved a good scolding from Isalia, but strangely enough, she never scolded them.

That evening, Roland made a call to both Raul and then to Pancho to let them know that he had arrived safely. He told both of them that the discussion with Isalia had gone well and that she had not scolded him. Both Raul and Pancho were glad to hear from Roland, Raul more so. Raul's family didn't have a phone, but their neighbors the Gonzalez family did, and Roland called the neighbors to go two doors down the street and fetch Raul to come to the phone.

The former Nashville publishing company still had several thousand copies of his book compilation and calendars stored in two places. On Roland's second day home, he made two trips to Nashville to carry the two truckloads home to the storage building.

Shortly after Roland's arrival back in Tennessee, he was called by several clients to ask him to come do some work for them. One of them, of course, was Isalia. She had plenty of yard work to be done, including planting more bulbs and flowers.

It was a few days after Roland arrived home that he went over to Isalia's residence to work. Roland told her all about Raul and his family and how great things had gone. He then also revealed something to her that he had not said in front of his parents the other day. He told her about Raul and Rigo's sister, Norma. Roland went on to tell her that he suspected that Norma might be his wife in the future. Isalia gave Roland a look of pleasant surprise, and her mouth dropped open when she realized the possibilities.

"You see, Roland," she pointed out. "There has been a subconscious reason why you've been going to Bustamante. The Quevalos ran you off because their subconscious minds caused them to give you a push toward Raul and Rigo's family because you were meant to know them. It's your destiny."

They talked about Norma some more and also about Raul and Rigo, and about the whole Zacatón family. As they continued working, Isalia thought for a few moments.

Suddenly, she said the key words: "Oh, Roland, I'm so happy for you, *I can't stand it!* What a great family!!"

Roland was glad that Isalia was happy for him, and he told her how great it felt to have finally made some close friends in Mexico and how much better he felt with Raul than with friends of the past, like Guillermo, the Quevalos, and others. It was so nice of Rigo and Raul to have asked Roland to stay longer.

The Poisonous Tongue

Roland felt appreciation for Isalia, and he gave her a signed photograph of himself for her to hang on her wall where some other male students' photos also hung. Isalia had been a good inspirational and spiritual advisor to Roland over the years, and she felt like she understood him very well, better than he realized, and she had helped him along in his life. Roland gathered more confidence in Isalia and he confided in her on several private matters and past relationships he had had with other people and past friends. He handed her writeups he had done on the relationships, and she made a file folder on Roland and kept it in her house. They had talked about Chip Collins, and now they were talking about Raul, Rigo, and Norma, the "future wife." Roland felt really happy about it, the first time he had felt good about a friendship in a long time. He really hoped this friendship would last and last, especially after the failure of so many over the past 6 years since he had graduated from Tennessee Tech University.

Several weeks went by, and Roland had plenty of work in Shelbyville, Tullahoma, Murfreesboro, and Columbia. Roland really missed his new friends in Bustamante. He wished he could go back before June. Then he thought, *Why not?* At the same time, he could loan Raul money to put in the bank in Mexico in his name to keep for several months to prove to the American Consulate that he had money so that he would stand a chance at obtaining a VISA. After all, Roland and his parents had been in recent contact with a Nashville native who was working in Mexico City's American Consulate office. He was very helpful on telling them about the procedure and requirements for obtaining a VISA. An article had come out about the Nashville native on December 27, 1996, which was Raul's 15th birthday, *quite by accident.*

Since having talked by telephone to the fellow in Mexico City and having been told that money in the bank would be a good idea to improve Raul's chances at a VISA, Roland had been thinking about it. He phoned Raul about it, and mentioned that he could wire money to his family for that purpose. Raul sounded agreeable to it. With that, Roland continued to think about returning to Bustamante sooner than June.

Another week went by, and Roland was surprised at the continuity of work. Isalia told him the Universe was helping him with his mission of helping out Raul and his family. When people have good intentions, money comes their way more easily, but at the same time, "God never makes things easy," which was one of Isalia's key beliefs. Roland did not agree with that phrase. Some things are made easy in life, and that is a fact.

One day, Roland drove up to Cookeville, one to see the university and to visit the library so he could copy some detailed topo maps of the Laredo region, and two to dig up some Hemlock tree seedlings to take to Mexico.

On the way, he stopped at the narrow truss bridge where State Highway 96 crossed the Stones River near Lascassas, and he took pictures of the bridge, which was built in 1945. The bridge was very narrow but was a classic landmark, and Roland wanted it to stay. However, due to increasing wrecks for the ever increasing traffic, the state highway commission recently had a referendum to consider replacing the bridge within the next few years.

One night a few years ago, Roland's aunt and uncle drove across it. They were shocked, and his uncle remarked, "My lands! The highway commissioner must have had a secret deal made with the funeral director!"

Roland thought back to the time when the bridge had been refurbished.

*   *   *

October 22, 1984

Roland Jocelyn had begun his first quarter at Cookeville's Tennessee Technological University. Each Friday on his way home to Longview, he drove along the Lascassas Highway, which in one place crossed the narrow truss bridge over the Stones River. Roadworks crew was refurbishing the bridge during this month, sandblasting and spraypainting the steel structure. They had installed a 3-minute light to regulate traffic, since one lane was open. They were also replacing the road surface of the bridge.

At 18½ feet for both lanes combined, the bridge was notoriously narrow. Every time Roland drove across it, he would cringe if he had to pass another vehicle coming the opposite way, hoping they wouldn't clash mirrors. There was no breathing room, and the bridge always demanded extra attention and caution from drivers. No one drove recklessly across that bridge, and those who did were punished straight away by the unforgiving truss rails on both sides! It was always tight getting through there, and the entire highway had been widened by 1980 . . . except for that one bridge.

Why is the highway department refurbishing this dangerously narrow bridge instead of replacing it? Roland thought to himself. He had no idea why, but it would make sense to him by the end of the millennium, when the bridge would finally be replaced.

October 21, 1945   Lascassas, Tennessee

It was a moderately warm, clear day in middle Tennessee.

It had been two months since the end of World War II. Roadworks crew had just completed and opened a new bridge across the Stones River to connect Lascassas to Murfreesboro. It was a fine truss bridge made of the best steel available. A masterpiece of its time, it was two lanes and had an ample width of 18½ feet, wide enough to allow two tractor trailers to pass by each other. It would serve the public along the Lascassas Highway for more than 50 years to come.

The last piece of the truss superstructure was being riveted into place. At both the north and south ends of the bridge, the ribbon cutting ceremony was about to take place. Murfreesboro's mayor came up for the event, and while he cut the ribbon on the southern end of the bridge, the mayor of Lascassas cut the ribbon on the northern end. They drove their cars (a 1940 Ford and a 1941 Buick) onto the new bridge and pulled up beside each other halfway across, where they stepped out of their cars and shook hands in triumph. Photographs were taken and documentation was made. Smiles could be seen on their faces for their pride in the new structure.

*   *   *

October 21, 1945

Sestrel was in the world of the spirits, and she was looking down through a special holographic crystal in the space-time continuum. Tears came to her eyes as she looked at the joyous ceremony of the opening of the new bridge. Molonco, the spirit whom she guided and protected through his lifetimes was by her side also witnessing the event.

"What's the matter down there?" he sharply asked her. "Why are you crying?"

"It's just that I'm really touched by that ceremony," she replied, still weeping with joy.

Suddenly, he sensed her feelings, and the genuine sadness of crying with joy overwhelmed him, just about being too much for him.

"They're doing it for you, Molonco."

"What for? I don't understand," he said, struggling to show a sneering face.

"Though they don't realize it, that bridge was built in memory of you," she informed him.

"Memory of me! What for?" he sneered at her.

Molonco was in such bad humor because he had just arrived to the other side less than an hour ago, having completed his past lifetime as Penn Yaskohl, who was one of many German Nazi officers who had been executed at the German war crime trials for their bad treatment of the Jews. He had been trained by his superiors to sneer and be sadistic. He was still adjusting to his new surroundings here in the world of the spirits again.

"Molonco, we do not make a practice of sneering here on the other side. We practice friendship, compassion, and love for each other. Those German officers were 100% in error for what they trained you, but it was a valuable experience for you . . . so that you will know, and *won't* be that way in the future! Now, take another look through that crystal and let the feelings wash over you. They'll do you good."

As Molonco looked through the crystal at the holographic image, emotions swept over him, and he felt the friendship of a friend who he would know during his next lifetime on Earth, more than 50 years into the future. Tears came to his eyes as he felt, for the first time in ages, genuine compassion and friendship. It had been so long since he had felt such kind feelings.

"Why do I feel a friendship with someone when I look at that bridge and ceremony?" he asked her, choking up on his words.

"Every bridge built represents a friendship with two or more people," Sestrel explained. "When a bridge is built, a friendship is born. For that particular bridge just built, born is a living friendship energy system between you and a future friend of yours who will live in that region. My superiors channeled the friendship energies into that bridge with their special forcefields as the construction crew riveted the steel truss together. They recorded the very forces of the friendship into the energy matrix system of the steel truss itself."

Molonco looked at Sestrel, then looked at the new bridge again through the holographic crystal.

"Keep looking at it. Don't be afraid," she reassured him.

He continued looking as the good feelings washed over him.

"You lived on Earth for 41 years this last time around," Sestrel commented. ". . . would have lived a lot longer had you remembered and followed your life's plan that you and I had discussed before you went down there in 1904."

Molonco now looked at Sestrel. Memories came to him of his discussion with her 41 years ago. She changed the scene in the holographic crystal. Now he saw the faces of more than 100 Jews who had been executed.

"Oh, no!" he suddenly exclaimed. "I completely forgot about that. Oh, how terrible! I could have saved them."

"That's right. You could have," Sestrel told him in a kind and loving manner.

"My goodness, how I wish I could have remembered that!" Molonco declared angrily. "Why is it so hard to remember my life's plans once I get to Earth?"

"They exist in a different dimensional frequency from us, as you know," Sestrel explained to him. "You have to remember through your spiritual goodness and your character being, integrated with your Earthly existence in any particular lifetime. Instead, you fell asleep."

"*That's* right," Molonco recalled. "Now I remember."

"You, as most people, got so caught up in Earthly events of the time, that it never occurred to you."

"I could have saved over 100 Jews from German slaughter." He started tearing up again.

"It's true, Molonco," Sestrel agreed in a consoling manner. "You were rather wealthy as a German Nazi officer."

"Why didn't I remember?" Molonco wanted to know.

"It comes from a character weakness that you have," Sestrel told him. "Your tendency is to follow the group and be one of them, instead of taking charge of your life and speaking out for yourself. You were too embarrassed to make the move, and for fear of repercussions, you squelched those feelings inside you."

As Molonco listened to his spirit guide, he knew she was right. He had indeed buried those feelings and, as a result, had never carried out his task and purpose. "Golly! Failed again!" he exclaimed, realizing the truth of Sestrel's explanation.

"I know it's painful for you, Molonco, and you will likely have lack of compassion for others in your next life as a means of avoiding the pain and guilt of your just completed past life."

He thought about her words and responded, "It just seemed like there was such a barrier for me to stick my neck out and speak out for myself."

"Speaking out for yourself and standing out are things you need to work on. As you now see, it's very important to carry out your tasks and missions when you live a lifetime on Earth," Sestrel told him.

"I know. I realize that now," Molonco admitted.

"When someone speaks up and takes charge of his life, great things blossom forth."

Molonco nodded a gesture of agreement. He looked through the holographic window. Sestrel caused the scene of the bridge to appear again. "Who is the fellow who I will know for whose friendship that new bridge stands for?"

At that moment in time, a spirit whose name was Kryphios appeared on the scene. He had that name because he liked to document everything, covering all topics. He was good at keeping records, and he had nearly everything tallied up and counted.

Molonco looked at him. Memories came to him, and a smile came across his face. "Kryphios," he called out as his name suddenly came to him.

"Welcome back, Molonco," Kryphios said to him.

"Oh, yeah," Molonco then recalled. "The South American Andes . . . 300 years ago."

"That's right. That's where we last knew each other in physical life on Earth. We were brothers there."

"Where have you been all this while?" Molonco asked Kryphios.

"I've been here on this side ever since then, keeping records and helping in that respect."

"Are you aware of what just happened to me in Germany?"

"Yes, I am," Kryphios replied with sorrow. "From this side, I was working with several people in Germany in efforts to save as many Jews as possible. Several of us transmitted thoughts and ideas, and those like Oskar Shindler who were tuned in and received them, acted accordingly. Unfortunately, Molonco, your spirit mind was closed. I was unsuccessful in penetrating your barrier and was therefore unable to deliver you any insightful ideas."

Molonco thought about that. "I realize that now, and I'm sorry."

"We on this side are, too."

"Is there anything I can do to make up for it?"

"Yes, there is," Kryphios answered. "Sestrel is going to whisk you back over to Germany, and I'm coming with you. There is still plenty of work to be done to neutralize the bad energy systems and negative energy patterns."

He then looked through the holographic window at the new bridge. "That's a fine bridge they've built for us and our next friendship."

"It looks very sturdy," Molonco commented.

Suddenly, a lively spirit named Awairna appeared before them. She went over to the crystal, looked through the holographic window, and saw the fine truss bridge. "Ohh . . . would you look at that fine bridge!" she declared with a smile. "It's time! There's my calling." She next looked at Kryphios. The two spirits knew each other.

"That's right, Awairna," Kryphios recalled. "You're about to start your next life, aren't you?"

"Indeed I am. It's time to go to the Earthly plane for another *lifetime*."

"Enjoy your time there."

"I will," she said. "We'll know each other in your next life. And remember base 12. It will be *important*." With that said, she whisked herself through the holographic window. Kryphios, Molonco, and Sestrel watched Awairna's spirit enter the Earthly plane directly above the truss bridge, after which she was seen to float away to the north . . . to be born in nearby Lascassas.

"That bridge is made of the finest steel available," said Kryphios, now talking to Molonco again. "It will last us through our next friendship on Earth. For more than 50 years that bridge will be in use . . . till nearly the end of the millennium."

Molonco could instinctively sense that Kryphios spoke the truth.

"All bridges out there are a physical manifestation of friendships among people," Kryphios went on, "and their durability and width parallels and dictates how well and how long they last. Our bridge is going to last a remarkable period of time, 20 years beyond the widening of that entire highway."

Molonco was filled with emotion and walked over to Kryphios. The two spirits shook hands, and Molonco showed him a smile of sincere friendship.

"It's good to have you back with us, Molonco. We have a whole new friendship ahead of us. Come. Let's get started."

The holographic window closed, and a forcefield arrived and whisked Sestrel, Molonco and Kryphios away to Germany.

May 25, 1982

It was a bright, whispy day in the world of the spirits on the other side. Molonco was talking to his main spirit guide Sestrel. She was helping Molonco review his most recent past life of having been a German Nazi Gestapo agent prior to and during World War II. He had been executed after the war during the war crime trials.

"Of course you realize," Sestrel explained to Molonco, "the reason you were executed was that you participated in Hitler's Nazi movement with his program of mass genocide of the Jews. You were insensitive and had no conscience. Your main job was to screen the mail and censor anything that was unsuitable, and it became second nature to you. You were also a spy."

"Yes, I realize my faults from that lifetime," Molonco admitted, "and I also realize that I was dishonest and that I was responsible for altering official documents under military orders from my superiors."

"That is all true, and that is good that you realize that," Sestrel told him. "One of your main life's purposes for your upcoming lifetime is to acquire more depth of feeling and compassion for your fellow man, humanity, and to respect and appreciate your friends. You will need to be honest with them to achieve true friendships with them. You will also need to be welcoming to them."

"That I will do my best to accomplish," Molonco assured her.

"That is excellent," Sestrel complimented him. "As your time of conception is almost here, I would like you to take a glimpse of some of those who you will see and know."

With her telepathic thought processes, she caused a holographic movie from planet Earth to materialize so that she and Molonco could view it.

"What are you showing me that for?" Molonco wanted to know. "It looks like a classroom."

"That's right," she verified. "That's a Spanish class at a high school in Tennessee. There's a student in that classroom who you will know very well and become good friends with. It is the last day of class and a happy time for the students to have social visits with each other and to wish each other well for the summer that awaits them."

"Who's the student I will know?" Molonco wanted to know.

"Can't you pick him out? You've known him before. He was your brother in an earlier past life," Sestrel reminded him.

Molonco pondered on the holographic movie and instinctively realized which one.

"Oh yeah," he seemed to recall as he felt the feelings of familiarity. "He's the fellow standing by that teacher."

"That's right," she verified. "You and he did a lot of walking and travelling together when you two were brothers in the mountains of South America."

"Yes, I recall that now," Molonco told her.

"Right, well his name is Roland Jocelyn, and when you're nearly grown, he will be sent into your life to help you come to realize what your main purposes are in this upcoming lifetime of yours. Roland is gifted with an astute awareness of things on that sort of level, and if you keep his friendship, he has a lot to offer you so that you can learn and also spiritually grow."

"That's good to hear," Molonco responded.

"And that teacher has her roots in the same town where you and your family will move to when you will be age six. Her name is Isalia Ives, and your mother will become her maid. She has also become good friends with Roland and his family. However, I must caution you to be . . . No, I better not say any more, except that her typewriter that you see on the corner table will eventually become yours . . . for a while."

"What are you telling me that for?" Molonco wanted to know. "The typewriter is irrelevant."

"That's what you think," she told him. "Those are pieces of the puzzle for you to figure out. If you can remember to ask Roland, he will be able to tell you the answer."

"Oh," Molonco calmly responded.

"Now, I will show you your family. They live in a town east of Monterrey, Nuevo León."

The holographic scene changed from the Spanish classroom to a scene inside a home. A young woman was inside making tortillas, and there were two boys in the family, ages 5 and 1. They were playing with some toys on the floor.

"Those two boys are soon to become your brothers," Sestrel told Molonco.

"The place looks so run down and poor!" Molonco complained. "Why do I have to go there?"

"That is part of your learning lesson in your next life," she explained. "Though they appear to be poor, Mexicans are rich in that they have a sense of family that you need, so you can be successfully taught the lessons you need in your upcoming life."

"Oh, I see," Molonco realized. "For my insensitivity during my past life, my next life in Mexico will help balance that out for me."

"Exactly," Sestrel agreed. "You see, Mexicans are hospitable in that they have a sense of friendship, which the people of your life in Nazi Germany lacked. In Mexico, you can relax and enjoy your friends and experience the rewards of the closeness of friendship, something Nazi Germany could not offer you. Now, if you will come with me, my friends and I will prepare you for the energy transference, for your time of conception is only hours away, and we still have much to talk about."

"What was it you were going to caution me about?" Molonco asked her as they wisped themselves away. "You told me something about . . ."

She went on to explain to him some characteristics of some other people he would know and interact with in his upcoming lifetime. It would be up to him to recall the necessary details at the appropriate times during his life. Further, they continued talking about the Mexican family he would soon join.

*   *   *

CHAPTER 5

LA SEMANA SANTA

March 1997

Roland decided he would visit Raul and Rigo and their family for their Easter vacation (La Semana Santa) which lasted two weeks. Roland was really looking forward to it. He called Raul to tell him the good news. When he got Raul on the phone, he was surprised to detect a sense of wishy washiness in him that had not been there before. Something had happened just in the past two weeks, since Roland had last called him.

He advised Raul that he was going to come around March 22, and he asked Raul if he could stay there. Raul answered, "No sé," saying that he didn't know. What sort of answer was that? So, Roland asked Raul if he came to stay with them, would he like it? Again, the answer of, "No sé." Roland thought Raul would have been glad to learn that Roland was coming, and it hurt his feelings that Raul thought less of his soon upcoming visit. Roland had given an orange Tennessee hat to Raul before leaving in February, and Raul told Roland that he had painted it black. Why did Raul say that, and much worse, why in the world did he paint it black?! What was going on?! That was downright insulting, and Roland now knew something was very wrong with his friendship with Raul. He finished the phone call with Raul, and went to bed, stewing over it all night. It really bothered him, especially the hat painting, and he couldn't sleep well.

The next day, Roland decided to call Isalia and consult her about it. This new problem had been bothering him a lot, and he couldn't shake it off. At first he didn't want to break the sudden news to Isalia because she had just told him a couple of weeks ago how she was so happy for him that she couldn't stand it and how great Raul's family was. He didn't want to devastate her. Well, he finally felt he had to, and since she had roots from Bustamante, he figured she would understand better than Americans.

Roland told her that Raul's attitude was suddenly changed, and he was acting wishy washy about his coming to visit. ". . . and Raul said something about a *maricón*. Do you know what that is?"

"Of course I do!" Isalia replied. She expressed her concern and said she could not figure why.

Then Roland told her for the first time about India's poisonous comment of, "Raul está enamorado a tí."

That struck a chord with Isalia. She flatly said, "That's what it is, Roland. That's made Raul embarrassed to be a friend of yours."

They talked a few more minutes, and Roland hung up, still feeling the terrible loss.

He called to speak to Raul that night to talk to him about staying there and confront him about the painting of the orange hat. Rigo was the one who came to the phone at their neighbor's house because Raul wasn't there. Rigo was nice and straightforward, glad to hear from Roland, and when Roland asked him if he could stay with them next week, Rigo gave the simple answer of, "Sí." There was no question in Rigo's mind. Roland was welcome as far as he was concerned.

The next day, Roland's parents relayed him the message that Isalia wanted to talk to him. Roland had been away at the time Isalia called, so he returned her call to find out what was going on. She asked Roland to come over and talk with them. So, he went over there. Both she and Clayton were there in the kitchen when he arrived.

"Roland, Clayton and I are going to gang up on you," Isalia began, "because we are very much concerned for you and love you. You know you're going to Mexico next week at great risk."

"Isalia told me what you and she talked about," Clayton added.

"Roland, when I told Clayton about your recent phone call to Raul, he got very upset and concerned for you, and that's why we called you to come over here and talk to you."

Though Roland didn't know it at the time, it was very rare that Clayton would get upset enough over someone else that he would come forth and express concern. It really surprised Isalia, and because of that, she realized this was something very serious. Clayton was very near the end of his life, and his intuition and psychic abilities were something that had greatly improved in his last few weeks of life. He was suffering from pancreas cancer, which was a sure death sentence to those who were unfortunate enough to contract it. It was inoperable and incurable. Clayton had lost a considerable amount of weight, but he was still thinking clearly, and his concern for Roland was genuine.

"Raul's peers are down there poking fun at him," Clayton told Roland. "They're calling him gay for being a friend of yours."

"Why would that be? Can't males be friends?" Roland pointed out.

"Yes, they can," Clayton agreed, "but the image of a man in his thirties going to a small town in Mexico to visit a *young boy* has strong implications that something strange or gay is going on."

"Now we know that you're not," Isalia assured him.

"Well, thank you," said Roland. "You mean that just for our age difference, the town would think that?"

"Yes! I'm sorry to say, but yes." Isalia answered.

Roland was shocked! It just hadn't occurred to him that people in Bustamante would think so badly. All Roland was doing was enjoying his friendship with Raul and his brother Rigo in Bustamante. One might say he was like a big brother to them. Why would the people make fun of that?

"People are really cruel animals when you look at the truth of things," Clayton informed Roland. Clayton knew about that. He had lived a lifetime and had experienced a lot of things.

"Yes, they are sometimes. I agree," said Roland.

"They'll ridicule and ruin a person's credibility and reputation," Clayton went on. "I'll tell you why Raul painted that hat black. The word *Tennessee* was written on the front of it, and he had to show his peers that he didn't care anything about you. Now in truth, he probably wants more than anything in the world to come up here to Tennessee with you, but he can't tell that to his peers."

"Why do you think Raul's changed?" Roland asked Clayton. "He was fine with me when I was there. India's comment didn't bother him then."

"Well, he had a chance to be away from you once you came back home," Clayton explained, "He's changed. Once his peers started poking fun at him, he became so embarrassed that he'd rather not have you come visit him to save him the embarrassment."

"Look, Roland!" Isalia pointed out. "Raul doesn't want you anymore, and you don't need him. We are telling you for your own good to *not* go down there."

"Roland," Clayton now suggested, "we think it would be best for your safety if you would wait three years before returning to Bustamante."

"Three years!" Roland exclaimed. "Everything will have changed by then."

"What about Pancho?" Roland now brought up, looking for a possible solution. "Maybe I could talk to him about this problem."

"You won't drop it, will you!" Isalia barked out angrily. She knew how stubborn Roland was, and she was trying to get the point across about how much danger he was getting himself into. Plus, she simply wanted Roland to do as she said. She wanted to mandate, Roland was beginning to realize.

"I know, but I'm tired of losing friends," said Roland, "and now when I finally make a really good friend, something happens to sabotage it!"

"Yes, and we feel for you," said Isalia. "Let me tell you something, Roland," she went on and explained. "People in a small town like that can gossip, freak out, and eliminate you, and if they do that, there would be no trace as to what ever happened to you. They'd bury you out there in the scrubland, and no one would ever find you!" She had fervor in her voice as she relayed these chilling possibilities to Roland.

That did indeed scare Roland, and he had second thoughts about going. "I don't know. I'll think about it. Maybe I won't go after all."

"And you know how the police pulled you and Raul over," Isalia added. "They've got your number."

"Okay, bring me the 4-page writeup I handed you telling the good news about Raul. I'm going to go ahead and burn it."

Isalia brought it to him. It was only a copy. Roland still had the original at home. Roland thanked Clayton and Isalia for their concern, said goodbye to Clayton, and stepped outside. He put a match to the 4 pages and burned them. Isalia watched him do it. Tears came to Roland's eyes, and he said, "Raul, ya no eres me preocupación." That struck a sense of familiarity with Roland. He had said the same thing about Chip Collins back at the Quevalos in January, and he did not want to place Raul in the same category.

Isalia told Roland, "Tell Raul that you forgive him and bless him."

Roland did that, too.

As Roland was leaving, she told him, "The Universe is strengthening you and making you tougher for what is yet to come."

"I know, but I don't like losing friends for it," Roland responded. "That's not fair."

He and Isalia said goodbye to each other, and Roland left and went on to his day's work. While it was nice of Isalia and Clayton in one sense to have genuine concern for Roland, it did not sit well with him either. Roland had a talk with several friends of his, some of them by telephone in other states. One friend of his, Paul, said the "devil" influenced Isalia and Clayton to think badly about Roland's friendships and to have unnecessary concern for him. Roland didn't believe in such things as the "devil" per say. That was just a concept the human race created to justify or give reason for bad events. It was also an excuse to explain bad behavior.

However, Roland did begin to think that some force, maybe even Isalia, was trying to put a halt on his friendships, but then there was no logical reason. Roland knew Isalia and Clayton genuinely cared for him and didn't want any harm to befall him in Mexico, but at the same time, Roland didn't like the opposition to his friendships. Isalia had told Roland in 1992 that Guillermo and Esalina didn't want him, that Chip Collins didn't want him, and now Raul?! What was going on, really?

Roland got angry at the situation and decided that there was no way he was going to forfeit his friendship with Raul and Rigo. He had lost enough friends, and losing Raul, and Rigo would be a bridge too far! He strengthened his decision that he was going to go. With that, he decided to go to Bustamante and that was that! After all, he had to make a stand and declare what was his. He wasn't going to lose any more friends!

Roland and his parents called Isalia about it, and Roland explained how he felt. Isalia was confused about some points and had thought Rigo had also said no. Roland corrected her and said Rigo had said yes without hesitation. Isalia explained that he was a year younger and wasn't yet under the influence of homophobia like his brother Raul was, and Rigo therefore had said yes. He was still a child, and it was perfectly all right with him for Roland to come. Isalia had a point, and she was entirely right about Rigo. Roland and Rigo had a good friendship coming.

Roland knew that Isalia would not consciously harm his friendships, but he did think there was some sort of a subconscious drive that caused her and Clayton to have that serious talk with him. He went over to Isalia and Clayton's place to do some more work for Isalia, and she said to Roland, "I don't know *what* that black cloud was that passed over us!" At least she admitted there was something that caused her to think badly about Roland's friendship with Raul and his family.

Incidentally, Isalia told Roland about a dream her brother had about her recently. He had called her on the telephone and told her. *He dreamed that he was walking along a trail in a forest, and he came upon a large blackish colored transparent glass enclosure, somewhat like a large glass encased cabinet, but made of pure glass. Inside it, to his surprise, was his sister Isalia! He asked her what she was doing inside there, and she answered, "God put me here for 1,000 years."*

Roland expressed surprise at her brother's dream about her, and he asked her what she thought it all meant. She answered that it probably had to do with karma, and she told Roland that she felt like she had been paying her karmic debts for the past 40 something years.

Isalia also told Roland she'd been having a recurring dream, though she didn't say what it was.

Roland also talked with some of his friends about the wiseness of his going to Bustamante. Prayers were said by some of them, and some of them wrote letters of good standing for Roland to take with him to Mexico, in case he were to get into any trouble.

He called the lady who went to the monthly meetings with him. She admitted to the dream Roland had had two months ago where she had said, "What are you standing on your head for?" She warned Roland not to go back to Mexico. She said the father Alejandro was not to be trusted, and she told Roland not to loan money to them in any form or fashion. She told Roland that there was someone in that town who didn't trust him and that he would likely be abused emotionally and physically, if he returns to Mexico. Roland listened to her, but he decided to go to Mexico anyway.

Roland also called Pancho on the phone and asked him if he would release Raul from his work to run around with him during his time in Bustamante. Pancho said sure, that it was no problem. After all, Roland would pay Raul in Pancho's place, and that certainly sounded agreeable to Pancho. Roland appreciated that Pancho was agreeable to it.

Roland loaded his Ford Fairlane station wagon with his luggage, including his old mountain bike, and he drove down there. Between Texarkana and Dallas, there was some sort of wreck, and traffic was backed up for two or three miles. Roland drove on the right shoulder in second gear, and drove around the whole section of backed up traffic, saving him probably more than an hour of waiting time. He wondered why no one else also did it. After all, he didn't see any cops, and he got away with it.

That night, he stayed with his cousins in Dallas. They were concerned for him and wished him good luck.

Roland drove his car into Bustamante in the late afternoon of his second day of driving. Customs had let him in easily enough, and the 180 kilometers of driving in Mexico to reach Bustamante was also easily done. Raul was working for Pancho when Roland arrived. Lavinia happily greeted Roland and was glad to see him. Rigo soon arrived from Felipe's carpentry, and he was also glad to see Roland. He helped him unload the car, including some Cedar lumber he had brought for Felipe.

They fed Roland some supper. He was glad to be here again, and it surprised him how soon he had returned. He felt like he was dreaming in a way, and it was hard for him to believe he was actually back here. Roland had brought some gifts for the family, including a toy schoolhouse for Norma and Irma. They were very glad to receive them. Lavinia asked Roland why he bothered with the gifts, and he said that was a gesture of appreciation for being friends. They thanked Roland.

Roland and Rigo went over to the Quevalos. Eliud had requested some computer disks, and Roland had a pack of ten to deliver to him. He asked Rigo to go into the Quevalo's residence to look for Eliud, which he did graciously. He found Eliud's mother India and gave them to her to give to Eliud later. As Roland waited in his car, he saw the Quevalo females' angry faces at a distance. Rigo came back to Roland, got in his car, and said that India had gotten angry. She had assumed that Roland was going to charge Eliud for the disks, and Rigo had answered that the disks were a gift. *What a shame that India thinks so negatively!* Roland thought to himself. He and Rigo returned home.

Roland had recorded some American pop songs onto a cassette tape and gave it to Raul and Rigo. Most of the songs were from the 1980's. Rigo put the tape into the stereo and played it. The first song to play was "A Good Heart" by the group, *Feargal Sharkey*. Rigo liked the song and continued listening to it, along with the other songs on the cassette.

Raul had still not arrived. He was working extra hours. He knew Roland was coming, and his thoughts were to continue working for Pancho and to spend as little time with Roland as possible. After all, he couldn't have the town thinking he had a *relationship* with Roland.

Roland looked around the room and saw that Raul had displayed photos of their hike up the Lion's Head Mountain. Then he saw the orange Tennessee hat. Only the hat bill was black. The word *Tennessee* was still there in its original color. Roland felt very relieved about that.

Roland went and talked to Lorenzo Quevalo. He let him know he was in town, and he asked Lorenzo to defend him if anything were to happen to him, especially if something were to happen with the police. Lorenzo said he would. Roland thanked him and returned to

La Semana Santa

Raul and Rigo's house.

Raul finally arrived, and he had already gotten cleaned up and dressed for the dance. He and Roland shook hands in a friendly manner, and Raul asked Roland if he would give him a ride to the town plaza. Raul went to the dance and stayed out till 3 AM. Rigo was away also and spent the night with a friend a few blocks away.

The next morning, both Roland and Raul got up at 11 AM. Roland talked to Raul about how he felt after his phone call last week, and he explained the conflicts he was feeling. Raul listened to him. Roland had another Tennessee hat, gave it to Raul and told him not to paint this one black because that was insulting. He also forgave Raul for having painted the first one.

Raul was very interested in Roland's bicycle, and he asked if he could buy it. Roland told Raul it wasn't for sale, but if he would go up into the mountains three times with him, he would give it to him. That sounded agreeable to Raul, and the deal was made. What Roland wanted to do was go and explore different canyons in the mountains, collect Flor de Peña and Siempre Viva plants, and be accompanied by a friend of his, like Raul, a person whose company he enjoyed.

Roland drove Raul over to Pegaso and then Angelo's house, and the four of them rode around town in Roland's Ford Fairlane station wagon. They circled the plaza several times and enjoyed the morning. In the afternoon, they went to the molino which was the swimming pool on the canyon road on the west side of town. It was situated within a grove of large Pecan trees with trunks up to a meter in diameter. It was a good day, and Roland also enjoyed visiting with Angelo and Pegaso.

That night, Raul went out to the plaza to be with Angelo and Pegaso and didn't invite Roland. Roland instead went to Lorenzo and visited with him and his family. Pancho had asked Roland to make a large photo poster of Lorenzo plowing the field with his ox, and Roland had obliged him. He had a 20 x 30 poster made from the negative. Pancho came over, and Roland gave it to him. He was glad to receive it and said he would hang it in the place of business. Somehow Pancho, as usual, had skirted around saying the word *gracias* by not saying it, and Roland noticed.

Later that night, Roland went to the plaza. He found Raul, Angelo and Pegaso who were glad to have him join them. There was a carnival set up right in front of the Presidencia with rides, games, and stalls where vendors were selling all kinds of knick knacks from pirated cassette tapes to jewelry to clothing. Roland liked some of the songs he was hearing, and with Raul's suggestions, he bought some cassette tapes to take home with him. The carnival had just begun and would last for the next ten days.

As Roland would find out, La Semana Santa was a time period each year when lots of tourists came to Bustamante. Many of them stayed in the hotel or rental houses, and many of them camped up in the canyon and at the Ojo del Agua. During that week, traffic was so congested along the main street, Calle Gral. Mier, that police had to direct traffic at each intersection. On the other hand, places of business thrived and sold their bread and baked goods to the tourists.

On Roland's second day of his visit, he and Raul went into the mountains. On the way up, Raul complimented Roland by telling him that he was a good man, and whenever he comes to Bustamante, he had his house to stay in with them. Those were kind words. Raul was a welcoming person, and Roland appreciated it.

Raul also mentioned that he wanted to go to the United States to work for a year. He had a goal of earning $9,800, enough to buy his family a house in town. Those were very noble plans of Raul, and Roland was hoping that Raul would be able to go with him to Tennessee this coming summer.

Roland had brought a couple of Hemlock trees, and after driving Raul to the cono at the end of the gravel road, he and Raul walked up the trail, passing by the caves, and continued further up the trail to the gully near where he had planted the Cedar tree. It was doing fine. Roland planted one of the Hemlock trees, and Raul planted the other one. Roland made an analogy and told Raul that these trees represented the friendship they had, and if both trees lived, their friendship would do the same.

Raul and Roland took a midday nap after eating some lunch. They also talked about the possible gossip going on. Roland told Raul about the scare tactics that Isalia and her husband Clayton had given him last week. Then Raul came forth and admitted that some people in town had indeed been kidding him about his friendship with Roland. Pancho and his other two workers, especially Pancho, had been kidding and poking fun at Raul, telling him that he and Roland were boyfriends and for Raul to send Roland a large signed photo of himself. Those comments had bothered Raul.

At least Roland now knew the truth. It wasn't as bad as Isalia and Clayton had said it was, but still it was a shame that some people were cruel enough to poke fun at Raul for his friendship with Roland! Not only did India have a poisonous tongue, Pancho had one, too!

Roland had contracted with Raul's brother Rigo to make him a Cedar *cuadro* (wooden tablet) with various designs on it, and they had agreed on N$100. As they descended the mountain, Raul told Roland that was too much to pay Rigo for that. He warned Roland to watch out and be careful about Rigo's taking advantage of him, because he didn't have the conscience that Raul had, concerning how much money to accept for work being done.

Raul and Roland returned to Bustamante, and Raul took a long nap. Roland went around town on his bicycle and showed photos of his previous trips to other friends of his, like Fernando, Daniel, and others. When he returned, Raul was still asleep, and Rigo was right by him doing the same.

Lavinia asked Roland to awaken them for supper, which he did. As soon as everyone had eaten supper, Raul and Rigo went out, again without Roland. Roland stayed home and had an early night to bed.

At midnight, Raul and one of his friends entered and woke Roland up, asking if it would be all right if Angelo came with them tomorrow. Roland said that would be fine, and he went back to sleep.

The next morning, Roland drove Raul over to Sabinas Hidalgo, and Angelo and Pegaso both accompanied them. Pegaso needed to pick up some books from an aunt's house, and Angelo came along just to do so. They inquired at the bank Banamex about having savings accounts, and Roland made a deposit in Raul's name. The amount was N$7,700 (US$990). Despite having been warned never to loan money to anyone in Mexico in any form or fashion, Roland went by his feelings and had enough trust in Raul that he would leave the money there and not use it out from under Roland. He did Raul this big favor to help him get a US VISA when he would return in June.

They did some more errands, including stopping by Raul's uncle's house on the west side of town. They also stopped by Roland's friends, the Velazcos at the Taller Electrico.

La Semana Santa

Mrs. Velazco was there and met Roland's friends. Roland had gone to the door first and told her he wanted her to meet his friends. They had been shy about entering, but with her coming to the car to invite them inside, they got out of the car and came in for a few minutes.

After the visit, Roland drove them back to Bustamante. Raul began kidding with his friends that he could now buy fiestas, a truck, clothing, luxury items, and treat all his friends to a grand trip to the beach down south, and so on . . . with Roland's money. Roland knew Raul was just kidding, at least he hoped so. Raul was like that. He liked to joke and play around, and he also liked to cause a worried look on Roland's face.

Back in Bustamante, they delivered Angelo and Pegaso to their homes and then went to the Quevalos. Roland and Raul talked to Pancho, and Raul told him that he had just opened an account in his name with Roland's money. They talked about the interest that it would pay. Pancho had more suggestions about how to go about getting the VISA this coming summer. Roland also bought three rocking chairs from Pancho, one for himself, one for Raul's family, and the other one for Isalia.

Later that day, Roland asked Raul who the other person was that had entered with him at midnight last night. Raul showed a look of fear and said that no one other than himself had entered. He told Roland not to talk like that because someone died in their house many years ago, and it could have been his spirit! Roland insisted that he had sensed that someone else was with Raul. He found it hard to believe that Raul had entered alone, and Raul again insisted that he had entered alone. Roland had not been fully awake and had not opened his eyes for the light Raul had turned on at the time. He had simply figured the other person was Angelo. It wouldn't be the only time Roland would think there was an extra person around.

Later that afternoon, Roland took Pancho and Mateo over to Villaldama. Pancho had a radiator to pick up. Roland talked to them about his friendship with Raul and his family, and Pancho asked Roland when he was going to get a girlfriend. Roland said no time soon, but he had an idea that his wife of the future, if he was going to have one, might be Norma. Pancho gave out a good laugh and a *Whoowee!* comment. He had suspected that Roland might have romantic interests in her for the future.

Later that evening, back in Bustamante, Raul informed Roland that Pancho had not paid him for the past two weeks' labor, and each time Raul went to ask Pancho, he would say, "Hasta mañana," (later, later). It was for that reason that Raul had so easily taken Roland up on his offer to hire him for each day he would run around with him. Roland was glad it worked out. Destiny was working in Roland's favor, and he was surprised that Raul was so easy to know and become a friend with. He kept wondering when the obstacles were coming. Any moment, he thought, but they never came. Raul was always available to be a friend. It was such a nice turnaround and compensation for the frustration Roland had suffered when trying to continue his friendship with other recently known people, like Chip Collins and Leonardo. The more days Raul could accompany Roland and the more times he could go up into the mountains with him, the better compensated he felt.

Roland was really hungry for friends, due to previous frustrations this decade, and as a result he came on a little intense with his wishes sometimes. Raul detected that, and he gave Roland a hard time by acting grumpy about it. Roland asked Rigo and Lavinia why Raul was sometimes grumpy because he couldn't figure out why. Rigo, who was very straightforward, simply explained to Roland that he was was coming across as possessive.

Roland didn't think so. He just wanted to make sure his friendship with Raul and his family stayed in place. After all, for the losses he had suffered in the recent past, Roland had every reason to behave in that manner. He didn't want to lose any more friendships.

The days went by, and Roland was really enjoying his time with Raul, Rigo, and their family. One day, a rancher named Jesús Lucio took Raul, Rigo and Roland to the other side of the mountains through the canyon and beyond the Ojo del Agua. Pancho had told Roland about some ancient paintings on the sidewalls and cliffs of a mesa in the middle of the desert. They were called Chiquihuitillos, and they were supposed to be very ancient. They were of much interest to some of the people of the region, and no one really knew what messages they really portrayed.

The three of them rode in the back of the truck while Lucio and his helper, Carlos, rode up front in the cab. After the pavement ended at the Ojo del Agua, it was another 12 kilometers down one-lane, rough, dirt and gravel lanes to Lucio's ranch where he fed and tended to his cattle. Along the way, he cut several Yucca bloom stalks with their white flowers from the Palma Real trees growing throughout the desert. He used a long pole with a hooked blade on its end to cut the bloom stalks in the tops of the trees. These he fed to his cattle.

After his ranch work, he took them the remaining 8 kilometers to the double mesa where the paintings called Chiquihuitillos were. They pulled up to a lone ranch house with a windmill nearby, stepped out of the truck, and talked to the rancher. He was the owner of the land and the mesa, and it was he who had given permission for the public to enter. All visitors were to sign the guest register log book, and then they could climb the cliffs to look at the paintings. The rancher told them to have respect for the paintings, not to mark them in any way, nor damage the area at all. All of them agreed to that, signed the guestbook, and paid N$5 each.

The mesa pair now stood clearly before them with its cliff walls clearly visible. From the base of the cliffs, the land sloped steeply to the desert floor. Lucio, Carlos, Roland, Raul and Rigo walked down the lane to the base of the mesa. They decided to climb up to the northeast face of the mesa on the left, and they would work their way around, following along the north face of the cliff. Then they would advance to the second mesa to the west. The dirt lane veered to the left and headed south as it passed by the east side of the mesas. They left the lane and immediately climbed the steep slope to the base of the cliff.

In addition to having to dodge various thorny bushes, Cactus, and Yucca plants, the soil was loose, and at times they slipped and fell. After some considerable effort and offering each other helping hands to make their advance, they arrived at the base of the brownish-beige cliffs. Sure enough, there the paintings were.

Most of the drawings were done with red paint, and some of the depictions contained orange, as well. There were drawings of what appeared to be people, tools, plantlife, animal representations, suns, and moons. There were also drawings of more exotic things like concentric circles, chains of diamond-shaped cross hatched squares, spacecrafts, and other vehicles.

As they moved on to the next area, the path along the base of the cliff was narrow and difficult. They had to negotiate Prickly Pear Cactus, Yuccas, Zotól, Agave, including Lechuguilla, and other thorny shrubs, and in places they had to climb over rocks and go up and down over ledges.

The paintings were very interesting, and Roland took several photos. He thought he might use some of his interpretations of these paintings to incorporate into his future artwork and calendars. There were drawings of more exotic things like rockets, energy fields, electronic circuitry, and even weapons of warfare, which indicated that whoever drew them was aware of technology, perhaps a recently lost technology, such as a devastating Earth crustal displacement that destroyed Atlantis along with their technology of that time.

Next, they walked on top of the mesa. It was covered with Lechuguilla plants and various thorny Mesquite shrubs. There were also pincushion Cactus plants of different types, and Roland and Raul collected a few specimens to take to Lavinia for her small flower garden.

On the way back, Raul and Roland including Rigo played with each other, vigorously at times. They sloshed water all over each other, and had the biggest time laughing. Even though they were somewhat rude to each other about how they played, Roland enjoyed it just the same. Lucio and Carlos were oblivious to what was going on, concentrating on the narrow gravel and dirt lane as he drove them along.

They arrived back in Bustamante by mid afternoon. Roland offered to pay Lucio something for the favor he had done for them, but he said that wasn't necessary. Jesús Lucio was a nice man who did things to help others. He had been a science teacher at the school there in Bustamante, and after teaching for 25 years, he had retired and was already on pension. However, he was still active on his ranch, going every day to feed his cattle.

Raul went out that night with his friends. Rigo decided to stay home. He and Roland sat in two of the rocking chairs that he had recently bought, and they chatted about different things. Rigo thanked Roland for his friendship with him and his family, and he was glad to have Roland stay with them. Roland appreciated that and realized that Rigo was a genuine friend.

Roland told Rigo that he wanted to save and buy a house in Bustamante, possibly this one, since it was for sale for only $8,000. The Cantu family was selling it, and Raul and Rigo's family had been renting it for three years. Roland would buy the house and let them continue to live in it, with the condition that Roland would have the right to come and visit any time. Rigo thought that was a great idea, and he said that Roland could designate the catch-all room to be his area to permanently keep furniture and his things, and he could stay with them like family. Rigo shook hands with Roland in triumph.

At one point in the evening, Lavinia was in the kitchen with her head between her hands and elbows propped on the table. Roland noticed that she was silently crying. He asked her what was the matter, and she said she was crying for her son Eduardo. It had been nearly a year since she had heard from him at all, the last time being when he returned to Salado wetback after his involuntary 4-day stay in Mexico.

Alejandro also came in. He had been drinking, and he smelled of alcohol. He was considerably drunk but could still talk in a reasonable manner, and he and Roland talked for a while in the kitchen. Alejandro asked Roland a favor. He said, "Si ves Raul tomando o fumando, que le digas que no hiciera eso," asking Roland that if he were to see Raul drinking or smoking, that he tell him not to do those things. Roland told Alejandro he would make sure and do that, and he appreciated the trust that Raul's father had in him to ask him that favor. Alejandro explained that he didn't want Raul to become like he had become, a heavy smoker and drinker. He wanted a better life than that for Raul, and also for Rigo.

Raul and Roland went up into the mountains again, this time to explore a different canyon, this one directly underneath the Lion's Head Mountain. They climbed and climbed through the gorge and gully until they ascended a very steep and slick section of limestone rock, a steep place in the creek. They took a seat on a ledge and ate lunch. Then they made their descent back to town.

Roland also talked to Raul about what his father had talked about last night. Raul said he only drank a little bit and that he didn't like to smoke. To a degree, that was good to know. It's that Raul didn't say that he doesn't smoke, just that he didn't like to smoke. Roland noticed and interpreted Raul's choice of words, and he would bring it up to him again, months later.

When they arrived back home, a neighbor, Arturo, was visiting with the family. He had a caguama (a 940 milliliter size beer bottle) in his hand. He was talking rapidly in his usual way. His son was Juan Carlos, a fellow the same age as Raul. Roland also knew him and would sometimes go to his house 100 meters up the street and chat with him at times.

Somehow, the conversation got onto girlfriends and wives, and Raul jokingly said some comment about marrying Roland's sister. Roland then joked with him and said that he might later marry Norma. Raul heard that and had an immediate reaction of anger, which surprised Roland. He showed his fist from a distance and said, "Hey, te pego en la cara," saying that he would hit him in the face! Raul also added that this was his house and told Roland to forget Norma!

That made Roland feel bad, and he and Raul argued about it. Roland firmly declared that he was kidding, and if he couldn't take a joke, then don't make one! He also reminded Raul about how they had also kidded with each other back in January about Raul's marrying Roland's sister in New York, and saying that they would be *brothers-in-law*. Raul had to admit that he had joked with Roland about that, and now he had second thoughts about the harsh comment he had just said to Roland.

Roland became worried that Raul's father Alejandro would find out, and Raul said with a certainty that if Alejandro found out, he would go after Roland for sure and run him off with anger! Roland asked him not to tell him, that he was only kidding. Lavinia had also been there when Roland told Arturo, and she said, "Rolando, con Norma no. Es una niña," telling him that with Norma no, explaining that she was only a child. Roland reiterated that he wasn't talking about now. Certainly not! He was talking about the possibilities ten years in the future. Even still, that wasn't agreeable to Lavinia. Nevertheless, the cat was out of the bag about Roland's thoughts about Norma in the future.

Roland left the house to do some afternoon errands. He was very worried that Alejandro would find out what Roland had only joked about. He went to visit Rigo at the carpentry business and talked to him about the Cedar cuadro and what designs to etch on it.

Then he went to Lorenzo and talked with him for probably an hour about what he had joked about. Lorenzo's wife Glenda was there, and she and Lorenzo stated to Roland that he was not wise to have said that about Norma, not even jokingly. Roland knew they were right, and he wished he could back up in time and correct that. What was done was done. He only hoped it would wash over and that nothing would get out of hand. It was then that Lorenzo said the real danger the psychic woman had predicted was not from his sisters; it was Alejandro. Roland and Lorenzo talked some more, and Roland expressed his worries. Every day, Roland came by to check in with Lorenzo as a precautionary procedure so that Lorenzo would know that he was all right. Lorenzo wished him the best with the situation and suggested that if Alejandro were to get angry that Roland simply offer to take his things and leave. Roland rode off on his bicycle, and Lorenzo jokingly said with a smile, "Ten cuidado con tu cuñado," telling him to be careful with his brother-in-law (Raul).

Roland saw Lorenzo as a good advisor. He knew how to make light of a heavy situation and in the right way. He was calm mannered and straightforward. Roland appreciated him for that and for the helpful advice he gave.

Raul went to the Saturday night dance. He asked Roland if he had an extra N$5. Roland brought it over to him and gave it to him. Raul asked Roland if he was giving it to him. He answered yes. The next thing Raul did very much surprised him.

He told Roland, "Caíste del cielo. Eres como un hermano," telling him that he fell out of the sky and that he was like a brother. Then Raul hugged him which surprised him even more! Roland was nearly at a loss for words, but he managed to say to Raul that he had fallen out of the sky for him also, because he was the first one to accompany him up into the mountains so many times and to be such a good companion. It was such a turn around for the better after Roland's joking comment about Norma earlier in the day. How nice that things had improved so!

Raul and Rigo went to the dance, and Roland slept in his car because Lavinia stayed up until 2 AM making lots of tortillas. That was part of her living, making tortillas and selling them to people around town.

The next morning Roland went to the ferretería (hardware store) in town and bought two new bike tires and tubes for Raul's old bike. Its tires were totally worn out, and he had seen him and his father attempting to fix them with more patches. They were just too worn out. He returned to their house with the tires and tubes in hand and surprised Raul and Rigo with them. Raul was worried that Roland had spent too much money for them, but then he was glad to receive them. He and Roland went to work fixing the old bike. After it was all fixed, Raul suddenly declared with a smile, "Llantas nuevas. ¡Que bueno!" saying, *New tires! How great!* He shook hands with Roland the Mexican way. That made Roland feel really good that a surprise gift was so well appreciated.

They went to the molino to swim that day. Everything went great. They swam in the large outdoor pool and played and splashed around.

Roland enjoyed running around with his friends. This was a great way to spend Spring Break . . . with some friends. Since none of his Tennessee friends wanted to do anything with him, he just came on down to Mexico to spend it here. In a way, he felt like these were his people and that he belonged here, more so than in Tennessee. He began to wonder if he had made a mistake at the time he was born. Maybe he should have been born in Mexico instead, if things like that were possible.

That evening, Roland talked to Norma about something. Her father, Alejandro was just leaving, and Norma went and talked to him. Then he came back in the house and talked to Roland. He approached him in a serious way, and Roland began to get worried for his safety. *Oh no! He's found out about Norma!* Roland thought to himself. He truly hoped Alejandro had not come to deck him. He could likely have dodged or blocked a blow, but he didn't want such a confrontation to occur because it would mean total curtains for his friendship with this family.

Then he spoke. "Dice Norma que me hablabas," telling Roland that Norma said that he wanted to talk to him. Roland answered no, that he didn't have anything to talk about. "Ah, bueno," said Alejandro calmly, and he turned and walked away. Roland was at a loss for words for the sudden relief he felt that Alejandro had not come to do what seemed most imminent. Thank goodness that had a good outcome! He could continue his friendship with Raul, Rigo . . . and Norma!

Roland spent the next week with them. They got to talking and decided that it would be best if Lavinia accompany Raul when he would leave Mexico this coming summer. She would also need a passport. They also decided to divide Raul's money into two accounts, part of it in his name and the other part in his mother's name. Roland made several trips to Sabinas Hidalgo to help them accomplish their wishes. The 5-year passport cost nearly $75, and since neither Bustamante nor Villaldama had a bank, all banking matters had to be taken care of in Sabinas Hidalgo, as well.

One day, Lavinia came home with groceries, and she had bought some perfume toilet paper. Roland commented that he didn't like perfume. When Raul heard that, he thought of a way to playfully tantalize Roland. He took bits of toilet paper, entered the catch-all room, and he casually dropped pieces into Roland's things, his totebag, and boxes. Roland kept extracting the perfumated pieces, and Raul, with a big smile, added more. Norma and Irma got into the fun, and they sneaked into the room when Roland wasn't looking, and then they ran out of there squealing with laughter when Roland chased them away. Raul did the same. Soon the game advanced to Roland chasing them into their room and playing vigorously with them, laughing all the while. They enjoyed tantalizing Roland and getting his attention.

Through the week, Roland ran around with Raul and his friends. They talked to various people who had crossed over the river and had visited the United States. One evening, they went to talk to a man in Villaldama about his experiences and how he was able to pass vehicles into Mexico so they could stay permanently and be legalized. Roland did nothing with drugs nor did this man, but he did want to take home some Flor de Peña and Siempre Viva plants to plant in the woods back at home. The man said he could take them to Laredo for him, but for a hefty fee. Roland opted to take his chances and take them across the border himself, which he later did successfully.

Raul and Roland went up into the mountains and collected numerous specimens of both plants from the left ridge going up the Lion's Head Mountain. It was a cloudy day, and they enjoyed the hike. They arrived to a little cove with a beautiful copse of Oak trees perched by a large limestone rock outcropping and cliffs. There were numerous Siempre Viva (*Echeveria*) plants growing in the cracks along the cliff walls, and many of them were in full bloom with their orangish-yellow flowers. They also collected some Flor de Peña (*Selaginella pallescens*). They turned around there and made the descent back to Bustamante, arriving in the mid afternoon. Roland set some of the plants aside for himself, gave others to Lavinia, and also gave specimens to numerous friends around town and also in Sabinas Hidalgo.

One day was rainy and cloudy, and Roland and Raul slept for the morning. They were going to go into the mountains again, but for the bad weather, they didn't. Later that afternoon, Roland took Raul, Pegaso and Angelo in his car around town. They stopped by some relatives of Angelo's, and also by the Cantu's store in the plaza.

On the way back to the house, Raul got playful and began blowing the horn in Roland's car while he was driving. Roland stopped his car and took Raul's hands off the horn and then also took part in the playing episode. They were just having fun, but it got a little more vigorous than intended. As they were laughing, they started bopping each other on the head, and Roland gave him what he thought was a normal playful bop on the head.

Suddenly, Raul stopped laughing, and his mood changed instantly to one of being hurt and angry. It was then that Roland realized that his fingernail had accidentally gotten Raul's eyelid. Immediately, Roland felt bad about it, but before he could say anything about it, Raul was already getting out of the car and walking home. Roland called out to Raul to ask him if he was all right, but he didn't answer. Roland drove his car to the house, parked, and walked inside.

Raul was already talking to his mother, explaining what happened, and Roland explained that they had gotten a little vigorous with their playing. Raul mentioned that he no longer wanted to go to Tennessee. Roland tried to sincerely apologize the best way possible, but Raul had his stereo playing loudly, and he wouldn't turn it down to give Roland a chance to speak. Well, Roland took matters into his own hands, and he pulled the plug out of the wall, immediately silencing the stereo. Then Roland made his apology, reiterating that they had just been playing. Raul answered in an angry manner, somewhat accepting the apology.

Lavinia explained the seriousness about playing too hard, and Roland knew very well about that. It's just that their playing got out of hand and the accident happened. Roland felt terrible about it the rest of the evening. He was so glad that it wasn't Raul's eye itself, just the eyelid.

Rigo came home from the carpentry, and he noticed that Roland wasn't feeling well. He asked Roland in a straightforward manner why he didn't feel well, and he told him why. Then Rigo went to Raul, who was still angry, and told him to forgive Roland. Raul answered yes, that he would.

The days went by, and numerous times, Raul had spells of blurting out to Roland that he had hit him in the eye. It only made Roland feel worse, which Raul gained from by acknowledging Roland's sorrow at what had happened. Nevertheless, Roland realized that Raul was having a big problem with the results of their vigorous playing episode.

There was another problem Raul was also having. Roland had unknowingly made another blunder. Raul had told Roland that Pancho had not paid him for the previous weeks of pay, and that Pancho owed Raul N$300. One day, Roland and Pancho were talking, and Roland mentioned that Raul was in need of that money that Pancho owed him. Later in the day, Roland mentioned to Raul that he had talked to Pancho.

Raul's reaction was completely unexpected. He started by commenting something about Roland being a *chismoso* (the equivalent of a gossiper). Then he went on to tell Roland that it was really out of order for him to have charged Pancho for him, and that in many ways, he was like a child. Raul made other disparaging remarks and scathing remarks to make Roland feel bad, and it really upset him. Lavinia heard Raul's outlandish remarks and intervened, asking them to stop arguing and to make up. She told Roland to ask Raul to forgive him. *For what?* Roland thought. *How about the other way around?* After all, Roland thought surely Raul would have appreciated his having talked to Pancho. Roland did what Raul's mother requested, and they shook hands, but Raul still steamed about it.

One day, Angelo took Roland and Raul with him in a horse and buggy to a remote ranch ten kilometers north of Bustamante. In Mexico, rural ranches were known as the *Ejido*. Angelo had to catch two horses that his father was grazing up there. They followed a gravel road all the way up there, and it took several hours. The horse Roland rode trotted in the most bumpy fashion possible, and it was most uncomfortable! Roland and Raul took turns riding the horse.

Raul, as it turned out, was basically a pill the whole day, and he kept saying things to make Roland angry, including foul language. As they ate lunch, Raul grabbed some of Roland's food and hid it, and when Roland reached into Raul's daypack to take it back, Raul said he was going to tell his mother. Roland angrily took back his food and ate his lunch. Angelo later came back, as he had been searching for the horse and had lassoed him. Raul cussed some more and said other things that intimidated Roland, including reminding him about the playing episode. Raul's uncalled for behavior made Roland more irritated, and he collected his daypack and water jug and started walking back to Bustamante. Raul called for Roland to come back, but Roland didn't answer. He just kept on walking. Angelo came after Roland on horseback, explained that it was a long way, and that he would tell Raul to be kinder and to quit being intimidating. Roland thought about it, and then returned.

Angelo had another horse to catch which took another two hours. After that was done, they spent several hours on the return journey to Bustamante. Roland now had serious second thoughts about taking Raul to Tennessee with him. He could envision Raul having lots of grief and anger, only days after getting to Tennessee, especially with the scenario of being away from his land, his people, and the culture of Mexico. Raul was mature in a lot of ways, but he still had to mature in the aspect of enduring being away from his own kind. After all, he was only 15, even though he and Roland were the same height and size. Near the end of their return journey, Roland noticed a most curious thing in the sky. It was a cloud in the shape of a ¿ (an upside down question mark). That was appropriate, because Roland was questioning the possibility within his own mind about whether or not to take Raul with him to Tennessee.

When Roland and Raul got home, Raul threw a tantrum and told his mother with quite a lot of anger what had happened today! He told about how Roland had begun to walk all the way back to town. He complained and carried on and said that he was no longer going to go to Tennessee with Roland, that he was going to go to his brother's in Salado, Texas. Roland said that would be fine, to just go there! At the same time, Roland reminded Raul by asking him when was the last time he and his family had heard anything at all from Eduardo in Salado. Raul knew it had been nearly a year. They were all sad about it, especially Lavinia, for not having heard from her own son! Why in the world had Eduardo not communicated with his family?

Lavinia asked Raul to be more reasonable and to calm down. Roland then thanked him, no matter what, for having accompanied him into the mountains so many times, a total of six times, more times than anyone else on Earth had ever done. Roland had already hiked more miles with Raul than with anyone else, he reckoned ever. Then he walked away and went into their catch-all room, the room where he was sleeping at night.

In a few minutes, Raul came into the room and extended his hand to make up with him, feeling sorry for the way he had been acting all day. He told Roland that it was all play, fun and games, and he told Roland not to believe that he had rejected him. Yes, he still wanted to go to Tennessee, and they would see what they could do about getting that VISA this coming summer. Roland was shocked with surprise to see Raul having come around so fast and to suddenly be content again. *Fine*, Roland thought, and he shook hands with Raul, putting the day's events behind them.

The next day, Roland decided to go into the mountains again. For the first time, he really was going to camp up there. He had never done it before for fear of wild animals like cougars, bears, and coyotes, but he had his spray container of Counter Assault, and he took his tent and sleeping bag along with five liters of water and enough food.

The walk from Raul's house to the ridge top at the grassy saddle took five hours, and he arrived in the middle of the afternoon. He set up camp there and decided to hike for the first time up the ridge south of the grassy saddle. It was nearly the same height as the Lion's Head Mountain, at around 1,850 meters in altitude.

He re-entered the Oak and Hickory forest that he had just walked through to reach the grassy saddle and soon veered right, leaving the small path as he climbed uphill. After having to push numerous tree branches aside so he could make his way, he came to the grassy ridge top. For the first few minutes, he continued to pass scrub Oaks. Then the ridge became steeper, and he was soon battling shrubs and bushes which made the going more difficult. In places, there were Lechuguilla and Nopal plants, and even though he watched his step, he occasionally got poked by their spikes and spines.

As the ridge further steepened, Roland climbed exposed limestone rock faces and had to carefully cross Lechuguilla laden gaps and spaces between rock boulders. In some places, he had to be very careful in his rock climbing because some of the limestone was loose, and rocks and footholds could easily have come off.

He started seeing Siempre Viva plants growing on small ledges and growing out of cracks in the rock faces. Numerous specimens were in full bloom with their orangish-yellow flowers.

Finally, the steep grade lessened, and he soon found himself on a flat table of limestone with numerous small crevices through it. The surface of the bedrock was not smooth. It had many lumps and showed that it had been worn down by wind and rain erosion. Cypress shrubs, some the size of small trees, could be seen here and there along the narrow ridge.

The going was easier as he made his way south along the ridge. He descended slightly and had to sometimes pick his way around large Cypress shrubs and scrub Oak bushes. There were gaps in the otherwise continuous run of bedrock, and again there were plenty of Lechuguilla plants occupying those spaces.

The views were magnificent. He could see the whole desert valley with its various ridges of mountains running in its northern section. The double mesa of Chiquihuitillos could be seen to the west and looked like nothing more than a couple of small mounds way below him. Bustamante in the other valley to the east of him now appeared very small. The road leading to it from the cono could be seen, and the whole valley appeared so far below him that he felt like he was viewing it all from an airplane.

To the south, he could see nearly to Monterrey, and there were numerous mountain ranges that were visible in the distance. One ridge not too distant had numerous Pine trees dotting its slope, and to the west, he saw another grove of Pines growing on the slopes below him near the large chasm. These views were equally as good as the ones he and Raul had seen from the summit of the Lion's Head Mountain back in January.

Roland reached a part of the ridge that had two large Cypress shrubs growing beside each other. He got between them and underneath their canopy. The views from within, cropped by the branches were spectacular, and Roland thought to himself that if there was ever a church for him, this was it. Roland had always thought of his church as being in the mountains, not some man-made building like most Earth people went to.

Roland decided to make some sincere wishes while he was there. As he looked across the ridge to the north, with a view of the Lion's Head Mountain in the distance, he wished for friends, true friends, and he wished for a travelling companion to travel with him and enjoy future trips with him, a reasonable and well expected wish. At that moment, a large eagle suddenly flew overhead and into the valley to the west. That somewhat surprised Roland, especially that the eagle had flown across him at just the perfect moment. Something was synchronized there, and that was impressive. Perhaps his wishes had been heard.

Roland made some other wishes, including his continued friendship with Raul, Rigo, and his family, and he made his way back down the ridge to the grassy saddle where he ate some supper.

He watched the great sunset, and as it got dark, he looked at the lights of cars and trucks of the distant highway from Anahuac to Monterrey down in the valley to the east. He wished for all negative influences from all levels to exit from him and his life, to leave his friendships and his life alone, and he wished to enjoy his friends without the sabotage he began to suspect was going on.

He also thought about Raul and Rigo's sister, Norma, and he thought again about her birthdate, July 11, 1986, and as he thought about that particular day and what he was doing at the moment she was born, he was suddenly spellbound when he realized what he experienced on that day at 9:20 AM. He had seen a small bouquet of flowers posted on the trunk of a Fir tree along the Pacific Crest Trail in Alpine Lakes Wilderness in Washington. Lavinia had told Roland that her daughter Norma was born at 10:20 AM, CST, which in Mexico was one hour ahead of Washington, since Mexico did not have daylight saving time. Norma had indeed been born at the same moment Roland had seen those flowers!

Roland just couldn't believe it! Never had he thought those flowers posted on that tree had any significance, and now he knew there must have been some sort of message for *him*, but *what*? This served as some sort of verification of destiny and things being predetermined. What an impressive coincidence! Could some manifestation or parallel life of Norma have chosen who her husband was going to be right before being born, at which time she would have left a sign for him to discover at that moment and then much later figure out? Roland wasn't sure, but he was certainly going to put his mind to work and figure out the rest of that puzzle. He knew he would tell Lavinia this impressive coincidence, as he now figured it was safe to do so.

He crawled into his tent for the night, and he had a peaceful night's sleep. Still, since it was Saturday night, there was a slight disturbance, the faint sound, mostly bass sounds, of the dance until 2 AM coming all the way up the mountain from Bustamante and from *within* the social center! To think that it arrived all the way to the top of the mountain! He knew the dances were loud, and he sometimes worried for Raul and Rigo's hearing, along with other Mexicans. Roland was always sensitive to loud sounds and carried earplugs, even when mowing the lawn back at home, but in time he would learn that the Mexicans, being a slightly different race and of a different genetic setup, were literally more durable in many respects than the frail Caucasian gringos. To the Mexicans, loudness was no more harmful than normal sound levels.

The next morning was nice and sunny. Roland ate some breakfast, packed up his tent, and walked the half hour back through the highland forest along the base of the ridge, and then he began his descent. The next thing he saw really surprised him . . . a tent!

Some other people had camped up here, and it would be the only time he would ever see other campers up here, apart from those he would bring with him in the future. Roland turned left off the trail and walked over to the tent to find a man and a woman in their 50's cooking some breakfast. They were Americans and were from Laredo, Texas. Roland chatted with them for half an hour, swapped addresses with them, and then he made his descent to Bustamante, arriving at Raul and Rigo's house in the late morning.

They had both gone to the dance, and they asked Roland how his camping trip went. Roland informed them that he didn't see a single bear, nor a snake, nor a coyote, nor any cougars. Rigo was most surprised that Roland had heard the sound of the dance up there on the ridge top!

Rigo was just preparing to leave. There were four young females outside the house waiting on him, and Rigo was shining his boots and had on a clean t-shirt. "Voy a andar con las *muchachas*," he proudly told Roland with a smile, saying that he was going to escort the four females. Without a hat on, he stepped out of the house, and Roland was impressed that someone who was barely 14 was already taking women out! He stood outside the house and just watched in amazement as Rigo perfectly escorted all four of them up the street with the greatest of ease, as if he had already done it 100 times! Raul commented that Rigo was a "muy hombre," a mature man, sure enough! Young men in Mexico matured faster than those in the United States.

As Raul got up and began his day, he kept talking, and suddenly Roland smelled something which made his heart sink. Raul smelled of alcohol! Roland immediately commented on it, and Lavinia, who was in the next room, heard Roland's words. She marched right in there, got close to Raul and smelled it also! She gave Raul a soft scolding smack on the face and said, "Voy a decir a tu papa," saying that she was going to tell his father.

Raul angrily answered, "¡Pues, díle! ¿Qué tiene? ¡Es mi vida!" telling her to go ahead and tell him, and that *so what*, it was his life! Raul went on to tell her that he only drank one, but in reality, he probably had plenty more than that.

Of course, Roland understood all of what was said, and he knew Lorenzo and Pancho were right. Raul was very likely going to be an alcoholic like his father. Roland talked to Raul about it on the spot, telling him that drinking a little was one thing, but increasing and getting drunk can lead straight to alcoholism. It is like a monster and can pull a person right in and clamp a vise on him. Roland also mentioned the story about the ranting and raving spell that took place at his cousin's house out West the previous summer. Alcohol makes people unreasonable, and Roland didn't want Raul to become like that.

Angelo and Pegaso arrived, wanting to go swimming at the molino. When they mentioned what time it was, they were an hour ahead of Roland. When Roland looked confused, Pegaso mentioned that today was the first day of daylight saving time. But Mexico didn't have daylight saving time. Pegaso said that used to be true, but beginning last year in 1996, they did.

Roland and Raul went to the molino with Pegaso and Angelo, and they went swimming, enjoying the day. They passed by Rigo and the four *muchachas*, already having arrived and sitting at a picnic table. Rigo was chatting with them with the greatest of ease, smiling and enjoying every moment of it. Pegaso and Roland had conversation with each other. They were becoming better friends, and Roland was glad to know him. To the best of his knowledge, neither Pegaso nor Angelo drank. They didn't smoke either, and Roland was glad to have some friends who were reasonably straight. They stayed at the molino well into the afternoon.

Behind the molino, there were lots of big Pecan trees. Strangely enough, the whole scene looked familiar to Roland. He commented the familiarity to Pegaso, who found that quite interesting. Perhaps Roland had had a dream years ago, Pegaso suggested. That could very well have been true. Perhaps Roland's parallel life had come here years ago, and the scene and information had crossed over when he was dreaming. After all, several years ago, the same thing had happened when he visited Norfolk Island in the south Pacific Ocean.

Angelo and Raul came over to talk to Roland and Pegaso, and they decided to do some arm wrestling. They invited Roland to join in. Roland declined, and they insisted. They wanted to see Roland arm wrestle Pegaso. So, he accepted. He and Pegaso sat across from each other at one of the picnic tables. It was a close match. Though Pegaso was strong and robust at the peak age of 17, Roland, who was 31, was stronger. Roland applied some extra force, and slowly but surely, he managed to put Pegaso's arm down, and he won the match. Everyone was surprised because Roland was somewhat lanky in appearance, but having grown up on a farm and having done plenty of hard work in his life, he was indeed strong. Raul proudly told Roland that Pegaso let him win. So, Roland asked Pegaso if that was true, and he said, "No. Tú eres fuerte," telling Roland that he was strong and that he truly won the arm wrestling match.

After Roland swam a while, he returned to Raul and Rigo's house. Not long after he got there, Rigo returned. Roland told him his concerns for Raul. Rigo told Roland that Raul doesn't drink. Rigo had just left with those four *muchachas* right before Roland discovered Raul's alcohol breath. Roland then informed Rigo what he had discovered right after he had left. Rigo was surprised and didn't make much comment. Roland also told Rigo about how drinking is like a monster that can pull one in like a vise.

That night, Roland told Lavinia and Rigo the coincidence about the flowers having been posted in the tree at the time of Norma's birth. Lavinia was certainly interested in that, and though she didn't let on, Roland knew she had more thoughts about it in the future. Rigo realized that it was a coincidence, and he asked Roland what he was doing when he was born, February 26, 1983. Roland remembered several things he did in that month, and he said he would check his calendar.

It was getting near time to leave. Roland's parents had called and said a friend of theirs had asked Roland to come and work with him on a house addition project to his parents' house in Fairview. Roland needed to go home anyway because he had already been staying with them for two weeks. Aside from Raul's spells, it had been an enjoyable two weeks, much better than being lonely back in Tennessee.

Raul and Rigo's vacation was over, and they were now back in school. Roland helped Lavinia by cleaning her backyard with a hoe and digging up all the weeds. In the afternoon, Raul and Rigo rode with Roland in his Ford Fairlane station wagon, and Roland let Raul drive it. He enjoyed that, and they rode around town. Raul was worried the police would see him, but he drove on some side streets to go around their trap, their favorite street corner to catch and ticket people.

They returned to the house. On the way back, Roland explained to Raul again about what drinking can lead to. Drinking a little is one thing, but if a person increases, it can easily lead to alcoholism, especially with teenagers, and Roland didn't want Raul to become a boracho (alcoholic). Raul and Roland also talked about the coming summer and about being business partners. Raul was looking forward to it.

That night, they visited some more. Raul asked Roland to hide his car keys, which he did. Then Raul went into the room, stood over Roland's belongings for a few seconds, and plunged his hand right down into one of the boxes, the correct one, and he brought up the car keys with the greatest of ease! Roland couldn't believe it and wondered how on Earth Raul could have done it! He knew he hadn't been peeking because Roland made sure of that when he hid the keys. On more than one occasion, Raul had known exactly where Roland's things were, including his green ex-army ammo box which had his money. That box was under the back flap in the back of his station wagon. He knew he had not told Raul, nor had he seen it either. Perhaps Raul was psychic and knew extra things. In actual fact, he was psychic in that respect.

On the last night, Roland slept in the same room with them. Raul and Rigo were talking to Roland about his being Raul's padrino of graduation from the secundaria school. Raul hadn't decided who would be his padrino, but he thought it would be either Pancho or Roland. He asked for an *esclava de plata* (silver bracelet for the wrist). Roland appreciated Raul for thinking of choosing him, but he asked Raul a question. It concerned Raul's possible embarrassment of being with Roland. Raul answered with assurance that no, he wasn't going to be embarrassed. Okay, good.

The last day came, and Roland had to leave. It had rained in the night, and the streets were wet. He said goodbye to them, and he thanked them very much. Norma and Irma said goodbye to Roland by saying, "Hermanito," which was a compliment declaring that they saw him as if he were a brother and a member of the family. Raul and Rigo made similar comments as they said goodbye to Roland in a genuine friendly manner.

Roland got in his car at 8 AM, and drove home. He turned in his permit at the Colombia Bridge and then drove to Nuevo Laredo for the sole reason of having an easier inspection because of the volume of traffic. Colombia Bridge on the U.S. side had always had Roland take everything out of his car, in addition to their annoying interrogation and personal questions! Since Roland carried Siempre Viva and Flor de Peña plants, he didn't want them found.

Using a detailed map, he entered the city of Nuevo Laredo and arrived at Bridge II. One block before arriving at the bridge, he saw a police officer standing at the street corner. Suddenly, the officer started waving at Roland, signalling him to pull over. Roland knew he hadn't broken any laws, and since he was only one block from the bridge, he just kept on moving and drove on by the cop. He looked through his rearview mirror at the cop waving his arms at Roland to pull his station wagon over. He had enjoyed his two weeks in Mexico without serious mishap, and he wasn't about to stop for this man! He had heard the horror stories. Roland turned left, very soon arrived at the toll booth, and he saw the sign for $1.40. The woman told Roland the fee was $2.40. Roland questioned it, and the woman repeated the same number $2.40. He quickly paid the woman without any further question, knowing that the cop might come after him. Immediately, Roland proceeded and drove across the bridge, breathing a great sigh of relief when he crossed the halfway mark, free of the cop's reign!

The officer on the U.S. side greeted Roland in a friendly manner, asked him if he had any trouble with the federales, and Roland said no. The officer said that was good. He directed Roland to one of the inspection bays where a different officer came and talked to Roland a few minutes. He had Roland open up the tailgate and lift up the back flap so he could peep under (to check for hidden Mexicans). That was all there was to it, and the officer wished him a nice day. Relieved, Roland closed his tailgate, rolled up the window, got back in his car, and drove away. He had his Siempre Viva and Flor de Peña plants. They had been hidden in his daypack with his lunch. How great that he got them in!

Despite the psychic woman's very plain and straightforward warning that things would go very bad for Roland in Mexico, the outcome was a lot better. But then, who knows what would have happened if he had stopped for that cop just one block away from freedom! He might have simply charged Roland N$20, or perhaps he could have thrown the book at him, made up lies, and hauled him off to jail, not to mention steal his car! Roland wasn't about to lose his 1970 Ford Fairlane station wagon, the first car he ever owned, a fine automobile with a V8-302 and a 3-speed on the column.

Roland's destination was Houston, Texas to stay with his cousins. When he passed the second inspection, the U.S. Border Patrol station at mile marker 14 on Interstate 35, the officer commented on the Fairlane station wagon, knowing that it was already rare that a car 27 years in age would travel that far from home. He spent the night with his cousins and drove all the way home the next day, using the Natchez Trace Parkway most of the way. He arrived home 16 hours after leaving Houston.

CHAPTER 6

WORK & TRIBULATION

April 1997

The next day, Roland drove his truck to Fairview and immediately started work for Malcolm Lassater. They had known each other since childhood, and it had been three years since he had last seen him. Their parents were just about the best of friends, having known each other for some 40 years. Roland was very tired after the long drive yesterday, but he needed to recuperate his money as soon as possible, which he did over the next two weeks.

When Roland arrived at mid day, he found that Malcolm's parents had a major project going on. They were building a two story fancy addition onto their house, complete with stone pillars. Malcolm was in the process of making the forms for one of the tall columns, and Roland helped him.

It was not easy for Roland to do the work since he was so tired. Since he would be working the next day also, he asked if he could stay overnight. They didn't want to accommodate Roland, but when he made it clear how tired he was after his long drive from Mexico, they consented. As he visited that night for a short while, he asked them if, while working on this project, he would be able to spend every other night there instead of doing the commute of over 40 miles every day. They said that would be fine. That was good.

The next day, Roland was more rested, and he worked more vigorously. It was cold that day, quite a change from Mexico. At the end of the day, Malcolm's father wrote the check for the two days' work. Roland would return on Monday. They left the house, and as they were walking down the driveway, Roland thanked him for his having consented that he spend some nights at their place to save on the driving and commuting. Well, the next thing surprised Roland, because Dr. Lassater said he had thought about it and said it would not be agreeable for Roland to stay with them on any night whatsoever! Roland appealed it and reminded him what he had consented to the night before. Dr. Lassater simply answered that he had changed his mind.

Roland turned around and went back in the house and approached Malcolm's mother and explained to her what her husband had just told him and that it was inhospitable. She started to respond, but then Malcolm came to Roland from another room, totally on the defensive and so angry that it scared Roland! He shouted at Roland, ranting and raving that he had thought about it too and didn't feel comfortable with his spending nights. He said he couldn't mix hiring someone and also being a friend to the same person, much less have him stay with him, visiting and keeping him awake, talking all night long! He shouted that he didn't appreciate it that Roland had approached his mother to appeal his father's decision.

How inhospitable and rude! Roland thought. They had given clear consent the night before. Roland certainly wouldn't have visited and talked all night long! He would have gone to sleep at nights. Malcolm shoved it in Roland's face that he wasn't family, and Roland reminded him that he was indeed a cousin on his mother's side! No matter what, Malcolm was totally against having Roland stay at nights. Roland wouldn't have wanted to now, especially with Malcolm's angry behavior, which was totally uncalled for! As a result, Roland no longer felt a close friendship with him. The root of the problem lay in the fact that Malcolm had had a couple of beers, and he was irritable!

Roland told him, "You know what I'm thinking? I thought you were a friend of mine."

"Okay, that's it! Go ahead and leave!"

Roland immediately walked out, but then Malcolm asked him to wait. He remembered that he didn't have any other workers. He and Roland now talked more peaceably, and Roland decided to continue to work for them only because he needed the money. It had very much upset Roland how Malcolm had acted, and even more so that he had insinuated that he couldn't be a friend with someone he was working with at the same time. How absurd!

Roland really and truly wished he were back in Mexico with his good friends, running around, laughing, and playing again, so much more enjoyable than being chewed out and resented by Malcolm. He really missed his friends in Mexico. He also wished Raul were the one working with him on this project instead!

Roland went ahead and made the commute for the next two weeks. The Franklin Road, which was part of the route he used to reach Fairview, was a very busy two-lane road, and he hoped he wouldn't have a wreck. He had already wrecked on that same road three years earlier. Everything went okay as far as that was concerned, and he successfully earned around $1,000 in that time. Three weeks after beginning, the work totally petered out, and another friend of his family needed his help because she had just bought a house in west Nashville to later move into. That work lasted a month, and her hospitality was so much better that the Lassater's.

Roland was glad to get away from Malcolm, who had been stressed out and agitated. Roland had unknowingly made a cutting error the final day he worked for him, which resulted in Malcolm's chewing Roland out, and with foul language! If Roland had ever been a friend of Malcolm's he certainly didn't feel it now. Their mothers met for lunch several months later and commented that Malcolm and Roland's friendship had definitely been fractured. Well, that was sad. While Roland appreciated the work for the money, he also felt punished, feeling the absense of friendship the whole time he was working there. Both Malcolm and his father seemingly had a sense of dislike for Roland, or they would have let their friend stay there every other night, if *friend* is the appropriate word.

Roland's new patron, whose name was Elizabeth, was a kind and understanding woman in her fifties, and she appreciated Roland's good work which he did with diligence and precision. He painted several rooms for her and painted bookshelves, assembled some greenhouse window attachments, and built a deck for her on the corner of her house. There was one chore after another, and Roland earned over $1,500. He was now financially set to return to Mexico and enjoy some of his summer with Raul, Rigo, and their friends.

Soon after arriving home from his March/April trip to Mexico, Roland had called Isalia on the phone and told her that he was home safely, and that things had gone for the most part all right, much better than she and Clayton had predicted when they strongly urged Roland not to go back to Mexico.

Isalia was very much relieved.

Roland told Isalia that Norma was excellent and also told her the coincidence about the flowers being posted in the tree the same day that Norma was born.

"Roland, that is *amazing*!" Isalia reacted. "The Universe is telling you something."

"I was very surprised when I figured it out."

"I know, and only you would figure something like that out, and have the phenomenal memory to remember the details in the first place."

Roland knew that was true, that very few people would have remembered that detail.

"By the way, Isalia," he now told her, "Raul is thinking of choosing me to be his padrino for graduation from the secundaria school."

"Ohhh, *Roland*. What an honor!"

Roland hadn't thought it was that big a deal, and he reacted to her comment with, "It is?"

"Oh, yes indeed," she told him. "They think very highly of you. They're courting you, and they love you."

Roland asked Isalia how Clayton was doing, and she told him that Clayton was not doing well, that he had been admitted to the hospital . . . to die there.

Roland expressed his sorrow. He knew Clayton was not going to make it.

Several days later, Isalia told her husband that Roland had safely returned from Mexico.

Clayton breathed a great sigh of relief and commented, "That is good knowledge."

In mid April, just a few days later, Clayton Ives went ahead and died of pancreas cancer. He was tired of life and was ready to go. Roland had seen that in Clayton for several years. His eyes showed it. He had also seen how Clayton and Isalia had bickered at times. Their relationship was not so close. No matter what, Isalia had faithfully been by his side as his wife, especially the last few weeks of his life. They said their blessings and forgave each other for everything.

Isalia called Roland and his family the day he passed away, and they expressed their proper sorrow for her. Her sister, Roma, came up from Texas to stay with her for a month, so that Isalia wouldn't be lonely. Isalia thought she had taken care of all her grieving six years ago in 1991, but now she found out that there was more. She panicked at times, and she commented that if her sister had not come, living there alone without Clayton would be unthinkable.

*   *   *

She was just weaving her way among a cluster of trees that wound their way between two hills to a valley below when she caught sight of a creature she knew to be extinct, or so she thought, for sitting on a solitary rock among deep purple flowers was a great hairy Neimas, whose startling blue eyes seemed to scan the sky as it sang a gentle song. She didn't understand but it made her want to laugh and cry all at the same time.

As she ran down the hillside, the Neimas must have heard her for it waved, beckoning with a great paw for her to join it. She stumbled down the last part and tripped, falling at the Neimas's dees. As she scrambled up she felt gentle paws lift her by the arms and place her on its lap, all the while singing its song. She felt no fear at the enormity of the creature, only joy at the touch of its silky fur on her skin. Feeling something underneath her, she laughed as she realised that it was a He. Very much so . . . . .

The Neimas seemed to like her laughter and it began to make a booming tone which shook his chest and with his right paw he patted her head. For a creature so strong he was surprisingly gentle, which had made them much sought after in past days.

She sat following the Neimas's gaze as he watched the few white, fluffy clouds drift across the sky. A sweet breeze made his fur dance, stroking her skin. He broke a piece of rock and began to shape it with his paws. She watched fascinated as a yellow glow began to seep out, slowly spreading until it engulfed his paws. He was still singing and watching the sky but she was held by the change that she could just see. Slowly the light died and with a nudge the Neimas indicated his paws, which he opened and there on his left was a piece of a cloud. That was what her ancient Elders would have called it and they were right, a cloud plucked from the sky.

Responding to his nudge she reached out and picked it up. The sensation was exquisite; it seemed to tingle with energy across her finger tips. But it was like holding nothing, because it was seemingly insubstantial. With great reverence she carefully put it in her mouth. That was her next surprise. Even though she might have seen images in the seeing crystal of dolphs eating this food it couldn't compare to the reality. It was like an explosion of colour which danced and played a wonderful tune upon her tongue. As it slipped down her throat she nearly passed out with the awesome feelings running through her. It was like an internally generated heat which massaged her from the inside out. It gave a glow which was unmatched by anything she had experienced before. And the stories were true; it was totally satisfying. She felt as if she wouldn't have to eat for a veul. She gave a contented sigh which made the Neimas laugh, his eyes looking at her with expectation. For a yen she was puzzled but then she remembered more of the Legend.

For after sharing their food, it was the custom to lie together and share a story.

Just as the Neimas began to lower her to lay with him among the purple flowers, the light of Danetar was snuffed out, plunging them into darkness. Suddenly a flash of white light streaked across the black sky, making the Neimas cry a terrible roar of pain.

He let go of her and she fell to the ground. Shaken she looked up to see the dark shadow of the creature go racing after the fireball that was falling towards the mountains.

One yen she was on the ground; the next she was swimming in the purple seas. She was holding her beak above the waves as again she saw the light, but this time from a greater distance away. Her mind cried out as she realised she was too far away to help. She was a Watersinger and the city she could just see on the far shore; in the opposite direction of the light was her home and its name was Malaroi. Her whole being was in pain at the hopelessness of it all. She didn't know. She was too young to know how to make the jump to the Neimas's home. The only thing she could do was to use her water-time to find her friends.

The scene shifted and she shared with the Neimas's water-time as he made it back to his home in time to see the destruction that the fireball had wrought. The grey shadows of the Mountain were broken by hot fire which crackled and roared into the night. The smell of burning flesh filled his nostrils as he tried to put the flames out of a fallen Neimas. She knew that it was his motherling and she cried with him. The area had been devastated by the fire, causing a side of the mountain to crash down, burning many of the Neimas. Those who escaped that had been burned alive by the flames as the Meteor had exploded into a thousand fragments. A single tree burned, wood spitting and crackling as the wood splintered. The surviving Neimas called out for her to help but she didn't know how and she cursed her water-time for the hopelessness of having a power which she had such little understanding of. The Neimas must have been aware of her sharing his plight for he became angry and bellowed, screaming for her into the night.

It was just too much. She couldn't stand it any longer, so she tried to free herself from his mind and as if he wanted her to know what she had failed to do, he climbed up the rubble, crying at every limb that he saw poking through, but relentlessly he climbed higher. He knew he was the last and he wanted to join them. No Neimas could bear the solitariness of *being without its own kind, so he climbed and climbed. When he reached the top he shook his paws at the sky and cried her name as he let go, falling through the darkness to join his bones with those of his loved ones. She felt the impact and was swept up by a wave of darkness which had her screaming incessantly.*

*   *   *

She found herself still screaming when she woke up and was greeted by her kind sister, Roma.

"Isalia, why don't you go and have yourself checked out by a psychologist?"

"No, I just want to put it behind me . . . just put it behind me!" she firmly answered.

"But Isalia, you keep having the same recurring dream," Roma insisted.

"I know, but I don't know what to do about it, much less, understand it!" Isalia was a very stubborn woman, and she reasoned that if she didn't pay it any attention, then it would eventually go away. She had been plagued by the same nightmare for the past twenty years, and she kept hoping it would just go away . . . and *never* bother her again! Roma didn't say any more to her, and she turned over and went back to sleep.

*   *   *

Roland called Raul via his neighbors, the Gonzalez family, a few times during the months he was home.

By late April, as it turned out, Pancho had decided to let Raul go because after Roland had been there, Raul didn't want to work so hard. He had been playing too much, and Pancho was also having a problem with money. He still owed Raul several weeks of pay, and he had not paid him.

Roland called Isalia and asked her advice on whether or not he would be doing the right thing to help out Raul and send him US $50. Isalia said that was a very generous and thoughtful thing to do, and she gave Roland the advice to help out Raul. Roland sent him a US $50 note in the mail.

So, Roland called Raul again on the phone. This time, Mr. Gonzalez answered the phone, and the newest phone bill from Teléfonos de México had just arrived. There was a charge for N$50 for a rejected collect call to Tennessee, which surprised Roland very much. Mr. Gonzalez was quite upset about it! Yes, Roland had called his parents collect a couple of times. They had said no, hung up, and called Roland right back. In the United States, there was no charge for doing that, but apparently there was in Mexico. Roland offered to pay Mr. Gonzalez when he would be coming to Mexico in June, but Mr. Gonzalez responded by ordering Roland to pay *de volada* (right then), or he would go to the police! One of his sons had gone and gotten Lavinia and her son Raul, and they now came on the line. Lavinia was gracious enough to pay the man the N$50 on the spot, and she was also worried about the whole problem.

Raul then talked to Roland, and he told him he had created a problem with the Gonzalez family. Roland explained that he didn't mean any harm, that he hadn't realized the detail about Teléfonos de México charging for rejected collect calls, and he apologized for the whole thing.

Of course, Roland felt somewhat put off by the whole situation. Surprises like that, he could just do without. He called Isalia and talked it over with her. She explained that most

127

Mexicans are just that way. They become unreasonable and freak out over small matters. He wrote Mr. Gonzalez a letter of apology, and he sent him a US $20 note to appease him. Roland much later found out that Mr. Gonzalez gave the $20 to Lavinia, which was fine.

It was now May 21, 1997. Roland decided to stop by Roger's house after working at Elizabeth's house, which was a mile from there. It was raining, and Roger was looking at and fixing his air conditioner that had quit. They ended up chatting 1½ hours. Roland brought up Chip by asking if he had talked to Chip at all this year, and Roger answered that he sees him all the time. Roland asked Roger if Chip had ever talked about him and if he got that postcard he had sent him from Mexico at the beginning of the year.

"Yeah he got your postcard, Roland," Roger flatly told him. Roger leveled with Roland and told him everything. Roland was impressed at how Roger remembered all of the details. He and Chip must have had a detailed discussion, right down to the fact that Roland had somehow found out where one of Chip's friends lived and had looked up Chip at that residence back in November. Yes, it was true. Roland had done that. After all, he had been frustrated at not having found Chip in late November to make him the business offer.

Roger said Chip told him back in January, "I don't want to go work for Roland! Why is Roland coming over here so much?"

Roger said he told Chip, "Why don't you go ahead and tell Roland?"

Chip said to him, "I don't want to have to tell him." Chip wanted to be polite, not straightforward.

Obviously, Chip didn't want Roland to come over there and chat with him. Even Chip's friend that Roland had also looked up when trying to find Chip had said that he didn't want Roland coming over. It's just that when Roland had last seen Chip on December 13, he answered Roland with an answer of consent that yes, he could continue coming over. However, the truth that Roger told Roland did not come as a surprise to him. Roland suspected that was the problem, which is why he had not been over there in the last five months to talk to Chip, anyway.

Roger explained that Chip had a tight knit group of friends and that he doesn't have any room for outsiders, nor for more friends. He is also living it up, enjoying his friends and always coming in late at night.

Regardless of Roland's not being surprised, this was more severe than he had suspected, that Chip found Roland *that* repulsive! Roland thought about it, and it irritated him, and he realized that he hadn't made very many, if any new close friends in the whole state of Tennessee since he graduated in 1991.

Well, the next day, he returned to Elizabeth's house to work, and at the end of the day, he (and it took a good bit of courage) went to the office supply store and walked in there to confront Chip himself. By golly, he was going to clear this up! He saw Chip and gathered his thoughts before approaching him, and when he was ready to talk to him, he had disappeared. Roland had the copy center page him. -No response- Chip was on break. Another employee kindly entered the break room for Roland and told Chip that he had a visitor. The employee came back over to Roland and informed him that Chip had given him a weird response and would not come out to talk to him, even though he wasn't told it was Roland who wanted to talk to him.

Finally, after more than half an hour, Chip came out of the break room, and Roland saw him start moving stuff in and out of the store. Finally, Roland cleverly positioned himself in one of the aisles where Chip could not avoid him and would have to pass by him. As he approached him, he called out, "What's up, Roland? What are you doing here?"

Roland answered, "I came over here to talk to you a couple of minutes."

He said, "I haven't got time to *talk* to you! Can't have you hanging out here, dude!"

Roland said, "I haven't seen you in 5 months. I figured I'd just come on over here." Chip passed by Roland as he said that, and Roland took off following him and called out to him, "I talked to Roger yesterday. You know, I didn't think it would hurt that I went over and chatted with you back in the fall when I was working at the Schultz."

Chip entered the freight room and said, "Wait up a second." He collected a parcel and returned.

Roland said to Chip, "You don't have to worry. I'm not coming over there anymore because I know that *you* don't want me over there."

He answered, "That's right! Look man, I don't mean to be a @*&# about this, but you wore out your welcome! I have my group of friends, and I don't have room or time for any more."

Roland quickly said, "I *know* you do!"

He continued, "I've got my own routine, and you threw a wrench in it!"

Roland replied, "Well I didn't know I threw a wrench in your plan!"

He then more calmly said, "I know, man."

Roland said, "If you didn't want me over there, Chip, you should have told me, but since I haven't been over there in 5 months anyway, it doesn't matter."

"That's cool, man. Don't worry, I'll see you over at Schultzes sometime."

"Look, I didn't want you to feel bad," Roland told him. "I just came over here to clear this up with you."

He and Chip were now walking toward the front of the store, and he said, "I've got 500 friends that I don't have time to do things with, so don't feel bad. Don't worry, I'll see you over at Schultzes sometime," he repeated.

Roland said to him, "I'm not worried about it, Chip."

He said, "Okay, that's cool."

As Roland left the store, Chip called out to him, "See you around, Roland."

Roland went to Isalia's place several times over the course of the next two months to do work for her. Her sister Roma was staying there. She was a very nice and genuine person who cared for others. Roland talked to her about how the Quevalos had run him off and had been so mean. Roma commented that it was one of life's strange mysteries how the more you help a family, the less they appreciate you. Roland agreed with that. It was a mystery indeed.

One day, several weeks later, Isalia told Roland that she had received more than one phone call from Luke Wiggins, the man who had thought of going to Mexico in 1991 to also stay with the Quevalos.

"Oh, really?" Roland responded with surprise.

"That's right," and Isalia went on to say that Luke wanted to send a bunch of tools and equipment down to Mexico to her cousins and that he had a mission to help the people of Bustamante. She expressed her approval of his kindness and went on raving about it.

"There you are, Isalia," Roland suddenly said. "That's your man."

"Ohhhh, Roland," she replied enthusiastically and with a smile. "I hope so."

"I think so," he told her in a matter-of-fact manner. "He keeps calling you, and he has that mission of wanting to help the people in Mexico. It sounds like he's a kind, caring man, just the man you've been looking for."

"Oh, I really hope so," she commented.

"My advice is, don't get too excited too quickly."

She laughed at Roland's comment and said, "Isn't this great how *you're* the one to now give advice. He's bringing the tools and equipment sometime next month."

"Oh, really?"

"Yes, and we're going to need a trailer to haul that cargo down there."

"As you know, I have a flatbed trailer." (He had bought one two years earlier.) "I'm going down there in June. I can take that cargo down there on my trailer, if you like."

"Oh could you? That would be super!"

"Now let me tell you," Roland pointed out, "you and I both know how your cousins, the Quevalos, ran me off and were ugly to me, but I'll take the cargo to them anyway because of the friendship my family and I have with *you*."

"I know they were mean to you, and I'm sorry about that, and that's very noble and kind of you to take that stuff down there for us, since you're going anyway, and we're also going to pay you something."

"Okay, good. That's fine," Roland said to her.

In late May, Isalia invited Roland over to meet Luke Wiggins. He was visiting Isalia for the weekend. Roland drove over there and met him. He came across as a kind and sincere man, somebody who had a mission to help the poor. He was a tall man, and he sort of reminded him of Mr. Mayfield, his science teacher from high school.

They now went inside the house to talk over plans, and Isalia looked like she was on cloud nine the whole time. She sweet talked Luke and was waiting on him hand and foot! Never had Roland seen Isalia talk so sweetly before, certainly not with Clayton. It looked ridiculous, but then when did being madly in love look entirely sane? Roland was happy for them. He could sense that they had found each other by some sort of destiny and that they were very happy with each other.

Indeed they had found each other by destiny, as Isalia would repeatedly tell the "story of the angels" to her friends.

It was a week later, and Isalia and Roland made a telephone call to Pancho about making arrangements for him to come to the border to meet Roland and receive the trailer cargo.

Pancho also mentioned to Roland that Raul's brother Eduardo from Salado, Texas had suddenly arrived unannounced in town yesterday with his truck, his wife, and child. *Curtains!* Roland could sense that over the phone. Eduardo's sudden arrival would very likely influence Raul to take a turn against Roland. He would likely now decide to go to Salado with his brother instead of come up to Tennessee with Roland.

U.S. Immigration had just granted Eduardo his residency, and he could now come and go to and from Mexico.

That night, Roland called Raul on the phone. Raul answered, and sure enough, he had quite a change for the cold in his voice. Raul asked Roland why he called, and he reminded Raul that he was calling according to the plans that they had made, to call Raul at the first of June to see if he wanted him to be his padrino for his graduation from the secundaria school. Raul answered that it had already been a good while since he had *chosen* his padrino! It was a teacher, and it wasn't Pancho either. Raul had obviously forgotten that he and Roland had talked over plans that Roland would be his padrino. Roland felt somewhat put off by Raul. The honor of being his padrino had been removed!

Raul went on to tell Roland that he wasn't going to go to Tennessee with him either, that his brother Eduardo had *taught* him to continue going to school in Mexico. Further, his mother was recovering from a recent operation. When Roland would come later in the summer, they would go to the bank in Sabinas Hidalgo and withdraw the money. On that, Roland thought, *Fair enough*. However, he was disappointed because that meant that Raul would not be getting a VISA, nor would they go to Monterrey to apply for one at the American Consulate.

Well, the next question Roland had for Raul was if he wanted to travel with him in the future, and he offered to pay Raul something to come with him, so he wouldn't lose work time, since he would have been working otherwise.

Raul laughed in a soft manner, implying that it was very strange for Roland to have invited him to travel with him. *Something that gay men do*, Raul must have thought. His voice also carried a sense of pride for his brother.

Roland asked him in a concerned manner why he laughed.

Raul answered by asking Roland why it was his obsession that he be the one to travel with him.

Roland explained why he wanted to travel with him because he enjoyed him.

Raul told Roland not to say it like that because it means a *relation*. Then he told Roland, "Hemos sido amigos." (We have been friends). Roland received a sharp sense of bad feelings and took it as meaning that they were no longer friends. He asked Raul why he said "Hemos sido," and further asked him if they were still friends. Then Raul modified his comment and answered that they were still friends, and he told Roland that he could still come and stay this coming summer, once Eduardo was gone. Roland thanked Raul for that much. Still, he felt like Raul had placed distance between them and he felt a friendship at arm's length, nothing closer, especially since Raul had chosen another padrino. Further, why couldn't Raul appreciate that Roland wanted to travel with him?

Roland asked Raul if he had received his letter and the US $50 cash. He said no, he hadn't. Roland was sorry to learn that, and Raul said he was going to inquire at the local post office.

Roland also asked Raul if he still had that mountain bike he had given him back in March. He said he did and went on to tell Roland that it was dirty, and that he had to clean it up. What sort of comment was that? What sort of appreciation did he have for the person, Roland, who *gave* him that bicycle! It really made Roland realize the influence that Raul's brother had on him. Roland's friendship was definitely put on the back burner. Again, somebody preceded Roland, and he felt like second place.

Roland didn't sleep well that night.

A few days later, Roland called Raul's neighbor and got Lavinia on the phone. She informed Roland that she had suddenly gotten sick a few weeks ago, had to be hospitalized, and operated on. She had a hysterectomy. She also told Roland that she looked forward to having him come to visit, and that Raul had come to her after his phone conversation the other night and told her that he did indeed want to continue his friendship with Roland. That made him feel a lot better.

Roland also asked her if the letter and $50 had arrived. She said it hadn't. Raul had gone to the post office to investigate, and they said no letter had arrived for him, as far as they knew. Sending cash to Mexico was risky. The $20 arrived to Mr. Gonzalez just fine, but the $50 to Raul was apparently intercepted somewhere in the system and never arrived to its destination!

Over the next few weeks, Roland continued doing work for Elizabeth in Nashville and also for others, like Isalia.

One day he was out at Isalia's place helping her with some yard work.

He talked to Isalia about Raul and his friendship with that family. She told Roland she understood him better than he realized, and she gave him the advice to not come on too strong and not to overstay. She expressed sorrow that Roland had been the subject of receiving mixed and tumultuous feelings from Raul, who wasn't so sure about Roland, but then that's the way a lot of teenagers were. They were just growing up. They were children in their minds and still had yet to mature.

"Yes, I understand all of that," Roland said to her, "but what I really want is a travelling companion to enjoy trips with, a friend who understands me and wants to be with me enough to enjoy the trips with me and to still be content with me and about the trip the day we return home, wanting to take more trips with me in the future."

"I feel sure the Universe will grant you your wish for a travelling companion," she reassured Roland. "As you know, for the past 46 years, I've been through #@%!! I had to wait till I was 63 to find my companion. Things don't always come right away. I've been praying for the past six years, and now I finally have my wish come true."

"Well, I'm happy for you, Isalia."

"Don't worry, Roland. It will all work out. You'll see. When Luke and I go later this year, I'll talk to Lavinia and explain some things to her about you."

"Thank you."

Later in the day, Roland brought up, "Isalia, I'm thinking of buying a used washing machine and taking it to Mexico to give to Raul's family."

"Roland! Raul's family is poor. They're used to being poor. It's giving them too much to take them that washing machine," she explained to him.

"Yes, but Lavinia's been sick, and they can't complete their chores washing all their clothes by hand. It's too time consuming. They need that washing machine."

"Don't take it to them, Roland!" she firmly told him. "They are used to having used and worn out towels, and that's the way they live their lives."

To avoid any further disagreement, Roland agreed and told her he wouldn't buy it. In his own mind, without telling her, he knew he was definitely going to buy and take that washing machine down there. He needed it for himself when he would be there, and he saw no harm in giving it to Lavinia's family. After all, when staying in Mexico, he had been washing all his clothes by hand, and he couldn't ask Lavinia to wash them for him, with all that she already had to do. Further, the washing machine was a used one.

And why in the world was Isalia so against Roland's generosity of taking a washing machine to his friends in Mexico? How *strange*! Roland was very puzzled by that one, but much later he would realize the true reason. Really, since Isalia and her new man were donating all that trailer cargo to her cousins in Bustamante, why couldn't Roland give his friends a washing machine? As it would turn out, that washing machine would be the best thing he would ever give them, as it proved durable and gave that family years of service.

Roland rang up the family that owned the farm where his former friend Ivanhoe lived, over in Scotland. He wondered how he was doing. They told him he was doing fine and that he had telephone service again, and they voluntarily gave Roland his phone number. That surprised Roland, and he called Ivanhoe right away. He was quite surprised, actually, to hear from Roland, and he responded with a cheerful, "Hello."

Immediately, Roland said, "Let's see if we can forgive each other, go on from here, and become friends again."

They talked quite a while, and Roland brought him up to date on what he had been doing, including Ivanhoe catching Roland up, as well. Roland told him about Chip and how he met him at the office supply store. He related all the amazing coincidences between them, how they seemingly became good friends, and then how Chip had suddenly brushed him off. Roland related the story about confronting Chip a couple of weeks ago by suddenly appearing in the aisleway.

Ivanhoe had a good laugh about that and said, "So, you ambushed him did you?"

"I had to. He kept avoiding me."

"See, that's one thing about you. When someone is nice to you, you expect it to continue. I do too, but unfortunately, most people don't live by that standard."

They talked about Chip for a while, then about Raul and Rigo and their family.

Roland also talked with Ivanhoe about the Quevalo family and how they ran him off back in January.

"Has Isalia told you the real reason why the Quevalos ran you off?" Ivanhoe decided to ask Roland.

"No, just something to the effect that there was a subconscious reason. She said the Quevalos ran me off because their subconscious minds made them give me a push toward Raul and Rigo's family because I was meant to know them, that it was my destiny."

"God dear! Let's get real about this. We don't need some *airy fairy* reason. I think the truth is, those Quevalo sisters still resent you for planting that tree for them four years ago, and they've been squabbling about you ever since."

They continued talking. Ivanhoe had some helpful comments and advice about how to handle the situations in the future.

They put the previous year's disagreement behind them, forgave each other, and became friends again. Roland was very pleased to have his friendship restored with Ivanhoe.

Before going to Mexico, Roland took the engine out of his 1980 Ford LTD station wagon, disassembled it, and loaded it into the back of his Ford truck to take to Mexico. Roland had plans of rebuilding it with Raul's help.

Roland drove over to Isalia's house with his 16-foot flatbed trailer. Luke came in from east Tennessee with a truckload of boxes, tools, spare tires, and other knick knacks, including a garden tiller, a well pump, and an air compressor. Luke and Roland loaded the cargo onto the trailer. Isalia came outside and gave Roland $130 to pay for the gas, which was voluntary on her part. Roland thanked her. He also noticed the strange way in which she happily released the money to Roland. She really was on cloud nine, and she was very happy to have her new man, Luke, with her.

Roland took the loaded trailer home.

*   *   *

Roland was still concerned about Raul, and he called Ivanhoe on the phone to talk about Raul and his family. Raul seemed so indefinite at some moments, and Roland mentioned what he thought the source of the whole problem was. He told Ivanhoe about India's comment of, "Raul está enamorado a tí."

"Now it all makes sense. You didn't tell me *that* before. That's devastating for a 15 year old. India has a very poisonous tongue, she does. She said the one comment she knew would wreck your friendship with Raul. India's comment was very wicked indeed. You see, the Quevalo sisters think you are gay, and that's part of the problem of why they don't accept you. In actuality, you're asexual. You're not bothered by the sexes, but none of the Quevalos understand *that*, nor Raul at times."

Ivanhoe went on to say that Raul had been stewing over India's comment ever since and that it was very unlikely that the friendship would ever be fixed, as a result. Roland knew that Raul was super nice *before* India's comment, and from that day forward, Raul had never been quite the same. Raul was suffering from recurring spells of her comment haunting him, and he was subconsciously angry at Roland, for his embarrassment and uneasy feelings. As a result, Raul was unsure about Roland and was also in conflict within himself about his fear of being gay. Back in April, Raul had put Roland through the wringer, like when they went with Angelo to the Ejido to catch those horses, and when Raul threw his tantrum in his house later that evening. The conflicts within Raul's mind caused him to choose another padrino instead of Roland. He couldn't shake his embarrassment at being good friends with Roland. Plus, Raul wasn't going to go to Tennessee because he wasn't sure about Roland, and was afraid that Roland might possibly attack him in the night. Absurd indeed if Raul thought *that*!

Ivanhoe suggested that Roland be very careful when staying with that family in Mexico, to be careful not to get too playful with Raul and Rigo, because his mother could easily turn up at the police station to report Roland for "molesting" her children. Ivanhoe told Roland that if he felt the instinct to flee for his safety, then go ahead and leave as quickly as possible. Roland took Ivanhoe's rather extreme comments seriously, nevertheless. On the good side of things, Raul had told his mother after the early June phone conversation that he indeed wanted to go on being friends with Roland, and he had told Roland that he could stay with them. On that much, Roland decided he would definitely go down there and stay with them.

Roland asked Ivanhoe what he thought about how Raul no longer wanted to travel with him and thought Roland was obsessed with travelling with him. How else was Roland supposed to plan a big trip with another fellow? It frustrated Roland considerably! Why couldn't Roland become good enough friends with another fellow he really liked and go ahead and make plans to travel with him, and *not* be laughed at nor be told, "Why is it your obsession to travel with me?" Ivanhoe said that it was arrogant of Raul to think that Roland was only thinking of him, and then Raul resented that Roland might! True friendships don't work that way. Ivanhoe said that Raul will not be a travelling companion, at least not until he feels better about knowing Roland and takes more pride and value in his friendship with him.

Ivanhoe told Roland that he felt confident he would actually find a travelling companion, but it would take a special fellow who would take Roland at face value and accept him for what he was. He would understand Roland very well, and he would also be of a free spirit. Roland asked Ivanhoe how all that was possible, because every time he got a new friend, the friendship would never get to the point where they could plan a trip out West or some big trip and travel together and *enjoy* it. Ivanhoe insisted that Roland would find one. Roland told Ivanhoe about the psychic woman, who he had the strange dream about in January. She thought there was one in Nashville. Ivanhoe didn't want to say one way or the other. Roland said that it would please him very much if he could take a long trip backpacking, hiking, camping, and travelling with a good fellow friend (a male), enjoy it, and return home the last day *content*! Then he would finally advance to a girlfriend. That's the way Roland wanted it, and he was very stubborn and would not back down on that. Ivanhoe said he knew who the companion was, but he would interrupt the course of events if he told him. Roland asked Ivanhoe to please tell him, and Ivanhoe told Roland he was fishing. He said several more things about it and something about how Roland would finally figure it out.

They talked a long while. Roland really appreciated Ivanhoe for being friendly and sincere. He was good about being with it, being tuned in to the conversations, and to what Roland was relating.

CHAPTER 7

THE FIRST CARGO

late June 1997

The day before leaving, Roland loaded his truck with his own belongings. To his trailer, he added some Cedar lumber, a folding bed, and the washing machine for Lavinia. He drove through Mississippi, Louisiana, and Texas to get to Mexico, and he arrived at the Colombia Bridge mid day on June 27. Pancho Quevalo was there to meet Roland, and they looked over the equipment. A Mexican Customs official came outside to inspect the boxes. He made them take off every tire that didn't have a rim with it, of which there were nine.

Then they walked inside, and Pancho and Roland paid importation duties to bring in the items. Roland paid to bring in the washing machine, bed, and lumber. He had hidden the 6 cylinder 240 Ford motor under everything in the front of the truck bed, since he already knew that bringing in car engines was prohibited. They overlooked it every time, thankfully, and Roland successfully sneaked his motor in.

Pancho followed Roland with his truck the 180 kilometers to Bustamante. Before entering the town of Anahuac, there was the second inspection, Aduana Anahuac. Roland pulled up to the inspection officer, showed his papers and his license, and the officer said, "Pásale," to go ahead. Pancho and his truck were also cleared through.

Then as Roland began to proceed, the inspection officer's chief came out of the building with a *Hey, wait a minute* look on his face. He asked Roland in English why he was carrying so many things, complete with a trailer load of knick knacks, boxes, and flapping tarps.

By that time, Pancho had parked and walked over to the chief officer, papers in hand, and he and the officer discussed the problem.

"Pero lleva muchas cosas," said the chief, stating that Roland was carrying too many things. Pancho showed the man all the letters of permission and duty receipts from the Colombia Bridge Customs, and he told the man that Colombia Bridge assured them they would have no inconveniences.

"Pero lleva muchas cosas!" said the chief, repeating his complaints. Pancho argued with him some more, and the man consented, saying OK this time.

Then the man told Roland, "Señor, when you come into my country, you bring your things and no more," as if that man was the owner of the whole of Mexico!

Roland said okay, and they were allowed to proceed. An hour and a half later, they arrived in Bustamante. By now it was late afternoon.

They first arrived at Lorenzo's house and unloaded from the trailer what was theirs. There were a few more boxes in the back of Roland's truck. He had put them up there to protect them from possible rain. Since the back of his truck was full with his own personal items, he drove to Raul's house to unload them, after which he would return to the Quevalos to unload their remaining boxes from Luke.

Raul and his mother Lavinia were at home, and they were both glad to see Roland. They were just preparing supper, and they, of course, welcomed Roland and fed him. Roland was a little concerned about how Raul was going to receive him, and he was glad that Raul was indeed happy to see him.

The weather certainly was hot, so different from past visits. This was Roland's first time to visit Bustamante in the summer.

Roland asked Raul how the rest of school went. Raul answered that it went well. He had graduated three days ago, and he and his mother informed Roland that the padrino Raul had chosen had, two days before the event, suffered a bad car crash, was presently in the hospital, and was unable to present Raul. The result was that Raul had no padrino.

Roland explained that he could have been Raul's padrino, if he had just advised him. He could have left home a few days earlier, to be in time for Raul's graduation. Since Raul's chosen padrino had failed to present him, Lavinia and her son now asked Roland to be his padrino. Roland commented that it was a little bit late for that now, wasn't it? They talked it over, and Roland decided to buy Raul that esclava de plata . . . to be his belated padrino.

After they ate supper, Raul and Roland went to the trailer and unloaded the folding bed, the Cedar lumber, and the washing machine. Then they unloaded Roland's personal items and took them into their spare room where Roland had slept before. Roland's motor and Luke's remaining boxes for the Quevalos were now revealed.

Raul looked at the disassembled motor with interest, and Roland said they could begin the rebuilding tomorrow. Then Raul looked at Luke's boxes intended for the Quevalos, and he asked Roland what they were. Roland explained that they were for the Quevalos and that he was about to take them over there. Raul looked at the boxes some more, and he asked Roland if he would let him have one of them.

Roland reiterated that the boxes were intended for the Quevalos.

Raul said something to the effect of: What do they need all of that for? Pancho already has a bunch of stuff, and they're not going to miss just one box. Further, Pancho still owed Raul $50.

Roland thought about it. *I don't see why not? After all, Luke is giving all of this stuff away, anyway.* So Roland chose a green plastic recycling box with worthless knick knacks in it, and he handed it to Raul, who showed appreciation. Raul carried it into the catch-all room, and with a smile on his face, he went through the contents of that green box as if it was full of treasures, more out of curiosity, if nothing else.

Roland drove over to the Quevalos and delivered the remaining boxes to them, and he returned to Raul's house. Rigo had arrived from working extra hours at Felipe's carpentry. He was glad to see Roland and greeted him with a friendly and welcoming gesture, including a Mexican style handshake. Norma and Irma arrived after playing with other children down the street. Alejandro came in later that night from the cantina.

Lavinia was so glad to receive that washing machine. She offered to pay Roland the $115 for it, and Roland said he didn't want any money for it. He explained that it was his washing machine for them, and he wanted to reserve the right to use it whenever he would come to Mexico in the future. She said that would be fine.

Since Lavinia had suffered an illness and an operation a month earlier, she had not been able to wash clothes, and her sons, Raul and Rigo had been having fights over which one had to do the washing. This automatic washing machine was a welcome relief to the whole family, and to Roland, as well.

Why Isalia had been so against Roland's bringing that washing machine to Lavinia remained a mystery indeed.

Roland also gave some other gifts to the family, including a wooden tablet he made for Raul. It said, "Compañeros de las Montañas," (Companions of the Mountains).

All of them visited for the evening. At this time of year, being so hot, they sometimes slept outside or if they slept inside, they used fans. Raul and Roland went up on the rooftop to sleep the night.

The next day, Roland and Raul unloaded all the engine parts and cleaned them. Roland delivered the Cedar wood to Felipe, and he charged him at cost, what it cost him. Felipe was glad to receive the Cedar and he would put it to good use in his carpentry business.

That evening, Raul had a fiesta to attend, one of the school graduation functions. Roland went and visited other friends of his, including Juan Carlos, a neighbor, Angelo's family, Pegaso, Daniel Mata, and Fernando.

On Sunday, they all got up late. Raul and Rigo invited Roland to come with them to the molino to swim. Pegaso and Angelo came along. They all played and splashed vigorously in the water like children. Raul was a little mischievous at times, but it was all enjoyable, just the same.

Roland got tired of the splashing and playing, however, and he went to another part of the molino to swim in a different pool. This one had some waterfalls entering it from a trough, and there was a diving board, as well. He dove in and swam around. There were some others in the pool, and before he totally realized it, he recognized a fellow who looked familiar and instinctively shook hands with him. Then they both looked at each other and realized they didn't know each other after all. They were somewhat taken aback.

Roland then remembered he had seen him riding his bicycle in the street near Pegaso's house. They got to talking, and they introduced themselves to each other. His name was Victor, and he lived on the same street corner down from Pegaso's house. He was age 14 and had finished his second year of the secundaria school.

* * *

The machine shop in Sabinas Hidalgo opened on Monday morning. Roland and Raul took the engine block, the head, and other parts to leave with them. Next, they visited Banamex and checked on Raul and Lavinia's account. It had earned a little interest, a total of N$90. They did other errands and returned to Bustamante to clean more engine parts.

Raul had things to do with his school friends the next day. So, Roland took the whole day and climbed the mountains all the way to the Cypress ridge, where he took some superb photographs. The day was perfectly clear and sunny. By 6 PM, he returned to town.

Raul had enjoyed a good day with his friends. Lavinia fed supper to them. Pegaso and Angelo came over, and they visited, talked about plans for obtaining VISAs, and what they had been doing.

Around a week ago, shortly before Roland arrived, Alejandro had wrecked his big 1974 Ford Country Sedan station wagon. Its top was crushed in. He was driving drunk, and a big truck had broadsided him, turning him over. The police had impounded the car and required a N$1,200 fine to be paid to release it. Alejandro had paid it with his government pension earlier that day, and it was now sitting in front of his house.

Raul, Angelo and Pegaso got inside the car and played, sticking their heads out of the broken window spaces. Roland took several pictures of them, some of them hilarious. Angelo and Pegaso were good people, and Roland was becoming good friends with them also. They talked over plans of going to Saltillo.

A month ago, a group of Mexican dancers had come to Tennessee to the International Folkfest, and Roland had made friends with several of them, including Sergio and his sister

The First Cargo

Lilia from Saltillo. They had told Roland to come and visit them, saying that their house was his house, a welcoming statement indeed.

To Raul, Angelo and Pegaso, Saltillo sounded like a nice excursion, a break from the normal routine of life, and they decided to go. The only requirement would be to obtain permission from their parents.

Roland and Raul returned to Sabinas Hidalgo where Roland picked up the block, crankshaft, and head, all machined and ready to go. All six cylinders had been sleeved and standard size pistons would be installed. He paid the machine shop N$3,300, equivalent to US $400.

While they were in town, they went to a jewelry store. Raul picked out a silver wrist bracelet and had his name engraved on it, and Roland bought it for him for N$390, around US $50. It was a nice gift, and Roland was now Raul's belated padrino. Raul did indeed appreciate it.

They returned to Bustamante. Roland looked for Lorenzo so he could loan him the piston ring clamp, but he couldn't find him. He did later in the evening.

Roland and Raul had not yet talked about it since his arrival, but Roland sensed that now was a time to discuss how he felt bothered by Raul's comments during their phone conversation at the first of June. Roland explained to Raul that his response of, "Why is it your obsession to travel with me?" was quite bothersome and unacceptable, when Roland was merely inviting him to travel out West with him. Raul answered that he wasn't Roland's life and that he sensed that Roland was thinking only of him. Roland corrected Raul, telling him that wasn't true. He was friends with several others in town, including Angelo and Pegaso, and Fernando, to name some of them.

Raul was still struggling within his 15-year-old mind over India's comment back in January. He was still feeling embarrassment at being friends with Roland as a result. Also, in early June, his brother Eduardo had been visiting, and for certain he had subconsciously influenced Raul's viewpoint of Roland at that time. Roland recognized all of that, and he explained to Raul that it had nothing to do with Raul's being his life. When two men want to take a long trip, they need to concentrate their thoughts on the trip long enough to make plans and then talk about it, and that it was very frustrating to Roland the comment that Raul had made.

Raul now saw reason and he realized his error in arrogantly thinking that Roland was obsessed with him. Plus, Roland reminded Raul about his enthusiastic response back in March about possibly going to England this summer. Their plans never materialized.

In a nutshell, Roland realized that making plans to travel with people was an incredibly mysteriously difficult feat! While very easy for some people to do in the world, it was not for Roland. What was going on? For nearly a decade, he had been looking for a travelling companion, but he just hadn't found one. Raul realized Roland's predicament now, and he showed compassion for him, commenting that he had suffered bad luck in that aspect.

That night, Roland set up his tent and slept in it. There were several nights that Roland slept in his tent because it was too hot to sleep inside the house.

The next day, Roland assembled the 6 cylinder 240 motor. Raul helped him with part of it. With help from others, they moved the assembled masterpiece over to the back wall of the house, placed it on top of blocks and tires, and covered it with several layers of plastic to protect it from dust and rain.

That afternoon, Lavinia's relatives from Salado, Texas came to visit. Raul and Rigo's brother Eduardo was supposed to come with his wife and family, but he had decided at the last minute not to come. Roland bicycled over to Felipe's carpentry to tell Rigo that his relatives had arrived. Rigo was making them a special chair. He asked Roland if Eduardo had arrived and Roland answered no. Rigo then said, "No quisiste que Eduardo venga," saying that Roland didn't want Eduardo to come. Roland admitted that was true because Raul would certainly have brushed Roland off, if Eduardo had arrived.

All of them visited in the evening. Alejandro and Lavinia let Roland continue staying with them despite the arrival of their four guests. Roland talked with them, as well. This family was well off. The husband, Sansovino, played in a band in Texas, performing every Saturday night in different places. Alejandro didn't go to the cantina with his friends. He stayed home and visited with his guests.

Raul and Rigo slept on the rooftop. Roland slept in his tent.

First thing in the morning, Rigo came to Roland, asking him to take them to Monterrey to visit Parque Sesamo, an amusement park. Sansovino offered to take them, but there wasn't enough room for everyone in his car, a Dodge Dynasty. Roland agreed to it, and they made the drive to Monterrey where they spent the whole day taking different rides. It was an enjoyable time, and they acted like children, which people are supposed to do in amusement parks. Amen. That night, they returned to Bustamante.

The next morning, Roland called Sergio and Lilia, and they said that would be fine to come and visit and bring his friends. Pegaso and Angelo came over. Raul and Rigo slept on the rooftop again. Lavinia's relatives were still visiting. They would be leaving later in the morning.

Rigo decided to come along, and he went to Felipe to get permission. Felipe was kind and understanding and gave Rigo the days off with ease. He was glad to come along also. Angelo's and Pegaso's parents both asked Roland to care for their sons and look out for them like a chaperone.

It was a three hour drive to Saltillo, west of Monterrey. They pulled up in front of Sergio's house in the early afternoon. His sister Lilia was there. Roland also met their parents and their younger brother Eloy.

After having lunch, Sergio took them on a tour of central Saltillo and of the university where he went to school. They visited the flea market and various shops. There were plenty of native crafts, and Roland bought some gifts to take back home with him. He took a few pictures at various sites, and in the evening, they returned to Sergio's house.

While Roland visited with Sergio and Lilia's family, Raul, Angelo and Pegaso, and Rigo who were more shy, entered the guest bedroom and did their own things. When suppertime came, Roland asked them to come down and eat. They wouldn't come downstairs. Sergio went to them and insisted they come out, or his mother would get angry. With that, they did. They came to supper, and they visited a little while.

That night, another member of the group came over to visit. Her name was Lyria, and she came across as friendly but also obsessive. Raul, out of her hearing distance had asked Roland to kiss her, but he wouldn't do it. She visited for an hour and then left. Lyria was obsessive because she wanted a husband, and she was looking for any opportunity available.

Raul, Angelo and Pegaso slept in the guest room. They pushed Rigo out in the hall. Roland chose not to sleep in there, and he and Rigo slept in a second guest bedroom.

Rigo was content with the trip and with his friendship with Roland.

They all had breakfast the next morning. Pegaso was more communicative than the others. He was thinking of going to the United States to work for a year, and he was considering going to Tennessee with Roland. They talked it over with Sergio who had been to Roland's house and farm to briefly visit in May.

After breakfast, all of them said goodbye to Sergio and Lilia's family, and Roland drove them over to Monterrey, where they visited the Macroplaza and the central flea markets. They drove north to San Nicolas and visited Angelo's grandmother, then Pegaso's uncle, and they stopped by the University of Monterrey where Pegaso would be going to school later in the year.

As they left San Nicolas, four of them were seated in the cab of Roland's truck with Rigo in the rear. Suddenly, a cop on the sidewalk told them to get over. Roland kept on going because the cop said, "Derecho," which means straight ahead. A few blocks later, the cop caught up with them on his bicycle, and of course Roland stopped then. The cop asked why he hadn't stopped, and Roland explained that he had said, "Derecho." The cop then told Roland that he had committed an infraction because there were four people seated up front. Roland told the man he must be joking and that the laws back in Tennessee clearly allowed up to four. He then told Roland only three were allowed in Mexico, absurd as it was! He directed Roland to follow him to the police station a few blocks away to pay the fine. It irritated Roland that such a law existed, and he knew it was in existence so cops could have reason to pull people over and write them tickets. But then that's how San Nicolas was, notorious for writing tickets for minuscule traffic violations.

As Roland would find later out, it was a common practice for cops to stand at numerous intersections throughout the city poised and ready, with ticket pad in hand. Sometimes they were so hungry for money that they would cleverly and strategically position themselves along the streets surrounding the arenas or stadiums, and right after a sports event, they would ticket everybody who was driving under the influence and with alcohol on their breath. Everyone who had two or three beers got ticketed, as well, but once wasn't enough. Every driver got stung once, then a couple of blocks down the street, they would be stung again, and then again, and again, up to ten times trying to get away from a game! The cops would make a fortune!

Angelo retreated to the back of the truck to be with Rigo, leaving three up front: Roland, Raul, and Pegaso. They drove out of San Nicolas. It was now night. Around 10 kilometers out of the city, Roland pulled over and ordered Angelo back up front. They were now a foursome again. Roland would be a monkey's uncle before he would allow somebody to tell him how many can sit in the cab of *his* truck! Roland proudly drove the remaining 80 kilometers back to Bustamante; Roland, Raul, Pegaso and Angelo, in that order. Rigo remained in the camper in the back.

They arrived back in town at 11 PM. Alejandro and Lavinia were still up. Raul and Rigo unloaded their things from Roland's truck. Angelo and Pegaso did the same, and they walked home.

Around five minutes later, Alejandro and Lavinia got into a serious argument, and they were yelling at each other. Raul was in the kitchen with Roland waiting for them to finish their argument before entering his bedroom. He asked Roland go in there and tell them to be quiet, but Roland said it wasn't his house. Raul and Roland were afraid the fight would become physical. Finally, after ten minutes, they stopped arguing. Raul now entered, and everyone went to sleep. Most of the time, Raul was a calm and peaceful person, and he didn't like arguments.

There were several nights during Roland's stay when Alejandro would come in drunk. One night he staggered in, severely drunk, and he lay down on one of the beds because he couldn't walk. Lavinia brought him some supper and placed it on a TV tray beside the bed. Alejandro propped his feet up on the tray to relax, oblivious to the meal. The flimsy table and tray toppled over, sending the meal and dishes crashing to the floor and shattering the plate and drinking glass. Roland was in the next room and heard the crash, and when he went into the front room to see what happened, he had to step outside so he could have a good laugh about it.

Roland spent the next two days in Bustamante. He and Raul worked on the truck. They repacked the front wheel bearings and replaced the front brakes. They went to Sabinas Hidalgo on errands. Roland realized that Raul was a good companion. His mother let him go do a lot of things with Roland. For more local travel, Roland had found his travelling companion.

Every night, the cockroaches came out, and dozens of them crawled the walls, especially in the kitchen. Raul and Roland talked about various things. Raul said that Sergio's family was rich, and they had a fine house to live in. Raul said it was such an embarrassment to be living in the house they lived in, there in Bustamante. Roland said that was true to some degree, but then they did have a house, which was better than nothing.

Rigo arrived from visiting with friends, and he visited with Raul and Roland in the kitchen. Raul and Roland had some bread on the table and they were eating some of it. Rigo made a comment and casually tossed a piece of bread on Roland. Roland answered and tossed Rigo a tiny piece of bread. This casual exchange occurred 3 or 4 times and Roland decided to toss Rigo a slightly larger piece of bread.

Raul immediately joined in. It was food fight time! The three of them had the best time hurling bread at each other, laughing all the while. In short order the bread on the table was used up, and they were picking pieces up off the floor to continue. Raul and Rigo soon entered their bedroom, still throwing pieces back into the kitchen toward Roland. Roland sent one last piece of bread flying into the bedroom, and then they called a truce.

*   *   *

Pegaso had made arrangements to go up in the mountains and camp with Roland. They would meet at his house at 9 AM. When Roland arrived, backpack loaded and ready to go, Pegaso wasn't there. He asked Pegaso's sisters where he was, and they said their father had called him to work today. He had left no message for Roland nor did his sisters even know he had planned to go camping in the mountains. That seemed strange. Evidently, Pegaso had completely forgotten his original plans.

Roland returned to Raul's house and talked to him about it. Normally, when making plans, if you can no longer go, it's appropriate to advise the other person instead of leaving him hanging, especially since Pegaso had asked Roland in the first place. Raul explained that here in Mexico, it was very common for people to make plans and then do something else. It wasn't even considered inappropriate. There was definitely a culture difference there.

That evening, Roland located Pegaso over at Angelo's house. They were in the backyard. Roland asked Pegaso what happened, and he explained that he had to go with his father. A third fellow was there. His name was Hector Cizneros, a big fellow, taller than Pegaso. They got to talking and became friends. Hector invited Roland over to his house around the street corner. He had a younger brother, Pablo, who was Rigo's age. Roland enjoyed the visit. Later in the night, Roland returned to Raul's house to go to sleep.

July 11 was Norma's birthday. She turned 11. Roland went to a pastel shop and bought her a birthday cake to surprise her. He brought it back to the house and set it on the table, surprising them all. Norma was elated, and everyone sang Happy Birthday to her. Roland took a picture of all of them.

In the afternoon, Roland drove by himself to Saltillo. Sergio had invited Roland to return so they could go into the mountains, something they couldn't do with the four others Roland had brought earlier.

After arriving, as it turned out, Sergio was busy, and his brother Eloy took Roland the next day. They went from Saltillo to a small town called El Tunal, situated high up in the mountains at 2,400 meters (around 8,000 feet). The place resembled northern Spain in the Pyrenees, minus the European Beeches. Here in this highland valley, there were Pinyon Pines and Junipers. The land was fertile and green with farms throughout. It wasn't even hot up here, but instead, there was a cool, mild breeze.

Eloy had brought a friend of his, Pancho, and while they lit a fire and had a cookout by the side of the dirt road, Roland took off hiking in the surrounding mountains for a couple of hours. He explored several places and enjoyed the adventure.

That evening, they returned to Saltillo. Roland visited with the family and the next day he returned to Bustamante. He would see Sergio, Lilia, and their family several more times in the future.

It was back to hot weather in Bustamante, with temperatures reaching 43° Celsius some of the days. Raul wanted to take a second chance at obtaining a US VISA, and Lavinia would come with her son this time. Roland had gone to considerable efforts to get his parents' bank statements copied, along with an official affidavit of support for both Raul and Lavinia while staying in Tennessee. He also had letters of recommendation from his congressman and from Isalia Ives.

Roland took them to Sabinas Hidalgo to buy two comprobantes, and they returned to Bustamante. At 2 AM the next morning they all got up, and Roland took them to Monterrey to the American Consulate where they got in a line of already 200 people. A man greeted them as Roland parked in front of the Consulate, and he offered to sell a front position in the line. Roland declined this time. He and Raul got more solicitúds and filled them out for him and his mother.

At 6 AM the Consulate opened their doors, and the line began to move. Roland got away from Lavinia and Raul so the Consulate wouldn't become suspicious, and a few minutes later he returned. Raul was outside! They hadn't even let him in!

With that, Roland intervened! He went straight to the officer guarding the entrance gate and told him that Raul had a comprobante in his hand, that he had paid the $20, and that he should be granted entry, and his mother was already inside. They told Roland the mother had carried both passports inside and that she would be getting the VISAs for both of them, and that it was best that Raul wait outside.

Raul was displeased about it, and he told Roland his prediction that they weren't going to grant the VISAs. At times, Raul had premonitions. Roland had gone to considerable trouble since February, and Raul explained that it was all to no avail. They were going to lose, and that was that! Half an hour later, Lavinia emerged with a long expression on her face. They had denied her the VISA. The young woman who had briefly interviewed Lavinia was very brief and curt. She had asked Lavinia some quick questions and didn't even give Lavinia a chance to open her notebook to show Roland's affidavit of support. The lady simply said No, and when Lavinia proceeded to ask for a VISA for her son, the woman replied, "No. ¡Retírese, por favor!" which means: No, and do me the favor of getting out of here!

After Lavinia said all that, Roland got angry. He told Lavinia and Raul he was going to talk to them. Lavinia didn't want Roland to do that, but Roland did it anyway. He took Lavinia's notebook, went to the reception desk outside the interviewing room, and he simply stated to them that he wanted a better answer. He told them who was denied the VISA (Lavinia) and they went and got the woman who interviewed Lavinia from the window and brought her out to the lobby. Meanwhile, Roland went back to his truck and told Lavinia and Raul to come quickly to the lobby. They were going to be given a second chance.

Upon entering the lobby, Roland talked to the woman, and he told her that Lavinia wasn't given a chance to show her paperwork, let alone the affidavit of support. The woman asked Lavinia how much she earned per week and what her job was. Lavinia answered that she makes tortillas, maybe N$400 per week. That was insufficient income. Roland told the woman that's why he secured an affidavit of support, complete with bank statement copies, so they could indeed obtain VISAs. The woman explained that if they don't make enough money, then they couldn't get a VISA. Roland asked her what good the affidavit of support was, and the lady now told Lavinia her apologies that she was unable to issue her and her son VISAs, said that's all she could do, and that was the end of it! Roland even had a letter from U.S. Representative Bart Gordon's office, requesting VISAs for Lavinia and her son, Raul.

Everything done was to NO avail. That's the last time Roland ever went to the Consulate to get VISAs for anybody. They're a brick wall. Only the rich can get VISAs, and that's the way it is! No wonder there are so many wetbacks and illegal aliens in the United States. It's the only way in.

Really, the Statue of Liberty in the New York harbor has a famous inscription carved on its base. Written by Emma Lazarus, it reads:

"Give me your tired, your poor,
Your huddled masses yearning to breathe free,
The wretched refuge of your teeming shore.
Send these, the homeless, the tempest-tost, to me.
I lift my lamp beside the golden door."

One would think with an inscription like that, on the *Statue of Liberty*, that the United States, that is, the American Consulate, would be kinder and more compassionate, instead of turning its back to the Mexicans.

While Roland appreciated Isalia's letter of recommendation for Lavinia, he couldn't help but feel envious that Isalia was always successful in having her friend, Mrs. Esquivel, from Taxco come up to Tennessee to visit. Isalia had sent Mrs. Esquivel bank statement copies along with a letter of recommendation, and she always got her VISA, no worries at all. Roland had gone to extra trouble. He was *here* in Mexico with Lavinia and Raul! Isalia always stayed home in Tennessee. Since Isalia had her way and enjoyed visits from Mrs. Esquivel, why couldn't Roland have his . . . with Raul? Was it too much to ask? And Lavinia could work for Isalia at the same time. Why was the system so blocked for Roland? It really frustrated him!

Roland drove them back to Bustamante. On the way back, they stopped by Banamex in Sabinas Hidalgo and withdrew the money Roland had loaned them. With that, their accounts were closed, and Lavinia was grateful to Roland for having gone to the trouble of setting up that bank account in their names so they would have a better chance of obtaining VISAs, which were impossible anyway, as they now knew. To help out Lavinia and her family, Roland handed her N$700 of the N$7,000 that was withdrawn. With that, she could pay some rent or buy groceries.

Roland was sad and disappointed. So were Lavinia and Raul. Roland suggested to Raul that he go to the United States by just crossing the river and entering. Eventually, that's exactly what he would do, and successfully.

One morning, Alejandro talked to Roland and told him his son Eduardo wanted to know him. Roland was surprised to find that out, having thought Eduardo was seemingly against Roland's knowing Raul and Rigo. With that, Roland asked for Eduardo's phone number and address. Alejandro went to Lavinia in the next room and asked her where it was written down. Suddenly, Lavinia and Alejandro were arguing and yelling at each other. It seemed that Lavinia didn't want to give it to Roland, but Alejandro insisted, which is why Lavinia got angry! A few minutes later, Alejandro came to Roland with the phone number and address, and he handed it to him. Roland thanked him.

Roland had so far been unsuccessful in finding anyone to go camp in the mountains with him. He had asked Raul several times, and he hadn't wanted to. So, Roland decided to increase the money offer to N$150 which is very good pay in Mexico, and with that Raul said yes. Then as it turned out, Roland found two more fellows, Alberto and Juan Angel.

Alberto had some work to do at his ranch, taking two truckloads of gallinaza (60 feedsacks of it) to their ranch from the *granja* (chicken farm) to be used for cattle feed. Roland decided to help Alberto so he would get finished sooner and would therefore be able to come along. Juan Angel and Raul also helped. Those two were paid, but Roland didn't charge Alberto anything. Roland used the trailer he had brought, and that facilitated the process.

At 4 PM the work was done, and the four of them drove to the cono at the road's end. Over the next two hours, they hiked into the mountains, passing the cave, and they arrived at the base of the cliffs where the narrow trail widened enough to allow the pitching of the tent. It was there that they camped. The others lit a small fire and roasted hot dogs and tortillas. They visited that evening. Roland and Juan Angel hiked further up the trail to the steep crevice where Roland had hung his rope. It was still there. Then they returned to the others.

Night arrived at 8:30 PM. They climbed in the tent, but everyone was restless. Raul was playful, but he carried things too far sometimes. The weather was hot, so the others went back outside to sleep, leaving Roland in his tent by himself. Raul decided to play, and he pulled up the tent stakes several times to annoy Roland. The tent fell over. Roland took it several times, re-inserting the stakes in the ground. Raul kept on, and Roland decided to be more firm about telling Raul not to bother him anymore and let him get some sleep.

He went to Raul and laid his hand on the sleeping bag. Raul was lying on his front. Right then, something got in the water. Suddenly, Raul turned around and leaped upward, grabbing Roland by the neck! Roland was beyond surprised, and he immediately grabbed both of Raul's arms, applied a decent amount of force and took Raul's arms and hands off of his neck, and he set Raul back on the ground again.

Raul was furious and invited Roland to hit him. Roland told him no, and that he wasn't going to pay him either. Evidently, Raul used the "opportunity" to lash out at Roland for his long, built up anger at India's comment from January, and of course, the two failures of getting a VISA. While none of that was Roland's fault, Raul had taken it out on him anyway, and his doing it up in the mountains was very dangerous! Roland was only a couple of feet from the edge of the dropoff where he managed to catch Raul's arms, restrain him, and put him back in his place.

Raul didn't try to hit Roland anymore. He knew who was stronger. Still, however, the campout was a disaster, and Roland was quite angry at Raul for how he behaved!

The next morning, Alberto got everybody up at 6 AM. He was a headstrong type who wanted everyone to return to Bustamante so they could continue the work of carrying more gallinaza to his family's ranch. Roland had thought the work was finished, but Alberto said there was more. Needless to say, Roland and Raul had bad feelings all day. They made the two-hour descent and worked nearly all day.

Later in the day, Raul decided to verbally light into Roland with a rash of complaints. Roland started to argue but soon firmly declared that the one who was at fault was Raul! Lavinia began scolding Roland, but he wouldn't have it. He instead started to take his things out of the house to leave. Seeing that, they became more reasonable and came to their senses somewhat. They didn't exactly want Roland to leave, for some reason.

Later that night, Roland and Rigo were talking about it, and suddenly Raul came to Roland offering to forgive each other, which was quite a surprise! Raul extended his hand with his offer to make up. Rigo urged Roland to accept. With that, what more could Roland do? He shook hands with Raul. That was somewhat relieving.

Roland knew the whole incident in the mountains, and the repercussions it brought, was mysterious. They had camped in nearly the same location where Raul had suddenly blurted out cuss words repeatedly back in February. Roland suspected there were bad energies in that particular region of the mountains, or perhaps there was some sort of malign force. Never did Roland camp there again. He would always camp much higher in the highland forest or on the grassy saddle at the ridge top.

The next day, Raul was back to his normal friendly self. Roland still felt uneasy, but he was glad the "black cloud" was behind them. Raul went to do some work for a client, an older man who needed some gardening done. Roland took a bike ride.

Later in the day, Roland took Raul, Rigo, Angelo and Pegaso to Sabinas Hidalgo. They visited the flea markets and other places. They returned by late afternoon.

Roland went to Pegaso's house, and they watched a movie. A big thunderstorm came in rather suddenly, and it rained heavily. After the movie, he walked back to Raul and Rigo's house. Raul was taking a nap, and Lavinia and Rigo were also home.

Lavinia decided to tell Roland that Raul had drunk four caguamas, the equivalent of one gallon of beer! He had just been to a fiesta. Roland didn't believe her. He got up and walked over to Raul to check his breath. Rigo warned Raul that Roland was coming over to him and told him what he was going to do. Roland leaned over and got near enough to smell his breath, a foot from his face, and Raul immediately smacked Roland in the face! He said, "Quítate! No me gusta que me acerques!" (Get away from me! I don't like your getting near me!) Roland managed to catch Raul's breath. No, there was no alcohol smell.

Roland said to him, "Que Feo!" (How ugly!)

Lavinia came over to them angrily and in a commanding manner told Roland to get away from her son. Never once did she scold her son, like she should have. Typical mother, protecting her son, even when he does wrong! That really made Roland feel bad!

Raul began ranting and raving, and his mother did also, and they chewed Roland out, saying he had no right to check his breath, despite the fact that Alejandro had requested to Roland back in March that if he sees Raul drinking or smoking, that he explain to him that this sort of thing is bad and not to drink nor smoke. Roland also told them that never in his 31 years of life had anyone told him that he didn't have the right to check someone's breath. Rigo sat by Roland and calmly asked him if he was a dog, and he joined in with his mother and his brother in ganging up on Roland. Roland was wondering why Rigo didn't bother to call his mother and his brother down instead for chewing him out. At least Rigo wasn't angry like Raul.

Raul said if he wanted to drink, it was his right, and he and Lavinia said Roland had to respect their house. So, now Lavinia totally supported Raul's drinking! How awful! Raul made sure and told Roland that this was not his house. He also made sure and told Roland that he was not like a brother, to cancel his kind remark on the contrary back in March. Raul just laughed, and his laughter was sneering and sadistic as he laughed off his embarrassment at having told Roland that he was like a brother back in March. He also told Roland that he doesn't have their blood in his viens, and he accused him of not knowing how to conduct himself. Roland told Raul that was a lie. Raul paced around the room very angrily, and Roland just sat in one of the chairs and took the awful insulting and scathing remarks! When Roland began to raise his voice to argue back, Lavinia told Roland he had no right to raise his voice in their house, and she went on to say that he could no longer sleep in the same room with her family. Of course, Raul was yelling plenty. He further said that going to Tennessee would be ridiculous, and he coughed up lots of things he didn't like about Roland. Further, Raul told Roland he didn't like people who stayed away from dances, drinking, and smoking!

Roland said to him, "¿Qué tiene? ¡Es mi vida!" (So what! It's my life!)

Raul ranted on and Lavinia started crying, seeing Raul and Roland arguing. Raul noticed and immediately blamed Roland for making his mother cry and said that if his older brother were here, he would have beaten him up. Raul put his brother Eduardo up on a high horse, made him look like gold, and continued making scathing, insulting remarks to make Roland feel like dirt. So, Roland told Raul that his brother can just come and *help* him get that VISA and that Roland wasn't going to do anymore about it! Raul continued ranting and raving in a very proud manner, and his face had a very arrogant look. He must have had a lot of anger built up in him and a lot of conflict to have acted so badly toward Roland. He told Roland that tomorrow they would take his things out of the house and that he would go somewhere else!

Raul and Lavinia were hysterical, and Roland firmly told them to calm themselves down!

Raul threatened to call the police and to tell his father. Roland told him to go ahead and tell them if he wanted to, and he would tell the police that he attacked him up in the mountains night before last. Raul offered to tell his brother Eduardo, so he would come to Bustamante and bust him up some.

Roland told Raul, "Hemos sido amigos. ¡Ya no! ¡Eres imposible! ¡Me caes feo!" (We have been friends. Not anymore! You are impossible! You come across to me as ugly!)

Raul walked out of the room. Rigo continued sitting by Roland. Roland was really angry, and he clenched his fists, got up, walked out the front door onto the sidewalk and gave out a scream which everyone in the neighborhood must have heard! He re-entered the house and walked into the kitchen.

Roland mentioned the esclava de plata to Lavinia and asked her what they were going to do about it. Raul already had it in his hand and immediately gave it back to Roland, saying, "Aquí está." (Here it is.) He plopped it onto the kitchen table.

Roland said, "¡Gracias!" in an impudent manner, and he took it up and immediately washed it with water under the faucet. There was no way Roland wanted Raul to have that esclava de plata after the way he acted. He did not deserve any padrino at all, and there was no way Roland could continue to be his padrino, not now. Roland felt really bad, but then the method that was used to get Raul that esclava de plata and the fact that Raul had already previously chosen another padrino said to Roland that he didn't want him anyway! Raul had used Roland to get that *esclava de plata*, and it didn't matter how he got it.

Raul prowled around the house with an angry face, and Roland gave him a very hard look of anger! After all, Roland had to tolerate all of their abuse this evening, which was certainly not deserved.

It was pouring down rain.

Roland went back over to Pegaso's house, told him what had happened, and asked if he could come over. He was very understanding, and he was sorry for Roland, and he said that would be fine for him to move over. He would have a word with his parents, who clearly consented. He thanked Pegaso for being a true friend, and they shook hands. In the morning, Roland would move over.

Roland returned to Raul's house and on his bed, he found the copy of his calendar he had given to Raul in friendship back on January 12. Roland knew what that meant, and he simply placed the calendar back among his things.

The others had gone on to bed. Roland wasn't in the mood for sleeping. He felt scared and nervous, and he walked to the back door and stared at the Pecan tree growing in the backyard. He picked a leaf and smelled it. Such a soothing, agreeable mintlike odor it had that Roland immediately felt more relaxed. To be a tree in the forest . . . such a *peaceful* existence.

Roland may have had faults in his character, but *never* did he deserve abuse like what Raul and his family had just given him! There just wasn't any happiness in Raul's family. Roland knew one thing for certain. He was NOT going to buy their house, because if he did it now, he would have to run this family off.

Needless to say, Roland couldn't sleep much of the night. He slept in his truck on the street side. Alejandro arrived at 2 AM. He didn't quite make it inside, and he fell asleep on the sidewalk by the house, his caguama of beer half used and fallen over beside him.

Golly! What a disgrace! Roland thought. He drove to another part of town to finish the night. No more interruptions.

When morning arrived, he told Raul he was leaving. He took his things and loaded them into his truck. When the truck was loaded, Roland told Raul he hoped he would learn one day how to appreciate. He drove over to Pegaso's house, where he stayed several days. He would have already gone back to Tennessee, but he wanted to return to the mountains to camp *by himself* and do it right!

The storm had cleared, and sunny skies were returning. Pegaso's family was friendly and welcoming. There was no bickering like at Raul's house.

That afternoon, Roland loaded his backpack and took off to the mountains. He drove and parked his truck at the cono. Ramiro, the cave guide, was there, and Roland talked to Ramiro about the incidents with Raul. Ramiro told Roland they, the Zacatón family, were *malagradecidos* (ungrateful). He gave Roland good advice and suggested he not do any more with them. He also suggested he collect that motor of his before it occurs to Raul to do harm to it.

In 3½ hours, Roland reached the highland forest where he camped for the night. He pondered on why the failure had occurred, and he realized the major reason could have to do with the fact that Raul and his mother resented Roland because they, under moral obligation, had returned Roland the money he had loaned them in March. Their accounts were closed, and they felt like failures as a result. Not until then had it crossed Roland's mind.

Lots of crickets were chirping through the night, but it was very peaceful indeed, so much better than the other night. No fighting, no threatening, no attacking, no ill feelings. This was the life. To camp overnight in the forest.

Roland made a sincere wish for a travelling companion, a good fellow who would be a true friend, who would travel long distances and be content in Roland's company. He really wished for that. Would it ever really come true? Ivanhoe was confident that one day Roland would finally figure it out. He hoped it would be soon.

He remembered all that Ivanhoe had told him before he came down here. Ivanhoe had made several predictions about Raul and his family, and an incredibly high percentage of his predictions came true! Unfortunate, but true! Roland then made a sincere wish for Raul to come around and be a good person again, and for their friendship to be restored.

The next day, he walked up to the Cypress ridge. The day was perfectly clear, and he took some excellent photos. Some of the scenes, he would definitely use in his artwork and paintings. He returned to where he camped at noon, took down his tent, and made the descent back to Bustamante.

The first thing he did was go to Raul and Rigo's house to collect his motor, which was next to the back of the house. Rigo was there. They got some neighbors, and five of them took the camper top off Roland's truck. Next, they lifted up the motor and carried it to the truck and set it on a couple of old tires in the front of the truck bed. Roland offered to pay them something, but they declined any payment, and they told Roland they were his friends. Next, they helped Roland place the camper top back on his truck. He thanked them.

Roland entered the house, and he and Rigo had a reasonable chat in the kitchen. Rigo explained several culture differences. Roland was impressed at how much Rigo instinctively understood and knew about people and their way of life. Rigo was remarkably straightforward, and he had the skill and expertise in negotiating and working out any problem that occurred. Roland realized that with that good trait, Rigo would go far in life and would be very successful. Rigo planned to be a teacher, and Roland predicted that he would be one of the best. He had passed his entrance exam for the Prepa, and he would be entering this fall, taking the bus to and from Sabinas Hidalgo each day.

Rigo explained the faults that occurred, both Raul's and Roland's in such a way that Roland didn't even feel bad. Roland told Rigo about India's comment from January. He had never told him before, and he asked Rigo if Raul had brought it up. Rigo knew about it, and he said Raul had come home that same night and had related India's comment to the family.

Suddenly, to Roland's surprise, Raul walked into the kitchen with a scowl on his face, and he brought the wooden tablet that said, "Compañeros de las Montañas," placed it on the washing machine, and gave a gesture of returning it to Roland. With that, he returned to his bed. Roland thought only Rigo was home. Raul had overheard the entire conversation with Rigo. No matter. It was probably best that way. Raul turned up the stereo loudly so that Roland would feel rejected and leave, which he did.

Roland and Rigo stepped outside where Roland thanked him for his friendship and sincerity, and they shook hands. He told Rigo to tell Raul that he wished the friendship had continued and that hopefully one day, he will learn how to appreciate. With that done, he drove over to Pegaso's house where he stayed a couple more days before driving home.

Roland went to the Quevalos and to Lorenzo to tell them the unfortunate turn of events. He also talked it over with his friend Alberto, who couldn't believe how awful Raul had behaved while camping the other night. He said if he'd been Raul, he would have been much more appreciating, especially of that esclava de plata, and he would have considered Roland like a brother.

Felipe Hernandez of the Hotel Ancira needed to send a load of chairs and tables to a client in San Antonio, and he asked Roland if he would do it for US $100. Roland said that would be fine. After all, Felipe was a kind and understanding man, even though he was in competition with Pancho Quevalo. Felipe had been kind enough to allow Rigo certain days off to spend with Roland and Raul, like when they went to Chiquihuitillos and recently to Saltillo.

Roland decided to accept some chairs as part of that payment, with some cash to cover the gasoline cost. Roland left his trailer with them overnight so they could load it, and the next day he went to recollect it. Felipe's business partner, Demas de León, accompanied Roland in his truck.

They stopped by the Quevalos before leaving town, and Roland bought a just-made rocking chair from Pancho. Pancho took Roland to one side and cautioned him to beware, especially when crossing the bridge at U.S. Customs, to make sure they have all their paperwork in order for the furniture Felipe was exporting. Roland told Pancho it was all in order. Roland also sensed that Pancho didn't trust Felipe, but then that's how it is in competition. Roland knew that Felipe was a good man.

He wished the Quevalos well, and he and Demas left town. Roland had done the Quevalos a huge favor by bringing all that trailer cargo to them last month, even though they had been so ugly to run Roland off back in January and report him to the police! He had done the favor more for Isalia than anyone else. Now it was time to do Felipe a favor, and he knew this favor would be better appreciated. After all, Roland helped others when asked to do so.

Three hours later, they arrived at the Colombia Bridge. Roland turned in his permit, and when they began to cross the bridge, they were told they would need to obtain an export permit from a different office, which happened to be closed today. Demas offered a bribe of US $20. The man walked to another office to check. Meanwhile, there was an ever increasing line of tractor trailers waiting behind Roland to pay toll. The minutes went by. The man didn't come back. Finally, five minutes later, the man returned, and he said $30 would work. Demas paid him, and Roland drove across the bridge with the cargo, and with Demas.

There was quite a line of tractor trailers to wait in on the U.S. side. Nearly an hour later, they arrived at the inspection point. The officer checked over the paperwork, which had Roland's name on it. Roland answered that Demas who was with him, was sending the cargo to San Antonio. The officer acted like he smelled a rat, and he asked Demas to go inside to Immigration to explain the situation. They thought Demas was lying, and he assured them he wasn't, that the cargo had a destination in San Antonio. Customs called the recipient in San Antonio, who verified that he was expecting cargo from Felipe and Demas, and with that proof, the problem was solved. Roland, Demas, and all the cargo were granted entry into the United States.

Several hours later, they arrived at the destination in San Antonio. They unloaded all the cargo, and Roland proceeded on his way to Dallas to visit with his relatives before going home to Tennessee.

Roland stopped in Salado on the way to Dallas, and he tried to call Raul and Rigo's brother Eduardo. The phone number was disconnected! Lavinia had supplied her husband with an old number! Roland tried to call Eduardo's uncle, that is, Lavinia's brother. There were two listings, and both of them were other people, not Lavinia's brother, who evidently had an unlisted number.

Roland was sad for quite some time, the failure of his friendship with Raul being totally inexcusable. He went to work at Elizabeth's house in Nashville for a few days. He built a small deck for her. She was concerned for Roland, and she asked him if he was all right.

He went and talked to Isalia and Luke about the whole thing. Isalia was sad for him, and Luke explained that Raul was only growing up. Luke used to be a guidance counselor in a junior high school over in East Tennessee several years ago. He said he understood the personalities, motives, and wishes of teenagers. "Teenagers have their own lifestyles, their own world. They're wishy washy, and they see things differently than adults," Luke explained to Roland.

"And in this generation, they're rebellious, since times are changing so fast," Isalia added.

"There's no telling what might have happened had Raul come up here with you," Luke pointed out.

"You see Raul wasn't meant to come," Isalia explained. "He was blocked from getting that VISA for a good reason, and it was for *your* protection."

They continued talking about Raul and everything else that occurred during Roland's stay in Mexico.

Luke had basically moved in with Isalia now, and she was exceedingly happy about it. Roland could tell by the way she talked. She felt content with her life, and she was now truly blessed.

Isalia told Roland that Luke had already proposed to her, that he had fallen in love with her, and wished to have her as his wife.

Roland told them congratulations. He was happy for them.

Isalia went on to explain to Roland that when two people live together, they have to work very hard to make the relationship work, and it takes a lot of effort from both parties involved. She pointed out to Roland how difficult it had been for him to stay with Raul's family for only three weeks, and to be married to a person is much harder than that. In reference to Roland's relationship with the Zacatón family, Isalia flatly stated, "It's over," and she had an unhappy expression on her face. That look also implied cancellation concerning Norma being Roland's wife, in the future.

"How is it possible for two people to stay married at all, seeing how I couldn't even last three weeks with the Zacatóns?" Roland asked.

"Well, you overstayed, Roland," Isalia answered. "I had told you, *'Don't* overstay.'"

"I know, but two people who are married *overstay* for a lifetime," Roland pointed out. "How do they possibly do it, and what about Norma?"

"It's like Isalia said," Luke then told him. "You have to work really hard to make a relationship work."

"You have to love people and forgive people," Isalia added. "Just keep forgiving."

To Roland, the Zacatón family failed in only a three week period. Marriage and living with the same person for a *lifetime* seemed an unfathomable feat. Still, he knew some married couples lasted, but how? Why was it seemingly, no literally, so much more difficult for Roland? He wasn't that different. The failure of his friendship with the Zacatóns was too mysteriously quick to be believable under normal conditions. He felt like some sort of malign force "got in the water" whether it was negative energy systems or demons of some sort.

"So, where are you two going to live?" Roland wanted to know.

"Oh, right here," Isalia answered.

"I've still got a few things to bring over from east Tennessee and some loose ends to tie up over there, and I'm going to live here with Isalia. We've got our whole life ahead of us."

"Even though we're in our 60's, we still feel young, and we've just located a really great natural foods company. They only sell what is the very best for you, and they sell specially processed organic herbs, designed to increase *longevity*."

"We plan to live till we're 125," Luke added.

"Roland, Luke wants to take his pickup truck to the Quevalos along with more tools and equipment."

"I've also got my eyes on a haybaler," Luke added, "if you could take that down there with your trailer?"

"Yeah, I can do that, if you think it will fit on the trailer," Roland answered.

"Oh yeah, it will," Luke assured him.

"Roland, we've all been chosen to play a part in this grand mission," Isalia explained, "called by God to take this cargo to Bustamante to help my family and the town. Luke has an agricultural mission to help the farmers grow better crops, with his years of awesome expertise as an agricultural professor in east Tennessee."

The truth was that while Luke had indeed been an agricultural professor, he also served part time for some of those years as a guidance counselor. He was a jack of all trades, and Roland saw him as a good man, an excellent husband for Isalia.

"Luke and I are going to get married in Bustamante this winter," Isalia informed Roland.

"Oh, really?" Roland responded. "Maybe I'll be in town then."

"I hope so, "Isalia said to Roland. "Of course, it goes without saying, you're invited to our wedding."

"Thanks."

"Roland, Luke and I have a major project here at home," Isalia brought up.

"What we want to do is build an addition onto Isalia's house . . ." and he explained all the details of an addition project for September and October. They asked Roland to help them. Roland accepted the job offer, and a few weeks later, they began the month long job.

When Roland was leaving, Isalia kindly told him that she and Luke loved him, that he was like a son to them.

Isalia had finally found her happiness. She had not been very happy with Clayton for the 46 years she was married with him, but then that was life sometimes. Isalia had married the father of her children, and a good father he had been. Clayton had been a good man, and now Isalia was moving on with life with her new man, Luke, a fine man who neither smoked nor drank. One of Isalia's grandsons came to visit for several weeks, and he commented that Luke was the perfect grandfather. He couldn't find a thing wrong with him.

Over the intervening weeks, Roland worked for various clients. There was plenty to do, and he earned the necessary money to return to Mexico later.

He also talked to his friend Ivanhoe over in Scotland, and he helped him analyze why the friendship had failed with Raul.

"You see, Roland, you're a person who lives and hopes things will improve, but it doesn't always work out that way, and you don't walk away fast enough. If you sense danger, *walk away* from it before it gets too hot. In the case of Raul and his family, energies kept building up, and things got very dangerous for you. Still, you did very well and managed to get out of there with your hide and pride intact."

Ivanhoe also had done some more excellent paintings, and he offered to send some examples over for Roland to see. He also told Roland some ideas and concepts that he could incorporate into his future artwork.

Ivanhoe was a fellow with an incredible amount of competence and understanding of the human species and their sometimes complex and weird ways of life. Roland was so glad he and Ivanhoe had ironed out the differences from the previous year.

CHAPTER 8

THE SECOND CARGO

It was early September 1997. Isalia called Roland on the phone, telling him that Luke had located and bought a haybaler for $300. It was an old New Holland haybaler, red in color. She asked Roland if he could take Luke up there in his truck and trailer. Roland said he could, and the next morning, he arrived at Isalia's house.

Luke was ready. He and Isalia hugged and kissed each other, and Roland took him over to Sweetwater, Tennessee. After going through Murfreesboro, Roland took the Lascassas Highway, crossing the narrow truss bridge over the Stones River on the way. It was indeed a narrow bridge, only 18½ feet wide, and whenever Roland pulled his trailer across it, he would cringe. Today, for the time he was crossing the bridge, no opposing traffic passed him.

They went through Smithville and Sparta to get to Crossville, after which they would take Highway 68 to Spring City, then more highways to Sweetwater. He and Luke talked about various subjects on the way over. Luke told him some stories about how wrong some of the people were to be racists, and how there are several east Tennessee towns where no blacks live.

Right about Pleasant Hill, Roland was telling him the saga about his loss of friendship with Raul. There was a slow moving vehicle going 30 mph and Roland passed him going down a three-lane hill and a straight stretch of road. At the bottom out, here came a state trooper car in the opposing lane.

"Watch that cop," Luke advised Roland.

The state trooper car swung around, parking on the right shoulder, and right as Roland and Luke passed by him, he turned on his blue flashing lights.

"Oh, what does he *want*? What did I do?" Roland asked Luke.

"You certainly weren't speeding," Luke advised. "I have no idea."

Roland slowed down and pulled over on the shoulder.

A cop who must have been near 60 years in age came to the side of Roland's truck, face angry, and blatantly asked for his license and registration. Roland handed them to the man who then said, "Wait here."

Roland then called out to the man who was already walking back to his car, "What's the matter? What did I do?"

"You passed on a double yellow line coming down that hill." He finished walking to his car, got in, and began writing the ticket.

Roland got out of his truck, anyway. He walked back to their vehicle and discovered that another officer was with him in the car. Roland asked the cop, "Is it possible you could give me a warning instead of a ticket?"

He said to Roland, "Can't do that on this one." The cop was bent on giving a ticket.

The cop's companion was friendly and calm and explained to Roland what he did. The cop came out of the car with the citation already filled out and asked Roland to sign it.

Roland asked him, "Where's the price? How much is it?" He presented Roland with a white piece of paper, and it said $107. Roland reacted with surprise but did *not* shout, "$107? You're joking."

The cop responded by saying, "I don't joke," in a very dry, non-humorous manner.

He asked Roland to sign the ticket, and Roland said that he would have to read it before he would sign it. The cop told Roland he could do that afterwards, that he would be given the pink slip. Roland reiterated that he wanted to read it first, and he saw the 3 lines of large print right above where he was supposed to sign. He didn't like what was written, because it was a threat with a year of jail and/or a $2500 fine. Roland mentioned that he was not comfortable with that, and . . .

Suddenly, the cop got extremely angry and began to scream at Roland saying, "NOW, YOU LISTEN TO ME . . .!!!"

Roland put his arm up over his head to shield himself and said, "Please . . . Don't get angry at me. Don't yell at me, or I will have to report you for abuse."

At the same time Luke, who was a tall and stout man of 6' 2", stepped out of Roland's truck and walked back there to see what all the screaming was about! The cop quit screaming right then, but he went on to threaten Roland that if he didn't sign it, he would haul him off to jail. Roland took the tablet over to the back of his trailer, read it first, and then signed it. Luke talked to them while Roland signed it, and Roland then calmly but firmly said to the cop, "Don't scare people like that. It's not right." The cop made no response. Roland handed him the tablet, and the cop handed Roland the pink slip copy of the citation and also returned his license and registration. Roland showed him an angry face and walked back to his truck to leave.

Actually, Roland was too disturbed and angry to drive, but he couldn't just stay there, parked on the roadside.

"Come on, let's go," Luke directed, approaching Roland. "Let me drive."

"But I can . . ."

"Roland, let's hurry and get out of here!" Luke directed more anxiously. Roland let him drive his truck. Luke was afraid the cop might change his mind and arrest them.

Needless to say, Roland was very angry at that cop!

"I'm going to report that man . . . very uncalled for, his screaming at me!"

"He even scared me, Roland."

While the cop did not hit Roland, his behavior was very unprofessional and uncalled for! Roland did not appreciate officers, who are sworn to *serve* the citizens, abusing them when they pull them over and cite them! He had really scared Roland, and Roland was *not* his private! What was the cop's huge hurry? Why couldn't he be kind enough and patient enough to courteously explain to Roland what he had to do, to sign the ticket, and he would have done it much more easily? He was getting $107 off of him, anyway. Roland had the right to ask him questions, and the right to *read* that ticket *before* signing it, and he knew he was right about that. Why was a cop like that, hothead that he was, working on the state trooper's police force? Why didn't the other officer in the car call his companion down and tell him he was out of order for shouting at Roland? Maybe he was of lower rank and couldn't, but had Roland been the other officer, regardless of rank, he would have commanded his companion to shut up and would have told him he was out of line. Roland wanted that cop fired or at least reprimanded.

When they reached Crossville, Luke parked in downtown, and they entered the courthouse where Roland paid the $107 fine. Luke loaned Roland cash to complete the payment. Next, they walked a block away to the district attorney's office and found out who to report that cop to. He was given the name of a lieutenant at the state trooper's headquarters in Cookeville.

Roland really felt punished for doing good. He was going to the trouble of getting a haybaler destined for the Quevalo family in Bustamante, and he was stung with a mean $107 ticket!

Roland now drove, and they arrived in Sweetwater by mid day. Luke arranged for a man to load the haybaler onto Roland's trailer with a bulldozer/backhoe machine. It wasn't easy, but they got it loaded and tied down.

Luke stayed with friends over in east Tennessee, and Roland returned alone. He stopped by his grandparents' house in Crossville and visited the people who bought it from them 20 years ago, and he took a walk along the "Bunny Trail" in their woods behind their house. Roland missed his grandparents, as his grandmother had passed away six years ago.

Roland drove back home. At Lascassas, he really hoped there wouldn't be an opposing car while crossing that narrow truss bridge because the left axle of that haybaler stuck out a foot beyond the trailer axle on the left. When he approached the bridge with caution, the opposing lane was clear. Excellent! He crossed it with ease, definitely occupying a portion of the opposing lane while doing so. That was certainly the widest load he ever took across that bridge. Whew!

When Roland got home, he called Isalia and let her know he got home safely, and he also told her about the unfair ticket and how the mean old cop had screamed at him. She said Luke had already called her and told her everything. She told Roland, "Well, you broke the law. You got a ticket. Those are the consequences, but that cop shouldn't have screamed at you. We're not second class citizens."

Roland wrote a two-page letter to the lieutenant in Cookeville, reporting the cop and how he had screamed at him. Luke did Roland the courtesy of writing a letter of testimony and while he didn't condone the cop's shouting, he wrote that, "Roland deserved the ticket, and he paid the fine." Roland didn't agree with that. He passed a slow moving vehicle with a clear view of the opposing two lanes on the three-lane hill. How else was he supposed to do it? Follow the man at 25-30 mph the half mile down the hill? In the cop's view, *Yes exactly*. Absurd, that would have been! Roland thanked Luke for the letter, and he mailed them both to Cookeville.

Roland called and talked to Ivanhoe on the phone, and he told Roland he wasn't surprised. That ugly incident occurred as a warning to Roland, a sign to let him know that he was helping out the wrong people. Of course, Roland realized the Quevalos were probably the wrong people to help out, but then he was doing it to help out Isalia and Luke. Ivanhoe gave Roland the suggestion of keeping on guard and to keep his thoughts on the road instead of going on and on about Raul. Roland took his suggestion seriously. He received no more tickets.

Ivanhoe also asked Roland if Isalia and Luke had offered to pay Roland for the ticket. Roland answered that no, they hadn't offered. Ivanhoe then pointed out that he would never have gotten that ticket if he hadn't been doing that favor for *them*. They should have offered to pay Roland for the ticket. Roland later went and asked Isalia and Luke, but they simply told Roland that he had committed the infraction and that he should therefore bear the cost of the ticket. Roland didn't push that any further since they were employing him to help Luke with that house addition. In Roland's view, Isalia and Luke should have at least offered to pay half of the ticket. So, during Roland's work, he paid Luke back for the cash he had loaned him at the courthouse in Crossville.

Later, Roland called the state trooper's headquarters in Cookeville. He talked to the lieutenant who said he wasn't going to issue any reprimand because it was Luke's and Roland's testimonies against the cop's and his companion's . . . two against two. Well, that wasn't good enough. Roland called the state commissioner's office of the Tennessee Department of Safety and reported the incident.

About three weeks later, that lieutenant in Cookeville called Luke on the phone, talked to him for 20 minutes, and he was very concerned about his sergeant's behavior. The lieutenant had even been riding with him to make sure his sergeant acted and behaved properly . . . no screaming, no abusing. After Luke got off the phone, he told Roland what the lieutenant had said.

That was music to Roland's ears. How had that turned around for the better? Why was the lieutenant now so worried about his sergeant? Roland never knew it, but after he called the state commissioner's office in Nashville, they had done an investigation. They don't like receiving complaints, and they handed down a reprimand from their higher level. Roland laughed. Justice had indeed been served! Of course, though Roland never knew it, that sergeant who had shouted at Roland was absolutely furious! More than once, he ranted and raved to his wife that if he could just get his hands on Roland . . . but he never did.

They now began the addition project onto Isalia's house. Luke and Roland worked hard on the project. One of his brothers came to help, and one of Clayton's former students came, as well. It took several weeks, but they successfully got it built. Luke commented to Isalia that he and Roland worked well together. Each day Roland came to work, Isalia prepared and fed him and Luke lunch. She was very pleased, and she praised them for their excellent work.

Roland put his rebuilt engine back in his Ford LTD station wagon. He connected all the accessories, started it, adjusted the valves, and it ran very well. He put a rebuilt carburetor on it at the same time. His car had been out of service nearly a year. How great it was to have it running and on the road again.

In September, Isalia told Roland about a book called *The Power of Your Subconscious Mind*, an excellent book about thinking positive and bringing forth favorable results. Roland read it, was very impressed by it, and he asked Isalia why she hadn't shown him that book years ago. She answered that she didn't know, that maybe he wasn't ready for it earlier on, that is, until now.

In early October, Roland looked up a fellow by the name of Steve Cason. He was the son of a good friend of Roland's parents, and he was going to Tennessee Tech University. As soon as Roland reached him on the phone, he instinctively recognized Steve's voice as very familiar, even though he had never talked to him before. Roland's father had recently told him about Steve because he also liked hiking. Steve was glad to hear from Roland, and they decided they would go hiking sometime. Roland said he could come up to Cookeville next week. Steve said that would be great.

The next day, Roland told Isalia about having talked to Steve and that he might be someone to travel with him. Isalia gave Roland a smile of surprise, being happy for him.

Well, Roland drove up to Cookeville the next week. He took his bicycle with him, and he pulled into the apartment complex where Steve was living. He wasn't there. He took his bicycle out of his car and rode around the backroads of Putnam County, stopping by the apartment every hour that day. The end of the day arrived, and not one of those times was Steve there!

When Roland got home, he called Steve and left a message on his answering machine. A couple of days later, he finally managed to reach Steve on the phone, and Steve apologized for being out of pocket. He said a crisis had come up, and he had to go home to Nashville for the day.

Roland talked with Isalia about Steve, and he told her he was feeling blocked from meeting him. As soon as Roland had heard Steve's voice on the phone, he instinctively realized that he should have met Steve years ago. He felt like he had always known him. Their father's had known each other since the late 1970's. How come it didn't occur to them to introduce their sons to each other years ago? They could have gone travelling and hiking. Back in 1993, Steve hiked the entire Appalachian Trail from Georgia to Maine. Roland would like to have joined him, if he had just known about him.

"Well, you can't cry over spilled milk!" Isalia commented in a flustered manner.

Huh! What sort of comment was that? Roland wasn't sure, but the fact remained that he was lamenting that he and Steve had not known each other in past years.

While Roland was working with Luke on the house addition project, they were in and out of the shop a lot. One morning, Roland needed to sharpen his machete. Isalia let him into the shop by opening the door and turning off the alarm inside, *before* letting Roland in. She accompanied him to the belt sanding wheel, and Roland spent five minutes carefully sharpening the machete. And you know, Isalia stood there watching Roland the whole time! He didn't say anything to Isalia about it, but he sensed a little bit of mistrust in her.

Isalia made arrangements with Pancho, telling him exactly what they would be bringing. Pancho meanwhile made appropriate visits to agricultural representatives in Monterrey and throughout Nuevo León. He got letters of permission and signatures.

Things got down to the wire before their departure date with finishing up the house addition. Isalia offered to pay Roland for his fuel cost to drive to Mexico, and then she offered to pay him something additional as rental of the trailer. Roland suspected she had $50 in mind, and he was about to say that amount, but instead he thought a moment. He knew Isalia had never offered to pay at least half of that stinging $107 ticket, so he added another $50 to the $50, and he said, "$100?"

"Uh, yeah . . . Yeah, okay," Isalia answered, "but keep in mind, this project's cost us enough already."

They agreed to that, and Isalia and Luke would pay Roland the $100 at his time of returning to Tennessee, after arriving to Mexico.

Luke and Roland made mad scrambles to finish the addition and close it in. Isalia's granddaughter would be living there while Isalia and Luke were away, and they planned on staying in Mexico until March. Roland would return home a couple of weeks after arriving, stay home a month, and then return to Mexico for the winter. He had plans and was looking forward to doing some more paintings.

On October 20, 1997, the three of them met at Isalia's house. She said a prayer for them, and they were on their way to Mexico. Roland led the way with his truck, trailer, and haybaler, and Luke and Isalia followed in Luke's white pickup truck, which was loaded with equipment and saws.

Roland took Highway 99 toward Columbia. Along the way, he took compensation into his own hands and passed a slow vehicle where there was a solid double line, even though the road was straight at that point and visibility was good. There! That was *better*. Roland got it in right, this time!

They turned left on I-65, took it to Birmingham, and took I-59 into Mississippi, where they found a hotel. Yes, Luke and Isalia paid for Roland's room and for his supper.

While they ate supper, Luke explained his philosophy on giving. He and Isalia expressed their appreciation of Roland for all the trouble he was going to by taking this second trailer cargo to the Quevalos. The cargo was heavy, and Roland had to drive carefully. There had been several hills between Nashville and Birmingham that required driving in second gear because the heavy cargo slowed him down.

"You see, you need to give till it hurts," Luke explained. "It'll come back four fold."

Roland understood to some degree the general belief that when a person gives, it comes back in a positive way, at a later time.

The next day, they convoyed to Isalia's sister, Roma, in Houston. Not long after leaving the hotel, Roland pulled off the interstate where there happened to be a Wal-Mart Supercenter. They pulled into the parking lot and parked.

Isalia and Luke stepped out of their truck, and Isalia said, "Rolando, you are perfect!"

"Thank you, Isalia."

They walked into the store and bought last minute items for Mexico.

They arrived in Houston by late afternoon. Roma and her husband and family received them well. They met Isalia's fiancé, Luke, and both Luke and Isalia, especially Isalia, related the most interesting and marvelous story about how the *angels above* caused them to be brought together.

Isalia explained that when Clayton was on his deathbed, he had told Isalia that another man would soon be coming into her life. There would be a key phrase of four words, "*C'est la vie, amour,*" that he would say to her, therefore verifying that he was the one. After Clayton died, Isalia's sister came to visit for a month, after which Isalia was alone. She began to suffer panic attacks, and in desperation, Isalia, you might say, spoke to the dead. She called to Clayton and said, "Clayton, I'm desperate. Send me somebody *now*." The next day, Luke called her and told her he wanted to send a bunch of equipment to Mexico to her cousins and with his agricultural expertise, he could teach some of the farmers better farming methods. This enchanted Isalia, a man with a mission. What a noble cause! He asked if he could come and visit her, and she said sure. He paid her a visit the next day and then returned home to east Tennessee.

Isalia suffered a sudden operation, a hysterectomy, and she called him to come and take care of her, which he did obligingly. The timing was perfect. They talked and talked for the week he was with her at her home, and she recovered very well. On the third day of his visit, he happened to mention the key phrase. Isalia was enthralled and said to Luke that he was the man for her. Quite by happen chance, (or was it divine destiny?), he had just settled a divorce with his third wife, with whom he was married for six years. He told Isalia she was just the woman he had been looking for all his life. The timing was indeed perfect, and the *angels above* had designed this divine union between Isalia and Luke. The best had been saved until last, and here it was. Isalia had been telling Roland that phrase for several years.

They went on to tell Roma and her family how everything was so perfectly in its place in Clayton's immaculate woodshop at the time he died. Clayton had saved materials over the years, and when Isalia and Luke began that addition project, exactly the right amount of materials happened to be left over to facilitate the construction of that addition. There were exactly the right number and sizes of nails, the right number of lag bolts and screws, and more details that turned out to be very precise! Isalia and Luke were both impressed at Clayton's intuition. On another level, he knew exactly what Isalia would need after his death, and as it turned out, he provided for her very well. In other words, everything was perfectly laid out for them. Clayton did indeed have psychic abilities.

Isalia and Luke both praised Roland for the help he had given them and for his excellent navigation skills and finding that Wal-Mart Supercenter so easily. Luke said Roland was the best travelling companion he had ever had.

Some of Roma's grandchildren came over to visit, and Luke played with them in a fun-loving way. Yes, Roland felt proud to be a part of this mission, and he looked forward to proudly introducing his Spanish teacher and her husband-to-be to his friends in Bustamante.

The next morning they left Roma's house and made their way to a ranch north of Laredo. It was there that Isalia had cousins living. While there was electricity, the phone company had never run lines down the road. So, they had a cell phone. Isalia had not seen her cousins since her youth, quite to Roland's surprise. They had an excellent visit, and Isalia and Luke related their marvelous falling-in-love story again.

The next morning, Isalia said a prayer for everyone and prayed for all the equipment to cross the border without mishap. She prayed for everyone's safety, as well. With that done, they stepped outside, said goodbye to her cousins, and they drove to the Colombia Solidarity Bridge, stopping for groceries and fuel on the way.·

Isalia was a little bit nervous, Roland noticed, but then that sort of thing is normal when a person is about to take a lot of items across the border. They reached the toll gate, and since Roland's trailer had that New Holland haybaler on it, they charged more toll. They also told Roland to step inside the office to pay, instead of just handing the man the $6 at the booth. Roland stepped down from his truck, walked to Luke's truck, and told him and Isalia they were charging $6. Isalia exasperatingly told Roland she would pay the $6, and she handed Roland the cash! He went inside the office. Right as he finished paying, Luke walked in with anxiety.

"C'mon, Roland. Let's go!" Luke urged, and he also asked Roland why he came in the office to pay instead of just paying at the booth.

"They told me to come inside to pay," Roland answered.

"Oh, okay," Luke responded.

Now, they drove across the bridge. Pancho Quevalo was outside and waiting for them. His brother Lorenzo was with him, and they happily greeted Isalia and her fiancé Luke.

Pancho and Lorenzo looked at the cargo, both in Luke's truck, and at the haybaler on Roland's trailer. They were intrigued.

". . . y no te preocupes. Voy a pagar todos impuestos," Isalia told Pancho, reassuring him that she was going to pay all importation taxes. (Then why was she so exasperated at paying that $6 toll for Roland?!)

A Mexican Customs official, the same one who inspected them in June with the first cargo, inspected both cargos. Then they all went inside and got their tourist permits. Customs gave them 180 days. Roland made sure to mention to Pancho that he didn't want any problem at Aduana Anahuac with that officer complaining saying, "Pero lleva muchas cosas!"

Pancho assured Roland there would be no inconvenience this time.

Roland, Luke and Isalia went back outside and waited by the cargo while Pancho and Lorenzo stayed inside to continue negotiating.

Roland looked at Luke's cargo and noticed a big spool of sandpaper used in floor sanders. He pointed to it and mentioned something about it to Isalia.

She coldly snapped, "¡Cállate!" telling Roland to shut up.

That hurt his feelings, but he said nothing.

There was a man and wife who had arrived in a big station wagon, and strapped on its luggage rack were 10 kayaks! They were going to Belize for a vacation, where they were supposed to meet a group flying in. Their station wagon was carrying the necessary kayaks to them. Mexican Customs denied them entry, and the man angrily got in his car with his wife. Then he looked over at Roland, who was standing by his truck, and commented, "I've got to go to Brownsville. These dumb *#%@! don't know what the #@%!! they're doing!" He drove away.

Get out of here and good riddance! Roland thought to himself. He was quite bothered, offended by the man's vulgarity! Why did Roland have to hear that?! The man was a negative thinker. His psyche reeked of it. No wonder he was denied entry, and sent back across the bridge to Texas!

Luke related a story to Roland about a time when he went to a town down south near the Yucatan Peninsula numerous years ago. It was a mission with his church. He stayed a couple of weeks in one of the small towns, and he fell in love with the country and the people. He didn't want to go back home to Tennessee, but of course he had to when the mission was accomplished.

Pancho and Lorenzo emerged from the building with the customs official. They had decided to waive all fees with no further inspections, and they were granted entry. Nothing was taken away this time. They drove (convoyed) to the second inspection station 40 kilometers away at Anahuac where they were quickly granted passage. No officer complained about carrying too many things. Colombia Bridge had called ahead to advise them. All of them drove on through. Roland led the way and arrived at Bustamante in the mid afternoon.

Since Isalia and Luke had fallen behind along the highway, Roland drove to Felipe's carpentry and delivered the Cedar lumber he had brought with him. Then he drove to Lorenzo's house and disconnected his trailer from his truck. They would unload the haybaler from the trailer later.

Roland drove his truck to Pegaso's house, and the Orolizo family received Roland well, telling him that he had his house there. That was kind of them. Pegaso was in Monterrey at the university, and he would be home for the weekend.

*   *   *

Nuevo Wimbisenho, October 23, 1997

Arfifra, Torxtalo, and others were gathered inside their secret and exquisite cavern well underneath a remote hillside on a ranch between Villaldama and Sabinas Hidalgo. The cave was called Nuevo Wimbisenho, named after its original location in the South Island of New Zealand. In January 1992, they had abandoned their old location, transferring to and taking up residence in the hills west of Sabinas Hidalgo, to enjoy a taste of new culture: Mexicans and Americans.

"What a grand and gracious mission Roland and his Spanish teacher are doing," Arfifra complimented.

"My protectee Pancho is so intrigued," Torxtalo added.

Sojornbloc and Sasjurech were also present along with Draaktra.

"Now listen," Arfifra told everyone. "Roland suffered a lot of grief back in July with that Zacatón family. We have to perform some . . . shall we say . . ."

"Arfifra," Torxtalo suddenly interrupted, "I don't think we should be doing any . . ."

"Hold your tongue there a moment, you stubborn Nyangshai," Arfifra quickly interjected. "I have some excellent plans for us to work a, shall we say . . . *miracle*, and furthermore, how's Roland going to return in December if we don't make things right? Plus . . ."

*   *   *

Roland called his parents to let them know he had arrived safely with all the cargo. They were relieved to know that. Roland wished his father a happy 70th birthday tomorrow, and he commented that he felt fortunate to still be alive and well.

Roland had brought some gifts for some people: a grease gun for Pegaso's father, Nacho Orolizo, a couple of used tires for Manuel, one of Raul's friends who Roland had met back in the summer, and some used pants and shirts for Raul and Rigo's family. He made the deliveries.

For the clothing, Lavinia told Roland, "Muchas gracias," and she told Roland that Raul was no longer angry at him, and that he was certainly welcome to stay. He thanked her, but he said he was already settled at Pegaso Orolizo's house. Nevertheless, Roland visited for a while. Norma asked Roland for some roller skates.

Rigo arrived home from the Prepa in Sabinas Hidalgo. He greeted Roland in a casual, calm manner, shaking hands with him. They asked each other how they were doing, and Roland invited him to go up in the mountains. Rigo explained that with work and homework, he wouldn't have the time.

Lavinia asked Roland how his family was. She explained that Raul was also working at Felipe's carpentry with Rigo and that Raul was also taking courses at night at Bustamante's tecnica. He was studying mechanics.

Since Roland had left in July, Raul had communicated by phone with his brother Eduardo about going to Salado, Texas to stay with him. Eduardo was, at that time, unable to take him in, more than that, pay the $700 to get Raul across the Rio Grande River and delivered to Salado by a coyote. So, Raul decided to study mechanics until Eduardo would come and get him.

As for Isalia and Luke, they spent the night at the Quevalos.

The next day, Roland took Pegaso's brother Leo and also took Manuel to Monterrey for the day. They visited the marketplace, called the Macroplaza, and Roland bought a CD of *Grupo Mojado*. The album was called *Sueños y Realidad* (Dreams and Reality). There were some good songs on that album, including one called "Piensa en Mí" (Think of Me). He also bought a couple of crystal display cabinets with assorted rocks and minerals displayed and labeled. They did other errands where Manuel bought supplies for their business of making dulces. They stopped by a bike shop called Julio Cepeda, a part of FAMSA, and they stopped by a grocery store called Soriana.

While Roland and his friends were in Monterrey, Pancho and the Quevalos moved Isalia and Luke into a rental house in the upper side of Bustamante, a couple of blocks up the street from the Orolizo family where Roland was staying. Pancho had found it for Isalia and Luke during the past month, and it was a nice two-room house, complete with a bathroom, shower and front porch. The rent was only N$300 per month, a great deal indeed.

They also needed a maid, and without Roland knowing, Pancho chose Raul's mother Lavinia, who at the time was without work and gladly accepted the job. She went to work immediately, helping Isalia and Luke by sweeping and cleaning the house and patio. Luke bought and connected a butane gas boiler for hot water and made some other plumbing repairs. His skills, being a jack of all trades, came in handy. Isalia was so proud of her fiancé and all he knew how to do.

Roland and his friends returned from Monterrey. He delivered them to their homes and then went over to Raul and Rigo's house. He visited with their family. Lavinia gave Roland the surprising news that she had been hired by Isalia and Luke to be their maid. Roland looked at her with surprise. Yes, he certainly wanted to introduce Isalia and Luke to the Zacatóns, but he never dreamed it would have occurred that easily and quickly.

Lavinia explained that when Isalia had introduced herself to Lavinia and found out her name, she had said to Lavinia, "¿La mamá de Raul?" (Raul's mother?) When Lavinia answered yes, Isalia was spellbound. In fact, she had never been so surprised in all her life! She and Lavinia began to talk about the friendship Roland had made with her two sons, Raul and Rigo, and she (Isalia) praised Roland on various points and explained to Lavinia many good things about Roland.

Lavinia was very content with her new job, and she took to Isalia and Luke right away. They had already met her daughters, Norma and Irma, who were already calling Isalia and Luke, "Tía" and "Tío" (Aunt and Uncle).

Raul arrived at 9 PM from the tecnica. He was glad to see Roland. He asked him how his friends Chip and Roger were. Roland said they were doing fine. Raul asked him how his family was, and he invited Roland to eat supper with them.

Wow! Roland thought. One of the two wishes Roland made up in the mountains back in July had come true. Amazing! The travelling companion wish . . . That remained to be seen. Roland and Raul talked, and Roland got to feeling better all the time. He felt a strong urge to forgive Raul and be his friend again. Raul admitted that they had treated Roland badly. He spoke with sincerity and there was absolutely no resentment nor grudges within him. Raul wanted to be Roland's friend.

They talked a while longer, and then Roland returned to the Orolizos to sleep. He was indeed spellbound by all that had changed for the better.

The next morning, he went to Raul and asked him if he wanted to spend the day with him. Raul accepted gladly. They went to Felipe, who gladly gave permission, and Raul had the day off. His father Alejandro had bought a car, a 1966 Chrysler Valiant with a slant 6 and a 4 speed. It ran pretty well, and Raul and Roland took it for a drive around town.

Roland felt the strong sensation of a miracle having come over him, his friendship with Raul totally restored. Peace and friendship prevailed in this situation.

They drove over to Isalia and Luke's house, and they met Raul, with whom they were impressed. They gladly welcomed him and Roland inside where Lavinia was cooking breakfast for them. Norma and Irma were outside in the backyard playing. Pancho was there, as well.

"You see, Roland, it's no accident that Lavinia was placed here as our maid," Isalia explained. "She was placed here . . . for you."

Roland had the most unusual feelings of happiness.

Next, Isalia really pleased Roland by explaining to Lavinia and her son Raul that Roland was a very fine person who was honest and straight. She explained that she had known Roland 17 years and was good friends with him and his family. Roland was very intelligent, a genius in some ways, but he had a lack of understanding of some of the cultural traits. Most of all, Roland was very sensitive in his hearing and his smell, a trait of autism, and he stayed away from smoke, perfume, and loud noises.

Raul listened intently, and Roland was very glad he got to hear that. Raul had not believed Roland on those sensitivity traits, but now he had verification from Isalia, and he gained more respect for Roland as a result. Raul had previously interpreted Roland's sensitivity as traits of being gay, but they weren't. They were traits of autism. Isalia went on to say that Roland needs to be wanted and loved as a friend, especially by those who he stays with. Amen.

Pancho and Luke, via Isalia's interpreting, were talking over the problem of a type of army worm insect that, in certain summers, not all, invaded the Pecan trees throughout the town and ate all the leaves off the trees, leaving the forming pecans totally exposed to the hot sun, and they would dry up, failing to form. Luke suggested a form of fumigation, however there was also a type of fly that would eat the insect larvae.

Roland and Raul left and spent the day together. Roland felt the sensation of a miracle all day. They drove over to a town called Potrero, which was 25 kilometers south of Bustamante. Raul introduced Roland to some friends in Potrero: Joel, Ramiro, and others. On the way back, Roland let Raul drive his truck for the highway stretch.

When they got back to Bustamante, Roland went to a shade tree mechanic. His truck's starter was very sluggish, and the mechanic took it off and disassembled it. He put some new bushings in it, and it was fixed.

As Roland took Raul home, he reached his hand over to him to shake hands, and he told Raul, "Te perdono por todo." (I forgive you for everything.) They shook hands.

Roland went over to the Quevalos in the evening. Isalia had worked a miracle there, as well. She praised Roland to all of them, and all of the Quevalos were now welcoming Roland. While they didn't actually apologize, at least they were now friendly to him. The Quevalos told stories to Isalia and Luke, and they had a lot of laughs. Of course, since Luke spoke very little Spanish, Isalia translated the Quevalo's comments to him. Luke fell in love with the Quevalos and said they were really funny.

The Quevalos made a joking remark about Roland having spent the day with his "brother-in-law." They commented on Roland eventually marrying Raul's sister, Norma. Roland admitted he had feelings that it may actually occur, depending on how her family continued to receive him.

Isalia and Luke called it a night. Roland offered and took them across town to their rental home. They made arrangements to go to Sabinas Hidalgo with Roland the next day,

The Second Cargo

Sunday.

Pegaso arrived home at night. They had a good visit and caught up with each other. Roland told him all the good news that had recently occurred, and Pegaso was happy for him. Roland had brought the book, *The Power of Your Subconscious Mind* with him, and he showed it to Pegaso. He was intrigued.

The next morning, Roland went over to Isalia and Luke's rental house to see if they were ready to go to Sabinas Hidalgo. They were eating breakfast, and Pancho was with them. Roland decided to talk about the meaning of: *A mí me gusta muchísimo mi mejor amigo*, which means, *My best friend is very pleasing to me*. Pancho explained that it meant that a person pleases someone sexually, and it is only supposed to be used in reference to boyfriends or girlfriends. Roland reminded Isalia that she had taught everyone in her class to say it that way in that *My Best Friend* recitation, and he asked her why she didn't have them say, *A mí me cae excelente mi mejor amigo*, instead of, *A mí me gusta muchísimo mi mejor amigo*, which has sexual connotations. Isalia didn't want to admit she had taught it that way, and Roland told her that's what she had taught. He said he had his notes up in the attic to prove it, if she didn't believe him. With that said, she admitted that she had taught it that way, and she somehow "hadn't realized" the sexual significance of that phrase. She asked Roland why he had brought it up, and he said he had unknowingly put his foot in his mouth, referring to Raul and other friends that way. It was very important, and why didn't she teach that to her students?

Later in the morning, Isalia and Luke arrived at the Orolizo's house. They met Pegaso, his brother Leo, and their parents, Nacho and Chela, and they also met Pegaso's sisters, Lumita and Mena. A great family they were, and Isalia and Luke were glad to meet them.

Roland took them over to Raul and Rigo's house where he found everyone at home. Rigo came outside, and Roland introduced him to Isalia and Luke. He politely shook hands with them. Then he drove them over to the cantina in another part of town where Alejandro was, and they met him. With those introductions complete, Roland took Isalia and Luke to Sabinas Hidalgo.

On the way over, Roland told Isalia and Luke, "I'm so glad to have my friend back."

"I'm happy for you, too," Isalia responded.

Roland told them all about the miracle, how he interpreted it, and that he was still in a state of surprise over the good happenings.

The first stop they made was Ricardo and Alicia Velazco's house and their Taller Electrico, electric motor repair shop. They weren't home. Next, they visited the Sunday flea market on the north side of town. Roland found Norma a perfect pair of used roller blades. Luke was very glad to know of this flea market, and he found a great tool display. The man at the counter spoke English, and he and Luke became friends right then and there. In fact, as Roland would later learn, Isalia and Luke invited the man to their upcoming January 1 wedding in Bustamante. Next, they ate lunch at a restaurant, after which they returned to Bustamante.

When they arrived back in town, Roland began to take Isalia and Luke to Daniel Mata's house to introduce them to him, but Isalia said she and Luke were suffering from stomach aches and asked to be taken straight home. Roland obliged and took them home. They never got to meet him nor his family.

Roland returned to the Orolizo's house where he found Pegaso, Rigo and Angelo watching a movie. Raul was visiting other friends at the time. After the movie, Roland took them over to Villaldama to a circus. He told the three of them on the way over that he appreciated them and that he considered them some of his best friends. They enjoyed the circus, watching all the different animals performing various acts.

*   *   *

October 26, 1997

Meanwhile, Isalia and Luke visited with the Quevalos.

That evening when it got dark, they drove back to their rental house on the other side of town. They were enjoying their stay very much, and Luke found Isalia's cousins really outgoing and funny. In his view, they had a great sense of humor. Isalia felt on cloud nine with her new man. After all, her past husband Clayton had died six months earlier, and it felt so good to her to be with Luke now. Though he had a sense of firmness about him, he was a kind and caring man to Isalia, and she was reveling in the delight of his feelings and protection toward her.

They had been talking with the Quevalos about Roland and his friend Raul, and all of them were amazed at how the two of them had restored their friendship so well that it was as if the problems of the past summer had not even occurred. They had absolutely no grudges whatsoever.

"Luke, isn't it just great how Roland and Raul have made up and become good friends again," Isalia told her fiancé.

"Yes, that's good," he agreed. "After all, Raul's just growing up."

"I'm really happy for them," she commented.

"What all did the Quevalos say about Raul and Roland?" Luke asked her, since he didn't understand nor speak Spanish, and therefore had not understood what the Quevalos had said.

"Well, India was commenting how it was a true miracle about how Raul and Roland forgave each other. She said they took to each other very soon after meeting and became good friends. Raul looks upon Roland as a guiding light. Lavinia was telling me that Raul appreciates Roland a lot."

"You know," Luke decided to mention. "I think Roland . . ."

*   *   *

During the week, Roland enjoyed his time with his friends. Things went very well.

One of the Orolizo family's neighbors was Victor, age 14. Roland had met him at the molino last summer. Victor asked Roland how things had gone for him. They talked a while. Roland also went to his residence and met his family. Victor Sr. and Marta were the parents, and Victor's two younger sisters were Mabel and Liliana. They lived in a one-room house just half a block away from the Orolizos.

Roland went up in the mountains to camp one night. So peaceful and quiet it was up in the highland forest. It rained a little bit overnight but cleared by morning.

Raul came home at lunch each day, and Roland would go over to visit with him. He was always welcoming and told Roland to come back again the next day, which he did.

One day, Raul took the day off with Felipe's permission, and they went over to Sabinas Hidalgo to enjoy the day. Roland let Raul drive the truck, as well. They did some errands, ate at a taco restaurant, and since Raul had no tennis shoes in good condition, Roland bought him a pair. They were only US $25.

They returned to Bustamante. Raul told Roland a little bit about his philosophy and belief about life, that each person has his/her belief system and that the *Bible* is not the final say. There is more to life than the exact wording of the *Holy Bible*, even though it's a very good book. Roland agreed with Raul. Raul gave a very reasonable explanation and analysis to the way he saw life and human character. No doubt, Raul was an intelligent, open minded fellow.

The following day, Roland took Pancho over to Sabinas Hidalgo. Isalia and Luke had driven there a little bit sooner in their white truck they were donating to the Quevalos. They were having mysterious trouble starting it, and they needed a mechanic to repair it. Pancho would stay with the truck while the mechanic would repair it, and Isalia and Luke would ride back to Bustamante with Roland.

On the way over, Pancho and Roland talked about the miracle that had occurred with his friendship with Raul. They also talked about the marvelous story of Isalia and Luke. Pancho mentioned that Luke had finally found the right woman, and seeing how he had three wives previously, it was evident that Luke had problems in being able to choose the right woman. Though Luke had stepchildren, he never had any children of his own. Isalia, however had several sons, numerous grandchildren, and one great-grandchild, and she was only 63.

Once they reached the mechanic, Roland took Isalia and Luke around Sabinas Hidalgo on errands. He took them by Alicia and Ricardo Velazco's Taller Electrico, and they were indeed home. Alicia was very pleased to meet Roland's high school Spanish teacher. Isalia struck up a friendship, and they talked for two hours. She made nice remarks about Roland, told the story about their bringing her cousins the trailer cargos, and of course, she told the marvelous story about how the *angels above* had brought her and Luke together earlier this year. Isalia was very glad to have met the Velazcos, and Luke commented that they were nice people.

They went to the plaza and walked around, and it was there that Isalia decided to tell Roland about something she saw as very important, concerning Felipe and his carpentry at the Hotel Ancira.

"Roland, Pancho mentioned to me that you took a trailer cargo to San Antonio for Felipe back in July."

"Right."

"And that you all just about got arrested?"

"No, they just gave Demas some trouble, but we got it across all right."

"I'm telling you as a friend to not have anything else to do with Felipe. He's not to be trusted."

Roland decided to be low keyed about Isalia's strange advice. She made a few more comments that made him feel uncomfortable, and then she and Luke said they were ready to return to Bustamante. As they walked to Roland's truck, he thought about defending Felipe's good character, but he decided to leave it at that. Still, for what Isalia had just said, Roland was in a state of frenzy because she had said that Felipe was dishonest and not trustworthy. Roland was mulling it over. He would bring it up to her, once back in Bustamante. No matter what, Roland was feeling squelched.

The three of them got in Roland's truck, and he began to drive them out of town. Luke had not fastened his seat belt. Roland asked him to put it on. So, he reached for it and put it over his shoulder.

"Luke, please make it click," Roland asked again.

"No!" he flatly answered.

Roland pulled the truck over on the shoulder.

"What's this?! You want me to get out and *walk*?!"

"No, Luke," Roland answered, quite taken aback at Luke's rudeness. As a result, Roland decided to snap back. "I want my passengers seatbelted. Now, dig it out! Dig it out!"

"Roland, calm down!" Isalia ordered him.

"I don't like the way he just talked to me, Isalia. Uncalled for that is!"

"Luke, go ahead and put on the seatbelt," Isalia asked him.

He showed Roland a mean look, made it click, and Roland then proceeded. Roland had an awful feeling in his abdomen all the way back to Bustamante, and none of them talked at all. Isalia placed her hand on Luke's thigh, caressing him as a means of keeping him calm.

When they arrived back in town and pulled up in front of their rental house, it was a relief to Roland to have them step down and *out* of his truck. Roland was unsure as to what to do, and he was still in a state of shock over Luke's sudden rudeness, which Luke never apologized for, Roland noted. Luke kept very quiet. He was angry inside. Roland could sense that, and it worried him.

Roland entered the house with them because he wanted to talk more with Isalia about Felipe and get to the bottom of why she was so against Roland's continuing to know him. Lavinia and her daughter Irma were inside cooking lunch. It was just ready.

Luke walked off to the other room while Isalia and Roland sat down at the table.

"Isalia, I was going to ask you more about why you feel the way you do about Felipe," Roland brought up, "but then for the seatbelt incident, we didn't talk."

"Luke's rather put out with you, Roland!"

"Well, Isalia, I'm sorry, but he made that remark about getting out and walking, and I snapped back."

"You need to control yourself better, Roland."

"I know, but what about Luke? You know how I want my passengers seatbelted. After all, my father lobbied for it back 20 years ago in Tennessee."

"But this is *Mexico*, Roland. It's not the same here."

"Well, my truck is the same, and so are my rules, and I've got to be responsible for my passengers' safety."

"Okay, okay," Isalia gave in. "Listen, it's like I was telling you, Felipe is not to be trusted. He got you in a lot of trouble, and you charged him a very low price, only $100."

"Well Isalia, I didn't charge you any more than that, and Felipe is a friend of mine, too."

"But then you bring him that Cedar lumber every time you come to Mexico, and you're not making any profit from it. You should charge him more, Roland."

"Isalia, I don't like to charge more than at cost, especially to Mexicans. They don't earn as much money as we Americans do, and I'm just not going to take advantage of them."

"Roland, Felipe just about got you arrested at the Colombia Bridge!"

"He didn't just about get me arrested, and who told you that, Pancho?"

"Yes, Roland," Isalia verified.

"Oh, Pancho *mentiroso* (lier), always making up stories and blowing things out of proportion!"

"Roland, DON'T have any further dealings with Felipe. He's a crook!"

"I don't think he's a crook, Isalia!"

"Okay, Roland. I don't think we ought to communicate anymore!"

Wow! What sort of final statement was that? Roland suddenly felt a sharp pain go through his abdomen.

"Sorry, what was that?" Roland asked in a surprised manner.

She repeated the sentence.

"You mean you're going to sever our friendship over just this discussion? I mean, I've known you for more than 16 years."

"Well, okay. We'll continue," she said.

"I would hope so. You don't throw away friends of many years." Next, Roland turned to Lavinia and told her what he and Isalia had talked about. He said Isalia had said Felipe was a criminal.

"Now, Roland, I didn't say criminal, I said *crook*."

"Well, that's the translation to Spanish, Isalia."

"Yeah, but don't go around town saying I said Felipe was a crook, or they could send the police after us."

"I wasn't planning to," Roland assured her.

"Isalia, haz de decirte que Felipe es patrón de mis hijos, Raul y Rigo, y es padrino de Rigo," said Lavinia, telling Isalia that Felipe employed both Raul and Rigo in his carpentry business, and that he was Rigo's padrino.

Isalia pushed the point no further. She never let on, but she knew she had really put her foot in her mouth.

"I guess I better leave, Isalia," said Roland, as he got up from the table. He looked at her. "You're not really going to sever my friendship, are you?"

"No, I won't."

"Okay, good. Can I still come over and visit?"

"Yes, of course, and Roland, no matter what happens, I will always love you."

"Okay, thanks. See you later."

When Roland left, he went straight to Lorenzo Quevalo and his wife Glenda to talk to them about what had happened and what Isalia had said.

Both Lorenzo and Glenda sincerely told Roland to be careful. "No le hagas enojar a Isalia," said Glenda, telling Roland not to get Isalia angry, that he didn't want to be on her bad side.

Roland left and visited other people in town. He was a bit concerned about what Isalia might do. After all, she had mysteriously severed her friendship with a Mrs. Tinkerton, a friend of 30 years, and that had been over a discussion of what color car she should buy. Mrs. Tinkerton had suggested the color red, but Isalia insisted on the color grey, and a grey car is what she bought, against her friend's suggestion.

For some time, Roland had known that the Quevalos were against Felipe, being in competition with him, but he never thought it would go so far that their cousin Isalia would approach Roland and literally order him to cease any dealings with Felipe! And who was Isalia to call that order? She didn't even know Felipe, let alone if what she said was true or not. The whole discussion made Roland have second thoughts about Isalia, a woman who had been a good friend to Roland and his parents for 17 years now. What motives did the

Quevalos have, or Isalia, or both, to attempt to wreck the friendship Roland had with Felipe? Roland didn't know, but what he did know for a fact was that Felipe had a good reputation, apart from the Quevalo's opinion. Felipe had never failed to pay Roland for the wood he had brought him, and he showed sincere appreciation. Plus, he was kind enough to allow Raul and Rigo to take days off work to go do things with Roland. In actual fact, Felipe was a kind, caring, and understanding man, who was, as best as Roland could tell . . . *honest*.

Roland thought back to March when Isalia and Clayton had sat Roland down and pleaded with him not to return to Bustamante for three years, and Isalia had told Roland that Raul didn't want him, among other comments. Until 1997, Isalia had never been this way, and now with her orders about Felipe, what was going on? Was there a malign force awakening or at work in Bustamante?

Roland visited others in town, and then he went over to Raul's house. Rigo and Juan Carlos, who also worked at Felipe's carpentry business, were outside talking to each other. They had gotten into a small skirmish at work and had thrown a couple of things at each other. Juan Carlos had come to Rigo to make amends, and they were talking over the whole incident, working it out. Rigo was entirely reasonable and talked through the problem like a mature man. So did Juan Carlos. Roland, without telling them, observed their negotiating skills at work, and he saw them as decent, straightforward and sincere fellows.

A little while later, he returned to the Orolizo's house, where he visited with Pegaso's parents, Nacho and Chela. At 8:30 PM, Raul and Angelo approached Roland. They wanted a ride to Villaldama so they could attend a dance there tonight. Roland decided to do them the favor, and he took them. Rigo came along also.

At first, Raul and Angelo were only going to be a little while, to peek inside and then leave. Rigo waited with Roland in the truck. Roland decided to mention to Rigo that it was possible that he was a brother in spirit. Rigo agreed it may very well be true. Half an hour went by. Roland stepped down, walked to the dance social center, and found Raul and Angelo. They said they were staying and would get a ride back to Bustamante much later. Roland returned to his truck and took Rigo home.

He spent the next day in town, went by Felipe's carpentry, and visited Raul and Juan Carlos. Rigo was at school at the time. Roland even helped them sand some chairs. At mid day, Raul had Roland over for lunch again.

Angelo's little brother Hugo had his birthday today, October 31, 1997. He was 12. Roland found a wooden toy truck from a vendor on foot by chance, bought it, and gave it to Hugo that evening.

Then Roland went to the plaza with Rigo and Angelo, who were becoming good friends. While they were there, a friend of Raul's came over to talk to them. His name was Roberto Enriquez, and he went by the common name of Beto. He was a friendly fellow, and he wanted to go up in the mountains to camp. He wondered if Roland would take him.

Later Roland, Rigo and Angelo returned to Raul and Rigo's house. Rigo and Angelo soon walked off together to do something else. Roland stayed and talked to Lavinia who said she and Isalia had been talking. They talked about all the trouble that had taken place back in July, and Isalia had told Lavinia that "Rolando necesita mucho cariño" (needs a lot of loving). Roland, having spent more than his fair share of childhood alone, felt somewhat deprived for friends. Lavinia was understanding to that and would see what she could do.

Norma and Irma were home, and they wanted to go visit their "Aunt Isalia" and "Uncle

Luke." Lavinia told them that she was too exhausted to take them. She didn't want them going alone, since they were ages 11 and 6. Roland offered to escort them over there, and Lavinia said that would be fine, except Alejandro might get angry. Then she thought about it. Her husband, who didn't work, was away at the cantina drinking. With that thought about her husband, she gave consent. What's it going to hurt, anyway?

Roland, Norma and Irma walked over to Isalia and Luke's. They visited on their front porch for half an hour. Luke was back to his friendly self, and so was Isalia. Roland told them in English, "First date." Luke and Isalia smiled, knowing that Norma didn't understand what Roland said in English.

"You know, everything's going great this trip. That book you loaned me sure must have worked."

"Keep thinking positive."

"That I will indeed. Have a good evening."

As Roland began to leave, Isalia said, "Roland, no matter what happens, I will always love you. You're like a son to me."

"Thanks, Isalia. So, no hard feelings about the other day?"

Isalia responded, "Let's all think positive and forgive."

"Good, I will," said Roland. "Have a good evening."

He walked Norma and Irma back home.

The next day, Saturday, Jesús Lucio took Roland with Raul and Angelo over to the desert valley on the other side of the mountains. They went to see another section of paintings at Chiquihuitillos. They had a great time. The section they saw this time differed in style from what they had seen back in March. Roland didn't know why, but the paintings seemed strangely familiar, and they seemed to depict an ancient epoch of technology. They probably had to do with Atlantis.

They stopped by Lucio's ranch on the way back, and he fed his cattle and did other chores. Then they returned to Bustamante. Roland gave Raul and Angelo N$40 each for the time they had spent with him.

That afternoon, Roland and Raul visited at his house. They listened to music on the radio. There was a really good song called "Chicas Chic" by a group of young fellows called *Mercurio*. He decided to later buy that CD.

Roland and Raul later talked about hiking and camping and going to the United States one day. Raul really wanted to go see California, and he and Roland talked about driving out there sometime in the future. They dreamed on and dreamed on, and they enjoyed talking about it. Who knows? Maybe they actually would travel out there together some summer.

Raul asked Roland if he could bring back that *esclava de plata* to give back to him. Roland told him if he will stay away from drinking and smoking, he would bring it back to him. That esclava de plata represented Roland's being Raul's padrino, and with that, he had a little bit of right to give advice to Raul.

They talked and visited a while longer. It was miraculous. Roland and Raul were good friends just like nothing had ever gone wrong. Forgiveness was performed 100%. If there was ever an example of true and complete forgiveness, this was it: the friendship between Raul and Roland.

Roland also brought his clothes over to wash them in the washing machine he had given

Lavinia. Yes, she let him use it, and Norma made a comment that Roland could use the washing machine as if he were in his own house. That was a nice and welcoming comment. After all, Roland had given them the washing machine, with the condition of reserving of his right to continue to use it.

In the evening, Roland bicycled around town and visited various friends. He also went to talk to Isalia and Luke. He told them all about Chiquihuitillos, and they reacted with interest. He also told Isalia that he and Raul are thinking of travelling out to California sometime.

"There you go again, Roland, He's *not* getting into your country!"

Roland didn't contest her sudden declaration like he did about Felipe, but Isalia's statement was a joy killer and a killer of positive thought! He would have defended his nice trip plans, but he didn't want to risk Isalia saying, "No more communication," which he felt she would have said. As far as Raul getting into the USA, Roland was glad Isalia was going to be wrong about that.

Roland, Isalia and Luke visited for a while longer, talked about other subjects, and then he returned to the Orolizos. Pegaso had arrived for the weekend. He was studying for a test and did not go to the dance. He and Roland talked with interest about the ancient paintings at Chiquihuitillos, and Pegaso showed him a book that had some of those same symbols in it. He wanted to go see the paintings, as well.

November 2 was Día de los Muertos, (Day of the Dead Ones), and it was a custom in Mexico to go to the cemeteries and visit loved ones who had passed away. People gathered and placed flowers on graves and performed rituals and ceremonies in respect for those ones who had passed. Roland took Raul and Pegaso over to Sabinas Hidalgo, and they saw the crowd of cars and people as they passed by the cemetery of Villaldama.

They visited the flea market in Sabinas Hidalgo. On the way back, they saw Luke and Isalia's white truck parked at a restaurant. Roland stopped, and he, Pegaso, and Raul walked inside to say hi to them. Pancho was with them, and they all said hi. Isalia offered them some of their food and to sit down and join them, which they did for a little while.

Before returning to Bustamante, Roland filled up with gasoline at a Pemex station. He always bought Magna Sin, after the low octane experience with his Fairlane station wagon back in 1991. As the attendant filled the tank, Roland realized that there was no Gasolina Nova. What they offered was Magna Sin and Premium. Roland asked the attendant, and he informed him that two weeks ago, they discontinued it. Well done, Pemex! Finally, and good riddance!

As it turned out, Roland stayed in Bustamante one more week. The Orolizo family was very kind and obliging to let Roland stay there, and he appreciated it. The week went very well indeed. Raul and Roland went up in the mountains one day. They got along with each other great, and they even walked by the spot where they had camped back in July. Thank goodness it went well, because this would be the final time they would ever go hiking in the mountains together.

They went to Sabinas Hidalgo the next day, and Roberto (Beto) Enriquez came along also. They did several errands, including Garza Morton, the flea market, and they ate at the taco restaurant. Then they went by the Prepa and collected Rigo and Pablo. There were now five of them, and was it ever a tight fit in Roland's truck cab. They visited the Turbina, a waterfall and swimming hole, and they visited the Ojo del Agua park on the west side of town.

Then they returned to Bustamante. Later in the afternoon, they drove to the Ojo del Aqua in the canyon, where they ate some snacks and took a swim. It was a nice and sunny day, and it wouldn't be long before cold weather would be arriving. Roland, Raul, Rigo, Beto, and Pablo enjoyed it. They all played like children and raced each other in swimming contests.

All in all, it had been an excellent day, and Raul and Beto commented likewise. Roland was grateful.

Lavinia told Roland he could come over and sleep tonight. She offered him to sleep in the same room with Raul and Rigo, which surprised Roland, after her comment back in July that he could never sleep in the same room with her family again. He decided to take her up on her offer, and that would correct the wrong done back in July.

Roland went over to the Orolizos, got his pillow and a few things, and he came back over. In the room where Raul and Rigo slept, there were two beds. The three of them: Raul, Roland and Rigo talked for a while and then drifted off to sleep. In the middle of the night, Lavinia turned on the light to observe them. She was proud of them and that the past wrongdoing was being corrected.

Morning came. Rigo got up and left the house to go to school between 5 and 6 AM. Near 8 AM, Raul got up to go to Felipe's to work. Roland got up simultaneously and returned to the Orolizos.

Beto Enriquez was supposed to go camping with Roland tonight. He didn't arrive. Roland loaded his backpack and at 11 AM, he took off hiking up the mountains. He hiked up to the highland forest and then made his way north to the grassy saddle where he pitched his tent.

He drifted off to sleep, feeling so happy to have his friends back, especially Raul. Roland felt truly appreciated and properly wanted. In fact, he felt loved by the Zacatón family. The awful incident of July was put where it belonged, in the past and also in the trash. How great it felt to forget that awful July event forever, forgive, and to now proceed with a great friendship with that family.

Roland really had become close friends with Raul and Rigo, and it made no difference that they were 16 and 17 years apart in age, respectively. The fact was that they had an inner understanding for one another, which could best be described as a sense that made them feel like they had known each other since time began. In a sense, Roland felt like he had found some younger brothers. Plus, Roland had a feeling that Raul and Rigo were going to be his future brothers-in-law, and Norma would make a great wife, as well. Of course, she was still a child, but Roland would happily wait 9 or 10 years, since he was in no hurry, anyway. Roland had triumphed. He had succeeded in making some good friends, and he really felt joy and happiness. Halleluyah! What a great family he had found!

That night, he had a dream that a young fairy woman visited him. Her name was Sorianis, and she told him about Psalms 6:26 of the *Holy Bible*. It had been cut from the *Bible* many years ago, and the Psalm stated: *Follow your own heart's desire. There are several routes to choose from. You won't go wrong.*

Clouds came in overnight. Fog was everywhere. Roland packed up his tent and hiked back down the mountain. Luckily, he had hiked through the highland forest several times, and he had no trouble finding his way back to the cono at the foot of the mountain.

Roland went over to Isalia and Luke's, and Isalia, with Lavinia being a witness at Isalia's request, gave Roland the $100 in an envelope that said "With Great Appreciation!" This was the money Isalia had agreed to pay Roland for the rental of the trailer. Luke had loaned Roland a flashlight, and he returned it to him with thanks.

Isalia and Luke were going to visit Esalina and her son Guillermo in Monterrey for a few days and Roland said goodbye to them, in case they would still be away from Bustamante when Roland would leave and go home.

Later in the evening, Roland went over to Raul and Rigo's house to visit.

Manuel was visiting, and he hadn't been able to pay Roland for the two tires he had brought him. Raul told Manuel to pay Roland for the tires, and Manuel got irritated at Raul for charging in place of Roland. Roland needed the money for those tires he had purchased. It would be several months before Manuel would be able to pay Roland. Roland observed what Raul did, and he told him thanks. Of course, Roland recalled the time back in March when he had charged Pancho for what he owed Raul and Raul had gotten so angry! Roland wasn't one to be egotistical, but he had to admit that he was a whole lot nicer about it than Raul had been. Roland was a truly nice person who helped others when asked to do so, and what he deserved was love and appreciation from people. He had certainly been of immense help to Isalia and Luke with those two trailer cargos, and of immense help to Raul and Rigo's family, as well.

Also at Raul's house, Roland went to look up Psalms 6:26 and to his amazement, the numbers didn't go up that high. That Psalm certainly was not in the *Bible*. A shame it wasn't because it was a good Psalm.

Alejandro needed to go to Villaldama, so Roland gave him a lift. He returned to Bustamante and found Rigo and Pablo near the center of town, and he gave them a lift home.

Rigo stayed with Roland, and he helped him collect some tossed out square shaped rocks to take back home with him. Rigo wanted to learn how to drive, so under Roland's instruction, he drove his truck. Rigo learned fast and he had a content smile on his face as he drove slowly up the road in first gear. He thanked Roland for the chance to drive his truck.

Roland spend three more days in town, enjoying his friends. One night they went over to Potrero on a Tlacuache hunt (a hunt for opossums).

Another evening Roland took Rigo and Angelo over to Villaldama. Angelo came out of the house, having just put on perfume or cologne, and he got in the truck with Roland and Rigo. Immediately the putrid smell went right up Roland's nostrils, and he stepped down, telling Angelo he couldn't take him along with perfume. He asked Angelo to change his shirt, and he did, but only reluctantly. A few minutes later he came back out of his house, and they went to Villaldama.

No matter what, for the brief time Angelo, all perfumed, had sat in Roland's truck, some of it had gotten on the seat. Later on, Roland had to wipe down the seat, seatbelts and doors with a wet rag and fab detergent to cut the awful perfume residual odor! Five times Roland had to wipe down that seat and the interior and the doors. There, finally! The nauseating perfume was gone!

Pegaso came home another weekend, and he and Roland enjoyed their time with their friends. It was amazing indeed. Roland felt just like one of them. He fit right in. He was realizing that he was now so fluent in Spanish that he never had to think in English to communicate. What good friends they were: Raul, Rigo, Angelo and Pegaso. Raul's new friend, Beto Enriquez was quickly gaining the same friendship status with Roland.

Roland made a wooden tablet that said the Spanish words for: *True Friendships, Happiness, Wealth, Success,* and he gave it to Raul and Rigo and their family. They appreciated it, and the tablet hung on the wall in their house for several years. Rigo, Lavinia, and Norma and Irma were home when Roland came over to deliver it.

Lavinia and Rigo suddenly remembered to ask Roland if he got their letter. He answered that no, he never received a letter from them. Rigo said he had sent the letter around three weeks ago, a week before Roland had arrived to Bustamante. Roland said perhaps it was at home now waiting for him. Lavinia said Rigo had requested a typewriter in the letter, that he needed one for writing school reports. Roland asked them the common sense question of . . . *Why didn't they use a telephone and call him?* Letters from Mexico can take up to a month to arrive to their destinations in the United States. He told them that eight years ago, Isalia had given him a typewriter, the one she used in Spanish class. He would bring that one and give it to his good friend Rigo.

The Zacatóns were in the process of looking for another house to rent and live in. The Cantu family had raised their rent to N$450 per month so they would vacate the house. They needed to do some restoration on it and sell it. Roland wanted to buy it, but unfortunately, he just couldn't muster up the $8,000. He really had wanted to buy it. Finding another house to rent was somewhat difficult in Bustamante. Yes, there were vacant houses, but most of them were run down shacks with twice as many cockroaches as where they presently lived, in addition to ants! He wished them luck.

Roland stopped by the Quevalos to say goodbye. The oldest daughter Lola told Roland there was something Isalia and Luke wanted him to take home to Tennessee, and to keep it in his house until they would return in March. Roland said he would be glad to. Lola went inside the house and came back outside with a beautiful framed piece of needlework. It measured 20 by 30 inches in size. When Isalia and Luke would arrive home, Roland would take it to them.

On Sunday morning, November 9, Roland was packed and ready to leave. He was sad to go home. He went to Raul and Rigo's house to say goodbye to them and his family. Raul asked Roland to come back soon and he named a date, December 12. Rigo placed his hand on Roland's shoulder and asked Roland to stay another day. "Monday, yes, Monday," they said. Rigo asked Roland to come with him to Felipe's carpentry to chat with him while he did a little work, making up for lost time. How could Roland say no? They wanted him to stay.

Roland and Rigo walked over to the carpentry, and he and Rigo talked about various experiences. Roland related some strange experiences he had had over the years, including some coincidences. Rigo listened with interest, and he asked Roland to tell some more stories, which he did. Rigo told Roland, "Nunca me ha pasado una coincidencia," saying that he had never experienced a coincidence. Famous last words, Rigo!

Roland didn't know it then, but there was a major coincidence on the platter, scheduled on the road you might say, between him and Rigo that had yet to come to pass. Roland would definitely be finding out later, and so would Rigo.

They talked a while longer. Roland enjoyed knowing Rigo. He was calm and reasonable. Perhaps Roland would become better friends with Rigo than with Raul.

In the afternoon, they went to the Orolizo's house. Roland saw Esalina and Guillermo's

GMC Jimmy parked in front of Isalia and Luke's rental house up the street. Roland, Rigo and Pegaso walked up there. Roland said hi to them and to Esalina, Guillermo, and his fiancée. He asked if they could enter and visit a few minutes. Isalia hesitated, asked Esalina what she thought, and then said that would be all right. A little strange, Isalia's hesitation, but nevertheless they entered. Roland introduced Rigo and Pegaso to the first homestay family he ever had in Mexico.

Esalina was glad to see Roland and meet his friends. Guillermo greeted them, then stepped outside to talk with Luke in English. Esalina was complimentary of Roland and how he had a phenomenal memory. Pegaso and Rigo had both made comments earlier about Roland's memory.

Before leaving, Roland took a picture of everyone. Something still wasn't quite right about Guillermo. Why was he outside talking to Luke instead of visiting with Roland? Surely he didn't still have grudges against Roland for his having walked in his underwear from the shower to the bedroom, back when he had stayed with them in 1983. Guillermo had a different look this time. He looked tired and sleepy. Maybe his fiancée would perk him up after getting married.

The date scheduled for the wedding was August 7, 1998. A grand wedding it was going to be. Guillermo and his mother had it all planned out in exquisite detail. Guillermo had asked Isalia to attend and had given her the grand honor of sitting by his mother's side at the wedding ceremony, since she and Esalina were like sisters. Isalia was flattered at the honor, and she definitely had plans on attending. Being absent would be unthinkable.

Roland, Rigo and Pegaso wished them well, said goodbye, and they walked back to the Orolizo's house. Later that evening, when Esalina, Guillermo and his fiancée had returned to Monterrey, Roland went to talk to Isalia and Luke one last time. He told them how great things had gone, and he thanked Isalia for having made him aware of the book, *The Power of Your Subconscious Mind*. Isalia told Roland how important thinking positive was. Luke was learning the way of Mexican culture, though it was difficult at times, but they were thinking positive. Roland told Isalia and Luke that he considered Raul and Rigo like brothers.

"And let me tell you, Roland," said Isalia, "Luke and I are thinking more and more positively every day, but at times it's difficult. Sometimes the negative *still* comes through."

"That book is an excellent book," said Roland.

"Oh, it is, and no matter what happens, I'll always love you," stated Isalia.

She and Luke also asked Roland to take some flower tubers (five of them) and plant them at their entrance and to also collect four gallons of clear varnish to bring to them in December. Roland agreed to it. They said goodbye, and he spent the final night at the Orolizo's house.

The next morning, he got up early, went to Raul and Rigo's house, said goodbye to them, and gave Rigo a lift to the plaza to catch the school bus to Sabinas Hidalgo. Then he returned to the Orolizos where he loaded his truck and connected his trailer. He said goodbye to Pegaso who was leaving to catch the bus to Monterrey. Roland thanked the Orolizos and drove out of town, headed for Dallas.

Customs gave Roland an easy inspection.

He stayed with his cousins in Dallas that night. They had a nice visit, and he told them how great everything went in Mexico.

The next day, he drove home to Tennessee.

The Second Cargo

There was a nice surprise awaiting Roland when he got home, a dial telephone from Italy! His friend Elton from Utah had sent it to him. What a nice gift! Roland called Elton on the phone and told him, "Bless your soul for sending me that phone from Italy," and he thanked him. Elton said he was glad to do it. He and his family had been travelling over there back in the summer, and knowing that Roland liked to collect telephones, they had found him one at a second hand store.

Roland told his parents and several friends about his stay and all the great news that went with it. They were happy for Roland. So was his friend Ivanhoe in Scotland, and he really hoped . . . really hoped that it was genuine. Roland said he felt for certain it was.

Also awaiting Roland when he got home was Rigo's letter. It had the strangest handwriting on the envelope, poorly written and done in two colors of ink because the first pen had evidently gone dry right as they were addressing the envelope. The name in the upper left of the envelope was not Rigo Zacatón. It was Lavinia de Zacatón, his mother. Roland opened the envelope with curiosity, and he was quite surprised to see that the handwriting was done by a child, perhaps Norma. It was full of misspellings and bad grammar, and words varied greatly in height and size from sentence to sentence. It was written as if Rigo wrote it because it was in his *voice*. Yes, he requested a typewriter, and the letter also stated to Roland that Raul was no longer angry and that he was welcome to come and stay.

Roland had been home a couple of hours. He called the Gonzalez family, Raul and Rigo's neighbors. Rigo came to the phone a couple of minutes later, and Roland told him he got his letter. He asked Rigo who wrote it. He answered that it was Norma. Rigo had dictated it to her and said she needed practice in writing letters, so that's why she wrote it. He told Rigo he would bring him the typewriter in December. They wished each other well, and they hung up.

Roland couldn't help but wonder, *Why didn't Rigo write the letter himself?* Didn't Rigo know how to write? After all, he was nearly 15 and was in the Prepa, and he was training to be a school teacher. Roland never forgot that strange letter, and much later, he would put two and two together and figure out why Rigo didn't write it.

The next day, Roland went over to Isalia's and he strategically planted the five flower tubers, just as she had asked him. Strange, she had asked him to. Why was she so enthralled by what in Tennessee was a noxious weed in barnyards? He also collected the four gallons of varnish and took them home. He would take them to Mexico next month in December.

Roland had some work to do. During the month he was at home, he did work for different clients, including Elizabeth. She said it was just great how everything had gone so well for him. He had brought home a rocking chair, made by Felipe's workers, and Elizabeth bought it.

Future Horizons was holding an autism convention in Nashville one Saturday. Roland took some boxes of his book compilation and calendars, and he sold 150 copies, the most he had ever sold in one day. Parents of autistic children were very intrigued that Roland Jocelyn, who had autistic traits as a child, had pulled through so well, done exceptional artwork, and had successfully compiled a book and several calendars. One woman said, "How can I resist?" and she bought several copies. A very successful day, Roland would attend several more Future Horizons conventions in the years to come.

Roland visited his relatives in Tullahoma and in Nashville. They were glad to know things had gone so well in Mexico, after what had happened in July. His cousin David was glad also, and he told Roland that any time he was in town, to stop by and visit. Roland felt fortunate to have such decent cousins. He appreciated them and he offered his cousins David and John a trip to Savage Gulf State Natural Area to go hiking this coming spring. They would see what they could do.

Yes, Roland appreciated and he appreciated. He appreciated his cousins, his friends, and of course, his friends in Mexico. He thought good things about them in more ways than one. Roland called Raul on the phone one day at lunch. Raul was glad to hear from him, and he asked Roland how soon he could come back to Bustamante. Raul suggested December 12, and then he went on to suggest an earlier day in December.

On December 1, around three weeks after Roland had returned home, he had a rather disturbing dream about Isalia and Luke.

In the dream, they were looking at parts in what seemed to be some sort of junkyard. Suddenly, Isalia picked up a long metal object and pointed it at Roland. She gave him a very mean look. Roland was quite taken aback, and he asked her what that was all about and if she was still a friend . . .

Suddenly, Roland woke up. He was sweaty and feeling nervous! He remembered their discussion about Felipe and how she had suddenly blurted out that they wouldn't communicate anymore. Of course, it was just a dream, but even still, it concerned Roland. Even though Isalia had said, "No more communication," that was just for the moment. After all, she had assured Roland that no matter what happens, she would always love him, like a son. Plus, she had continued to talk to Roland until the time he had left to come home. With those thoughts processed, Roland eased his mind and went back to sleep. It had just been a bad dream and nothing more than that.

Yes, Roland wanted to spend the winter in Mexico. He had some good ideas for some more paintings. Plus, he could enjoy more time with his friends. He really missed them.

A couple of days before leaving, Isalia's granddaughter Missy called and said Isalia and Luke had called her and told her to call Roland and tell him not to take anything. *Oh my goodness! The dream!* Roland thought. He told her to tell Isalia and Luke that he had already been by there, collected the cans of varnish, and that they were already loaded in the car ready to go with him to Mexico. He asked her why they had called her. She didn't have an answer. Something strange was going on, and Roland knew it. Had it not been for that dream, he would have been a lot more surprised.

On the 10th of December, he drove his Ford LTD station wagon to Mexico, stopping by his cousins in Louisiana and also spending the night with Isalia's cousins north of Laredo.

Mexican Customs let Roland enter easily enough, and he even got to bring in his Black Cypress-Pine from Australia. In just over two hours, he was driving into Bustamante. Snow was falling, and further south toward Monterrey, it snowed several inches.

His first stop was Raul and Rigo's house. They were still in the same house. Raul and Rigo came outside, and they happily welcomed their friend Roland inside to eat lunch and stay with them.

Roland brought his things in, including the Black Cypress-Pine. That was going to Daniel Mata.

It was December 12, and Raul told Roland he thought he was coming today. He asked Roland if he had brought the *esclava de plata*. Yes he had. Raul and Rigo helped Roland bring everything inside. He handed Raul the esclava de plata. Isalia's typewriter was still out in the car. He brought that in, placed it on the washing machine in the kitchen, and he told Rigo it was his. Rigo looked at it, observed it, and tried out some typing on a piece of paper. Back in 1989 when Isalia had given it to Roland, she had told him she thought he deserved it. Now Roland was passing it on to Rigo, who he thought now deserved it. It would serve him well in school.

Raul and Rigo said they might be moving tomorrow. Roland asked them if they could stay in the same house a while longer. Their parents had not been able to pay rent. Roland offered to pay that for them if they would stay on in this house. Raul appreciated that, and he told Roland he was their salvation.

About that time, Alejandro walked in with his bicycle. The car was without gasoline. He was staggering drunk, and he had a real complacent look on his face. He greeted Roland and then lost his balance, catching himself against the wall.

"¡Vamos!" said Raul, advising Roland that they leave. "Anda boracho," saying that Alejandro was staggering drunk. They quickly left the house.

Raul and Rigo got in the car with Roland, and they drove down to the Cantu's store in the plaza. There, Roland gave the Cantu family N$450.

Next, they drove up to Isalia and Luke's rental house. They were both there, and so were Lavinia, Norma and Irma. Roland, Raul and Rigo brought in the four gallons of varnish. There was a gas heater going inside. Isalia had on a night robe. She had not been feeling well. She had been suffering from stomach pain. They greeted Roland and asked him if he could help Lavinia with the move tomorrow. Raul then told his mother and sisters the good news.

Isalia told Roland they were grateful to him for having brought the varnish.

Luke explained that they had called Isalia's granddaughter to intervene and ask Roland not to take anything because they decided they didn't want Roland to trouble himself over it, and they might be the wrong cans. Roland assured them it was right where they said it was, in the yellow covered trailer outside Clayton's shop, and they were indeed the right cans.

Isalia asked Roland if he had planted the flower tubers, and he said that yes, he had.

"Okay, well . . . we'll see if they take to and grow," Isalia commented. She had remembered the flower tubers. They must have been more important than Roland realized.

With that, Raul, Rigo and Roland walked out of the house, got into Roland's car, and he drove them to Sabinas Hidalgo to do errands. Raul commented to Roland that Isalia didn't look very happy. Roland really hoped his December 1 dream had just been a dream, but now hearing Raul's observation, he knew there was more to that dream than its just being a dream. He told Raul and Rigo he wasn't surprised by Isalia's sullenness, and he told them about the disturbing dream he had two weeks ago. Plus, he had the phone call from Isalia's granddaughter to ponder.

It was a cold day. All the hills were covered in ice, and the clouds were lying low. They arrived in Sabinas Hidalgo, visited Garza Morton, visited the tape and CD store, and visited Raul and Rigo's uncle, as well. They returned to Bustamante by evening, and they went looking for a house for rent.

Even though Roland had helped them with the rent, Lavinia wanted to move, especially since the Cantus had the house for sale. Raul's friend Manuel had a house for rent, as it turned out, but it was too small for them, plus Manuel's family didn't want to remove their furniture.

CHAPTER 9

THE TRIP TO ZACATECAS

December 1997

That night, as they were eating supper, Raul and Rigo proposed plans of Roland's taking them and their friends on a major trip to Pinos, Zacatecas to visit Alejandro and Lavinia's relatives and Lavinia's parents. Raul and Rigo told Roland various stories from their native homeland in the state of Zacatecas.

Raul and Rigo were not originally from Bustamante, even though they had lived there for the past eight years. Before they moved to Bustamante, they lived on a beautiful remote ranch located in the middle of the Mexican highlands in the state of Zacatecas. There were no native trees, except for the Palma Real trees, and also the large Nopal plants (*Opuntia lindheimeri*) which in Zacatecas, grew to the size of small trees. In the past, Eucalyptus trees had been brought in from Australia, and they could be seen in the town of San Miguel a few kilometers from their ranch.

Raul and Rigo said they and their parents used to live with their grandparents on a large estate ranch situated at least a kilometer off the road. The terrain was beautiful, and their father and grandfather used to farm it by growing various beans and running goats and cattle. It was hard work, but it was a peaceful and tranquil lifestyle.

Fifteen kilometers away was Pinos, a small town the same size as Bustamante, and it was situated on the southwestern slopes of a dry, treeless mountain towering above the surrounding plains. They used to go there for supplies and ride with their grandfather in his pickup truck. Each time he went, he would take his cylindrical shaped LP gas tank and have it filled. In town, he would buy them toys and give them treats, and they used to go visit their relatives.

They lived in an adobe house built in the configuration of the letter U, and to go from one room to the next, you had to go outside, since the rooms were not connected by interior doors. There was no electricity nor running water. They didn't even have telephone service. Nearby, there was a spring that seeped out of a small hillside, and their mother and grandmother spent a lot of time there, collecting water from a hand dug well and washing clothes. Their aunts and cousins would gather there and gossip about life as they washed their clothes on washing boards, after which they would hang them to dry on the spines of Nopal plants.

One of their aunts used to enjoy playing hide and seek with them, and they used to run up and down the narrow dirt lane and hide behind Nopal bushes. Those were good days for Raul and Rigo, and they had good memories of those times.

It was eight years ago that their father, Alejandro, got offered a good position at a large chicken ranch ten kilometers outside of Bustamante, and he moved up there, taking his wife and children with him. Raul and Rigo longed for the days of their childhood, and they missed their homeland. They had not been back to Zacatecas since the time they had moved away from there.

Roland enjoyed listening to their story. He said he would take them there. He was interested in going himself, and they decided they would drive down there on the 18th.

Raul and Rigo invited Roland to sleep in the same room with them. They could talk about Zacatecas as they drifted off to sleep. For the next six nights, Roland slept in the same room with them, until they would drive down to Zacatecas. They made Roland feel welcome, just like part of the family.

This was really great. Roland had found his family in Mexico. They were his favorites, and Raul and Rigo really were like brothers. He sincerely appreciated them.

The next day was sunny with a cold north wind. Raul wanted to go to Monterrey, and Beto came along with them. Roland drove them along the highway. Halfway to Monterrey, there was around four inches of snow on the ground. Roland pulled over, and he, Raul and Beto played in the snow. They threw snowballs at each other. It was the only snowball fight Roland ever had in Mexico. They had the best time and plenty of laughs.

They got back in the car, hands cold, and drove on to Monterrey. Raul drove part of the way. They visited the Macroplaza, where Roland bought some CDs including *Mercurio*, with their song "Chicas Chic". They visited the flea markets in central Monterrey, the Gigante store, and then drove back toward Bustamante.

Roland decided to talk to Raul about the issue of smoking. Raul had told Roland that he doesn't like to smoke, but the fact was that Raul didn't say that he does *not* smoke. Roland explained that smoking was just *not* something good to do. Raul got defensive and told Roland that not even his father corrects him on issues like that. Roland told Raul that his father should come forth and talk to his children about that, and Roland reminded Raul that since he was his padrino, he did indeed have a little right to talk to Raul about it and give his advice to stay away from tobacco and liquor. Raul saw some reason with that, said that he had smoked on occasion, and Roland pointed out to Raul that if he didn't like to smoke, then *don't* smoke. Simple as that.

When they came to the turnoff for Potrero, Raul requested that Roland drive into the town, which he did. Raul, Roland soon realized, had special interests in Potrero, and he would be bringing Raul here several more times. Raul was a sociable type and he had prospective girlfriends in Bustamante, Villaldama, and in Potrero. Finally, more than an hour later, Raul and Beto were ready, and they returned to Bustamante after dark.

Roland went to say hi to the Orolizo family. Pegaso had arrived. He was home for Christmas holidays. He was glad to see Roland and asked him how things had gone. They visited for a while. Pegaso wanted to go see Chiquihuitillos, and Roland said he would see what he could do. He also told Pegaso that Raul and Rigo wanted to go to Zacatecas. Pegaso expressed interest in coming along.

Raul and Rigo went to the baile. Roland went to sleep at 10:30 PM. Raul and Rigo got in at 2:30 AM.

The next day, Roland took Raul, Rigo, Angelo, Pegaso, and Beto to Sabinas Hidalgo. They visited the flea market and then ate out at the taco restaurant. Roland treated them all to lunch. For so many, it was rather costly. They went to visit Raul and Rigo's uncle and family, and they also visited one of Angelo's aunts, a friendly but rather outspoken young woman who had spunk.

Her name was Nancy, and at her request, Roland took all of them on a cruise of the strip, the stretch of the Carretera National, the main highway through town. It was getting dark, and everybody was doing the same thing, as Roland soon found out! Traffic was terribly congested and slow! Roland drove the stretch one time and took her home. It would be the only time he would drive that stretch at night. They returned to Bustamante.

That evening, Roland imitated Alejandro to Raul, Rigo, Lavinia and Norma. They all got a good laugh as Roland imitated the staggering. Later that night, Alejandro arrived, and Norma, in front of her father, asked Roland to imitate him. Roland declined and said that would offend her father, but she insisted. Roland asked Alejandro if that was okay. He said no problem. So, Roland did the staggering act again. Alejandro had a good laugh. He asked Roland to do it again, so he did. The whole family roared with laughter!

With a few trusted friends, Roland had joked that Alejandro works out, that he does weights . . . with caguamas (940 ml beer bottles) as he drinks them. He and other friends had enjoyed some good laughs. One night back in the summer, Alejandro had "worked out" too hard, and he couldn't even make it from the car into the house. He was asleep, drunk on the sidewalk.

Monday was very clear and warm sunny weather. Roland quickly decided to hike up in the mountains to go to the Cypress Ridge for more photos. He left at 8 AM from the cono. In places, there was snow on the ground, and in the highland forest, there was 3 to 4 inches on the forest floor. He hiked up the ridge, which was somewhat treacherous with snow, and the views were indeed excellent. To the southeast, he thought he could see the Gulf of Mexico, well over 160 kilometers away, and he could see parts of Texas to the north, way in the distance.

It was perfectly quiet up here, except for one lone honeybee buzzing annoyingly. That was a little surprising, seeing there was snow on the ground. At least the bee didn't sting.

Roland made the several hours' descent back to the cono. He felt really content with the day.

He found some flowers growing, and since he knew that Isalia and Luke would be getting married next week, he dug them up for Isalia. When he got back to town, he stopped by their house and called out her name. She came out from the house. He told her he had brought her some flowers as a wedding present and that they were from the mountains. Since Isalia liked flower gardening, she thanked Roland. She asked him how things were going for him and where he was staying. He told her he was at Raul and Rigo's house and that things were going fine.

The next day, Raul, Beto and Roland spent the day together. In the early afternoon, they went by Isalia and Luke's. Raul needed to talk to his mother Lavinia about something. They casually entered the premises, and Lavinia asked them not to enter the patio (yard and premises). She told them that Isalia had ordered her not to let anyone enter, or Isalia would scold her.

Roland felt taken aback. So did Lavinia's own son Raul. Raul commented to Beto and Roland about how untrusting Isalia and Luke had become. Roland decided he was going to go talk to Isalia and Luke and get the truth from them, straight up. What was going on? Why were Isalia and Luke cooling off with Roland? He asked Raul and Beto what they thought he should do. Both suggested that he go talk to them.

Roland drove them over to the Quevalos. Both Isalia and Luke were there. Raul and Beto waited in Roland's car while he entered the Quevalo's premises. Luke was in Pancho's workshop in the backyard, and he was looking over the equipment, all now installed and in working order. There were various sanding machines in place along with routers and guides for making tongue and groove lumber. They had quite a wood shop installed, and Pancho and his workers were busy making chairs. None of them paid any attention to Roland, let alone say hi to him. Luke ignored Roland entirely.

Isalia walked over to sit with the Quevalos near the kitchen. She was ignoring Roland's presence. Roland was waiting for an opportunity to talk to her, but she was busy talking to the Quevalo sisters. After several minutes of waiting, Roland finally interrupted and blurted out, "Isalia, can I talk to you?"

". . . About what?" she responded, finally.

"About you and me," Roland told her.

"I don't want to talk to you!" she suddenly blurted out.

"What?!"

"We're not going to communicate anymore. It's over, Roland!"

"You have got to be kidding! Look, I've only been your friend. I brought two trailer loads down here for you."

"You charged me," Isalia told Roland with an expression of accusation and disgust.

"No, I didn't! You only paid me for the gasoline, and at your offering."

She started to walk off, and Roland followed her a few steps to continue talking.

She turned around. "Don't follow me!" she shouted at Roland.

"Isalia, I had a dream a couple of weeks ago that you gave me an angry look, and I told you I only wanted to be a friend, but now I see your anger is for real."

"It's over, Roland!" she declared emphatically. "I don't need you in my world!"

"Isalia, that is thinking negative. I haven't done anything to you, and I just gave you some flowers for your wedding."

"You can dig 'em up if you like."

"No, I don't do that. I'm not an Indian giver."

"Roland, I don't need you in my world!" she repeated. "Don't follow me! Don't bother me!"

"Well, good riddance, Isalia!" Roland angrily declared. "That book you told me about, *The Power of Your Subconscious Mind*, read it again."

Roland walked away, feeling hurt and rejected. A friend of 17 years, how in the world could she have done that? She had such a wretched look on her face. As he walked through the Quevalo's vending area, they asked Roland what had just happened. Since Roland and Isalia had their final conversation in English, the Quevalos hadn't understood what they said, but they sensed something was very wrong.

"Isalia me rechazó," Roland told them, saying that Isalia had rejected him. The Quevalos were surprised.

Roland walked to his car, where his two friends, Raul and Beto were waiting for him. He told them it was even worse than he had suspected. His dream had spoken the truth to him, only it was worse. Roland thanked Raul, and also Beto, for being friends of his. He shook hands with them. He started his car and drove away, taking Beto and Raul to their houses.

Roland took his Black Cypress-Pine over to Daniel Mata's house. He was very glad to receive such an exotic gift, all the way from Australia. Raul was with him, and Daniel invited them both inside to visit a little while.

That night, Roland went over to the Quevalos to ask them why Isalia and Luke had taken such a mysterious rejection of him. India was there at the vendor's area. She told Roland he had lost a great friendship with Isalia and Luke, and she gave Roland the impression that he had done something very very wrong and had offended them. Roland insisted that he hadn't done anything wrong. With a somewhat stern look, she told him, "Pronto vas a saber," telling Roland that he would soon know why. She didn't tell him what it was.

Also, India recommended that Roland no longer associate with the Zacatón family. Roland explained that Raul and Rigo were his friends, like brothers to him, and India said, "Pura conveniencia," saying that they were only friends of convenience.

Roland answered, "Como quiera, estoy disfrutando mi tiempo con ellos," that no matter what, he was enjoying his time with them.

Later that night, Rigo and Roland went over to Angelo's house to see if he wanted to go to Zacatecas with them. His parents weren't going to let him, and with that, Rigo said he wasn't going to Zacatecas, since Angelo couldn't go. So, Roland intervened to change the situation. He went to talk to Angelo's parents to ask them to let Angelo come along. His father asked Roland to pay for Angelo's food because Angelo had no money. Roland said he would do so. With that, Angelo's parents consented, and Angelo was granted permission. Now, most importantly, Rigo was able to come along. After all, for Roland, unless Rigo came along, the trip was off. Both Raul and Rigo had to come along for Roland to make the long trip, since it was Raul and Rigo's family they were going to visit.

The next morning, Raul and Rigo loaded their stuff into Roland's car. Roland brought along $120 to pay for the trip. Pegaso and Angelo came over, each with exactly two meals in a lunch sack, and no more. Beto also came along. The six of them left at 10 AM. They made a stop in Potrero at Raul's request, then proceeded, driving through Saltillo and Concepción del Oro. Roland let Raul drive part of the way.

The next part of the highway straightened and crossed a huge flat plain of desert plants, Mesquites, and various Cactus shrubs, including one variety called Coyonoxtle. For nearly 300 kilometers the highway headed southwest to the city of Zacatecas. Finally, just short of Zacatecas, they turned left and took other highways over to Pinos, arriving at 10 PM.

There were small businesses on both sides of the road and a Pemex station on the left, the only fuel station in town. They crossed a bridge, and the road narrowed as they entered the central district with streets lined by She-Oak trees, Eucalypts, and tall narrow Cypress trees.

They entered the town center at the plaza with a cathedral on their right on the downhill side. Large Cypress trees grew in the plaza's interior grounds, and park benches lined its perimeter. The whole plaza, actually the whole town, was perched on a sloping hillside with the bottom of Pinos at the foot of the mountain where it touched the desert plains.

The whole region was at a high altitude, more than 2,500 meters (nearly 9,000 feet). Most of Zacatecas sat on the high desert plains in central Mexico, and not far to the west of them was the continental divide.

Raul asked some people if they knew his uncle, Antonio, and if they knew where he lived. It wasn't long before he found someone who knew him, and he gave Raul directions.

Raul directed Roland to take the narrow street by the cathedral, and he drove them down the somewhat steep street to the lower part of town. When they neared their uncle's house, Raul and Rigo recognized it. Roland parked on the streetside while Raul went to the door and knocked.

His uncle Antonio ran a motorcycle mechanic's garage. Antonio, who was in his house beside his garage, came to the door and opened it.

"Ah, sí, mi sobrino. ¿Cómo estás?" Antonio greeted him, recognizing Raul and asking how he and Rigo were doing. "Pasa con tus amigos," he said to Raul, telling him to bring Rigo and his friends and come inside.

Raul motioned all of them to enter. Everyone got out of the car and walked inside.

Antonio pulled up some chairs for them to have seats. He called for his wife to come forward from the back of the house where their kitchen was. Her name was Eustolia. Both of them greeted Raul and his brother, followed by everyone else. They talked and visited for a while. Raul did most of the talking, and he and Rigo related to them their recent adventures and their trip down from Bustamante.

Antonio's wife, Eustolia, soon returned to what she was doing in the kitchen. He now led them across the street to another building. It belonged to his brother-in-law. He opened the door to the front room, and there were several double beds inside, enough to sleep all six of them. Antonio told them they were welcome to sleep here during their stay in Pinos.

With that, he left them to it and said for them to come over tomorrow morning to eat breakfast with them, and he walked back across the street. Raul and Rigo started preparing the beds while the other four took their bags out of Roland's car and brought them inside the room.

The exhaustion had caught up with them after the long drive today. They lay down on the beds and relaxed. Some of them talked, and some of them fell asleep. Before they realized it, all of them had drifted off to sleep.

The next morning was cold and sunny. They awoke to the sound of Antonio and his mechanic starting and running a motorcycle engine. Antonio and his wife Eustolia had all six of them over for breakfast.

Then they drove out of town to the ranch called San Miguel to visit Raul and Rigo's relatives and grandparents. Raul gave Roland directions. In a short distance after leaving Antonio's house, they were at the edge of Pinos at the bottom of the mountain. Roland turned left on the highway, and they proceeded for several kilometers, after which they turned left on a rough dirt road that took them to the village of San Miguel. He had to drive slowly, as no section of the road was smooth.

As they were on their way, Raul decided to shout at Roland unexpectedly and quite to Roland's surprise! Roland barked back, ordering Raul not to treat him that way! Raul asked Roland if he wanted him to get out and walk, and Roland told him that would be fine. Raul stepped outside, and since he did, Beto stepped outside to accompany him. Roland drove on 100 meters, stopped, questioned Rigo, Pegaso and Angelo about what he should do, and he backed up for them. Several times, Roland asked Raul and Beto to get back inside, but they wanted to walk. Both of them walked back to Pinos.

Roland drove on to San Miguel along the bumpy dirt road. Rigo told Roland that he, Pegaso and Angelo were his friends and would travel with him in the future. When they arrived, they were greeted by various aunts and uncles on both sides of Raul and Rigo's family. They were glad to see them, and they commented on how handsome they were.

After visiting relatives in San Miguel for the day they returned to Pinos in the afternoon. Raul and Beto were at Antonio's house. Roland talked to them, and he directed his comment more toward Raul, telling him he wanted to be his friend but that he kept making it difficult. Raul was that way at times, temperamental with flare ups, and it made it difficult to be his friend. Rigo was calmer and more easy going, and Roland's friendship to date had been easier with him. Rigo was indeed a good friend and was one of Roland's favorites.

The six of them visited with Antonio's family and later took a walk to the central plaza. Raul and Beto, more than the others, started up conversations with some of the young girls.

Roland felt a bad cold coming on. He hadn't slept well, being in the company of the others, all six of them sleeping in the same room across from Antonio's house. Plus, walking in the snow-covered forest up above Bustamante the other day hadn't helped matters. He returned to get some sleep. Half an hour later, the other five returned.

Roland was still somewhat in a state of shock about his Spanish teacher Isalia's rejection of him. He was pondering, *Why in the world did she reject me?* He talked to the others about it, and he mentioned to Rigo the absurdity of Isalia severing a friendship of 17 years over whether or not Felipe was a *ratero* (crook). Of course, Roland knew Felipe was a decent honest man, and he knew he had done the right thing to defend him to Isalia. Pegaso and Angelo suggested to Roland to just forget about it and move on, but Roland was stubborn. He was going to figure this one out, even if it took a year or two of thought! Isalia never liked stubborn people, but there are times when being stubborn is beneficial and rewarding to the person who is stubborn and persists.

The next day they returned to San Miguel, and they proceeded on to Rancho El Conejo. This time Raul and Beto successfully stayed with them. Roland drove on through San Miguel, and they proceeded for another two kilometers to the entrance of the ranch.

After turning left, Roland drove them for a kilometer down the narrow dirt lane. The scenery was truly beautiful here in the rural Mexican highlands of Zacatecas. Although the terrain was in one respect generally flat, there were some rolling hills. Further in the distance, they could see some small mountains clearly visible and standing above the terrain. No trees grew on them, but their colors of beige, brown, and red made them appear to stand out.

Like Raul and Rigo had told them, there were beautiful Palma Real trees here and there, along with some of the largest Nopal shrubs they had ever seen. Some of them were indeed the size of small trees. There were also some large Maguey plants, and some of them were in full bloom.

Roland drove them down through a gully and up the other side, and they pulled up to the adobe ranch estate of Raul and Rigo's grandparents. There were many goats, a few dogs, and chickens that ran loose everywhere. Their grandfather, Arturo, heard them arrive, and he stepped outside. Their grandmother, whose name was Eliza, soon followed, making her appearance from within the U-shaped enclosure of the adobe buildings.

The whole house showed signs of age and was in much need of repair. All of the cement had fallen off the walls, exposing every one of the brown dirt adobe blocks. The roof was basically flat and was also made out of adobe blocks resting on top of numerous horizontal poles made out of Maguey bloom stalks.

Arturo and Eliza were pleasantly surprised to see their grandsons.

Raul and Rigo were the first ones to step out of Roland's car. "Abuelitos," Raul called out, saying Grandparents.

"Son nuestros nietos," Arturo said to his wife, commenting that they were their grandchildren.

Eliza and Arturo walked over to them, glad to see them. They gave each other hugs, and they invited them and their four friends to come inside. All of them got out of the car and walked inside, following Raul, Rigo, and their grandparents.

They talked about the fact that it had been a long time since they had seen them, and they commented that they were no longer children and were now grown up.

Raul handed his grandparents a letter his mother Lavinia had written them. They read their daughter's letter with interest and laughed at some of her comments about Raul, Rigo, Norma and Irma. They talked about life here at the ranch, and Raul and Rigo told them how things were going for them in Bustamante.

After visiting for a while, Arturo and Eliza took them over to a neighboring house so Raul and Rigo could also visit with their aunt Catalina. Arturo and Eliza also had a son, their oldest, who still lived on the ranch. His name was Miguel, and he had a son named Ramiro, who was a year older than Raul. All of them were glad to see each other, and they talked about what they had been doing since they had last seen each other.

Soon Arturo, Miguel, and Ramiro had to go to the back of the farm to harvest beans for the rest of the day. They invited them to walk back there later to see their operation. Meanwhile, Eliza and Catalina took everyone to the spring. Raul and Rigo laughed with their aunt as they reminisced about their childhood days when she used to play hide and seek with them among the Nopal bushes.

While Eliza and Catalina tended to some washing by the spring, Raul and Rigo took Roland, Beto, Angelo and Pegaso on a tour through the Nopal bushes, and they went up and down the hillsides of the gully on the narrow, winding dirt lanes. They told them childhood stories of how they used to play with their cousin, Ramiro, and also with more cousins from San Miguel and Pinos. Those were fun days for Raul and Rigo, and they wished they had never left this place. It was great to be back in their homeland again.

They spent a couple of hours walking around and exploring the ranch. Then they walked to the back of the farm and found Arturo, his son, and grandson tending to a crop of beans. They talked for a while, and then Raul and Rigo took them to another area where they used to run and play. The back of the farm had another gully which was a deep dry creek bed. It had steep banks and dropoffs in some places.

Rigo showed them his favorite climbing tree, a large Nopal. Rigo, Angelo and Pegaso climbed up into the large shrub, being careful not to be stuck by the spines on the thick, succulent leaves. They waved to everyone below them in the gully where they were exploring. Afterwards they climbed back down and caught up with the others who were now on their way back to where Arturo, Miguel, and Ramiro were working.

They were nearly ready to return to the house for lunch. A few minutes later, they dropped what they were doing, and all of them walked the half kilometer back to the house. Arturo and Eliza had a small woods of Nopal trees on the east side of their house, and they walked through those woods on the way back. It felt really strange to be walking underneath those strange plants with their branches overhanging the multiple paths made by the goats that ran through there.

Eliza was in the kitchen preparing lunch. The LP gas tank was empty, so she was cooking over a fire. The kitchen was in the back portion of the U-shaped house, and access to it was through a low door. Actually, each room of the house was accessed through a low door from the outside. The kitchen walls were jet black from years of fireplace smoke and soot. There was no running water, nor was there a sink. Water was obtained from the spring down the lane. Also, there was no electricity. Another feature of the kitchen was that every ledge was occupied with brush, firewood, and twigs. Chickens entered and left as they pleased, and they were sometimes a nuisance the way they would walk in looking for food scraps and then leave in a fluster when Eliza would run them off.

Eliza gathered up enough bowls and served them all lunch. Roland and his friends along with Raul and Rigo took seats on some of the dilapidated chairs in the kitchen. Others remained standing. Two of their dogs came up to the kitchen entrance, hoping to be thrown a few morsels of food.

They finished lunch, and Arturo announced that they were going back to work. He told Raul and Rigo that it was great to see them. With that, Arturo, Miguel, and Ramiro said goodbye to them, wished them a safe journey back to Bustamante, and they returned to the back of the farm.

All of them thanked Eliza for the lunch. She wished Raul and Rigo well, told them it was great to see them, and said goodbye to them. Everyone walked to Roland's car and climbed in. Catalina happened to come down the lane at that moment, and she walked over to them.

"Que les vaya bien," she said to Raul, Rigo and their friends, wishing them well.

They said goodbye to her.

Roland started the engine, and he drove them back to the San Miguel Road.

They visited some more relatives in San Miguel before returning to Pinos that night.

On the way back to Pinos, Roland's car began sputtering, and it worried him. That evening, he checked over his car and couldn't figure it out. Antonio's son Pablo came to him and checked the spark plugs. One of them was defective and not firing.

The six of them walked to the plaza, and Roland bought them some chicharones. He was about out of money, and he realized he hadn't brought enough. He had $60 left, but most of that was gasoline money to return to Bustamante. Roland remembered Angelo's father's comment about his son not having money, and Roland wished he'd brought more money. In fact, Rigo mentioned that. Why hadn't the others packed more food when they all left Bustamante? Now they were hungry, and Roland felt for them.

The next morning was Sunday. Roland went to a ferretería and bought spark plugs. He replaced his fouled spark plug, and his car's performance was restored. He replaced the other five plugs, as well. Then he and Rigo took it for a small test drive. Roland let Rigo drive his car. Rigo was a bit more nervous than Raul, but he did quite well.

Antonio and Estolia fed all of them lunch and supper. All of them started becoming ill. Roland had been the first one with a bad cold, and it had now spread to the others. In the middle of the night, Roland had to step outside to throw up twice, first time he had thrown up in 11 years.

On Monday morning, everyone said goodbye to Antonio and his family, and Roland, though he felt quite ill, drove them away. Raul was the only one who was not ill, and Roland let him drive more than 50% of the trip back home. Beto, Pegaso and Angelo were suffering from the flu, and they were very quiet in the back seat, so different from their liveliness on their way to Pinos the other day.

It was 10:30 PM when they arrived in Bustamante.

The next day was Christmas Eve, and it was a day of recovery for everyone, except Raul, who became ill with a bad cold. Rigo wasn't so happy with Roland anymore, and he blamed him for having pegged everyone else with his bad cold in the first place.

CHAPTER 10

THE GREEN BOX SCANDAL

late December 1997

On Christmas morning, Roland gave Raul and Rigo an old Voigtlander camera he had bought some time ago from a camera shop in Tullahoma. They were pleased to receive it, and they were feeling better. Roland took Raul, Rigo, and Beto over to Sabinas Hidalgo to visit the flea markets and the plaza. They visited some of Alejandro's relatives. One of them ran a radio and TV repair shop in central Sabinas Hidalgo.

That evening, Raul was out somewhere with friends, and Roland was talking to Lavinia and Rigo about why Isalia had taken such a mysterious rejection to him. He was telling them it was so strange, that he couldn't figure it out.

Lavinia finally came forth to admit something. "Roland, yo no te iba a decir, pero India me dijo que Isalia y Luke les faltaron cosas," telling Roland that she wasn't going to say anything about it, but the other day India had mentioned to Lavinia that Isalia and Luke were missing some items . . . from the June trailer cargo that Roland had brought to the Quevalos.

Roland looked at Lavinia with surprise and concern and asked her how that could be.

"Pues, la caja verde que regalaste a Raul," Lavinia pointed out, reminding Roland of the green box of Luke's that he had given to Raul instead of to the Quevalos.

"Ohhh . . ." Roland reacted. He had completely forgotten about the green box. So, *that's* what India was going to tell Roland!

Lavinia went on to mention that Isalia and Luke were so angry at Roland about missing some items that they didn't want to talk to him again.

Roland asked them if they already knew specifically about the green box.

Lavinia answered that no, they didn't. She said they had come over to visit during Thanksgiving in late November, but they hadn't ventured into the back room where the green box was stored, thank goodness.

"Lavinia, tengo que decirles," said Roland, telling Lavinia he was going to have to go tell Isalia and Luke and to make things right and straighten out the misunderstanding.

"No . . . No!" Lavinia quickly said and fervently.

Roland wanted to know why not.

Lavinia said they couldn't tell. For one, her job with Isalia and Luke was at stake. Plus, she already knew the two of them well enough to know that they were not the reasonable type. She explained to Roland that if he went over to Isalia and Luke to explain the misunderstanding, Isalia would take him straight to the police, have him arrested, and the police would likely haul him off to the federal prison in Monterrey for five years! Lavinia pleaded fervently with Roland not to say anything because Isalia and Luke could accuse Alejandro and Lavinia of being accomplices, for having kept that box of knick knacks.

"Haz de cuenta que no vas a decir nada a nadie," Lavinia told Roland, telling him not to say anything to anybody concerning that green box. Rigo chimed in and in a very straightforward manner, stressed the importance to Roland to keep his mouth shut about that green box.

Lavinia went on to say that they were protecting him. If Roland were to tell, he would be severing his own fate. Isalia and Luke would have Roland arrested, and Lavinia stated that she would not rescue Roland from the jail under that situation. Roland promised them he would never tell anybody about the green box, and he never did. After Lavinia and her son Rigo drove the points home about the importance of not telling, he obeyed their wishes for his own safety, and for theirs.

Roland asked them what they were going to do with the box. What if Isalia and Luke came to visit again and happened to see it? Lavinia said she was going to hide the contents in an old feed sack. Again, Roland asked her about the box itself, and she answered that it was just a green plastic box. How would they ever know? Roland calmly pointed out that the box had the words OAK RIDGE RECYCLING stamped on it in white letters.

"Ohhh . . . Uhhh . . . !" Lavinia reacted with a look of alarm on her face! Now, she was worried!

Roland mulled it over in his mind. The box only had knick knacks, nothing of importance. Now he finally had a reasonable answer as to why Isalia and Luke had rejected him. Lavinia explained that right at the end of November, Isalia and Luke inventoried all the items, and they came up short. Isalia, as a result, had felt so awful, so tricked, that she couldn't bring herself to call Roland and ask him if he delivered everything.

Instead, on December 1, Roland had his nightmarish and mysterious dream of Isalia's pointing a metal object at him and glaring at him in anger!

Lavinia explained that Isalia became quite ill with a stomach virus for the next week, and she had a lot of anger at Roland. As Lavinia worked for Isalia and Luke, she received all of Isalia's negative comments about Roland for that whole time period. Poor Lavinia.

Roland now realized how lucky the situations were that he hadn't already let the cat out of the bag. When he had approached Isalia last week, she somehow didn't accuse him of stealing nor did she mention any missing items, only that he had charged her. When he went to the Quevalos that evening, India had only mentioned that Roland would soon know why. Plus, he had tried unsuccessfully to find Pancho at home, and he most certainly would have told Roland about some missing items, at which time Roland would have remembered the green box and would have told. Whew! Somehow, the sequence of events and timing had never brought the details of the green box forth into conversation. What coincidental and miraculous luck that was indeed!

Roland would go and talk to Pancho and Lorenzo as soon as possible tomorrow, and he now knew not to say anything at all about the green box.

Though Roland never knew it, there was another detail that occurred between Lavinia and Isalia, a confidential conversation. Back in early November Lavinia had invited Roland to sleep in the same room with Raul and Rigo, and again for the six nights before their trip to Zacatecas, reversing her July decision of never again doing so, for *more* than just genuine reasons. Isalia had taken Lavinia to one side back on October 27, and she quietly slipped her US $50 to invite Roland to sleep with Raul and Rigo. She had asked Lavinia to be very discreet about it, to not let on that anything was being conjured up, and then report back to Isalia. Now, Isalia didn't realize it, but in the room where Raul, Rigo and Roland slept, there were two beds, and Raul and Rigo were in one of them.

It was for the above secret between Isalia and Lavinia that they had been so welcoming to Roland, and they used that high level of welcoming to their advantage, knowing that it would greatly increase Roland's chances of saying yes to taking Lavinia's sons to Zacatecas.

The Green Box Scandal

Make the visitor, Roland, feel at home like one of the family, and he will likely do more for us, was what Lavinia thought, and it was their philosophy, as well. It worked like a charm, and Roland took her sons to Zacatecas. Lavinia was grateful, also.

It was now at this time that they asked Roland to set up his own bed and roll pad in the spare room where he used to sleep. They didn't tell Roland why, but he knew. They assured him he was still welcome, and they explained that their reasons for sending Roland back to the spare room to sleep had to do with the bad colds they were suffering, and since Roland was still sneezing some, they didn't want any contamination. Roland didn't have any problem with it. He already got what he wanted, the reversal of Lavinia's July decision, even if it was just temporary.

*   *   *

Meanwhile, behind Roland's back, two months earlier: **October 26, 1997**

It had now been a few days since Isalia and Luke had arrived in Bustamante. It was already dark, and at the moment, they were driving back to their rental house on the other side of town. They had been visiting and chatting with the Quevalos this evening. They were enjoying their stay very much, and Luke found Isalia's cousins really outgoing and funny. In his view, they had a great sense of humor. Isalia felt on cloud nine with her new man. After all, her past husband Clayton had died six months earlier, and it felt so good to her to be with Luke now. Though he had a sense of firmness about him, he was a kind and caring man to Isalia, and she was reveling in the delight of his feelings and protection toward her.

They had been talking with the Quevalos about Roland and his friendship with Raul, and all of them were amazed at how the two of them had fixed their friendship so well that it was as if the problems of the past summer had not even occurred. They had absolutely no grudges whatsoever. Even though Isalia's family and roots were from Bustamante, she didn't always understand the usage of words, and the Quevalos had made some comments about Roland and Raul that made Isalia begin to wonder if there were more things going on than just a good friendship.

"Luke, isn't it just great how Roland and Raul have made up and become good friends again," Isalia told her fiancé.

"Yes, that's good," he agreed. "After all, Raul's just growing up."

"I'm really happy for them," she commented.

"What all did the Quevalos say about Raul and Roland?" Luke asked her, since he didn't understand nor speak Spanish, and therefore had not understood what the Quevalos had said.

"Well, India was commenting how it was a true miracle about how Raul and Roland forgave each other. She said they took to each other very soon after meeting and became good friends. He looks upon Roland as a guiding light. Lavinia was telling me that Raul appreciates Roland a lot."

"You know," Luke decided to mention. "I think Roland is gay, Isalia."

Such a blunt comment came as a complete surprise to Isalia. She could feel the "truth" of his words, and a chill went down her back. Her face suddenly changed, and her mouth started to feel dry. Tingling sensations could be felt in her fingers and hands.

"Uh, how . . . Luke?" she finally managed to ask.

"Isalia, I know my sudden comment comes as a total shock to you, but we need to view the truth of the situation, here."

"Like what?"

"Well, I mean think about how Roland went on and on about Raul after their falling out this past summer. You saw how grief stricken he was."

"Yes, but that's just the way Roland is. I've known him for more than 16 years. Friendships mean a lot to him."

"Look, I've served as a guidance counselor for teenagers for several years, as you know," Luke pointed out, "and I understand them very well. Normal guys just don't make such a fuss nor worry about friendships like Roland does."

"Well, Raul means a lot to him," Isalia stated.

"Which is a trait of being gay," said Luke, adding to her comment. "I mean, look at the situation. Roland is twice Raul's age, and don't you think it unusual for a man Roland's age to come here and visit a . . . young boy?"

With that said, more chills went down Isalia's back. Nervous energies were within her, and she felt beside herself. The "truth" rang out in her, and Luke's final comment drove the point home and reminded her of the comment Clayton had said seven months earlier when she and Clayton had sat Roland down and urged him not to return to Bustamante back in March. She had told Roland that she knew he wasn't gay, but that the town might think so. Now, she was beginning to wonder. Maybe Roland really was gay. In addition to that, her love for Luke was so complete that she couldn't go against his speculation.

"Oh my god," she commented. "Oh my God!" she said more strongly. "Oh, my GOD!!" she yelled. She was beginning to freak out.

"Isalia, calm down!" Luke firmly told her. "It's okay. It's okay."

"No, it's not okay, Luke!" Isalia snapped back. "I hadn't really considered it before. Oh, Dios mío! Oh, Dios mío!" she repeated in Spanish several times, trying to come to terms with what she now believed to be the truth.

"Isalia, calm down," Luke told her again.

"Luke, we've got to do something!" she declared.

"Don't worry, we'll figure something out," he assured her.

"Luke, I can't continue to know him . . . Not now!"

"I know it's hard to take, Isalia, but we've got to see if we can prove it."

By now they were pulling up in front of their rental house. As they stepped out of their truck and walked into the house, they continued to talk about it.

"So, how are we going to prove it?" Isalia said to Luke.

"Start by talking to Lavinia," he suggested.

"Okay, I'll have a word with her, but how am I going to brush him off?" She had to figure out some way to get Roland out of her life and keep a lid on this whole thing.

Luke thought for a minute, but before he said anything, Isalia came up with an idea. "I know. Let's talk to Roland about Felipe. You remember how Pancho was telling us how Roland almost got arrested by U.S. Customs when he helped Felipe take that trailer cargo of chairs and tables to San Antonio. I think it's best if Roland not do dealings with him anymore. After all, the Quevalos have told us several stories of his dishonesty. Roland and Felipe are on good terms with each other, and Roland will probably defend him. He and I will disagree, and I'll sever it *right then.*"

The Green Box Scandal

"That's a good start," Luke agreed, "but if that doesn't work, we'll just make up a story that we're missing some items from that trailer cargo Roland . . ."

Luke and Isalia continued talking and making plans in efforts to sort out the problem at hand.

For the whole evening, she was under such shock that she felt beside herself. Roland, who she had known for so long and thought so much of, just couldn't be gay. Now she was thinking differently. Isalia had a real intolerance for gays. After all, she had a high ranking gung ho son in the military, and her husband Clayton had also served in the military and was a righteous man of good credentials.

Though Luke had said nothing of it, he had taken a dislike to Roland, as well. Even though Roland had helped with bringing two of his trailer cargos to Isalia's cousins, that project had been completed, and Roland had already been of use to them. It was now safe to brush Roland off, and Luke had an idea of how he was going to do it.

It was the next day when Isalia approached Lavinia and slipped her that US $50.

Over the intervening weeks, Isalia also had some detailed discussions with Pancho to find out what was really going on? Pancho, being the mentiroso type that he was (lier), told Isalia some whoppers and tall tales about how Roland and Raul were "in love" and the "real reason" they had gone up into the mountains so many times was to "make out." He even went on to say that Roland performed various *ceremonies* and *rituals* while up in the mountains. Pancho, though his claims were entirely false, made his stories sound so believable that Isalia's hair was standing up on the back of her neck! Pancho had a very poisonous tongue indeed! As a result, Isalia also had some very inappropriate dreams about Roland and Raul.

*   *   *

The next morning was the day after Christmas. Roland went to the Quevalos to talk to Pancho about why Isalia and Luke had rejected him. He indeed found Pancho in the backyard, making chairs. Pancho told Roland that they were missing items from the trailer cargo of June and that Isalia and Luke thought Roland had stolen them. Thankfully, Roland had been primed the night before by Lavinia and Rigo, and he showed surprise to Pancho.

"Pancho, no agarré nada. Entregué todo," Roland said, telling Pancho he didn't take anything and that he delivered everything. (Yes, Roland did indeed deliver everything, even the green box, except that it was delivered to Raul instead.)

Pancho responded by saying they were missing three pulidoras (sanding machines) and a mandril (jackshaft). Roland told Pancho he definitely didn't take those items, and he told him the fact that he didn't even remember seeing any pulidoras. However, there might have been a mandril on board. Without saying anything to Pancho, Roland had confirmation that Isalia and Luke hadn't even thought about the green box, much less miss the items, seeing they were blaming Roland, via Pancho, for taking three pulidoras and a mandril, none of which were in that green box of knick knacks he had casually given to Raul. Roland was safe to declare that he didn't take anything, and he was also safe to say that perhaps some items got stolen in route, likely at the Colombia Bridge when he and Pancho went inside to pay duties. Roland suggested that possibility to Pancho, and he agreed that could have been very possible, especially concerning the missing mandril.

Pancho assured Roland he was very grateful and content with what was brought, and he couldn't fully understand why Isalia and Luke had taken such rejection to Roland. Pancho mentioned that there was a valuable lesson to be learned. Don't trust anyone, not even your best friend when hauling goods for them. Make out a detailed list of items and take before-and-after photos of everything, so they would have no room to make false accusations. Pancho decided to call Isalia who, with Luke, was in Monterrey at Esalina's house. Pancho told Isalia that Roland said he didn't steal the items. Isalia answered that Roland had never stolen from her before, at her house, nor the whole time he'd known her, but her wording, according to how Pancho later told him, showed that she still believed Roland stole some of the trailer cargo!

Since Isalia was accusing Roland of stealing, couldn't she and Luke have at least gotten the missing items *right*? A missing green box! Roland honestly didn't remember seeing three pulidoras nor a mandril on the cargo at all, and he thought that perhaps those items were still at their place in Tennessee. Since Isalia and Luke had gotten the missing items wrong, Roland knew they had made it up and that there must have been some other underlying and more subtle reason(s) for their rejection of Roland.

The missing trailer cargo was just an excuse to cover up the real reasons, or perhaps the Quevalos had already sold some of the items, thereby innocently causing Isalia and Luke to think they had never arrived, and therefore must have been stolen by Roland! What ill logic Isalia had, if she really honestly believed that Roland had stolen from her, but if there was some other more subtle underlying reason for the rejection, then the ill logic made perfect sense . . . as an excuse for rejection! Isalia thought Roland was gay!

Roland now realized that Isalia and Luke were mean and dishonest people who didn't want to reason nor work out a misunderstanding. If they really were good people, they would have been straightforward and would have called Roland in late November to directly ask him if he lost any cargo in route or if he kept anything. They did nothing of the kind, which furthered the reality that they made up the whole conspiracy and were now trying to frame him!

Roland told Pancho thank you for making that call to Isalia. He assured him again that he didn't take anything, and he walked away, confused by the whole mess. He returned to Raul and Rigo's house and ate lunch.

Rigo was very grumpy, and Roland asked him if he was angry with him. Rigo answered that he wasn't. Raul was giving Roland a cold shoulder today. How strange! Roland asked them what was going on.

Roland walked into the spare room. He looked over at the green box . . . but it wasn't there anymore! So, he called out to Lavinia who came in from the kitchen, and he asked her what happened to the green box. Had she hidden it? She answered that she had just burned it out in the backyard an hour ago. She had slid it into a big feed sack, taken it outside, covered it with grass and limbs, and had lit a match to it! She had put all of the contents in another feed sack and had hidden them in a large cylindrical shaped cardboard food storage container. Lavinia had covered her tracks and her fears, and she had protected her sons, as well.

Roland would have preferred to have talked with Isalia and Luke to clear the whole misunderstanding, but seeing how strangely unreasonable they had been acting recently, being straightforward was no longer an option. Lavinia, under the circumstances, and with her job and sons' reputations at stake, had no other choice than to burn the green box and hide its contents.

Roland went around town on his bicycle visiting different friends. Daniel Mata had already planted the Black Cypress-Pine, and it looked good. It would grow successfully into a fine tree.

In the evening, Roland told Raul, Rigo, and Lavinia what Pancho had said. Roland assured them he had said nothing of the green box. Raul seemed indifferent to the whole matter. He went to the front room to listen to the stereo.

The next day was Raul's birthday, December 27. Neither Raul nor Rigo cared to speak to Roland this morning. So, he moved his stuff over to Pegaso Orolizo's house. Raul and Rigo went to Felipe's to work. The Orolizos happily received Roland.

It was appropriate for Roland to move for another reason. The Zacatón family was about to move to another house in Bustamante. Lavinia had found a place over in the north side of town just a few houses down from Raul's friend, Manuel.

Roland was back over at the Zacatóns, taking the last of his things with him when Raul and Rigo walked home from Felipe's carpentry. It was only 2 PM. Raul told Roland that Felipe had just closed the business till the new year . . . no more work. Raul had a scrape on his arm. He had gotten into a strong scuffle with one of the other workers. Upon entering, Raul explained to Roland that he had nothing against him. He hadn't talked to him this morning because he was just tired. Rigo was more content also.

That evening, the three of them played and wrestled. Beto Enriquez joined in the fun and they all acted like children.

Roland went to Pancho the next morning and asked him if he could use the blue 1981 Ford truck and the trailer (all which Roland brought the Quevalos in 1991) so he could move the Zacatón family to their new location. Pancho loaned the truck and trailer but charged Roland N$50. They spent most of the day moving the items. Isalia and Luke were still in Monterrey, and they therefore did not help one iota with the move. Beto helped them with the moving.

Late that afternoon, Roland talked with Pegaso and Angelo, inviting them to take another trip sometime, to the south of Mexico. They told Roland they were disgusted with him because he didn't give them enough to eat. Roland asked them why they hadn't brought more food in the first place, and he explained that he had to spend nearly the whole $120 on gasoline, leaving less than $40 for food. While Roland had given them food out of his food box, it had not been enough, and he regretted that they were hungry. Thankfully, Raul and Rigo's relatives had given the six of them some meals, as well. No matter what, Pegaso and Angelo did not ever want to take any more trips with Roland.

Roland went over to Raul and Rigo at their new residence and he talked to them about it. They weren't quite so dissatisfied, but they weren't interested in any future trips either. Rigo told Roland he should have brought more money along. Yes, Roland had several hundred more dollars, but that was in reserve for the rest of his stay in Mexico, until February.

Lavinia hadn't realized the hunger the others had, and now she took an untrusting stance and told Roland that she wasn't going to let her sons travel long trips with him anymore, let alone to Australia or England some day. While Lavinia had earlier expressed gratitude at his having carried her sons to Zacatecas, now she was completely different, and she also said she wouldn't have let Raul and Rigo go to Zacatecas with Roland unless Pegaso had been along on the trip!

Roland said the equivalent of: Well, *excuse* me for having taken your sons to Zacatecas!

Lavinia was like that. She went through phases of not trusting people, and then she was fine again. She was rather inconsistent, and she would sometimes worry about what neighbors would say in regards to Roland's friendship with her family. Even though Roland was now staying at the Orolizo's house, Lavinia came around soon enough, and Roland would come over to eat supper with them, at times.

Raul and Rigo became ill with the flu, which followed the bad colds they were having. Alejandro asked Roland to take them over to Villaldama's Centro Salud and doctor's office. The next morning, he took them. While they visited the doctor, Roland drove the few blocks over to Leonardo's house, and he was actually at home, just preparing to leave on a trip with some friends. Roland had not seen him for a full year, because every time Roland had stopped by, Leonardo had been gone or had just left. Leonardo was glad to see Roland and asked him how he'd been. They visited 10 minutes, and Leonardo left on his trip. Roland returned to the doctor's office where Alejandro was outside.

He talked to Alejandro about Lavinia's mistrust, especially concerning Raul and Rigo's one day travelling with Roland to Australia or England. Alejandro said it would be fine with him and that he would have a word with his wife Lavinia about her lack of trust in Roland.

That afternoon, Roland took it easy. He washed clothes in his washing machine he had given to the Zacatóns back in the summer. He wrote in his diary over at the Orolizos where he was staying. He visited with Pegaso and Angelo. Pegaso again expressed interest in seeing Chiquihuitillos, the ancient paintings in the desert valley on the other side of the mountains. They made plans to go sometime next week.

The next morning, Roland drove over to Raul and Rigo's house and offered them a trip to Sabinas Hidalgo. They climbed into Roland's car, and he took them over there. They were feeling better now, after the doctor's medicine. They did several errands and ate at the taco restaurant again. Roland felt really satisfied taking only Raul and Rigo, *without* others as "protectors" like Pegaso or Angelo. Lavinia had not been at home this morning, as she was over at Isalia and Luke's, working. They were back in town from Monterrey. Therefore, Roland took Raul and Rigo *without* permission, thank you very much!

By early afternoon, they returned to Bustamante. When they pulled up in front of the house, there were visitors, none other than Raul and Rigo's brother Eduardo and his wife Millana! They had suddenly shown up, on their way home from Monterrey. Eduardo's little boy, who was age two, was with them, as well.

Raul was thrilled! Roland walked into the house and met Raul's much talked about brother, Eduardo. Why, he was a decent man, friendly enough, and Roland was glad to meet him! He ran for his camera at the Orolizo's house and hurried back, and he took a picture of the entire Zacatón family, a classic picture it would turn out to be.

Lavinia happened to be home for lunch when Eduardo and his family had arrived, and she took the afternoon off! She was glad they had come by.

Lavinia never got after Roland for taking her sons to Sabinas Hidalgo. Roland didn't know it, but Alejandro had already talked to her. She was glad they had returned in time to see Eduardo.

Anyway, Eduardo and his family needed to return to Salado by morning, and since the drive was nearly 500 miles, they decided to leave. Roland heard Eduardo talking to his father Alejandro about Raul, and Alejandro told him that Raul had been quite a night person and had gotten into some scuffles with other teenagers in town on late nights. Eduardo was concerned and started making plans to have Raul moved up to Salado later in the year.

After Eduardo and his family drove away, Roland told Raul that he perceived Eduardo as a decent friendly fellow.

Raul responded, "¿Qué tiene?" meaning, *So what*. He was disappointed because he wanted Roland to be afraid of Eduardo.

Roland had brought a kitchen sink for future use in Mexico, as he had plans of building a house in Bustamante to come stay in, but the fact was that Roland just didn't have the extra $5,000 it would take to buy the materials, land, and labor to make it. Since the Zacatón's new residence had no sink, Roland took it to them and gave it to them, for their having received him at their other house.

In Mexico, it was a common occurrence for a house to be absent of a kitchen sink. In fact, many houses had no sink at all, only a faucet or spicket outside the house, and sometimes not even that. Roland wondered how it was possible that families could live their whole lives without going to the trouble of installing a kitchen sink to make life easier for them. They weren't that hard to install and not that expensive either. Plus, there were plenty of used ones. Another thing that really bothered Roland was the fact that nearly all the houses lacked a decent flushing commode, and they almost never had a commode seat! More than once, Roland had taken commode seats to Mexico to install in the houses where he was staying.

The next day, Roland went over to Felipe's carpentry, although closed, and he used the equipment with Felipe's permission and made a table for the kitchen sink. Demas helped Roland take it over to the Zacatón's house upon completion.

That afternoon, Roland loaded his backpack to go camp up in the mountains. It was New Year's Eve, and he didn't want to be in town during the wild parties and dances. Pegaso wished him well, and Roland made it to the highland forest by 7 PM, half an hour after dark. Since Roland knew the way along the trail he had cleared, he arrived just fine.

The music from the dance could be faintly heard along with the fireworks and explosions at midnight. It was now January 1, 1998, a new year.

Roland got up at the crack of dawn, 7 AM, and he hiked back down the mountain, arriving in Bustamante just before noon. Isalia and Luke were getting married at the Quevalos, and Roland made sure he was going to go to that wedding. He got cleaned up, put on some new jeans, some new Asics Gel 120 tennis shoes, a clean t-shirt, and he bicycled over to the Quevalos in time for the 1 o'clock wedding.

Roland knew Isalia and Luke had long ago invited him to come, but he had a feeling he wasn't welcome to attend, after his recent falling out with Isalia. However, he was going to the wedding for sure, since he had been a friend of 17 years and had helped them immensely by bringing two trailer cargos to her cousins in June and October. He had attendance rights, and even the Orolizos had been invited. Roland looked for the Orolizos right before going to the wedding, but they were gone. They didn't come to the wedding. They had forgotten about it.

A lot of people were attending, including many of the Velazcos from Monterrey. Esalina and her son Guillermo were there, and they were glad to see Roland. Guillermo's sisters were all there along with all their children. Even the tool vendor from Sabinas Hidalgo's flea market was there. It was a grand event, and Lavinia, along with her daughters Norma and Irma, were doing all of the major cooking over a fire, out in the backyard and partially out of sight.

Even Isalia's sister Roma was there from Houston.

Isalia and Luke were inside the main room of the Quevalo's house, getting dolled up for the ceremony. Lorenzo came over to Roland, who was talking to some of the Velazcos, and he informed Roland that Isalia had not invited him. Roland corrected Lorenzo by telling him that yes she did, back in the summer. Lorenzo went on to say to Roland that she didn't want him attending the wedding. He could stay long enough to get some pictures and then he would have to leave. Roland firmly stated that he was staying, and over his dead body would they remove him from the wedding! He told Lorenzo to tell Isalia that he was going to report her orders back to several mutual friends in Tennessee. Lorenzo consented, very well then, go ahead and stay, and Roland stayed.

Roland noticed that the Quevalos, with Isalia and Luke's financial help, had spruced up the area. They had painted the house and walls, and the place looked nicely refurbished.

As everyone was looking on, Isalia and Luke emerged from the back of the house onto the concrete patio. Isalia had an artificial appearance, sure enough, and she had the most joyous, cloud 9 appearance imaginable, like she was walking with the man of ecstasy! Luke had a normal appearance. They took a seat at a table where Pancho and Lorenzo, with the assistance of a pastor, performed the ceremony. Luke signed various documents and agreements.

Roland took several pictures of documentation.

Over to the left were the wedding presents, nearly all of them from the Velazco family. They were exotic gifts: ceramic bells and displays of various adornments . . . *material items*. There was a three-layer cake nearby on another table. Isalia was very quiet and kept her smile of ecstasy on her face through the whole ceremony. She would look over at Luke, with such a smile of dedication and love, every once in a while.

When that was done, Roland retreated to the back area of the yard, where Lavinia, Norma and Irma observed the wedding. This was the area of second class citizens, and Roland felt like one, due to the message Isalia sent to Roland through Lorenzo. Second class citizens did the cooking and preparing of the wedding feast and they were not to be present in the first class area, where all of the Velazcos were and, of course, Isalia's friends.

When another round of pictures was being taken by other photographers, Lavinia urged Roland to go take more pictures, because his Olympus OM-1 camera took excellent sharp pictures. With that, Roland retreated no longer. He got up and joined the others, by golly! All of the Quevalos, every one of them, gathered and Roland took three group photos. He had never seen all of them gathered together at one time, and he made very sure he got several pictures of them.

The wedding feast was served. The Quevalos invited Roland to join in and eat lunch, which he did. He took a seat at the same table as Guillermo, talked with him, and found out how things were going for him. Guillermo looked strangely pale, but otherwise he looked okay. He had his fiancée with him, and they were scheduled to get married August 7 of this year.

Isalia's sister Roma came over to Roland. "What happened?!" she asked Roland. Obviously, Isalia had told her.

"Your sister thinks I stole cargo off the trailer," Roland replied, "but I stole nothing."

"I know you didn't," Roma kindly told him. "I know you're an honest man."

"Thank you."

"You need to *talk* to her," Roma urged him. "Fight for what you believe in."

"I know, but she won't talk to me, and she won't reason with me."

"Then write her a letter and explain."

"Okay, good idea. I will."

"Good man. Don't let her walk all over you," Roma advised him. "Dios above knows the truth. You know you didn't steal anything."

"Thank you, Roma."

She wished him well.

Roland then took pictures of the attendees, a group picture. He also took a picture of Lavinia and her daughters. They were his friends, and he was totally against a class system, quite the contrary to Isalia, who considered herself and Luke to be very important people who were helping the town, and obviously of supreme first class rank.

The truth is, the sun rises for everybody, not just for those of the first class.

Roland talked to the Quevalos about what Roma suggested, and he wanted to talk to Isalia before she and Luke left. Lydia told Roland not to bother them, but to talk to her later. Roland kept quiet and let them leave.

That night, Isalia and Luke stayed at the fanciest hotel, Hostel La Casita, and Roma and her husband stayed at Isalia and Luke's rental house. You can imagine that Isalia reveled in ecstasy with her new man that night, and she certainly wanted the *finest* optimum conditions for just such an occasion.

The next day, when the ecstasy had passed, Isalia couldn't help but think negatively. Roland didn't know it till days later, but she was absolutely furious that he had attended her prize wedding! To her, his presence had jinxed it, even though he never spoke to her at all. Yes, he took pictures, but then other photographers did, too.

She made a phone call to Roland's parents in Tennessee. They were not home at the time she called, and she left a disturbing message.

"Dr. and Mrs. Jocelyn, this is Isalia Wiggins here in Bustamante. Your son *attended* my wedding with Luke yesterday. I asked him to leave, and he stayed, and he took *lots* of pictures! It's as if he was a professional photographer! I told him not to come! Plus, I'm tired of his quirks. If he keeps following me and bothering me, we're going to have to call the *police*. I know you'll understand, at least I hope so . . ."

With that said, she hung up. Her voice had a chill and hollowness in it that Roland's parents had never heard before, and the way she ended the phone call and hung up left his parents hanging, and with chills down their backs when they later listened to the message! That message made Roland's parents angry, not at Roland, but at Isalia!

*   *   *

The next day, Roland went with Pegaso, his sisters, and some of their relatives in a pickup truck to the other side of the mountains to visit Chiquihuitillos. One of them was named Angelita, a woman in her 50's who was also a friend of the Orolizos. Upon reaching Chiquihuitillos, they paid the rancher N$5 each, and they spent several hours there looking at all three sections of paintings on the mesa sidewalls. Pegaso found the paintings interesting, and one section was very interesting indeed.

It had a story specifically for Roland. He stared at it and counted 37½, that is, 37.5

diamonds hanging in seven chains in one depiction, the last three digits in Chip Collins' phone number. Amazing! Coincidences with that guy back in Tennessee were still showing up in Roland's life. Pegaso said that back in the summer when he took that preliminary course at the University of Monterrey, his room number was 375. There was a lot of significance in that depiction for Roland and Chip, and now for Pegaso? What did it all mean? Somehow, Roland hadn't noticed the significance of this set of paintings the two times he had come here before.

They returned to Bustamante, and Roland went to visit Raul and Rigo. He also visited his friend Victor. He wanted to go hiking up in the mountains with Roland. So, he asked his mother and father for permission, and they reluctantly consented, but he would have to be back by 3 PM, so they wouldn't have time to reach the top, nor the highland forest.

The next morning, Roland took Victor in his car at 8 AM to the cono. They had exactly 7 hours, and they made tracks, reaching the highland forest in just over two hours and the grassy saddle in 2½ hours. The clouds were covering the valley to the west, but here on the ridge, the sun shined. Using his self timer, Roland took a picture of both of them, both in the grassy saddle and also in the highland forest.

They made their return by 2 PM, and his mother was quite surprised at his early arrival. As far as she knew, they only went a little bit above the caves. A great day it had been, January 3, 1998.

On the way down the mountain, Victor talked to Roland about Pegaso's sisters, Lumita and Mena. He said they were pretty and attractive. However, he advised Roland not to tell Pegaso that, because he would run him off in a heartbeat! Victor explained that Pegaso was very protective of his sisters, and he told Roland to be careful with him. Roland thought that was strange, and he appreciated Victor's warning. He would make no comment about Lumita or Mena to Pegaso.

A few days later, when Roland developed the pictures, Victor told his parents the truth. They were really surprised, and they were also glad for him. A couple of days later, Victor's legs really were sore from all the hiking.

Roland went to the Quevalos the next day to attempt to talk to Isalia and Luke. They were inside the house. Pancho was in the backyard making chairs, and Roland went to him to ask him to make him three rocking chairs to take home. Then he asked him to accompany him to talk to Isalia and Luke and straighten out the whole misunderstanding. Pancho expressed his fear in doing so and in taking the risk. Isalia might get angry at him, too! After all, they had just brought him all the equipment and he didn't want them getting angry and recollecting it. Roland pleaded with Pancho to help him.

Suddenly, Lola emerged from the bakery. "Pancho! Díle a Rolando que se vaya. Dice Isalia," telling Pancho to tell Roland to leave at once because Isalia said so.

So, now Isalia had set herself up as *Queen of the Quevalos*, telling them what to do, and they better hop to it and do as she says!

Roland told Pancho to forget about the chairs! He'd go have them made by Felipe's people. Pancho told Roland to do as he wished, but he just couldn't cross Isalia and risk losing all she had brought him. Though Pancho had earlier made that one phone call, he had failed to defend Roland now at a very crucial moment. Back when Pancho's sisters had gone hysterical last year and India had gone to the police, Pancho had meekly failed to defend Roland in that crucial moment also, due to fear that they might kick Pancho out of his home. For some reason or another, Pancho had fundamentally failed to defend Roland, and Roland had had enough. He took Pancho's friendship and laid it to one side.

Roland went to the Orolizos and wrote Isalia and Luke a letter. It read as follows:

To: Isalia Ives and Luke Wiggins   January 4th, 1998
From: Roland Jocelyn

It has taken me a while to find out the real reason you brushed me off, Isalia. It was Pancho who told me last week that sometime in November, you discovered or at least thought that you were missing some items that were supposedly on my trailer cargo of June 1997. Pancho told me that they were 3 pulidoras and a mandril of a grinding stone and wirebrush. Pancho and I suspect that the mandril was stolen at the Colombia Bridge when both of us went inside to pay duty and taxes. As for the pulidoras, I promise you, I didn't take them, didn't sell them, nor do I remember your even loading my trailer with any said pulidoras in Tennessee. I think your pulidoras are still in Tennessee, and that you all failed to load my trailer with them. Pulidoras would have had serial numbers, and they are not listed on the list of items.

I did not steal your stuff. As far as I know, everything you loaded on my trailer (except for the above said mandril) arrived to Bustamante, and I immediately delivered all. I don't make a practice of stealing items. My conscience is at stake, and I must keep it clean. I'm strictly honest.

It surprises me and insults my dignity that you were such fair weather friends. Obviously my friendship with you was one of convenience and no more. You sent Lorenzo to tell me to leave your wedding. I felt like a 2nd class citizen. I now realize why that cop pulled me over and ticketed me in Pleasant Hill. I was punished for helping out two malagradecidos.

Isalia, why didn't you come to me when you discovered the discrepancy in November? I knew something was wrong when I had my dream of your giving me an angry glare. My subconscious mind knows the truth. It serves me well. You could have phoned me and asked me, but instead you held it in, thought negative of me, and still have yet to approach me about the missing cargo.

Like I said, I did not steal your stuff, Isalia and Luke, but if you think I did, then I will pay you for the missing items, *after* we are back in Tennessee and *after* you have searched for the pulidoras at your place in Tennessee. My checkbook is in Tennessee, and I will write a check. I hope this will appease you.

I made one mistake. I failed to write a complete list of items down to every last bloody screw and bolt, and I failed to take before-and-after photos of every open box, exposing the items.

This is a bridge you two have burned yourselves, falsely accusing me of stealing! I want my file folder of my writeups returned to me, Isalia. They are none of Luke's business. I also want my signed photo returned to me hanging on your wall, since you are not my friends. You two, Pancho, and I need to have a serious sit down discussion.

Sincerely,
Roland Jocelyn

Roland went over to Raul and Rigo's house to visit in the afternoon. They watched a movie on TV. While he was there, he noticed that the kitchen sink and table were gone. Lavinia told Roland that Luke and Isalia had collected it a couple of days ago, so they could make improvements to it. Wasn't Roland's work good enough?!

While they were watching the movie, Isalia, Luke, and Pancho rolled up in Luke's white pickup truck. Roland and Raul went outside, and he, Pancho and Raul carried the sink and table into the house and placed it in the back room, of which part was the kitchen. They had replaced the entire top that Roland had made. Roland had used Eastern Red Cedar, but Pancho and Luke used Pine, which they sanded and varnished. An insult to Roland's workmanship it was indeed! Though he said nothing, he was not best pleased by the "improvement"!

Neither Luke nor Isalia stepped down from the truck to talk to Roland. Though Roland thought about walking up to the side of the white truck and shouting at her that he didn't steal any trailer cargo, something told him not to. Actually, he was afraid to. The "barrier" was too much for him to "cross".

Pancho got into the truck, and Luke drove them away.

Roland rode over to the Orolizos, got the letter, made copies at a corner store nearby, and took the original by bicycle to Isalia and Luke's place. They had just arrived. Roland rode up to the side gate and called out, "Luke?"

"Oh, hey," Luke responded to Roland, surprisingly in a friendly manner. Then he suddenly remembered, and his face turned angry.

That answered a lot of questions! So, Isalia was the one who had instigated the main rejection, not Luke.

"I've got this letter for you." Roland handed it to Luke. "We'll talk later," and Roland rode away on his bicycle.

Isalia said nothing. She had an angry face.

As Roland rode away, he heard Luke call out, "No talk."

Roland returned to the Orolizos and he hoped Isalia, Luke, and Pancho would soon respond, so they could straighten out the whole mess.

Meanwhile, minutes after Roland hand delivered his explanatory letter, Luke took a chance to begin reading it.

Isalia saw him. "Luke, what did I tell you? We *don't* communicate with Roland."

"Isalia, I'm sorry, but I think it's appropriate to at least read it."

"Tear it up, Luke. It's over between me and Roland. He's gay, I tell you!"

"Yeah, I had thought that, but I don't think Roland's that bad a . . ." He continued looking at Roland's letter.

"Luke, *don't* read the letter!" Isalia snapped.

"Isalia, he's offering to pay us for the missing cargo."

"That's not an option, Luke! You and I know he didn't really steal from us, but we had to cover up the truth."

"Yeah, I know, Isalia, but this has gone far enough. We need to talk to . . ."

"Luke!" she interrupted. "There are some things about Roland that I've never told you. I've known him for 17 years. Let's go inside and talk about it."

"Like what, Isalia?" Luke asked. He folded the letter.

"Tear it up!" she snapped again.

Luke was so flustered by Isalia's commanding ways, and her will power was so strong . . . that he tore Roland's letter up. He would have resisted more, but then he was in Mexico, and since he didn't speak Spanish, he was very much dependent on his wife, Isalia, to translate. Therefore, he obeyed her wishes and did what she said. Yes, Luke had gotten irritated about the seatbelt incident in Sabinas Hidalgo, and while he didn't exactly like Roland, he at least somewhat believed in talking through the problem. Isalia had been the main instigator of the problem, and it was she who urged Luke to provoke the incident in the first place, by not putting on the seatbelt. He began to realize there was a lot of truth buried between them, and now he began to wonder what sort of woman he had just married. He decided to go along with her unreasonable decision, if nothing else to avoid confrontation with his *fourth* wife!

They walked inside, and Isalia began to relate a story from the fall of 1981. "Luke, Roland's of a different sort, a genius in many ways. He has a remarkable amount of energy and intelligence. Back when he was in my Spanish II class, something happened. By the way, it's no accident that he does paintings and artwork, including scenes from alien worlds! Listen, I've kept a lid on it until now, Luke, but there is something about Roland that you don't know . . ." and she told Luke about the day she nearly fainted in class and how she was absent the following day, recovering at home. ". . . I always suspected it was Roland, and after reading all his weird analyses of life in those stories he's loaned me, that file folder, and the *weird* paintings he does, who else could it be?! Things have come together. The *angels above* have made me aware of it, and I've put two and two together, Luke. Never, NEVER am I going to forgive Roland for that incident! It took me 36 hours to put my psyche back together."

One may wonder why Isalia continued to be Roland's friend for 16 more years. Though she suspected Roland was behind the mysterious energy blast she received in class back in September 1981, she was not sure, and she had no proof. It could have come from one of several others in that class. Plus, she saw a vision, a premonition about the future, and she knew she would be able to secure various favors from Roland up through and including the carrying of those two trailer cargos to her cousins, the Quevalos. Plus, for Roland's intelligence, it convenienced her to maintain her mental connection and friendship with him. From 1981 forward, she had reinforced her personal protection and she could afford to wait until late 1997 to reject him.

Luke sat across the table from his wife, mouth dropped open, wide-eyed in amazement.

"Roland is *not* to come near us!" Isalia declared. "I'm sure you understand . . . at least I hope so."

". . . I'm working on it, Isalia," Luke admitted.

Luke had considered later going to Roland and talking with him behind Isalia's back, but not now, after what Isalia told him. He was afraid to!

One fragment of truth that Isalia kept buried between her and Luke was the fact that when she and Luke began living together half a year ago, mid 1997, she turned in her lifelong membership to a club she used to belong to in Eagle Pass, Texas . . . and as a result, she now had less protection from "upstairs" than she used to have. Isalia had a long history with that club, none of which she would ever communicate to her husband, much less so to Roland. That was extremely confidential information that neither Roland nor Luke had any business knowing about!

*　　*　　*

The next morning, Roland went to Felipe's carpentry to hand them the job of making three Oak and Poplar rocking chairs, to be ready by the time he leaves. Rigo and Sotero were the only two working for Felipe, and after being closed for a week, he was starting back up slowly. Rigo and Sotero would do part of the work on the chairs, with the help of two other fellows, Pancho Gonzalez and Victor Ramirez, who ran another carpentry business nearby.

Roland then bicycled over to Isalia and Luke's house to talk to them. Surely, they must have read the letter. They weren't there. Only Raul and Rigo's mother Lavinia was there. When Roland arrived at the gate to the front yard, Lavinia immediately gave him a warning. "Dice Isalia y Luke si sigues molestándoles y siguiéndoles, te van a llevar a la policía," telling Roland that Isalia and Luke said that if Roland kept bothering them and following them, then they would call the police on him! A rush of fear went through Roland with that comment from Lavinia, and she said it to Roland in such a way that implied she would do nothing to talk to Isalia and convince her to communicate with Roland. After all, Lavinia needed her job, and she couldn't afford to lose it. Lavinia advised Roland not to come around there anymore, and she also informed Roland that Luke got angry and tore the letter up.

Roland was shocked that Luke and Isalia had acted so irrationally. He thanked Lavinia for telling him, and he left. Roland bicycled over to Lorenzo's house, and as he was getting off his bike, Lorenzo gave him a disgusted look, telling him he was angry at him and didn't want him coming around anymore!

Roland told Lorenzo to hold on just a moment, that he needed to talk to him about Isalia and Luke. Lorenzo, who still did have the belief system of giving a person a chance to explain, decided to let Roland speak. He told Lorenzo what Lavinia had just warned him about. Lorenzo told Roland that was true, that he needed to quit bothering them and to leave them alone.

Next, Lorenzo said that Isalia told him last night that when Roland had come over to deliver Luke that letter, he had shouted a bunch of phrases at Isalia and Luke and threatened to report the white truck that Luke was planning to leave in Mexico with the Quevalos.

Roland looked at Lorenzo with surprise, and he told him that was an outright lie! All Roland did was call out Luke's name, hand him the letter, say, "We'll talk later," and rode away, hearing Luke say, "No talk."

Lorenzo saw Roland's reaction of surprise, and with his accurate judge of character, he was now inclined to believe Roland. They talked about the problem for an hour. Lorenzo explained that Isalia felt so awful, so shocked when she and Luke discovered missing items, so much anger at Roland for "doing" the unthinkable, that she wasn't able to face him and be straightforward about it to ask him if he had delivered everything.

Roland had forgotten to tell Isalia back on December 17 when she verbally rejected him, that he wanted his file folder of stories back, that they weren't for Luke to read. The letter he handed Luke yesterday requested that, but since he tore it up, Isalia still had yet to be told to give it back to Roland upon her arrival to her home in Tennessee. He asked Lorenzo to talk to Isalia, and he said he would see what he could do.

Roland asked him if he was still angry, and Lorenzo answered that he wasn't anymore. He had believed Isalia's lies, but now he believed Roland instead.

It was at this time that Lorenzo decided to tell Roland something else. He told him he and Isalia had been talking, and they had arrived at the conclusion that perhaps the reason Roland liked to go to the mountains so much was to perform rituals and ceremonies, that is, along the lines of witchcraft! He asked Roland if that was really true.

Roland answered that of course it wasn't, and he explained that he went into the mountains because he enjoyed nature and the wilderness. Yes, he had had a few strange experiences and coincidences over the years, but none of that was his purposeful doing, and he certainly didn't believe in doing witchcraft. Lorenzo was glad to hear that, and he admitted that at times he had wondered what was really going on.

Lorenzo then brought up the second part of his concern. He and Isalia had also talked about Raul and Roland's past excursions to the mountains. He told Roland that Isalia had talked to Pancho, and she was especially concerned that Roland might have made "advances" at Raul and that they might have been "making out," among other things that would be considered even more inappropriate! No, Roland had never done anything of the kind. It hadn't even crossed his mind to do such things! Roland was shocked that certain people thought he did! They were malignant in their thinking, and Roland suspected that most of the stories and inappropriate speculations had originated from the poisonous mouth of none other than Pancho Quevalo!

Really, couldn't Roland and his good friend Raul go explore and enjoy the mountains, without such malignant speculation?! What was this world coming to?

Roland thanked Lorenzo for talking to him and for being reasonable.

He went to the Orolizos and fixed himself some lunch. No more than he had begun to eat lunch than one of the police trucks showed up in front of the Orolizo's house. Only Pegaso's sisters were home at the moment, and they went to the door to talk to the police officer. He requested to speak to the gringo staying with them. That was Roland, of course. So, he went to the door.

"Nito que vengas a la estación para hablar con nosotros," telling Roland they needed him to come to the police station to talk over a problem.

Roland asked him what it concerned, and he said they had a serious complaint from Isalia and Luke, and the comandante was down there waiting for him. More fear went through Roland, and chills went down his back. It was no longer a threat that Isalia and Luke were going to call the police, like Lavinia had warned Roland. They had already *called* the police!

Roland told him he'd be ready in just a second, and he went into the room where he was staying where he grabbed his photo album of his trips and stays in Mexico, and a copy of the letter he had written Isalia and Luke. He came back to the door, went outside with him, and got into the Dodge police truck with the officer, whose name was Juan. Roland was nervous during the short ride to the station. They stepped out of the vehicle and walked inside the station.

The comandante, whose name was Valentín, was waiting for him. They shook hands and began the conversation. Juan took a seat on the other side of the table by Valentín.

Roland was now talking to the head law enforcement officer at Bustamante's police station, the comandancia. Valentín informed Roland that Isalia and Luke had visited the station early this morning to complain about Roland's following them and bothering them. They had reported that Roland had shouted at them and threatened them yesterday afternoon, and they no longer wanted his friendship. Roland looked at the comandante and swore that wasn't true. He explained the scenario that actually happened, and he presented Valentín and Juan the photo album to look through, which they did.

Valentín asked Roland some questions, which Roland answered truthfully. He asked Roland what he did with the 3 pulidoras and the mandril, and Roland insisted that he didn't steal anything. He showed them the letter. Valentín asked Roland if he had left the pulidoras with Raul, and Roland truthfully answered no. (They were not part of the green box.) Valentín gave Roland a look of mistrust. They weren't believing Roland's story, even though Roland had photos to back him up. Needless to say, Roland was quite worried for his safety, and he certainly didn't want to go to jail for something he knew he wasn't guilty of. He was innocent.

For someone, Isalia, who had been a good friend for so long, Roland just could not believe that this "friend" had accused him of stealing, and for the accusations to have reached him third party (via Pancho Quevalo) last week made matters even worse. Neither Isalia nor Luke wanted anything to do with Roland now. It had come as an absolute shock to him two weeks ago when he had approached them, because he intuitively sensed that they were being sullen with him, and was suddenly told by Isalia, "I don't want to talk to you!" He had no idea why Isalia and Luke had mysteriously rejected him until a week later, which was now one week ago, when he heard first from Lavinia, then from Pancho, that Isalia and Luke were spreading gossip that he had stolen from them.

Yesterday, Roland had written Isalia and Luke that letter to appeal their shrewd tactics and accusations and to explain to them and assure them that he did not steal any of the trailer cargo. Instead of receiving the letter properly, reading it, and coming to Roland to discuss the problem to make amends, which people in their right mind would have done, they tore the letter up, likely without even reading it, went to the police station, and reported Roland for following them, bothering them, and for stealing!

Valentín, the chief police officer, kept interrogating Roland with questions, and he was also believing that Roland was a drug trafficker, which he certainly was not. Roland sat there across from the officers, still explaining his story, and Valentín continued to respond by looking at Roland in a manner of disbelief. Roland was silently praying for reason to prevail. He was in serious danger!

At the same time, he thought of a good way to get revenge on his two "friends." He no longer had any mercy for them. The friendship was definitely ruined for their having reported him and for putting him in this type of danger. He swore that if he made it through this, he was definitely going to proceed with action and serve them what they now deserved. Roland didn't normally believe in "an eye for an eye" tactics, but for what his "friends" had just done, he would make an exception.

He just hoped more than anything that the police officers would soon release him.

Roland explained that he had come to Bustamante several times, as his picture album proved. He asked Valentín to talk to some others in the town, if he didn't believe him.

Valentín asked Roland to choose two people, and he chose Mr. Cantu, and Mr. Orolizo, who were both well respected individuals in the town. Valentín asked Roland to wait at the station, and he sent two of his officers to go out and fetch Chilo Cantu and Nacho Orolizo. Half an hour later, both of them arrived, alarmed and also concerned for their friend Roland.

Both Chilo and Nacho, bless their souls, spoke highly of Roland, saying he behaved himself well. Never, not even once, had they seen Roland traffic drugs in any form or fashion. He didn't even smoke or drink. They explained that Roland was honest and trustworthy, and that the missing items likely took wings and flew away at the Colombia Bridge when Pancho and Roland paid duties inside the customs house. Nacho brought up another point and suggested that perhaps Isalia's husband, Luke, "el viajito", was jealous and protective of his new wife.

Valentín and Juan both had a good laugh at Nacho's sharp and accurate analysis of the problem. They looked at Roland and said there was no longer any problem. He was free to go. Valentín asked Roland not to go visit Isalia and Luke anymore. Yes, he could use the public streets, but he wasn't to step up on the sidewalk and try to talk to them. Plus, since they were foolish enough to have torn up the letter Roland had written them without reading it, he was no longer responsible for the "missing items."

Valentín and Juan wished Roland a safe stay and told him they were his friends.

Roland thanked them very much, gave special thanks to Chilo and Nacho for having come to the station on his behalf to defend him, and he walked away with his photo album under his arm.

Whew! That was close! He would do as the police said and not go over to talk to Isalia now, but he still had to get the message to her about returning his file folder to him upon her arrival to Tennessee in February or March.

Over the next several days, Valentín talked with the other police officers in town, as a means of double checking Roland's validity. All of them gave a good report. One of them, Jorge, told Valentín that he had never seen Roland trafficking drugs, nor did he do them, and he never smoked nor drank. Yes, he ran around with *chavos* (teenage fellows), but then they were the straighter ones who had not yet taken up smoking or drinking. Jorge explained to Valentín that a lot of fellows Roland's age had become borachos, and Roland therefore preferred to run around with the younger ones who were straight. Jorge had a good point, and with that, Valentín was convinced without a doubt that Roland was a good and straight fellow.

Roland went back to Lorenzo's house and talked to him. He told Lorenzo he was very angry at Isalia for her having reported him to the police! All Roland had done was try to reason with her, but she wouldn't give him a chance to talk to her. Lorenzo explained that Roland was going to have to accept it as it is, and to quit being so stubborn by insisting to talk to her to straighten the whole mess out. That wasn't Roland's way, to walk away, not for a friend of 17 years to him and his parents. Isalia was going to have to answer to Roland, especially with his file folder at stake. However, that would wait until he would go home to Tennessee. He had to obey the police in Mexico, and he really felt squelched by Isalia and Luke!

Roland returned to the Orolizos. There he wrote three pages documenting the problem he had with Isalia and Luke, and including the copy of the letter he had written them, he copied the four pages and sent them to various friends of his who were also friends of hers. He also sent a copy to Danny, one of the young fellows whose pictures were hanging on the wall in Isalia's house.

It occurred to Roland that Isalia and Luke might get the bright idea and send a search warrant to Lavinia's house to search Raul and Rigo's belongings for the missing items. Immediately, he bicycled over to their house, and he told Lavinia his concern. Raul was there, and he, Lavinia, and Roland discussed the best possible way to get rid of the items (knick knacks). Lavinia suggested placing the feed sack of contents under one of the bridges crossing the river near Sabinas Hidalgo. Raul suggested stuffing the whole thing in a garbage container over in Sabinas Hidalgo. Roland explained that someone might take note with all the contents still consolidated, and he suggested tossing the contents piece by piece out of his car, along the highway between Villaldama and Sabinas Hidalgo. They liked Roland's idea. That was good. Raul gave Roland a pat on the back, and Lavinia shook hands with Roland for his ingenuity. As it turned out, Rigo needed to go to Sabinas Hidalgo tomorrow morning to check his results from his final exams in December. They agreed that Rigo would ride with Roland first thing in the morning, and that he would help Roland throw out the knick knacks along the highway.

That evening, Roland talked with the Orolizos. Pegaso, who was home most of January on winter break, suggested that Roland forget the whole problem and not worry about it. Isalia and Luke no longer wanted anything to do with Roland, and that was the end of it. Nacho was telling his wife Chela about the incident at the police station, how they didn't want to believe Roland's story. He also told her that Isalia and Luke tore Roland's letter up without reading it. Chela reacted in a surprised manner, commenting how crazy Isalia and Luke were by saying, "¡Que sonso!"

Nacho said he had thought Isalia was a good woman, but not anymore, and he asked Roland if she were a school teacher, right? Roland verified, yes, and Nacho pointed out that since Isalia was a school teacher, she ought to put forth an example like one, instead of acting like a little 5-year-old child. Nacho was entirely right. School teachers are leaders, and they are not supposed to turn their back to anybody!

Early the next morning Roland drove his car over to Raul and Rigo's house. It was a cold morning, and it was still dark at 7 AM. Lavinia had the feed sack full of knick knacks ready to load, and Roland heaved it over his shoulder and took it out to his car, where he placed it in the back seat. Rigo was ready to go, and he got in the car. Lavinia and Raul wished Roland good luck, and he drove away.

They went to Villaldama. Dawn was arriving. Once through Villaldama, Roland pulled over to sort through the knick knacks. He had brought along a cardboard box to facilitate the tossing out process, and he transferred the contents to the large box.

Next, he asked Rigo to help him toss out the pieces, but he didn't want to. Roland explained that it was important, but Rigo still didn't want to. What was with Rigo this morning? This was no time for a bad mood. Roland then offered him N$10. Rigo said he'd help him for N$20. Okay, deal! He gave Rigo N$20, got back in the driver's seat, and he drove them to Sabinas Hidalgo.

A few kilometers east of Villaldama, when they had just passed a small community called Santa Isabel, Roland announced it was time. Rigo reached back and grabbed some pieces, among them an orange hard hat. He rolled down the window. Whoosh! The hard hat hit the ground. Roland never forgot the sound the hard hat made with the Mesquite shrubs and branches before it made a whack sound against one of the shoulder road posts. He started laughing. Rigo smiled and threw more pieces out the window.

Both of them started laughing. Rigo was enjoying it. He reached behind the seat into the box for more knick knacks and tossed them out. Roland rolled down his window. Rigo handed him some pieces, and he tossed them out, as well. They were having great fun!

They kept on the lookout for other vehicles from both directions, to be sure no one saw them. Along a 10 kilometer stretch of the highway, Roland and Rigo casually tossed out every last piece of the knick knacks that was originally in that green box. The last piece was tossed out where the curves of the highway began nearer Sabinas Hidalgo.

For the way Isalia and Luke had treated Roland, being so unreasonable, and calling the police on him, they deserved the loss of that green box and its contents. It was such a relief to Roland to throw out those materials, worthless as they were. If they had just been reasonable, Roland would certainly have admitted his mistake, and he would have returned the green box and knick knacks to them. However, under the circumstances, and with Lavinia's job and sons' reputations at stake, what Roland and Rigo did was the only solution to resolve the problem.

Those who are unreasonable . . . end up losing, and Isalia and Luke lost the green box! For their irrationality, Roland and Rigo had done justice to Isalia and Luke, and to the Quevalos.

*   *   *

Meanwhile, a group of beings inside a nearby cave were telepathically observing Roland and Rigo and their actions . . . from their vantage point behind a holographic window.

*   *   *

They arrived at the Prepa where Rigo checked his exam results. He passed all his exams fine. Smart fellow! They did other errands in town and then returned to Bustamante. It was the first time Rigo had come along with Roland by himself. Roland wasn't quite sure what to think of Rigo for charging him N$20 to help throw out the knick knacks. Nevertheless, the evidence was gotten rid of, and Roland was grateful to Rigo for his help.

When they returned to Rigo's house, Raul, Beto, and Angelo were there watching a movie. Roland spent the afternoon with them. Beto asked Roland if he wanted to go to Potrero to go hiking in the mountains around there. He also told Roland about some mines up in the canyon where there were some interesting rocks. He could add them to his collection. Roland said he'd like to go, and they made plans to go later in the week.

That night, Roland called his parents and told them all that had happened. His parents said they already knew something was up because they got a very disturbing message from Isalia on January 2, four days ago, and the strangeness of the message and the lack of compassion in Isalia's voice had very much irritated Roland's parents.

Roland was quite angry to find out that Isalia had done that! Roland was a mature adult, already in his 30's, and Isalia was way out of line to have called and frightened his parents with a threat that they were going to call the police on Roland and especially in a foreign country like Mexico! How could she?!

Roland told his parents everything that had happened and how cruel and unreasonable she was being. He pointed out that, ". . . and you know, Isalia is the one who used to talk about loving people and forgiving people, and she said she will always love me, that I'm like a son to her. Hog-wash!"

"She's casting aspersion on you, son," Roland's father told him. "Please come home."

"Yes, come on home and get out of that hot box," his mother advised.

"Yeah, I see your point," Roland partly agreed, "but Isalia doesn't mandate me. She has no right to scare me out of this town, and I'm staying! I have my artwork and paintings to do, and it's cold back in Tennessee."

"Okay, son," his father said. "We really wish you'd come home, but you do have a point."

"Just be careful, Roland," his mother advised.

"If it gets any more dangerous, you come on home," his father added.

"Roland, something terrible happened."

"What?"

"Your third grade teacher died last night."

"What?! How?!"

"She became mysteriously ill, a rare blood disease, had to go home at Thanksgiving," his mother informed him.

"They admitted her to the hospital. She went steadily downhill and died," his father told him.

"Oh, how terrible! She was my favorite teacher." Roland was quite surprised about it.

"Oh, we're in shock," his mother said. "We just can't believe it."

Roland thought and then said, "She was 52, wasn't she?"

"That's right," his mother said.

"I'm very sorry to hear that," said Roland.

They talked about some other things. Then they wished each other well, and they hung up. Roland told the Orolizos what Isalia had done. They were shocked by the whole thing. How dare Isalia call and frighten Roland's parents like that!

What more could Roland do? He had made reasonable efforts to reason with the irrational, which is what Isalia and Luke now were. By force of the police, Roland was squelched from even so much as talking to Isalia and Luke, much less straighten out the mess with them! Roland found the whole thing hard to believe. It was like a nightmare, but this was real life, not some dream.

Had Roland suddenly, back in November, slipped into a parallel universe? He thought not, because everyone else was still the same.

Isalia and Luke had changed so much. They had only been in Bustamante a week or so, and by early November, the seatbelt incident with Luke had occurred. That started the ball rolling, and one thing led to another. Why was Isalia, especially her, so changed for the worse? It just didn't add up and made no sense to Roland. Was there some malign force existent in the Bustamante region that, a few days after arriving, woke up a dark side within Isalia? It was possible, and Roland couldn't help but remember Isalia's strange falling out with Mrs. Tinkerton last year.

Roland had done so much to help out Isalia. He had *given* her three pickup truck loads of gravel back in 1990, and when he worked for her from 1994 through 1997, he had charged her for his labor at less than the going rate. He had helped her and Clayton immensely on that deck beside their creek, and of course he had helped Luke with their addition, not to mention the two trailer cargos he had brought her cousins. Who else but a really good friend would have done all that? Roland really felt like a sucker now, and he knew he had been used. She and Luke had been friends of convenience and that was for certain.

It remained to be seen the showdown that would occur between Isalia and Roland's parents, when she and Luke would return to Tennessee. Roland's mother would likely tell her off! Perhaps Isalia believed the danger she put Roland in would not jeopardize her friendship with his parents, but it did, and she would later realize that!

*   *   *

Holographic Window, Jan. 6, 1998
Nuevo Wimbisenho

As Roland and Rigo were tossing the knick knacks onto the highway, a group of spirits was observing them through their holographic window from their secret cave under the hills between Villaldama and Sabinas Hidalgo.

Draaktra, young whipper-snapper that he was, enjoyed peering into the black holographic crystal ball, observing Roland and Rigo. He was the youngest brother of Sojornbloc.

"Mmm! They have such a good friendship, I can't stand it."

"Such a grand opportunity," Sasjurech commented with savour in his voice.

"There he is. There he is!" Draaktra declared with vigor and enthusiasm as he observed Rigo. I want that one," he now told his brother, Sojornbloc. "Can I? Can I?"

"Now hold your taste buds there, just a moment!" Sasjurech said to Draaktra.

"I've waited long enough! I'm ready for my first mission," Draaktra told them with an energetic smile on his face. "Plus, we'll gain ranking with this one."

"We may have to get permission," Sojornbloc pointed out.

"We might not have to on this one," Sasjurech replied. "He charged Roland N$20."

"Ah! You and your permission rubbish!" Draaktra, now complained. He calmed down and observed the scene through the holographic crystal ball. A few seconds went by. "Who do those materials belong to?"

"They belong to Luke Wiggins and his new wife, Isalia Ives," Sojornbloc replied. "Of course, we know Isalia's protected by our great friend, Arfifra, who . . ."

"Well, what are we waiting for?" Draaktra suddenly asked impatiently. "Call her over here!"

In a period of five seconds, Arfifra materialized. Her favorite "pet" Torxtalo accompanied her, as well.

Sasjurech and Sojornbloc immediately gestured for her to look through the crystal ball.

"Oh, my GOD!" Arfifra declared, upon seeing Roland and Rigo's actions.

"Those knick knacks were supposed to go to my protectee Pancho," Torxtalo declared.

"We need your permission concerning that young friend of Roland's . . ." Sojornbloc began.

"Oh, by all means! He's all yours," Arfifra quickly consented, anger in her voice.

"Just like that? No hassles? No haggles?" Sojornbloc checked.

"Have at 'em," Arfifra approved. "Roland totally failed to talk to Isalia to straighten out the problem. Of course, I made her reject Roland and made her . . . shall we say . . . *hard* to get!"

All of them cackled with laughter at Arfifra's clever choice of words and subtle implications that went with it.

"Arfifra, you never cease to amaze us with your sharp wit and humor," Sasjurech complimented her.

"Not to mention the inappropriate dreams you sent Isalia about Roland and Raul," Sojornbloc added.

"Isalia fell for them, hook, line, and sinker!" Draaktra added with a snicker.

"Oh I made them very believable, and with *pleasure*," Arfifra boasted with a smile.

The cave was quiet for a few seconds, and when they caught on to the pun, the place became filled with laughter!

"To be totally honest," Arfifra carried on, "you win some, you lose some. Isalia and Luke lost a green box of knick knacks, but they can't have their cake and eat it too, you know. After all, I made sure they successfully smuggled in all those special herb powders, hidden within that big roll of sandpaper, not to mention Luke's disassembled revolver, cleverly hidden inside the metal motor housing of the bandsaw he brought in with him. In other words, the bandsaw had a . . . shall we say . . . *false* motor."

"Let's just say that motor had a built in . . . *defense mechanism*," Torxtalo cleverly added.

They roared with laughter!

"Of course you know," Arfifra told Draaktra, "Miss Isalia is adept and possesses certain skills in the occult arts, you might say. She was a fine student, having studied and practiced a branch of black magic, our most prominent one, which we call *Carifrajariflaquestrav*." Arfifra now filled Draaktra in on important information concerning Isalia, Roland and Rigo. "Yes, Isalia was a refined woman in the arts, a long time member of that club in Eagle Pass. She could see the future and premonitions. She was absolutely brilliant in establishing and maintaining mental connections, without anyone realizing it. She took energy off of 12 of her select students, Roland and his sister both being unsuspecting victims in her Spanish classes. She also knew how to pass off her ailments and arthritic pains to her students, all in efforts to improve herself. The energy responders she left in her students would in the future trigger mysterious aches and pains in each of them, like knee inflammation, tendonitis, arthritis at young ages, abdominal pain, and a whole nother slew of problems."

"That's right. I jumped in, in February 1981," Sasjurech recalled.

"And so did I," Sojornbloc added, "straight from her energy responders installed in Roland at that time."

The two of them shook hands in triumph.

Meanwhile, Torxtalo was listening intently to Arfifra. He had high regard for her. She was like a mentor to him, and he looked upon her as a guiding light.

"Draaktra, this is confidential," Arfifra continued, "but what's it going to hurt for you to know? Isalia wasn't all "hunky-dory" with her work. She suffered some setbacks."

"Really, what happened?!" Draaktra responded with all ears. He always enjoyed confidential gossip.

"One of them had to do with her son in 1972. He was ready to leave the nest, you might say, and Isalia tried to establish a strong mental connection with him so he wouldn't leave . . . Pity she didn't realize you can't do that to close blood kin.

Those mental energies turned right around and whacked her mind with devastating results. Her sharp clear mind was partially fractured, and she never was the same again.

"In February 1981, she took energy off of Roland, including some intelligence and mental clarity, to better herself, and she also passed off certain rheumatic ailments to him. Roland remembers the day his mind was dulled. He was sitting right across from her the day it happened, but he never realized she was the reason. When Roland arrived home that afternoon from school, his parents' archangel protectors realized it, and they immediately located and assigned Roland a full-time protector, a guardian angel by the name of Selím. He is swift and powerful and still looks after Roland to this day.

"In September 1981, when Roland was in his second year of Spanish, Isalia tried to take energy off of Roland again, and some other students, as well. Her energy sapping was not permissible by any means, not while Selím was present! He wasn't about to let her get away with it! He took a bundle of energy and delivered her a resounding blow, a scolding blast of energy, so as to teach her never to take energy off of others, in his view. It took her 36 hours to recover!

"Of course, I planted some temptation thoughts in her mind the next year, when Roland was no longer in her class, and she was back at it again."

"Well done, Arfifra!" they complimented her.

"Of course, we all know she turned in her membership six months ago," Arfifra continued, "when she started living with her new man, Luke. As a result, she now fears Roland because she thinks he did it, but the culprit was Selím, who she has NO access to! Of course, I'm not going to correct Isalia. I always enjoy seeing a good rejection take place, anyway," she remarked with a smirk.

"As you know," Arfifra warned, "we must exercise extreme caution around guardian angels, especially those like Selím. Keep your stealth devices intact at all times, because if he detects you and gains knowledge of your existence, he will send an order upstairs to have you zapped right out of existence."

"He hasn't got us yet!" Sasjurech declared with a happy shout.

He and Sojornbloc shook hands in triumph again.

"Draaktra, your mission is with Rigo," she told him. "You do a good job with him and you'll achieve high rank advancement . . . to be admitted into the school of . . . *Carifrajariflaquestrav*," and she smiled.

Feelings of thrill and excitement flashed through him, and he looked at her with even more enthusiasm. He was speechless with honor.

"That will be all," Arfifra told everyone. "I'll return to Isalia's conscience now. Come along, Torxtalo," and she vanished.

"Can I get in? Can I get in?" Draaktra asked Sojornbloc and Sasjurech.

Sojornbloc was observing Rigo. He shook his head.

"What? Don't tell me he's clean!" Draaktra exclaimed.

"I'm afraid so," Sojornbloc responded. "You want somebody else?"

"No, I want him!" Draaktra insisted. "How soon can I get in?"

"The first opportunity is 3:56 AM, Sunday, August 9. He will be with a young muchacha. You be poised and ready, and at the moment they . . . *do it* . . . you take that brief opportunity and jump through that open door."

"I'll go through the formalities of clearing it with Roland's two spirit guides . . . Sarlo and Malluck," said Sojornbloc. "They're very lenient. I'm sure they'll consent. They're pretty easy to buy off."

"Don't you worry about a thing, Draaktra," Sasjurech told him. "We'll get you into Rigo."

Meanwhile Sojornbloc established telepathic contact with Sarlo and Malluck . . .

*   *   *

CHAPTER 11

LA CUETONA Y SU FUERZA MALIGNA

January 1998

The Cantu family had two empty houses for sale, one of them the house where Raul and Rigo used to live. The other one was up Avenida Independencia, and at Roland's request, they loaned him a key and let him use the house to set up his equipment and drawing pads and do some paintings. On several days, Roland went there and got some paintings successfully completed. However, it was sometimes difficult for him to concentrate, due to passing traffic, chickens and roosters calling out, dogs barking, as well as neighbors playing music from time to time. Still, Roland enjoyed what he was doing. Friends and neighbors would sometimes happen by, and they were always intrigued with some of the scenes Roland had painted.

As it turned out, Chilo and Mina's vacant house was around the block from the house Isalia and Luke were renting. Mina Cantu told Roland that Isalia and Luke had recently looked at it and were interested in buying it for US $20,000. Roland thought that was good, and the house would serve Isalia and Luke very well.

Over the course of the month, Roland did his best to forget about Isalia and Luke, but he was still baffled by their very mysterious rejection. At times, he passed by them on the road, and Roland instinctively waved. No, Isalia and Luke didn't wave back. Instead they both, especially Isalia, gave Roland angry stares.

He wrote his friend Ivanhoe in Scotland a postcard and let him know what was going on. Surely Ivanhoe would be surprised.

Roland visited different friends around town. One evening, he visited Hector and Pablo, and they watched the cartoon *The Simpsons* on TV.

Pegaso was busy with his father working and didn't have much time. On occasion, he and Roland talked and visited. Angelo came over, and Roland did things with him.

Roland visited with Raul and Rigo at times, and he took them to Potrero or Villaldama. Raul accompanied Roland to Sabinas Hidalgo from time to time.

Roland took Beto Enriquez to Potrero one day, and they went hiking several hours in the canyon approaching the mountains. Beto was a decent, straightforward fellow, a little bit mischievous and playful at times, but basically a kind fellow. Raul had introduced Roland to him back in November.

Beto told Roland stories as they walked along. He and his younger brother and sister were living with their grandmother in Bustamante. They lived in a one-room adobe house. His parents had gone. He told Roland of some mines up above the canyon back in Bustamante, and after hiking several hours in Potrero, they returned to Bustamante. They climbed the steep canyon slopes to reach the mine, and they collected some interesting orange rocks. Beto had worked various jobs over the past few years. He had manned the goats along the hillsides, tough work indeed.

Roland enjoyed Beto's company, and he was calmer than Raul, even calmer than Rigo.

Raul found a part time job with a fellow named Juan who sold Snaky Fritos to different corner stores in town. He drove a VW van, and Raul rode with him and helped him.

Victor, neighbor of the Orolizos, did things with Roland. They played basketball together at times. Roland used to go to their house to chat with him and his family.

Roland also checked on the progress of his three rocking chairs at Felipe's carpentry where now Rigo, Sotero, Juan Carlos, and a fellow named Pedro worked. He used to visit with them, shoot the breeze, and he enjoyed their company.

There was a special family in Bustamante who did artwork and crafts. They were Sebastian and his wife Bertha. Roland had intended for some time to go over and meet them so he could show them his artwork and calendars. Plus, wanted to talk to them about Chiquihuitillos. One afternoon, he got his photos of Chiquihuitillos together, plus his calendars and walked out of the Orolizo's house. Just as he was mounting his bicycle to ride over there, he heard the sound of the 6 cylinder motor of Sebastian's vehicle approaching. Sure enough, it was Sebastian. He had come to talk to Nacho. Roland went to his vehicle's side and introduced himself to Sebastian, and he told him he was just leaving to go over to his house! Sebastian was impressed (so was Roland) at the coincidence, and he told Roland that telepathy had certainly been at work there. He carried Roland over to his house. There he met Bertha, and the three of them had an interesting discussion about Chiquihuitillos. Sebastian was an investigator of odd phenomena, as well. Roland was impressed with some of Sebastian's artwork, and so were Sebastian and Bertha with Roland's. Sebastian lacked photos of Chiquihuitillos, as it turned out. So, Roland offered to have copies made and later mail him the pictures.

They talked for a while about the culture between Mexico and the United States, and Sebastian said he had travelled several times to art shows up in Dallas. Roland asked him how he had managed to obtain a VISA, and he stated that he never got one. Since he happened to look very much like a native American Indian, he would just tell U.S. Customs, "American Indian," and they would immediately say to go ahead and that he was free to enter.

Roland expressed surprise and asked how that could be, and Sebastian explained that there are various native American tribes of people that live in reservations along Mexico's frontera, and not being U.S. nor Mexican citizens, and for recognition of their rights as native Americans, they are always free to go back and forth across the border. In other words, they are exceptions and do not fall under the rules and guidelines that U.S. and Mexican citizens have to obey. What an interesting concept!

Roland enjoyed visiting with Sebastian and Bertha, and later that afternoon he returned to the Orolizos.

One Saturday, a fellow named Sergio, who was a friend of Raul's, accompanied Roland up in the mountains. They were going to clear a trail up in the highland forest, the only section Roland hadn't yet reached. They did a few hundred meters of trail clearing, but Sergio was suffering from what seemed to be high altitude sickness. Roland was surprised, and he asked him if he'd been to Saltillo which sits at 5,000 feet (around 1,500 meters). No, he hadn't. In fact, this was the highest Sergio had ever been! They made their way back down the mountain, and Sergio felt better and better.

*   *   *

Roland also met more people in the plaza, among them Luis, Julian, Olí, and Francisco. They introduced themselves to Roland and quizzed him later on their names. Roland got their names right. They asked Roland where he was staying, and he told them he was at the Orolizos. One of them made a comment about the young girls in town.

"¿Y las muchachas?" Luis brought up with a smile on his face, asking Roland what he thought of the girls in town.

"Sí, son bonitas," Roland answered, saying that they were pretty.

Luis next asked him what he thought of Pegaso's sisters.

"¿Quién, Lumita y Mena?" Roland said, asking if he was talking about Lumita and Mena.

"Sí," answering yes.

"Pues, Lumita es bonita, y me gustaría por una novia, si yo quisiera," Roland casually told him, saying that Lumita was pretty and would please him for a girlfriend, if he wanted one.

"Ah, *cuñados* . . . tú y Pegaso," Luis declared with a smile, joking with Roland that he and Pegaso could be brothers-in-law.

"A lo mejor sí, pero quien sabe," Roland admitted, saying that maybe so, but who knows.

Luis gave out a good laugh. Julian laughed heartily while Olí and Francisco joined in, and soon everyone was laughing.

For the next half hour, they talked about various subjects of culture and travel. Roland enjoyed the chat with them.

*   *   *

In mid January, Pegaso went to Monterrey to take some exams for the previous fall semester. Roland asked him if he was going to go to the Macroplaza, and if so, could he buy the CD, *Maná: Sueños Líquidos*. Roland handed him N$125 and asked him not to open or unwrap the CD. Pegaso said he would buy it for him. Roland said gracias and wished him well on his exams.

Roland was enjoying his friends and things were going fairly smoothly. The Orolizos were good people, and they were calm and friendly.

Roland also visited Raul and Rigo, and Lavinia sometimes fed him supper. Lavinia told Roland how Isalia and Luke were doing. They never had found out about the green box, thankfully. Lavinia said Isalia had been wishing Roland well by saying, "Que te vaya bien." Though Lavinia didn't know it, what Isalia really and truly said was, "Que te vaya bien, a *fuera* de Bustamante," (May you go well, *away* from Bustamante.)

Lavinia told Roland that Isalia had been struggling with Roland for the past 16 years, with culture differences and his having problems with people, like when he walked from the shower to the bedroom in his underwear at Esalina's house in 1983, among other things.

Roland was surprised and asked Lavinia if Isalia actually told her that. Lavinia verified a yes, and she told Roland that was very bad. Roland said of course he later knew that, but that was 15 years ago, and what business is it for Isalia to have told Raul and Rigo's mother, Lavinia?!

Lavinia went on to say that Isalia was disgusted with Roland because he charged her for everything he did for her, and he never did anything for free. Isalia and her negative thinking! Obviously she had totally forgotten the time in December 1990, when Roland delivered her, free of charge, three pickup truckloads of gravel for her driveway. Plus, he had given her plants and trees, including two Western Red Cedars, Siempre Viva, Flor de Peña, and some Mexican Rain Lily bulbs.

Roland decided to write her a short note to ask again that they communicate and straighten out the whole misunderstanding. That wasn't violating police order, and he asked Lavinia to take it to Isalia. Roland wrote it in Spanish so Luke wouldn't be able to read it.

The next day Lavinia delivered the note to Isalia. No more than Lavinia told Isalia who the note was from than Isalia got angry. She handed the note to Luke who diligently and immediately tore it up. Next, Isalia threatened Lavinia that if she brought any more messages from Roland, she would be fired on the spot! Lavinia, for fear of losing her important job, never again lifted a finger on Roland's behalf. In other words, Lavinia couldn't afford to lose her job, which paid an extra N$100 per week, above other jobs. That evening, Lavinia told Roland what Isalia and Luke had done.

Pegaso arrived from Monterrey on Friday night, that same night. He had passed his exams very well. However, he looked a little bit different. Roland playfully asked him for the *Maná* CD, and Pegaso gave him a serious look which made him think twice. After Pegaso got settled, he pulled the CD out of his bag and gave Roland his change. It was N$5. The plastic wrapper was off the CD, and as Roland noticed it, Pegaso immediately acknowledged that yes, it was open because it was the last one in the store, and it was their demo copy. He said it had cost him N$113, and he told Roland he took N$7 because he had to buy something and also pay for the city bus fare to get to the Macroplaza.

Roland reminded Pegaso that he thought he was going to the Macroplaza anyway. Pegaso corrected him and said he had made a special trip, as it turned out. Roland asked him how much the bus fare was, and Pegaso said it was N$3. Immediately, he said he would *later* give Roland the N$4 remaining, and he walked out of the room, nearly leaving Roland hanging. Roland was about to thank him anyway, but Pegaso was already . . . gone.

The next day, Roland did things with Raul and Rigo. He also visited Victor and his family. That late afternoon, Raul and Angelo, including Hector and Pablo, requested a lift to Potrero to attend a baile there. Roland took them.

When he returned to Bustamante. Pegaso was getting ready for the baile in Bustamante. It was Saturday night. Roland asked him for the N$4 balance. Pegaso had N$3 and gave them to Roland, who said thanks and that it was close enough. He went to the room where he was staying. Pegaso followed him and entered behind him, closed the door, and stood in front of it. Roland asked him what was the matter. Pegaso said his parents had overheard Roland charging Pegaso for the N$4. They wondered why Roland bothered charging such a tiny amount of money, and they advised Pegaso not do any more favors for Roland. Pegaso was upset and went on to compare the situation to Raul, pointing out to Roland that he didn't charge Raul to take him and his buddies to Potrero. Basically, Pegaso made Roland feel guilty for charging him the balance, which didn't sit well with Roland at all. Pegaso wasn't keeping his agreement, and as far as Roland was concerned, Pegaso was shortchanging him.

Yes, Roland was staying with him and his family, but that was a different matter. Roland had brought them gifts, such as the grease gun, which cost more than the CD, and he had paid to have their butane gas tank filled. Plus, he had replaced, free of charge, a broken window in their house.

Pegaso scolded Roland some more, then walked out the door to go to the dance. Mr. Orolizo then walked in and gave Roland the remaining money, N$1.

What was with Pegaso? He had always been a good friend. The look in his eyes wasn't right either. Something had happened. He passed his exams. Why was he so bothered, seemingly with Roland more than anyone else? Roland slept over at the Cantu's vacant house. He felt like Pegaso was tired of having him stay there.

La Cuetona Y Su Fuerza Maligna

The next morning, Roland had a talk with Mrs. Orolizo who told Roland that Pegaso felt bad for being charged that minuscule amount of money. Roland was exacting at times . . . down to the peso. After all, he was an engineer. He always wanted things to add up, but his preciseness with things like money caused problems. Mrs. Orolizo said there was a saying that said, "If you want to lose a friend, charge him money." Roland couldn't understand why Mexicans were so sensitive about being charged money. Yes, problems had occurred back home in Tennessee, for example with one friend concerning wiring up some electrical boxes and being paid on time for the work, but here in Mexico, it was much more prevalent. Why? Mrs. Orolizo explained that Pegaso assured her he had intended to pay Roland the remaining N\$4. He wasn't just going to keep it.

Suddenly, Mrs. Orolizo started to cry. She gestured as if she had a premonition, and when Roland asked her what was the matter, she said it was nothing.

Roland wanted to know why the CD was unwrapped. He didn't believe Pegaso's story. He didn't say anything, but he was just about sure that Pegaso had bought the CD brand new, had unwrapped it, and played the whole thing to record it onto a cassette tape. Later that day, he heard Pegaso playing a cassette tape with those songs on it, and he hadn't had that tape before. What bothered Roland was that Pegaso wasn't being entirely honest about the whole thing. Perhaps Pegaso had a motive: *Instigate a problem so Roland would leave.*

Raul, Rigo and Angelo came over to Pegaso's house in the afternoon. He left with them, and they did not invite Roland to come with them. Evidently, Pegaso had communicated the problem to them at the baile last night, and now they looked at Roland in a different way.

The next day, Roland went over to Raul and Rigo's to talk to them about Pegaso. Raul kept fairly quiet about Pegaso's reasons for getting upset. Then Raul asked Roland if he wanted to go to Potrero with him and his buddies to go camping in the foothills of the mountains. Roland said he would be glad to.

Roland returned to the Orolizo's house. Pegaso was sullen, and Roland felt impeded or somehow prevented from asking Pegaso what was the matter. Actually, Roland sensed that Pegaso might flare up, and he was a little afraid to approach Pegaso. Roland just kept his distance and didn't bother him.

Later in the week, January 22, Roland took Raul to Potrero. Once there, they rounded up some of Raul's friends: Joel, Ramiro, and two others. They packed some backpacks, got permission from their parents, and Roland drove them into the canyon foothills. They followed an old gravel road, opened a locked gate, and then proceeded to a turnout where Roland parked his LTD wagon.

From there, they walked a couple of hours to a beautiful area of Nogal and Walnut trees, complete with a running creek. They built a fire and roasted food over it.

One of the others took Roland up higher in the mountains on an afternoon hike. The views were quite good. Here in Potrero, the mountain foothills were more sprawling than up north in Bustamante. In some ways it was more beautiful.

They all visited that evening around the campfire and slept that night out in the open.

At 7 AM, they got up, packed their things, and walked the two hours back to Roland's car.

The better part of the camping trip went well, and Raul had not fought with Roland this time, which made up for the horrible incident last summer.

He drove them back through the big gate and back into town, where Raul's friends stepped down from Roland's car. Then Roland and Raul returned to Bustamante, arriving late morning. He delivered him to his house and drove to the Orolizos. Upon arriving, he saw Pegaso and told him the camping trip went well.

Pegaso replied, "Ah bueno," in a manner as if he couldn't care less. He was still cold toward Roland.

Roland didn't say anything else to him, and he entered the house with his backpack, showered, and cleaned up.

Raul and Beto wanted to go to Sabinas Hidalgo, so Roland took them over there. He asked Raul why Pegaso was continuing to be cold shouldered. Five days had gone by since Roland had charged Pegaso that remaining N$4, for which he had gotten irritated and scolded Roland, and he was still sullen. Why wasn't he coming around? All Roland wanted to do was straighten out the misunderstanding with Pegaso, shake hands, and go on being friends with him. He ran all that by Raul to see what he thought.

"Es lo que dijiste de sus hermanas," Raul suddenly mentioned, telling Roland the problem had to do with what he had said about Pegaso's sisters.

"¿Qué?" Roland asked Raul in a confused manner.

"Dijiste que son bonitas y que te gustarían por novias," Raul said, reminding Roland that he had told several fellows in the plaza that Pegaso's sisters, Lumita and Mena, were pretty and would please him for a girlfriend.

"Ohhh . . .!" Roland exclaimed, recalling what he had said to Luis, Julian, Olí, and Francisco, in the plaza last week.

Then Roland asked Raul the obvious question: Why was Pegaso upset about that? What's the big deal?

Raul explained that in Mexico, saying a girl pleases you is a no no, because to say *gustaría* means the girl pleases you sexually.

Roland asked Raul what could be done to clear the misunderstanding, and Raul shook his head in a way that let Roland know that he had gotten himself into a hornet's nest without realizing it.

Roland asked Raul and Beto to accompany him in confronting Pegaso, upon returning to Bustamante, for Roland's protection, in case Pegaso might get angry. Raul and Beto said they would be glad to.

While they were in Sabinas Hidalgo, Roland developed a couple of rolls of film, and he gave Raul and Beto extra copies of the pictures from the trip to Zacatecas. Among those pictures were photos of Roland and Victor's hike up in the mountains, and 12 photos that he took of Isalia and Luke's wedding. They came out great! Roland would proudly show those pictures to various friends of his in Bustamante.

Japan had a Nissan car parts factory in northern Sabinas Hidalgo. It was a big factory that gave employment to numerous people, including some from Bustamante, and they paid around N$450 per week (US $55), which was better than average pay in Mexico. Raul and Beto wanted to apply for work, so Roland took them by there.

By evening, they returned to Bustamante, and the three of them entered the Orolizo's house. Pegaso's father Nacho was in the kitchen with a couple of other visitors, and he told them Pegaso was in his bedroom.

Roland, Raul and Beto entered. Pegaso was listening to music at the moment. He turned around, saw Roland, and he immediately leaped up from the chair he was sitting in. His face went angry, and he grabbled Roland by the shirt and firmly asked him, "¿Qué dijiste sobre mis hermanas? Díme la verdad. ¡Eh!" asking Roland what he had said about his sisters and to tell him the truth. He then shoved Roland away, knocking him down!

Roland had not had a chance to react, and Pegaso was quick. He jabbed Roland in the ribs several times, repeating the questions, and Roland was not quick enough to deflect his jabbing. Roland tried to leave, but Pegaso blocked the door.

Roland answered Pegaso, telling him the truth fair and square, which only made Pegaso angrier. He jabbed Roland in the neck! Now Roland was angry, and he began to wait for a good opportunity to give him a swift kick in the balls! Pegaso kept on interrogating Roland, and Roland asked Raul and Beto to intervene, but they stood aside in fear because Pegaso was hopping mad! Roland asked Pegaso to sit down and be reasonable, but nothing doing.

Then Roland blurted out, "¿Qué tiene? Ya tiene 15 años." (What's it to you?! She's already 15.)

Pegaso got angrier, and he jabbed Roland in the ribs again. Roland lay down on the bed and raised his feet and legs toward Pegaso. He was poised and ready to kick him.

Raul laid his hand on Pegaso's shoulder and told him, "Pegaso, ya," which meant enough. Pegaso flung Raul to the side of the room! Then Pegaso grabbed Roland by his ankles, and dragged him off the bed! Raul quickly managed to rush to Roland's rescue, caught him by his arms and prevented him from falling on the hard concrete floor. Beto stood to the side and simply watched.

Roland was considering delivering Pegaso some serious blows, but he refrained from doing so, because the fight would have escalated into serious violence with injuries to both parties, which Roland did NOT want.

At that moment, it occurred to Roland to scream for Pegaso's father, who he hoped was still in the kitchen. He yelled several times for him to come and help him and get his son off of him! Nacho responded immediately, and his two fellow visitors wondered what on earth was going on! Nacho threw open Pegaso's bedroom door and saw the fight escalating. He immediately laid his hands on his son, jerked him away from Roland, and he asked Pegaso what sort of devil had gotten into him.

The two of them went to the front porch, and Pegaso told his father. Roland got up and defended his side of the story. Nacho wasn't angry, but he sided with his son. Roland asked them since when was it wrong to say that some young female is pretty and would please somebody for a girlfriend? Roland stated that he had said they were pretty, but he had not made any sexual remarks whatsoever, much less had he ever touched them!

Suddenly Victor, bless his soul, arrived running to Roland, Pegaso, and Mr. Orolizo. He said he had heard Roland screaming out for Pegaso's father, and he wanted to be sure everything was okay. Roland said he managed to squeak by unscathed, that he was lucky, and he thanked Victor very much for coming over . . . very kind of him.

Pegaso said he had been Roland's friend, but now he had such rejection that he wanted nothing to do with Roland. Some sort of demon had gotten into Pegaso, and *how*! His eyes glared, nothing the same as the calm and friendly Pegaso that Roland had known before. He was so changed.

Nacho suggested Roland leave tomorrow because Pegaso was angry. Roland offered to leave immediately, and he said if he stayed one more night, for certain Pegaso would attack him in the night. In front of his father, Pegaso admitted that he was planning just that!

Roland took his things out of Pegaso's room and left. Roland told Nacho thank you for having rescued him. Roland also mentioned that he didn't feel a part of this world, that where he came from (different star system) people are reasonable and friendly. Nacho showed understanding.

After Roland left, Nacho told Pegaso to leave Roland alone, that he had already gone, and there was no need for further fighting. Though Pegaso said nothing of it, he was afraid to do Roland serious harm, because he knew very well that Roland had won their arm wrestling match last year.

Roland took his stuff over to the Cantu's vacant house which was only one block away from Isalia and Luke's house. It was around 2 AM before he finally could get to sleep. At times, he shuddered, equally as much as he had after escaping the harrowing descent out of the mountains two years ago!

Roland turned on his radio and tried to receive stations. He picked up WBBM from Chicago, and briefly received WLS, which was no longer on clear channel, like it had been up to 1985.

If that was the norm about how young females' brothers protect and defend them, then Roland wanted absolutely nothing with having a girlfriend! Roland really hoped Raul and Rigo wouldn't turn on him the day he would want Norma. Roland was really flustered, and he was angry at Pegaso for days. Over the next few days, he would tell numerous people around town so that Pegaso would feel embarrassed. In short order the whole town would know. That would serve Pegaso right!

Roland also really needed to talk to Isalia and Luke about the whole thing, but then the police had prohibited Roland from doing so, and Roland couldn't approach them. He really needed their help, especially Isalia's, in talking to the Orolizo family to straighten out the whole misunderstanding, but the reality was that Isalia and Luke had removed their hand of friendship. While they were there physically, they were not there for Roland. He thought about approaching Isalia and Luke anyway, but he didn't want to risk being arrested. So, he didn't go to them. Ironically, Isalia had a ceramic plaque hanging on her kitchen wall that said: *Love is a friend who never once removes his hand.*

The next morning, Roland went to the police station and reported Pegaso's actions last night. The policeman, whose name was Jorge, said he would go have a word with him and his family.

Roland went to collect his three chairs from Felipe's carpentry. The three chairs, including Rigo and Sotero's sanding services, had cost a total of US $100. He would keep one for himself and sell the other two.

That afternoon, Roland took a three hour nap to catch up on his lost sleep last night.

During that nap, *Roland dreamed that he was over at Longview High School, and lo and behold, there was Isalia by the front office! Roland started to speak to her, but she gave Roland an awful and angry glare, and then she rushed toward him!* The dream ended just before she reached him. Roland woke up flustered and angry! What was Isalia doing now? Was she performing some sort of telepathic witchcraft?

*   *   *

-Meanwhile-

"Drat!" Isalia exclaimed to Luke. "Roland still hasn't left town! Now he's moved into the house we wanted to buy!"

"Well, you prayed for Pegaso's rejection . . ." Luke began.

"Yeah and *now* look what it's brought us!" Isalia complained. "Roland's right around the block from us, now. We've got to get him out of there, and *out of town*, Luke!"

"I know, Isalia," said Luke. "I want him gone, too."

"Luke, let's say a prayer. *Right now!*" Isalia directed.

*   *   *

Roland went over to Raul and talked to him about Pegaso, and he asked Raul to talk to Pegaso and get after him about how harsh he was to Roland. Raul said that Pegaso would get angry at him if he did that, and he didn't want to get into the middle of it and cross him. Raul explained that Pegaso was his better friend, and he told Roland that he shouldn't be telling people in town about the incident, or Pegaso might get angrier.

Raul's father Alejandro was sorry about the way Pegaso had treated Roland. He told Roland that he had never offended him, and though their new residence was small, they would receive him well. He could bring his things over. Roland thanked Alejandro, but since he was already set up at Chilo and Mina's vacant house, he would stay there.

That evening, Roland asked Victor and his parents to let him sleep in their house for the night, so that the last night he slept in a house roofing others would not be Pegaso's and his family's. They understood Roland's reason, and Victor went with Roland for his blue bed and brought it into their house for the night. There Roland slept from 10 PM to 6 AM.

The next day, Victor and Roland moved the blue bed over to Chilo and Mina's house. They came later in the morning to plant Pecan trees. Raul came by to visit and see where Roland was now staying. He told Roland he would have intervened to prevent Pegaso from doing serious harm, if it had gotten to that. Roland appreciated that much.

For the rest of Roland's stay, he slept at Chilo and Mina's vacant house. He visited various friends around town. He went to Nacho and Chela and asked them if they would still be his friends, and they said yes. That was good to hear.

That night, Roland had another dream about Isalia. Again, she gave him an angry glare and rushed him! This time, Roland stood his ground and glared back. She did not quite reach him.

*   *   *

Nuevo Wimbisenho

"Whew-wee!" That was quite a show!" Torxtalo declared, having thoroughly enjoyed it.

"We really had Pegaso on the rampage," Sasjurech commented.

"That's my telepathic witchcraft at work!" Arfifra proudly boasted. "Just answering Isalia's prayer, my dears."

"Brutoxlo responded like a charm," said Sojornbloc.

"I'm telling you!" Torxtalo agreed. "Brutoxlo guides and protects Pegaso well."

"We set up an excellent chance for rejection, didn't we?" Sasjurech boasted.

"So rich indeed," Sojornbloc added.

They cackled with laughter.

"Dashed that friendship to the wall," Torxtalo remarked, and he laughed inappropriately.

"Not to mention the dreams I've sent Roland," Arfifra added. "Of course, Isalia can't have her cake and eat it too, you know. Roland's now staying in the house she and Luke want, but we'll soon fix that . . ."

* * *

Roland took a hike up in the mountains and had a peaceful night's sleep up in the highland forest. It was not cold. Roland made a sincere wish for compensation to arrive and for Isalia and Luke to be punished.

The next day, Roland spent 6 hours clearing the rest of the trail through the forest over to the grassy saddle. It was hard work, but Roland was determined, and he accomplished what he wanted. So peaceful it was to be among the trees, who never took mysterious rejections against Roland, never yelled at Roland, and were always peaceful to be with. The trees never transmitted bad feelings like people did, who in Roland's view, were extremely strange for the majority of them. Trees were always the same. They were dependable and predictable, quite the contrary to the temperamental ways of the people of Earth.

That afternoon, Roland descended the mountain and returned to Bustamante. As he was arriving, he saw Angelo's brother Hugo with some friends of his, one of them Fabian. Hugo was carrying a rooster with him, and they talked to Roland.

Roland slept well that night, no bad dreams about Isalia.

One day, Luis and Juan Angel came over to visit Roland. They looked at his pictures in his album and also at his paintings.

Alberto had been working on his ranch, feeding all that gallinaza collected back in July to his cattle on his father's ranch. Suddenly, Roland saw him in town one day. He wanted to go up in the mountains to the ridge top with Roland. So, they made plans to go.

That night, which was a Friday night, Roland went to the plaza to talk to friends. Pegaso was there with several friends of his, including Angelo. With safety in numbers, Pegaso strutted over to Roland and asked him why he had gone all over town telling people about their fight the other night. Roland stated that he told people because he wanted to. Plus, people were asking Roland why he was no longer at the Orolizos.

Roland had his bicycle with him, and he placed it between him and Pegaso so he wouldn't get any closer. Pegaso didn't touch him. He'd already been talked to by the police a few days ago. Roland walked over to the police station with his bike, at which time Pegaso and his buddies all arrived. Both Pegaso and Roland entered the station where Pegaso complained that Roland had been telling everyone what happened and that they were looking at Pegaso in a bad way. The comandante, Valentín, asked Roland why Pegaso had gotten angry in the first place, and Roland said that he had commented that Pegaso's sisters were pretty. Valentín looked at Pegaso in a strange way and told him that Roland was a good fellow, and he asked Pegaso why he had gotten angry over that. Pegaso went on to say that he also was a good fellow, and he continued complaining. They were there several more minutes, and Roland left, followed by Pegaso. The police made Pegaso assure them he was going to continue to leave Roland alone, and they told Roland to not say any more about the incident.

The next day was the last day in January. Roland took Alberto over to Sabinas Hidalgo to obtain what is known as a Cartilla Militar, basically a military release after age 19 to be able to get a Mexican passport. Any Mexican male while age 19 cannot legally leave Mexico. Those are military requirements. Alberto had everything in order except his birth certificate, and upon arriving in the central plaza, they saw the military men set up. Several civilians were waiting in a line outside to obtain their releases. When Alberto reached them, they refused to give it to him for lack of his birth certificate.

They returned to Bustamante. It would be until next year before the military would visit Sabinas Hidalgo again to grant military releases.

They quickly packed some food and water and left for the mountains at 11:30 AM. In 2½ hours they had reached the grassy saddle. Alberto was impressed by the scenery. They hiked or climbed for another hour and reached the Cypress ridge. Views were spectacular today.

Alberto told Roland he wanted to go to the United States to work several months. He also expressed interest in going to Tennessee with Roland and possibly travelling with him to places like California, Oregon, and Washington.

Roland and Alberto enjoyed the views, took some photos, and they began the descent. It was 7:15 PM and already dark by the time they reached the cono. It had been a great day.

Roland went over to Raul and Rigo's house. Lavinia asked Roland if he would take them to see their godfather in the town of Pesquería. Rigo wanted to go, but Raul expressed that he was ready to go to the United States to be with his brother Eduardo. He went on to say that going to Pesquería was of no interest to him. Lavinia was not pleased by Raul's nonchalant attitude.

Roland told them he better stay out of it, and he returned to the Cantu's vacant house. It had been a long day. He went to sleep and slept well.

The next day, Roland rode his bicycle along the old gravel road 10 kilometers to Villaldama. He stopped by Leonardo's house. His sister was the only one there at the time.

Back in the old days, before 1970, the state highway from Anahuac to Monterrey didn't exist. There were roads, but they were old one-lane gravel roads designed for horses and buggies. The old road from Bustamante to Villaldama was one of these. People mostly travelled by train from Monterrey to Villaldama, Bustamante, Lampazos, and Anahuac. One day, Nacho Orolizo had related the past history of Bustamante to Roland, saying that in those days, there were a few taxi drivers who took people to and from the train station, 5 kilometers east of Bustamante. Of course now, there was regular bus service, (ZuaZua, Tamaulipas, and Grupo Senda), with the highway in full use, and the train station was disused. Trains still passed regularly, but most of them were freight trains.

In the later afternoon, once Roland had returned to Bustamante, he went over to Raul and Rigo's house. Roland bought some tortillas from Lavinia, but he didn't have exact change. He needed change for a N$10 note. Raul playfully grabbed the note from Roland and didn't want to supply him the N$5 change. Roland thanked Lavinia for the tortillas he, as a result, paid N$5 extra for, left it at that, and rode away.

That night, Roland had another nightmare about Isalia suddenly appearing and rushing him again! He awoke, somewhat terror stricken thinking, *What is wrong with that woman!?*

The next morning, Roland returned to Raul's house. It bothered Roland that Raul had collected N$5 extra off of him. Raul was not very receptive when Roland arrived. Perhaps he was upset at Roland for the discussion at the police station with Pegaso. Roland asked Raul why he didn't feel very happy, and he answered that he didn't know.

Roland asked Raul for that N$5 from yesterday. Raul looked at Roland and said, "Si te doy, ya te vas," which meant that if Raul gave it to Roland, then he better get up and leave. With that said, Roland's feelings were hurt. So, he asked Raul to go ahead and give it to him, which he did. Raul then told Roland never to come back, not to eat supper with them, not for any reason! Roland got up and left, and Roland pointed to his bicycle that he had given Raul last March, and he reminded him of that fact. Raul told him to go ahead and take it, and he would call the police, and he started cussing at Roland repeatedly!

With Raul's threat of calling the police, Roland rode straight to the police station, quite angry at Raul's sudden wickedness, and he reported Raul's actions to them. They sent out a car, found Raul, and hauled him in to the station where the police and Roland were waiting.

Raul walked in, and he had that sneering, scoffing look on his face again, the same face he had back on July 20 during that awful argument they provoked! The police did indeed scold Raul, telling him he ought to respect people better than that. They also asked Roland why he charged for a measly N$5. Roland explained that it was the principle of the thing. They talked a few more minutes and were then released.

Roland went over to Felipe's carpentry to talk to Rigo about it. He said he couldn't do anything about it, but he told Roland that if he wanted to go on being friends, then he would be his friend, or if not, then he wouldn't.

Roland then rode back to Chilo and Mina's vacant house, in a state of disbelief for the argument he and Raul had suddenly had. It had now been 20 minutes since the discussion at the police station, and as Roland rode up Avenida Independencia, he looked to the left and saw Isalia and Luke in the backyard with Lavinia. Lo and behold, there was Raul, talking with Isalia and Luke! Roland arrived at the Cantu's house to cool off!

*　　*　　*

-Meanwhile-

"We'll figure out another way to get him out of town," Luke assured Raul.

"Vamos a fijar una táctica para que Rolando se vaya asustado," Isalia translated, saying they would figure out a tactic so that Roland would get frightened and leave.

Next, Isalia took a N$100 note out of her pants pocket, and she handed it to Raul. She apologized to Raul that Roland had reported him to the police, and she praised him for his good work in running Roland off and severing his friendship with him. Maybe now, Roland would feel so sad, he would decide to pack his things and drive home.

Raul, though he didn't say it, was having mixed feelings of anger and guilt at what he had just done. He had run Roland off, at Isalia's request and offer of N$100. He needed the money or he wouldn't have done it. Thoughts were going through Raul's mind, and he wasn't comfortable with how he had just treated Roland.

"Raul, te pagamos otro N$300 más si puedes . . ." Isalia began to say, offering him an extra N$300 if he could . . .

"No . . . No," Raul declined, feeling more guilty.

Isalia saw Raul's sad face, but she was unable to understand.

Raul walked away and returned to his house.

Lavinia, Raul's mother was quite displeased at the whole incident, and she and Isalia talked about it. She asked Lavinia if there was anyone she knew who would like N$300 to scare Roland out of town. Lavinia, with her anger at Roland for having taken her son to the police, decided to be in on it, and she told Isalia about one of Raul's friends, Beto, down the

226

street. Translating their conversation to Luke, they decided that if Roland was not out of town within 24 hours, they were going to implement their next tactic.

*   *   *

Roland was quite sad at the sudden loss of friendship with Raul. Having seen Raul talking to Isalia and Luke made Roland suspicious. Granted, Raul's mother Lavinia worked for Isalia and Luke, but Roland smelled a rat. They were up to something.

Beto and Angelo were very nearby as it turned out. They were helping a man build a fence. Roland went and talked to them about what Raul had just done. Angelo said it was ridiculous for Roland to have charged Raul that N$5, even though he had taken it from Roland the day before.

Roland was too flustered to paint today. He went and visited different friends.

In the afternoon, he visited the Cantus at their store in the plaza. Roland asked them if they had sold the house to Isalia and Luke. Mina answered that they hadn't done anything yet. Then she told Roland that she and Isalia had been talking, and Isalia had made some bad remarks about Roland, how she didn't want his friendship, and how she still thought he stole some of the trailer cargo. Isalia had also told Mina something more, that Roland was out walking in his underwear!

Roland was shocked as he heard Mina tell him what Isalia had said to her. Roland assured Mina it certainly was not true. He knew better than walk outside in his underwear. Neighbors might see him.

Really, how far was Isalia going to take this . . . now defaming tactic?! How many others in town had Isalia told this new rumor? A considerable percentage of the people might believe it and as a result turn against Roland. He was very irritated at Isalia for spreading that malicious rumor, and he began to figure out a way to counter that.

The next day, Roland took Alberto to Sabinas Hidalgo. They went searching for an agent who knew how to get VISAs and border crossing cards for a fee of US $100. They were unable to find him.

Alberto told Roland that back last year he had gone to McAllen, Texas, with his passport and VISA, and the U.S. inspection officer asked him how much money he carried. Alberto knew it was somewhere near $80, and he gave them that answer. They requested to see his wallet, and they counted the money. It was $76, which was not $80. They accused Alberto of lying, and they ripped up his passport and VISA right there in front of him! That had made Alberto quite angry, but there wasn't much he could do about it, and U.S. Immigration had been very cruel to have literally stolen and destroyed his passport and VISA over a matter of exactly how much money he was carrying in his wallet! That was very unfair treatment indeed!

Roland told Alberto that some of the inspection officers are very sarcastic and sometimes downright ugly! He related to him the story of the black agricultural inspector taking away his Fan Palm leaves two years ago.

They returned to Bustamante in the afternoon. Roland ate supper over at Victor's house.

When Roland got up the next morning, February 4, he knew what he was going to do to counter Isalia and Luke's malicious rumor of Roland walking in his underwear. He went to the police station and asked them to accompany him to Isalia and Luke's house to confront them about the whole problem. Two of the police officers, Juan and Pancho, accompanied

Roland. They took him there in their Dodge pickup police truck. In addition to the underwear problem, Roland wanted to straighten out the whole mess from last month and come to some reconciliation. This was his last effort to reason with them, and this time he was confronting Isalia and Luke with the protection of the police officers.

They pulled up in front of Isalia and Luke's rental house, and the three of them stepped down from the police truck. Roland stepped up to the front yard gate. Isalia and Luke were both there, and so was Lavinia with a worried look on her face. She had *reason* to be worried.

Isalia approached Roland with an extremely angry look on her face. She had a look in her eyes that made her look like the devil woman! The police officers were taking their positions beside Roland.

"What did I *tell* you, Roland," Isalia declared. "You *don't* come over here!"

Roland managed to squeeze in the words, "No me gusta que . . . (I don't like it that . . .) in attempts to scold her for spreading malicious rumors, but he was unable to continue under her vicious spellbinding willpower!

Isalia screamed her head off, saying "Now get away!! Muy lejos!! *Muy lejos*!!" (very far away!!)

Roland stood his ground, but upon Juan and Pancho's advice, he retreated away from the front gate. Roland had the most awful feeling of nervous tension inside him, and he was shocked beyond belief at how cruel Isalia was!

Roland only slowly moved away, and suddenly Luke shouted, "*Get* over there to that pole!"

Juan told Isalia, "Este hombre viene para pedir disculpas," saying that Roland had come to request their forgiveness.

Luke complained in English that Roland had passed by several times on his bicycle during the past few weeks.

Isalia then translated that to Spanish, and she went on to complain and complain as Roland listened to this now nothing other than a woman who was severely mentally deranged . . . or possessed by some demon!

The police officers scolded Isalia for having rumored that Roland was walking in his underwear. He told her, "Ya no andas diciendo eso," saying to not go around saying that anymore.

Isalia responded, "Okay, okay, pero díle que ya no moleste a nosotros," saying, Okay, okay, but tell him not to bother us anymore.

The police officers went on to explain that the streets are public, and it is everyone's right to use them.

After that, the officers called Roland to come to them, and they got back in their truck. Juan told Roland that Isalia and Luke didn't want any kind of friendship with him, and they didn't want to clear any misunderstanding, basically no communication. Roland thanked the officers for their efforts. Juan admitted to Roland that it certainly was strange how Isalia was so unreasonable, and he told Roland he had done the right thing, by trying to reason with the woman.

Roland couldn't believe it! He thought surely Isalia would have been more reasonable, but instead she, and in the presence of two police officers, had screamed her head off at Roland as if he were some ogre or scary monster about to attack her! That was his third and final attempt to reason with her, and the misunderstanding would go, forever unresolved between them. Isalia lost her chance as a human being. She acted like a little immature 5-year-old child! Isalia had been a teacher. She should have known how to be reasonable, and to put forth an example like a school teacher!

Roland had felt guilty that he had not gone to Isalia and Luke to tell them about the green box in the first place, but now he realized that Lavinia had done the right thing by burning the box, and he and Rigo had done the right thing by tossing out that box's contents along a 10 kilometer stretch of highway between Villaldama and Sabinas Hidalgo.

Never, never in all his life had Roland seen a person be more unreasonable than Isalia! Why had she changed so much? In a way, he pitied her, but he would not excuse her bad behavior. He would have to figure out a way to get back his file folder from Isalia's house, either call her granddaughter, or obtain a court order back in Tennessee, if it became necessary! The way Isalia and Luke acted really made Roland angry. They were extremely ungrateful for those two trailer cargos!

Roland went to the Cantus and told them how unreasonable Isalia and Luke had been. He told Mina he had told the police about the malicious rumors Isalia had been spreading and that the officers had scolded Isalia for that. Mina agreed that was well done.

Roland went to Alberto's house, and they visited several hours. Alberto was sorry for Roland's bad luck with Isalia. Roland wrote out a note requesting his file folder back and expressing his disgust at Isalia and Luke. He wrote it ten times and asked Alberto to toss those ten copies into their yard at night, once Roland was safely away from Bustamante. He agreed he would do that for him. One of the copies was in an envelope addressed to "Isalia and Lucifer Wiggins." Roland and Alberto had a good laugh at the clever use of names.

That evening, Roland went to three places in attempts to be received for supper, but none of them would have him, not even Victor's family. Roland felt a sense that it was time to go home. He kept having disruptions every time he sat down to do his artwork. Maybe it would be best to go on home and finish his projects there. He returned to the Cantu's vacant house and fixed himself some supper.

There in the bedroom, he got out his drawing pads and began painting an excellent alien scene dealing with the origin of the Liriodendron (Tulip Poplar). He was painting a multileafed Poplar, the Poplar Reale he had seen in his dream of June 1996.

In the kitchen, he suddenly heard what sounded like a piece of tin roofing falling down. A couple of seconds went by.

POW!! Roland saw a white flash of light! Instantly, Isalia and Luke entered his mind as being behind it!

"What in the world?!" Roland commented. He stood very still, afraid to go into the next room. He wasn't sure if the explosion had been in the living room or kitchen. He also hadn't seen or heard anybody enter or leave the premises. After a couple of minutes, he walked into the living room and kitchen to investigate. He smelled gunpowder!

There was a piece of broken grey cardboard wrapper in the living room near his bicycle, and when he went into the kitchen, he found the rest of the stick, equal to the size of a stick of dynamite! The wrapper was grey in color, and there was white chalky powder within it. Then Roland noticed that the kitchen window was slid open. That was the sound of the "tin roofing falling." Somebody had sneaked up to the house, slid the window open, and tossed the firecracker/bomb inside.

Roland stepped outside, talked to the neighbors to see if they had heard it. Yes, they had, but they hadn't seen anybody. He checked his car, and it was fine. Of course, Roland was shaken up. He thought about going to the police, but he knew they wouldn't be able to do anything till morning. So, he went to bed, but before he did so, he locked all the windows.

Of course, Roland didn't sleep very well. He was nervous and worried that something else might happen.

The next morning, Roland went to the police station to report it. They agreed it was bad to toss a firecracker, and that later in the day, they would come and investigate. Roland also went to Alberto's house and told him what happened. Alberto suggested that Isalia and Luke were probably behind it.

Roland began to pack his car that morning. He went to Angelo's house. Beto was there, as well. Roland told them what happened and that he was leaving today. Beto asked Roland to stay, but Roland said he was afraid for his safety. He was sending up his surrender flag and going home.

He also called his parents. His mother answered, and he told her he was coming home. He told them about the firecracker, that Isalia and Luke were likely behind it, and that Isalia had been spreading malicious rumors about his walking in his underwear!

Roland's mother was very irritated to hear that. She said that was it! Isalia was no longer on her list of friends, and she would not be forgiven. Plus, she had put Roland in a lot of danger with the police several weeks ago, and she had accused him of stealing. Isalia should have known Roland better than that. Roland's mother told him to pack his car and get out of there as soon as possible.

Alberto came over to help Roland finish packing his station wagon. The police came over to investigate, and they looked at the firecracker/bomb. Juan, the same officer as yesterday was present, and he thought it was Beto, Raul's friend. They left in their police truck and ten minutes later, they brought both Beto and Raul to the scene.

Next, they searched the grounds for footprints. Beto had on boots, and his boots perfectly matched the boot prints on the ground leading to the kitchen window. The evidence was there. It was Beto.

Juan offered Roland to have Beto arrested and taken to jail, if he wished. Beto denied it entirely. Roland explained that while the boot prints matching Beto's boots was a form of evidence, his conscience wouldn't let him have Beto arrested because he hadn't actually seen anyone entering and leaving the premises last night. Plus, Beto was one of Roland's friends.

Roland talked to Raul about their argument the other day. Raul actually talked to him, but he was showing resentment.

Juan and the other police officer told Raul and Beto they were free to go. They walked away. Beto had an angry look on his face, and Roland assured him that they could go on being friends.

Roland thanked them for their investigating. He handed Juan N$50 so he could buy sodas for everyone. Juan commented that it certainly was strange how vicious Isalia had been yesterday when they had arrived at their front yard gate. Juan, though he said nothing to Roland about it, had some other ideas and investigating to do, concerning that firecracker/bomb. The police drove away and wished Roland well.

As Alberto and Roland packed the last item, a little brown car arrived, and a woman in her 40's got out of the car and walked up to Roland. She introduced herself as Elisa, and she told Roland that Victor's mother had told her about him. She wanted to buy several copies of Roland's artwork and calendars. He was quite surprised, and he showed her what he had. She picked out several calendars, some intended as gifts for her family members in Monterrey, and she bought a copy of his book compilation, as well. She offered him retail price, which would have been N$500 for all that she bought, but he told her that N$300 would be fine. After all, Mexican wages were miserably low. She handed him N$300, and he thanked her very much. Roland specially autographed the book for her, and she returned to her little car and drove away.

Alberto looked at Roland and pointed out that he had experienced a stroke of good luck.

Roland was now ready to leave. He locked the house door, and Roland wished Alberto well on getting a passport and VISA. He would see if he could return for him in April, to take him up to Tennessee with him. Alberto rode away on his bicycle.

Roland drove to the plaza and turned in the key to Mina Cantu. She looked very displeased at Roland. He asked her what was wrong.

Mina told Roland that Isalia and Luke had come by this morning to say they were no longer going to buy the house because Roland had entered the house to stay, and his bad energies had contaminated the house forever! Mina was quite angry, and she told Roland that he had ruined the sale of the house!

How cruel of Isalia to have said that about Roland! Now Isalia had succeeded in turning the Cantu family against Roland also. Very clever and shrewd tactic that was! The truth was, Isalia and Luke had never really intended to buy the house in the first place.

Roland told Mina good luck with selling the house, and he thanked her for letting him stay there. She repeated her complaint, telling Roland again how he ruined the sale of the house! Of course, Roland felt sad about it, and he walked out of the Cantu's store.

Roland went over to Felipe's carpentry and told them goodbye. He handed Rigo an envelope with a N$200 note and a written note saying he appreciated him for being a friend and that the money was to help him with school. Rigo sincerely wished him well, and they shook hands, Mexican style. Roland got in his car and drove out of town.

He reached the Colombia Bridge by late afternoon, where he turned in his tourist permit and cancelled his car permit.

Now was his time to get even with Isalia and Luke. He wrote a one-page letter to Colombia Bridge authorities, reporting Luke's white truck, that he planned on leaving it with the Quevalo family forever, and that he was violating Mexican law! He wrote down the license plate number, type of truck, and he gave necessary and sufficient addresses and phone numbers, including the police's phone number in Bustamante. Customs was rather irritated to learn about Luke's plans. They said Luke had a serious problem with them, and that what he did carried a big fine.

They told Roland he was all right with them. He could come and go as he liked because he always took his vehicle home with him and always turned in his permits for cancellation.

Roland thanked them. They wished him well by saying, "Dios te bendiga."

Roland wasn't going to report the truck, not even for their having reported him to the police for "following" and "bothering" them, but after they screamed their heads off at him, he had changed his mind. And then to add injury to insult, there was the firecracker/bomb explosion!

Suddenly, Roland realized he had left Bustamante without telling the most important detail to the police this morning, and Alberto had even suggested the possibility. Somehow, it did not occur to anybody at the crucial time to mention to the police that Isalia and Luke likely paid Beto to toss that firecracker/bomb! How could that have slipped their minds? How in the world?

Roland crossed the bridge and underwent inspection. The officer was friendly and courteous, inspected most of Roland's baggage, made a nice comment about the three chairs, and then said he was free to go. Roland thanked the officer, loaded his car again, and drove to Laredo.

From a payphone, he made a call to the Bustamante police to tell Juan the important detail about Isalia and Luke being behind the firecracker/bomb. Juan came to the phone and told Roland it had dawned on him only minutes after they had finished investigating the site. They were in the process of trying to locate Beto to question him concerning that detail, and then they were going to pay Isalia and Luke a visit to try and get them to confess to the conspiracy.

Juan was a police officer on the ball, a good detective indeed.

Gossip was already spreading about the firecracker incident and how the gringo left town as a result. Since the Spanish name for firecracker is *cuete*, and since Isalia was the one truly behind it, she earned the nickname: *La Cuetona*, a defaming name that would put her in her place for years to come.

*   *   *

Meanwhile Isalia and Luke were celebrating with the Quevalos. Roland had successfully been run out of town.

"He's gone, Luke!" Isalia told her husband and grinning a smile from ear to ear.

"Hot dog!" Luke shouted with joy.

Their selfish and malicious tactics had gotten Roland out of "their" town.

"It was his destiny to leave!" Isalia declared.

"With his being gay, he had no right to be here, anyway!" Luke strongly agreed. "Isalia, how many friendships did we have to wreck for him to leave town?"

Isalia paused and diligently counted silently. She said under her breath, "Pegaso, Raul, Beto, the Cantus, and of course the Quevalos . . . *Five*. Oh, how perfect!" She gave a smile that showed she was reveling in delight. Luke took her into his arms and kissed her. "Oh, I love you, Luke. Now we can enjoy our time in Bustamante . . . in *peace*."

Famous last words! Little did they know what was to come, a visit from Juan, and for certain a larger problem from the Colombia Bridge!

*   *   *

Roland never realized it, but those five flower tubers that Isalia sent to Tennessee with Roland back in November, represented more than just five flowers in her front yard entrance. Roland had recognized them as a type of noxious weed that is common in barnyards, and he wondered why Isalia had been so enthralled by them. The truth was that Isalia performed a "ceremony", said a special prayer, and programmed those tubers with a special energy, that once planted in the ground, would grow and seek to destroy one friendship each! Isalia's black magic experiment had worked like a charm, and Roland lost five significant friendships in Bustamante, just the magic number to run him out of town and back to Tennessee! That was exactly her intent!

Roland felt satisfied with his retaliation. After all, Isalia and Luke were getting away

232

with everything, and even though Roland sincerely wished for natural law to punish them, it just never happened! It was not fair at all. So, Roland took natural law into his own hands, and he reported that truck to Mexican Customs.

It was two days later when the police finally resolved the problem. They found Beto easily enough, but Isalia and Luke were "playing hide and seek" when they got wind that the police were looking for them. The police stationed themselves at the entrances to the town, and eventually, Isalia and Luke drove by. Immediately, they were pulled over and hauled in for questioning. They steadfastly denied it.

Poor Beto was charged a N$100 fine, even though he confessed to having been paid N$300 by Isalia and Luke. Isalia and Luke received a stiffer penalty. They were both sentenced to three days in jail . . . that or pay the bail of N$1,200 each. They paid the bail and were released. And no, Isalia and Luke were not gracious enough to reimburse Beto for his N$100 loss. After all, they were the same ones who never offered to reimburse Roland for that mean $107 ticket he got back in September, while helping out Luke with the trailer and haybaler!

Roland drove back to Tennessee angry and sad. All the good and miracles and everything that had occurred back in October and November had now been shattered! Roland only went to Mexico to enjoy his friends. Never was it his intention to lose friends, but by the time he left, his friendships were dropping like flies! His stay in Bustamante ended in disaster! What was going on?! More and more, Roland was becoming aware of some sort of malign force that was ruining his life, and now he had reason to believe that Isalia (La Cuetona) was behind it all.

On the way home, Roland had a dream about Raul. He had a look on his face with an expression of: *What have I just done?* He seemed to be regretting the loss of friendship that had so quickly occurred the other day. In the dream, they were standing on a narrow bridge on a curve of a highway.

Upon arriving home two days later, he called up his friend Ivanhoe in Scotland. They talked for two hours. Ivanhoe told Roland he was not surprised, that he had seen it coming. Roland thought surely Ivanhoe would have been surprised, and he asked Ivanhoe if he had heard him right. Ivanhoe verified that yes, he had seen it coming but had kept it to himself. Ivanhoe wasn't the only one who had seen it coming, Roland would later find out.

He asked Ivanhoe if there was anything he could do to protect him via his powers, and he offered to pay Ivanhoe for the favor. Ivanhoe named a price of £200, which equaled $330. Roland agreed to it, as he was really afraid of what else Isalia and Luke might do, especially once they returned home to Tennessee.

Ivanhoe told Roland he had rubbed energies the wrong way in certain situations, and that the whole problem began when he delivered that green box to Raul back in June. The energy grew straight off that box, and Roland was on a fine line as a result of that mistake. He also told Roland his reporting that truck was like poking a bear with a stick, and he was really asking for it. At the same time, Ivanhoe could understand Roland's reasons for reporting Luke's truck, and he and Isalia deserved it.

"Now, listen," Ivanhoe advised. "You and Isalia became totally incompatible. If you do as I say, no more contact with them, you'll be fine anyway, but you're on a fine line about . . ." and Ivanhoe gave Roland the rest of the advice.

Roland asked Ivanhoe what it was that he was going to do.

"I know what to do. Don't worry about it. If I tell you, it won't work. I'll tell you this, Roland. You're extremely lucky that you got out of there with your hide intact. I saw you in jail down there for two years, with no court, and no bail!"

"In jail!?" Roland reacted. "How would that have happened?"

"Raul's mom likely would have reported your for touching her son."

"But I didn't," Roland said.

"I know you didn't, but Raul would have told his mother you did," Ivanhoe explained. "Plus, you would have had serious intimidation tactics from Isalia and Luke. Let me tell you how close you were. The next night, had you stayed in town any longer, they would have tossed a petrol bomb under your car, and you would never have been able to prove it. They have no conscience, and they cover their tracks well."

Roland was shuddering, realizing how close it had been for him.

"Roland, are you all right, there?"

". . . Uh . . . yes, I'm fine, Ivanhoe. Just shell-shocked. That's all."

"Don't worry. You'll be fine. Just take my advice. When you sense danger, just leave. Don't linger around . . ."

They talked a while longer.

Roland went to the bank the next day and bought ten £20 notes. He took with him the very same copy of the book compilation and the calendars that Isalia and he had used in August 1996, when she had "blessed" them on her deck by the creek. He placed the £20 notes between various pages of that book, wrapped it and the calendars up in a cardboard box, secured it very well with tape, and sent it by airmail to Ivanhoe. He received it a week later.

Roland later realized that the amount of money he had sent Ivanhoe (US $330) exactly equaled the extra expense Isalia had to make two years ago to buy the extra materials to complete her deck by the creek, since Roland had miscalculated the amount of materials needed.

No matter what, the amount of money Roland had sent Ivanhoe was money well spent. The protection was worth it. Plus, they had had extensive conversations by telephone, talking about various concepts and interesting ideas, in addition to Ivanhoe's helpful and philosophical analyses of various situations, all of which Roland appreciated.

Roland was glad to be safely back at home, and he told his parents everything that had happened. They were shocked and disappointed at what Isalia and Luke had done.

"The very idea of Isalia casting aspersion on you!" Roland's mother declared. "How cruel and wicked of her to spread malicious gossip that you were walking in your underwear!"

"And she dumped poison on your friendships," Roland's father added.

"How would Isalia like it," his mother pointed out, "if we went around saying, 'Guess what? Did you know that Isalia runs a prostitute business here in town?!'"

"She would be furious, wouldn't she?" said Roland, laughing.

"Of course, but it would only be fair," Mrs. Jocelyn continued. "She betrayed you, and therefore betrayed us, and she put you in serious danger! If she ever calls out here, I'm going to give her an earful, and I'll hang up on her!"

"I thought she was our friend," Roland's father added. "She's no friend of ours!"

Roland's parents weren't just put out with Isalia and Luke. They were furious!

Roland called two of Isalia's friends. One of them was quite surprised, and said she would never have been crazy enough to take all that trailer cargo down there! The other one, Mrs. Tinkerton, was not so surprised, since she had a falling out with Isalia over what color car to buy. Roland asked both of them to ask Isalia to return his file folder to him. Mrs. Tinkerton, bless her soul, obliged him.

Mrs. Tinkerton said it wasn't she who had said, "I don't need you in my world!" It was the other way around, and it was Isalia who had suddenly snapped, "It's over!"

Roland also found out something else that was totally unreasonable. Several years ago, around 1993, Isalia's granddaughter, Missy, was spending the summer with her. She had a new boyfriend, and she wanted to date him. Isalia had consented but told her to be back at a certain hour of the night. Well, her granddaughter got in an hour later, and Isalia threw a fit! Not only did she scold her, she used the police to have her granddaughter removed from the premises, taken to the airport, and flown back to California where she was living! Now, why couldn't Isalia have taken her granddaughter to the airport herself and said goodbye to her properly? The woman was truly unreasonable and was over extreme in her punishments! One can imagine the angry words Isalia and her son must have had over the telephone, once his daughter arrived home!

Roland talked to some other people about Isalia, including Longview High School's principal, Mr. Wallace. There was an underlying reason why she and Mr. Wallace had gotten into it, back in 1990. One of Isalia's Spanish students smarted off to her, and she slapped the student! His parents came to the school, and they came down on her like a bear! In other words, they had a serious discussion with her. They really got after her, and they didn't let her off, either! Mr. Wallace handed Isalia a formal reprimand, and he was on her back, as well. He watched her like a hawk, driving her into frustration. Since she had tenure, they couldn't fire her, but they did make her transfer to another high school in the system. Yes, Isalia was very angry at Mr. Wallace for having intimidated her by watching her like a hawk for weeks, but then there are consequences for slapping a student, and Mr. Wallace was right!

Several cats were being let out of the bags, one might say. Truths were being revealed. Roland verified the student slapping incident with several teachers who knew Isalia at Longview High School.

Over the next several weeks, Roland started up his carpentry and painting business again. He did work for Elizabeth in Nashville and for several others in Shelbyville and Murfreesboro, and he also painted the house where he lived on his parents' farm.

Being the month of February, work was somewhat slow. So, he made up for lost time, did some more paintings, and compiled several more calendars. He included scenes from Mexico in one of the calendars, complete with semblances of his friends there, as well as portraying some of the weird incidents that had occurred. He was so mad at Isalia that he did one painting of her and her husband being scared out of town! He did it like a cartoon sequence of events, and he showed them fleeing town as fast as they could go . . . in their old white truck, complete with lots of white smoke coming out of the tailpipe! Roland thoroughly enjoyed doing that painting, and it gave him a good laugh every time he looked at it.

One day, Roland was in the kitchen eating lunch, and he suddenly zeroed in on an object. "Oh, yeah! The piece of needlework!" he exclaimed to himself. He had been home a week already, and it had somehow not caught his attention . . . until now. When Roland had arrived home in November, he had placed it upright in the kitchen, and there it sat, still decorating his kitchen.

Of course now, Roland no longer had Isalia and Luke's friendship. How in the world was he going to take it to their house, without being accused of stealing and trespassing! Why did they send the piece of needlework home with Roland, anyway? And it was delivered to Roland's hands third party, via Lola Quevalo. Roland was suspicious. Perhaps Isalia and Luke had plans to frame him, accusing him of stealing the framed needlework!

He took it straight to his parents, and they called another one of Isalia's friends, this one being Cason Butler. He and his wife were really sad to learn about Isalia's rejection of Roland and all the cruel and malicious actions she had done. They were afraid to touch that piece of needlework, and they suggested that Roland take it straight to the sheriff's office. Good idea!

Roland's father called the sheriff himself, explaining what had happened. He asked him if he would receive the needlework, and deliver it to Isalia. The sheriff said he'd be glad to. Roland wrapped it up in brown paper, wrote Isalia's address and phone number on it, and took it to the sheriff. Roland also wrote a note to Isalia, directly on the brown paper, asking her to return him his file folder. The sheriff's office wrote Roland a receipt, verifying reception of the needlework, and Roland went home. The sheriff called Isalia's house and left several messages, and Isalia's granddaughter Missy responded and picked up the item a week later.

Roland also reached Isalia's sister Roma on the phone. She was very sorry about it all and wondered why it had to get so ugly. Roland explained that all he tried to do was reason with Isalia, but she would not give him a chance to talk to her. Roma assured Roland he was a good fellow. She explained that Isalia was not a church goer, and she had always viewed life differently. Roland then said he didn't frequent going to church either, but he certainly was reasonable and friendly. Why couldn't Isalia be reasonable and friendly anymore? Roma explained that people change and that we have to accept those things. *No we don't*, Roland thought to himself. Roma talked to Roland a few more minutes and wished him blessings, but best of all, she told Roland to feel free to return to Bustamante and that Isalia has no right to tell him anything, much less, mandate him! Roland thanked Roma for those words.

Ivanhoe received the money and the "blessed" copies of Roland's book and calendars, and they talked on the phone. Roland said he was feeling better, and Ivanhoe was glad to know that.

*   *   *

At the end of February, Pancho received a call from Mexican Customs pertaining to Luke's white truck. Isalia and Luke were there at the time and came to the phone. They were horrified to find out that Roland had reported it! The customs official ordered them to either come to the Colombia Bridge and pay the fine or come and cancel the permit and return the truck to the United States.

Nervous feelings went through both Isalia and Luke! They were furious at Roland! Yeah, but what did they expect, after all the danger they had put Roland in, plus the friendships they helped destroy by different shrewd tactics. They now had to admit that Roland had caused them to be bitten in the tail! Never would they forgive Roland for that! *Never*!

The three of them, including Pancho, went to the Colombia Bridge where they made up excuse after excuse. Customs would not let them off, and they were forced to pay a fine equivalent to US $500. Luke deserved the ticket, and he paid the fine! He was shaking in his boots, too!

La Cuetona Y Su Fuerza Maligna

As they walked out of that building, Luke told Isalia, "I tell you what! The day I get my hands on Roland, I'm gonna . . ."

"Luke," Isalia interrupted, "let's join hands and say a prayer, right now."

Pancho joined hands with them also, and Isalia said the prayer both in English and in Spanish.

She prayed hard for Roland to be punished (as if he hadn't suffered enough already) for his having reported Luke's truck. She declared Roland dangerous to be around, for his special abilities and talents, namely the energy blast she received back in September 1981, that she was blaming Roland for! She prayed very hard for Roland's friends to take rejection to him, for their own safety, and most of all, she prayed for anyone who had serious intent to travel with Roland, to experience numerous problems, sufficient to drive them into poverty, so they wouldn't be able to travel with him. In other words, she prayed for Roland to be alone so that he would always have to travel . . . alone!

The three of them climbed into the old white truck, and they returned to Bustamante.

Though Roland knew nothing of the fine Isalia and Luke had just received, *Roland had a dream that he was with them back in Tennessee. Luke was hopping mad at Roland, and he reached out angrily to grab Roland by the arm. Roland dodged him and said if he touched him, he would call the police on him! Luke was unsuccessful in reaching Roland.*

Roland later told the dream to Ivanhoe, and they had a good laugh about it.

"Don't worry. You'll be all right," Ivanhoe confidently told Roland.

Roland recalled back last year when he had told Isalia his thoughts about Norma. Isalia had said, "Oh, Roland, I'm so happy for you, *I can't stand it!*" Of course, that's just a figure of speech to emphasize your happiness for someone. Not so for Isalia. She meant it . . . to the word! Isalia really couldn't stand it that Roland had made so many friends in Bustamante, and she set out to destroy those friendships by her cruel and malicious tactics, so cleverly shrewd they were hard to detect.

More than that, Roland was helping his friends by giving them things, like bicycles, a washing machine, money, among other things. He helped Felipe and only charged him at cost. As a result, Roland was slipping away from Isalia's mental grasp. It was not convenient to her that Roland was out there on his on, befriending people and helping them. Roland's continued benevolence and goodness would liberate him from her mental connection, and for her own selfish reasons, she tried to stop him.

Roland really felt like his friendships had been jinxed by Isalia in one way or another, especially those friends that he had told her about. He had told her about Leonardo back in 1996. Yes, he had enjoyed a good visit on December 28, 1996, but after that, he was mysteriously blocked from ever seeing him again, except for one visit of less than ten minutes! He had told her about Chip Collins, and look where that went! He told her about his friend in Spain, and he was too busy studying for final exams to visit with Roland when he was there. Roland got wind of something mysterious going on last year because the loss of friendships was becoming more frequent, and of course, the awful experiences in Bustamante during the past month provided proof without a doubt!

It was a great relief to Roland to have Isalia out of his life, and he would never tell Isalia about any new friends of his. Still, it was far from over. Roland still had friends he had previously told Isalia about, and it remained to be seen if those friendships would stay intact.

*   *   *

Nuevo Wimbisenho

Meanwhile, Sasjurech and Sojornbloc were making remarks down at Nuevo Wimbisenho.

"And wasn't that hilarious, that dream I sent Chris in London back in 1994," Sasjurech laughed.

"Scared the stuffing out of him, didn't it?" said Sojornbloc.

"You could have heard his screams all the way to Harrow."

"Rather *harrowing* experience for him, wasn't it?" Sojornbloc pointed out, gesturing a pun.

Both of them roared with laughter!

"And that dream we sent Roland about dialling Ivanhoe's number . . ." said Sasjurech.

"Not to mention all those coincidences we sent him and Chip Collins," Sasjurech added.

"Roland and Chip became great friends, didn't they?" said Sojornbloc.

"Until we sent Chip that *special* dream about Roland that scared the pants off of him!" and Sasjurech poked Sojornbloc in the side.

They roared with laughter again!

"Never did it occur to Roland who his travelling companion was," Sojornbloc proudly boasted with a smile.

"I tell you what," Sasjurech complimented Sojornbloc. "You were on the ball on that one . . . shifted Roland's thoughts every time, didn't you?"

"Amen, brother," and Sasjurech poked Sojornbloc in his side again.

They both cackled with another round of laughter.

"We sure got Leonardo out of the way every time," said Sasjurech.

"Just at the right moment, we always reminded him of something he had to do," Sojornbloc added.

"And we really took Raul for a spin back in July."

"I tell you, we got that Roland under our thumb."

"Knock off a few more friendships of his, and he may be ours," Sasjurech told him.

They shook hands in triumph.

About this time, Draaktra and Arfifra walked in. Arfifra's favorite "pet" Torxtalo also walked in. He was right by her side, following her like a piece of candy.

"Time for the feast, everyone!" Arfifra announced with a smile.

"Isalia really came through for us this time," Sasjurech commented.

"You really worked a number on her, didn't you?" Sojornbloc praised Arfifra. "How did you do it so well?"

"Just a telepathic twist of dark energy and a sprinkle of our special black magic," Arfifra boasted.

"You're amazing!" Draaktra also praised.

"Take lessons, my dear," Arfifra advised him. "That is the way it's *done*. Your mission is Rigo."

"Piece of cake!" Draaktra spouted off. "I'll have him fall for me, hook, line, and sinker. You'll see."

"Isalia really sent the energy to us, didn't she?" Sasjurech told the others.

"A surplus indeed. I tell you!" Sojornbloc agreed.

"That firecracker/bomb scared Roland to death. That was hilarious!" Draaktra said, and he cackled with laughter.

"And did you hear Isalia's prayer?" Sasjurech pointed out. "She's insatiable, isn't she?"

My protectee Pancho was right in on it," Torxtalo commented. He laughed inappropriately.

The demons had a special energy capture apparatus which they used to capture angry energy. Isalia had unknowingly sent them a surplus, and their mouths were watering as they waited to feast on it. Feasting on concentrated energy in special surges was so much more exhilarating than taking it in as it came from angry and possessed people. Arfifra's father, Denlamter had invented it some 30 years ago, and now demons throughout were using them. It gave them much more incentive to wreck havoc than in times past.

The "meals" were prepared and served on special energy disks.

"Hail to Arfifra!" they chanted. "Our queen of black magic."

In less than 15 seconds, the energy was . . . "eaten".

"Oh, scrumptious!" Sasjurech remarked with savour in his voice.

"Ecstasy to perfection!" Draaktra declared.

"All from prestigious rejections, my dears," said Arfifra, and she cackled with laughter.

They finished their feast and put away their energy disks.

Before anyone else spoke, Arfifra announced, "Now to more serious matters," and she looked at the other three. "I've got bad news. Roland had a conversation with his friend Ivanhoe, who has a very swift and adept guardian angel named Martoncíon, who is Selím's father. Roland requested a protection from Ivanhoe, and he has weaved a very complex and intelligent quantum energy system, which will endure for exactly six months and will protect Roland. Sasjurech and Sojornbloc, you may as well take a six month vacation. You're not getting through that barrier. It's too strong! Not even I can get in. Draaktra, as for you, you be poised and ready on August 9. Rigo will be available for you. Until then, all three of you keep your distance from Roland. Martoncíon knows how to see right through stealth cloaking shields.

"However, there are some things we can still do in answer to Isalia's prayer, and furthermore . . ."

*   *   *

Roland missed those in Bustamante who were still his friends. Somehow, despite Isalia's jinxes, Rigo had faithfully remained a friend. Roland appreciated Rigo a lot, and he hoped he would be able to return to Bustamante to continue knowing him.

Roland had his pictures developed. They came out great! He mailed copies to Alberto of their hike in the mountains, and he also sent a packet to Rigo with pictures of him, Raul, and the Zacatóns. Roland also typed out a short letter to Rigo and sent him a self-addressed envelope, and in the letter to Rigo, Roland asked him to use that Royal 440 manual typewriter that he gave him and type him a letter.

Later, Roland would find out that in addition to the protection energy system Ivanhoe weaved for him, he also sorted out the energies rubbed the wrong way in Bustamante. People's anger toward Roland was being alleviated. Things were changing for the better. Plus, Ivanhoe installed a new program on Roland that caused people to take a turn for the better in his presence, that is, take a liking to him. That program would provide Roland the good compensation he deserved, and it would be sufficient to at least partially override Isalia's wicked prayer.

As the weeks went by, Roland continued doing more excellent paintings on rainy days and evenings. Some days he worked for clients. Other days he worked at home.

Spring arrived, and some friends of his in North Carolina needed some painting done. Roland drove over there. On the way, he decided to happen by Steven's parents' house in Jefferson City. Steven was a friend from Tennessee Tech University. Lo and behold, Steven was actually there! It was the first time Roland had seen Steven in more than four years. They were glad to see each other, and they had a good visit.

Later that afternoon, Roland continued to Asheville, feeling really content.

One morning, while over there in Asheville and while half asleep in bed, Roland felt a tendon pull in his left knee. Discomfort resulted from that, and it lasted for several months before it finally went away. Mysterious it was indeed!

Roland painted for four days, and then returned home.

On the way back, he decided to stop by Cookeville to see if he might catch Steve Cason at home. Back in October, he had fundamentally failed to ever find Steve at home. Just as Roland drove into the apartment complex, Steve was arriving. They finally met each other, and they visited and made plans to go hiking. Steve's fiancée was with him, and so was his brother.

Things were indeed improving. Roland had felt mysteriously blocked from finding Steve at home, and now he had found him. That was good.

When Roland arrived home, his parents handed him a big envelope. Inside it was his file folder. Isalia had returned it. Well, Good! She did something right! Roland's father said he got a call from the office where he used to work. They told him there was a big envelope there for him, and that it had been delivered by a woman. He had gone to his former office and picked it up yesterday.

Isalia and Luke had just arrived back in town the other day. One of Isalia's friends had picked them up from the airport. They had enjoyed (apart from the truck reporting) the remainder of their stay in Mexico. Isalia complained to her friend about Roland's having *attended* her wedding. She also complained about the truck reporting and that they would never forgive Roland for that! When they got home, they found the wrapped up piece of framed needlework, delivered via the sheriff's office, and of course, she saw Roland's note requesting his file folder.

The next day, Mrs. Tinkerton called and told Isalia that Roland wanted his file folder back.

Isalia became flustered and answered, "Yes, I'm going to take care of it!"

La Cuetona Y Su Fuerza Maligna

She had been reminded enough times! After all, she couldn't help but read the ten copies of Roland's note that were tossed into the yard of their rental house, a few days after Roland had left Bustamante, and she could sense that if she didn't return that file folder to Roland, she was going to receive a lot more interrogation: letters and phone calls from Roland and more phone calls from people she knew. Yes, she got that problem over with. She returned that file folder promptly! Smart move, Isalia!

Shortly after that, Roland had a dream about Raul. He had come to the United States wetback, and Roland was visiting with him. Raul said he was getting adjusted to life, now in the USA and so on. Roland woke up from the dream, missing his friend, and he realized that he had, at that moment, forgiven Raul.

Roland called Alberto on the phone and told him he wasn't going to be able to come for him in April like he had wanted. There wasn't enough extra money at the time, but in August he would be coming for sure.

The leaves were beginning to come out on the trees. Roland noticed the Sugar Maple in the front yard was not putting out new leaves. Alarmed, he walked over to the trunk and placed his hand on it. The bark was loose and separating from the trunk! The tree had died. That Maple tree was Roland's favorite climbing tree when he was a child. He must have climbed it over 100 times. He was very sad to realize it had died.

For more than two years, Roland had been making numerous efforts to take his cousins: David and John on a hike to Savage Gulf State Natural Area, a beautiful canyon with a section of virgin forest. Every time he had invited them, they always had their weekends full and were never able to go. As a result, Roland was unsuccessful in ever getting on their schedule. He had a solution. He took a stone slab, wrote: *Trip to Savage Gulf to see the virgin forest, Spring 1998*. He put their names on it and signed his own. Then he mailed it to them in a box.

A few days later, Roland received a phone call from them. They named a day in April, during their Spring Break, and they *finally* put Roland on their schedule. Amazing!

Two weeks later Roland drove to their house to pick them up, and from there they drove on to Savage Gulf, and they went hiking. John had to be back for a family ballgame at 6 PM sharp. So, that cut the time short, but nevertheless, they had a good hike with nice sunny weather all day. He took several pictures.

Roland felt satisfied. He had finally done some activities with his cousins, and they had finally gone hiking. After all, Roland rightfully believed that friendship and activities with family members is very important. Roland's stone tablet was taken seriously. The hiking trip had been written in stone, and it *occurred*.

Isalia's curse was over! Halleluyah!

Roland happened to meet another young inspiring artist in Shelbyville. His name was David, and he was very impressed with Roland's artwork and paintings. Roland was impressed with David's artwork, also. They got along very well and became friends. David, like Roland, was competent, very precise, and did an excellent job with his drawings and paintings. David also had a keen interest in scenes from alien worlds, and he and Roland even talked about collaborating and doing a calendar project together.

As the weeks went on, they also talked about travelling together, but as it turned out, David's old Nissan Sentra went on the blink, coughing and sputtering. He had it towed to numerous mechanics, and none of them were able to fix the car. They replaced numerous expensive parts including the brain box, and the car only ran worse! Roland suggested replacing the car's distributor, but mysteriously, none of the mechanics could ever understand nor believe that was the problem piece on the car. David had to abandon his Sentra, and he bought a newer one, resulting in his having to take a second job to complete the car payments. Travelling was out of the question now. He barely had enough time to do any paintings at all, much less collaborate with Roland to do a calendar. Roland realized David's sudden bad luck, and he told him he was sorry about his car. No matter what, they had enjoyed getting to know each other, and they would remain friends for some time.

On April 16, the weather across Tennessee became very dangerous. All TV programs were cancelled for the whole day, and every station became a weather channel. Hundreds of tornados were passing across the region, touching down in every county in west Tennessee. Bedford and Rutherford Counties were right on target, and everyone was on tornado warning!

Oddly enough, that afternoon, just before the mass of tornados reached Bedford and Rutherford Counties, they lifted upwards, no longer touching down. Debris from Columbia and Hohenwald literally fell out of the sky. There were pieces of tin, building material, newspapers, magazines, and photos, and they were scattered across the whole countryside like litter. Roland later went up in the woods and found a bunch of items.

Never had he seen anything like it.

East of Murfreesboro and Shelbyville, the mass of tornados began touching down again, and they caused more damage to east central Tennessee.

Nashville had suffered severe damage, and the counties to the south had also been hit. In fact, as it turned out, northern Bedford County and Rutherford County was the *only* region that was spared tornados.

Murfreesboro's newspaper had a front page banner headline the next day saying:

Angels . . . worked overtime! County dodges storm damage.

"Miraculous is the best word to describe Rutherford County's good fortune Thursday, after it escaped a rampage of at least 10 tornadoes across Tennessee," an emergency official said. "If the county had guardian angels, they worked overtime yesterday . . ."

As soon as Roland saw that, he thought of Ivanhoe, and he mailed him a copy of the newspaper front page and article. A week later he called him.

"Ivanhoe, did you have anything to do with that?"

"See, Roland? There's your proof. I actually wove an energy system for you, and it looks like your whole surrounding region benefited from it." He chucked in a friendly way.

"I'll say it did. Thank you."

"So, you believe me now, don't you?"

"With that I believe I must," Roland admitted. "I'm impressed."

"That energy system, or bubble you might say, is one of the best ones I ever did. When I build energy systems, I just set them up, put them in motion, and forget about them. They have a life of their own."

Roland was indeed impressed. Ivanhoe had done a great favor. Bedford and Rutherford Counties would never know it, but the fact was that Ivanhoe was the counties' guardian angel for that one. Amazing!

That £200 Roland had sent Ivanhoe was money well spent, indeed.

La Cuetona Y Su Fuerza Maligna

As the month of May arrived, work was picking up, and Roland was getting plenty of calls for carpentry and painting.

The International Folkfest occurred in May, and groups came from various countries.

Roland went to the dormitories at Murfreesboro's MTSU where the groups were staying for the week. He visited with several from Lithuania and from Spain, and by prior e-mail communication, some of them had brought Roland some telephones. He gladly bought them. One was from Russia and had the hammer and sickle symbol on it.

The groups performed at various schools and one night at MTSU's Boutwell Center for the Arts. Roland and his parents attended, and when Roland walked into the auditorium, he suddenly felt strange, like something wasn't quite right. His mother saw it first.

"Roland, there are some people we used to know," and she pointed.

He looked into the audience. There sat Isalia and Luke! They sat around 20 feet away and behind Roland and his parents. The two hour performance from various countries took place. A couple of times, when the dancers made more noise, Roland looked toward Isalia and Luke's direction and firmly said, "¡Pídame disculpas, ya!" telling them to apologize to him!

After the performance, Roland went to the display tables out in the hall where various countries were selling native crafts. Isalia and Luke went to the tables. Roland thought about chewing them out, but he opted to avoid confrontation, and he went to some other tables. He had nervous feelings crawling inside him.

Isalia and Luke left, and Roland's mother had an angry look on her face. He asked her what was wrong, and she said Isalia had walked by her and smiled at her. Roland's mother had been talking to somebody else at the time, and she had instinctively smiled back at Isalia without thinking. Roland's mother was mad at herself for having smiled at Isalia. She had intended to tell Isalia off, instead!

That was the last time Roland saw the faces of Isalia and Luke. They were out of his life, and good riddance! Roland's parents were so surprised at Isalia's rejection that they called it the *surprise of the century*. It was obvious that Isalia had been a friend of convenience, and her goodness of character had been faked. What was really strange was that after Clayton had died last year, Luke came into her life literally within weeks! The fact of the matter was that Isalia never did her grieving. Granted, she was having panic attacks, and her son Laurence sent one of his sons to spend part of the summer with her. Plus, her sister Roma came, but the fact remained that Isalia just didn't wait long enough before she and Luke started living together.

Isalia just didn't know how to suffer grief properly. Roland remembered that Isalia had done all her grieving ahead of time, six years before her husband died, and wasn't it a little strange that Isalia told Roland that she had been praying hard for six years, and she finally got what she wanted, her new man Luke? What were her real motives, and what was her prayer? It didn't take a genius to put two and two together, you might say.

Roland called his former high school science teacher, Mr. Mayfield. He hadn't talked to him since last summer, and he wanted to talk to him about Isalia.

"Yes, it's true. She slapped a student," Mr. Mayfield verified. "Isalia has a dark side. When you told me last year that you were going to take that trailer cargo down there for her, I thought about warning you, and I'm sorry I didn't, Roland."

Mr. Mayfield was a good man who Roland appreciated.

"I guess you heard about me, didn't you?" Mr. Mayfield said to Roland.

"No, what?"

"I've been diagnosed with pancreas cancer."

"Oh, no!"

Mr. Mayfield told Roland he had been diagnosed back in February and was in dire pain at that time. Pancreas cancer is inoperable and is always a death sentence, but Mr. Mayfield had gone to an herb store and was taking herbs and vegetable drink mixes, and he improved. The cancer retreated. He told Roland he was going to prove the doctors wrong.

Roland went over to visit him and his wife. He showed him his picture album from Mexico, and he told them everything Isalia and Luke had done.

Mr. Mayfield was a very perceptive man. He knew a lot more than he let on, and by his psychic sense, he knew things about Isalia that very few, if anyone else, knew about her. Roland had been naive in comparison. He really wished he had Mr. Mayfield's good judgment of a person's character.

"Isalia should have known you better than that," Mr. Mayfield told Roland. "I know you didn't steal any trailer cargo. With you, I could leave money lying all over the floor, walk out of the house, and I know you wouldn't take it."

What a kind compliment from Mr. Mayfield! Now there's a person who trusted Roland. It was true. Roland wouldn't have taken that money. His conscience was very strong, and stealing was against his beliefs.

Mr. Mayfield went on to tell Roland that Isalia was likely involved in some form of black magic, probably down there in Mexico. She had used that magic to get what she wanted. Roland started putting two and two together on several counts. He remembered the time Isalia had told him about a force that was trying to strangle the life out of her when she was at a "beautician" in Taxco. That beautician was probably somebody else, somebody of the occult life.

Yes, it was very likely that Isalia had jinxed Roland's life in more ways than one, both financially, and socially. Roland, for being the kind fellow that he was, had undeservedly lost far more than the usual number of friends.

The Sugar Maple in the front yard had indeed died, a shame really. Roland, with sadness, cut it down, and he hauled the limbs to the brush pile with the tractor. Though Roland never knew it, there was a very good reason why that tree died. When Roland had arrived home in February, he was contaminated with bad energies. Via her witchcraft, Isalia had cleverly and telepathically sent him those bad energies through those nightmarish dreams: the dream about Isalia's angry glare and several dreams of her rushing him. That Sugar Maple sensed Roland's problem. At the time it was doing fine, but since Roland was in trouble, more than he knew, and since that tree had more of a connection to Roland, since he had climbed it all those years of childhood, the tree decided to die for Roland. It absorbed much of Roland's negative energies he had brought home, became contaminated, and died. Trees have a life force too, and they have an intelligence existent on another level of reality. As Roland was an *Alquzok*, the Maple sacrificed its life so that Roland could continue his. In the literal sense of the word, that tree saved Roland's life. Bless that Sugar Maple tree's soul.

CHAPTER 12

COMPENSATION VISITED

summer, 1998

Roland gave Rigo a call in late June. He was somewhat apprehensive that Rigo might be mad at him for what happened between him and Raul. Manuel was Rigo's nearest neighbor with a telephone, and he went down the street and brought Rigo to the phone. Roland asked Rigo how he was doing, and he answered that he was doing fine, and he asked Roland how he was doing. Immediately, Roland felt at ease. What a good fellow Rigo was, and a faithful friend, as well.

Rigo said he received the packet with the photos, letter, and self-addressed envelope. He was glad to have the photos.

They talked for half an hour. Roland told Rigo he regretted the incident that occurred with Raul back in February, and he asked Rigo if Raul was in Salado with his brother Eduardo. Rigo answered that Raul was in Guadalajara with an uncle. Roland knew that wasn't true. Manuel had earlier told Roland that Raul went to Salado wetback in late March.

Rigo also told Roland that Raul said he wanted to make up with him, to forgive the incident. Rigo didn't know about Beto and Pegaso, but yes, Raul was regretting the loss and wanted to renew his friendship with Roland. That was good to hear about Raul. Roland had dreamed about Raul some months ago, and now he realized that the feelings he picked up were true and accurate.

He asked Rigo for Raul's address and number at Eduardo's, but Rigo reiterated that Raul was in Guadalajara.

Rigo wanted to know when Roland was coming and if he could bring a bicycle with him. He told Rigo he was planning to come in August, and he may very well be able to bring a bicycle.

They had a nice and friendly conversation, and Roland slept well that night.

Some more things occurred to Roland a few days later, and he called Rigo again, who took his phone call in a friendly manner.

Yes, Roland was looking forward to going down to Mexico now. He called up Alberto and talked about bringing him into the United States and travelling out West.

Roland called his friend Ivanhoe to see what he advised about his going to Mexico this August.

"No, don't go to Mexico, especially if Isalia and Luke are going to be there," he advised Roland. "Go to Canada instead. There's something interesting waiting for you there."

"Yeah, but I want to go back to Mexico," Roland responded. "I have my friends there, like Rigo and others, and I want to see them."

"I know you do, but it might be too dangerous there."

"Plus, I have the right to be in that town, even if Isalia and Luke are there, and I have the right to have my friends there."

"Yes, that's all true and good, but there's still some residual resentment going on down there, and that's not in your favor, but then if you're bent on it, you'll go down there, won't you?"

"That's right," Roland answered.

"Well, I really hope all goes well with you down there. I wish you the best, but don't be surprised if something blocks you from going there, and if you do make it down there to Mexico, don't be surprised if something bounces you out while you're staying there."

Roland thought about Ivanhoe's advice, especially that last comment with his two predictions.

As for Isalia and Luke, they were bound to be there. After all, Guillermo's wedding was taking place August 7, and Isalia had the most honored position at the wedding, to sit by his mother's side. Roland wrote out a letter on a 10 inch piece of aluminum, telling Isalia and Luke he was going to be in Bustamante also, that there was enough room for both of them in the town, and that they better leave him and his friends alone. He told them not to do any shrewd tactics with the police and that he had the right to enjoy his friends.

Next, he called Mrs. Tinkerton to tell her he was going to mail Isalia and Luke the piece of aluminum.

"No, you don't need to do that, Roland," she told him, laughing. "They're not going to be there."

"They're *not*?" Roland asked with total surprise.

"I know that for a fact," she answered. Roland was about to ask her about Guillermo's wedding, but Mrs. Tinkerton carried on to say, "And as for the wedding, they decided not to go to it."

"They're not going to that important wedding?"

"Nope, they're going to California with her son, Laurence."

"Well, I will say! That's great!"

"Have a great time in Mexico," she told Roland.

"Thank you! Thank you very much!"

Roland hung up, feeling like he was on cloud nine! Isalia and Luke were not even going to Mexico. Halleluyah! Roland danced a jig right then and there. He really looked forward to going to Mexico now, and with Mrs. Tinkerton's good news, he was definitely going.

Roland had plans of talking to Rigo's employer, Felipe, and paying Rigo for his time so he could accompany him to different places, including Monterrey, Saltillo, and hopefully the mountains. He looked forward to a great time, and he hoped Alejandro and Lavinia would receive him into their home.

Around late July, Roland and his parents found a new and promising distributor. He ran a wholesale outlet distributorship over in South Carolina. He was very reassuring, and he and Roland signed a contract that he would sell his products for him. Roland took the man 250 copies of his book compilation and 100 copies of each of his previous calendars, personally delivered them, met the distributor, and saw the facilities. Finally, Roland's books and calendars were going to move, and possibly be mass marketed.

Also in the month of July, Roland paid a local printer to print 100 copies each of his newest calendars, which he delivered to friends and relatives who had supported his endeavor and had bought one or more copies from him. He gave a copy each to the new distributor, who expressed interest in publishing them for him. Plus, he offered to compile a new book of his more recent paintings. Great news! That distributor looked really promising.

In early August, Roland loaded his truck with his goods, including Cedar wood for Felipe and a bicycle he had bought for Rigo, and he began his trip to Mexico.

He drove to Murfreesboro's Wal-Mart Supercenter to buy some last minute items for the trip. While he was there, he went to fill up with gas. He bought a gift card from Wal-Mart and went to one of the gas pumps. As it turned out, the satellite was down, and it wouldn't recognize the card. Roland went back in the store, got a refund on the card, returned to the pumps and paid cash for the gasoline. It was 7:30 AM now, and he proceeded to take Highway 96 to the west toward Franklin. As soon as he left town, quite to his surprise, the highway was mysteriously congested with traffic, leaving town. Normally, it would have been congested, entering town at this hour. How strange, indeed! Roland took a side road and got on the Eagleville Highway further south, completely going around Franklin on other small highways and backroads, finally accessing I-40 nearly 100 miles west of Murfreesboro.

So, *that* was what Ivanhoe predicted! Roland had managed to drive around the blockage anyway, probably using up some of his good luck to do so. Life and its destinies are very strange sometimes.

He drove on to Bustamante in two days, staying overnight at his cousins in Dallas. They were concerned for Roland, and they wished him well.

There were no more mysterious blocks, and around 4 PM on August 4, Roland pulled in to Bustamante. It was hot and sunny. He decided to first drive over to Felipe's carpentry to talk to Rigo. Before Roland even got there, he happened to see Rigo walking out of a different carpentry business operated by a man named Gonzalo. Roland had found Rigo already. He stopped, stepped down from his truck, walked over to Rigo, and they shook hands, glad to see each other. Rigo had grown. He was very nearly Roland's height now.

Rigo was just finishing his day's work, and he asked Roland when he had arrived. Rigo was somewhat surprised when Roland answered that he had at that moment just arrived. As it turned out, Rigo was the first one Roland saw and talked to in Bustamante this trip.

Roland entered the carpentry business with Rigo and looked over the facilities. Just six months ago the building used to be a grocery store.

Rigo asked Roland where he was going to stay, and he told Rigo he was hoping to stay with him and his family. Rigo suggested that Roland stay in the hotel. Roland didn't like that suggestion, and he explained to Rigo that in a town where he had friends, he would rather stay with friends than in a hotel. Again, he asked Rigo if he could stay with him and his family, and he invited Rigo to accompany him to various places in the coming week, for which he would pay him for his time.

Rigo somewhat harshly commented, "Cada vez vienes esperando quedarte con nosotros," telling Roland that each time he comes to Bustamante, he always expects to stay with Rigo and his family.

Roland felt some resentment from Rigo by the way he said it, and Rigo again suggested that Roland go to the hotel. Roland explained again why he didn't want to stay in the hotel, and Rigo responded by telling Roland that he was arguing with him.

Roland walked to his truck to drive away, and suddenly something caused Rigo to remember, *Oh, yeah, maybe Roland brought me a bicycle.* He followed Roland to his truck, and he asked him if he had brought a bicycle. Roland answered that yes he had indeed, and he told Rigo he was going to give it to somebody else, since he wasn't going to receive him into his home. He got into his truck to drive away.

Rigo asked Roland to wait, and he asked him to come back inside the carpentry business. Once inside, he asked Roland what that was about his offer to accompany him to various places? Rigo had also just recalled that Gonzalo was about to close his carpentry business.

Felipe's carpentry had closed several months ago, and carpentry in general was suffering a lull this summer. As a result, Rigo needed the money, and he now asked Roland with interest how much he would offer per day. Roland asked him how much Gonzalo paid per day, and Rigo told him it was N$100. Roland looked at him with disbelief, knowing Rigo was joking. He looked at Roland and couldn't help but smile, and then he gave him the truthful answer of N$35. Roland offered him N$40 per day, and Rigo accepted it.

Bad feelings were quickly vanishing, and Roland was quite surprised at how things were taking a turn for the better. He and Rigo talked about how they were going to get permission from Gonzalo. Roland offered one of the three pieces of Cedar lumber for Gonzalo, who was not there at the moment, and Rigo would also get his permission, which he felt nearly certain he would grant, especially with Roland's offer of a 3" x 8" x 8' piece of Cedar.

Next, Rigo told Roland he could come on over to his house with him, and he would get his parents' permission for Roland to stay with them. Amazing! Things were improving for sure.

Roland never knew it, but his friend Ivanhoe, as part of the work he did for him concerning that quantum energy system, had installed a positive energy responder, to activate moments after Roland and Rigo would meet again. An ingeniously designed installation, it would serve Roland well for several visits in the future.

Rigo got in Roland's truck with him, and they went to his house. Lavinia, Norma and Irma were there, and they happily greeted Roland. Rigo kindly explained to his mother that Roland had just arrived in town, and he asked her if he could stay with them. She consented and said that would be fine with her, but he would need to get the final say from Alejandro. He was down the street at the cantina.

Rigo continued talking to Lavinia while Roland walked down the street. Alejandro saw him and came outside. Roland shook hands with him the Mexican way. Alejandro didn't look very pleased, however. Roland asked him if he could stay with his family. It was then that Alejandro brought up that he was quite displeased at the problem that had occurred with Raul back in February. Roland told Alejandro he regretted what had happened and he wanted to make up with Raul. Alejandro explained that he had talked to the comandante, Valentín, about the problem, and he told Roland he should have come to him first before the police. Roland admitted he had done wrong in that aspect, and he apologized.

Alejandro pointed out that Roland had first become friends with Raul and later on with Rigo, and he didn't want any more problems. Roland assured Alejandro there wouldn't be any more problems, and he told Alejandro that Rigo was always more friendly and understanding in comparison to Raul.

Alejandro went on to explain that he and his family were financially drained, but if Roland could supply food for the house and help when necessary, then it would be okay for him to stay. Roland thanked him, shook hands with him again, and returned to their house. He told Lavinia that Alejandro had said yes.

Rigo was glad to find that out, and he helped Roland unload his things, including that prized bicycle, and they took them into the house. They also unloaded one of the three pieces of Cedar. Rigo showed him where to put his things, and he offered him a bed to sleep in at night. He shook hands with Roland in a very friendly and sincere manner.

Roland told them all thank you. He felt welcome indeed. He knew he almost didn't get in, but he certainly was thankful to the forces that be that things had so much improved for the better, since his arrival half an hour ago. Raul and Rigo were Roland's favorites anyway, and he was so glad to be staying with Rigo and his family, instead of with others.

Rigo asked Roland if they could go for a drive. So, he and Roland drove over to Villaldama. For part of the road, Roland let him drive. Roland told Rigo that he had thought Raul was his best friend in all of Mexico, but in truth, Rigo had been the best friend. Rigo appreciated that kind comment from Roland. It was true. Roland had a lot of appreciation for Rigo, and he was glad to be back in Mexico to enjoy more time with him.

They returned to Bustamante, and Lavinia fed everyone, including Roland, some supper.

Rigo went out with some friends for a while, and Roland drove over to Felipe at the Hotel Ancira, and he delivered him the remaining two pieces of Cedar. Felipe explained that sales had been slow this year, and they had closed for that reason, and also because they had a surplus. He said they hoped to be opening again in the fall. He paid Roland at cost for the wood.

Felipe asked if Isalia had ever apologized, and Roland told him he hadn't heard a peep out of her. Felipe seemed a little bit surprised, and he explained his viewpoint on it. He said that once Isalia found her new man Luke, she had become so involved with him that her head was full with all the adjustments to make in her life. As a result, she didn't have time to deal with other people so much, especially those who she knew in the days she was married to Clayton. Felipe explained that she no longer wanted Roland's friendship because he was a friend during that time (when she was married to Clayton) and that her seeing Roland reminded her of her former husband and perhaps caused her grief. He went on to say that Isalia likely severed numerous past friendships so she would be able to forget her old husband, and proceed with her new one.

Felipe gave a good analysis, but Roland knew that he was the *only* one of Isalia's past friends who she rejected, and permanently. However, there was some truth about Isalia's severing past ties in reference to avoiding grief and avoiding being reminded of her past husband Clayton. Granted, Isalia was somewhat one-track about how she handled matters in general, but the truth was that her problem of dealing with grief stemmed from that recurring dream that had haunted her for many years, instead of from normal circumstances.

Roland drove over to Victor's house. He had a bed mattress/sofa to give to him. They were glad to see Roland and commented what a miracle it was that he had come back to Bustamante, after all the problems he had back in January and February. He said he was glad to be back, that he had decided that Isalia had no right to keep him away, and that he was going to exercise his right to have his friends in Bustamante!

A few days before Roland left home, he designed a special flyer and had 75 copies of it with him. The flyer had a very appropriate photo of Isalia and Luke, and it announced their "prostitute business" with a breakdown of costs for all the services rendered to men, women, and gays. Roland took great delight in designing the flyer with hilarious comments, and he knew it would be a real bombshell to Isalia and Luke, if they were to intimidate Roland in any way at all! Even though they weren't in town, Roland still brought the flyers to hand out all over town as a retaliation means, if it were to become necessary. Russia and the United States had their nuclear weapons. Roland had his flyers.

He also made a poster with a note that said, *Aquí tengo mis amigos. Es mi derecho. No somos de la segunda clase, y esta calle es publica!* (Here I have my friends. It's my right.

We are not second class citizens, and this street is public!)

Roland went up the street, passing by the Orolizos, and he arrived at Isalia and Luke's rental house. It was vacant. He slid the poster board under the front yard gate, and he spoke out loud, telling them they better leave him alone! Even though they weren't there, he still said it. He climbed over the gate and proudly walked all around the premises. Then he climbed back over the gate and walked back and forth in front of the house, *many* times, exercising his right to use that public street and sidewalk. Back and forth he walked in front of that house, and he whistled a tune from the movie, "The Wizard of Oz": *The Wicked Witch is Dead.* Yes, Roland whistled that tune several times, and he felt more relieved every time he whistled it. The very idea of Isalia thinking Roland didn't have the right to pass in front of her rental house! The street is public, and she has *no* right to control who uses it.

Roland returned to Rigo's house and visited with his family for the evening. Rigo was still out with friends. Lavinia told Roland that Raul was no longer angry at him, and that whenever he may see Roland, he would content himself with him like a friend again. Roland asked them how Raul was doing. They showed Roland some pictures of Raul, having arrived in Salado. There were pictures of his brother Eduardo. There were pictures of a vacation trip to the beach at Corpus Christi, and more.

Yes, Raul had really gone to Texas with his brother Eduardo. Roland realized he had just not been first choice. He had really wanted Raul to go to Tennessee with him, but they had kept having falling outs! The pictures made Roland remember the dream he had back in March. He really missed Raul, and he really wanted to see him again, to make up for the nasty surprise of that incident that took place back in February! The pictures made Roland just about cry. Lavinia looked at Roland in a confused manner, not knowing what to make of Roland's reaction. He had to get up and leave the table.

A little while later, he asked Lavinia for Raul's address at Eduardo's. Lavinia said she would look for it, that she had it somewhere.

Rigo came in later that night. He and Roland talked for a while, and they drifted off to sleep.

The next day, Roland took Rigo and his neighbor Manuel to Sabinas Hidalgo for errands. They returned by mid day.

Roland had brought a bunch of clothing to Mexico to give to people, including Manuel, who had previously requested clothing. People back in Tennessee, friends and clients, donated clothing to Roland to take down to Mexico. Part of the clothing was going to Rigo and his family, and the rest was going to Manuel.

However, there was one problem. Lavinia informed Roland that Manuel's family had charged Rigo a total of N$10 for taking both of Roland's phone calls back in June. Roland wanted to know why in the world that was, because Roland had dialled direct, and Manuel's family had not been charged a single penny by Teléfonos de México. Roland went to talk to them, and he told them he objected to their having charged Rigo for those two phone calls he merely received. They explained that they were charging N$5 per call for the use of the phone instrument. Why on Earth did it occur to them to do that?! Roland told them he was not all right with that, and that if they wanted that bag of clothing they had requested, they would have to refund that N$10 to Rigo. They acted quickly and rounded up N$10. One of Manuel's sisters took the money to Rigo's house and refunded him immediately. With that problem cleared up, Roland then sorted through the bags of clothing. Manuel came over and chose what he wanted and filled one of the bags full. He said thank you with sincerity and carried the bag to his house up the street. That worked out fine. Roland was glad they had been gracious enough to refund Rigo the N$10, because if they hadn't, Roland wouldn't have handed them the clothing.

Roland and Rigo loaded the remaining Cedar into the truck and drove over to Gonzalo's carpentry. He was there, and he gave Rigo permission to take the whole week off so he could accompany Roland. That was great. Roland was really feeling compensated now. With that permission granted, Roland unloaded the piece of Cedar and gave it to Gonzalo as a token of appreciation.

Rigo had a little bit of work to do on a bed he was repairing for a client. Roland helped him. While they were working on it, Rigo said he had talked to Beto Enriquez. He told Roland the police had charged Beto a N$100 fine for the firecracker incident. However, if Roland would like to reimburse Beto that N$100, he would become his friend again.

Roland thought about it. If all it took was N$100 (US $11) to fix his friendship with Beto, he would give him that money. Roland was glad to know that Beto was the forgiving type. He told Rigo he would go and talk to Beto this evening. At the moment, Beto was working, and he was involved in building concrete block houses in town, tough work indeed.

Roland asked Rigo about Pegaso. Now that was a different story, Rigo informed him. Pegaso had absolutely no intention of ever *ever* becoming Roland's friend again!

Rigo finished his work. He appreciated Roland's help. They returned to his house. Of course, Roland had brought several copies of his calendars with him, and he showed them to Rigo, who was impressed with them. His mother Lavinia walked over to them and looked at the calendars, as well. Both of them complimented Roland by telling him he had a lot of imagination, and Lavinia asked Roland where he got so many ideas. He answered that they just came to him as he thought about things, and also from dreams.

Rigo proved his intelligence and gave Roland some helpful ideas of what he could paint, more scenes from Mexico, adventures, culture scenes, and of course Chiquihuitillos. Rigo knew the culture very well, and Roland was amazed at his competence. He very much appreciated Rigo's suggestions, and he would do some new paintings accordingly. Rigo was training to become a school teacher, and Roland predicted that he would become a good one.

However, Rigo was of a very poor family, and it was possible he would have to drop out of school to work full time to make ends meet. Roland told Rigo if it became necessary, he would pitch in and help pay his way through school, a very generous gesture of friendship on Roland's part.

That evening, Roland went to Beto's house. He was still living at his grandmother's house. He was there, and Roland told him he had come to see if they could forgive each other. Beto was friendly and receptive of Roland's offer and they started talking. Roland asked Beto if he thought Isalia and Luke had paid him or someone else to toss Roland that firecracker/bomb. Beto admitted they were behind it and had paid him N$300 to do it. That was what Roland suspected. Beto had been in dire need of money, and the offer had been presented to him by Lavinia. Of course the police, as it turned out, got one third of the money.

Roland told Beto what Rigo had said, and he gave, that is, reimbursed Beto the N$100, and he thanked him for telling the truth that Isalia and Luke had put him up to it. Roland told

Beto that he forgives him. Beto did the same. They shook hands and became friends again. Beto had felt guilty about what he had done. He learned from it, and he was glad Roland had come to him and had forgiven him.

Next, Roland and Beto walked over to Pegaso's house. Roland wanted to see what he could do to fix that past friendship, too. Pegaso was not there, but his mother and his sisters were. In front of Mrs. Orolizo, Roland apologized to Lumita and Mena for having said they were pretty and for having said they would please him for a girlfriend. They accepted the apology with ease, and their mother told Roland thank you. Later, Mrs. Orolizo told Pegaso about Roland's apology to his sisters, and Pegaso said that was good. Still, he never ever became Roland's friend again.

Beto and Roland walked over to Rigo's house, and they spent the evening visiting. They walked to the plaza and talked to others. Beto also had a girlfriend now, and her name was Clarisa.

The Feria de Agusto (August Fair) or carnival was taking place. Plenty of tourists came at this time of year. There were lots of market stands set up and plenty of children's rides. It was set up down the street from the plaza, and all the tractor trailers that had brought the rides were parked on Calle Escobedo, occupying two blocks of it. Roland, Rigo, and Beto looked it all over and talked with other people they knew. Roland saw Alberto and talked to him. He saw Valentín, the police officer, and they shook hands.

People were selling all kinds of knick knacks, food, clothing, and pirate cassette tapes of different music. Every August, Bustamante hosted this carnival.

The next day, Roland took Rigo with him to Monterrey. Roland wanted to buy himself a bicycle to replace the one he had given to Raul last year. There was a large bike shop called Julio Cepeda within FAMSA, and Roland found a new Magistroni 18 speed for US $100. He bought it, and he also bought some steel bike pedals.

Upon Roland's purchase of that bicycle, Rigo asked Roland if he was indeed giving him the mountain bike he had brought from Tennessee. He wanted to be sure. Roland told Rigo yes. Rigo said gracias and gestured sincere appreciation. Then Roland then said to Rigo, "No me vas a desafanar en el futuro," telling Rigo not to brush him off in the future. Rigo assured Roland he wouldn't and that he was his friend.

Roland and Rigo visited the Soriana store, the Macroplaza, and the downtown flea markets. On the way back, before leaving Monterrey, Roland purposefully drove down Simón Bolívar Boulevard and stopped by the house where Esalina and Guillermo Velazco used to live. They had moved to the richer colonia of Río Nilo back in 1991.

Roland pulled over, and he and Rigo stepped down to walk around. The Velazco's house had been converted to commercial real estate. The house had not been torn down, but it had been converted to a small bank and a Cedetel, to do with telephones. Roland told Rigo that he had stayed here back in 1983 with Guillermo, who was scheduled to get married tomorrow evening on August 7.

Roland and Rigo returned to Bustamante by mid afternoon.

Around 5 PM, a very special event took place. Every August 6 during the Feria de Agosto, they have a big celebration where they have a devout marching procession and carry the church's statue of Jesus on the cross throughout the streets of the town. It is such an important event, that each year all of the residents are notified ahead of time so that they will know what streets are used, and they hang decorations on the front of their houses in honor of Jesus.

Today was the day, and part of the procession passed right in front of Rigo's house. All vehicles had to be moved out of the way ahead of time.

Roland, Rigo, and Beto, who came over, got up on the roof to watch the procession. It was quite an event. The police led the way with their newest vehicles, two new red original style VW bug police cars, and then some people carried a sort of white mattress with palm leaf lacing around it. This they set down on the street every so often as they carried it along. Next came five people dressed in white robes. They were carrying long poles with candles. Next was a parade with children in Matachines costumes followed by other groups playing drums and other instruments, and then came various parade floats.

After all that came the special items, a specially made stand, a framed structure carried by 12 people, which carried the statue of Jesus Christ on the cross. They set the structure down every so often, and people would go up to the statue and touch it, of course crossing themselves three times before doing so. Everyone showed super respect for Christ on the cross.

Next came literally thousands of people, an absolute crowd of them occupying the street from side to side and one block long. Most of Bustamante's residents were there, along with people from other towns, as well.

Roland took numerous pictures to document the event, including a picture of Rigo and Beto up on the roof.

That evening, they went to the fair again. Roland saw more people he knew. The Feria de Agosto was a week that was full of fiestas and bailes (dances). Rigo went to the bailes each night, and he spent the days with Roland, accompanying him on his errands or visits.

They went to Sabinas Hidalgo again, and they went to Saltillo to visit the central district, the flea market, which was full of native crafts, and to visit Sergio and Lilia and their family. Eloy was there also. While they were in Saltillo, Roland and Rigo visited a shoe store. He bought Rigo a new pair of tennis shoes for N$330 as a gesture of friendship. As they left the store, Rigo put his hand on Roland's shoulder and sincerely told him *gracias* for the pair of tennis shoes. Roland was glad that Rigo appreciated them.

Roland and Rigo also visited a department store called Del Sol. In one section, they sold tapes and CDs. *Mercurio*'s new album "Tiempo de Vivir" had just been released a couple of weeks ago. It had just arrived and was on special for N$99. All five fellows were clearly pictured on the front, and knowing how good their previous album "Chicas Chic" was, Roland bought "Tiempo de Vivir" right then and there.

They returned to Bustamante. Roland let Rigo drive part of the way.

Rigo got ready for the big Saturday night dance, the grand fiesta of dances at the end of the special Feria de Agosto. Pegaso came over in his father's pickup truck carrying Beto, Angelo, and Christian. Rigo got in the truck with them, and they drove away.

Roland got on his bicycle and rode to different houses to visit friends like Victor. A little while later, he happened to see Pegaso and his buddies. They were in front of one of the numerous corner stores, and Pegaso bought several cases of beer. Angelo and Christian were smoking and drinking. Beto told Roland that Rigo had just had a beer, and he told Roland to scold him. Roland answered that he wasn't sure if Rigo drank or smoked and that it wasn't his place to scold him. The others laughed. Roland rode back to Rigo's house.

A little while later Rigo arrived. He had forgotten something. Upon arriving, he told

Roland, that is, assured Roland that he doesn't drink nor smoke nor does he smell of beer. He told Roland in a sincere, believable manner, and Roland told him that was good and that he was glad to hear that. Rigo laid his hand on a cassette tape and then left, kissing his mother on the way out the door.

Lavinia fed Roland and the rest of them some supper. Alejandro was away at the cantina. Lavinia said that Raul had called within the hour. He was doing fine in Salado and was working plenty. Roland said he'd like to have talked to him. Lavinia said that Raul had asked about him and wished he were back in Bustamante to run around with Roland and Rigo. He had asked his mother if Roland was behaving himself, and she said he was indeed. He also told her to make sure Roland leaves some money at the end of his stay, to pay for food costs. Roland was amenable to that.

Roland went to sleep for the night. Lavinia, Norma and Irma slept outside where it was cooler.

Just before 4 AM, Sunday, August 9, Roland woke up feeling a tight sense of nervousness. Rigo had not yet arrived. The feelings Roland had were *not* good at all. For some reason, he was very concerned that Rigo was going to come in drunk. Roland couldn't go back to sleep either.

Finally, at 5 AM, Rigo came in and briefly talked to Roland. He was sober, and he had no alcohol smell either. That was good.

The next morning, Roland woke up at 8 AM. Rigo tried to sleep later, but Lavinia, Norma and Irma were already up and at 'em. Norma and Irma were playing with each other and they made plenty of noise and laughter. Rigo, as a result, was grumpy and he more than once told them to be quiet.

At 11 AM, when Rigo did get up, Roland asked how things went last night.

Rigo immediately took offense and answered, "¿Por qué quieres saber todo?" asking Roland why he wanted to know everything. Rigo had resentment in his voice, too.

What sort of answer was that? Roland thought. He was taken aback by Rigo's curt manner and didn't know what to say. He asked Rigo to accompany him to . . . but Rigo was quick to remind Roland that it was *Sunday*, and he showed absolutely no interest in being with Roland! Roland would have said more, but he felt mysteriously prevented, or you might say, a little afraid to ask Rigo anything else, because it seemed that he was touchy and might get angry.

Over the next several minutes, Rigo prepared himself and left for the day, to spend it with *his* friends.

What had Rigo done last night? Roland thought, especially since Rigo had asked him why he wanted to know everything.

Today was a different day. There was a tight, nervous feeling inside Roland that lasted all day, and he could not shake it. The feeling carried a sense of danger, but he had no idea what.

It was a hot and sunny day. Roland got on his bicycle and went riding. He visited friends. He went to the molino alone and went swimming, and he talked with those he knew there.

Still, the nervous feeling persisted, and that evening he told Lavinia, Norma and Irma about it. They had no idea either. They ate supper, talked and visited. Roland looked at the pictures of Raul again.

Rigo briefly arrived at 9:30 PM and had a bite to eat. Roland asked him when he would be getting in tonight. Rigo repeated the same question, and Roland assured Rigo that no he didn't want to know everything, but he didn't see anything wrong with asking that! Rigo didn't answer and took off again, to be with *his* friends.

Roland resumed looking at the pictures of Raul. He asked Lavinia for Raul's address and phone number. Lavinia coldly answered that she had decided not to give it to him! Roland asked her why not, and she stated that she had her reasons. Roland asked her what they were, and he explained that he wanted to see and talk to Raul on the way back home, to apologize, forgive each other, and become friends again. Lavinia answered that one day, perhaps three years from now, when Raul might be in Bustamante, he would content himself with Roland again and run around with him, but not before, and NOT in Texas! Again, Roland asked her what her reasons were for not giving him her son's address. She didn't want to tell. Yes, Roland asked nicely and now for the third time he asked her again. She answered that Raul's brother Eduardo was angry at Roland for the police incident in February, and he was protecting Raul. She said he wanted nothing to do with Roland, and that's the way it was! Roland asked her why she didn't tell him last night, and she said she hadn't wanted to, and she said her brothers in Salado were even angrier!

Next, Lavinia scolded Roland for having taken Raul to the police, that it was bad, and so on. Roland answered by reminding her that Raul had run him off, cussed at him repeatedly, and told Roland he was going to call the police on him. For that reason, Roland went to the police. Lavinia pointed out that the police could have hit Raul, because at times they were abusive. Roland stated his reasons, said it was bad what Raul did, and walked out of the house.

He rode over to Alberto's house and talked with him for an hour. Alberto still wanted to go to Tennessee with Roland but he had a major problem aside from not being able to get a passport and VISA. He had a girlfriend. She had told him she had just become pregnant, and he was concerned about future child support. He wasn't sure how he was going to tell his parents, and he had other worries, as well. Roland was now unsure if he wanted to take him to Tennessee. He had also wanted to take Alberto out West before going to Tennessee. Plus, if Alberto went wetback, he would need to go to Tennessee right away and get to work immediately to save some $900 to give to his girlfriend. It was complicated.

Roland returned to Rigo's house. Rigo got in at 12:30, just past midnight. Roland told him he had been feeling strangely nervous all day. He also told Rigo that his mother Lavinia refused to give him Eduardo and Raul's address and number, and he told Rigo what he told Lavinia after she scolded him.

Rigo warned Roland not to get angry at his mother Lavinia. Roland wasn't sure if that warning meant what Lavinia would do or what Rigo would do, if Roland one day got angry at her. Roland leaned toward what Lavinia might do, hoping that was what Rigo meant, anyway. Rigo was more complacent now. They talked a little while longer and then went to sleep.

It was Monday, August 10. Roland somehow felt much better. The tight, nervous feeling was gone entirely, and good riddance! Lavinia was much more content. In fact, she was grateful. She told Roland a thousand thanks for paying Rigo for his time with him and for the gifts he had brought. Roland was pleasantly surprised at Lavinia's turn for the better, but he still wondered, *What was the matter with yesterday?*

Lavinia was preparing to go to Pinos, Zacatecas to visit her family. She was going to take Norma and Irma with her. She sold some tin roofing and an old table to a neighbor, and with that money, she was able to complete the bus fare. As Lavinia and her daughters walked out the door, she told Roland to behave himself with Rigo. He said he would do his best to.

Roland had other plans today. He was going camping up in the mountains with two other friends: Juan Angel and Fabian. They had expressed interest in going, so today was the day.

Roland went for them in his pickup truck, and the three of them loaded their backpacks and daypacks with food and water. He drove them to the Cantu's store and bought them fruit, avocados, and drinks. Then he drove them to the cono, and they left at 10:30 AM. It was a four hour hike to reach the highland forest and grassy saddle at the ridge top. The weather was moderately hot, but the forest provided nice cool shade.

Roland set up his tent in the highland forest, and they crawled in and took an afternoon nap. Juan Angel and Fabian were more tired than Roland. While they continued to nap, Roland took a walk along his trail through the highland forest. Bustamante could be seen way below through the Oak and Hickory trees, some of which were more than a foot in diameter. He really felt at peace among the trees of the forest, and whatever that strange nervous feeling of yesterday had been, it was totally gone.

Though Roland didn't realize it, the quantum energy system Ivanhoe had set up for him back on February 8 had expired in the wee hours of the morning of August 9. Its six month duration was up. However, under the conditions for where Roland was at the time (with Rigo and his family in Mexico), Selím and his father Martonción, and Selím's right hand man Igor, all sensed a need for an extension. They communicated telepathically with Ivanhoe across the waters, who under the circumstances gladly obliged and granted the extension. It wasn't as powerful as the original one, but it would be enough to prevent danger and harm.

Half an hour later, Roland returned to Juan Angel and Fabian. Roland had something to do and he wanted them to be witnesses. Back in 1992, when Roland took some chairs home from Mexico, U.S. Customs had made Roland promise not to sell any of the chairs, as if three chairs were considered commercial cargo! They had been sarcastic with Roland and interrogating and mistrusting! So, out of spite, Roland *sold* one of the three chairs, upon arriving home, to Isalia for 1¢. Roland wrote her a receipt, as well. He had kept the penny all this time, and he brought it with him on this camping trip. Roland took the penny out of his backpack, told Juan Angel and Fabian what it had to do with, and they walked to the edge of the major dropoff on the west side of the ridge in the grassy saddle. Roland threw the penny off the cliff. There! That severed another connection with Isalia.

The three of them explored around the area, later had some supper, and when it got dark, they crawled in the tent and slept for the night. This was the first time anyone had ever camped with Roland in the highland forest, and the whole night went peacefully . . . no fights, such as what had occurred with Raul the summer before, halfway down the mountain. Roland was really glad to replace that sour campout of the year before with this one. Excellent compensation!

The next morning, they made their way back down the mountain, arriving at the cono by 11 AM. Juan Angel gathered some Oregano herb and Laurel leaves along the way.

They got in Roland's truck, and he drove them back to Bustamante. Before delivering Juan Angel and Fabian to their homes, Roland took them over to Isalia and Luke's former rental house. He reached for the poster board sign under the gate, and he held the sign in front of him while his two friends stood on either side of him. A passerby on the street took a picture of them. Roland had wanted at least ten people in the picture, but it was too difficult to get them all rounded up for the picture. Nevertheless, three was better than none, and Roland would consider mailing the photo to Isalia out of spite, so she could read his sign!

Roland delivered Juan Angel and Fabian, gave them N$40 each, and told them thank you for having camped with him. He drove to Rigo's house.

Rigo was alone. Festivities were over. He was just getting up, having now caught up on lost sleep from the week before. He told Roland that his mother and sisters had successfully left yesterday and were by now likely in Zacatecas. Alejandro was down at the cantina as usual.

Roland told Rigo the camping trip had gone well, but Rigo seemed a little bit grumpy. Roland asked him if he was upset with him about something.

Rigo's answer was something to the effect of: *Did I tell you I was upset with you?* and he was combative the way he said it. Roland answered no, and Rigo stated the equivalent of: *All right then.* Roland realized that Rigo's answer was not straightforward. Since two days ago, something about Rigo had changed. He was 15½, and as a standard practice for teenage fellows on planet Earth, his personality had become more complex. It was one of life's strange mysteries why so many teenagers became more complex at Rigo's age. In general, something caused more than 90% of teenage fellows to lose their sincerity and straight-forwardness. No, not with all, but with a grand majority, this unfortunate scenario was known to take place, and it looked like Rigo had suddenly taken a turn down that complicated road.

Roland showered and got cleaned up, and he ate some lunch. He asked Rigo if he wanted to go to Sabinas Hidalgo. He said yes, and they went. They went to Garza Morton where Roland bought food. Rigo asked for a cassette tape, and Roland bought it for him. Before they went to check out, Roland handed him a N$50 note to pay for it, of which there was supposed to N$6 change. Rigo said he would give him the change once they got in the truck. That way, it would look like Rigo paid for it.

When they got to the truck, Rigo didn't hand Roland the N$6 change. Roland began to sense a trap, and he knew better than remind Rigo to give him that N$6 change, which would in essence be charging him money. They ate lunch at the taco restaurant and then went to the Centro Comercial San José store. Roland hesitated a moment to see if it would occur to Rigo to pay him the N$6 change. So, Roland told Rigo that about that N$6 change to just forget about it, to just leave it. Roland walked in the store while Rigo waited in the truck. A few minutes later, Roland returned to his truck with more groceries, and he started the truck, ready to return to Bustamante.

Rigo seemed unhappy about something. So, Roland asked Rigo the equivalent of: *Now what?* Rigo asked Roland to look in the ash tray, so he did. There was the N$6 in coins. Rigo got after Roland, expressing disgust at him for not trusting him to pay him back and for blaming him indirectly for wanting to keep the N$6. Roland took the scolding, which he was quite displeased to receive, and to avoid confrontation, he apologized to Rigo. Roland also mentioned that no, he didn't charge Rigo for that money, and he asked Rigo to think more positive.

Roland could sense that Rigo's subconscious mind had designed this trap for Roland, as a means of retaliation for his having charged his brother Raul that N$5 back in February. So, therefore, he knew not to fall in it, and then Rigo had made the trap so complex that it was impossible to get out of it without a scolding, anyway! Golly! What was the matter with Rigo?

One of Roland's philosophical beliefs was about bridges representing friendships. It seemed that the friendship Roland had with Rigo was dangerously narrow. Drive with caution. If you slightly deviate from your lane, the unforgiving truss rails will quickly let you know about it!

They returned to Bustamante and once at home, Roland asked Rigo in a straightforward manner if he still wished to continue being friends. Rigo answered yes, and Roland asked him for how long. Rigo answered that he didn't know, because one day they might have a fight, and that would be curtains. He appeared to be contemplating. *Wonder why Rigo was contemplating?*

Roland walked off for a moment to think about how to respond. He came back to Rigo and told him he didn't wish to ever fight with Rigo, that he considered Rigo a good friend, like a brother, and that he always had the good intention of wanting friendships for a lifetime. He also told Rigo he would help in whatever way he could, but he certainly never wanted any fights. With that, Roland walked back into the other room.

Rigo thankfully listened to Roland's words. He thought it over, and a few minutes later, he came over to Roland, who was sitting at the kitchen table adding to his diary, and he placed his hand on Roland's shoulder with a sincere gesture of friendship. Roland turned around, and Rigo shook hands with him. It was like a spell had been lifted.

*   *   *

Nuevo Wimbisenho

"Oh drat! I missed!" Draaktra bitterly declared.

"Nice try, anyway!" Sasjurech declared, patting Draaktra on the back.

"For a first go at it, you almost got him," said Sojornbloc.

"I lost contact!" Draaktra complained.

"You certainly jumped in his aura at the right moment," Arfifra complimented him, "but you just got bumped out."

"I didn't know how to play Roland's kind gesture to Rigo!" Draaktra ranted and raved.

"That's all part of the learning process," Arfifra explained, "and there are ways to play that. You're still young at this. Keep working at it. Practice makes perfect."

"Arfifra, the door's closed pretty tight," Sojornbloc pointed out to her. He had a dismayed look on his face.

"Martonción just gave Roland another extension," Sasjurech added.

"Oh, that Martonción!" Arfifra exclaimed. "Comes in and wrecks all our plans!" She looked at Rigo through the black crystal ball on the table in their cave. "He's sealed Rigo off from us!"

Draaktra looked on, as well. "When can I get back in?" He was impatient with his question.

Arfifra firmed up, looked Draaktra straight in the eyes, and declared, "I will have you back in there within a month. God knows how, but I will make *sure* of that, or my name isn't Arfifra!"

"Hail to Arfifra, our queen of black magic!" Sasjurech, Sojornbloc, and Draaktra all three chanted.

"Now, Draaktra," Arfifra advised, "here's what you need to do. I have a friend named Druxtrli, and I'm going to get her in on this. You be ready at . . ."

*   *   *

Beto and Angelo came over, and the four of them watched a movie on TV. Alberto came over, as well. Roland took him into the kitchen and quietly showed him one of the 75 prostitute flyers with Isalia and Luke's photo on it. Alberto read it, looked it over, and burst out laughing. He made an exclamatory remark in Spanish, and he kept on laughing. Beto came in and looked at it, and he had a good laugh, too. Rigo and Angelo stayed by the TV.

The next day, Rigo and Roland went for Alberto, and they looked for two different people who would be able to get Alberto across the border wetback. They found one of them who said he would get Alberto and Beto both to the other side of the second inspection station for a total of US $900. That was more than Roland wanted to spend.

They went to the carpentry of Gonzalo's, where Rigo had a little work he wanted to do, off of Roland's clock, of course. Meanwhile, Roland went around on his bicycle and visited other friends. He went to Victor's house and asked him who the lady was who had bought his book and calendars right as he was packing his car to leave in February, and where did she live? Victor took Roland over to Elisa's house a few blocks away, and she was home. She happily greeted Roland, glad to see him.

Elisa was a school teacher there in town. She taught Spanish to 6th graders. Roland wanted to talk to her to see what she had done with the calendars she had bought and what her relatives in Monterrey had thought of them. He also showed her his newest artwork and calendars, and she was rightfully impressed. She told Roland her family was awe inspired at the calendars, and they realized that he had a lot of imagination. Plus, Elisa's visitors there in Bustamante had made raving comments about the calendars. She suggested that he enter some of his paintings in galleries in Monterrey. He could even display a few copies at the Hotel Ancira gift shop.

Elisa was separated from her husband, had been so for 7 years. She had three children ranging in ages from 15 to 10. Their names were Carinda, Carlos, and Lalo respectively. The house belonged to her mother's family, who all now, except Elisa, lived in Monterrey.

Rigo finished his project by late morning. He and Roland ate lunch at home, and for the afternoon, Roland took Rigo, Angelo, and Angelo's brother Hugo to the canyon to the Ojo del Agua. They went swimming, splashing and playing with each other in the water. There was an old Ash tree at the water's edge, and some of them dived off of it.

After the swim, Roland told them them several entertaining stories, which they enjoyed hearing. They too told Roland he had a lot of imagination.

In the evening, they returned to Bustamante. Beto came over and Roland took him, Rigo and Angelo over to Sabinas Hidalgo. Beto tried to find a fellow named Placas who passed people over the border. He was not at home.

They ate supper at a fried chicken restaurant, (not Kentucky's). Roland asked Rigo for Raul's address and phone number, reminding him that his mother wouldn't give it to him. Rigo said no, unless Roland wanted to pay him $1,000 . . . then he would. Roland didn't push him about it. It wasn't necessary. He had another tactic in mind about how to go about finding Raul.

They returned to Bustamante. Rigo and Beto watched a movie on TV. Roland went over to talk to Manuel, and he asked him if he could see the phone bills for March and April. Lavinia had come to them to use the phone to call Eduardo in Salado, and their private phone number was bound to show up on the phone bill. Manuel said the phone belonged to his uncle, and he was afraid to go through his things. Roland explained the importance of it, that he wanted to find Raul in Salado. No, Roland didn't have plans to turn Raul in to Immigration like Lavinia, Rigo, Eduardo and his wife must have thought. Roland wanted to see his friend Raul again and restore the friendship. Was it too much to ask? Manuel said he just couldn't do it.

Roland returned to Rigo and Beto and watched the rest of the movie. The next time he goes to Sabinas Hidalgo, he would go by Teléfonos de México and request a copy of the March and April 1998 phone bills for Manuel's phone number. They would likely give it to Roland. They had done so before concerning Mr. Gonzalez and the collect call charges the year before. One way or another, Roland was going to jump the obstacles and find Raul!

The next morning at 9 AM, Manuel came to talk to Roland. They stepped out into the backyard out of Rigo's hearing distance, in case he might be listening. Manuel asked Roland to give him N$75 so he could have enough money to buy an alternator for his car. A smile came across Roland's face, and Manuel knew exactly what Roland was thinking. The *phone bills.* Manuel said he'd pull them. Roland told Manuel that when he has the March and April phone bills in hand and the Salado numbers secured, he would give him the N$75 and *not* the other way around. Manuel needed the money, and he agreed to the deal. He didn't want to have to take the risk of being caught by his uncle, but now he was financially pressed to do so.

Rigo cleaned house. Alejandro surprisingly made a batch of tortillas this morning, since his wife and daughters were in Zacatecas. Of course, they weren't as good as his wife's, but they were fair. He made around 20 packages and took them to the corner store and sold them. Roland was quite surprised. Alejandro must have needed the extra money.

Roland washed his clothes in the washing machine he had brought them last year.

Later in the morning, he went to friends, including the Orolizos, and he showed them his latest calendars.

Then he went to the Cantus. They were glad to see him. Mina Cantu was actually friendly, no longer angry at Roland for the shrewd tactic Isalia and Luke had done, causing the failure of the sale of their house where Roland had stayed. Mina told Roland she had forgiven him and said there was no reason to have gotten angry at him. After all, the failure of the sale of the house had not been his fault. Plus, it was totally unacceptable how Isalia had commented that she no longer wanted the house because Roland's "bad energies had contaminated it." Roland accepted Mina's forgiveness.

Chilo came over to the counter. He pointed to a sign hanging up above. It read: *No fio porque cobrar es un lío, y el negocio es mío.* (I don't sell on credit because charging is a complicated matter, and the place of business is mine.) At first, Roland thought Chilo was serious. So, Chilo pulled another sign out of a drawer below the counter. It read: *Se fía solamente a personas mayores de 90 años, y acompañados de su abuelito!* (We sell on credit only to persons above 90 years in age, and accompanied by their grandfather!) A smile came across Chilo's face. Roland quickly realized it was a big joke, and both of them had a good laugh, realizing that, if serious, it would be literally impossible! After they finished laughing, Chilo put the sign back in the drawer.

Later in the afternoon, Rigo and Beto were talking to Roland about the mountains. They decided to go up there with him. Roland was quite surprised that Rigo wanted to go. He had never wanted to before. They decided on tomorrow. Both of them went out for the evening. Roland was alone in the house.

Manuel came over half an hour later. He had the March and April phone bills in hand. Great! Roland ushered him into the kitchen, got out a pen and paper, and read over the bills. On March 24, three calls to Salado showed up, two of them for 1 minute each, and the third call for half an hour. All three numbers were different. Roland wrote down the numbers in more than one location, put one set in his metal ex-army ammo box, and the other set in his file folders, well hidden. He then took N$75 out of his wallet, handed it to Manuel, and told him thank you. Manuel was grateful for the money, told Roland thanks as well, and he left.

Roland had the numbers! They were bound to lead to Raul. One major obstacle jumped. Roland knew better than to call the numbers himself. He would have a friend, likely Beto or Alberto, do the calling to secure that address.

Rigo came in later that night, and they went to sleep.

Roland and Rigo got up early, 6:30 AM. They went to pick up Beto and then drove up to the cono. At 7:30 AM, they had their daypacks loaded, and they began hiking up the mountain. It was Rigo's first time to go up in the mountains with Roland, apart from a trip to the caves a year and a half ago. It was a hot and sweaty climb, for the hot sunny weather, but they made their way. Once in the forested gully, it was cooler, and Roland took pictures of Rigo and Beto standing by trees and standing on ledges and rocks.

At 11:30 AM, they entered the highland forest. For a long time, Roland had wanted Rigo to come up here, and he was very thankful for his wish come true. In actual fact, not even Raul had been to the highland forest with Roland. He had stopped and turned back several hundred meters short of reaching it.

The difference with Rigo, as compared to Raul, is that Rigo would not have come into the mountains at all with Roland, unless there were a third party along, such as Beto or any other good friend of Rigo's. This implied a sense of mistrust on Rigo's part. For six times, Raul had gone alone with Roland into the mountains last year, but not Rigo. Nevertheless, the requirement was met with Beto, and Rigo had made it to the highland forest. It was for real. They walked through the forest to the grassy saddle.

They were impressed with the great scenery. Rigo wondered why he didn't come up here before. Both he and Beto were surprised at how far below them Bustamante was.

Rigo and Beto, especially Beto, decided to have some adventures. They tossed some rocks off the cliff, hurling some of the smaller ones toward the west. Some of them took 7 seconds to hit the ground way below. Beto lived on the edge and eased himself over to an outpost of rocks, where he overturned a couple of them. They crashed way below, and a couple of minutes later, white dust came back up with the updrafts, along with the smell of broken limestone rocks.

They looked around the area some more, took pictures, and re-entered the highland forest. They ate lunch. Then the three of them took a nap for a while, after which they began the descent.

The hot sunny weather was changing. A cloud mass could be seen over in Villaldama, dropping rain, and the skies were now overcast. They were worried they might get rained on, but they were lucky. At 4:15 PM, they arrived back at the cono in good condition.

It had been a really good day, and the three of them had gotten along great with each other. Good friends indeed they were. Roland thanked them for going into the mountains with him.

Beto had taken a day off from work to come with Roland and Rigo. So, Roland paid him for his day. Of course, he was paying Rigo anyway, according to their prior agreement.

Later that afternoon, well . . . evening, after showering and cleaning up, Rigo took Roland over to a friend of his, Pedro, the one who sometimes worked at Felipe's carpentry. They talked and visited for a while. Pedro knew Pancho Quevalo, and Roland asked him what Pancho had to say? Pedro answered, "Puras mentiras," that Pancho told total falsehoods! They all had a good laugh at that comment.

They later went to visit Alberto and others.

The next day, while Rigo was still sleeping and recuperating from the major hike yesterday, Roland went around town on his bicycle visiting different friends. He talked to the Cantus, to Victor and his family, and to Elisa. She had been thinking about Roland's artwork, and she had some helpful ideas about doing some more paintings and what types of scenes to include in them. She told him stories of her younger days when she visited the mountains over in southern Tamaulipas, and she talked to him about a treacherous and narrow mountain road that accesses the higher mountain reaches. The scenery was spectacular up there, and she invited Roland to go with her and her family there sometime.

Roland also went to visit with the police, and he talked with them about how things had gone after he had fled from Bustamante in February. Juan said he had indeed gone to talk to Isalia and Luke about the firecracker incident, and they had denied the fact that they had paid Beto to toss that firecracker/bomb into the Cantu's vacant house where Roland was staying. Roland was so glad to know that Isalia and Luke had been questioned. Roland wasn't as naive as they had thought.

That afternoon, Roland took Rigo, Angelo, and Beto over to Sabinas Hidalgo. Beto had finished his work early. Roland had his pictures of yesterday's hike developed. They came out great. He had copies made for Rigo and Beto, and some for Angelo from the Ojo del Aqua. Then Roland took them out to eat at the Centro Comercial San José restaurant. They also visited the flea market.

As they were returning, a big rain came, and the streets soon filled with water.

Upon returning to Bustamante, Beto called a man in Monterrey from the Orolizo's house. He was a coyote who said he would take Beto and Alberto to Encinal on the other side of Laredo, and that they were to meet at the bus station in Sabinas Hidalgo tomorrow at 2:30 PM. Beto was interested in going, to stay in San Antonio with some relatives.

The next day was August 16, Roland's birthday. He spent the morning riding around Bustamante visiting friends.

By early afternoon, Roland, Rigo and Angelo went looking for Beto, and they couldn't find him at the crucial moment. If they couldn't find him soon, they were going to be late to

Sabinas Hidalgo. Half an hour later, they found Beto walking down the street with his girlfriend Clarisa. He saw them, said goodbye to her, and then he ran to them and got in Roland's truck with them.

Roland drove them to Villaldama, where they found Alberto cooking chicken. That was where he worked on certain days. He had forgotten that he and Beto were going to meet the man in Sabinas Hidalgo to take them to Texas. Immediately, he dropped what he was doing. His working partner continued working, and Alberto climbed into Roland's truck with the others. Seems like a part of Beto and Alberto didn't want to go.

There were five of them now, and it was a tight fit with all of them in the cab! Roland drove them to Sabinas Hidalgo, and he went rather fast (100 km/h) along the highway, where conditions permitted, the straighter stretches.

At 2:29 PM, one minute early, Roland arrived at the bus station along the national highway. The coyote was supposed to arrive on the Monterrey-Laredo bus. He wasn't there, and neither was the bus. Perhaps it hadn't yet come in. Roland went to inquire inside the station, and they informed him that the bus had come in 15 minutes early, and it had already gone! The coyote, who was likely on the bus, had not waited for them, and he had gone on to Laredo. Couldn't he have taken a later bus out of Sabinas Hidalgo?

Roland and his four friends made the best out of a lost situation. They went to the flea market, visited one of Alberto's sisters, went to eat out at the taco restaurant, went to Angelo's aunt's house, and to the Ojo del Agua in Sabinas Hidalgo. All in all, they had a great afternoon with plenty of laughs. Roland enjoyed the day with them, and he had a good birthday.

They returned to Bustamante by evening. Beto tried to call the coyote who had stood them up, but he couldn't be reached. That plan was gone.

Roland talked to Alberto about what he wanted to do. As he needed money to give to his girlfriend who was going to become his wife, he decided to come with Roland. They would try to call the man named Placas tomorrow.

The next day, Roland went over to Beto, and he was sleepy at 7:30 AM. He didn't want to call. So Roland went to Alberto's house, and they later went to Beto's house, and the three of them went to the Orolizo's house to ask to use the telephone to call Laredo, Texas. Nobody was home. They went to the Gonzalez's house. They didn't want to loan the telephone. They went to Manuel's house. He didn't want to loan the phone because it was his uncle's phone, and he wasn't there at the moment. As there were no payphones in Bustamante, they couldn't call. Yes, the Hotel Ancira had phone service, but it didn't occur to any of the three of them at the time.

Rigo had taken a bus to Sabinas Hidalgo to register for school this morning. Roland took Alberto and Beto to Sabinas Hidalgo, picked up Rigo, and they enjoyed the afternoon in town. Roland bought them lunch again, and he also bought Rigo a cassette. They returned to Bustamante.

In the late afternoon, a big rain came, a gully washer. Roland rode around town on his bicycle that evening after the rain. The streets were flooded with up to a foot of water! He bought some food at Chilo Cantu's store, made last minute arrangements with Alberto and with Beto, and he returned to Rigo's house.

The next morning, Roland loaded his truck with his things. He wrote a note to Lavinia, who was still in Zacatecas, thanking her and Alejandro for having him. He wrote that he was leaving N$330 with Rigo to help pay expenses, in addition to the new bicycle he left with him, as well. On top of that, Roland paid Rigo an additional N$500 for the time he spent with him. Roland put the note up in their glass encased dish cabinet.

He thanked Rigo and his father for everything. They wished him well, and Rigo told Roland that it was a pleasure having him in his house for the past two weeks. Roland said thanks and told him the pleasure was his. They shook hands in a sincere manner.

Roland really felt like he had a great friendship with Rigo. He was like a brother. Roland had been able to stay with Rigo and his family, and Rigo had kept him company, as well. To top it all, there was an extra added bonus. Rigo had gone into the mountains with Roland and Beto. What more could Roland ask for?

Rigo was one of the best friends Roland had ever had, and they had an inner sense of understanding that made it seem as if they had known each other since time began. Yes, Roland really appreciated Rigo, and now he felt properly compensated for the ugly events that had occurred back in January and February.

Roland couldn't help but go over to Isalia and Luke's rental house. In a sneering manner, he walked back and forth numerous times in front of that house, and he took great delight in whistling the same tune from "The Wizard of Oz." There! Serves Isalia right!

CHAPTER 13

THE CROSSINGS

August 1998

Next, Roland went for Alberto and Beto. They each threw a handbag into the back of the truck, and at mid morning, they drove out of Bustamante to go to Laredo. It had really rained, and the creek, which was normally dry, was running swiftly and was muddy. Perhaps the Rio Grande River would be up as well, and crossing it might not be possible.

In a little over two hours, they reached the Colombia Bridge. Roland turned in his permit at Mexican Customs. Roland, playing it safe, checked under his truck and under the hood for drugs, to be sure no one had planted any drugs on his truck. The best he could tell, it was clean.

He drove Beto and Alberto over to Nuevo Laredo. He had a detailed map with him, and they arrived at Bridge 1. Roland parked a few blocks away from the bridge, and they walked to a parking lot next to the bridge. Next, they crossed the parking lot and reached the fence where they took a look at the rain swollen and muddy river. It looked iffy.

A couple of Nuevo Laredo cops on mountain bikes came by, and they asked Roland, Beto and Alberto what they were doing. They answered that they were just looking at the river. The cops didn't want to believe that story, and after they asked some further questions, Beto and Alberto admitted that they were thinking of crossing the river. The cops gestured that was what they thought. Next, they did a quick inspection, checking the pants of each of them to be sure they weren't carrying knives or weapons, and then they said they were free to go. Whew! Thank goodness that didn't get complicated.

Roland, Beto and Alberto returned to Roland's truck several blocks away, and he drove them to some sort of a forested roadside park along the river three kilometers east of the two bridges. Beto and Alberto each took an extra change of clothing and a hand towel, and they walked toward the river. Roland wished them good luck.

Literally only hundreds of meters away was the back of one of Laredo's HEB supermarkets. If they could cross the river, walk through the monte (scrubland) for 200 meters, and reach the store, they would wait for Roland there.

Meanwhile, Roland drove along the highway by the river, soon reaching Bridge II. He reached the toll booth, paid the correct toll this time, that is, he wasn't overcharged, and he drove across the bridge. He reached one of the initial booths where the officer asked Roland the standard questions of citizenship, where he had been visiting, his reasons for going, and what he did for a living.

Then he asked Roland if he had any fruits or plants. Roland said he had two avocados. The officer asked Roland where they were, and Roland said they were in the back in his food box. The officer asked Roland to step down, *right then*, go to the back of his truck, and retrieve the avocados, which he did obligingly. Roland opened the back door to his camper top, got the two avocados and handed them to the man.

"These *don't* come in!" he told Roland, as if they were contraband, and he asked Roland if he had any more hidden. Roland told him no.

Next, the officer sent Roland and his truck to one of the many inspection bays. Everyone driving in from Mexico had to be inspected there by a different officer. Normally, prohibited items are surrendered to the second officer at the inspection bays, but *not* those two avocados. They were such a *hot* item that the first officer at the initial booth wanted them handed over right then and there!

A tall militaristic type gringo who had a crew cut came to Roland's truck. He asked Roland if he had any drugs, and that if he did have any, to admit it, hand them over, and he would be free to go. However, if he were to say no and they find drugs, he would have a very big problem.

"I don't do drugs nor do I have any," said Roland.

"Are you sure?"

"I'm sure. I don't have drugs."

"Okay," he said in a mistrusting manner. "Just don't say I didn't give you a chance to admit it."

By now, Roland thought the officer was very strange. Roland stepped down, went to the back of his truck, and opened the tailgate. The officer explained that there was too much #%$@! and that he would pick certain items to inspect. One of the items was Roland's box of water jugs in former orange juice containers. Roland always carried several gallons when travelling.

"What the #@%!! is that?!"

"My water jugs," Roland answered.

"I think it's liquid cocaine."

"Liquid cocaine?!" Roland asked, surprised at the term.

"Yes, liquid cocaine!" the officer answered.

"No officer, it isn't any liquid cocaine!" and he handed the officer one of the jugs.

The officer sniffed and then poured a little of it on the ground. It was water!

Suddenly, something mysteriously calmed down the officer as he saw both of Roland's photo albums.

"Are those picture albums?" he asked Roland.

"Yeah, they're of my trips to Mexico," and Roland handed them to the officer.

"Let's have look at them. A picture says a thousand words." He looked through them. "Looks good. Nothing incriminating to me." He looked through them some more, handed them back to Roland, and told him he was free to go.

Roland thanked him. Whew! Thank goodness that was over. That officer must have been sure he was going to find drugs in Roland's truck, but as Roland had nothing to do with drugs, the officer, of course, didn't find any. It was strange how he had been so mistrusting, but thank goodness he had calmed down and decided to believe in Roland.

He drove away and drove several miles southeast to the HEB store, and he got out of his truck and walked into the store. Neither Beto nor Alberto were there. Next, Roland walked around the store to the back, and he looked across the several hundred yards of monte, across the river, and the forest park beyond that. There was no one.

There were not even any fences. No wonder so many Mexicans crossed over. It was easy, and there were no lookout officers checking at all.

Roland got in his truck. He would wait another 15 minutes. Suddenly, Beto and Alberto arrived to the side of Roland's truck in desperation to get in. Roland immediately let them in the cab with him. He was glad to see them, and he asked them how the crossing was.

They said the river was a little swift but they managed it. One of them fell and swam for a tree overhanging the river, and he grabbed hold of the limb, stopping himself from being carried much further downstream. They changed their clothing and hid under some Mesquite trees, waiting for Roland to arrive. They hadn't seen him pull in, but when he had walked to the back of the store to look across the scrubland, they saw him then. They emerged and crossed the parking lot to Roland's truck.

They had really made it across the river! Beto and Alberto also said a cop on the Mexican side tried to arrest them for leaving Mexico, and the only way he released them was if they each gave him $30, which of course they did. The cop then told them to have a nice crossing, and it's for certain he went home and ate steak that night!

Roland started his truck, and he drove them to the western side of Laredo where Beto's contact, Placas lived. They didn't find him, but they found his buddies. Beto and Alberto talked to them, asking them how they could get around the second inspection at mile marker 14 on Interstate 35. They said it was difficult, and they would take them for $1,200. That was way too much. Roland asked them how much they would charge to take Beto and Alberto to the last exit before the inspection station, that is, exit 13. They wanted $200!

Why, Roland could do that! Why did he need these other men to do it? They left.

Roland took Beto to his aunt's house where he stayed overnight, and then Roland and Alberto went over to a house where some cousins of the Quevalos lived. They accommodated them overnight.

That night, Roland had Alberto call the most likely number of the three phone numbers Roland had gotten off of Manuel's phone bill. Alberto reached Eduardo's wife Millana. He told her he was from Bustamante and was a friend of Raul's, that he was on his way to Dallas and would like to stop by and visit. He made no mention of Roland. She gave the address with the street number and name. Alberto asked her to spell the name. Roland was sitting by Alberto, and he handed Roland the phone so he could listen to her spell out the address. Roland wrote it down and then handed the phone back to Alberto, who continued talking to Millana about when he might come by.

Secured! Second obstacle jumped! Roland now had Raul's phone number, an unlisted number, *and* his address. Lavinia and her son Rigo were unsuccessful in blocking Roland from finding out. Evidently, Roland was meant to find it out, and he did. The very idea, really, of Lavinia and Rigo refusing to give Roland Eduardo's number!

After Alberto hung up, Roland laughed. So did Alberto. They shook hands in triumph. Roland really was elated to have found out Raul's address. Both of them laughed some more.

The next morning, Roland and Alberto thanked the Quevalo's cousins, and they went to Beto's aunt's house. Beto came outside and got in the truck with them. Roland drew them a map of the highways and put a dotted line along the proposed route they were to walk. He told them he would turn them loose at exit 13. They would walk for 5 miles parallel to I-35, and arrive at Highway 83, 500 meters west of exit 18, where Highway 83 and I-35 intersected. Roland would pick them up there on the side of the highway.

Roland drove them to exit 13, pulled off the interstate to the right, turned left, and drove under the underpass, where he pulled over. Beto and Alberto anxiously got out of Roland's truck. Roland managed to hand them one of his jugs of "liquid cocaine". No, really it was water. The two of them bolted to the fence on the west side of the exit, and they ran into the scrubland, soon being out of sight.

Roland drove back to Laredo and went to Auto Zone and other places, doing errands to let three hours go by, while Beto and Alberto were walking 5 miles in the hot, 100° sunny weather.

At high noon, Roland left Laredo. He drove through the U.S. Border Patrol inspection station at exit 14. They waved him through without even talking to him. Great! Roland drove on to exit 18. Along the way, he saw a helicopter flying south, parallel to the interstate. They were looking for Mexicans. At exit 18, he turned left on Highway 83. He drove along, hoping to see Beto and Alberto, but they were not to be seen. Roland really hoped that helicopter hadn't found them, nor one of the numerous 4WD Border Patrol trucks, driving through the scrubland.

Roland drove his truck a few miles down the highway and turned around at a tavern/restaurant. On the way back, he found a gravel lane and pulled in. A van was there with a Wisconsin plate, and its hood was up. They were faking being broken down. Of course, they were waiting for some Mexicans. Roland waited there ten minutes to give Beto and Alberto a chance to arrive.

Then he drove away to return to the intersection at exit 18. He drove along the kilometer of the highway, worried for his friends. Suddenly, they made their appearance, crossed the fence, and ran to the side of the highway. Roland pulled over, and they quickly jumped in. Miraculously, the whole highway was clear. No one saw it. They were nervous, including Roland. Immediately he proceeded, soon reaching the intersection, where he turned left on I-35 and drove them to San Antonio.

They talked along the way. Alberto pulled a few Nopal spines out of his legs. They had drunk all the water and were very thirsty. Roland gave them another jug of his water, which they drank down pretty quick. They had seen that helicopter and had immediately taken cover under a Mesquite tree. All in all, their 5 mile walk had gone well, and they were glad to have made it.

Roland was glad they had arrived. Out of fear of being caught, Roland wasn't going to pass by that stretch of highway a third time. Thank goodness they had made their appearance then, or they would have been abandoned.

All three of them were very lucky. Alberto and Beto were grateful to Roland, and Alberto said Dios cleared the highway of all vehicles at the time they had made their appearance and gotten in Roland's truck. That was indeed lucky.

Months later Roland would find out from another Mexican friend what the penalty would have been, had he been caught picking up two Mexicans off the highway: six months in jail, a $5,000 fine, and confiscation of the vehicle and contents! How awful and severe!

Evidently, Beto and Alberto were meant to make it through, since Alberto had undeservedly had his passport and VISA confiscated (stolen) by U.S. Customs over a matter of how much money he had in his wallet. Roland deserved compensation as well, since the U.S. Consulate had sneered at Raul and had scribbled through his solicitúd in defiance, and also for the fact that the Consulate wouldn't recognize any of Roland's paperwork, such as the affidavit of support for Lavinia and Raul.

There was still danger of being caught. I-35 between Laredo and San Antonio was crawling with Border Patrol vehicles and police cars, and they were known to pull people over at random to check anyone for documentation and paperwork. Fortunately, no one pulled Roland over.

They arrived in San Antonio where Beto's madrina (godmother) lived. Beto called her, and they stopped by her house. She and her sister lived there, and they were kind people. They invited Roland, Beto and Alberto inside, and they fed them a meal. They were glad to see Beto, and they were surprised they had gotten around the inspections without being caught.

Beto asked if he could stay with them and work in San Antonio. They answered that they didn't have any extra bedrooms. So, they couldn't accommodate him. Roland told Beto he was welcome to come with him and Alberto, and that's what he decided to do. Beto's godmother gave them both advice, saying the United States was much more strict than Mexico, that you couldn't go shouting and drinking in the street like back home in Mexico. She advised them to respect Roland and wished them well in whatever work they would find.

Roland took pictures of them. They said goodbye, and left.

Their next stop was Salado. As they drove along, Roland told them he wanted to drive out West. He had told them before, and now he was telling them again. Roland really wished to take a travelling companion out there, and he asked them to go out there with him. They said okay to it.

Along the way, they talked about different things, and Beto and Alberto slept part of the way also. Their three hour walk had made them tired.

They arrived in Salado at 9 PM. Roland consulted his map of Salado and found the street where Eduardo and his wife Millana lived. He drove them there, and they pulled up in front of the house. Roland asked Beto and Alberto to knock on the door, but they felt shy. So, Roland decided to knock on the door but with his two friends being by his side. All three of them went to the porch. Roland was concerned about how Eduardo might react, that he might get angry.

Eduardo answered the door, and he and Roland greeted each other in a civil manner. Roland introduced Beto and Alberto, who Eduardo recognized from Bustamante. Roland immediately said he regretted what had happened between him and Raul back in February, and he asked him how Raul was doing. Eduardo thanked Roland for that, and he invited the three of them inside.

Roland went and got his two picture albums from his truck and brought them inside. Eduardo and his wife Millana looked through the photos with interest. Beto and Alberto talked with them. Things relaxed, and soon they were laughing and telling stories from Bustamante.

Beto and Alberto said they were thinking of going to California with Roland before going to Tennessee. Millana mentioned that they have inspection stations entering that state and that they check everyone for their papers.

Eduardo said Raul was doing fine and was working at a wood mill around a mile away.

Eduardo and Millana offered them to sleep out in their garage/house. There was an extra bed and mattresses out there. That was kind of them.

Eduardo offered to go with them to see Raul where he was working. So, he got in Roland's truck and Roland drove them over to the wood mill. Upon arriving, Eduardo entered and found Raul. Roland, Beto and Alberto waited outside the fence and gate.

Raul came. He was ecstatic! He had a smile on his face as he eagerly greeted Beto, Alberto, and even Roland with an enthusiastic Mexican style handshake. He was so glad to see them.

Roland was quite surprised that Raul greeted him too, and he responded by saying, "¿Cómo estás?"

Raul asked them how they were and told them he'd be home at 4 AM when he gets off work. He would enjoy a visit then and in the morning also.

What Rigo had initially said was true. Raul did indeed want to make up with Roland. Once Roland saw how glad Raul was to see him, nothing would do but that Roland had to forgive him. Roland was really glad to see his friend Raul, that they met again in their lifetimes. Yes, he had found him! Thank goodness Lavinia and Rigo were unsuccessful in blocking him.

Raul had to return to his work. Eduardo went with Roland, Beto and Alberto to a fast food restaurant, and they ate a late supper. Then they returned to his house, and he and Millana set them up in the garage/house to sleep.

They slept until 4 AM when Raul arrived and chatted with them a while. Then they all went back to sleep.

When they woke up at 9 AM, Eduardo and Millana had already gone to work. Raul invited them into the house for a while. Then they went to different stores. Raul had bought a car, a 1984 Buick Century, and the motor had just quit in it. Roland took them to Raul's friend's house where the car was, and he showed them his car. It looked in pretty good condition.

Also Raul, along with Beto, said that the culprits behind the firecracker incident were indeed Isalia and Luke. They had paid Beto N$300 to do it. They had offered the money to Raul first, but he had refused. Since Beto had needed the money, he took the dangerous job, and he made sure to toss the firecracker/bomb in a different room from where Roland was. Roland told them that's what he had thought. Oh, if only Isalia and Luke could be sitting in Monterrey's prison right now.

Roland realized that, regardless of Immigration, Raul had become a good 'ol American. Yes, he was lonely for his past friends in Bustamante, but he had relatives in Salado, and he was beginning to make friends, as well.

They returned to Eduardo and Millana's house. Raul asked Roland, Beto and Alberto to stay until tomorrow. They could goof off again tomorrow and enjoy another day. Beto decided to stay.

Alberto told Roland he wanted to go to Tennessee right away to begin work, not out West to travel. Roland wanted to go out West first, and Alberto said they could go out there in November or December. Roland explained that it didn't work that way. It wasn't like Mexico. The mountains out West were covered in snow after September, and they didn't thaw out until the next June! Alberto didn't want to understand, and he insisted on going to Tennessee now, not later. Roland insisted on going out West, and Alberto then said he would stay with Beto and Raul and return to Bustamante instead.

Plus, Alberto was afraid to go to California for what Millana had said last night. Roland insisted that there is no Immigration. It's a fruit inspection, and that's all. Plus, there are some highways entering California that are free of inspection stations, and Roland knew of one. Still, Alberto was afraid to go.

Alberto got disgusted and took his things out of Roland's truck. Raul came over to Roland and explained that he was about to lose his friendship with Alberto. He explained that Alberto was tense because he was away from his homeland, and he suggested to Roland that he accommodate Alberto and take him to Tennessee for the time being. Raul told Roland that he had to endure a lot of loneliness to adapt to his new life in Salado, and now Alberto was experiencing the same.

Roland took Raul's advice, and he went to Alberto and said okay, they would go to Tennessee. Beto, who was one of Raul's best friends, stayed in Salado with Raul for two days. Eduardo and Millana happily *accommodated* him and let him stay.

Beto was without money, and he would need money to return to Bustamante by bus. Roland took $70 out of his wallet and gave it to him. That would sustain him.

Raul asked Roland if he had bought any CDs while in Mexico. Roland said he had bought *Mercurio*'s "Tiempo de Vivir." Roland brought it in from his truck and Raul played it in Eduardo's stereo system. No more than three notes of the song "Tiempo de Vivir" had played, and Roland was struck with a sense of familiarity that made him feel like he had heard that song many times before, but he knew he hadn't. So familiar that song was, that Roland took a liking to it right away. He felt tingling sensations or goose bumps. Why was it so familiar? He didn't know.

Eduardo and Millana came home in the afternoon, a break from work. Roland said he was taking Alberto to Tennessee, and he thanked them for taking them in overnight. Roland asked Eduardo if he could come to visit Raul in the future. He said that would be fine, and he could stay in the garage/house. He said he could come and visit Raul whenever he wanted to. Eduardo was an understanding and reasonable fellow. In fact, he was glad Roland thought enough of Raul to actually stop by and visit, as well as having apologized and made up for the incident back in February.

Roland and Alberto said goodbye to everyone. Raul was just leaving to go to work at 2:30 PM. A friend of his came by to pick him up. He shook hands with Roland and Alberto, thanked them for stopping by, and rode off to work with his friend. Roland and Alberto drove away, headed for Tennessee.

For six hours, Roland drove, skirting around Dallas and driving to Arkansas, and they stopped at exit 83 to sleep in a service station parking lot. Early the next morning, Roland drove them to Tennessee, and around 11 AM, they arrived at Roland's farm.

Though Roland didn't know it, Millana had just had a dream last night. Plus, Raul called several muchachas in Bustamante the next morning by telephone and told them Roland had come by, a pleasant surprise indeed. As it turned out, one of the girls knew Rigo. She was friendly with Rigo, and she worked at the Hotel Ancira. Rigo went by to visit with her, and when she told him, he nearly blew his top! He was quite irritated, offended actually, that Roland had penetrated the obstacle he and his mother had placed in front of him! She began to explain that Raul had been glad that Roland visited . . . but Rigo stormed out of the hotel angry!

Rigo bicycled straight over to Manuel's house, riding of course the new bicycle that Roland had given him, and he immediately told Manuel that if Roland were to call for any reason, to just hang up on him! The very idea that Roland had jumped the obstacle and found Raul, and the tricky manner in which he did it!

Further, women in town found out before Rigo did . . . embarrassing indeed!

* * *

Nuevo Wimbisenho

Meanwhile, in Nuevo Wimbisenho, Arfifra and Draaktra were talking things over. Millana's spirit guide Druxtrli was present, and so were Sasjurech and Sojornbloc.

"Draaktra, I believe we have an opportunity for you," Arfifra told him with savour in her voice.

"Roland succeeded in finding Raul, didn't he?" he guessed.

"That's right," Arfifra said with a smile. "You see, Draaktra, Roland broke a few rules. He must suffer the consequences!"

"Amen!" Druxtrli agreed. "How dare Roland do what he did! He's going to pay!"

"Did you do what I suggested?" Arfifra asked Druxtrli.

"Oh, by all means, and more," she proudly boasted. "I planted a dream in her last night. She dreamed that Roland did witchcraft, that he was an alien from another star system, and that he could appear and disappear, that is, teleport."

"Did you really?" Sasjurech reacted.

Druxtrli cackled with laughter. "Yeah, I did a good number on that dream . . . made her hair stand up with fright!"

All of them roared with laughter!

"Now, Draaktra," Arfifra advised, "concerning Rigo, there's going to be an opening at . . ."

*   *   *

Roland's parents, Dr. and Mrs. Jocelyn, greeted him and Alberto. Roland took Alberto up to his house, where he set up an extra bed for him. Alberto took a nap, and Roland mowed the lawn, which his father had not had a chance to do for the hot weather.

That afternoon, they made some phone calls. Alberto called Bustamante and said he would be staying till December. He called his family and his girlfriend. Roland called a Mexican he knew in Nashville who had become legalized, and he informed them he had had to pay $10,000. Wow! That's way too much. Then he "dropped a bomb" and told Roland and Alberto that U.S. Immigration had just arrived for a two week period and had set up various roadblocks throughout Nashville checking everyone, especially Mexicans, for legal paperwork. Alberto really tensed up! He was scared to leave the Jocelyn's farm now. Roland said there was a few days' work to do here on the farm, cleaning fence rows, and Alberto could do that. Meanwhile, Roland would find work for them.

They called Raul and talked to him. It was his day off. Beto was with him and was enjoying his stay. Raul was, no doubt, grateful to Roland for having brought Beto up to Salado to visit. Raul had been lonely and missed his friends from Bustamante. What a nice treat Roland gave him.

That night, Roland called Manuel and asked him to go down the street, get Rigo, and bring him to the telephone. Manuel answered that he wasn't going to bring Rigo to the phone, nor would he pass messages to him. Plus, it was pouring down rain in Bustamante. Actually, it was flooding there. Roland was taken aback, and he asked Manuel why. He evaded direct answers. Roland reminded Manuel about the clothing he had given him and the N$75, and he said he was coming across as someone who was not a friend. Manuel said he was Roland's friend, but his uncle, the owner of the phone, had said no. Roland told Manuel he had gotten permission from his uncle before he left town. Manuel said that's the best he could do. Roland left it at that. He thanked Manuel anyway for having given, well . . . sold Roland those three phone numbers off the phone bill, and he told him he had indeed found Raul. They finished the conversation. Roland was left confused. What was going on? The truth was, Manuel didn't want to level with Roland and tell him how angry Rigo actually was.

For the next three days solid, Alberto swung a machete, cleaning fencerows. He was a workhorse for sure! Roland went to Alberto from time to time to see how he was doing and to give him instructions. Roland's father gave instructions also, and Roland translated.

Alberto was extremely lonely. He missed his own kind back in Mexico. He missed his mother and his family. He missed his girlfriend. He told Roland he wanted to go back home, and Roland explained that they had just arrived. He wanted to take Alberto hiking in Savage Gulf, take him to visit his cousins, and other places. Roland stated that they would need to stay at least a couple of months.

"¡No aguanto! ¡No aguanto! Entienda, entienda. ¡No aguanto!" Alberto exclaimed, telling Roland he couldn't endure, and for Roland to *understand* that he just couldn't endure, here in Tennessee. He wanted to go home. "Se metió en mi mente mi mamá," saying that his mother was constantly on his mind. He also explained that he couldn't go hiking nor visiting Roland's relatives because swinging the machete helped him endure the pain and sadness of being away from his family. Alberto was borderline freaking out, and he felt like he was on another planet. Desperation was an understatement.

Roland had to give in. He couldn't endure Alberto's desperation, anyway. He told him they could leave in two days. He had some errands to do in town. He also had to adjust the valves. One of them was clicking. He reloaded the truck, leaving his new Magistroni bike at home.

On the day of leaving, Alberto worked for two hours while Roland got his food together to load into his truck. He also listened to his new CD by *Mercurio*. The songs on that CD were amazing, and for some reason, Roland kept having the idea that they had been channeled from another star system where humans also live. To Roland, that album was one of the best he had ever heard, and the five members of *Mercurio* represented peace, love, and friendship.

Roland and his father both paid Alberto for his time working. They climbed in the truck at 10 AM, and Roland drove 13 hours, reaching Salado that night at 11 PM. Eduardo and Millana's house was dark. They had gone to bed. Roland drove Alberto over to the wood mill. Raul saw them and came to them to greet them. He said he would be getting off work at 2 AM.

As for staying at Eduardo and Millana's house, Raul said he couldn't give them the consent to stay there, since it belonged to Eduardo and Millana. If it were Raul's house, he would have given them the key and told them to go to his house and make themselves at home. He suggested a park nearby and told them how to get there, and he asked them to come by and visit at 9 AM.

If only Roland and Alberto had arrived a little earlier, perhaps Eduardo and Millana would have still been up and would have let them stay.

Roland and Alberto found the town park and slept in the truck the rest of the night.

Mosquitoes were somewhat bothersome.

In the morning, they went to Eduardo and Millana's house. They were away at work. Raul was just getting up, and he let Roland and Alberto inside. Roland asked if he could shower, and Raul said it wasn't his house, thus he couldn't give permission. Roland looked at Raul in a strange way.

Raul said in English, "I'm sorry."

That wasn't hard, was it, Raul? Raul had just now apologized to Roland for the awful incident in February. That finally made things right.

Roland walked back to the garage/house and without permission helped himself to the shower. He was all sweaty feeling from yesterday's drive. There. That was better. Raul knew what Roland did, but he didn't mind. Raul was a genuine welcoming person, but here in Salado, his "hands were tied" to some degree.

The three of them went to a major shopping mall and walked around different stores. Alberto used part of his money and bought a $90 pair of tennis shoes. They would last him a long time. Roland took pictures of Raul and Alberto, and Alberto took some of Roland and Raul.

Yes, Roland and Raul ran around together in the United States of America. Raul yes, got into the USA, against Isalia's declaration, and there wasn't a thing Isalia could do about it! If one day they went to California, that would make it complete. The very idea of Isalia having said, "There you go again, Roland! Raul is *not* getting into the United States!" Well, Isalia was just *wrong* about that! Amen!

Yes, Roland, Raul, and Alberto enjoyed their time together. How good that their friendship had been fixed, and so soon! How ridiculous it would have been to wait three years, like Lavinia had suggested!

They returned to Eduardo and Millana's house and visited a while longer. Raul wanted Roland and Alberto to stay overnight. So, he called Millana at work to ask her if that would be all right. She told Raul that Alberto would be fine, but she didn't want Roland in the house at all! Raul hung up and told Roland and Alberto that she didn't want them spending the night because of Roland.

They continued visiting. Roland tape recorded Raul and took his message to his family in Bustamante.

Around 3 PM, Raul went to work. Roland and Alberto said goodbye to Raul. He enjoyed having their visit. Roland took Alberto south to McAllen, Texas to a ranch near there, where his sister and family lived.

On the way, Roland and Alberto talked. Roland asked him why Millana had suddenly seemingly turned against him. Alberto was clueless about Millana's sudden change. While Alberto could have stayed with Raul, leaving Roland out, he decided not to, for his respect for Roland. Roland wondered if he had offended Millana somehow, but if he had, he had no idea how.

They talked about Raul and Rigo. Roland asked Alberto which one was the better friend, and Alberto reckoned it was Rigo. Roland agreed. He and Rigo had never had any big problems. Rigo was more complacent, not so hot tempered as Raul. Rigo had received him in his house for two weeks, had spent time with him, accommodated him nicely, most of the time, and had told him it was a pleasure having him in the house. Yes, Roland really appreciated Rigo for a friend.

They arrived around 9 PM at Alberto's sister's house and ranch. She fed them some supper and set them up with bed mattresses and fans in a new concrete block house next to theirs.

The next morning, Roland parted ways with Alberto. A rash of poison ivy had broken out on both his arms. He had done all that fence row cleaning in a short sleeve shirt, against Roland's suggestion of long sleeves.

Alberto thanked Roland, and Roland drove his truck to a bridge northwest of McAllen.

CHAPTER 14

COMPENSATION REVISITED

late August 1998

That morning, Roland and Alberto saw the news on TV. The Rio Grande River had really flooded. Up around Del Río, Texas, it had rained some 16 inches yesterday and the water all came barreling down through Laredo, flooding both Customs houses and carrying trash of all types. The bridges were closed at Laredo for two to three days, as a result. However, there was a huge man-made lake further downstream before McAllen, and all the floodwaters were caught there and filled up the lake. Downstream from that, the river was normal. Roland crossed at Miguel Alemán, Tamaulipas, and the river was not up at all, just a clear creek way below.

Roland got his permit from Mexican Customs. Little children were going around begging for money. Roland gave some of them some coins, and he gave Corn Flakes and fruit to one of them who looked nicer and more genuine than the others. After an hour of obtaining his permit and having copies made across the street, he drove out of there and drove west toward Sabinas Hidalgo.

Around 30 kilometers into the country, he drove through a town called Mier, Tamaulipas and drove out of town headed west. He continued along the two-lane highway going around 40 mph.

Suddenly, a pickup truck began to pass him, and it drove along beside Roland. It was a police truck! What did they want?! Roland pulled over, had to pull completely off the highway at the next available ranch entrance.

The two policemen stepped down. So did Roland, and they greeted him at the back of his truck. They introduced themselves in a friendly way, and they were impressed that Roland knew Spanish as well as he did. They walked with Roland to the cab and pointed at his speedometer, telling him he had been speeding. The speed limit was 60 km/h, and Roland was doing probably 70 km/h. They said one of them was going to ride with Roland in the cab of his truck, and they would follow the police truck back to the comandancia (police station) in Mier. So, one of them got in Roland's truck and Roland began to drive back to Mier. The police truck passed them and took off toward Mier and was soon out of sight.

The policeman in Roland's truck talked to Roland. He had a small book of laws and section codes on his lap. He told Roland the fine was high for speeding. Roland asked him how much, and he said it was around N$600. Roland said he thought it would be around N$130.

As they approached the edge of town, Roland asked the policeman, who called himself Tonio, which way to the station. It was 1:20 PM. He told Roland the station had just closed at 1 PM, and he asked Roland to pull over next to a cantina. Roland did. Tonio explained that it would be tomorrow before the station would open. If he would just hand over the keys, they would take the truck and impound it till tomorrow when he could pay the fine.

No . . . No way! Roland knew if he gave in to that, the police would take his truck and belongings, and he would never see his truck again. And what about Roland? Where would he spend the night? In their jail, for certain! That cop was lying out of both sides of his mouth. Roland reminded Tonio that the other cop had said for them to go to the station

276

where he would pay. How could they be closed? Tonio reiterated that they had just closed at 1 PM.

Roland then said he just wanted to pay right then and there, and be on his way to Bustamante. How much? The cop said it would be high! Roland reiterated that he wanted to pay. So, Tonio said with US $60 he would conform and step down, and Roland would be free to leave. Roland took three $20 notes out of his wallet and handed them to Tonio.

As a "courtesy" Tonio pulled a US $10 note out of his wallet and gave it to Roland as a "rebate." He told Roland "Que te vaya bien," and he stepped down.

Roland told the man, "Sí," and that was all. Whew! That was close!

Tonio walked into the cantina, and Roland turned around and drove straight out of town. He saw a hitchhiker, and yes he picked him up so he wouldn't be alone. He took the man 20 kilometers down the road, told him the corruption that had just happened, and let him out at his destination.

Roland drove on for 160 kilometers, no more mishaps, and he reached Sabinas Hidalgo. He exchanged money, bought groceries, and he also visited a flea market stand where he bought a pirate cassette tape of *Mercurio*'s "Tiempo de Vivir".

After that, he drove on to Bustamante, arriving in the late afternoon. He arrived at Rigo's house, where he parked under a Mesquite tree across the street.

Rigo was not there at the moment. School had begun, and Rigo was away for the day at the Prepa in Sabinas Hidalgo. He was expected home any moment.

Lavinia and her two daughters were there. They nicely welcomed Roland. They were surprised to see him, and Roland told them that Alberto had not lasted. They had gone all the way to Tennessee where Alberto worked at Roland's family's ranch for three days, and he had just driven him to his sister's place in McAllen, where he would stay for a couple of weeks. All in all, Alberto had cost Roland $330, including the gasoline to Tennessee and back and including the $70 he had given Beto to return to Bustamante.

Since Roland had to bring Alberto all the way back, well that is, to McAllen, he had decided to return to Bustamante for a while to enjoy his friends again. At least that would be some consolation for the extra time, effort, and money spent on Alberto's behalf.

Roland told Lavinia that he had found Raul and that he, Beto and Alberto had a good visit with him.

"Ves, ya no está enojado contigo," Lavinia kindly responded, telling Roland that Raul was no longer angry with him. Lavinia was glad Roland had found her son and that things had gone so well. Somehow, she was not the least bit irritated that Roland had jumped her obstacle.

Roland unloaded his things from his truck, and he walked up to Manuel's place to talk to him about why in the world he would not cooperate and bring Rigo to the phone. Roland could only speculate that perhaps Manuel was jealous of Roland and Rigo's friendship. But why would he be? After all, Roland was a friend to Manuel, too.

Manuel wasn't there, and as he was asking about his whereabouts, Rigo happened to arrive. Roland looked at Rigo, standing there on the patio. Rigo's arms were crossed, and he had a confrontational look on his face. Roland instinctively sensed that it had to do with Raul.

"¿Cómo le encontraste?" Rigo quickly said, asking Roland how he found Raul.

Roland received nervous feelings of tension, and he answered that he had just . . . found him.

"No. ¿Cómo le encontraste?" Rigo reiterated.

They left Manuel's family's patio and began to walk to Rigo's house. Roland told Rigo he just got lucky and found Raul.

Rigo was rather combative and asked Roland a third time.

Roland answered, now a little more firmly, that he had his ways of doing it and he had succeeded!

Rigo then accused Roland of going to Juanito, Manuel's uncle, and getting the numbers off the phone bill.

Roland didn't want to admit it to Rigo, and Rigo began a scolding. They entered his house. Lavinia, Norma and Irma were in the backyard hanging up clothes.

"No me vas a regañar," Roland firmly told Rigo, telling him not to scold him. "Y no me gusta que tú y tu mamá me bloquearon. Soy su amigo," telling Rigo that he didn't like it that Rigo and his mother blocked him from finding Raul, and that he was Raul's friend. Amen!

"No te estamos regañando," Rigo said, now suddenly more friendly and assuring Roland that he wasn't scolding him.

"Pues bueno," saying, *Well good*.

"Fue Eduardo que nos dijo que no te diéramos," Rigo now said, calmly explaining that it was Eduardo who had told Rigo and his mother not to give Roland his address nor phone number.

Roland nodded a gesture of understanding.

"Entonces arreglaste con Beto y con Raul. Falta Pegaso," said Rigo, telling Roland in an approving manner that he had made up with Beto, with his brother Raul, and there was still Pegaso lacking.

Roland felt like he just stepped off a roller coaster. The tense, nervous feelings were quickly leaving, and he felt much relieved.

Rigo then welcomed Roland back to Bustamante. He and Roland shook hands, greeting each other finally. He showed him which bed he could sleep in, and he asked Roland what they would be able to do. He was without work. Gonzalo's business was virtually closed.

Roland told Rigo about how Alberto didn't last and how he refused to go to California with him. Rigo explained that Alberto had used him simply as a means of getting across the border, and not entirely for genuine reasons

*   * . *

Nuevo Wimbisenho

"Oh drat! I almost had him!" Draaktra angrily declared.

"Curse that energy system of Martonción's!" Arfifra exclaimed, her voice trembling with anger.

"He blocked me from getting in!" Draaktra complained.

"System kicked in and shielded you off," said Sojornbloc, "minutes after Roland and Rigo met again!"

"Oh that blasted Martonción!" Sasjurech added. "We can't get in either."

"Just ruined my frequency synchronizers!" Draaktra shouted.

Compensation Revisited

"I've got a plan," Arfifra proposed. "I'll talk with my good friend Druxtrli . . . let her spur some ideas, plant some false memories, if you know what I mean . . ."

*　　*　　*

Roland and Rigo drove over to Angelo's house. Angelo greeted Roland normally, and they started talking on the sidewalk in front of his house.

They looked down the street. There came Beto Enriquez in the distance. He approached them and greeted them. He had just arrived from Laredo today, said they had just opened the bridge to pedestrians this afternoon, and he had taken a bus from Nuevo Laredo.

Roland said he had just arrived half an hour ago.

Beto asked Roland how things went with Alberto, and Roland told them about how Alberto didn't last, how he couldn't psychologically endure being away from his family and friends.

"¡No aguanto! ¡No aguanto! Entienda, entienda. ¡No aguanto!" Roland ranted and raved, copying Alberto.

Rigo, Angelo, and Beto all had a good laugh, and so did Roland.

Roland told various stories about Alberto working on his farm and about their visits with Raul. He told them about the police incident over in Mier, Tamaulipas. They told Roland he did the right thing to pay on-the-spot cash to that wish washy cop and leave, or he could have stolen his truck.

Later that evening, Rigo and Roland returned to his house, and Lavinia fed them supper.

Alejandro came in later that night from the cantina down the street. He sat on the sidewalk just outside the front door and watched the TV inside the front room. It was cooler outside. Alejandro would make a regular practice of that, and some nights, he would arrive so drunk that he would pass out on the sidewalk and sleep there through the night.

Rigo got up at 5:45 AM and left to take the 6 AM bus to school in Sabinas Hidalgo.

Roland went to the police station there in Bustamante and reported the incident in Mier yesterday. The police said that was out of their jurisdiction, being a different state, Tamaulipas. They suggested Roland call that police station in Mier. That's what Roland did. He went to the Hotel Ancira and paid them for the call, first getting the phone number from Mexican directory assistance and then calling the comandante in Mier. Roland told the story in three minutes, and the comandante offered Roland to come over, and they would refund him his $50. That surprised Roland, and he thanked him and said he would see if he could come over. For what the comandante said, he must not have approved of his subordinate, Tonio, acting the way he did, literally stealing US $50 off of Roland and being so wishy washy about it!

Roland would later find out that Mexican police disapprove of people like Tonio, and they run them off, that is, fire them from their police force, because it's a bad maneuver to scare people like that, especially Americans who come as tourists.

Roland thought it over in his mind about going to Mier. He didn't want to drive alone. He would have to take another one along as a passenger. Plus, after they refund the $50, they might pull Roland over again, as he would be leaving town, and they would make up some infraction and either ticket him or put him in jail. Another option would be to take a bus, but since Roland would take a friend with him, the bus fare for two would not be worth the trouble, in addition to the day's pay (around N$50) to whomever would go with him, not to mention the scheduling and connections which would make the trip to Mier and back take all day! With those time consuming and expensive options, Roland decided not to go to Mier. He let the whole thing drop.

However, he was glad he had reported Tonio, who likely got fired as a result.

Roland talked to the Cantu family about it. They asked Roland if he got the patrol vehicle number and license plate number off that police truck. Roland said it hadn't crossed his mind. Also, they assured Roland they could not have taken Roland's truck, not unless they went to the station and brought Roland an order, a police order, which they hadn't done.

That afternoon, Roland took Beto and Angelo over to Sabinas Hidalgo. They picked up Rigo from the Prepa, and they did errands. They asked Roland for some cassette tapes of Mexican music. Roland obliged and treated them to the cassettes.

They returned to Bustamante, and Roland took them to the Ojo del Agua in the canyon. They went swimming in the natural water hole, splashing and playing like children. They dived in several times, and raced each other in the water.

Then they dried off, changed clothes, and went climbing up one of the ridges. Roland took pictures of them at their request, several pictures, and an hour later they returned to the Ojo del Aqua. The four of them got up in a leaning Willow tree. Roland used his self timer on his camera and took a picture of everyone.

Yes, it was really great having friends in Mexico. Though they were a good bit younger than Roland, it didn't matter. He felt like he was one of them and fit right in. They returned to Bustamante later that afternoon.

That evening, Rigo went out with friends. Roland went to sleep early.

Alejandro arrived later and watched TV out on the sidewalk in front of the house until 3 AM. Roland opened a package containing a brand new pair of foam earplugs, put them in his ears, and got some sleep. During the night, the fan quit, the motor having burned up.

Rain arrived in the wee hours of the morning. By 7 AM, it cleared out and became sunny.

It was now Saturday. Rigo had a special test at 9 AM. The Prepa was gung ho and sometimes had tests and classes on Saturday, something that was against Roland's religion.

Roland agreed to take Rigo and his friends to Sabinas Hidalgo. They would leave Rigo at the Prepa to take his test.

As they were getting ready to leave the house, Roland happened to see the note he had left Lavinia a couple of weeks ago when he left to take Beto and Alberto to the United States with him. He picked it up because part of it looked black. The middle paragraph was entirely blacked out with a big black felt marker! That was the paragraph that told Lavinia that Roland had left his bicycle with Rigo as a gift, and had left him N$330 to help him with school. Roland showed it to Lavinia and Rigo, and he asked who had marked through that paragraph? Rigo answered that he had. Roland asked him why in the world he'd done that? He didn't answer. My goodness! Did Rigo not appreciate the help Roland had given, not to mention the bicycle?! Next, Roland asked Lavinia if she had read it. She hadn't been able to, said there wasn't any problem with it, and she told Roland not to be like a child. Roland proceeded to tell Lavinia exactly what the deleted paragraph said, so she would *know*! Further, Roland told Rigo that what he did was insulting! Really, what was going on?! Rigo took the note and wadded it up in a surprisingly casual manner, and he threw it away.

He and Roland walked out of the house and got in Roland's truck. Roland told Rigo he didn't appreciate that at all, and what did he do it for? Rigo made up an excuse that he was testing out a new marker he had bought. Hogwash! Roland suspected Rigo spent the money for something else, but Rigo insisted he had used it for school. Three weeks ago, Rigo had gotten after Roland over a matter of N$6. Now it was Roland's turn, only he had a lot more reason.

They picked up Beto and Angelo and drove over to Sabinas Hidalgo again. They delivered Rigo to the Prepa, and they went to Farmacia Benavides to have the pictures from yesterday developed. They came out great, and Roland gave them extra copies.

Later, they returned to the Prepa, picked up Rigo, and went to the flea market. Roland also took them out to eat at the Centro Comercial San José restaurant, and they ate well. Roland would take them out to eat at that restaurant several times during the coming week.

Roland bought Rigo and his family a new fan, to replace the one that had quit. They were glad to receive that.

Roland asked Rigo to apologize for blacking out the paragraph on that letter. He wouldn't do it. That didn't please Roland at all. He told Rigo he wouldn't be letting him drive his truck anymore.

Roland thought about why Rigo had done that. Perhaps Rigo was a German Gestapo agent in a past life, and his job was to censor mail to the Jews. Part of Rigo's past life characteristics were coming to the surface. After all, Rigo was a little bit severe at times, with his sisters and with his mother.

They returned to Bustamante by the mid afternoon. Roland rode his bicycle around town visiting different friends. One of them, Juan Angel, wanted to go to the USA with Roland, and they talked over plans.

Roland returned to Rigo's house for supper. Rigo came over to him and apologized, saying, "Disculpe lo que hice." Roland looked at Rigo as if he didn't mean it, and Rigo put his hand on Roland's shoulder and repeated his apology, "Discúlpeme." Okay, Roland accepted it, but he would never forget the incident, not to mention its strangeness. Roland could tell that Rigo was feeling embarrassed for what he had done, and he also realized how much it had bothered Roland. That incident bothered Roland so much that he never had the same level of trust in Rigo again.

That night, there was a baile as usual, and Rigo got dressed for it. He never missed a dance, anymore. Rigo couldn't find his new pants, and he got angry with his mother, shouting at her very aggressively. That made Roland feel bad and awkward, and he told Rigo he didn't like to see him talk to his mother that way. A couple of weeks ago, when Roland was with them, Rigo was much more friendly and kissed his mother goodbye before leaving the house, but not tonight. Rigo left the house disgusted!

*   *   *

August 29, 1998

Though Roland didn't know anything about it, a childhood friend of his, Joseph Ruffner, was serving on the Lascassas Volunteer Fire Department back in Tennessee. He and the crew were answering an emergency call. The siren was sounding, and Joseph was driving the fire truck down the Lascassas Highway at a pretty good rate of speed. He was fast approaching the narrow Stones River bridge. Here came a tractor trailer rig in the opposing lane! There was no way Joseph was going to be able to stop that fire truck in time, and he quickly realized he was going to have to pass that tractor trailer on the *bridge*!

"Ayyyy . . .!" he exclaimed as he entered the bridge. He hoped and prayed for the best.

Whoosh . . . Clash!! Their mirrors clashed and shattered. Everyone on the firetruck had cringed and shut their eyes at the moment of passing, not to mention the tractor trailer driver! Their hearts skipped a beat, and then they proceeded, except for the broken mirrors, which stayed behind on the bridge.

"Whewww . . .! That was close!" Joseph declared as he wiped the sweat from his brow with his shirt sleeve. He breathed a sigh of relief and continued racing to the housefire.

*   *   *

Things were beginning to change. Roland woke up when Rigo got in at 1:55 AM. Both of them talked a while before drifting off to sleep for the rest of the night.

Sunday was a rest day for nearly everybody. Rigo slept late. Roland went around town visiting friends. He visited Daniel Mata and his family, Victor and his family, Fernando, Elisa, and others. He also visited Juan Angel who was playing baseball in the field, one block behind Rigo's house. It was a nice and sunny day.

In the afternoon, Roland found Beto and Angelo visiting some of Beto's cousins. Rigo was there too, including Pablo. They asked Roland to repeat the ranting and raving that Alberto had done.

"¡No aguanto! ¡No aguanto! Entienda, entienda. ¡No aguanto!"

Everyone laughed and laughed, especially at the way Roland gestured it. Even Rigo laughed. He was no longer feeling agitated, like he was yesterday.

Roland enjoyed his time with his friends. This was the life. There was no smoking, no drinking, and no drugs.

Beto brought up a problem he had. He owed a man, a señor, N$230. He had borrowed it from him before going to the USA with Roland and Alberto. The señor was a loan shark, and he was driving all over town today, charging the people the money they owed him, with threats of taking to jail whoever didn't pay. Beto said he needed the money urgently. Roland found it hard to believe, and he asked Beto why he didn't tell him about that before. Beto explained that the N$230 was stolen by that Mexican cop right before they crossed the river in Nuevo Laredo. Roland said he would give Beto the money, but what he wanted was the total truth. Beto assured Roland it was true, and he hadn't seen it necessary to tell Roland earlier. Roland said he and Beto would look for the man, and Roland would pay him.

A little while later, they went over to Angelo's house. Angelo's father happened to bring up to Beto that the loan shark señor had come by, asking for Beto. Angelo's father had paid the man the N$230. With that said by Angelo's father, Beto had indeed told the truth. Roland took N$230 out of his wallet and handed it to Angelo's father. Beto saw it, thanked Roland, and the debt was cleared. The problem was gone.

Later that evening, back at Rigo's house, Roland was talking to Rigo and Lavinia about driving on out West for several weeks to hike in Arizona, California, and Oregon. Roland really wanted to go out there, with or without anyone.

Rigo said, "¿Por qué no quedas aquí? Aquí tienes amigos," saying for Roland to stay with them there in Bustamante, since he had friends there. Now, that was a nice and welcoming comment from Rigo, and Roland really appreciated that. He would never forget it.

Compensation Revisited

Rigo was feeling much better than the previous night.

Lavinia now dropped a bomb. She suddenly announced that they were moving. She had talked to some neighbors and had found a slightly larger house for rent for N$150 per month, N$50 cheaper than where they were presently staying. Rigo was content with where he was, and he didn't want to move. In fact, he offered to give his mother N$50 per month if they could just stay put. No, Lavinia was stubborn. She was bent on moving, and over the next several days, arrangements would be made.

Lavinia was working part time for a lady named Diana, who had a 90-year-old mother that needed taking care of. Lavinia also cooked and cleaned for Diana. As it turned out, Lavinia stepped on a nail the next morning, and it punctured her foot. The move was delayed several days.

In the afternoon, after Rigo got home from school, Roland went with Lavinia and Rigo over to the vacant rental house. The place smelled musty and moldy. It was an old adobe house with ancient wooden doors. A huge Palm tree grew on the streetside directly across from the house. The back room had tin roofing and was heaping full of old furniture and junk, not to mention, a few rats. Large chunks of paint and plaster were separating from the walls. Rigo told his mother the house was run down and poor, and he didn't want to move. What if a piece of wall fell on them during the night? Rigo was right, but his mother was bent on moving.

There was another friend of Roland named Julian, and he wanted to go up in the mountains and camp, like Juan Angel and Fabian had done. On September 1, Roland got his backpack loaded for the overnight trip. At 1 PM, when school was out, Julian arrived at Roland's truck with his cousin Gilberto. Born October 22, 1984, he was nearly 14 in age, and was an energetic young fellow, still not fully grown. Immediately, he met Roland's approval, and he drove them to the cono, stopping by the Cantu's store on the way to buy food supplies. Roland loaned Julian a spare backpack, and a daypack to Gilberto.

At 2 PM, Roland, Julian and Gilberto began the hike to the highland forest. They enjoyed the hike. Roland took pictures of them, including himself, using the self timer. They were impressed at the trail Roland had cleared last year, and they enjoyed the rope climb through the steepest part of the ravine.

At 6 PM, they arrived at the grassy saddle. Roland chose two sites, and he pitched his green tent for Julian and Gilberto to use. Then he pitched his smaller tent around 30 meters away, climbed in, and went to sleep. He slept 12 hours, and he needed it. That Zacatón family he was staying with were a bunch of night owls! Alejandro watching TV till 3 AM, and Rigo never coming in before 11 PM, and *much later* on dance nights.

Apart from hearing the chatter of Julian and Gilberto's conversations from the other tent, it was a nice and peaceful night.

The next morning was cloudy, and fog was prevalent. The temperature was around 10° C. Gilberto came over to Roland's tent at 7 AM. He was cold. Roland loaned him an extra shirt. They got up, ate some breakfast, and they packed to leave.

At 8 AM, they began the hike back down the mountain, arriving at the cono at 11 AM. Julian and Gilberto both thanked Roland for taking them up there. They had really enjoyed it.

Roland returned Julian and Gilberto to their homes. He met Gilberto's mother, Gloria, and she informed Roland that her son had not gotten her permission. Roland apologized for that, and he explained that he thought Julian had taken care of that before bringing Gilberto along with him. She had been very worried as to her son's whereabouts last night, and she certainly was relieved that he was home safe. Gilberto lived with his mother and older brother in a one room adobe house. It was amazing how they fit in and lived in that one room.

Roland returned to Rigo's house. No one was at home, but since Roland was a guest, and since the door was never locked, he let himself in and took a nap for 1½ hours. One would have thought 12 hours of sleep last night would have been enough, but it wasn't. Roland wasn't feeling 100% well. He felt like he had a mild case of the flu, and this extra sleep was enough to run it off.

At 3:30 PM, Rigo, Norma and Irma arrived. Roland had been up for some time. He had washed some clothes in his washing machine and had written in his diary.

They told Roland that the power had gone out last night for 3 hours, and without the fans running, the mosquitoes invaded and pestered them to frustration. Fans were very necessary in the summer to keep them away, as Roland learned.

Thank goodness Roland hadn't been there last night. He certainly picked the right night to go into the mountains with Julian and Gilberto.

Rigo wanted to go to Sabinas Hidalgo again, and Roland took him, Beto, and Angelo. Rigo wanted a cassette tape, and Roland bought him another one. He also gave N$15 to Beto so he could complete the purchase of one. Angelo asked for a cassette, and Roland obliged him, as well.

They went to the Tokyo plant on the north side of Sabinas Hidalgo. Beto and Angelo applied for jobs. Rigo wasn't interested, even though he wanted and needed part time work. Beto and Angelo weren't in school any longer.

They ate out again at the Centro Comercial San José restaurant. Roland was going through his money. He had spent more than $1,000 since last month, but at the same time, he was enjoying his friends. They saw Roland as a great friend, and as far as Roland was concerned, he was treating himself to his compensation. He had worked hard for his money, and he deserved to enjoy it. And he still had enough left to drive out West and back.

1998 had been a good year for income. The economy was good. Plenty of clients had called Roland to work. Gasoline prices had really dropped since 1996, and it sold for only 78¢ per gallon. Here in Mexico, it was only a little bit more. Money went a long way. Food was decently cheap, and the exchange rate was good, at nearly 10 pesos per dollar.

They returned to Bustamante by nightfall.

Lavinia announced that tomorrow they would be moving, and she asked Roland if he would help them. Roland said he needed to get on out West, but if they needed the help, then he would help them. He didn't want to use his own truck, and he suggested to Lavinia that she go ask the Quevalos. Lavinia didn't want to bother them. So Roland explained that as far as he was concerned, Pancho owed him some favors, after all that trailer cargo he had brought them, not to mention bringing them the blue Ford truck in 1991. Roland offered to accompany Lavinia to ask the Quevalos. Okay, she would go and ask them, but she doubted they would say yes. Granted, Pancho had loaned the blue truck and flatbed trailer in December when they had moved, but he had charged Roland N$50.

That evening, Roland also went to the Orolizos, and he asked Nacho if he could help the Zacatóns move to their new residence. He said he would be able to from 3 PM till dark. As

Compensation Revisited

Nacho had a Ford pickup truck, it would be useful. Roland would have used his own truck, but then it had a camper top, and if there was some other truck available, he wouldn't have to detach his camper.

Rigo went to school, left at 6 AM. Roland drove Lavinia over to Diana's house to her job, then returned to the house and slept till noon. He was feeling somewhat tired and ill, and with that extra sleep, he ran off the flu like illness.

Rigo arrived home at 2 PM. They went over to Angelo's house. He helped with the move. They went to Lavinia at Diana's house. Lavinia had asked the Quevalos, and they had said no. Roland was not pleased to hear that. He drove Rigo and Angelo over to the Orolizo's house. Chela was there, and she came to Roland with the keys to the truck, which surprised Roland. He asked her where Nacho was, and she said something had come up and he couldn't help, but he had said Roland could use the truck, but only Roland. What a kind gesture of trust, and Roland very much appreciated it, but he had to decline for one simple reason. The truck was automatic, and never in his life had he driven an automatic truck, and he was a teenager the last time he had driven an automatic car of any sort. It had been at least 15 years, and he didn't want to take any chances with something he was unaccustomed to driving. Roland thanked Chela anyway, and he, Rigo and Angelo left.

At Angelo's house, Roland took his camper top off his truck and set it in the backyard there. Next, he drove them over to Rigo's house where he unloaded everything. They made several trips between the two houses, which were four blocks apart. Rigo was irritable because he was against the move taking place. Roland had suggested to Lavinia along with Rigo that they stay put, but stubborn Lavinia was bent on moving. That was it!

Rigo was so irritated with his mother that he just about cried. He was embarrassed to be moving into this old looking run-down house. What would his amigas say? And a girlfriend later on, what would she say? Roland felt like he was between an acorn and its hull because he was obliging Lavinia by helping her and her family more, but at the same time, Rigo was against it, and it was possible he might hold it against him. Roland thought about driving on out West, but he didn't want to abandon Lavinia. After all, she and her family had received Roland to stay in their home.

That evening, Roland went over to talk to Nacho, and he thanked him for his offer of loaning his truck. Nacho asked how the Zacatón family was doing, and Roland told him about them. Roland mentioned that Rigo was without work at the moment and would be needing work soon, especially since Roland was leaving. Nacho said there was plenty of work gathering Pecans, and he knew who was hiring for part time work. Roland was glad to know about that. After all, Roland had served as Rigo's "employer" for the past several weeks, part time, and he felt obligated to set Rigo up with a different job before leaving town. He would tell Rigo the good news this evening.

Roland returned to Rigo's house. As only some of the furniture had been moved, they still slept in the same house this one last night. Lavinia fed supper to everyone and Roland told Rigo the good news.

"¿Dijiste a Nacho?!" Rigo suddenly shouted, angrily asking Roland if he had told Nacho. Roland was quite taken aback and surprised, to say the least. He answered yes.

"¿Te *dije* que estoy buscando trabajo?!" Rigo shouted, angrily asking Roland if he told him he was looking for work.

Rigo jumped all down Roland's throat, scolding him for handling other people's business and getting into things he shouldn't be getting into.

Roland was shocked at Rigo's behavior and his outlandish accusation. He responded and firmly told Rigo he had just done him a favor, finding work for him! Plus, he had felt obligated since he was soon leaving town.

Lavinia asked them to calm down, but Rigo continued ranting and raving, and he said he didn't even want to understand Roland's reasons for having found him work. He accused Roland of being a *metiche* and a *vieja*, which basically means a person who meddles in other people's business, something a woman would do, according to Rigo's viewpoint.

As far as Roland was concerned, why would a woman be more apt to meddle in other people's business than a man? But then Mexicans, with their macho image, believed that way.

Rigo stayed disgusted for quite some time. How ungrateful of him!

They went to sleep for the night.

When Rigo got up at 5:30 AM for school, Roland told him he felt unappreciated, and he told Rigo not to be so combative in general. Rigo nodded a gesture of some sense of understanding, and he walked out the door to go to school. Rigo would stew over it all day.

Norma and Irma got up late and missed school. They tried to enter but the school didn't admit people who were late. They always closed the gates at 8 AM sharp. Roland hadn't known they were that strict about being on time.

As it turned out, Norma and Roland worked all day together moving the items. Julian came for a while and helped them with some of the bigger items like the refrigerator and beds. Basilio, Chilo Cantu's son, came as well and helped.

Alejandro, for the first time in two years, had begun to work again. Right across from the house they were moving into, there were several workers building a stone patio and fixing up a big stone house and arched stone underpass. Alejandro was working with them. Each time Roland and Norma arrived with a truckload, he broke away from work, came across the street, and helped them unload and move the furniture into its place.

Roland enjoyed the day with Norma. It was the only compensation Roland was receiving for this grand favor he was doing, helping the Zacatón family move. Roland and Norma got along great. At lunch, they played some cassette tapes in the stereo, including *Mercurio*'s "Tiempo de Vivir" which Norma also liked very much. Norma was easy going and complacent, and Roland could sense that she was indeed the destined one to be his wife in the future. Hopefully, Rigo would get over his anger at Roland, because Roland had hopes of knowing this family the rest of his life.

Yes, there had been problems, but they had been ironed out, and how great it was that Roland and Raul had already seen each other, made up and become friends again.

Roland thought Norma was a great person. Of course, she was still a child at only 12 years in age, but in two years she would be grown. Of course, Roland also knew to keep quiet about everything until she would be age 18, which would be the year 2004, July 11th.

After the 15th trip, Roland and Norma got everything moved. Roland still had more to do. He had to go over to Angelo's house where he thoroughly washed and swept out the back of his truck, after which he put the camper top back on. Then he drove back over to the house, showered and got cleaned up. He loaded his things back into the truck and drove over to the Zacatón's new residence, an old and run-down adobe house.

Rigo had an extra class this Friday, and he arrived at 7:20 PM. He didn't even greet

Roland, and he walked into the house in an angry mood.

Roland told Rigo he wasn't like he was before. Rigo was now an angry hothead.

Lavinia fed them all supper, and Rigo and Roland had a discussion at the supper table. Rigo was having recurring anger at Roland for having talked to Nacho about work for him. In addition to that, he got after Roland for his having jumped his and his mother's barrier to successfully find Raul in Salado. Further, he told Roland he was acting like a maricón or gay for the sneaky manner he went about in finding Raul.

Of course, Roland defended himself, telling Rigo he was being very ungrateful, and as far as finding Raul the way he did, Rigo and Lavinia had given Roland no other choice, except of course never look for Raul and therefore let the falling out stay fallen, for years! On the contrary, Roland had located Raul incredibly fast, considering the circumstances, and their friendship was happily repaired. Amen!

Roland reminded Rigo that he had given him that mountain bike and that he had told him not to brush him off in the future.

"¡Si quieres, llévatela!" Rigo blurted out, telling Roland he could take it with him, if he wanted.

Roland said he wasn't an Indian giver, and he demanded that Rigo apologize to him. He explained that he came to Bustamante for friendships, and he expected those friendships to last for a lifetime!

Rigo laughed in a sneering manner at Roland's philosophy. He had a proud look on his face, which Roland had never seen before. That hurt Roland's feelings.

Next, Lavinia did what she should have done long ago. She told Rigo that friendships were indeed meant to last a lifetime. Roland thanked her, and he asked her if it was good or bad that he had found Raul and visited with him. "Está bien." Good answer, Lavinia. She was glad Roland had been resourceful enough to find her son, Raul. The reason Rigo didn't like it was that he didn't trust Roland, in that he might turn Raul in to U.S. Immigration.

Roland stepped out of the house and went to his truck for something. Rigo, at his mother's urging, came outside, went to Roland, and he apologized to him. He also told Roland not to go around finding work for him anymore. Roland accepted the apology, and they shook hands. Rigo's anger was gone, and he was calm like he used to be. Roland asked him if he wanted to go on being friends, and he said yes.

They re-entered the house.

*   *   *

Nuevo Wimbisenho

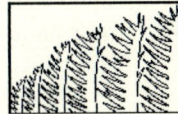

"Frequency phasing techniques," Arfifra commended Draaktra. "That is ingenious!"

"You always have been good at figuring out a way in," his older brother Sojornbloc told him.

"I became aware that Millana is fuming mad, and I tapped her essense, you might say," Draaktra boasted.

They all cackled with laughter!

"You almost latched him that time," Sasjurech reckoned. "Rigo really was on a rejection rampage, wasn't he?"

"That blasted energy system of Martonción's kicked us out again!" Arfifra exclaimed.

"But take note," Druxtrli pointed out, "not as easily. I've been working on Millana's conscience."

They snickered with laughter.

"Draaktra's frequency phasing is whittling that positive energy down," Sojornbloc explained to the others.

"You are right about that," Arfifra admitted. "Keep working at it. Practice makes perfect!"

"Wait till tomorrow . . ." Druxtrli began, and she had an enthusiastic look on her face.

*   *   *

Roland went to visit other friends for a while. Juan Angel was not home. His mother said he had just taken a job at a factory in Monterrey and wouldn't return home for three weeks. Roland wouldn't see Juan Angel until January, as a result.

Rigo was friendly now. They watched a movie later that night on TV. All was calm and tranquil. Whatever the black cloud had been, Roland was glad it was gone.

They all slept peacefully for the night.

The next morning was Saturday, September 5th. Rigo had another Saturday class! What was wrong with that Prepa? Wasn't Monday through Friday enough? Rigo asked Roland to take him. There was no bus service on Saturdays. So, Roland obliged.

Lavinia asked Roland to buy some plumbing supplies so he could help connect the sink and repair the toilet this afternoon. She gave Roland a N$100 note and asked him to bring back the receipt and the change. He said he would do so, stay overnight, and leave in the morning. Lavinia said that was fine.

Roland took Rigo, Angelo, and Beto to Sabinas Hidalgo one last time. They waited outside the school while Rigo attended his class. Then they went around town some and also to the Centro Comercial San José restaurant where Roland treated them to lunch.

Roland saw Fernando and talked with him for a while.

While they were going around town today, he heard Angelo call Rigo by his nickname: *Molonco*. Interesting name that was, indeed!

They returned to Bustamante by 2 PM, and Roland gave Lavinia the receipt, along with N$19 in change. He took the parts to the bathroom, along with some tools, to begin installing the parts when . . .

CHAPTER 15

WRENCHES ARRIVE

September 1998

Surprise! The sound of a V-8 automatic truck pulled up in front of the house and stopped.

"Llegó Eduardo!" Norma happily announced, saying that Eduardo had arrived.

Everybody rushed outside in front of the house to greet them. Roland dropped the plumbing supplies, picked up his own tools, and he walked to the front door. Eduardo greeted him and shook hands with him. He had brought his wife and son, and his stepdaughter. The two little ones rushed inside and immediately began to play dollhouse with Irma.

They had also brought some gifts. In the back of the truck were an extra bed, a fan, and a dinky electric typewriter.

Thoughts went through Roland's mind. Now he would have a chance to talk to Millana and ask her why she had told Raul that Roland wasn't welcome in her home. At least here, she wouldn't be able to kick Roland out. After all, Lavinia had given Roland consent to stay until morning. Plus, he was helping them with plumbing repairs to connect the sink and toilet.

Millana was still inside the truck, and Lavinia and Norma had gotten into the cab to greet her and visit with her. Roland walked up to the cab to say hi to Millana. She made some *scoff* of a remark to Roland that he didn't understand. With that said, Roland walked away from the truck.

Rigo walked up to the cab to greet Millana. They kissed each other (Whoo-wee!) and talked for a minute. Eduardo got into the cab and they drove away.

Angelo and Beto had not yet left, and Roland started talking with them.

Rigo walked over to Roland and told him he wouldn't be able to stay tonight, because Millana didn't want it.

Roland looked at Rigo and quickly reminded him that his mother had given him consent to stay overnight, and Millana didn't mandate here.

Rigo told Roland more firmly that his brother Eduardo and Millana and the others had gone for a half-hour excursion in the canyon. He told Roland to take his things out of the house and load his truck. Millana had said she refused to step down from the truck because Roland was there, and she sent a threat via Rigo that when she and Eduardo return in their truck half an hour from now, Roland better be cleared out and gone, or there were going to be serious problems! (That sounded like a threat!)

Roland didn't take kindly to that at all. He reminded Rigo that his *parents* say what goes, and NOT Millana! Plus, Roland was here first.

"Mira, Millana es familia, y tú no eres nada," said Rigo, telling Roland that Millana was family and that Roland was nobody. That was a hurtful comment!

"¡No me digas que yo no soy nada!" said Roland, firmly telling Rigo not to tell him he was nobody! Roland told Rigo he was inhospitable, and he said he was going to tell his father.

Alejandro was right across the street working on that stone patio. Roland walked over to him and asked if he could stay overnight.

"Pues sí. Ya sabes," Alejandro replied, giving clear consent.

Roland returned to Rigo and politely told him his father Alejandro gave him permission. The matter was settled. Roland picked up his tools to re-enter the house and start the plumbing work.

Well, Rigo took matters into his own hands, which proved to Roland that he didn't want him in the house and was using Millana's music-to-his-ears mandate as a convenient excuse to get rid of him. Rigo marched straight over to his father, told him what Millana had said, and with that, Alejandro came over, entered the house, and talked to Roland.

"Hay un problema . . ." Alejandro began, saying there was a problem. He admitted he hadn't realized that Millana hadn't wanted Roland in the house, and he kindly told Roland he would have to leave.

Roland told Alejandro that his daughter-in-law doesn't mandate, but instead he and Lavinia do.

Alejandro asked Roland what more could he do, and Roland suggested he tell Millana that he was staying overnight as well, and that he would be away in the morning. Plus, he was doing the plumbing that Lavinia had requested.

Alejandro pointed out to Roland that Millana didn't want him in the house, and that he and Lavinia had to serve family and in-laws before serving friends, like Roland. He told Roland not to worry about the plumbing. That was fine with Roland, and he wouldn't have done the plumbing now, even if they had asked him to!

Roland went to Rigo and told him he was leaving now. He asked Rigo to put himself in his place and asked him how he would like it. He took his things out of the house and loaded them into his truck.

Once Roland had his truck loaded, Rigo wished him well, shook hands with him, and stated that they go on being friends. Well, Roland would hope so. Beto and Angelo explained that Rigo was still his friend, but he was somewhat over a barrel by Millana's mandate.

Well, maybe he was, and so were Alejandro and Lavinia, but why couldn't they simply defend Roland and declare that he would be staying overnight, also? After all, he had just helped them painstakingly move, having donated his time and services, not to mention the use of his truck to move all of the items! Outrageous it was indeed!

Beto and Angelo got into Roland's truck, and he drove them away. Angelo said Roland could stay over at his house tonight. That was kind of him. Roland arrived there. He would be away in the morning. He told Angelo's parents what had just happened.

"¡Que afrentoso!" they exclaimed, commenting how outrageous it was!

Roland went over to the Orolizo's house and he told them, as well. They said Rigo and his parents should have defended Roland. They were quite ungrateful to run Roland off because another guest, even though a daughter-in-law, mandated it.

An hour later, Roland walked over to the Zacatóns. Eduardo's truck was there. He called for Lavinia, who came to the sidewalk and talked to Roland. She assured Roland that they always appreciated him for all he did, helping them move, and more. She also assured Roland he was welcome to stay with them the next time he would come to town, but at the same time, he had to understand the situation that Millana didn't want him in the house, and that she had refused to step down from the truck because Roland and his truck were there.

Roland said he was trying to understand her reasons, but the fact was, Millana, also a guest, didn't have any right to order her hosts, Alejandro and Lavinia, to throw out other already staying guests! That's what was so outrageous!

Lavinia explained to Roland, asking how else they were supposed to do it? Roland pointed out that they could have defended him and told Millana that he was welcome to stay, too. Lavinia said they could have done that, but Millana didn't understand reasons, and she would never have stepped down from her husband's truck. Plus, they would have left, to go stay with other relatives in Monterrey. Or it's possible that Millana might have thrown a tantrum right there in front of everyone. That would have been interesting, watching a 22-year-old woman act like a little 4-year-old child.

Roland somewhat understood Lavinia's reasons and the serious consequences that would have resulted if they had defended Roland. Still, they should have done it, if nothing else to tell Millana that Roland was a decent person. He still would have taken his things and left, because he didn't want to see Millana either. No matter what, Roland really resented it. While he would forgive the Zacatón family, Millana was a different story. He would definitely be sending her a letter expressing his disapproval of what she had done!

Roland thanked Lavinia for having him, and he said he would return in December.

Eduardo came outside to talk to Roland. He explained that his wife was weird. He said he could have gotten after her and forced her to tolerate him, but then she would have gotten her own back with Eduardo later, and they would have had problems. Also, he said he appreciated Roland for having visited Raul. Roland wouldn't be able to stay overnight in his house in Salado, since Millana had taken such a dislike to him, but Roland was welcome to come by during the day and visit with Raul whenever he wanted to . . . when Millana was away at work.

Roland thanked Eduardo for that much. Rigo was out in the street, playing with his little nephew.

Roland walked back to Angelo's family. He visited some other friends, like Victor.

*   *   *

Nuevo Wimbisenho

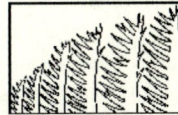

"Mmm . . . Mmm!! Those energy disks are *good*!" Draaktra remarked with total satisfaction.

"Delectable!" Arfifra commended, and she cackled with laughter.

"Esctasy is an understatement," Torxtalo chimed in.

"Ingenious rejection tactic," Druxtrli praised Draaktra.

"You played Rigo very well," Sasjurech also praised Draaktra.

"A pro," Sojornbloc added.

"After all," Draaktra pointed out, "Roland's continued goodness in helping install that plumbing set up an excellent chance for rejection."

"Excellent chance for *prestigious* rejection, my dear," Arfifra corrected.

"What about me, Draaktra?" Druxtrli protested. "I pulled Millana's strings for you."

"Rigo took to Millana, hook, line, and sinker," Sasjurech remarked.

"Did you see them *kiss*?" Draaktra brought up. "Whew doggie!"

They roared with laughter!

"Rich rejection if I ever saw any," Sasjurech told her Druxtrli.

"And so subtle and clever," Arfifra added. She cackled with some more laughter.

"Here Druxtrli," Draaktra offered. "Have one of my energy disks, for your contributing efforts."

"That's more *like* it," said Druxtrli. "Mmm . . . beautifully done!" She reveled in delight, feeding off the rich rejection energy Roland had suffered.

"I want some of this, too," Torxtalo stubbornly insisted.

"Here you are, my dear," Arfifra offered. "Have part of mine." They shared a disk.

"I tell you," said Sasjurech, "with you experts, we'll never go wrong!"

"Hail to Arfifra, our queen of black magic!" they all chanted.

"How about some credit for our friend, Druxtrli?" Arfifra told everyone.

They chanted some praise for her, too. Then Druxtrli went on and said, "Now for our next line of action. Roland's heading out West. He's bound to write my protectee a letter. Draaktra, I need you to conjure up some false memory programs to install on . . ."

*   *   *

The next morning, Roland drove out of Bustamante, reaching the Colombia Bridge at noon. He turned in his permit and crossed the bridge. U.S. Customs officials gave Roland's truck and belongings an inspection. At least they were friendly with their routine inspection. Roland opened the hood for them and they checked for drugs both there and under the truck with mirrors.

Roland briefly bought more groceries in Laredo. Then he drove northwest, headed toward Van Horn, Texas. As Roland was going northwest on Highway 83, 20 miles after clearing the mile 14 checkpoint north of Laredo, a cop in a Chevrolet Camaro passed Roland, then slowed down and turned on his flashers. Roland pulled over, and the cop came up to Roland asking if he owned his truck and that he found the plates registered to a station wagon. Roland told the man that the state of Tennessee was supposed to have those plates registered to the truck, and he showed him his registration papers showing the valid license plate number. With that, the cop said okay and for Roland to go ahead.

Several weeks later when Roland arrived home to Tennessee, he inquired at the County Court Clerk's office. There was an error. The state of Tennessee had it listed wrong in the computer. They made the correction, apologizing for any inconveniences.

As for the cop pulling Roland over, thank goodness he hadn't been carrying any Mexicans at the time. They would have been caught, and Roland would have suffered severe penalties. That cop was a U.S. Immigration official in disguise, and he randomly pulled people over, checking for illegal aliens.

Roland made it to west Texas by dark, and he found a backroad where he pulled off the highway and slept in his truck overnight.

The next day, while driving through El Paso, he stopped at an Office Max store, and he wrote Millana a letter right then and there. He also wrote Eduardo a letter and included a copy of the letter to Millana, in case she were to tear up her original. Plus, he wrote Raul a letter, telling him how glad he was to have seen him again and to have fixed their friendship. He walked into Office Max and copied all the letters, put them in envelopes, and mailed them.

Wrenches Arrive

Millana sure did deserve Roland's letter to her. It stated as follows:

Millana,   Sept. 7, 1998

I was still staying with my friends the Zacatón family because Lavinia and Alejandro had requested I stay to help them move, which I did with my truck. You and Eduardo arrived unannounced suddenly on Saturday afternoon. You insulted me by not greeting me and further really irked me by ordering Eduardo's family to have me leave the premises under your vice that you would not step down from the truck until I was gone!!

Look, I was there first!! I had just immensely helped them move at their request. You were way out of line and very wrong to have Eduardo's family remove me from their house for your convenience.

For your own house in Salado, you have the right to prevent me from spending the night there, but for other houses, the hosts mandate. You don't. You just cannot expect your hosts to remove their already staying guests for your convenience. When you stay in other people's homes, you have to tolerate the ones already staying there.

I highly resent what you did Millana, and I do not like it one bit. You ought to be ashamed of yourself.

When and where had I offended you? I don't recall any incidents. What is your problem with me? I'm not an ogre, and I'm not a 2nd class citizen.

Roland

It was bad enough for Millana to have done what she did, but what was worse was that she had gotten her way! There was one detail about Rigo that bothered Roland considerably. After Roland had talked to Alejandro across the street and gotten his consent to stay overnight, Rigo angrily went to his father so that Roland would indeed be made to leave! Not once did it cross Rigo's mind to defend his friend Roland so that he could stay and finish that plumbing work! As far as Roland was concerned Rigo wanted him gone. A real friend would have told Millana that Roland was his friend and that he wasn't going to oblige her and run him off. Until Roland arrived home to Tennessee he had doubts, and he was unable to shake them. He recalled every positive thing that occurred, to think positive that is, in efforts to justify that Rigo still welcomed Roland in the future. At one point, Rigo had asked Roland to stay in Bustamante instead of drive out West. That was kind of him. Then why had he promptly and faithfully obliged Millana without thinking twice? In truth, Roland felt punished for having been such a good friend to that family. He had been very generous with his money, his giving, and he had helped them immensely with their move!

Roland drove on to Flagstaff. On the way, he called his cousins the Hodges in Los Angeles. They were glad to know Roland was coming to visit. Mrs. Hodges informed Roland that her mother-in-law, Lilly, who was Roland's great aunt, had suffered a sudden stroke and was expected to die in the next day or two. She was 95 and was the oldest sister of Roland's grandmother. She was the record holder for longevity. Roland was sorry to find out that she was dying.

Though Roland didn't know it, someone else he knew was dying exactly at that moment. A month later, he would find out.

That night, Roland reached a national forest picnic ground north of Flagstaff, Arizona, and he slept in his truck.

The next morning, he drove to Grand Canyon National Park. At 6:30 AM, a huge elk stepped across the road in front of his truck. He got out of the way just in time. Roland barely missed him! It would have been disaster for his truck, had he run into him.

Grand Canyon no longer charged $2. They charged $20! Roland paid the hefty entrance fee and drove to the north rim. All day long, he hiked the Bright Angel Trail, arriving at the Colorado River in 2 hours and 40 minutes. He ate lunch and made the climb back out, reaching the rim 3 hours and 20 minutes later.

Whatever that flu like illness Roland had suffered from last week was now returning. He felt nauseated, now back up on the rim. Roland lay down in his truck for a while, then drove out of the park. He knew a good place to sleep, a backroad off of I-40, and he drove there.

Roland drove to Los Angeles the next day and spent two days with his cousins. It was good to see them. Aunt Lilly had indeed died, and they were preparing to fly to Georgia for her funeral. She had died at the moment Roland was nearly out of the canyon, coinciding with the moment he began to feel nauseated.

Also, while in Los Angeles, Roland telephoned Lavinia over at Diana's house in Bustamante. Irma answered, happily saying, "Rolando."

Lavinia came on the line. "¿Qué quieres?" she said, greeting Roland by saying the equivalent of, What do you want?

Roland was noticing more and more that every time after Eduardo came to visit, Lavinia and her family were somewhat cold shouldered for several days.

Roland ignored Lavinia's less than friendly greeting and said, "¿Cómo estás?" He told her he was calling from Los Angeles, and he told Lavinia that he had written Millana a letter. Lavinia said Millana would simply tear it up, and Roland said not *that* one. He sent a Xerox copy separately to Millana's husband Eduardo. Lavinia sounded a gesture of surprise, knowing how resourceful Roland really was. She told him he shouldn't have written her a letter, and Roland responded by saying how could he not?

They talked a few minutes, and Lavinia assured Roland he could stay with them the next time he comes to Bustamante. Roland kindly told Lavinia that he forgives them for running him off. She asked Roland what else they could have done, and Roland suggested that they could have defended him. Lavinia then said that Millana would have thrown a tantrum, a hysterical tantrum! Roland left it at that and thanked Lavinia for having received him into their home for the time they had. They said goodbye, wished each other well, and hung up.

After his visit with his cousins, Roland drove north to Sequoia and Kings Canyon National Parks. He wanted to do some hiking along the High Sierra Trail, plus see the big trees, the Giant Sequoias. Roland knew of a backroad that accessed the high forest and got him by the entrance station. Roland didn't believe in paying park fees. After all, he paid income taxes, and government funds should pay all park costs. Parks were supposed to be natural pristine wilderness. They couldn't require that much money to run them.

There was a beautiful grove of Sequoias along the backroad. Roland pulled off on one of its side roads and slept in his truck overnight. It was totally peaceful and quiet. Roland spent the entire next day there, enjoying the peace and serene beauty of the forest.

He took a long nap in the middle of the day, still feeling the flu like symptoms.

Also, he wrote a long letter documenting his August/September stay with the Zacatóns, his having Alberto in his home, and his fiasco in being dismissed from the Zacatón's house by Millana! It was nine pages long. Roland later Xeroxed a copy of the letter and mailed it to his friend Ivanhoe in Scotland. In that letter, Roland mentioned that he had still not figured out nor found a travelling companion. He also wrote, "Was it too much to ask for me to have found a travelling companion?" He really wished he had found someone.

Roland had another peaceful night's sleep in the Sequoia forest.

The next day was September 12. Roland drove over to the Lodgepole Visitor Center, got a permit, and drove to the Giant Forest, where he parked his truck. He put all his food in several layers of plastic garbage bags and covered all his things in the back of his truck to make his vehicle look as plain as possible, for the bears.

For the whole afternoon, Roland hiked 9 miles. Scenery along the High Sierra Trail was spectacular, and the weather was warm and sunny. He reached a campsite at Nine Mile Creek at dark, and he set up his tent and placed his backpack and food in the metal bearproof box, supplied by the park service. He was the only one to camp here this night.

Roland had a strange dream around 2 AM. He dreamed that Millana came to his tent, declared that it was hers, and she expected him to leave! Roland told her no way! So, she proceeded to struggle with Roland in efforts to remove him. He felt himself sliding out of the tent, a possible out of body experience, then he was back in his tent again and woke up. She was gone! Roland in real life unzipped his tent, stepped outside, and he shouted out loud, "And you better know this is my tent, Millana! And if you have me thrown out again, I'll write you another letter!" He got back inside his tent and went back to sleep.

Roland realized that with that dream, Millana had received his scolding letter. She must have really gotten angry, for her essence to have come all the way to California to annoy him in his tent! For her spirit guide Druxtrli, that was a piece of cake. It was she who had easily located Roland and had brought Millana's spirit to him.

Roland was very satisfied that he had written Millana that letter. No one else had ever told Millana off before, but Roland did! She had succeeded in having Roland run off, like a second class citizen. She had gotten what she wanted, and she sure had that letter awaiting her when she arrived back to her home in Salado. She had it coming, a scolding, and it served her right!

For the manner in which she had attempted to kick Roland out of his own tent, he could tell that she had no respect for other people's basic rights. She acted like a queen of first class status, and the rest were of lower rank!

When morning came, Roland packed *his* tent and *his* backpack and hiked the 9 miles back to Giant Forest. When he reached his truck, he ate lunch, put his backpack inside, and took a several mile day hike over to Moro Rock. The size of some of the Giant Sequoias was impressive. How great it was to be here in California, and in the forest.

Roland drove back to the place where he had camped in his truck, enjoying another peaceful night's sleep.

The next day, he drove down out of the Sierra Nevada Mountains and across the San Joaquin Valley to Oakland, where his friends, the Strauss family lived. He had visited them several times over the years, and they were always hospitable and glad to receive him. It was just getting dark when he arrived.

Roland related his adventures to the Strausses. Roland spoke as positively as he could, and he told about how he felt compensated for the problems which had occurred back in January and February due to Isalia and Luke. He told them about Beto and Alberto, and when he mentioned that he had given $70 to Beto to return to Mexico, Mrs. Strauss said, "You certainly are generous, Roland."

What a nice comment! It was true. Roland was quite generous, probably too generous at times, sometimes to the point of causing him to run out of money. For those who give till it hurts, and Roland was certainly one who did, it's supposed to come back ten fold, or at least several fold. At least he hoped so. What Roland really liked was the thanks and appreciation he received from some of the people he had given to.

Roland spent two nights at the Strauss' house. He called Raul on the phone and they had a nice half hour chat. Roland asked Raul if he and his brother had received their letters. He said yes. They talked about the incident that Millana caused, and Raul assured Roland that it wasn't a matter of their running him off, per say, but more of a situation that Millana had them over a barrel and had coerced them into dismissing Roland.

He and Raul talked about Bustamante and how things had gone, and they had some laughs. They wished each other well, and as they were saying goodbye, something occurred to Raul that really made Roland's day.

"Gracias por haber ayudado a mi familia en Bustamante y por haberles movido," Raul said, thanking Roland for having helped his family in Bustamante and for having moved them to their new residence.

How kind of Raul to thank Roland for his help. He was the only one who gave proper thanks. To Roland, that kind compliment from Raul was worth more than the money he could have been paid to move them.

Roland went to the Oakland zoo and had a look at the animals. That evening, the Strauss' son Daniel came over and visited. Roland played him his cassette tape of *Mercurio*'s "Tiempo de Vivir."

Yes, Roland had a good visit with the Strausses. The next day, he drove over to San Francisco and walked around Golden Gate Park, then drove north, visiting Sausalito, and Muir Woods National Monument, where some Coastal Redwoods grow.

He drove north to Crescent City along US Highway 101 and the "Avenue of the Giants" which was part of the original US Highway 101.

There was a state park east of Crescent City that Roland always liked to visit, and he knew of a huge, hollowed out Redwood tree, where several times he had slept inside it. To sleep on the ground literally inside a tree. What an experience! The park prohibited camping, but Roland always sneaked in and out of there, hiding his gear over behind some trees and numerous fern plants and driving his vehicle to a parking area several miles away. Never did he get caught, and since the tree was off the trail, the chances were minimal. He slept successfully in the tree for the 7th time.

The next morning, Roland enjoyed the immense peacefulness of the old growth Redwood forest. The trees stood so tall and graceful, like queens of the forest.

From there, Roland began to make his way home, crossing the states of Oregon, Nevada, Utah, Colorado, and Oklahoma.

He stopped by the house of his friend, Elton, in Pleasant Grove, Utah. It was raining, and his wife and 8-year-old son were home. As soon as she answered the door, she flatly stated to Roland that he couldn't stay. Roland looked at her in disbelief and explained that he was passing through, needed only one night, and that it had been three entire years since he had been here. She told Roland he always asked for one night but stayed more, and the way he had stayed three nights while attending that computer software-training course (though he slept in his car) was totally unacceptable! She stated that it was *her* house and that there was no way he was staying, and she mentioned to Roland that perhaps he thought she was rude. Roland said he had to admit she was being rude, and he asked her if it was not also Elton's house? She admitted that it was. Roland was disgusted with the inhospitality, and he simply left. He would call Elton upon arriving home and have a talk with him. Golly! What was going on? Wasn't the incident Millana caused enough rejection already? Roland really had wanted to see his friend Elton. Unfortunately, he was still at work, though it was 7 PM. Had he been home, they might have made better arrangements. Plus, they were Mormons, and all Mormons have a tendency to feel guilty unless they are constantly overworked by their employer companies. In many respects, Mormons are great people, but couldn't they have taken in Roland for one night? After all, he was 2,000 miles from home.

Roland drove out of the rain, crossed the mountains at Price, Utah, and pulled off the highway in the Juniperus desert terrain to sleep in his truck for the night. The next day, he drove on to Arches National Park and over the next three days, he made his way home.

Roland visited Danny, one of his better friends from school and scouts, and he was glad to have him stay overnight. He lived in Colorado Springs. He was also one of Isalia's former students, and his picture hung right by Roland's on the wall of Isalia's house. Danny sure was sorry about the way Isalia had turned so ugly against Roland, and the danger she had put him in! Danny and his wife were still Isalia's friends, but at least Danny and his wife had been kind enough to tell Isalia by phone that they were frustrated about the way she had treated Roland, and that she would have to work it out with Roland and his parents.

Roland had a good visit, and he was away in the morning. Two days later, he arrived home. Overnight, he stayed at some more friends in Oklahoma. They too were glad to see Roland, and they took him in for the night.

That flu like illness never really went away. It lasted for two more weeks. For the last two days coming home, Roland's ankles and feet swelled some. That had never happened before. In that year, there was a flu virus going around that caused leg swelling afterwards. Roland called a doctor who didn't have any real suggestions except to let it run its course. Roland took a 20 mile bike ride . . . made no difference. He went to a health food store, and they suggested and sold him *Viraplex*, and it cured him within two days after he began taking the tablets.

When Roland arrived home, he had some mail awaiting him, including a letter from Millana. He laid his hand on the letter. Immediately, he received bad and nervous feelings. He opened the letter and read it. It read as follows:

Roland,   Sept 11, 1998

You have some nerve! To be writing me and insulting not only me but Eduardo and my family. You know what my problem is with you? You're just plain <u>weird</u>! You make the hairs on my neck stand up. Not one person that I know that you know likes you. I'm going to tell you straight up! Not even <u>Raul</u>. They would give you up in a second if there were a price on your head if there isn't one already!

Lavinia told me she would rather have you leave than me. I told her I would rather stay with my grandmother in Monterrey because she has more room and is air conditioned. I told her I was going to leave. But how the #@%!! do you think she would pick you over her own son? Because if I were to leave, Eduardo and her grandson would have to go with me. Do you have no brains? And besides I'm sure Lavinia would have been just fine if you would have not helped her. She would have found a way, like she always has. So don't play this good samaritan !@*%$! with me.

Eduardo doesn't have to announce himself for any reason to show up at his own mother's house. I don't know what the #@%!! you're trying to pull, but I DON'T LIKE YOU. I don't like the way you tricked us into giving you our address. Because you put Alberto on the phone so that one of us could give him the address. Because Raul didn't want anything to do with you anymore. That's why Lavinia didn't want to give you our phone number and address. Eduardo don't like you either because you keep but'n into stuff that doesn't even concern you. You don't know what family is. You don't understand it. Because that's what Mexican culture is made of, unlike white folk.

I don't have to be ashamed for any reason when I'm in all my right. Don't give me any !@*%! about being a 2nd class citizen because all my life I have been treated as one living in this country. You don't know. You will never know what it is like to be rejected. You don't know what it is like to be denied a joke for the only reason of being a <u>Mexican</u>. I didn't ask my family to bring me to this country. I didn't ask to go to school here. I was brought here for the sole so called reason to live a better life!

Lavinia wouldn't have made it this far if it hadn't been for Eduardo and now Raul. You know why Raul don't want anything to do with you? Because he is afraid that you will turn him in to Immigration. What does that tell you? It should tell you something, but you have no brains. I'm going to tell you. He doesn't trust you. I don't want you to be calling my house. I don't want you to write ever again. I don't want to see your ugly face again. If you keep bothering us, I am going to file charges against you for stalking.

X- Millana -X

Why that no good cabrona! Her letter had threats! Good gracious! How unreasonable does a person get?! She was a jerk, no two ways about it!

The next day, Roland took her letter, minus her address, to the sheriff's office to file a complaint on her.

They assured Roland that there wasn't a thing she could do to Roland for his calling to talk to her brother-in-law, Raul, since she was out of state. Roland had perfect right to call him.

That was good to know. Plus, Roland was going to see his friend Raul any time he liked. Amen, brother! And if it were to ever occur to Millana to take serious action against Roland in efforts to block his friendship with Raul, he would just quietly and anonymously set off a spectacular fireworks display in front of her house at 3 AM some morning in the future, needless to say with a very long fuse! Of course, he didn't mention *that* detail to the sheriff's office.

On Saturday afternoon, September 26, nearly two days after Roland got home, he called Rigo in Bustamante. Roland needed to talk to Rigo about a drawing he had requested, to be made by Roland's artist friend, David, a drawing of the Lion's Head Mountain with the names of Rigo's best friends written in the skyline, a clique known as *Los Chukys*. Why didn't Rigo want it done by Roland?

Well, it took three calls to reach him at Diana's house. The second time Roland called, which was 15 minutes after the first call, Rigo had still not come to the phone. Though Roland didn't know it till much later, Rigo didn't want to come to the phone. Since Roland had left Bustamante, Millana had bad mouthed Roland quite a lot, not to mention the dreams that Draaktra and Druxtrli had sent Rigo on certain nights, in addition to false memories. As a result, Rigo had been stewing over Roland considerably!

Between Roland's second and third call, Irma told Rigo again that Roland wanted to talk to him and she urged him to come to Diana's house to take his phone call. Rigo was watching TV, and he reacted angrily to Irma, shouted a rash of complaints and foul language in Spanish, and he left the house. He knew Roland wouldn't give up until he took his call. Rigo, with angry face, walked into Diana's house to wait by the phone.

Meanwhile Roland, totally unsuspecting and friendly, called Diana's house for a third time. Rigo answered and Roland greeted him saying, "¿Cómo has estado?"

"Bien. ¿Por qué?" Rigo quickly responded, answering, *Good. Why?* That was NOT a good answer. Roland immediately received a rash of negative and nervous feelings.

He kindly asked Rigo if he had any work, and he answered that he only had a little bit. Roland began to tell Rigo that he sent a letter to Millana, and . . .

"¡No tuviste porque para escribir una carta a Millana!" Rigo quickly interrupted, angrily telling Roland he had no right to have written Millana a letter. Obviously, Rigo already knew.

"¡Mira, me disgustó bastante!" Roland managed to firmly respond, despite a dry mouth, telling Rigo that Millana disgusted him considerably!

Rigo told Roland that Millana considered him like dirt, and he went on to tell Roland he was no longer welcome in his house. Roland asked Rigo why, and he told Roland he had meddled in other people's business, like when he had talked to Nacho and found work for Rigo. Plus, Rigo was still hopping mad that Roland had located Raul, despite the barrier Rigo and his mother had put before him.

Roland then told Rigo that the only people he was going to let drive his truck would be those who considered Roland a good friend and properly welcomed him into their home. Rigo then agreed he wouldn't be driving Roland's truck anymore. He *never* did again.

Roland, thoughtful and friendly as he was, began to ask Rigo what he wanted him to do about that *Los Chukys* drawing? Rigo snapped back that he didn't want it anymore! He went on to tell Roland that he thought he had called for something important, and obviously the drawing wasn't!

With that, Roland asked to speak to his mother Lavinia. Rigo called his mother to the phone, and Roland overheard Rigo telling her that Roland wanted to stay with them the next time he comes to town and for her to tell him no!

Roland then asked Lavinia why Rigo was being so hateful. She didn't have much to say. Roland asked her if he could stay with them, like she had earlier said. Rigo, in the background was repeatedly urging her to say no. So, instead of defending herself, like a woman with a backbone would have done, she gave in to her son, and she told Roland he'd be better off in the hotel. He asked her again, and she stated no.

With that, Roland said goodbye and hung up. What in the world was wrong?! Boy was Rigo angry! New definition for the words, *holding grudges*. It had been three entire weeks since Roland had left Bustamante, but that was no time in Rigo's view. As Roland was realizing more and more, some Mexicans were extremely resentful. They held grudges for years and years, sometimes for lifetimes!

Roland called right back a few minutes later, and he told Lavinia he would likely never come back to Bustamante, because he did not feel wanted. Lavinia wished him well.

Roland felt absolutely terrible! How could Rigo have been so awful? Did he not one bit appreciate all the good Roland had done for him? Plus, Roland was nice to call and ask Rigo how he was doing. He would have told him he had a nice trip to California, but what did Rigo care?!

*   *   *

Nuevo Wimbisenho

"Mmm . . . Mmm! Ecstasy to perfection!" Draaktra savouringly remarked.

"I've got to hand it to you, Draaktra," Arfifra told him. "You implemented that royal rejection program on Rigo better than I could have done it myself."

"You successfully made Rigo forget every good thing Roland did," Druxtrli commended him, and she patted him on the back.

"You've definitely earned your keep," his older brother Sojornbloc added.

"That is some of the richest rejection energy I've ever seen," Druxtrli told everyone, with a smile.

"Roland's in a bad way," Sasjurech observed. "He may become ours very soon."

"Whittle him down some more," Arfifra advised.

"Now do you see why I wanted Rigo so much?" Draaktra asked everyone.

"You certainly know how to play his rejection chords," Sojornbloc recognized.

"Rejection chords," Druxtrli said to the others. "What a nice phrase. I like the sound of that!" She laughed.

"Draaktra," Arfifra announced, "you've just earned entry status into our special school of black magic, the school of . . . *Carifrajariflaquestrav.*"

"Whew, doggie!! Chop chop!" he exclaimed with vigor and excitement. Then he calmed down and asked, "But there's nothing else I can do with Rigo. His friendship with Roland is over."

Arfifra looked into their black holographic crystal ball in their cave. "That's what you think. Roland is very stubborn. There's more. Their bridge is still standing."

Draaktra took the energy disks out of the special energy capture apparatus. Torxtalo happened to arrive at just the perfect moment. He had been visiting their original site under New Zealand. Including Torxtalo, six demons enjoyed one of the richest feasts ever to take place at Nuevo Wimbisenho.

"You know, that was hilarious those dreams I sent Rigo?" said Draaktra with an irresistible smile on his face, and he told them what they were.

They roared with laughter!

"Aren't you going to credit me with the dreams I sent him, too?" Druxtrli asked, faking a hurt look.

They roared with laughter some more!

"Mmm . . . Mmm! These energy disks are scrumptious!" Torxtalo declared.

"Delectable!" Draaktra agreed.

After their feast, they were stuffed.

*   *   *

Wrenches Arrive

Sept 26, 1998

A truck pulling a pontoon boat on a trailer and a landscaping crew driving their pickup truck pulling a flatbed trailer were driving in opposite directions along the Lascassas Highway. Here came the narrow bridge over the Stones River. Both of them entered the bridge, and they proceeded to pass by each other.

SNAG! . . . CRASH!!

The back axles of their trailers hung each other, jerking them to a halt and causing them to crash into the siderails of the bridge . . . a spectacular wreck indeed! Some of them were killed and the rest of them seriously injured. Police and ambulances soon came to the scene to rush the injured to the hospital and clear the wreckage.

When the state highway department learned of the tragedy, they decided to take measures and action, and replace what should have been replaced when the highway was widened nearly 20 years ago.

Molonco and Kryphios had just suffered a major setback in their friendship, and work would now be placed in action to replace their bridge . . . and their friendship, as well.

*　　*　　*

Roland called Elton on the phone the day after he got home. Elton wasn't too pleased, and he apologized to Roland that his wife had not received him. He regretted that he had not been home when Roland arrived, because he would have at least paid for Roland to stay in a hotel overnight. That was kind of him, and Roland appreciated that gesture of friendship. They talked for a while on the phone, and Elton explained that there had been a lot of things going on, and his wife was tired of having visitors as a result. At least Elton wanted to continue his friendship with Roland, and that was what was most important. He was sorry to hear about the rejection from Rigo and his family in Mexico.

The next morning, Roland called Raul on the phone. He said the rest of his stay in California had gone well, that he had slept inside a big Redwood tree, and had enjoyed part of the drive back home. He liked the West and hoped to return another summer for more hiking and adventure.

Also, Roland talked to Raul about Millana's absolutely ugly letter, and he told Raul about how awful Rigo had been on the phone. Raul was sorry to find that out, and Roland read Millana's letter to him. Raul told Roland he could continue to call and also stop by to visit, because Eduardo had given prior consent. Raul didn't exactly like Millana either, but since she was married to his brother, he had to be nice to her.

Also, Roland assured Raul that he would never report him to Immigration, like Millana and others like Rigo must have thought! Raul admitted to Roland that he had been concerned about that, and he really appreciated Roland's assurance that he wouldn't report him. Roland told Raul he could ease his mind on that. After all, he was in the United States for good reasons, working and making money to send back to his family in Mexico. Plus, Mexicans are human beings, too!

Also, by this day and time, Mexicans were becoming so integrated into the American culture that the American economy depended on them. In fact throughout the nation, they were becoming the staple of the manual labor workforce, such as brick and block laying, fruit picking, lawn care, carpentry, painting, and even industrial labor.

Despite this fact, the American Consulate still had in place their rigorous (sometimes impossible) requirements for Mexicans to obtain VISAs to visit the United States. One would wonder why the Consulate still made it so difficult for Mexicans to visit legally, with literally millions of illegal Mexican residents already on U.S. soil. Actually, it was a deliberate American policy, designed that way so that Mexicans would realize the impossibilities of coming to the Unites States the legal way, and therefore be encouraged to cross the river wetback, that is, immigrate illegally. They could therefore be paid lower wages, that is, cheaper labor, and they wouldn't be subject to all the benefits requirements that legal U.S. citizens must have from their employers. It was a very clever system that actually helped the U.S. economy. Plus, it was less paperwork for the government because the illegal Mexicans could stay as long as they wanted to, without having to go through the bureaucratic and expensive hassle of applying for VISA extensions every six months.

Roland also called Ivanhoe on the phone. He commented how awful Millana had been. Plus, the friendship between Roland and Rigo was mysteriously dead, a shame really. Ivanhoe wasn't surprised, and he reminded Roland how he had predicted he would somehow get bounced out of that family.

Roland remembered Ivanhoe's prediction, and he also remembered his prediction about some sort of mysterious block while attempting to go to Mexico back in August. He told Ivanhoe about the mysterious roadblock of congested traffic on Highway 96 *leaving* Murfreesboro at 7:30 AM that morning.

"You've definitely used up all your luck on that one, Roland. You definitely did, and you went right around that roadblock and succeeded in getting there, anyway!"

Ivanhoe strongly recommended that Roland simply not return to Bustamante, at least for a year, that things might get very dangerous, since Isalia and Luke would almost certainly be there. He explained that Luke and Isalia have no conscience, and they could easily pay someone to eliminate Roland. No one would ever find him, and no one would ever be able to prove it! Ivanhoe also said if Roland went anyway, he would have no sympathy for him if he fell into a big problem. Well, actually, that wasn't totally true, but Ivanhoe said it that way to keep Roland from going, simply to avoid danger. He cared for Roland's well being and safety. Roland took Ivanhoe's advice and he thought long about it. Make no mistake, Ivanhoe wasn't against Roland's having friends. The main concern was Isalia and Luke's potential danger.

Roland looked at his pictures. He thought of all his friends, like Victor, Fabian, Fernando, Daniel, Juan Angel, Alberto, Beto, Hector, Pablo, Angelo, Hugo, the Orolizos (minus Pegaso), Elisa, Manuel, Julian, Gilberto, the Gonzalez family, and more still. The more Roland thought about it, the more he realized he just couldn't throw aside those friends, especially over danger from Isalia and Luke, who had *no* right to keep Roland out of Bustamante! After all, most Mexicans were good people.

To Roland, friendships were gold. He valued them as such. He took his friendships seriously, and never had he done anything intentionally wrong to ruin a friendship. It really appalled Roland how people like Rigo, Pegaso, Isalia, Luke, and previously Raul, had taken an insane amount of rejection of him! Fortunately, in the case of Raul, for his having left Bustamante, he learned the very valuable lesson in life that friendships are worth their weight in gold. Raul had seen the light, you might say, but since Rigo was still in Bustamante, he had never learned the value of friendships.

Roland also called up Mr. Mayfield. For a while, he had considerably recovered from his pancreas cancer of February, but it had come back, and he was now on his way out. Roland went over to talk to him, and they visited for an hour. Roland talked to him about several subjects, and his experiences and adventures in Mexico. They talked about Rigo. Mr. Mayfield told Roland that Rigo blacked out that paragraph because he spent that N$330 on something else. He explained that it wasn't really Rigo's fault for how badly he had acted. That was an interesting remark. Mr. Mayfield was psychic, more than Roland realized, though he said nothing of it, and he knew that evil sources, such as those of Nuevo Wimbisenho, had used Rigo as a tool to make Roland experience awful rejection!

Mr. Mayfield suggested that Roland read the *Bible* entirely, not just certain sections. He read some verses out of the *Bible*, and he told Roland it had taken him a lifetime to figure out the true meaning of the *Holy Bible*, a whole lifetime of 65 years for him.

Roland also asked Mr. Mayfield *to send him a travelling companion*, once he steps over to the *other side* or at least cause Roland to realize who he was, since Ivanhoe had told Roland, ". . .when you finally figure it out." He asked Mr. Mayfield to contact him, as well.

"Oh, I'll contact you," he told Roland.

Yes, Roland had known his high school science teacher for 18 years. He was sorry he was dying now. Later, his wife Mrs. Mayfield would tell Roland that he really enjoyed that last visit he had with him.

Mr. Mayfield had been an interesting man of different and unique ideas. He knew many things that he didn't tell people in general. There were several stories he told Roland that he had not told anyone else except his wife, because people would think he was crazy. He had written down plenty of notes of astral travels he had taken and he had derived mathematical formulas and conceived many ideas that were prodigal by normal standards. The world wasn't ready for much of what he knew, and during his last month of life, he burned his numerous notebooks.

Roland got to feeling better. Clients called him to work, and he earned a decent amount of money, enough to return to Mexico in January.

On October 7, Roland decided to call Lavinia at Diana's house to see if Rigo was feeling better. She said he was feeling more content now. That was good, and yes, she told Roland he was welcome to stay with them. Roland thanked Lavinia, and he told her that she and her family were his first choice of who to stay with in Bustamante. Lavinia thanked Roland and then mentioned that Rigo needed money and wanted to sell the Royal 440 manual typewriter Roland had given him. After all, Millana had brought Rigo that dinky electric one. Roland asked Lavinia how much Rigo wanted for it, and she said N$600. Roland told her those Royal 440's were worth around US $40, approximately N$400. He told her he'd give US $50 for it. Lavinia said that would be fine. If Rigo didn't want that typewriter, Roland would rather buy it to recollect it and just take it back home again. Rigo could have the $50, but he didn't deserve that typewriter, especially since he preferred Millana's, which to Roland was an insult!

Next, Lavinia said she had talked to the Quevalos, and she had news. She told Roland that Esalina Velazco's son Guillermo had died. Roland reacted with disbelief, and he told Lavinia she must have misunderstood them. The news about Guillermo was that he had just gotten married, not died. Lavinia then told Roland that she knew that. Yes, he had gotten married, and then he died a month later! Roland made another response of disbelief, and he told Lavinia he was going to hang up and call Esalina right then to see if it was really true, and then he'd call Lavinia right back and let her know. They hung up.

Roland called Esalina's house in Monterrey. Guillermo's sister María answered with sadness in her voice. Roland asked them how they were and how Guillermo was.

"¿No supiste?" said María, expressing surprise that Roland didn't know.

He told her that a friend in Bustamante had just minutes ago told Roland that Guillermo . . . died.

María verified that it was true, that he had died one month ago on September 7. He was almost age 34.

Roland expressed his sincere sympathy to María. Esalina came on the line. Roland expressed his sympathy to her, as well.

Esalina thanked him. Then she asked Roland how on Earth he didn't know? She had notified Isalia the day her son had died, and she had specifically requested that Isalia notify Shannon, the Creighton family, and Roland.

Roland let Esalina know that he would have called right away to express his sympathy, if he had just known. Isalia had not informed him. She had completely left Roland out! Esalina was not pleased that Isalia had purposefully neglected to inform Roland. Granted, Roland was out West, but his parents were home, and Isalia could have told them.

Esalina was also aware of the major problem that Roland and Isalia had gotten into and that it was a major misunderstanding. Roland explained that Isalia wouldn't reason nor give him a chance to talk to her, to try and resolve it.

Esalina asked Roland why he announced that white truck to Mexican Customs at the Colombia Bridge, and he answered that Isalia and Luke had reported him to the police in Bustamante, putting him in danger! That part of the story Esalina hadn't heard. She said Isalia and Luke were never going to forgive him. Evidently, Isalia had told Esalina the story about her falling out with Roland, but she left out crucial details that were not convenient for her to relate!

Roland said that not only did Isalia lose her friendship with him, she also lost it with his parents. Esalina now saw more reason to Roland's side of the story . . . the truth. She expressed her sorrow that the misunderstanding had occurred, and she thanked Roland for having phoned her to express his sympathy for her son's death.

They finished their conversation, and Roland then called Lavinia right back to let her know that it was really true about Guillermo's death.

Roland typed out a five page letter to Esalina in Spanish. It told the whole story about Isalia and Luke. He bought a sympathy card and mailed it and the letter to Esalina. That letter, Roland later modified in his computer/word processor, and he made 40 to 50 copies of it to take to Bustamante on all future trips, to hand all over town if such an occasion occurred that Isalia and Luke intimidated Roland.

For years, Russia and the United States had added to their nuclear weapons arsenal. Roland now had his letters, which he added to his "arsenal" of 75 prostitute flyers.

Roland called Shannon and her family. Yes, they had been notified on September 8, and they were quite surprised that Roland hadn't known. Roland told them the whole story in a nutshell. They certainly were sorry.

Shannon informed Roland that three months ago, they had received Guillermo's wedding invitation. They hadn't had any contact with him since 1984, and they certainly were pleasantly surprised to be invited to his wedding.

"Well, I will say!" Roland reacted. "I certainly didn't receive any invitation."

"You *didn't?*" Shannon responded with surprise.

"No, I didn't," Roland replied.

"That just doesn't make any sense," she went on. "Didn't you keep up with him?"

"Oh, yes," Roland answered. "I saw him several times, even twice within the last year."

"If anyone should have gotten a wedding invitation from Guillermo, it should have been you," said Shannon.

"Yes, I agree."

"I tell you what, Roland. You can have the invitation he sent me."

"Are you sure?"

"Oh, yes. I think you deserve the invitation. I want you to have it."

"Thank you. Thank you very much," said Roland. "I'll put it in safe keeping with my things."

They finished the conversation and hung up. Shannon had been one of Roland's better friends in high school. He had known her and her family since childhood. Of course, now she was married and had a family of her own, and Roland was a friend to them, as well.

Imagine that! Guillermo did not invite Roland to his wedding! That was downright insulting! Shannon was right. Roland deserved that invitation more than anyone else. Isalia had stood Guillermo and his mother up by not even coming to a wedding where she was going to be so highly honored by being allowed to sit by Esalina's side! Plus, Roland was actually in Mexico on August 7, and he could easily have attended the wedding, had he simply been invited. Guillermo knew good and well that Roland was the only fellow Tennessee classmate who frequented coming to Mexico and had maintained friendly contact over the years, and yes, or course Guillermo had Roland's address. Yes, there had been the underwear incident 15¼ years ago, but that was not reason enough to sever a friendship, at least the way Roland saw it. Guillermo seemed like he had forgiven it, but maybe not? Perhaps Guillermo had sent Roland an invitation in the mail and it had gotten lost, but then Shannon's invitation arrived, so that was unlikely. Guillermo's purposefully neglecting to send Roland a wedding invitation was inexcusable on all counts. Perhaps he was now being reminded of that, on the *other side.*

Roland met some Mexicans living there in middle Tennessee. He was buying supplies at a paint store, and got to talking to a fellow named Jaime. Right there was a new door that led to many great things. Jaime was impressed at Roland's Spanish, and took a liking to him right away. He invited Roland over to his apartment where his wife and three children lived. Also in the apartment complex lived two of his brothers, a nephew, and other relatives and friends. Roland went to visit them. They were really good people, and they came from several ranches north of the town of Matehuala. Others came from areas further south.

Roland told them about his travels to Mexico. They enjoyed his stories, and they offered their friendly hospitality by telling Roland to come and visit them in Mexico this coming January. He could stay with them for several days. Jaime's nephew Francisco lived in Monterrey at the foot of Cerro de las Mitras, and he said he and Roland could go up that mountain, if he liked.

Jaime came from a big family. His youngest brother Margarito was also living with him.

Jaime also wanted to start his own painting business, and he expressed interest in Roland's working with him. They would talk that over more and more as time went on.

Yes, autumn came, then winter. Roland was getting plenty of work from friends and clients.

Roland went over to Asheville, North Carolina to do some work for some friends one weekend. While out of state, he called Raul and had a nice visit with him by phone. His sister-in-law had no idea who in the world the caller was when she later looked at her caller ID. Let her rack *her* brain for a while! After all, Roland wasn't supposed to have brains.

Raul talked to Roland about his calendars, and then he came forth with a good suggestion: that Roland write a book about his life, that is, a novel about an American in Mexico with all the strange events that Roland had experienced. Raul explained that it was very rare that an American like Roland spend considerable time in Mexico. Roland said that it had crossed his mind also, even though he had never written a novel before, but he said he would seriously consider it. He thanked Raul for his suggestion, and he would soon begin his novel.

Raul was concerned about Roland for something, and he told him that since his mother Lavinia was Isalia's maid in Bustamante, it was possible that it would occur to Isalia to tell Lavinia not to receive Roland into her home, and if she did, her position as Isalia's maid would be terminated! Now Roland was concerned. He really hoped Raul's prediction would not come true.

Something also occurred to Roland, and he advised Raul to forewarn Lavinia not to tell Isalia where her son Raul was living, because Isalia, vicious as she is, might report Raul to Immigration, and she might go so far as to frame Roland and make it look like he did the reporting. Roland again assured Raul that he would never report him to Immigration, but the most important thing was to tell Isalia that Raul was in Guadalajara with his uncle. Raul very much appreciated Roland's warning and advice, and he would call his mother and warn her.

Mr. Mayfield, Roland's high school science teacher, passed away on Thanksgiving Day, and the funeral was in Woodbury where he had grown up. They had a picture display with photos from childhood right through his whole life. Roland called Mr. Mayfield's wife and expressed his condolences.

In his last days, he had talked about Roland, that somebody was going to be contacting him. He had been reading a book called *Parallel Universes*, a very interesting book indeed. Mrs. Mayfield loaned it to Roland to read so he could tell her what it was about. He took great care of the book, read it, and later returned it to her.

Roland decided to call Isalia's son, Laurence, out in California, so he could tell his mother that Roland would be going to Bustamante for the month of January and for her and Luke to leave Roland alone. He also told Laurence to be sure and tell her that he would also leave her and Luke alone, and he didn't want any problems.

Roland wasn't sure how Laurence would receive him over the telephone, and he started the conversation by asking him if he knew what had happened between him and Isalia and Luke.

"A blowup, right?" Laurence asked.

"That's right . . ." and Roland briefly explained how Isalia and Luke would not reason with him nor give him a chance to talk to them to straighten out anything. ". . . and every time I handed them a letter, they just tore it right up."

Laurence knew how his mother was. After all, she had removed his daughter from her premises by force of the police, but of course Laurence didn't tell that to Roland, nor did he know that Roland knew about it.

"I have my friends down there in Bustamante," Roland told Laurence, "and I have the right to visit them and be in that town, too. There's enough room there for all of us."

Laurence told Roland that he would tell his mother and said for him to call him back in a week or so.

Roland also asked Laurence if he could still remain in contact with him, and he said sure. He didn't have anything against Roland.

Meanwhile Roland started a big deck project on the shores of a man-made lake on Elizabeth's farm out near Columbia. The work lasted for two weeks, and the pay was good.

A week later, Roland called Laurence to find out. He asked him what his mother had said.

"None of your business!" he rudely snapped.

Roland faltered for a couple of seconds and then firmly said, "You know, I want to be sure they're going to leave me alone down there!"

"Well, I guess you probably think I sounded rude."

"Yes, I have to admit, you were."

"Okay, okay I'll tell you this," Laurence decided to inform him. "My mother said for you to keep your distance and not to bother her."

"Does that mean they're going to leave me alone?" Roland persisted.

"Yeah, you just do as she says."

They talked another minute or two and finished the conversation. Roland had Laurence's word that his mother and step father were indeed going to leave Roland alone.

That was the last time Roland ever called Laurence. He was really taken aback by the "None of your business!" comment. It was very much out of order and uncalled for. Roland was just about sure that Isalia had specifically told her son to say that to Roland when he would call, and he did just as his mother told him to. And to point out, it was very much Roland's business to check with Laurence about what Isalia and Luke had said, because it concerned Roland and his safety!

Roland felt a little less apprehensive now. However, his friend Ivanhoe had strongly advised him not to return to Mexico because Isalia and Luke could easily hire someone to take Roland out to the countryside, do him harm, and eliminate him, and no one would ever be able to find him. Ivanhoe had explained that Luke and Isalia have no conscience. Roland realized those possibilities, but he was willing to take those risks because he had friends there he wanted to visit.

Several more weeks went by before Roland left. The distributor over in South Carolina made a good offer on publishing Roland's artwork calendars and book compilation. He said that he would be a little bit "creative" and do a small print run of 100 copies of each.

At the same time, Roland had incidentally found another book and calendar publishing company in Nashville. They had recently opened and had collaborated with a local printing company where they could store books electronically in their databases, and they could therefore print books and calendars to supply orders as necessary. Roland called them up and went to visit them. Their setup was impressive, and their prices were good. They catered to smallhouse publishers by offering low number print runs. Roland could self publish his books and calendars, and all he would have to do would be to purchase a block of ISBN numbers to obtain his publisher's prefix and register each title with the Library of Congress.

Then he could pay the company a certain amount per copy printed.

Roland told the distributor in South Carolina about his competition, and he told Roland he could beat their price plus get a Library of Congress catalog card number in an hour over the *Internet*, among other good offers. Roland sounded impressed, so he sent his original artwork along with the proposed calendar and book layouts.

Three days later, he called the man on the phone to check and make sure he received the valuable documents. The distributor said he wouldn't be able to help Roland out. He made himself seem real busy, saying he didn't have time to talk. Roland asked him to please not send the materials back until they would have a chance to talk it over. Well, the next thing the distributor said really surprised Roland. He told him he had already put it back in the mail to him!

"Look, I haven't got time to talk to you!" the distributor repeated.

"Arghhhh! I'll talk to you later," Roland said as calmly as he could, and he hung up.

That was the last time Roland and that distributor ever talked to each other. He couldn't believe how quickly the distributor sent his materials back to him! It was too quick, actually, and Roland was suspicious. He tried numerous times to call the man after that, because he was still the distributor for his first set of calendars, and he still had exactly 250 copies of his book compilation in stock. Irritatingly, he was *always* unavailable to take Roland's calls. Either his wife or one of the secretaries always answered.

Still not a single copy of Roland's book compilation had sold, even though the color artwork inside it was fabulous. However, Roland decided to leave them with him a while longer in hopes that one day, at least some of them would move.

Roland talked to a friend of his, Mark, about the distributor's sudden cold shoulder, dropping his materials like a hot potato, and sending them back to him in the mail before he could even talk to the man about it.

Mark asked Roland, "You don't think he needed them electronically, do you?"

Suddenly, Roland received a strange feeling that he had been tricked.

"Maybe he did," Roland told his friend. "Do you think he might have sold my artwork under the table . . . to Japan, for example?"

"No, I don't think he would do that. You've got it copyrighted, don't you?"

"Oh, yes," Roland replied. "Since last July."

"That was a smart move. You're safe then. I wouldn't worry about it."

Needless to say, Roland made arrangements with the new publishing company in Nashville, told them he was going to publish his future calendars and book compilations with them, and he began the process of buying his block of ISBN numbers, and obtaining his publisher's prefix. By spring, he would have more calendars and another book compilation in print. Plus, he got his Library of Congress catalog card number by normal mail, thank you.

Roland loaded his truck with his belongings, and he drove down to Mexico at the end of December. He was a little apprehensive, but he was looking forward to his stay. Plus, he was looking forward to visiting with Jaime's family further south near Matehuala.

CHAPTER 16

NEW DOORS OPEN, NEW FRIENDS

late December 1998

In Salado, Roland visited Raul at his brother's house. Millana was luckily not at home. Raul took Roland in his 1984 Buick Century, which he had recently repaired. They went to a mall in Salado, and they also went to a restaurant. He was glad to have Roland visit him for the day, and when Roland was leaving to drive on to Laredo, Raul sent some items with him for his family, including $20.

Roland spent the night in Laredo, and the next morning, the last day of the year, he drove to the Colombia Bridge. He passed Mexican Customs easily enough, and he drove toward Bustamante.

While driving through the city of Anahuac, an old police car followed him through town and pulled him over. He told Roland he entered a little fast and started out being persistent about fining him. Roland kindly insisted that he was going 30 km/h, as the signs said.

The cop thought about it, and then said, "Bueno, que te vaya bien. Pásale," wishing Roland well and telling him he could proceed.

"Gracias, igualmente," Roland responded, thanking the cop. He breathed a sigh of relief, and he drove his truck out of town. The cop turned around and drove back into town.

Roland drove on to Bustamante, and he drove very slowly through Lampazos. Later, around 2 PM, he reached the intersection and turned right to drive the five kilometers into Bustamante. He soon crossed the railroad track, and a white truck approached Roland's truck in the opposing lane and passed him. It was Luke's white truck. Mexican Customs had never confiscated it.

Roland drove on in to Bustamante. The first place he went was to Victor's house. He had mailed him $50 in the mail last month, and he wanted to know if it had arrived safely. He pulled up in front of the house and walked to the door. Victor was at home, and he opened the door, greeted Roland in a friendly manner, and immediately thanked him for the $50. That was kind of him.

Roland told Victor how Rigo had acted over the phone back in late September. Victor wasn't the least bit surprised. He knew Rigo, and he told Roland that Rigo was only Roland's friend for special interests in what he might bring him. Roland now answered a question that Victor had asked him back in September about who was more sincere, and he told Victor that he was far more sincere than Rigo. Victor appreciated that kind comment, and it was well deserved because Victor was always Roland's friend, and not just for the $50 Roland had sent him either, but for genuine reasons, and he would prove to be a lasting friend, as well.

Roland decided not to even go over to Rigo's house until tomorrow. He wanted to do something else first . . . go up into the mountains and camp on the ridge top for New Year's Eve, to be away from the sound of the dance, and the fireworks at midnight. With his truck still totally loaded, he drove over to Daniel Mata's house and asked if he knew of a place he could park his truck for the night, near the cono, but not right at the cono, because it was possible that certain drunks might bash in his windows and steal from him.

Daniel said that Jesús Lucio had a corral, a small shelter and parking area, off to the left of the main cono road. Daniel was sure Lucio wouldn't mind. Roland thanked Daniel, and he drove over to the Cantu's store in the town's central plaza.

There Roland saw Chilo and Mina Cantu, and they happily greeted him, asking him how things had gone since September. Mina asked Roland where he would be staying, and he said he planned to stay over at Rigo's house. Mina voluntarily brought up that it was possible that Lavinia and her family might not receive him, because Isalia might try and prevent it by threatening to terminate Lavinia's position as her maid, if she took Roland in. Roland told Mina the thought had also crossed his mind, and he just hoped that it would *not* cross Isalia's mind.

Next, Roland bought some tortillas and some fruit from the Cantus, and he drove up the gravel road toward the cono, easily finding Lucio's corral, and he parked there. He loaded his backpack, locked his truck, and took off walking at 4:30 PM.

For 3½ hours, Roland hiked up the mountain. It got dark at 6:30 PM, and for an hour and a half, Roland hiked up the mountain in the dark. He had two flashlights, and since he knew the way very well, he continued just fine. He reached the highland forest, hiked through it for 20 minutes, and reached the grassy saddle.

He set up his tent on the top of the cliff in a small grassy area, putting the top of the forested ridge between him and the town. There! That would block any annoying sounds of the dance for the night! He crawled into his tent and slept peacefully. At midnight, Roland faintly heard the sounds of the fireworks going off. He was glad he was up here instead of down there where all the wild activity was sure to be taking place.

It was now a new year: January 1, 1999.

At 8 AM, Roland got up, had a bowl of cereal, and he hiked back down the mountain. He passed the cave. It was open, and he walked over to the entrance and looked inside. The lights were on, and there were tourists. Rogelio, who was now the cave guide again, was taking them on a tour of the cave.

Roland continued back to the cono. Parked at the road's end at the cono was, quite to Roland's surprise, Luke's white truck! They and possibly some of the Quevalos were taking a tour of the cave. Clayton's Ford pickup truck was also parked there. It had a new camper top. Luckily, Roland had not seen Isalia and Luke, but they were lurking nearby! Roland really didn't want to see them, not their faces, not at all. Evidently, Isalia and Luke had driven to Mexico in Clayton's Ford truck.

Roland walked the several hundred yards to where he parked his truck at Lucio's corral. Smart move Roland had made, now that he saw that both Luke's and Clayton's trucks came up here this morning! Luke could have done some sabotage to Roland's truck, had it been parked at the cono.

Back at his truck, Roland took a couple of water jugs out of his box, and he gave himself a bath. He placed his backpack inside, closed his camper top door, and drove into Bustamante.

Now he decided to stop at Rigo's house. He wasn't sure how he would receive him. Roland stepped down from his truck and knocked on the ancient wooden door of the old and run down adobe house. Rigo answered, surprisingly showed that he was glad to see him, and he asked him to come inside. His sister Irma was there also. Rigo asked Roland how he had been. He looked okay, and the resentment he had earlier had was gone. Well, good. Roland started talking to Rigo.

In addition to the $20, Raul had sent some items to his family, including some cassette tapes to Rigo, and Roland had Rigo sign for the delivery. That signed note, Roland would later show Raul to prove that he delivered the items.

Rigo eagerly asked Roland if he would buy the typewriter that he had given him the previous year. Roland told him he would think about it. Rigo had been unsuccessful in selling it for the N$600 they were asking for it.

"¿Dónde vas a quedarte?" Rigo said to Roland, asking him where he was going to stay.

Roland casually answered that he planned on staying right here with them. Rigo wasn't so sure about that, and Roland decided to say that he would indeed buy that typewriter, offering N$500, but with the condition that he could stay here with them. Rigo also wanted to sell a windup wrist watch he had been using, and Roland told him he would think about that also.

Lavinia and her daughter Norma arrived, and they greeted Roland nicely. She said that would be fine for him to stay with them, just that he behave himself well. This time she didn't need her husband's permission. Roland talked with them for a while, catching them up on everything. He told them he had just visited with Raul and that he was doing well. They were glad to know that.

Roland and Rigo went over to Angelo's house, and they visited there for a while. It seemed like Angelo had become Rigo's best friend. They always did things together, and it's like they knew each other since time began. There were some other people over at Angelo's house, and one or more of them suddenly made kidding remarks to Rigo about his being gay and what he and Roland might be *doing* together. Rigo didn't appreciate the comments, and neither did Roland! And no, they weren't gay!

That evening, Roland decided where in the house he was going to sleep. Lavinia said he could stay with them but not in the same room, like he had done before. There was the back room with all the junk furniture in it, and there was a run down bed back there also. Rigo was away at the time. Roland and Norma lifted some couches and other furniture off the bed and carefully placed them on top of some of the other furniture, freeing up the bed. Next, Roland took the extremely dusty blankets off the bed, placed his plastic tarp on it, followed by his roll pad and sleeping bag. He was now set up, and he appreciated their taking him in.

The next day, Roland took Rigo and Angelo over to Sabinas Hidalgo.

On the northern side of Villaldama, there was a new Aplicación de la Ley Federal, a federal inspection point where they stationed soldiers who checked all passing traffic on the highway for drugs. As it turned out, they would be stationed there just about the whole year, and every time Roland went to Sabinas Hidalgo, he had to pass by their inspection point and undergo an inspection where they looked through his belongings that were in his truck. Though they were always courteous, Roland still didn't like having to undergo inspections. As a result, on some of the trips to Sabinas Hidalgo, Roland would take the old one-lane gravel road from Bustamante to Villaldama to bypass the inspection.

In Sabinas Hidalgo, Roland, Rigo and Angelo stopped by the stores, and Roland bought food and supplies. They stopped by a boot store, and Rigo decided to buy a new pair of black shiny boots. Roland gave him N$440 to pay for them, plus an extra N$60, and he had Rigo sign a receipt that Roland had given him N$500 (US $50) for the Royal 440 manual typewriter. Rigo signed it, went inside the store, and bought the boots. He was satisfied. So was Roland. He was glad to get that typewriter back because it was not properly appreciated by Rigo, and when Roland would go home in February, he would take it back home with him.

Roland treated Rigo and Angelo to lunch at the taco restaurant, and then they returned to Bustamante. They delivered Angelo to his house.

Back at Rigo's house, Roland decided to talk to Rigo about their phone conversation back in September. Roland told him he was made to feel very bad by how Rigo was so angry and rude. Rigo reacted grumpily about it, and he didn't like talking about it. Lavinia told Roland to drop it, and he said he would, but he still insisted that Rigo thank Roland for the N$200 worth of cassette tapes he had bought him back in August and September. So, Rigo said, "Gracias." Roland responded with the Spanish words for *finally* and *miracle*.

Rigo stayed grumpy the rest of the afternoon and evening, and Roland went around town on his bicycle, visiting other friends of his.

He stopped by the Cantus, and they asked him if Lavinia took him in. Roland said yes. Chilo said what a miracle it was that they took him in, and it was even more of a miracle that it had not occurred to Isalia to try and block it. Roland was very grateful. Despite the trouble that had occurred between him and Rigo, he still wanted his friendship and wanted to stay with his favorite family in that town, the Zacatóns.

The next morning was January 3, and Roland went to a telephone to call Leonardo's house in Villaldama. His sister answered and said he was there. Roland was glad to hear that, and he asked her to tell Leonardo that he was coming over in 20 minutes and for him to not go away. Roland immediately left in his truck. He hardly ever got to see his friend Leonardo, and he was looking forward to it.

Well, after the delaying drug inspection on Villaldama's north side, Roland arrived at Leonardo's house 22 minutes after having called. His sister came to the door and said that Leonardo had just left. Roland was surprised, and he asked her if she had told him he was coming over and for him not to leave. She said she had told him, but he had pressing matters that could not wait, and he had to leave. Leonardo's brother Julian was there, and they talked a few minutes. Then Roland wished him and his sister well, and he left. As he walked back to his vehicle, he then suddenly heard Julian talking to another fellow. Immediately, it occurred to Roland that it was Leonardo. He had not left! He was hiding instead. Roland quietly walked back around to the back porch where they were talking to make sure, but he saw only Julian and his sister. Julian was somewhat surprised, and Roland mentioned that he thought he had heard Leonardo speaking. Julian denied it. Roland left it at that, walked back to his truck, and drove away. Something was not quite right about Leonardo. It seemed that he was mysteriously avoiding Roland.

Roland drove back to Bustamante. Suddenly, the valves in his 6 cylinder motor started clicking considerably! He had to clear another drug inspection leaving Villaldama, as if they didn't remember inspecting him 15 minutes earlier, and he drove, quite worried about his truck, back to Bustamante.

Once back in front of the Zacatón's house, he got out his tools and took the valve cover off of the motor. He found several valves mysteriously loose. It was amazing those nuts didn't back off thousands of miles earlier. He replaced all 12 nuts with new ones that he happened to have with his spare parts, and these nuts were interference thread nuts that would *not* back off! Once he adjusted the nuts properly, the valve clicking was solved, no more clicking.

Rigo put on some of his putrid perfume and went to Angelo's for the afternoon. He was still grumpy from yesterday. Roland wasn't pleased with that at all, but he said nothing to him about it.

After Rigo left, Roland talked to Lavinia and Norma about Rigo and asked them why Rigo was so ill content with him. Lavinia said that since Rigo had accompanied Roland so much back in August and September, the town's people had been kidding Rigo about his "gay" friend Roland. That very much displeased Roland, and he mentioned that yesterday over at Angelo's house, one or two visitors had kidded Rigo right there in front of Roland, and it must have been quite embarrassing for Rigo. It was like the "devil" had won, and Roland sensed that certain people had been caused to think that way in efforts to ruin his friendship with Rigo!

Roland mentioned to Lavinia and Norma that he was going to go on down to Matehuala to visit Jaime's family for several days, and he would return to Bustamante after that. However, if Rigo didn't want to come around and be friendly, then he would just head on back home to Tennessee.

Rigo arrived in the evening and was watching TV. Roland was in the back room of the house organizing his things and deciding what he would take with him to Matehuala. He didn't want to take everything of his because there were bound to be more drug inspections, and he didn't want to go through the hassle of their inspecting any more of his belongings than was necessary.

Suddenly, Rigo called Roland over to him, and he surprised Roland by asking him if he wanted to go to Monterrey tomorrow. *An outburst of friendliness! Miracle!* Roland looked at him strangely, and Rigo insisted on his genuineness about wanting to go to Monterrey with him tomorrow.

Roland thought about it a moment and then said fine. Then he thought to ask Rigo what about his work. He said he had not gone back to work with Felipe nor anyone else for two reasons. He had his studies in school, and the second year was harder than the first. Plus, he was tired of working for what paid next to nothing (miserable Mexican wages). So, he just wanted to rest from work in general.

The next day, Roland took Rigo to Monterrey with him, and they did various errands, including visiting the Macroplaza and Soriana. They also went over to Santa Catarina, a suburb on the south side of Monterrey, and they looked up Jaime's sister and brother-in-law, Cecilio. They had four children, the oldest one being Francisco, who Roland already knew. Francisco's younger brother was Chilín. Rigo was glad to meet them, and as it turned out, Roland enjoyed the day very much. Rigo was in good spirits, as well. Cecilio and his wife made plans for Roland to come for them the next day, and they would go straight to the ranch north of Matehuala.

Roland took Rigo back home to Bustamante. He was feeling better all the time. Their friendship was coming back to life again, and that was good. Plus, he was looking forward to visiting with Jaime's family in Matehuala.

The next morning, Roland loaded his truck, and he thanked Rigo and his family. They all wished him well and also a safe journey, and they told him to be careful.

On the way out of town, Roland went to the Quevalos to buy a Rosca de Reyes since tomorrow would be January 6. He paid the N$40 for it and drove south to Santa Catarina, arriving there in the early afternoon.

Cecilio and his family were ready, and they put their bags into the back of Roland's truck, and several of them, his wife and younger children, rode in the back under the camper top. Around three hours later, 25 kilometers north of Matehuala, they turned off the dangerous 2-lane Highway 57, and Roland drove them along a rough gravel lane for 15 kilometers to reach the "rancho" which was actually a small town by the name of Rancho San Miguel. Part of the road to get there was quite treacherous, and there was one ascent that was extra bumpy with annoyingly large rocks. Roland took life into his own hands as he drove up it. He had to ride the clutch a little bit, but his truck handled it fine. How any car could get through that section, Roland would never understand, but they did.

They pulled up to the adobe ranch house, and Jaime's parents greeted Roland, Cecilio and his family. Jaime was away further south in San Luis Potosí with his wife's family and would be arriving later tonight. His younger brother Margarito was there, and he was also glad to see Roland.

The adobe house was situated on the lower end of the town, and the yards throughout the "rancho" were just dirt. The terrain was desert like, and there were plenty of large Nopal trees, Palma Reale (Yucca) trees, Cactus shrubs such as the Coyonoxtle, and other plants, as well. This was also part of the Mexican central highlands, and the altitude here was 5,600 feet, (around 1,700 meters). Jaime's family had plenty of goats running around, and they also had some pigs. There was electricity supplied to the town, but there was no water supply and therefore no running water. The town had a central well, called a *presa*, and people would draw water up in buckets. Green algae grew in the water! Also there was a large pond with water for the animals to drink from. Roland had brought his own jugs of water and he would be buying purified water from Matehuala.

Jaime's mother had supper ready for everyone, and they entered the kitchen to eat tortillas with rice and beans. Roland shared his Rosca de Reyes with everyone. It was a real treat for them. That Rosca de Reyes had 4 monos in it! Everyone had the best time laughing as they blamed the finders of those monos and told them they would have to give a fiesta sometime in the next year. Plus, Roland told them stories from Bustamante and what he had done during his various stays there. They listened with interest, and they reacted with surprise at some of what Roland said.

That evening, there was a visitation ceremony for a señor, a man in his 60's who had died suddenly. Roland went with Margarito, Cecilio, Chilín, and other cousins whose names were Omar, Enrique, and Ramiro. They one by one entered the small room where the black wooden casket was sitting on a table in the middle. There were around 10 women dressed in black. They were gathered around the edge of the room, and they were crying and sobbing over the death of their loved one. Roland briefly looked at the man inside the casket. He had on a collared shirt, no tie, and no suit. Roland didn't feel right in that room, and he promptly exited. Margarito and Chilín asked Roland what was the matter, and he commented that something scared him in there. Plus, he felt really uneasy for the excessive grieving by those 10 or more women.

Roland visited with Margarito and Chilín. They were teenagers and were easy to talk to, and Roland was quickly becoming friends with them. Strangely enough, they seemed familiar to him from the first moment he saw them, not so much as Leonardo, but there was something there.

Later that night Jaime arrived in his white Chevrolet pickup truck. He walked inside the house and greeted Roland, and he told him he was glad he had come to visit his family. Roland thanked him for his having invited him. Roland and Jaime went outside, even though it was dark, and he looked at Jaime's truck. Jaime told Roland that the running boards had just been knocked off along that extra bumpy, treacherous section of road coming into the ranch. He took the plastic running boards out of his truck bed and placed them on top of the roof out of the way so the goats wouldn't be able to reach them and gnaw on them.

It was a cold night and frosted. Margarito and Chilín worked with the goats the next morning, rounding them up and feeding them. This was a daily chore that members of the family took turns doing. There were several horses to be branded, as well. Jaime's father and other companions rounded up several of them, got a big fire going, and heated up their branding irons to mark their horses. It was a big chore because they had to catch the horses one by one with a lasso.

That afternoon, they had the funeral for the man who died. All the cars and trucks drove up the hill along the dirt lane leaving the town rancho. Lo and behold, there was another town on the hilltop with streets and plenty of houses! It was also a "rancho," and while they had electricity, there was no phone service nor running water.

The cemetery was on the other end of town, and when they reached the cemetery, Roland began to feel apprehensive. He didn't want to attend the funeral. To him the whole thing was too symbolic, and he felt like he was being led to his own death. He told Jaime and the rest of them that he was going to return to their house on foot, and with all due respect, he was not going to attend the funeral, because he felt afraid. It took Roland an hour to walk back through this upper ranch town, down the hill, and back to the house.

While no one was in town, Roland used two of his water jugs and took a bath. He could not find a bath house on the premises, and of course there was no running water. So, he hid behind some Nopal shrubs and took his bath there.

Later that afternoon, Margarito, Chilín and Omar wanted to go to Matehuala. They had another house there where they ran a billiard room. Roland drove them out of the rancho along the rough gravel road and back to the national highway. He turned left and drove the 25 kilometers to the town of Matehuala. It was around the same size as Sabinas Hidalgo. Margarito gave Roland directions, and they arrived at their house.

That evening, Roland drove them over to the carnival that was taking place. There were plenty of rides including a mini roller coaster. There were plenty of flea market stalls selling all kinds of items. There were events taking place, including cock fights. Roland, Margarito, Chilín and Omar took different rides and walked all around the carnival for several hours.

At 11 PM, Roland said he was going back to the house to sleep for the night. Margarito gave him the house key and said they would arrive later in the night. Roland returned to the house.

At 4:20 AM, the other three arrived and knocked on the door. A friend had brought them home. Roland got up, let them in, and went back to sleep.

They got up late. In the early afternoon, the four of them went to the town center and looked around. They visited several markets and a grocery store called Chalita. Then they went to several salvage yards where Roland found a replacement glove compartment door for his truck.

Later in the afternoon, Roland washed clothes with their EASY brand washing machine. The separate gyrator that spun dry the clothing didn't work, and Roland had to manually wring out the clothes before hanging them up on the line.

This house, although it served people who came and played billiards next door, had no kitchen sink, and the bathroom was an outhouse in the very back corner of the yard with what used to be a functional flushing toilet. It was eternally stopped up, and there were three or four extra failed toilets stacked up to the left! To add to the difficulty, they had an old mangy dog who jumped up and down all over Roland with excitement every time he walked back there. Also, there was no shower.

Some workers were adding on to the house, that is, an upstairs which was finally going to include the above items they had always been missing. Thanks to Jaime and his brothers working in the United States, they had the money to fix up the house.

Jaime and his brothers and sisters were actually legal in the United States. Their parents thought ahead and crossed the Rio Grande River every time Jaime's mother was about to give birth so that their children would be born in the United States. As a result, Jaime and his siblings were legal U.S. citizens. Roland found out that it was a common practice for Mexican mothers to cross the border right before giving birth so their children would have U.S. priviledges and the right to exist in the United States of America.

That night, they went to the carnival again. Roland went back to the house, and the others, who had enjoyed seeing more cock fights, arrived again around 4 AM.

The next day, they went to the town center and looked around the central flea market. They ate lunch, returned to the house, and Roland drove them back to their ranch north of Matehuala.

Roland spent several more days with them on the ranch. People had returned back to their normal lives after the death of one of their long time residents and the funeral the other day.

Jaime had gone back to San Luis Potosí, and Roland spent time with Margarito, Chilín, and Omar. They watched some novelas on TV one evening. During Roland's stay, he met more cousins of theirs.

He also took a walk around the countryside, looking at the desert flora and plants. He took some pictures, as well. Throughout the highlands in this area, there were various groves of the big Yucca trees (Palma Real trees), and there were other groves of the large Nopal trees and shrubs.

The last morning on the ranch, Roland woke up with stomach pain, even though he had brought all his own water. It was so hard to stay well in Mexico, it seemed. With a Treda tablet, he soon felt a lot better.

In the late morning, Roland packed his truck, and he thanked Jaime's family for receiving him so well. They said he was certainly welcome back anytime. That was a kind comment, and Roland appreciated it.

Cecilio, his wife, and family were returning by bus from San Luis Potosí, and they made arrangements to meet Roland at the highway intersection at 12 noon. Roland drove his truck the 15 kilometers out the gravel lane and found them all waiting under a Mesquite tree. They got into the back of Roland's truck again, and Cecilio got in the cab with Roland, and he drove them back to Santa Catarina.

By 4 PM, they were home, and Roland stayed with them for two nights. They watched a Mexican movie on TV that night.

Francisco came in at 1:30 AM. He had been visiting with friends.

It was the morning of January 12. Roland and Francisco went to the foot of Cerro de las Mitras. For the whole day, they ascended and descended that mountain. It was Francisco's first time ever to go up it. Roland had climbed it a long time ago, back when he had stayed with the Velazco family in Monterrey.

The ascent followed the left ridge, was tedious, and took 3½ hours. It was steep but well marked along the limestone rocks. There was plenty of Zotól, Lechuguilla, and Nopal plants to have to negotiate, along with other plants and shrubs. Higher up the mountain, they started to see Oak trees and other hardwoods, including a small grove of rare Hophornbeam trees at the base of a beautiful cliff.

They arrived at the main ridge, now affording them a view of Santa Catarina to the south. Along this ridge grew mountain Fan Palms, Lechuguilla, Zotól, Espadín, Nopal and other shrubs. There was no forest as such. Between the limestone rocks were several Siempre Viva and Flor de Peña plants, and there were the green blades of Mexican Rain Lilies (*Zephyranthes drummondii*). None were in bloom since it was January.

They turned right, and made a more gentle ascent for another kilometer to arrive at the peak, called Pico Apache, elevation 5,900 feet, according to the altimeter Roland brought with him. There were two more peaks beyond, and they were inaccessible without technical climbing gear because there were deep chasms between each one of them. At the peak, there was a log book in a small metal box on top, and Roland and Francisco signed it.

The views were great, and other mountains like Cerro de la Silla (Saddle Mountain) were visible across the city. The general rumble, hustle and bustle of the city of Monterrey could be heard constantly for the whole day. Even though some 5 million people lived in Monterrey and its suburbs, there were absolutely no other hikers who ascended this mountain today. Granted there were a few university students hiking the trail along the mountain's lower reaches, but almost no one ever went any higher.

After eating some lunch and appreciating the mountainous scenery, Roland and Francisco began the long descent. It was 5:30 PM when they reached the bottom. They entered the colonia (subdivision) where Roland had parked his truck, and they returned to Francisco's home in Santa Catarina.

It had been a great day. They were both somewhat tired and weary, but they had really enjoyed it. Roland had taken several pictures, and he would later get copies for Francisco.

The next morning was January 13. They got up at 8 AM, and later in the day, Cecilio and Francisco accompanied Roland to the flea markets in central Monterrey. Roland bought some Levi's jeans and some other items. They also went to the Macroplaza.

In the later afternoon, Roland thanked them for their kind hospitality, and he thanked Francisco for going up Cerro de las Mitras with him. They were glad to have Roland stay with them, and they told him thanks for gracing them with his visit. That was a very kind comment.

They said goodbye, and Roland drove back to Bustamante. He didn't go through the center of Monterrey to leave. Instead, he went around the west side of Cerro de las Mitras, turning right on Highway 40, and later turning left on the highway to Anahuac. He reached Bustamante by 6 PM.

The Zacatóns were at home. Lavinia greeted Roland in a friendly manner. She and Rigo were applying cement to the bathroom walls to keep out mice and roaches. They were also stapling cardboard and plastic over the windows to keep out the cold air of winter. Roland helped them, and Lavinia soon realized that Roland knew what he was doing with handling cement.

Rigo was in a bad mood. Roland asked Rigo to greet him, and he wouldn't do it. Rigo responded by asking the equivalent of, *What for?* Roland decided to make a game out of it. He had brought along a Giant Sequoia cone from California. So, he took it out of his belongings and gave it to Rigo, placing it in his hand. Rigo immediately scoffed at Roland, and he placed it on the shelf with his stereo. A few minutes later, Rigo asked Roland if he would buy his windup watch. Roland extended his hand. Still no handshake from Rigo. Roland walked out of the house, commenting to the others that Rigo wouldn't greet him!

An hour later, he returned from visiting with some other friends. He ignored Rigo this time. Lavinia fed them supper. A few minutes later, Rigo came to Roland and asked him for a second time if he would buy his watch. Roland looked at Rigo, smiled and extended his hand. Rigo knew the requirement, and he finally shook hands with him. With that done, Roland told Rigo he would consider buying it. Roland would have told him a definite yes, but the fact remained that Rigo had not yet apologized for how rude he had been over the phone, back on September 26.

Later that night when Roland was getting ready to go to bed, he was at the bathroom sink cleaning his contact lenses. Rigo barged right in and began to use the sink, and he suddenly said, "Quítate," telling Roland to get away!

"¡No, hombre! Tú vas a esperar tu torno," Roland firmly said to Rigo, telling him he refused to get away from the sink and that he would have to wait his turn!

Rigo didn't like that at all, and he stated that he was in his house and had the right to use the bathroom whenever he wanted to!

Roland told Rigo to have some respect for his guests, and he did *not* get away from the sink! He stood right there and finished cleaning his contact lenses. Rigo stayed there also and washed his face simultaneously, making more ugly and scathing remarks to make Roland feel bad.

"¡Cállate!" Roland said to Rigo, telling him to shut his mouth!

"¡Cállame!" Rigo angrily responded, daring Roland to shut him up! He repeated his dare ten times!

Roland didn't push any further. He didn't want to get into a knock-down drag-out fight with him. Rigo walked into the front room and went to bed.

Roland entered the front room and told Rigo off, telling him how rude that was of him to barge into the bathroom on his guests! He told him he's not a friend and to forget about selling him that watch. How would he like Roland to barge in on *him* like that sometime?

Rigo angrily made some complaints about Roland to his mother Lavinia, and she defended her son, telling Roland that Rigo was right.

Roland told her no way was her son right! Rigo was very bad the way he barged in on Roland. He told her that Rigo obviously didn't want his friendship and that he hadn't wanted him in the house since September.

Lavinia answered by telling Roland to behave himself well, and she said she didn't want him arguing with her son.

Roland told her to tell her *son* to behave himself well. After all, Roland wasn't the one picking fights. He offered to take his things and leave the house right now, if she wanted.

"No, acuéstate," Lavinia calmly said, asking Roland to go to sleep. She didn't want him to up and leave.

Roland went to bed, but he didn't sleep well. He couldn't, after such rude inhospitality!

Some demon was on the rampage somewhere! At least Roland had stood up to Rigo and defended himself and his rights as a guest! Of course, Rigo thought Roland had no rights. It was so obvious that Rigo had done what he did as a tactic to make Roland leave. By the way, it happened to be Isalia's birthday. She was 65 today.

The next morning, Lavinia approached Roland and told him that when her son wanted to use the bathroom that he would have to step aside and let him enter. Roland told her he didn't think so! Her son was going to have to wait his turn, like everybody else in the world! Roland never needed more than just a few minutes in the bathroom, anyway, and he didn't barge in on anybody. He expected the same respect from them!

Then Lavinia got after Roland for leaving the light on in the back room while he entered the bathroom, resulting in the light bulb being on for a few extra minutes per day. She explained that it cost them extra electricity. Roland explained that the bulk of their electric bill was the refrigerator, and after that, the TV and stereo.

Why in the world was Lavinia so bothered over the usage of the light bulb? That was plum inhospitable! So, while no one was looking, Roland took a piece of tape and pasted two N$1 coins to the electrical cord the light bulb was hanging from. There! That would be more than enough to cover the extra electrical cost. Plus, that would put Lavinia in her place when she would later discover the coins!

Later that morning, Roland took Rigo and Angelo over to Sabinas Hidalgo. They did some errands. Rigo behaved himself reasonably well.

Before returning to Bustamante, Roland stated to Rigo that if he wanted to go on being friends, he would have to apologize for his rudeness by phone on September 26, and for last night! He was giving Rigo the chance to make up and forgive those incidents.

Rigo said, "Te pido disculpas," asking Roland's forgiveness.

They shook hands, and then Roland asked Rigo to respect him as a friend and guest. He assured Roland he would not barge in on him anymore, that he would wait his turn. Roland asked him if he could feel welcome and at ease in the house, and Rigo said yes.

Thank you Rigo! Miracle! Amazing!

Roland drove them back to Bustamante, delivering Angelo to his home.

That afternoon, Lavinia showed Roland some broken dresser drawers that needed repair. Roland got the message, and since he was a guest in their house, he offered to take the drawers over to Felipe's carpentry to have them repaired by Pedro. Lavinia was happy with Roland's offer, and he took them over there in his truck.

At the same time, he asked Pedro to make him a wooden rocking chair out of Oak and Poplar wood. He said he would do the work for N$300. Roland said that would be fine.

Later that afternoon, Roland went to Fernando's house and visited for a while.

Then he went over to Elisa's house. She had some interesting books on trees and plants of Mexico. She hadn't showed Roland her books before, and he was now impressed. He could tell she was very intelligent, indeed. Roland looked at her tree books with amazement. One was especially interesting, and he asked her if he could get a Xerox copy of the entire book. She said that would be fine, but first she would see if she could find another copy of the book at used bookstores in Monterrey. They visited for a while, and then Roland returned to Rigo's house.

He slept more peacefully that night.

Roland had a strong urge to begin his novel about an American in Mexico. He went over and talked to Jesús Lucio about the possibilities of staying at his ranch house in the desert valley, so he could have the peace and quiet necessary to write. After all, things were always too hectic in town. There were too many distractions to be able to write, such as the noise of passing vehicles, dogs, chickens, roosters, and stereos playing all over the place, especially the one that almost always played in Rigo's house.

Lucio said that would be fine for him to stay at his ranch house, and he and his son Gerardo kindly took Roland with them to the other side of the mountains. Roland rode with them in his Chevrolet pickup truck. As Lucio backed out of the driveway, the truck sounded different. Roland looked at the steering wheel and saw that the column lever for the automatic was gone. There was a big stick on the floor!

"¡Ohh! ¿Lo cambiaste a estandard?" Roland commented, asking Lucio if he had changed it to standard.

He answered yes. The automatic transmission had failed him, and he installed a standard shift with a granny low first gear. Plus, he mentioned that he had welded a chain under the front of the driveshaft so that in case the driveshaft were to break loose, it would be caught by the chain and therefore not bury itself into the ground like a huge nail. That was good thinking.

Lucio drove Roland through the canyon, passing by the Ojo del Agua, and continued 12 more kilometers along the one-lane dirt roads to reach his ranch. He had a small concrete block building and several sheds where he tended to and fed around 80 cattle and a few donkeys.

The house was built around 1983 by Lucio and his workers, soon after he had acquired the land on this side of the mountains. It was situated in a small yard that was surrounded by a good woven wire fence, complete with Ocotiyo stakes. Lucio showed Roland the features of the house. There was a 4-burner stove that ran off of butane gas, and there was even a butane gas refrigerator, which cooled with liquid ammonia instead of freon. The house had two doors and two windows, and it even had a good fireplace. There was a back porch, as well. There was no electricity. The end of the line was at the Ojo del Agua, 12 kilometers away. There was no telephone service, nor running water.

Without electricity, there would be no lights, but Roland had flashlights. In addition to that, Lucio had battery powered electric lights, and he had an old lamp that used special lamp oil, similar to kerosene. Lucio showed Roland his concrete water tank, covered by several wooden boards nailed together. It held around 250 gallons of water. Plus, he had a windmill, called a *papalote*, which pulled water out of a well that was 27 meters deep. That was what supplied water to the cattle via an underground water line that fed several concrete tubs over by the sheds, when it was windy enough. On other days, Lucio brought water in large 55 gallon plastic drums, similar to oil drums.

There was no bathroom, but if Roland wished, he could bring his post hole digger and create a pit privy. That he would definitely do. He would dig a hole one meter deep, place 4 concrete blocks around it, and place a wooden pallet over that. The privy would be around 100 meters away from the house and surrounded by Mesquite shrubs.

Despite the lack of normal luxuries that one would normally take for granted, Lucio had this house well furnished. He had two beds, one inside the house, and the other one outside under the back porch. There were two kitchen cabinets and a counter. He also had a white metal table that was good and sturdy. It was in the middle of the room and would also serve as the kitchen table to fix and eat meals.

Roland would bring food with him to last for a week and plenty of drinking water, as well. He thanked Lucio very much and would plan to come over in a few days and begin staying.

Lucio assured Roland there was no danger. No one ever came to steal. No one ever came to shoot anybody. Dangerous events like that didn't take place in the countryside of northern Mexico. The place was safe, no worries at all. Roland was glad to be assured on that.

He returned with Lucio and his son to Bustamante after they finished feeding the cattle.

The next day, Roland went into the mountains to do maintenance on the trail. It was somewhat overgrown, and Roland did a good job in civilizing it again. He returned to Bustamante by late afternoon.

Rigo had gone to Sabinas Hidalgo for the day to take exams at the Prepa. He didn't return till evening.

While Roland was at the Zacatón's house that late afternoon, Alejandro was out in the backyard very worried about something. He was pondering and pondering. Roland didn't know until later what it was about. Alejandro had a major decision to make about where he was going to take his next job. He was contemplating driving cargo vehicles as a courier or taking a factory job at the Tokyo car parts factory north of Sabinas Hidalgo.

That evening after eating supper, Roland bicycled to the town plaza to visit with friends. Julian and Fernando were there, and Roland was quite surprised to see Fernando drunk! He was in a daze as he shook hands with Roland, and then he hopped along to join Rigo and others who had just arrived from Sabinas Hidalgo.

Instead of sleeping on the bed in the Zacatón's back room, Roland took his tent and pitched it in the backyard, and he had a good night's sleep. Dogs could be heard barking all over town, and roosters called out from 3 AM onward, but earplugs solved that problem.

The next morning was January 17. Rigo, Angelo and Christian wanted to go to Sabinas Hidalgo. Roland took them in his truck, and they did several errands.

At mid day, Roland treated Rigo, Angelo and Christian to lunch at the Centro Comercial San José restaurant. Quite to Roland's dismay, Angelo and Christian took the liberty of ordering beer. In fact, they ordered two each.

While leaving Sabinas Hidalgo, they stopped by the Turbina and Ojo del Agua.

Later that afternoon, they returned to Bustamante. On the way, they stopped by Angelo's aunt's house in Villaldama. Nancy was now married and living with her husband. She used to live in Sabinas Hidalgo. Upon arriving, they discovered that her husband was partying with a bunch of his buddies. He was a party animal, as Roland would later realize, and he drank a lot. He insisted to everyone to take a beer. Roland flatly refused. Rigo reluctantly accepted one, but Angelo and Christian were both delighted, enchanted actually, and they took two beers each!

More than that, Roland felt bothered by Rigo's drinking a beer. He knew that Angelo and Christian were drinkers, but he was surprised at Rigo because only five months ago, he had told Roland that he didn't drink nor smoke nor did he smell of beer. Well, five months is a long time for a 15 year old, and things can change.

Then Angelo and Christian accepted cigarettes and began to smoke them! What next?

Roland urged them to leave this party. He wanted to return to Bustamante, and he told them he didn't bring them along to drink and smoke. After several minutes of urging, Roland got the three of them into his truck, and he drove them away. He told them they had changed, that they were taking the habits of drinking and smoking, and if that's the way they were going to act, then he wasn't going to take them around with him anymore.

They stopped by the town plaza in Villaldama and visited Alberto, who still had his job of cooking and serving chicken. Roland bought one to take back to Alejandro and Lavinia. Alberto told him that once he returned from his trip to Tennessee last August, they had given him his job back, cooking chicken. Also Alberto mentioned that he developed a terrible poison ivy rash, had to see the doctor, and take medicine to cure it! Roland had told him to use a long sleeve shirt when he did all that fence row clearing for three days, but he wouldn't do it.

They chatted about things for a while, and then Roland drove them back to Bustamante.

Roland went to visit different friends, including Nacho and Chela Orolizo. He looked for Beto Enriquez but couldn't find him. In fact, he had yet to see him since he had arrived this trip. Roland learned that Beto was courting Clarisa. In fact, he had asked her hand in marriage, and they were scheduled to get married next month.

Roland returned to Rigo's house and had supper. Quite to Roland's surprise, Rigo was talking to his mother Lavinia about having had one beer. In fact, he told her voluntarily and amended his previous convictions of not drinking to state that he does drink, but only a little bit. Somehow, his mother was approving of it. At least he didn't drink a lot, but then how long would that last? Roland expressed his concern to Rigo that for teenagers, it was really easy for them to increase their amount of drinking, and if they're not very careful, they can become borachos (alcoholics). Roland also asked Rigo if he wanted to become like his father, Alejandro, and he said he didn't. That was good to hear.

They talked about other subjects. Rigo showed Roland his payment receipts for going to the Prepa each year. There were subscription payments, bus fares, and books. All of it added up to around US $1,000 per year to go to school. Rigo's brothers, Eduardo and Raul, were helping by sending money to him from time to time.

Lavinia and Rigo talked about Eduardo and his wife Millana, and how Millana had taken such a mysterious dislike to Roland. Lavinia told Roland that Eduardo and Millana go to church regularly and that they take Raul with them. Roland looked at Lavina with surprise, and he was about to make some comments, but Rigo said them for him.

"¿Por qué va a la iglesia? No ama a la gente. No perdona a nadie. No sabe como tolerar. ¿Es lo que pensaste, verdad?" and Rigo looked at Roland.

Translated to English: "Why does she go to church? She doesn't love people. She doesn't forgive anyone. She doesn't know how to tolerate. That's what you thought, right?" and Rigo looked at Roland as he said the last part.

"Sí, exactamente," said Roland, verifying that's exactly what he thought.

"Leí tu mente," said Rigo, telling Roland he read his mind.

How did Rigo do that? Roland thought. He was quite surprised at Rigo's ability to sense the truth. Somehow Rigo seemed more atuned than usual this evening. With what Rigo said about Millana, Roland knew that Rigo realized the trueness of character in her, and that she wasn't so goody two shoes as people might think.

Lavinia went on to mention that she knows her daughter-in-law Millana very well, and that she doesn't understand reasons, like why Roland was a friend to the Zacatón family, and why he helped them move last September. Millana was basically an unreasonable woman who had unnecessary dislike for Roland.

They continued talking. Roland was surprised at how talkative Rigo was. In fact, he was more reasonable than usual. Usually he would just turn on the TV and not talk to others, but this evening was different. Rigo had his intelligence when he wanted to.

Rigo told Roland it was a great idea that he was writing a novel of his adventures in Mexico. He could include the time Beto and Rigo went up in the mountains with Roland. Rigo said a novel about Mexico would sell very well, considering the number of Mexicans living in the United States. Roland told Rigo he was about to start it and that Raul had suggested it also.

Rigo went out with his friends for the evening and came in later that night.

Roland prepared his things to go to the ranch the next day. He visited with Lavinia and her daughters while she kneaded dough to make tortillas. Norma was quickly growing up, becoming more attractive all the time. She was of happy spirits and enjoyed Roland's company. Her younger sister Irma always enjoyed Roland and his staying with them.

Later on, Roland and Rigo talked some more about drinking and smoking. Rigo explained that he has no pleasure in drinking, and would only drink one beer on occasion to accompany the others, his friends who invite him to drink, but he wouldn't drink more than that. He also added that what he doesn't like is cigarettes, and he never smokes. Roland saw Rigo as a good and reasonable fellow after all, nearly as straight as his cousins, David and John, back in Tennessee. It remained to be seen if Rigo would stay true to his revised convictions.

The reason it remained to be seen was that Rigo had suggested something to Roland that made him wonder. What Rigo said to Roland was that if he drank, he would have more friends. In other words, he suggested that Roland drink, so he would have more friends. No, nothing doing! Roland didn't drink at all, and he would still have friends, and those who would be his friends would be more genuine ones indeed!

Roland also decided to go ahead and buy Rigo's watch, since he needed the money to help pay for school. Roland told him not to run him off and never to tell him he wasn't welcome in the house. Rigo assured Roland he was welcome to stay.

The next morning, Roland drove out of Bustamante toward the canyon and Ojo del Aqua to stay at Lucio's ranch. He took his typewriter that he bought (recollected from Rigo) so he could write his Mexico novel, plus do some more artwork. 12 kilometers beyond and southwest of the Ojo del Aqua, he arrived at the ranch, where he opened the flexible fence/gate and backed his truck into the yard by the concrete block house.

He was tired. Staying at Rigo's house had been a bit of a roller coaster, and now he could enjoy some peace and quiet and get some serious work done on writing his Mexico novel. After taking his things inside the house, he placed his sleeping bag on the bed under the back porch, and he took a nap. He wrote out some notes and ideas that occurred to him and began to organize the first chapter of the novel.

Later in the afternoon, he took a walk along the main gravel lane, which they called, "La Brecha." The views of the desert valley and surrounding mountains in the distance were spectacular, especially during sunset. A few kilometers to the east stood the towering mountains between him and Bustamante, its main feature being the reverse image view of the Lion's Head Mountain.

Most of the terrain consisted of shrubs and small trees, including many varieties of Mesquite and Acacia, Gobernadora shrubs, Nopal, Coyonoxtle, Ocotiyo, Anacahuita and

Desert Willow trees. Of course, there were the Yucca trees called Palma Real, and there were lots of Lechuguilla and Maguey plants.

At times, the wind would blow, sometimes fiercely, and other days were quiet and sunny. Coyotes occasionally called out their howls at night, and at times, Roland could hear a little bit of the activity from the next ranch over, which was one kilometer away.

At night, the stars were so clear. They were easier to see here than back in Tennessee. The skies were usually clear and blue, but there were days when the south winds blew, and white smog would drift up from Monterrey, which was 100 kilometers due south of here. Plus, at night, one could see the visible glow in that direction, of the lights of Monterrey and its suburbs.

The next day, Roland rode his bicycle south to Chiquihuitillos, which was around 8 kilometers to the south. He would have taken his truck, but there were parts of the gravel and dirt lanes that were too rough, in other words, impassable. Lucio's truck could make it because it sat up higher and had 8-ply tires. Plus, it had a granny low first.

The ranch owner for Chiquihuitillos was there, and he had Roland sign the guest book and pay N$5. When he went to put his name and date in the guest register, he was quite surprised to see that Isalia and Luke and many of the Quevalos, including Pancho, had been here only yesterday! Thank goodness, Roland hadn't come to Chiquihuitillos a day earlier, or he would have encountered them!

Roland had no wish to see Isalia and Luke, and so far he had not seen them since his arrival December 31. He didn't want any further problems with them, nor did they with Roland.

After signing the guest book and paying, Roland climbed up to the mesa cliff walls and observed the paintings, studying their features to see if any more ideas would occur to him for his artwork and future paintings. He spent several hours there and ate his lunch he brought with him. He visited all three sections. Plus, he had a look on top of the double mesa.

After seeing Chiquihuitillos, Roland talked to the rancher about the ancient paintings and what they might represent.

Then the rancher said that Isalia, Pancho, and the Quevalos talked to him for quite a while yesterday. Isalia had talked as if she was a very important woman, *chosen by God* to help the poor in Bustamante, in other words, a woman of supreme first class status. She had a sense of pride about her, and her favorite cousin Pancho was right by her side, adding his carefully savoured comments. The rancher, who was in his right mind, went on to say that all people are created equal, and while she has the right to help people in need, there are no set guidelines for who are first or second class citizens!

After all, the sun rises for everyone. Amen.

Later in the afternoon, Roland returned on his bicycle to Lucio's ranch where he stayed several more days.

Lucio and his son Gerardo would come each morning and feed the cattle, among other chores. Meanwhile, Roland made good progress on his novel.

One of the afternoons, Roland walked over to the neighboring ranch to introduce himself and see who they were. They were the children and grandchildren of Romulo Uvalle of Bustamante. Word was that he had special powers for curing people, and every morning, people with strange illnesses would arrive at his house in town, so they could be cured.

New Doors Open, New Friends

Some even came from out of state, as far away as Chihuahua. On occasion, Romulo himself would drive to the ranch in his old red Ford truck, carrying hay or corn stalks for his cattle.

Roland visited with them, and over time he became friends with them. One of the young fellows was named Kena. He was the age of Raul, and he used to know him before he left to go to Texas last year. They usually brought meals with them, which they cooked over a fireplace and grille inside the small, one-room adobe house. Sometimes, they invited Roland over to have lunch with them.

While Lucio only had cattle and a few donkeys, Romulo and his family also had goats. Each day they would come to release them from their fenced in enclosure so they could drink water, and they would feed them grain and hay.

Also, a common practice among the ranches was to collect the prickly succulent leaves of the Nopal Cactus, growing in the scrublands, load the pickup truck with them, and feed them to the cattle. However, there was a process that had to be followed so they would be edible. After picking them, they would unload the cargo of Nopal and let it sit in a fenced in area for a day or two, after which they would burn the needles off with a hefty flame thrower apparatus connected to a standing butane gas tank, just like the tanks used for the stoves. Then they would take a machete and, one by one, chop all the leaves into slivers while holding each leaf with the left hand. Care had to be taken to be accurate because a slight error would mean a serious cut to the left thumb and forefinger. Some of the ranchers used gloves for protection, but not all.

Such was the rural ranch life. At least it was more peaceful and quiet than in town. Roland wondered why he hadn't come on over and stayed here earlier. He was grateful to Lucio for letting him stay here.

Roland spent several days at the ranch. One morning he woke up with an annoying stomach ache that wouldn't go away. It was one of those bad stomach aches that occur only in Mexico. Roland had had them before, but this time he decided to go to the doctor. It was time to go back to town anyway and restock for another stay. The awful abdominal pains made it hard for Roland to load his truck, but he managed it okay.

He closed up the doors to the ranch house, closed the windows, turned off the gas to the stove, and drove back to town. On the way, he had to pull the truck over and throw up.

He drove straight to the doctor's office, the Centro Salud, paid the N$10 consultation fee, and the doctor prescribed him some Buscapina and Eritromicina. By night time, Roland would feel better. The Centro Salud sold him the medicine for less than N$100, and when they were out of stock, they sent people to the pharmacy in town.

Roland arrived at the Zacatón's house. Rigo and a friend of his were there, and they were painting a new Pine and plywood wardrobe with brown wood stain. Roland asked Rigo where they got that from, and he answered that Isalia and Luke had made and given it to them.

Really?! Roland was in disbelief. So, Rigo indicated to Roland to look at the back of the wardrobe. There inscribed were the words: *Para Lavinia de Zacatón y familia. Cariñosamente, Luke e Isalia Wiggins, 21 de enero, 1999.*

"Well, I will say!" Roland commented to himself. This, Roland had to admit was a nice gift, for Lavinia's being Isalia's maid. Roland was glad to know that Isalia and Luke were kind enough to have done that. If Isalia liked someone, she would do anything in the world to help them, like she used to do for Roland.

Rigo and his friend, whose name was Rogelio, continued with their painting and staining. They were playing one of Ramón Ayala's songs on the stereo, and Rigo was whistling the tune in unison.

Rigo asked Roland how things had gone at Lucio's ranch, and he answered that he got a lot done, including seeing Chiquihuitillos. Apart from being sick earlier today, things went fine. Rigo was glad to hear that, and he expressed interest in seeing Chiquihuitillos before Roland goes home to Tennessee.

Lavinia arrived home with Norma and Irma, and they greeted Roland, asking him how his ranch stay went. He answered that it went fine, and he expressed his surprise at the wardrobe.

Lavina was proud of it and appreciated it very much. The wardrobe stood nearly 6 feet tall, was 5 feet wide, and 2 feet deep. Though rustic and simple in appearance, it served its purpose very well and was very sturdy. Isalia and Luke had noticed that the Zacatón's old particle board wardrobe was falling apart, and they had therefore built them a new one. Lavinia had taken the pieces of the old wardrobe out into the backyard, piled them into a heap, along with some other garbage and junk, and she lit a match to them.

Roland slept on the bed in the back room that night. Alejandro got in late from the cantina. He was about to take another job.

The next morning, Rigo accompanied Roland over to Sabinas Hidalgo, and they did errands. Roland stocked up with food and supplies for another week at Lucio's ranch.

Once back at Rigo's house, Roland had lunch. Rigo took off with Angelo and other friends for the rest of the day.

Roland went to Pedro and collected the wooden dresser drawers he fixed for Lavinia. Pedro was a good carpenter, and he was making good progress on the sturdy wooden chair Roland had ordered. Roland paid him N$50 for the labor, and he brought them back to Lavinia. She was pleased, and they thanked Roland.

When she later told Isalia, she remarked that that was good. When Roland stayed with people, he needed to pitch in and help.

Lavinia told Roland that Isalia and Luke had begun their house next to the Quevalo's bakery, that is, on Quevalo property. For this winter's stay, they were staying with Lorenzo and his family, and they were paying all their utilities and meals for them, more than enough, in Roland's view. Roland believed in paying his portion, but he didn't want to spoil his hosts by giving too much.

This afternoon, Roland went around town visiting different friends, among them Fabian, Victor, Hector, Pablo, and the Orolizos.

Also that afternoon, someone mentioned to Roland his opinion that Isalia and Luke were convenient to the Quevalos, and that Pancho and other Quevalo members were following them around like pieces of candy, wondering what else they might bring them in the future. The way he said it and the gestures he made gave Roland a good laugh.

They also talked about the fact that Isalia and Luke were building on Quevalo property. There was an old saying: *El que siembra en tierra ajena hasta la semilla pierde.* (He who plants on other people's land loses everything right down to the last seed!) Roland laughed some more, and he knew that if he were Isalia and Luke, he would *never* have built a house on Quevalo property. Who knows? They might get angry one day, run them off, and claim it for themselves.

New Doors Open, New Friends

Roland also went to visit Elisa. She was about to go to Monterrey to search for a spare copy of that book on trees and plants of Mexico. Roland handed her N$100 to pay for it in case she were to find one at a second hand bookshop.

It was Saturday night, and Rigo went to the dance. Roland began a tradition of leaving town for Lucio's ranch right before the dance and wild night activities began. Roland was just finishing loading his truck when Rigo emerged from the house to go to the dance. He walked over to Roland, wished him well, and shook hands with him, Mexican style. Roland was quite surprised, and he wished Rigo a good week, as well. Rigo was a good friend after all.

At 10 PM, Roland arrived at the ranch house and parked by its side and within the fenced in yard. He got a good night's rest.

During the course of the week, Roland made more progress on his novel. Lucio and his son or a different helper would come each morning to feed the cattle and do other chores.

The weather was warm and sunny with slightly chilly mornings, milder weather than back in Tennessee.

Jesús Lucio's son Gerardo was getting married this Saturday, and they invited Roland to come to the wedding ceremony and fiesta/dance following. They handed him a wedding invitation.

On January 28, Roland drove back to Bustamante. He took Rigo and Alberto over to Sabinas Hidalgo to do errands. Roland needed money, so he went to a bank to take out a cash advance on his VISA card. The bank couldn't do it personally. The only way one could take out a cash advance was through an ATM, which Roland had never ever used. He didn't even have a PIN number on his credit card. Roland visited several banks and inquired. None of them could do the transaction personally . . . ATM only. How strange! In the United States, any bank could do that personally, and two years ago, Mexico still could. Why not now? Well, Roland had to call his VISA card company and request an ATM PIN number, which they established for him, effective in 24 hours.

The next day, Roland took Rigo with him to Saltillo, Coahuila for the whole day. They had a good time and visited the flea markets and also visited Sergio and Lilia and their family. They were glad to see them and told Roland it was a pleasure. Roland and Rigo visited the flea markets some more, and they bought some pirated cassette tapes, other gifts, and they found a vendor who was selling windup wrist watches.

Roland succeeded in using an ATM for the first time in his life, and he took out a cash advance.

At 7 PM, they arrived back in Bustamante. Roland gave Rigo N$80 for the day (US $8), a day of 13 hours. Rigo had enjoyed the trip. Lavinia fed them supper, and Rigo went out with his friends for the evening.

Roland went to talk to Elisa. She had not had a chance to go to Monterrey, and she gave Roland back the N$100. However, she said she was going to drive her car there tomorrow, and if Roland wanted to come with her, they could search the stores. Roland agreed to it. They would leave at 8 AM tomorrow.

Elisa's daughter Carinda was going to the Prepa in Monterrey, and her two sons, Carlos and Lalo were living there in Bustamante and going to the secundaria there. They were ages 14 and 12 respectively. Carlos was a somewhat sullen lad, and Lalo was more enthusiastic and friendly. He emerged into the front room where Roland and Elisa were visiting and asked him various questions. Lalo was interested in Roland's way of life and his repeated visits to Bustamante. Elisa enjoyed knowing Roland, and she looked forward to the day tomorrow.

Roland went to the plaza and talked with various friends there. Rigo and Rogelio were talking to some others, including Fernando. At it turned out, Rogelio was working for the Quevalos, and Isalia and Luke were employing him to help them build their new house by the Quevalo's bakery. Rogelio mentioned that Isalia was very pragmatic at times, the way she would bark out orders like a commanding chief. After all, Isalia was a very important woman of first class rank, and she was helping out the poor with her various *missions*.

Roland talked with Rogelio about Isalia. Since Roland used to work for Isalia back in Tennessee, planting bulbs, doing landscaping, building rock walls, the deck, and the house addition, he and Rogelio had something in common. Roland decided to mimic some of Isalia's pragmatic ways, and he said the Spanish equivalent of, "Forget it! Just build them straight!" among other comments that Isalia had said back in Tennessee.

Rogelio and Roland laughed till their sides hurt, and Rigo and Fernando joined in on the laughter, as well.

After the laughter, Rogelio informed Roland that Isalia and Luke had just left this afternoon and were on their way back to Tennessee. Roland looked at Rogelio, questioning him if the good news was really true. He verified it was true.

Roland danced a small jig right there and shouted out several times, "Ya no hay peligro, ya!" meaning there was no longer any danger. Rogelio, Rigo, and Fernando laughed some more.

Roland also visited others in the plaza. He saw Fabian and went to talk to him. A friend of his, whose name was Gazdi, was with him. They got to talking to Roland, and for something Gazdi said about his family coming over from the country of Lebanon, Roland put two and two together.

"¿Eres el hermano de Moises?" Roland said to Gazdi, asking him if he was Moises' brother.

"Sí," he answered yes with surprise, wanting to know how Roland knew that.

Roland answered that he knew Moises back in 1992 and that his family came from Lebanon. Plus he saw the strong resemblance in Gazdi to how he remembered Moises, back when he and Eliud used to play together at the Quevalos.

Roland proceeded to ask about Moises. Gazdi said that his brother was 16 and was at a technical school in Monterrey, training to be a mechanic. Roland somehow hadn't seen him since 1992, and he wanted to see him again. He had good memories of him and his cheerful smile. Gazdi told Roland that Moises was the same height as Roland, which meant that he was grown. Roland asked Gazdi where they lived, and he gave him the address and location in Bustamante. Roland would stop by some weekend and see if he could find Moises at home.

Roland met someone else in the plaza. His name was Rolando, the same name as Roland's. Rolando was 14 and looked very familiar to Roland, but he didn't know why. He had just left Monterrey to come live with his grandparents in Bustamante. Rolando was looking for new friends as a result, and he was now going to school here in Bustamante.

Roland told Fabian and Gazdi that Isalia and Luke had just left town. So Fabian and Gazdi started chanting the phrase, "Ya no hay peligro, ya!" several times. They were hilarious as they started marching around the plaza in a manner as if they were cheerleading.

Roland enjoyed the evening visiting friends in the plaza, and he returned to the Zacatón's house to go to sleep.

The next morning, Roland rode with Elisa in her little brown car. He had asked Rigo to accompany them to Monterrey, but Rigo didn't want to, not with Elisa along. That was strange.

Anyway, Roland rode with Elisa, and he told her that Rigo hadn't wanted to come along. Elisa knew why, and she explained that Mexico portrayed more of a macho image than the United States. It was embarrassing for men to ride in a car with a woman driving. That's why Rigo didn't want to come along . . . culture barrier. Well, Roland had ridden with plenty of lady drivers in his life, and it never crossed his mind that Rigo would be embarrassed to come along, because Elisa was driving.

Roland enjoyed the day with Elisa. They stopped at her mother's house in San Nicolas. Her brother ran a computer parts business upstairs. They went to several second hand bookshops, but they couldn't find the book they were looking for with the trees and shrubs of Mexico. So, Elisa said she would loan Roland the book so he could copy it. They went to the Macroplaza where Roland found and bought an original "15 Exitos" version of the *Mocedades*.

They left Monterrey and arrived back in Bustamante at 4 PM. On the way back, when passing Villaldama, Elisa saw three men needing a lift to Bustamante. They were standing by the bus station. She offered them a lift, but they politely declined. So, Elisa drove on. It was true! In Mexico, men didn't want to ride with lady drivers.

Once back in town, Roland returned to Rigo's house. Angelo was visiting, and they were listening to cassette tapes in the stereo. They asked Roland how his day with Elisa had gone, and he answered that it went fine. Then both Rigo and Angelo made some gestures and *Whoo-wee* comments, implying that Roland and Elisa might have done more than take a normal excursion to Monterrey. Perhaps they had *made out*. Roland laughed off Rigo and Angelo's gestures, telling them he and Elisa didn't do anything like that. Rigo and Angelo soon left the house to do other activities.

Tonight was Gerardo Lucio's wedding. Roland decided he would go to it. It would be at 7 PM at the central church by the plaza, followed by the fiesta at the social center building.

Roland entered the bathroom to take a shower and clean up. He happened to look at the small trash can by the commode, and something caught his attention. He walked over to the trash can with a puzzled look on his face. There was one wadded up piece of trash in the can, and it looked very familiar. Roland retrieved it. It was the wadded up manila mailer, addressed to Rigo, in which he had mailed him some pictures and a letter last spring. Roland unwadded the mailer and checked for anything remaining inside. Quite to his dismay, he found the self-addressed envelope he had sent Rigo, the envelope he was supposed to use so he could send Roland a letter that he was supposed to type out on that Royal 440 manual typewriter, (the typewriter Roland had subsequently bought off him for $50 earlier that month).

With the piece in hand, Roland, in a serious and calm manner went to the kitchen to talk to Lavinia about it. Norma was in the kitchen with her. Roland showed them the mailer, and he extracted the self-addressed envelope. He gestured them a look of: *What's this all about?* They acted clueless, and Roland told them he had just retrieved this from the bathroom trash can, and that it was the only thing in the can.

Lavinia asked Roland, "¿Para qué sirve?" wanting to know what use it still had.

Roland told them the self-addressed envelope was inside the wadded up manila mailer and that the envelope was intended for Rigo to mail Roland a letter, which he had never done.

Lavinia then took the self-addressed envelope from Roland and placed it on the kitchen glass encased cabinet.

Then Norma, in a defiant, mocking manner, stated, "¿Para qué sirve?" repeating her mother's question.

Roland repeated the importance of the self-addressed envelope, and he asked why Rigo hadn't used it to send Roland a letter. Lavinia got on the defensive and crossly asked Roland why he was so obsessed with Rigo's corresponding with him. After all, Rigo knows if he wants to send a letter or not! Well, Roland defended that accusation by saying he was justified to expect a letter from him, if nothing else for the gratefulness he should have had toward Roland for having given him that typewriter in the first place, last year. Was that too much to ask?

Norma repeated the same defiant question of, "¿Para qué sirve?"

That disgusted Roland and made him feel bad, and he scolded Norma by saying, "¡No me insultes, ya!" telling Norma not to insult him. He walked out of the kitchen.

Roland re-entered the bathroom to take a bath. In 20 seconds, Lavinia stormed in hopping mad at Roland, and she began a chewing out, telling Roland he had no right to scold Norma. Lavinia pointed out to Roland that they were doing him a *grand favor* by receiving him into their house, and if he had a problem with anything, the best thing to do would be to stay quiet about it! After all, he was in *their* house.

No, Roland didn't stay quiet about it! He firmly told Lavinia that her daughter had just insulted him, and that he also felt rejected and unwanted, for that wadded up manila mailer being the *only* piece of trash in that can.

"¡Pídame disculpas, una vez en tu vida!" Roland angrily stated, telling Lavinia to apologize to him for once in her life!

Both of them walked out of the bathroom as they kept arguing, and Roland asked Lavinia not to shove in his face about the "grand favor" they were doing by receiving him, and if they wanted him out of the house, he would gladly take his things and leave!

By this time, Lavinia could see that Roland was really upset. She quieted down, and she and Norma stepped out into the backyard to talk in private. Lavinia was between a "rock and a hard place" about the whole thing.

It was a complex issue. For one, Rigo had mixed feelings about wanting Roland in the house. A part of him liked him, but a part of him disliked him, too. However, the root of the complexity was as follows: Last week, though Roland knew nothing of it, when Isalia and Luke had given Lavinia and her family that fine wooden wardrobe, she had asked Lavinia how Roland had been behaving. Lavinia explained that Roland had done pretty well, but that he and Rigo had gotten into it a couple of times. As a result, Isalia asked if Roland had made any advances at Rigo, and Lavinia answered no. Isalia, still remembering her disgusting and inappropriate dreams the year before, in addition to believing Pancho's tall tales, predicted that Roland would make advances at Rigo sooner or later. Isalia also pointed out that Roland had taken several friends of his up in the mountains. Some of them had even camped with him, and most of them were teenagers! What might they have done up there? Perhaps they had "made out" and Roland had paid each of them US $50 to keep quiet. Though Isalia's claims were entirely false, she told Lavinia in such a convincing way as to make Lavinia's arms and hands feel tingling sensations!

Lavinia was quite worried now. So, she decided to consult with Rigo and provoke a problem, make Roland feel rejected, and then he would leave! Lavinia, now believing her son Rigo to be in potential danger from Roland's future "advances," thanked Isalia for her warning and advice. While it was malignant thinking for Isalia to believe dreams were reality, she had no right to request that Lavinia and Rigo provoke a problem.

(Of course, Roland didn't do any making out up in the mountains, nor anywhere else! It didn't even cross his mind to. As for paying them to be quiet, that was a fallacy in itself. Not even $3,000 would have kept a teenager from telling his mother, who would subsequently have gone straight to the police! In short order, Roland would have been serving time in Monterrey's prison facilities. No, Roland wasn't foolish. He respected his friends!)

Anyway, as a result, while Roland and Elisa were gallivanting around in Monterrey for the day, Lavinia took Rigo to one side and explained the "serious" situation. Rigo, not being in 100% trust of Roland anyway, welcomed his mother's advice. They thought and thought about what they could do, and like a light bulb being turned on, Roland's self-addressed envelope entered Rigo's mind. He promptly took it out of the cabinet and still being in the manila mailer, he wadded it up. Then he casually emptied the bathroom trash can and placed the one piece in it. He and his mother would play normal, like nothing was out of the ordinary, and so Roland wouldn't be suspicious. Norma was also at home when Lavinia and Rigo made their plans, and Lavinia had asked her to go along with it, as well. All of this occurred at 3 PM, one hour before Roland returned from Monterrey.

Lavinia and Norma continued talking in the backyard. Lavinia didn't quite have the heart to run Roland off. Plus, if she did so, she would forfeit the amount of money that Roland would give her at the end of his stay, which was only a week away. Also, Roland's friendship was convenient to her. She might have a use for him in the future.

Lavinia and Norma walked back into the house, and they made an effort to make up. Lavinia knew it wasn't going to be easy, and she offered to Roland that they just forget about the incident that just took place here. Roland responded by asking if he could continue to stay, or did they want him out? Lavinia said he could stay. Norma apologized, but Lavinia managed as always, to skirt around it, by not apologizing. But of them extended their hands to make up, and Roland shook hands with them.

Roland, for the third time, entered the bathroom to shower.

Lavinia would have to tell Rigo that Roland was staying a while longer. After all, Rigo wasn't the one who mandated. Alejandro and Lavinia did. As far as Isalia was concerned, Lavinia would tell her that she couldn't quite go through with it.

Roland went to Gerardo's wedding. Many people Roland knew were attending. The pastor (padre) performed the ceremony, pronounced them man and wife, and finished by shouting that it was time for the fiesta!

Roland entered the social center with everyone else. Jesús Lucio was at the entrance greeting everyone. The first event was the wedding meal. It was taking a while before everyone would be served, and Roland was seated with others upstairs at the tables. After 20 minutes went by, Roland could endure no longer. The cigarette smoke was building up, and he therefore had to leave.

It was now 9:30 PM, and Roland returned to the Zacatóns and went to sleep. He was somewhat nervous and still upset for the envelope incident, and he smelled a rat as far as his friendship with the Zacatón family was concerned.

The wedding fiesta ended at 4:30 AM, and the music was loud and clear, penetrating right into the Zacatón's adobe house, which was 3 blocks away from the social center, and keeping Roland awake despite earplugs.

Rigo walked in at 5 AM. Roland asked him in a surprised manner if he had gone to the wedding fiesta. No, he had gone to a dance in Villaldama.

*   *   *

Nuevo Wimbisenho

"We really had them stirred up that time, didn't we?" Druxtrli remarked.

"Not as much as the night Rigo tried to dismiss Roland from the bathroom," Draaktra added, laughing.

"I know," Arfifra agreed. "We enjoyed a good feed off that one. Plus, it was my protectee Isalia's birthday."

"Well done, giving Rigo the idea about that manila mailer," Druxtrli praised Draaktra.

"Throw a few more wrenches in, and we'll finish this friendship off for sure!" Arfifra stated.

"Yeah, but let's prolong it as much as we can," Draaktra requested. "I enjoy the rejection feeds, and Roland keeps coming back for more."

"Draaktra, you can't have your cake and eat it too, you know," Arfifra told him.

"What do you . . .?" he began to respond.

"Now hold your mouth there a moment," Arfifra directed. "I have an announcement. We have a new member. Her name is Arce-fera, and she guides and protects Roland's new friend, *Elisa*."

"Hi, everyone," said Arce-fera, introducing herself. She was gorgeously self-centered in appearance, beautifully intelligent in many respects, and she liked men. "Roland and Elisa are quickly gaining a good friendship. There are various interesting plans you can help me implement over the intervening months, and furthermore . . ."

*   *   *

Roland got up later that morning. Rigo slept till nearly noon.

When Roland served himself some breakfast, he talked to Lavinia and Norma some more, including mentioning that Isalia and Luke had just left to go back home to Tennessee.

Lavinia decided to tell Roland something. Back in late November, when Isalia and Luke had arrived and begun their stay at Lorenzo's house, they had a talk with Lavinia about Roland. They were very very irritated at Roland for having reported the white truck to Colombia Bridge Customs, and they were even more irritated when the police had trapped them last February and blamed them for hiring Beto Enriquez to toss that firecracker/bomb into Chilo Cantu's house where Roland had been staying. Isalia and Luke had to pay a

N$1200 fine each or be put in jail for three days. Wow! Roland didn't know they'd been punished that severely. He thought the police had just questioned them.

"Por eso, menos te hablan," Lavinia said to Roland, telling him that Isalia and Luke had even less reason to talk to Roland, for the fact that the police had punished them for being behind the firecracker incident! Lavinia also added that Isalia and Luke didn't want any further problems with Roland and for him to just keep his distance.

Roland started laughing. He laughed and laughed. After a while Norma couldn't help but laugh, also. Rigo woke up and asked Roland why he was laughing. Roland was so satisfied to know that Isalia and Luke had suffered a decent penalty for their malicious action, which they thought they could get away with! They hadn't counted on Bustamante's police being so on the ball . . . and catching up with them! Served Isalia and Luke right! The very idea that they hired Beto to toss that firecracker! Beto didn't mean any harm by it, which is why he tossed it in a different room. He just needed the money, since he was poor. As for Isalia and Luke, their intentions against Roland were wicked and uncalled for. Yes, Roland laughed some more. Isalia and Luke had been punished. Excellent! And they better continue to leave Roland alone, or they might be punished some more!

Roland went to visit Beto Enriquez this morning. He finally found him at home, and they talked and visited for a while. Beto asked Roland to be one of his padrinos (sponsors) for his upcoming wedding February 20. He needed $35. Roland agreed to it and would give him the money before leaving Bustamante to go home.

It was good to see Beto. Roland told him what all he had done this past month, some of which gave Beto a good laugh.

Later in the morning, Roland drove over to Villaldama, and he visited with Alberto for a while. He was busily cooking and serving chicken to the public. Roland bought one from him, and he went over to Leonardo's house.

Of course, he wasn't home, but his brother Julian was. He was glad to see Roland and asked him inside. Julian and a friend of his were watching a movie on TV, and Roland joined them. He enjoyed the afternoon visiting with them, and Roland shared the grilled chicken with them as they watched the movie.

Julian said Leonardo was doing fine and was busy working as an architect in Monterrey. It had been more than a year since Roland had seen him.

The next day was the first day of February. Rigo and Roland were going to go to Sabinas Hidalgo to do errands. Roland was in the truck at 8 AM ready to go. Rigo walked by Roland and his truck, and he asked him to wait just a few minutes. He walked up the street to the corner store, and a couple of minutes later returned with a pack of cigarettes in his hand. Rigo walked by Roland again, entered the house, handed the cigarettes to his father, and then climbed in Roland's truck with him.

Roland asked him why he just did that favor for his father. Rigo got defensive and said his father had told him to go fetch a pack of cigarettes for him. So, he did. Rigo then told Roland it was none of his business. That got Roland a bit irritated. He told Rigo that since he was paying him for his time with him, it was very much his business, and he told Rigo that in the United States, the stores wouldn't have sold him those cigarettes, because he was still under 18. It was against the law. Further, why couldn't Alejandro go get those cigarettes himself, instead of teaching his son Rigo the bad habit of buying them, which would greatly increase his chances of becoming a smoker! All of those ideas Roland told Rigo, which did nothing but make Rigo more irritated. That was Rigo's problem and insecurity with himself for getting angry and defensive. No matter what, Roland told Rigo those ideas and advice, in hopes that he wouldn't be a smoker. Roland finished the "argument" by telling Rigo that if he'd been in his place, he would have told Alejandro to buy those cigarettes himself. Why was Rigo so afraid to make a stand and tell his father no? While Rigo wasn't always so kind to his mother, he was to his father. He was afraid of Alejandro, and whatever he told Rigo to do, he hopped to it and did it right away!

Rigo stepped down out of Roland's truck disgusted, and he entered the house. Roland then entered and offered to leave. Rigo then asked him to go fetch Alberto and return here for him.

Roland went to Alberto's house, found him at home, and they returned to Rigo's house, picked him up, and the three of them went to Sabinas Hidalgo. They did errands and had lunch there. The day went well, and Rigo was in happier spirits.

While they were there, Roland left Elisa's book on trees and plants of Mexico with Garza Morton and had them copy all of it. The lady wasn't very willing, and when Roland offered to do the copying himself, the store said that only authorized store workers could operate the machine. In fact, as Roland realized, there was no such thing as self-service copying in Mexico at all. So, the lady had to consent and make the copies for Roland. After all, she was being paid for the copies.

That evening, back in Bustamante, Roland went to the plaza with Rigo and others. Fernando, Rogelio, and another fellow named Juan Roberto were there, and they were playing vigorously with each other, acting silly. Rigo and Fernando wanted to see Chiquihuitillos. Roland agreed to take them there tomorrow.

In the plaza, Roland saw another young fellow he recognized. He looked sad, so Roland went over to talk to him. He said his parents had gotten angry and had kicked him out of the house! He didn't know where he was going to stay, and he commented that he felt very sad. Roland offered to go with him as a friend to talk with his parents to see if they could work it out. After all, he was still a minor, and it's a moral obligation for the parents to raise their children until they become age 18. He thanked Roland for the offer, but he would see if he could work it out himself, but if he couldn't, he would come back to Roland to seek his help.

Later that evening, Roland talked to Rigo, and he asked him what he thought about it.

"¡No sé! Es su problema," he quickly answered, telling Roland that was his friend's problem, not anyone else's!

Good gracious! Did Rigo have no compassion at all?! Roland really wondered sometimes.

A few days later, Roland saw his friend again, and he asked him how things went. He had indeed worked it out, and he was back at home living with his parents again. Good news, because family is important.

The next day, Roland drove Rigo and Fernando over to Chiquihuitillos, and they saw all three sections of paintings. It was a good day, and Fernando, more than Rigo, found the paintings intriguing and of interest. They brought some food along and had a cookout at the base of the double mesa, after which they returned to Bustamante.

Roland decided to offer Fernando some advice, as well. He told him that having seen him drunk in the plaza the other night made him feel sad. Yes, Fernando has the right, but since he was training to become a school teacher, it would be good to put forth a better example as a teacher. Fernando took Roland's advice a lot better than Rigo, and while he had a little bit to drink at times, he didn't get drunk anymore. Now, that's more like it.

New Doors Open, New Friends

Roland's advice finally fell on some good ears. Fernando was a good and reasonable fellow, and he had a good sense of responsibility and a reputation to establish with the people.

It was late afternoon when they arrived back to Bustamante. Fernando thanked Roland for the day, and he walked home. Rigo and Roland entered the house. Lavinia was just fixing supper, and she soon fed them. Roland and Rigo had a good day, and Roland began to peacefully eat supper with his friends, the Zacatóns.

Roland had his hat on, and Rigo asked him to take it off. Roland took it off and placed it on the table. Then Rigo told Roland to put the hat on the glass encased cabinet over to the side. Roland obliged him, but started smelling a rat. Next, Rigo told Roland to chew every bite with his mouth closed, as if Roland didn't know how! With that said, Roland told Rigo not to mandate him. Rigo said he had every right to, since he was in his own house, and he began to yell at Roland. Roland retaliated, and he ordered Rigo not to yell at him. Further, why was Rigo picking a fight, anyway? Roland got up from the table, abandoning his meal. Lavinia followed him out of the kitchen, and she began to tell Roland how they had done him a "huge favor," receiving him into their house, and if he didn't like it, he could just leave!

Right you are, Lavinia! Roland told her he was leaving, taking his things with him, and he wasn't leaving a single penny with them, since he was leaving disgusted! Roland first took his food box to his truck, came back in the house, and took some other bags to his truck. When Roland began to make a third trip to his truck, Lavinia stopped him with a *Wait, wait* look on her face. She and Rigo both now stated that they weren't running him off. Roland told them the equivalent of: *You could have fooled me!*

Roland looked at Rigo and, in a straightforward manner, told him that he picked that fight on purpose to get Roland back for telling him it was bad to buy cigarettes for his father. Rigo glared at Roland with a gesture verifying that was why, and Roland told him that's what he thought.

Lavinia and Rigo told Roland he could stay the several more days he was planning. Roland said okay, he would, but he didn't want any more picking of fights, nor being shouted at, nor being run out of the bathroom! He would leave them some money upon leaving, but if he left disgusted, he would take his money with him instead. Rigo assured Roland he would be nice to him and yes, he could feel welcome in their house. Good then! Roland stayed.

They shook hands and forgave each other, even though Lavinia, as always, managed to avoid apologizing. Roland didn't like to have to be so petty, but if he hadn't threatened not to pay them for his stay, they might have continued their abuse schemes. Things went all right. Roland stayed four more days, and he visited different friends in town.

One night, Roland went to camp in the mountains. He went to Fernando to see if he wanted to go camp with him. Fernando said he couldn't go because his father Mateo wouldn't let him. Roland reminded Fernando that he was already 19. He realized that, but in Mexico, if you live with your parents, they still mandate. Plus, Mateo was quite angry at his son for having gone to Chiquihuitillos. Even though Fernando had obtained his mother's permission, that didn't count. He had to obtain his *father's* permission.

So, Roland went to the mountains by himself.

Rigo, Alberto, and Roland went over to Sabinas Hidalgo again, and Roland bought N$220 worth of bicycle parts to repair and refurbish the yellow mountain bike he had given Raul two years earlier. As Roland was repairing the bicycle, Rigo showed appreciation, and he placed his hand on Roland's shoulder in friendship, and he said thank you. Roland was pleasantly surprised.

Roland also gave N$400 to Lavinia and got a signed receipt, and he thanked them for letting him stay with them.

Roland and Rigo talked some. Roland asked him to send him a letter, but Rigo didn't want to. However, Rigo did give Roland a piece of paper with his various signatures and insignia on it. Then later, without Rigo knowing about it, Roland took the signatures and placed them in the self-addressed envelope he had retrieved from the trash, went to the local post office, purchased a stamp, and mailed it home. He may never get a letter from Rigo, but after the awful envelope incident the other night, by golly that envelope was going to be mailed home! Roland was determined, and he made certain of that!

Roland bicycled over to the Quevalo's bakery, now that Isalia and Luke were gone. He bought some empanadas to take home, and he talked to Lorenzo and Glenda. Glenda was friendly, but Lorenzo was cold shouldered and indifferent. He never forgave Roland for reporting the white truck. Roland had thought Lorenzo was his friend, but now he was observing that Lorenzo was more contaminated than before and that he had taken on the habit of holding grudges and not forgiving.

Roland went over to Pedro and picked up the fine wooden chair he had built for him. He paid him N$300 and thanked him for making it.

Roland said goodbye to certain people in town, and then he drove back home.

He arrived at the Colombia Bridge, turned in his permit, and drove across to the U.S. side. The officer at the booth asked Roland some basic questions. Another fellow inspected the bottom side of the truck with a mirror on an extension pole. Then he tapped some metal several times and declared, "Clear!" The officer asked Roland a couple more questions and then said, "Go ahead."

Roland proceeded to leave slowly, checking in his rearview mirror, just about sure they would wave him over, but they never did. No inspection, first time ever! That was great!

Roland drove on to Salado and visited with his friend Raul. Roland told him all about his stay in Mexico, including his stay at the ranch down south with Jaime's family. Roland also talked with Raul about Rigo. Roland had mixed feelings about continuing his friendship with Rigo. Every few days, Rigo had flared up about something, and in addition to that, he had thrown tantrums with his mother and his sisters. Rigo wasn't nearly as calm as before, and Roland just didn't feel so good around him. Raul was upset to know that, and even more so about the tantrums his brother was throwing to his mother and sisters. Raul said he was going to call Rigo and have a talk with him or at least write him.

Raul looked at Roland's pictures from his stay, and he discovered something that very much displeased him. There was a picture of Rigo and Angelo, and Angelo had on one of Rigo's expensive baseball caps that Raul had recently sent him and given him. Rigo hadn't cared anything about the hat and had given it to his best friend Angelo! Raul explained that his brother Rigo had done what is known as a *desprecio*, which means to have lack of appreciation for something and just casually give it away or toss it aside in a scoffing and sneering manner. Desprecio also means lack of respect for the person who gives you something. Roland noticed that even Raul was experiencing the ungrateful characteristics of Rigo.

Roland enjoyed the visit with Raul. Luckily, Millana was away at work the whole time.

Roland spent the night at Wal-Mart's parking lot, and the whole next day, he drove back home.

His parents welcomed him back, and he unloaded his things, including a fine wooden TV table he bought from Felipe. The table was a gift for his parents. Roland took the wooden chair up to his house.

The next day, Roland wrote Rigo a letter, telling him his mixed feelings, and he asked him why he couldn't have been more stable, that is, content with Roland's stay. Rigo had become more aggressive. Roland explained that he had come for genuine reasons and that his first choice family to stay with was the Zacatón family.

Roland also called Ivanhoe on the phone, and they talked a while. Ivanhoe had strongly suggested to Roland that he not go to Mexico this past winter, but he went anyway.

"So, you've been to Mexico, I presume?" Ivanhoe asked Roland.

He answered yes and told him all about the trip and events. He told him about his new friendships with Jaime and his family and his stay on their ranch near Matehuala. Ivanhoe was glad to know that Roland took some different avenues and didn't go just to Bustamante.

Roland told him about Rigo, how he acted, and how his stay went.

"God dear, he did have some flare-ups, didn't he?!" Ivanhoe remarked.

"Yeah, but he was nice part of the time," said Roland.

"I know, but that still doesn't justify Rigo's abuse every few days, does it? Not to mention, the grief that comes with it."

Roland had to agree.

"Roland, I think as far as your continued friendship with Rigo is concerned, it can be compared to beating a dead horse."

It was true. Ivanhoe was absolutely right about that.

"I had thought Rigo was my friend."

"It's a shame really," Ivanhoe went on. "He obviously took a dislike to you back in September, and he never really came around after that. Plus it was so petty the way you had to threaten not to pay them so they'd be sweet to you, and still they weren't that nice to you, were they?"

"No, they weren't," Roland agreed.

"You see, Rigo is a type who is extremely impatient and acts on impulse."

They talked about the Zacatóns a while longer and then talked about Isalia and Luke. Roland told Ivanhoe about the wardrobe they gave Lavinia and her family. He told Ivanhoe that he didn't even see Isalia and Luke, not even once during his stay in Mexico, and that they left him alone.

"So, they didn't do you any harm?" Ivanhoe checked.

"No."

"That's good. They'd have certainly paid for it if they had! I'd have made *sure* of that!"

"Oh . . . thanks Ivanhoe."

"Not a problem. I look out for my friends."

"That's very kind of you. So, how would they have paid? I'm just curious."

"Back in December, I set up a program that if they did you any harm, the harmony of their marriage would have been dismantled."

"Oh, really?"

"Oh, yeah. They'd have paid dearly. So, they can thank themselves that they left you alone. Anyway, it looks like you handled yourself very well, considering the potential danger. It could have gotten a lot nastier between you and Rigo and his mother. You're to be commended. I think your trip to Mexico this time has taught you how to deal better with people, and you have progressed in your spiritual growth."

"Thanks."

"But it's like I've said before, if you sense danger, walk away from it. It's not always good to continue hoping things will improve because they don't always do, and in some cases things can get very dangerous."

"Yes, I understand what you're saying," said Roland, "but I like to continue my friendships."

"Oh, I know you do. I do too, but I'm afraid there are some people who just don't, and Rigo is one of those, I'm sorry to say. So, my advice is to walk away before it gets too dangerous, if you choose to continue knowing him."

"I think Rigo has become more complex this past year," Roland mentioned.

"Exactly," Ivanhoe agreed. "You've gained an awareness of the subtleties of complex family relationships, and . . ."

They talked for several more minutes and then wished each other well.

Roland called his cousin David right on his 18th birthday and he invited him and John to go to Mexico with him some time. As of today, David was no longer under the requirements that he would have to get his parents' permission, and John would soon be of age also. Hopefully, David and John would take the opportunity of Roland's kind and gracious invitation within the next few years, while they still had time, because after that, a 40-year work career, plus raising families, would never permit it. Roland was different than the norm, of course, in that he worked for himself in his carpentry and painting and in his artwork. Plus, he had never married, let alone have kids. He had the time.

During the coming spring, several clients called Roland, and he got plenty of work. He helped somebody finish the inside walls and ceiling of an old barn. He was converting it to an old antique shop. Also, he finished the deck project near Columbia.

Roland made the necessary steps to successfully self publish another artwork calendar and a book compilation with that new publishing company in Nashville. It cost nearly a thousand dollars, including the $195 for the ISBN block of numbers, paying a local typesetter for layout fees, paying set-up fees at the Nashville publisher, and the cost of printing around 100 copies.

From time to time, he checked with the distributor in South Carolina. The owner/president was always unavailable to talk to Roland, but his wife or workers did. The answer was always the same. No sales on his previous books and calendars.

Roland called Ivanhoe on the phone again and talked to him about how things were going. He was pleased to know that Roland had managed to self-publish his artwork, and Ivanhoe began to contemplate having his special artwork published via Roland and the Nashville publishing company.

Roland also talked to Ivanhoe about the fact that for more than two years now, he had still not figured out who his travelling companion was. He was frustrated about it, and was ready to throw in the towel on the whole thing.

"I think that would be a good idea," Ivanhoe agreed. "That way you'll release your fixation on it, and the energy will be able to do its work."

"I will then," said Roland. "Ivanhoe, do you think if I'd gone to Canada instead of Mexico that I would have found someone?"

"Yes, you would have. I didn't tell you this before, but I saw a vision of your happening into a fellow you already know. There was a 90% chance you would have crossed paths, and you and he would have travelled to Alaska together."

In some ways, Roland was now regretting that he had gone to Mexico anyway, last August. Why hadn't he taken Ivanhoe's suggestion?

They finished their conversation, and Roland grabbed a towel, stepped outside, declared he was throwing in the towel on ever finding someone, and he threw the towel on the ground. Then he recollected it and walked back in the house.

That night, while half awake at 3 AM, Roland thought, *What if I'd gone to Canada?* He thought about driving to Alaska along the Alaskan Highway. He was thinking about the Firs and Spruces through Saskatchewan and Alberta, pulling over on the roadside for a . . . Suddenly he was thinking about Brad Carlson and how his parents had been strict on him and made him go to a private school. They had yanked him out of Longview High School. He had been the first date for Roland's younger sister, etc.

Wait a minute! Roland thought. *Why did my thoughts shift?*

"He's the one!" Roland suddenly shouted, completely waking himself up. "Brad Carlson! How did that not occur to me ages ago?!"

Roland lay awake an hour thinking about his sudden revelation. He hadn't seen him in 15 years, and he was just about sure he was the fellow Ivanhoe was not telling him about and had said, ". . . when you finally figure it out." Now, Roland knew exactly what that meant. He had finally figured it out! Golly! 15 years had gone by. The last time Roland had seen Brad was at a high school basketball game. They visited and chatted during that game, and somehow it had never occurred to either one of them to look each other up again. For the way Roland remembered him, he would have met all the basic requirements of a travelling companion, complete with a sense of compatibility.

Roland called Ivanhoe back on the phone the next morning, and he explained what he had realized. He told Ivanhoe he was 95% sure it had to be Brad Carlson, and he explained how he used to know him, how he was his sister's first date, his characteristics, etc. Ivanhoe while listening was verifying Roland's analysis with his feelings.

"Okay, okay," Ivanhoe suddenly admitted. "I'm going to go ahead and tell you. I'm going to put you out of your misery and tell you . . . It was him."

Roland felt a flash of feelings as if he'd wasted years of time, and he told Ivanhoe, "That's what I thought." He thanked Ivanhoe for telling him (verifying), and he said he was going to contact him and invite him to Alaska by writing him a letter.

Ivanhoe wished him success and they finished their conversation.

Roland started by calling Brad's parents, and he asked them how Brad was doing. His parents said Brad was single, with no children, doing freelance work, and living in Nashville. He had experienced some ups and downs, but he was doing okay. Brad's father thanked Roland for calling and asking about him.

After the conversation, Roland realized his mind had finally located the hidden data and figured it out.

Not married. No children. Freelance work, that is, self-employed. Brad might actually have the time. Roland wrote him a letter immediately, inviting him to Alaska, and he mailed it to Brad's parents, since he didn't see Brad listed in Nashville's phone directory.

While Roland went about his work the next week, eagerly waiting for Brad's response, he thought a lot about the past 15 years since he began looking for a travelling companion. How is it possible that Brad being the travelling companion had never once occurred to

Roland? He must have thought of Brad 1,000 times, but never in the right context! Roland did what could best be described as soul searching. He was just about sure something had blocked him from ever thinking of Brad in the right way, and he lamented the loss. They could possibly have enjoyed several trips together out West, backpacking and hiking and enjoying America and its sights, not to mention what they could have enjoyed in Mexico. Brad definitely would have been able to travel with him, especially between 1985 and 1990. Roland felt sure of it.

Ten days went by. Roland decided to call Brad's parents. He hadn't received a response from Brad, not a peep.

"Yes, Roland," Mr. Carlson answered, "we got your letter to Brad. We saw him and gave it to him. He thanks you for the invitation, but he can't go. Plus, he's just started work for a company, began this past Monday, and he hasn't got the time now." Roland was sorry to find out that Brad said no, and he thought to ask Mr. Carlson if Brad happened to travel to Canada last summer.

"Yes, he sure did! Went up there by himself. Anyway, thank you for calling Roland. Goodbye."

-click-

"Oh . . . that was quick," Roland commented to himself.

Brad was the one! Roland realized it at precisely the moment of expiration, that is, precisely too late! The 15-year window of opportunity had just closed, as of this past Monday! Shoot the luck! Why hadn't Roland thought of him in the right context? Why hadn't he? It really bothered Roland a lot. How many other opportunities had also passed Roland by?

He and Rigo didn't get along that well, anyway. Roland realized he should have gone to Canada instead of Mexico.

Brad never responded directly to the invitation letter, and Roland couldn't call him because his number was unlisted. He would have asked Mr. Carlson for the number, but then it seemed inappropriate, seeing how he wrapped up the conversation so fast. Months later, Roland saw Mr. and Mrs. Carlson in town. They said that Brad was doing well with his new job. Life was moving on.

Roland subsequently wrote letters to several more people inviting them to go to Alaska with him. He even wrote his friend in Spain. Not a single one of them responded to Roland's invitation, and he had to call every one of them by phone to follow up. Strange really, the lack of interest and response!

Roland's friends in Asheville, North Carolina called him in March and asked him to come do some work for them for a few days. So, he loaded his truck with his things, his tools, a ladder, and he drove over there.

He drove through Murfreesboro to get there and just before reaching Lascassas, he rounded the gentle curve on the highway where the narrow Stones River truss bridge came into view.

"Uh-oh!" Roland declared to himself as he saw the bridge. There was a huge crane erected to the left of it, and the shrubs and trees that used to grow there were cleared out. As he drove by, he saw that concrete footings were already being installed. Roland had known the Lascassas Bridge his whole life, and he felt sad that it was soon going to be replaced.

He drove on to Asheville and did several days of work for his friends, and then he returned home.

CHAPTER 17

TEMPORARY MIRACLE

April 1999

Roland wanted to return to Mexico for La Semana Santa. He decided to drive his Ford Fairlane station wagon instead of his truck. His friend Fabian had requested a bicycle. Plus, he wanted to have a wooden wardrobe made by Pancho Gonzalez, who ran a carpentry business out of his home. While it may have been an unnecessary trip, Roland made the decision to go. Besides, he would stay at Lucio's ranch part of the time and work on his Mexico novel.

In early April, Roland drove down there. He stopped by and visited his friend Raul in Salado. He was glad to see Roland, and he sent $125 with him to give to his family in Bustamante. Raul trusted Roland, and knew he would follow through and safely deliver it to them. Eduardo was at home and happily greeted Roland, also. Eduardo's wife Millana was miraculously away at the mall with the two children.

Roland offered to take Raul with him to Bustamante. Raul said he wished he could go with him. It had been more than a year since he had left Mexico and come to Salado. He missed his family and friends. Getting there would be easy enough, but the return to the United States was the dangerous and expensive part, and Raul was afraid to cross the river again. So, he opted to stay in Salado.

Roland stayed at Wal-Mart's parking lot, and he drove away the next morning. He pulled in to Bustamante at 3:30 PM, and he first arrived at the Zacatón's house. Lavinia was home, and she greeted Roland. He said he had a delivery from her son Raul, and he went back to his car and took out his tablet, a piece of paper, and the money. He handed Lavinia the money and had her sign for it, so he could later show the receipt to Raul in case there were any discrepancy later.

Norma and Irma were home, and they happily greeted Roland. Lavinia asked him in, and she kindly fed him a meal of rice and beans with tortillas.

Roland hadn't yet gotten to the part about asking if he could stay with them when . . . in walked Rigo! He entered with an inhospitable, angry face. Roland's feelings suddenly tightened. Something about Rigo looked very different, and the look in his eyes was a look Roland had never seen in Rigo before. Roland verbally greeted him, though he suddenly felt nervous to do so, and as Rigo approached, Roland extended his hand. Rigo barely shook hands, and he didn't even talk to Roland, let alone ask how he was doing!

Roland was saddened by Rigo's gestures, and he could instinctively sense that Rigo had increased his amount of drinking. He now drank several beers every weekend at every baile, but he had not yet been drunk. Not only that, he had started smoking, though he always kept that secret away from his family! Adjusting and revising convictions had become Rigo's first passion. The vicious look in Rigo's eyes said a lot. Roland felt suddenly so bad, that is, so unwelcome that he handed the unfinished meal to Lavinia, thanked her, and he left.

He drove over to Victor's house. They were glad to see Roland. Victor shook hands with him properly. He had grown! Now, he was the same height as Roland. They were about to move to their newly built house in the upper part of town, having lived in the same one-room rental house for over 14 years. In three days, they were going to move, and until then, they said Roland could stay in the house and sleep there. That was kind of them, and Roland drove his car up there, arrived at the house, and carried his things in. The house had three rooms and was well furnished, but it had no kitchen sink.

This upper part of town was a new colonia being built. It was up in the monte (scrubland) of Mesquite shrubs and Nopals. The streets were most of them dirt with some gravel, and the houses were still sparse and scattered, many lots not having been built on yet. Bustamante was growing, and it sometimes worried Roland how much Bustamante might grow in the future.

Later that afternoon, Roland delivered to Fabian the bike he had bought him. It was a used bike from a yard sale. He was ecstatic, and he thanked Roland.

The next day, Roland looked up Alberto, and he offered him to come with him to Sabinas Hidalgo. They decided to go fetch Rigo, and they pulled up in front of the house. Rigo greeted Alberto and somewhat greeted Roland, and he shook hands better this time. Roland took them to Sabinas Hidalgo to do errands.

While they ate at one of the restaurants, Roland asked Rigo why he was being so resentful. He asked him what he had done to him that was so bad. Rigo didn't have an answer for that. Roland also asked him why he wasn't a good friend, like he used to be. Rigo gestured an *I don't know*, and he told Roland not to come visit him at Felipe's carpentry, where he now worked again. With that, Roland sharply responded that he would go by there any time he liked! After all, he had other friends who worked there, like Sotero, Juan Carlos, and Pedro.

After lunch they did some more errands and then returned to Bustamante. As Roland delivered Rigo home, he wished him well, and he asked him to see if he could appreciate and be more grateful. Next, he took Alberto home.

It was a very windy night, the windiest night Roland had ever seen in Mexico. Winds probably howled at nearly 100 mph! Plus, this April was a hot one, with day temperatures being in excess of 40° C (near 110° F)!

Roland took Alberto and Beto to Monterrey for the day. Beto was working for ZuaZua bus lines, also known as Tamaulipas or Grupo Senda, and he had the week off, due to being in a bus crash. Fortunately, he was uninjured, except for a bump on the head. Beto needed to go by the company headquarters in Guadalupe, the eastern suburb of Monterrey, to fill out some paperwork related to the accident. Roland and Alberto visited the Macroplaza and other sights, and that evening they returned to Bustamante.

Victor's family moved into their new house, which meant that Roland moved out. He thanked them for the place to stay, and he gave them an American Elm seedling that he had brought from home. It would grow and do well, being the only American Elm in the whole of Bustamante.

Roland moved his things to Angelo's house and stayed there a few days. They were friendly and received Roland well. Angelo and Hugo were glad to see Roland, and they visited and talked about different things. Angelo also told Roland the good news that both he and Christian had stopped smoking. Well, great!

Over the next few days, Roland visited his friends. He placed his wardrobe order with Pancho Gonzalez and paid him US $150 for materials and labor. He ordered a painting to be made by Sebastian, and he also had a carburetor cleaned and refurbished by a shade tree mechanic.

On April 7, Roland went hiking up in the mountains to camp overnight. He couldn't find anyone to go with him, so he went alone. He left the cono at 11 AM and reached the grassy saddle at the highland forest at 3:30 PM.

Up here, the weather was nice and sunny, and the cooler mountain temperature was a relief in comparison to the hot 40° C weather in town.

Roland put up his tent in the forest and took an afternoon nap. The leaves of the Oaks and Hickories rustled in the steady breeze. As he drifted off to sleep, he suddenly became aware of two spirit beings standing by a tree outside his tent. Their names were Alfra and Tabra. Immediately, Roland became wide awake. There was no one. He wrote their two names down and went back to sleep.

Wednesday, April 7, 1999

Oyamel, one of the chief spirits of high ranking, was overseeing and presiding over the court case of two spirit guides named Sarlo and Malluck.

"But we didn't do anything that bad," said Malluck, appealing the charges that were brought against him and Sarlo.

"Besides, he needed to learn some important lessons in life, karmic debts, and that sort of thing," Sarlo added.

"That's a miserable excuse for the grief you've given permission to be wrought upon him by other means!" Oyamel roared at them. "Lessons in life . . . yes, to a degree, but NOT to the point that he is caused to lose every new good friendship he ever made, the last one being the one we know as Molonco."

"That's crazy!" Sarlo argued. "Roland and Molonco had a lot of good times."

"They did, but the bottom line is they've still lost their friendship!" Oyamel pointed out. "That's totally unacceptable!"

"Well, he wasn't supposed to become such good friends with Molonco, anyway," Sarlo stated. "He was going down the wrong road and was supposed to find his *real* travelling companion . . ."

"Your statements are false!" Oyamel firmly told Sarlo. "After you and Malluck gave permission to several evil spirits, namely Messofilo, who subsequently subcontracted Sasjurech and Sojornbloc to plant bad energies and programs on Roland, how could you have expected him to ever figure out who his travelling companion was really meant to be?"

"Uh . . . well, you know . . ." Sarlo began.

"He only just figured out who he was two months ago," Oyamel told them. "*Fifteen years ago* Roland was supposed to figure that out. Every time since then when Roland was at the brink of figuring out who he was, Sasjurech and Sojornbloc threw thoughts at him (or the programs installed upon him) always caused him to shift his thoughts and never realize who his travelling companion really was!"

"Well, he finally did *realize* who he was," Malluck declared, defending himself.

"How can you expect that to work?!" Oyamel roared. "It was entirely too late, in addition to the homophobia and resentment programs, not to mention the false dreams you allowed your evil comrades and clients to plant on Roland's friends, causing them to turn against him. Others were caused to become depressed while more still were caused to feel uncomfortable. And then, as if *that* wasn't enough, every time Roland sincerely appreciated a friend, he lost him, due to the devious programs, especially the inverse reality virus, which added more resentment to those who he highly appreciated."

"Like I said, he had important lessons to learn in life," Sarlo reiterated.

"Oh, you thick headed estúpidos!" Oyamel shouted. "Roland, as everyone does, has the right to make and keep his friends and enjoy them, *without* corruption and grief caused by guides turned evil like the two of you. Sarlo and Malluck, you two are wicked task makers who enjoy watching grief and frustration."

"We are not wicked!" Malluck stated, defending himself.

"You have no ground to stand on anymore!" Oyamel told them. "Having given permission to others to tamper with him is just as bad, and it is punishable under the same severity. Not only were you wrong to have given Messofilo permission to do what he did for those ten years, you were even worse to continue giving permission to others who said they'd help you teach Roland his lessons in life. The job was yours and NOT for others! Messofilo never told you, but when he made that attachment on Roland 18 years ago, he also subconsciously made deals with that Spanish teacher, via her demon Arfifra and her friends Torxtalo, Draaktra, and Druxtrli, who were in cahoots with Sasjurech and Sojornbloc. They caused Roland to miss several important opportunities in his life . . . by being *prevented* from thinking of them!"

"Messofilo didn't subconsciously make deals with the Spanish teacher!" Malluck shouted.

"Yes he did, and I've had that confirmed!" Oyamel shouted back. "You two have broken one of the highest spiritual laws, and you two are therefore charged with corruption, interference, sabotage, and neglect!"

"Roland has permanently lost his chance to the travelling companion he was meant to have. He had to take nearly all those trips alone, except for one where he was accompanied by a much less than satisfactory companion who, on the final day of the trip, complained until the cows came home! Most people would not have survived the grief Roland has had to undergo, and pain now sometimes wracks within him."

"He wasn't ever attacked nor beaten up," Sarlo pointed out.

"True," Oyamel partially admitted, "but only thanks to the protection measures that were given to him by Martonción, Igor and Selím, who detected your malicious actions and reported you to me. The grief you allowed is still bad. For Roland's loss of his travelling companion, he must be compensated. His friendship with Molonco must be restored immediately, and the resentment thoughts that were planted in his mind must be wiped clean, but that task I will assign to others who *know how* to protect and care for, those who will *replace* you, effective immediately! Away with you two!"

At that moment, Martonción, who was a valuable spirit of high ranking, appeared on the scene.

"Deliver them their bill," Oyamel said to Martonción. He telepathically transmitted the entire court scene to Martonción, who would then know how to administer their punishment.

Next, Martonción grabbed the arms of both Sarlo and Malluck, who by this time were wailing in protest! He dragged them out of the courtroom, and they were now outside.

"As Oyamel said, it is now time for you two to pay for your wrong actions," Martonción calmly told them. "Your sentence is to be doomed to a remote, cold, icy, dead planet, to be buried alive within its confines for an eternity of eons to come." A forcefield arrived, plucked Sarlo and Malluck from their existence, and it instantly took them away, teleporting them to their destination.

Martonción returned to Oyamel in the courtroom, clapping and wiping the dust off his hands, signalling that he had successfully completed the task.

"Excellently done!" Oyamel commended. "Good riddance to those two!"

"Amen," Martonción agreed.

"Martonción," Oyamel asked him, "there's a hefty reward for the capture of the demons of Nuevo Wimbisenho. Arfifra is of special concern to us for the havoc she has wrought."

"With all due respect, Oyamel, I cannot locate them. They must have gone into hiding."

"They slip away from my grasp every time!" Oyamel complained. "Martonción, I'm asking you to put it on a high list. Find and capture them!"

"I will do my best to find them and bring them before you."

"You can see through their stealth cloaking shields, right?"

"Yes, I can, but they're very clever and very slippery. However, I will make their missions difficult in hopes that they'll just lose interest and go away."

"The first priority is to *capture* them and bring them to me," Oyamel reiterated. "With Selím and Igor by your side, I have confidence that you'll accomplish the task."

"I will do my best," Martonción reassured him.

There were two other spirit guides now in the room. Their names were Alfra and Tabra. Prior to the court trial, Oyamel had telepathically given them Roland's complete history.

"Martonción," Oyamel now told him, "these two are to be the new spirit guides and protectors for Roland. They are genuine, loyal, and honest. Please take them to Roland. He is presently in the mountains of Mexico. At the same time, would you go into Roland's mind and decontaminate him of any bad energies and programs, as well as doing the same for the one we know as Molonco, and for anyone else you deem necessary, who are important friends of Roland."

"I will make sure and accomplish those tasks, also," Martonción assured him.

Martonción was a valuable spirit who was a great help to his good friend, Oyamel. He, his son Selím, and Igor were trustworthy and dependable, and Martonción was especially valuable for his expertise in being able to go into the minds of contaminated humans and removing their bad energies and unwanted harmful programs.

Alfra and Tabra, of male and female essence respectively, left the courtroom with Martonción. He teleported with them to Mexico, and from a higher dimensional reality, they looked down through an opening or window from the spirit world and observed Roland who was by himself in the high mountain forest.

"So, this is our new person to protect," Tabra said to Alfra.

"Looks like a kind, considerate fellow who deserves to have friends," Alfra said to her.

"Indeed so, I agree," she responded.

"It's a miracle he's lived through the onslaught of grief and loss of friendships," said Alfra.

"Treat him nicely," Martonción told Alfra and Tabra. "I know this one well. We go back eons of time."

"We will indeed," Alfra assured him. "Tabra and I are not like those other two."

"Very fine," said Martoncíon. "I will decontaminate Roland tonight. I will also seek out his friend Molonco when he's asleep tonight and will remove the resentment and bad energies he was contaminated with, along with other important friends in Roland's life."

"That's good to hear," said Alfra. "We will do our best."

"Roland deserves some decent friends," Martoncíon went on. "I became aware of Roland's problem several years ago. I'm going to tell you, it was my son and I and Igor who discovered the corruption, gathered evidence in those several years, and took our case to Oyamel."

"You've done very well to report Sarlo and Malluck," Tabra told him. "If you hadn't stepped in, those two scoundrels could have gotten away with a lot more!"

"And might have led to his suicide from chronic grief," Alfra added.

"It's more like he would have been either killed by violent actions or unfairly put in jail," Martoncíon clarified. "If I hadn't placed the protection energies within him when I first discovered the corruption, things would have been far worse for Roland."

"Oh! How severe that could have been for him!" said Tabra, realizing the chilling possibilities.

"At the same time," Martoncíon also told them, "over the past two years, Roland himself was becoming aware that some sabotage had been going on."

"Things really were getting out of hand," said Alfra.

"Anyway, those days are now over," Martoncíon said with confidence. "His friend Molonco is good at heart. I'll have his contamination removed in less than five minutes, tonight. They have a very strong friendship which will bounce back into place within days. Molonco will also be sent a dream tonight to help the process along."

"Roland's previous losses are unfortunate," said Tabra, "but at least we're in time for this last one."

"Anyway, I better get started," Martoncíon told them. "Take care, and all the best."

"Thanks. That we will," both Alfra and Tabra assured him.

The changeover process for Roland's guides was complete. His life could, from that day forward, run more smoothly. *Peace and friendship* could finally prevail.

*   *   *

Roland had a good night's sleep, and the next morning, he packed his tent and sleeping bag and hiked back down the mountain to the cono. He drove back to Bustamante where he arrived at Angelo's house, showered and cleaned up.

It was time to wash some clothes. So, Roland took his clothes to the Zacatón's house. Norma and Irma were there, and they asked Roland why he hadn't come over. He answered that he hadn't liked the way Rigo had "greeted" him the other day, and he didn't feel comfortable in Rigo's presence. For that reason, he went to stay elsewhere, like at Victor's and Angelo's houses.

Norma and Irma asked Roland to come over and stay with them. They enjoyed his company, and they told him as for Rigo, he doesn't mandate. Alejandro and Lavinia do. Roland appreciated that kind invitation, but he was already set up this time at Angelo's house, and tomorrow he was going to Lucio's ranch, anyway.

346

Norma told Roland the washing machine was in the back room, and it went without saying that he could use it.

Roland put his clothes in the machine, and as they ran through their cycle, he continued visiting with Norma and Irma in the front room.

Norma was quickly growing up. Of course Roland knew she was still a child in age, but she had matured fast. She was 12 going on 18, one might say. She was around 5' 6" and nearly grown, and her legs . . . they were *attractive*! Roland wasn't usually one to notice beauty in women, but when he caught sight of her legs . . . Wow! Roland kept his surprise and thoughts to himself, but his eyes and mind registered the fact that Norma was very pretty. He realized to himself that she was indeed the predestined one to be his future wife, and his feelings were turning on for her. It had been a long time since he had found a woman so attractive.

Roland's clothes finished washing, and he hung them on the line outside.

Norma said Lavinia was up the street at Diana's house working, if he wanted to visit with her.

Roland went over there and talked with Lavinia for a while. Lavinia told Roland he was welcome to stay with them, and she asked Roland why he had left so suddenly. Roland answered it was because of how Rigo "greeted" him when he arrived. Lavinia said Raul had called yesterday to see if Roland had delivered the money. She had told him yes, and no more than she had signed for it than Roland left.

Roland asked why Rigo was being so resentful and cold shouldered, and Lavinia answered that, like she had said back in January, various people in town had been rumoring that Roland was gay, and since he and Rigo had run around so much together, the town's people had been poking fun at him. Rigo, for his embarrassment, and to prove he wasn't gay, had given Roland the brush off, as a result.

That's what Roland thought, and he told Lavinia he wasn't surprised.

Roland later visited Manuel who had talked with Rigo in the last few days. He had told Rigo that Roland was in town, and Rigo blurted out, "¿Para qué lo quiero? ¡Que se larga, ya!" meaning, Why did he want Roland, and for him to keep his distance. Roland was sad to learn that, but he wasn't surprised.

Roland found Victor later that afternoon, and he wanted to go to Sabinas Hidalgo. Roland had some more errands to run, anyway. As they were driving out of town, they happened upon Fabian. He saw them, and a smile came across his face. He hopped in Roland's car and they were off to Sabinas Hidalgo. They ran some errands, and Roland took them out to eat at the Centro Comercial San José restaurant. They visited some of Fabian's relatives and then returned to Bustamante.

Roland later that evening went to visit Elisa, showed her his photo album and latest pictures, and they talked about life in general. Elisa played a recording of a bird she had heard down south in the high mountains. Roland recognized it, and he told her he had heard that type of bird call up on the ridge top. She was quite surprised to learn that. Elisa's son Lalo came over to Roland and talked a while.

That night, back at Angelo's house, Fabian and a friend came over, and they looked at Roland's photo album.

The next morning, Roland rode up to the clinic, the Centro Salud. He heard they were building a larger facility next to the old one. It was more than twice as large, and the workers had already put the walls up. It was scheduled for its grand opening in September.

Roland met the doctor. His name was Luis, and he was doing a year in residency here in Bustamante. He spoke fluent English, and he and Roland talked for an hour during his break. He was very interested to know of Roland's artwork and paintings and of his experiences, and he believed in life on other worlds, as well. They enjoyed their visit, swapped addresses, and they would remain in communication.

After that, Roland went to the Zacatón's house to collect his clothes off the line. Rigo answered the door, looked at Roland and gruffly said, "¿Qué?" meaning, Now what?! Roland explained that he came for his clothing, and Rigo let him in. Roland got his clothes off the line in the backyard, bagged them, and promptly left. He took them to his car parked in front of Angelo's house.

Later that afternoon, Roland went to Felipe's carpentry to visit with Sotero, Juan Carlos, and Pedro. Rigo was there working. Roland showed them some articles from Tennessee, proving how the people of Tennessee help the Mexicans and welcome them instead of running them off. Nashville had no Immigration office, the nearest one being Memphis.

Somehow, Rigo was friendly and talkative, and he and the others asked Roland how work was up in Tennessee. Roland answered that there was plenty. People like Jaime needed more painters, and there were jobs offered in other areas, as well. The standard pay was $10 per hour, better than the $6.50 presently offered in Texas. They talked for a while.

Right before leaving, Roland looked at Rigo and asked him "¿Amigos?" (Friends?)

He answered, "Sí, hombre." In other words, yes.

They shook hands. Rigo's resentment was somehow gone. That did indeed please Roland.

Later that evening, Roland drove his car to Lucio's ranch to stay a few days. He wrote another chapter in his Mexico novel, making good progress. The weather was hot and sunny, almost unbearable. Lucio and his son came to tend to the cattle each day, and some days Roland went and visited Romulo's people at the next ranch over.

Four days later, Roland returned to Bustamante, and he spent one last night at Angelo's house.

Pancho finished the wardrobe, and he and another worker helped Roland carefully load it into the back of his station wagon. He did a good job on it, and once at home, Roland would add a central divider and install some shelving to his liking. Pancho wished him a safe trip back home.

Roland went over to Rigo's house. He greeted him kindly, and he asked him inside. They talked for a while. Rigo admitted he had been thinking badly of Roland, and he said little things had gotten to him, like Roland's not liking loud stereo music nor perfume.

"Pero como quiera, seguimos siendo amigos," said Rigo, telling Roland no matter what, they will continue being friends.

Rigo told Roland when he returns in August, he would be welcome to stay, not continuously for weeks, but to come and go.

Roland thanked him and said he would indeed be returning in August, and he would spend the bulk of his time at Lucio's ranch, writing more of his Mexico novel. Of course, he had interest in going in the mountains at least once. Rigo said he would like to come along and take Angelo and Hugo with him. Roland said that would be fine.

Rigo's mother Lavinia came home from various errands and walked in the door. She greeted Roland, and the three of them talked. Rigo said he was interested in going to Tennessee with Roland next year before beginning his next phase of schooling, the Normal. He mentioned how they paid $10 an hour.

Rigo asked Roland how his Mexico novel was coming along and he showed interest in it, too.

All in all, Rigo had really come around for the better. The resentment was finally gone. Halleluyah! As Roland left and said goodbye to them, Rigo sincerely wished him well and shook hands with him properly, that is, he made Roland feel good. They said they would see each other in August.

Well, miracles never cease, when they want to occur. Roland was really grateful to have Rigo's friendship back. Amazing!

*   *   *

Nuevo Wimbisenho

"Oh, that Martonción!" Arfifra screamed to the others. She was throwing a tantrum, and she was wringing her hands in anguish! "Took every one of our programs out of Rigo!"

"And he's fenced us off!" Druxtrli added.

"But he's mine!" Draaktra insisted.

"Oh, shut up, you stubborn mule!" Arfifra yelled at him.

"You all heard Oyamel's order from upstairs," Druxtrli told the others. "We better clear out of here for several months."

"They're on the warpath after us," Sasjurech declared. "We better clear out of Roland's psyche for a while, too."

"Not before I leave a trigger/responder on that highway near us!" Sojornbloc angrily stated.

"The very idea of they're wanting us!" Druxtrli complained. "We don't have to be ashamed for any reason, since we're in all our right!"

"Not to mention, our missions to accomplish," Draaktra added.

"Arfifra, you are aware that Martonción simply hopes we'll go away," Torxtalo pointed out.

"Right you are, my dear." She thought a moment. "I have a plan. We'll do just as Martonción hopes. That way, he won't have any reason to hunt us down and kill us, and *then* . . ."

*   *   *

The next morning, Roland loaded his car, thanked Angelo's family, and he drove home.

At the Colombia Bridge, he turned in his permit, crossed the bridge, and underwent inspection. They spot checked some items but didn't make Roland unload everything thankfully, especially with his wardrobe in the back. The inspection officer said Roland must have a pretty good motor in his Fairlane to be able to make it to Mexico and back, all the way from Tennessee. Roland thanked him and said this car runs better than his newer ones, and he was glad he had kept it. A sniffing dog was unavailable at the time, and the officer said he was free to go. Roland said thanks and drove away.

On the way home, Roland looked up a Tennessee Tech friend who was living in Austin. His name was Mike, and they had been pretty good friends. He was working for a company in Austin, and thanks to the TTU Alumni Directory, Roland had his address and phone number. It had just become dusk when Roland reached Austin. He called him and asked if he could stay overnight.

Mike didn't remember Roland, but he agreed to meet him at a Taco Bell. Half an hour later, they met each other, and Mike somewhat recalled Roland's face upon seeing him. It had been ten years since they had seen each other. Mike's hair was already partially grey and he had aged. They entered Taco Bell where they talked for a while, and Mike bought him a couple of tacos.

Mike was making efforts to place Roland. So, Roland named several details of what they had done. They asked each other what they were doing with their lives, and Roland enjoyed the visit. However, one thing was very strange. Every so often, Mike's face would go cold, that is, expressionless and he was repeatedly thinking: *Who is this guy?* The look in Mike's eyes would change, too. Then Mike would snap back out of it and be friendly again. Several times that occurred.

They finished their meal and walked out of Taco Bell. Mike told Roland he was welcome to stay overnight and to follow him. Well, a mile down the road, Mike suddenly pulled over at a convenience store. So, Roland pulled in also, and when Mike got out of his car, Roland asked him what was the matter.

"Roland, I'm having second thoughts. I just don't know you that well."

"You haven't placed me yet, have you, Mike?"

"I'm sorry to back out. Can I put you up in a hotel?"

"No, that's okay. Don't worry about it."

"No, please. I want to help you out. I feel bad about backing out."

"Well, okay, if you're totally sure about it."

They talked about it and came to an agreement, and Mike gave Roland $60. Roland told him thanks, and he gave him a couple of his artwork calendars. Plus, he showed him his photo album of pictures from Mexico. After that, they wished each other well. Roland told Mike it was good to see him, and Mike drove home.

Mike had second thoughts about his and Roland's brief meeting. He had a sense of mistrust, and while Roland accepted the $60 with thanks, it still didn't make right the unwelcoming, untrusting stance that Mike had, not to mention his face repeatedly going cold and expressionless the way it did. The meeting had been awkward, mysterious as it turned out. Roland began to realize that it wasn't so wise to look up old friends, mainly because some of them can't remember. Roland really did have a phenomenal memory, and he sometimes forgot that some others didn't.

Roland drove straight to Salado and slept in his car overnight at Wal-Mart's parking lot. He visited Raul the next morning. Raul laughed about Mike's uneasiness, and he jokingly suggested Roland look up more friends. He could make some money. Each friend could give him $60. They both had a good laugh about it.

Roland enjoyed the visit, and then he drove on home and got busy with several projects.

Somebody else appeared in Roland's life, a fellow from Central America. His name was Abraham, and he had a wife and little boy named José. He had answered an ad for work that

Roland had earlier posted, and he began working different jobs with him over the intervening months. He was an expert philosopher and quite a storyteller, a fellow who was full of imagination. He told many stories from his homeland and why he came to live in the United States.

Numerous jobs came in, and Roland stayed busy. In addition to that, Ivanhoe came forth and asked Roland to publish his artwork in the form of calendars. Suddenly, one day, the group of artwork drawings arrived by email, in 19 attachments! Quite a surprise! Roland got right to it, and in a couple of months, 100 calendar copies with Ivanhoe's unique artwork came off the press. It was quite an accomplishment, and they were very pleased indeed. In addition to that, there were various marketing techniques that Ivanhoe suggested, most of which Roland implemented.

Roland attended another autism conference and sold a good number of his calendars and book compilations there. Parents of autistic children were quite interested in scenes from alien worlds.

During the spring and summer, Roland also worked various jobs with Jaime and his family members, brothers, and nephews. They were great people and Roland became good friends with them.

A couple of times during the summer, Roland drove over to Lascassas to check on the bridge. The new and much wider bridge to the left was quickly taking shape. They were pouring the concrete surface already. It wouldn't be long before the old narrow truss bridge would be history.

On August 7, Roland drove back to Mexico. He took some extra bicycles he had bought at the Goodwill Store in Nashville.

He looked up and stayed with Raul overnight. He was no longer at Eduardo and Millana's house. He was now living with his uncle, who received Roland graciously and was friendly. Roland appreciated the hospitality and he enjoyed visiting Raul, without the apprehension of Millana suddenly arriving and throwing him out!

Raul took Roland to Salado's flea market, and they also went over to Wal-Mart, where Raul bought $80 worth of notebooks and other school supplies for Roland to take to his younger siblings in Bustamante.

The next morning, Raul wished Roland well, and he drove to Bustamante, arriving at 5 PM. As he turned the corner to arrive at the Zacatón's house, Rigo pulled up on his bike, just arriving from Felipe's carpentry where he worked. Roland drove to the house and pulled up in front of it.

As Roland stepped down from his truck and arrived at the doorstep, Rigo greeted him in a kind manner, glad to see him. They shook hands, Mexican style, and Rigo asked Roland how he had been. Roland was so glad that Rigo was being friendly, and they talked for a while. As it turned out, Rigo was the first person Roland saw and talked to in Bustamante this trip . . . just like last year.

Lavinia and her two daughters, Norma and Irma, were home and they happily greeted Roland, as well. All of them, including Rigo, welcomed Roland to stay, and he brought his things in from his truck.

Now, that's more like it, a friendly greeting from Rigo and a decent handshake with good feelings. That wasn't hard, was it, Rigo?

That evening, Roland set up initially to sleep on the bed in the back room, but since there were no extra fans, the mosquitoes would be bothersome. Roland set up his tent out in the backyard. He was tired after the long drive, and he slept till 8:30 AM.

Roland took Rigo and Angelo over to Sabinas Hidalgo, and they did errands. Roland bought food and supplies to stay at Lucio's ranch. They stopped by one of Angelo's friends for a while.

Then they returned to Bustamante, visited the Ojo del Aqua, went swimming, and they also went to Angelo's family's ranch just outside of town. They had a swimming pool sized concrete holding tank of water, and they all went swimming there. They all played and splashed around, and Rigo and Angelo did some "cannon balls" as they jumped in. At their request, Roland took some pictures.

That evening, Roland went to the plaza to visit with other people. Some new items had been added . . . payphone booths! Bustamante had never had actual payphones before, and these were pushbutton and used a plastic card with a microchip. There was a slot to slide the card into, and the phone would subtract a certain amount for each minute used. Plus, there was a display telling the exact amount still left on the card. Calls to the United States were expensive at N$10 (around $1.10) per minute, and calls to Sabinas Hidalgo and Monterrey were also very expensive, at N$4 (around 45¢) per minute! The alcalde (mayor) had decided to have the payphones installed, and Roland kept discovering them on street corners all over town! Wow! Bustamante was going "uptown" with their upgrades, but their telephone exchange was still on crossbar. However, that was soon to change. Teléfonos de México was presently digging a trench from Sabinas Hidalgo to Villaldama and to Bustamante, and they were burying a fiber optic cable. Plus, they were installing a new digital exchange in Bustamante, to be cut over before the end of the year, that is, before the new millennium.

Not only that, Pemex was finally installing a small fuel station at the entrance to the town. They had started it last year, and they were building it little by little, and even though it was small, it would take them nearly two years to complete it, quite the opposite of how a fuel station and convenience store are built within weeks in the United States! It would be next year in May of 2000 before it would finally open. This station was a unique one because it had the luxury of shade, being situated under some large Pecan trees.

The next day, Rigo and Angelo worked. Roland looked up Victor, and he gave him one of the bikes. He was very appreciating and glad to receive it. He said it was *perfecto*. Roland also gave one to Angelo's family, and they thanked him by saying, "Muy amable." Another bike went to Irma, Rigo's sister.

Later in the day, Roland looked up Fabian and other friends, and he also saw the ranch house several kilometers out of town where Fabian and his parents recently moved. They had a nice place, and Fabian's father was a welder who was making metal flower pot stands and other wares.

That evening, Rigo and Angelo and his brother Hugo said they wanted to go into the mountains with Roland. Rigo had gone last year and Angelo and Hugo had never been. Roland was quite surprised that Rigo wanted to go again.

Early the next morning, Roland drove them to the cono, and they hiked up the mountain, passing by the cave on the way to the highland forest above. Roland and Hugo led the way while Rigo and Angelo were slower. Every so often Rigo and Angelo called out to Roland and Hugo to wait up.

Nearly four hours later, they reached the grassy saddle at the ridge top. The views were good today. The others took a nap for a while. Roland walked around the area and did a little maintenance on his trail. They got some pictures, and then they made their descent, arriving at the cono by 4:30 PM. Roland drove them all back to Bustamante and paid Rigo and Angelo N$70 each for their day. Hugo didn't charge Roland anything, since he wasn't yet working. Angelo thanked Roland and said he was going to buy a shirt for the next baile.

The next day, Rigo was back at work at Felipe's carpentry. Roland went by there a while and visited with them. Sotero and Pedro had plenty of jokes to tell, and Rigo was in happy spirits, too. They told story after story and had plenty of laughs.

Over the last two years, more and more young fellows were putting in earrings, which in Roland's view, were only for women. No, Rigo never did so, but Angelo had done so two years ago, being one of the first in Bustamante. The fad spread, and some were even piercing their eyebrows, tongues, noses, belly buttons, you name it!

Roland decided he'd make fun of it, right then and there, and he drew a young man with all kinds of rings and piercings complete with coil spring chains connecting his belly button to his nose! He put lots of tattoos on him and gave him weird hairstyles. Pedro, Sotero and Rigo got the best laugh out of Roland's absurd drawing. They called the drawing, "Hombre del Futuro," (Man of the Future).

Roland went to look up Dr. Luis who he had met back in April. He was unable to find him. Someone said he was at the Hotel Ancira. So Roland bicycled over there, and when he arrived, they informed him that Luis had just driven away, never to come back. His year of residency was up. Roland had just missed him!

He also went to look up Moises, not having seen him since 1992. His parents said he was in Monterrey and would be home the end of August for the weekend. He was doing well in mechanic's school.

When Roland had arrived the other day, Elisa's house was closed. Her little brown car was parked in the patio, and the gate was locked. She came home Saturday, having been in Monterrey. Roland stopped by, and she was glad to see him. They caught each other up on what they had been doing. Roland began to sense that Elisa had her eye on him. Her three children were home, and they greeted Roland, as well.

Roland also looked up Juan Angel, and they made plans to go camping in the mountains.

That evening, Roland thanked Rigo and his family, and he drove over to Lucio's ranch to stay a few days and continue writing his Mexico novel. The weather was hot and sunny, and it was hot inside the ranch house. No matter what, he made some good progress on his novel.

Four days later, he drove back to Bustamante. Juan Angel was ready to go camping. He said he would see how far he could get, but he wasn't sure. Two days ago, he had been accidentally knocked down during a soccer game.

Roland drove with Juan Angel to the cono, and they began the hike up the mountain. Juan Angel's leg was bothering him, and when they reached the cave entrance nearly an hour later, he gave up. Roland continued to the highland forest alone, reaching the grassy saddle three hours later. He set up his tent in the forest and had a good night's sleep. The wind blew considerably, and the summer crickets chirped through the night.

The next morning, on the way down the mountain, he used his clippers and did some trail maintenance, trimming some annoying Poison Oak out of the way.

Rigo had not passed one of his final exams at the Prepa, and he needed to retake it.

Roland took him over to Sabinas Hidalgo early one morning and left him at the Prepa. Meanwhile, Roland did errands at Garza Morton and Centro Comercial San José, and he returned for Rigo, who said the teacher didn't even show! The exam was postponed.

Roland had his photos developed at Farmacia Benavides, and he had extras made for Rigo and Angelo, pictures of them swimming and of their hike in the mountains.

They returned to Bustamante. Roland visited other friends and returned to Lucio's ranch by dark.

One day, he took a nap, and he surprisingly had a detailed dream about Isalia and Luke. *Roland was walking along the Eagleville Highway, and they pulled up to Roland in Luke's white truck. Both of them were passengers, and there was no driver at the wheel! They talked to Roland and told him they had a project for him. Isalia grabbed Roland by the arm, and she and Luke took him to her son Laurence's house to begin work . . .*

Roland suddenly woke up, sweaty! What did they want?! They were not Roland's friends anymore. Couldn't they stay out of his dreams?

A few days later, Roland returned to Bustamante for the day to do Rigo a favor, to take him to his rescheduled final exam at the Prepa. Rigo took a shower before going with Roland, and Angelo also came along. They waited outside the school while Rigo took his final. He barely passed it, but he made it.

It was a major turning point for a lot of decisions in Rigo's life. If he hadn't made it, he couldn't have gone on to the Normal to train to be a teacher, and he would have gone wetback either to Texas or all the way to Tennessee with Roland.

However, since he did make it, he would be granted entry into the Normal for a four-year teacher program. He was to enter at 2 PM today.

So, Roland said he and Angelo would go on back to Bustamante, leaving Rigo here, or they could eat lunch there in Sabinas Hidalgo and wait for him during the afternoon.

No, what Rigo wanted to do was return to Bustamante for lunch. Roland didn't understand why, but he obliged him. They went home for lunch. As Roland drove them back, he kept smelling something bad. Rigo took a bath again and put on different clothes of the same style. Then they had lunch, and Roland took him and Angelo back to Sabinas Hidalgo again. Angelo's father also came along, and once they reached the Normal school, Rigo stepped down and entered his first day at a new school.

Roland took Angelo and his father on a couple of errands and then drove on back to Bustamante. Rigo took the bus home later that evening.

Roland couldn't understand why Rigo had to return to Bustamante for lunch. Rigo didn't say anything about it, but he had to shower and change clothes because he had an accident in his pants while taking the final. You see, he had been nervous during the test.

* * *

The new clinic, the Centro Salud was about to open. Roland met the new doctor, whose name was Roberto. He too spoke fluent English, and they became friends.

Late that afternoon, it rained. There was talk of a hurricane coming in and possible flooding. Rigo came home in the evening, and as they were eating supper, Alejandro and Lavinia urged Roland not to return to the ranch, for risk of getting stuck in mud. They asked Roland to stay.

Roland thanked them for their concern, but he had only come for the day, and nearly all of his things were at the ranch. So, that evening, he drove back to the ranch. Around a kilometer after the Ojo del Agua, the rain quit, and everything to the west was clear skies. He arrived at the ranch just fine.

He spent several more days there, and he was making good progress on his Mexico novel. Plus, he did some more paintings.

On August 27, Roland returned to Bustamante, and he rode around town on his bicycle, visiting friends. Dr. Luis was supposed to arrive and so was Moises this weekend.

Roland visited his friends at Felipe's carpentry. Rigo was there with them, and they all had some good laughs. It was really great how Rigo was such a good friend. He didn't drink nor smoke, had not done so since April, and Roland was thankful to him and his family.

Though Roland didn't tell anybody, he could sense that Ivanhoe had done something, having cleaned Rigo of his contamination, and restored him to the good and kind hearted person he really was. Rigo's resentment was entirely gone, and it was like the slate was cleaned from April forward. It was a miracle indeed, and Rigo was benefiting from it, as well. He was straighter and friendlier, and he was more loving with his family, and with his mother, also.

After all, Roland felt like the Zacatón family was the predestined family for him to know and eventually marry into, seeing how he had seen those flowers posted on that tree in Washington's Alpine Lakes Wilderness on the day that Norma was born. Plus, Raul and Rigo were like brothers to Roland, since he didn't have any of his own.

Whether nor not Ivanhoe was behind the miracle, Roland was grateful that it had occurred.

That evening, Rigo was out visiting friends, and Alejandro was at the cantina as usual. Lavina and her two daughters were at home, and Roland said he was going out for a while to visit friends. In case they were asleep when he returned, would they leave the door unlocked? Lavinia was iffy, and she expressed concern about Roland entering the house without Rigo or his father being here. Why was Lavinia being iffy? After all, Roland was their guest. Irma immediately came forth and assured Roland that when he returns later tonight, she would open the door for him to let him in. Thank you, Irma. Roland visited friends for an hour, and when he returned, Irma was true to her word and let him in.

The next day, Roland took Rigo and Angelo over to Sabinas Hidalgo. Rigo bought clothing, his uniform for the Normal school. Then Roland treated them to lunch at the Centro Comercial San José restaurant. Prices had gone up 150%, and as a result, the meal for the three of them was more, a total of N\$89.

While leaving Sabinas Hidalgo to return to Bustamante, the police had a road block, and they were checking everyone for alcoholic beverages. Roland stepped down, went to the back of his truck and let them inspect his things. Of course, there was no beer nor liquor. There never was. The police told Roland and his two friends to have a nice day and to go ahead.

Roland drove them out of Sabinas Hidalgo, and as they were going along the narrow winding highway, heading toward Villaldama, Roland asked Rigo when he would have his winter vacation from school.

"¡No sé! ¡No sé!" he answered, gruffly telling Roland he didn't know.

What?! Roland thought. He was quite taken aback at his sudden rudeness, and he asked Rigo why he answered like that.

"¡No sé! ¡No sé!" he repeated.

Roland told him not to talk to him like that, and he proceeded to tell him that he asked that question because he wanted to take him and Angelo down south to southern Mexico this January, if they had the time.

"Es que quieres saber todo, Rolando!" Rigo angrily snapped, telling Roland it's just that he wanted to know everything!

That wasn't true. Roland merely wanted to know Rigo's schedule in January so they could plan to go down south.

Before he knew it, Angelo suddenly began to rant and rave, accusing Roland of not having fed them nor having given them anything during that trip to Zacatecas 20 months ago!

Roland corrected Angelo and said he did too give them food and bought some for them, as well. No, it wasn't a lot, but he did. Antonio, Lavinia's brother, also fed them all several meals.

That didn't matter to Angelo right now. He continued to rant and rave, shouting at Roland repeatedly that he didn't give them anything, that they were dying of hunger the whole trip, and he carried on with a rash of outlandish accusations and complaints. Rigo just sat there and let Angelo go on and on about it!

Roland was taking Angelo's annoying complaints, but his shouting was distracting him considerably while trying to drive his truck down the road. There was a gravel turnout just ahead on the highway, and Roland decided to pull the truck over, firmly applying the brakes to do so.

"Angelo, ya me disgustaste. ¡Bájate ya!" said Roland, firmly telling Angelo he had already disgusted him and to just get out and walk.

As soon as Roland stopped his truck, Angelo proudly and promptly stepped down from Roland's truck.

"Si Angelo baja, yo también," said Rigo, telling Roland that since Angelo was stepping down, so was he, and Rigo diligently stepped down, to faithfully accompany Angelo.

Roland stepped down from his truck as well, and he watched them walk down the edge of the highway. He figured they'd turn around, but they kept on walking.

Roland hadn't literally intended for Angelo to walk, but then he made Roland so frustrated that he pulled the truck over and said, "Bájate," before he knew it.

Since they kept on walking, Roland got back in his truck and drove up to them, and as he slowly drove beside them, they kept on walking. "Súbense," Roland said to them, telling them to get in. They kept on walking. Roland told Angelo not to treat him that way and to apologize. Nothing doing! They kept walking. "Súbense," Roland repeated, telling them to get in.

They were on a dangerous curve of the highway, and two or three cars had gathered behind Roland. He waved them around him, and he continued trying to get Angelo and Rigo back inside his truck.

Twenty times he asked them to get back inside, but they were stubborn. Okay, they left Roland no other option. He drove away. Words wouldn't sufficiently describe how terrible Roland felt, not to mention the feelings of betrayal that Rigo and Angelo had just caused him to suffer. Why in the world didn't they get back in his truck?! Five minutes earlier, they were Roland's friends, and like a light bulb being turned off, they had suddenly taken what was nothing other than severe dislike to Roland . . . for his having invited them to travel to the south of Mexico!

Temporary Miracle

Roland drove fast. He was in anguish and very worried about what Rigo and Angelo and their friends might later do to him. When he reached Villaldama, he asked Alberto who was serving chicken to go back with him to collect Rigo and Angelo off the highway. Alberto was willing to drop what he was doing, and he asked Roland to loan him his truck, because if Roland was in the truck, they wouldn't get in. Roland said he couldn't do it that way. If Alberto would just accompany him to return for Rigo and Angelo, that would work. Alberto insisted on borrowing Roland's truck, but Roland said no to that. So, Alberto decided to stay with his chicken.

Roland drove on to Bustamante, immediately arriving at the Zacatón's house. He quickly took all his things out of the house and loaded them into his truck. Lavinia and her daughters were there, and Roland told them the bad news, and if they wanted to take him to the police, he was prepared to go with them and explain that Angelo was shouting at him considerably, and even after he and Rigo had stepped down, Roland had asked them 20 times to get back inside his truck.

No! No, Lavinia didn't want to get the police involved in the problem. Okay, good!

Roland thanked her, gave her US $20 for having kept him in their house, and he told her he hoped she understood.

She answered by saying she wasn't angry, just worried. She said she was always going to believe her son over Roland, and she told Roland it was his fault, not her son's.

Roland drove his loaded truck over to Victor's house in the upper part of town, and he briefly told them what happened. Victor told Roland he did the right thing to leave them on the highway. If they didn't have enough sense to get back in Roland's truck, then just let them walk!

Roland took his bicycle out of his truck and rode to Angelo's house to explain to his parents what had just happened.

Then he rode over to Moises' house. Gazdi came to the door and said Moises didn't come. Their father had mysteriously become ill and was rushed by ambulance to a hospital in Monterrey! Roland told Gazdi he was sorry to hear about his father and hoped he would be all right, but he was by now feeling blocked from ever seeing or knowing Moises again!

By now, an hour had gone by since Roland had left Rigo and Angelo. He was standing on the sidewalk with Gazdi by his house, and he told Gazdi what had happened. Gazdi could see that Roland was quite worried. A ZuaZua bus pulled up to the street corner and stopped. It had just arrived from Sabinas Hidalgo, and several people stepped off the bus, including Rigo and Angelo!

Roland was glad to see that they were alive and well, but he didn't like the look on their faces. Gazdi saw their faces and acknowledged to Roland that they looked very angry.

Roland said goodbye to Gazdi and bicycled away. Rigo and Angelo slowly walked up the street together. They had looks on their faces like they wanted to deck Roland. Seeing that, Roland fled in fear and bicycled right back to Victor's house, got in his truck, and drove straight to Lucio's ranch. It was Saturday night, and who knows who they might have rounded up against him during the dance and other wild activities!

He arrived at dark, and he took a walk through the desert with the star-filled sky above. He spoke out loud and asked why that awful event had taken place. The friendship between Roland and Rigo had been fixed and was running just fine . . . until this afternoon! Roland did not deserve having that rug pulled out from under him. Who had caused it, some bunch of demons?! It seemed that way. Roland thought and thought, trying to figure it out. The downfall had occurred so quickly! Why were Roland's better friendships this past decade the subject of such sabotage?!

Roland tried to get some sleep that night but couldn't sleep well.

*   *   *

August 28, 1999

Alfra and Tabra were sent reeling in grief and desperation as they watched through the holographic window from their location in the spirit world. They telepathically called for their friend, Martoncíon. In less than a minute, he arrived, appearing before them.

"Yes, Alfra and Tabra?" Martoncíon responded. Then he looked through the holographic window. He shook his head with disappointment. "I'm not the least bit surprised."

"What's happened?" Tabra asked Martoncíon with concern.

"We thought we had everything fixed back in April," Alfra added.

"We did," Martoncíon agreed.

"But look at what's just happened," Tabra stated. "Roland's devastated! He didn't deserve that."

"No, he didn't deserve that," Martoncíon agreed again. "Let's just put it this way. What does Molonco care?"

"What's that supposed to mean?" Tabra asked.

"It means just that," Martoncíon replied.

"I thought you set up the energy system, the dream . . ." Alfra began.

"Yes, I set up the energy system, sent the dream, and the rest of it," Martoncíon broke in and made clear, "but there was a clause in the program."

"A clause? What?" Tabra asked.

"Look at the scene yourselves!" Martoncíon directed. "If Molonco were a faithful friend of Roland's, he would have defended him. He did nothing of the kind. Instead he stepped right down out of that truck with his friend, Angelo, and never gave even a second's thought to Roland, much less his feelings. He's failed!"

"Can't the problem be fixed?" Tabra asked.

"Look, the clause stated that if Molonco failed to defend his friend, the energy system would detach and flee!"

"Why did you have to put that in?" Alfra asked, somewhat disgusted.

"It's like this. All energy systems have to have safety valves, right?" Martoncíon explained. "Deep down, Molonco is of cold heart, full of hate and sneer, in addition to being ungrateful."

"What harsh comments!" Tabra declared.

"Yes, but it's only true," Martoncíon told her in a matter-of-fact manner. "Look, he's been draining on the cosmos with his negativity, and with this failure, it was too much for the positive energy system. It abandoned him and flew away. Molonco doesn't deserve Roland's friendship."

"But Roland's devastated!" Alfra reminded Martoncíon.

"He will be all right. I know him. Events will come together properly, and he will figure it out."

"And you had told us that Molonco is good at heart," Tabra added.

"Yes, I did tell you that. That was *then*. Things have changed, and unfortunately, so has he. I'm sorry if I have misled you."

"I have to admit you did," Alfra told him.

"At that time, I thought it too," Martonción said to them, "but I was sadly mistaken."

"Isn't there something you can do?" Tabra asked.

Martonción probed the atmosphere for feelings. "Look, I'll do this much. I'll weave a temporary system for a few days, until Roland exits Mexico and goes home, but it will only work if Molonco has enough goodness in him to cause it to work for him. If that will make Roland feel better, then it's worth that much."

"Thank you, Martonción," Tabra told him. "We know Roland will also appreciate it."

"Fair enough, but the important lesson in life is that people like Molonco, who make you think they are your friend and then turn their back on you in betrayal, do not deserve Roland's genuine friendship."

"Yes, we both agree with that," said Alfra.

"If it will ease Roland's grief, then fair enough. I will temporarily weave the system, but I must dismantle it as soon as Roland returns to his country."

"Martonción," Tabra brought up, "while what you stated is true, do take note that Molonco and Angelo stepped down from Roland's truck within spitting distance of Nuevo Wimbisenho."

"And have you captured the demons there?" Alfra added.

"No, I haven't been able to locate them," Martonción admitted.

"Then we believe they provoked this problem," Alfra speculated.

Martonción, who hadn't probed that area of thought, began to send his feelings out in that direction. Suddenly, his face went cold as his mind latched the data and registered the chilling truth of the situation, and the culprits . . ."

*   *   *

Nuevo Wimbisenho

"Mmm . . . Mmm! Draaktra, I've got to hand it to you," Druxtrli told him.

"You are super excellent," Arfifra praised him, "a champion collector of rejection energies!"

"Complex variable integration phasing techniques," Sasjurech praised Draaktra. "Never have I seen it better done!"

"Complete with an appropriately timed frequency responder and cue, left on the side of the highway," Sojornbloc added praise.

"See if Martonción can clean Rigo *this* time," Draaktra boasted.

They roared with laughter!

"Roland's really in a bad way, now," Torxtalo pointed out.

"He's very ill and is soon to be ours," Arfifra remarked presumptuously. "He's in pain."

"We complied with Martonción's wishes to get *bored and go away*," Arfifra pointed out.

"He didn't think we'd sneak back up and slide one in on Rigo so fast," Draaktra boasted again.

"After all," Torxtalo pointed out, "Roland's continued friendship with Rigo and his family, and his staying with them set up an excellent chance for rejection." He finished his statement with a look of ego and pride.

"Excellent chance for *prestigious* rejection," Arfifra added, correcting Torxtalo's carefully savoured statement.

Torxtalo turned toward his mentor Arfifra and faked a hurt look.

Everyone roared with laughter!

"We thought last year's feast was the richest one we ever had," Sasjurech commented.

"Oh, that was just a practice run," Draaktra proudly stated. "I've upgraded Denlamter's energy capture apparatus, and these energy disks are super charged!"

"Whew-wee!" Torxtalo exclaimed, and he laughed inappropriately.

"Let's call in some more of our friends and have the grandest feast ever to be known to . . . *Nuevo Wimbisenho!*" Arfifra announced with joy!

Others soon arrived, magically making their appearances. Among them were Brutoxlo, Arce-fera, Ferúpsula, Zepita, Agüantano and Farbula, the last two having come in from Florida!

They had a major feast, and the cave was full. All night long, they partied and feasted on Draaktra's energy disks until they were exhilaratingly drunk beyond reason!

* * *

That program that Draaktra suddenly managed to spring onto Rigo was horrifyingly malignant! It immediately became so integrated within Rigo's psyche that it would be nearly impossible to remove, and it came complete with a subconscious training course that would teach Rigo how to become an expert at turning his back to and being indifferent to certain people like Roland. Rigo would still go on leading a mostly normal life, but from this day forward, the road would be bumpier. Plus, the friendship between Roland and Rigo would forever remain a guaranteed loss, even though it was never Roland's fault.

* * *

The next morning, Roland bicycled over to Chiquihuitillos and looked at the ancient paintings some more. He talked to the family who owned the ranch there and lived there. The owner was an older man who saw life as it was, and he decided to mention to Roland that in this day and age, the man who is well accepted in society is he who drinks, dances, and smokes! Society doesn't care much for people who think differently and analyze, like Roland and also this ranch owner.

Roland laughed at the way the man put it, and he told him he was right. It was true. In fact, Rigo had told Roland that if he drank, he would have more friends. It was not good that Rigo believed and thought that. Roland still had plenty of friends, and he didn't want friends who drank a lot.

Roland gave the ranch family a couple of his calendars, for which they were very thankful.

They talked a while longer about philosophy and life on this side of the mountains. It used to be wetter and rain more often in past years, but now it was dry, and even the Mesquites and other Acacia shrubs were dying.

Roland bicycled back to Lucio's ranch, and he decided to drive into Bustamante to talk to Rigo and Angelo, to see if they could apologize and forgive each other for the awful event yesterday.

Roland wrote out a short note to each one of them, and he drove into town. He first arrived at the Zacatón's house. Lavinia was out front, said Rigo was over with Angelo and other friends, and she told Roland he must find Rigo and take him to the clinic to cure him. He had serious blisters on his feet from having walked 10 kilometers along the hot pavement of the highway! Roland was sorry to hear that, was apologetic, and he reminded Lavinia that he had told them 20 times to get back in his truck. He handed her his note to Rigo. She took it, read it, and would give it to him.

Roland drove over to Angelo's house. They weren't there.

An hour later, Roland found Rigo and Angelo over at the Zacatón's house. Lavinia and her daughters were there and so was Alejandro. Roland began to tell Rigo and Angelo that he felt bad about the event yesterday, and he wanted to see if they could make up. Plus, Lavinia had told Roland he must . . .

Rigo and Angelo said nothing, showed Roland angry faces, and Rigo turned on the stereo. He put his back to Roland and turned the volume up! That hurt Roland's feelings even more, and he felt a terrible tightness of nervous feelings, combined with anger, indifference and sullenness coming from Rigo's back. Lavinia tried to tell Rigo to go to the clinic with Roland, but he just shunned her.

Alejandro came to Roland, and they stepped outside to talk. They had to go down the street to hear each other, due to Rigo's loudly playing his stereo. Alejandro explained that Rigo was very angry at Roland. Roland asked him why? It was totally Rigo's decision to step down with Angelo. Roland hadn't run him off. Now, Angelo yes, Roland had run off, but that was for the moment's frustration, which is why he had told them 20 times to get back in. Alejandro explained that not even 100 times would have convinced them to get back in. No matter what, Roland told Alejandro he was sorry it had happened.

Roland felt so awful that he went to one of the new payphone card phones, and he called up his friend Ivanhoe in Scotland. The call yanked N$20 per minute off his N$50 card, so he only had two minutes.

"Oh, hey Roland! Gee, you sound funny! What sort of phone are you on? Are you in Mexico?"

"Yes, I am. Listen, I . . ." and Roland told Ivanhoe in a nutshell that Rigo and Angelo had gone mad on him, etc.

"Don't worry about it. It's been taken care of. You should be seeing results within the day's time."

"You mean you already knew about it?"

"Yes, I felt it all yesterday, and I've taken care of it . . . don't know how long it will last nor how well it will work, but I've sent some positive energies down your way."

"Why, thank you, Ivanhoe."

"That's quite all right. So, have a word with your friends to see if you can sort it out, and then I suggest you clear out of there and make a beeline home."

"I will, and thanks again, Ivanhoe."

"You take care of yourself, Roland."

"You, too."

They said goodbye and hung up. Ivanhoe was quite concerned for Roland.

He went to visit other friends that afternoon. Later, he went back over to Angelo's house and talked to his parents. Angelo, Rigo, and another friend were hidden in the next room. He had read Roland's note and he refused to talk to Roland at all. Angelo's father explained that writing a note like that was something that *maricóns* did, that is, gay people. Roland responded by looking at him in disbelief, and he asked him since when was it considered *gay* for a man to write a note or letter to another man, especially in matters of resolving a problem? Angelo's father told Roland that's the way it was in Mexico. That was the culture. Roland asked him how it was possible that he never knew that, seeing that he had been coming to Mexico for several years, and no one had ever told him. He had been writing letters and notes to friends here and there and everywhere, and never once did it cross his mind that they would consider it something that gay men do!

Roland explained that he had letters from men from various parts of the world, and Angelo's father asked him if he had any from Mexico. Roland answered that as a matter of fact, he did. He had a letter from Mr. Esquivel from Taxco. He also had the nice letter from Leonardo three years ago, and no, Leonardo wasn't gay. He had a serious girlfriend in San Nicolas who he would soon be marrying.

Roland talked a while longer with Angelo's father about the problem, and he wished he had known that culture flaw a long time ago. Roland had already learned that one cannot say *disfrutar* nor say *gustar* in reference to enjoying a friend or that a friend pleases you, because that carries sexual connotations, but when would he have ever thought that writing a note to another male would be considered *gay*? How absurd does one get?!

He left Angelo's house and went to talk to other friends. He thought about the culture flaw some more, and he remembered when he had received that letter in November 1997 from Rigo's family and how Norma had written the letter instead of Rigo.

Ohhhhh! That's why Rigo had not written that letter! Roland suddenly realized. It was now making sense for the first time. *Ohhhhh! No wonder Rigo wouldn't type out a letter on that Royal 440 manual typewriter and send it to Roland.* Another realization!

Roland also went and talked to Roberto, the doctor in town, during his off time. (By the way, the former doctor, Luis, had never come back to town.) Roberto was from Monterrey, like most doctors were, and Roland wanted to see what big city people thought about writing letters. Roland explained to him about Rigo and Angelo and how he had written them a note to try and resolve the problem. The doctor explained that in a big city like where he was from, they have more culture and understanding than small town folks, who in many ways are still superstitious. People like Rigo and Angelo just don't understand the definition of friendship, nor the advanced culture of writing letters. Rigo, more than anybody, should have understood, since he was now training to be a teacher. They talked a while longer, and he recommended to Roland that he just turn the page on it and move on. Eventually he would, but not until he would figure it out.

Roland went to Elisa and talked to her, as well. She seemed somewhat surprised about the whole thing, and they talked a while about the whole problem. She could sense that Roland was quite bothered about it, and she saw that he valued his friendships. Elisa said she had few friends in Bustamante. Most people she just said hi to, but that's as far as it went. There were some people she had been better friends to, but as soon as a disagreement occurred, that was it, right then! They never talked again, and she would just put it to the past and not worry about it. They would walk by each other on the street and have no past feelings about it. Roland said that he was always more hopeful and that he was one to hold onto his friendships whenever possible. Elisa explained that one has to let things go sometimes. Well, Rigo and his family had been such special friends, that he wasn't going to let them go so easily. Besides, those flowers were posted on that tree on Norma's date of birth for a very good reason, a good sign for the future.

Roland also went to the Quevalos. It had been a long time since he had talked to them. He saw Pancho and asked him how things were going for him. He answered that making chairs was hard work, and little by little, his business was growing. Most of the equipment Luke had donated was still working. Pancho then showed some anxiety and told Roland he needed to get back to work. He quickly returned to the backyard. Roland also saw Eliud. He told him he had always seen him as a good fellow, and he had always thought good of him.

No more than Roland managed to tell Eliud that, than one of the Quevalo sisters, Olana, shouted a directing comment to Eliud, "¡No le pongas atención!" telling him not to pay any attention to Roland. That was not very nice, but then Olana had never liked Roland, anyway.

Roland then added a comment saying that he was not gay. After all, Roland was sure the Quevalo sisters thought Roland was gay and that he was also loco.

Roland said goodbye to Eliud and left.

That evening, Roland went to the Zacatón's house and talked to them some more. Rigo was at home and on the bed watching TV. Roland brought up the November 1997 letter, and he asked Rigo why had hadn't written it himself. He got extremely defensive and quickly shouted some reasons at Roland as to why he hadn't written it. Lavinia made some comment that she had written it, and Roland reminded them all that it was Norma who had written it, instead of Rigo, and it was in Rigo's voice.

Rigo asked Roland what importance it carried, and he shouted at Roland, accusing him of picking a fight!

Roland quickly told Rigo that he had his sister write that letter because he was embarrassed to write it himself, wasn't he? Further, the people might say that he was *gay*!

Rigo shook his head up and down, admitting and verifying a *yes*, and Roland asked him why he didn't tell him that culture detail a long time ago? He had not been straightforward on that one at all.

Rigo angrily shouted some phrases, stating that he didn't have to tell those details to anybody!

Roland said goodbye to the Zacatóns, and he told Rigo he realized that he was not going to ever feel content again, that the devil had won, and that it was nice having known him in the past. Roland walked out of the house.

As he was getting into his truck to drive off, Irma came to him, saying that Rigo wanted to talk to him. Roland thought, *About what?!*

He re-entered the house, and Rigo quite surprisingly wished Roland well, shook hands with him in a sincere manner, and he assured him that they go on being friends! *Why, miracle!* Roland thought to himself. Okay, he shook hands with Rigo. They said goodbye, and Roland walked out of the house, feeling much better.

*   *   *

Nuevo Wimbisenho

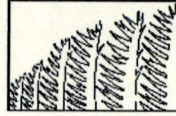

"Oh how sick!" Sasjurech remarked, almost throwing up.

"There, there, let 'em have their little moment of compassion," said Arfifra. "It's all in the game, you know."

"After all, we want Roland to come back for more," Draaktra pointed out.

"Draaktra and I have some plans to announce," Arce-fera brought up.

*   *   *

Roland spent the night somewhere else that night, and he drove away the next morning. He reached the Colombia Bridge, turned in his permit, and crossed the bridge. They gave him a quick and easy inspection at the booth, checking underneath with mirrors and declaring, "Clear!"

CHAPTER 18

PERFUME AND THE SKUNK

fall, 1999

On the way home, Roland visited with Raul, his uncle and family in Salado. He had a good visit, and Raul reckoned that Rigo would come around and remain Roland's friend.

The next day, Roland drove home, and he began working carpentry and painting jobs again.

He called Ivanhoe on the phone, and he told Roland that putting Angelo and Rigo out on the highway was the best thing he could have done for them. Angelo had decided to rant and rave to Roland, and he soon realized that he didn't get away with it. Roland was right to have a firm hand on that one. Still, he felt bad for their having stayed on the highway, and he had told them 20 times to get back inside. Of course, for their pride, they hadn't. Ivanhoe pointed out that if Rigo had been a real friend, he would have stayed in the truck with Roland and would have told Angelo to get back inside with them. Instead, he was silent complacent, and he diligently stepped right down with Angelo. Never once did it cross Rigo's mind to defend Roland.

Roland wrote Rigo a letter, explaining how he felt about the whole thing. He apologized again, and he reiterated that Rigo had stepped down by his own decision. He asked Rigo why it hadn't crossed his mind to defend him, and to tell Angelo to get back inside. He enclosed US $20 to help him with school. He enclosed the letter in an envelope which he addressed to Rigo, enclosed that envelope in another envelope, and sent it to Elisa's house, asking her to deliver the letter and envelope within to Rigo. He would have sent the letter directly to Rigo, but then they didn't have a telephone, and remembering how unwilling Rigo was to take Roland's call last year, not to mention how rude he had been, Roland didn't want to call him and verify. Elisa had a phone, and he would verify with her.

Not long after arriving home, Roland drove through Lascassas one afternoon, and he saw the old narrow truss bridge. It was still in use, but the new and much wider bridge to its left was very near completion. Traffic was somewhat heavy that afternoon, and Roland saw two dump trucks approaching the bridge from opposite directions. One of them stopped to avoid passing the other truck on that bridge! That's how narrow it was.

In late September, Roland drove over that bridge one last time while still in use. He had Jaime with him as a passenger. They were out in that area looking for painting work.

On Saturday, October 2, 1999, the narrow truss bridge was taken out of service and closed. For 54 years, it had served its purpose, spanning the Stones River. A few days later, there was an article in Murfreesboro's newspaper about its closing. It read:

"Bridge to Lascassas: New $1.8 million structure gives drivers breathing room."

With the opening of the new Lascassas bridge over the East Fork of Stones River on State Route 96, area motorists no longer have to worry about swapping mirrors with other drivers. Notoriously narrow, the just-replaced bridge had caused more than one driver to grip the steering wheel a little tighter . . ."

Simultaneously, Rigo had just received Roland's letter and the $20 via Elisa, and late that afternoon, he rounded up a bunch of his friends, bought $20 worth of beer, and they went to the canyon. There, Rigo drank 9 beers, and he got drunk for the first time! Some of his friends drank more! They laughed at Roland behind his back and sneered at him for being so naive at mailing Rigo that $20.

Well, Roland wasn't so naive as they thought. That night, he had a dream about Rigo drinking 9 beers and spending Roland's money the wrong way! Roland got right to it and wrote him another letter, and this time he sent it directly to his house. He told Rigo about the dream, and that if it was true, he was going to be like his father Alejandro after all. Though Rigo never told Roland, he was very surprised when he received and read that second letter!

On Sunday, October 3, Roland called Elisa to verify if Rigo had received the first letter and the $20. She said it had arrived October 1, and she had delivered it to him yesterday morning, October 2. However, she decided to bring up, without apologizing, that her son Carlos opened the envelope addressed to her, and as a result, opened up both envelopes and *read* the letter to Rigo! Roland asked her about the $20, and she said that was intact, and she had delivered it to him, as well. Roland told her the disturbing dream he had just had, and she stated that dreams weren't always reality.

Roland called up another friend in town, and he happened to mention that he had seen Rigo and his friends in the canyon Saturday afternoon, and they were drinking! Dream was reality this time. What more proof did Roland need? That was the last time Roland ever sent Rigo and his family money!

What was more interesting was that the Lascassas Bridge had closed right when Rigo and his friends were having their sneering fiesta with Roland's $20! Maybe that narrow bridge really did represent the friendship Roland and Rigo had.

Along about this time, the distributor from South Carolina wrote Roland a letter stating that they have yet to make the first sale on his materials, and for him to come over and collect his books and calendars as soon as possible. Roland looked at the contract, and from the time the letter was written, he was obligated to be the distributor until November 8. Roland called the distributor, reaching someone else of course, and he said he would arrive punctually on that date to collect his books and calendars.

He drove over there on that date, and once he loaded his 250 books and his various calendars, he drove all over the city where that distributor lived, and he delivered them to residents at random. In other words, he gave them away. He delivered door to door, in parking lots, and he even delivered to the dormitories of a nearby college. In each book and calendar, he included flyers and order forms about his more recent calendars. There! That got those materials *distributed* finally! Why couldn't that lazy bum distributor do the same? It irritated Roland how lackadaisical he was!

Roland kept two copies of the book compilation and one copy of each calendar to take home. On the way back home, he drove through Lascassas, and when he arrived at the new bridge, he pulled over and parked. He got out of his car, and he walked across the old truss bridge, which was still standing. It was night, and the star-filled sky could be seen through the truss rails above. Roland had the bridge to himself, and he enjoyed the walk across it. He walked those two books and calendars across that old bridge, the same bridge he had crossed when he took them to the distributor last year. Once having crossed the bridge, he set them down on the highway shoulder, and he walked back across the old bridge to return to his car.

Perfume And The Skunk

Now, he drove across the new bridge, stopped, collected his two books and calendars, and he drove home to Longview. There was no way those remaining materials were going to cross that new bridge to return home again, and 248 of those books, plus numerous calendars, were now being enjoyed by residents in South Carolina!

Also, during this fall, Roland made two phone calls to his friend in Spain, the one who he had visited back in 1996. Each time he had reached him, he was too busy to talk to him, and Roland began to smell a rat. He wrote him a letter stating that he felt brushed off, and he asked him what was up. He had wanted to talk to him by phone to make arrangements about going over to Spain to visit next summer. Plus, he had invited him to Alaska and never got a response. Well, that "friend" wrote Roland back a surprising letter and stated that he didn't wish to continue knowing him, and that he didn't feel comfortable with him. He further stated that he wasn't the one Roland should contact in Spain. However, he did agree with Roland on one point, that Mexicans were very mistaken about their concept of men who write each other letters being *gay*! Roland thought that fellow and his family were his friends. They were his first chosen family to contact whenever he might be in Spain. In previous years, they had been glad to hear from him. What was going on?! It made Roland quite sad.

Roland talked with his friend Abraham from Central America, and he was quite surprised at the way the fellow from Spain had acted. Roland also talked to Ivanhoe about it, and he sensed that something had recently scared him off. Perhaps his "friend" had recently had a strange dream!

He and Ivanhoe also talked about Rigo, and Ivanhoe predicted that Roland would more than likely sort out the problem with Rigo, and they would continue being friends.

In mid December, Roland packed his truck to return to Mexico for a while. He planned on staying a good while to make good progress on his Mexico novel, plus do some more artwork. He had no idea if the Zacatón family would receive him this time, but he would be staying the majority of the time at Lucio's ranch, anyway.

He had bought several bikes at the Goodwill Store in Nashville, and he would take them with him to give to various people and friends in Bustamante.

The day before leaving, Roland drove over to Lascassas to check on the bridge. Yes, it was still there. Roland parked on the shoulder, and he walked across the old truss bridge for the last time. He had known that bridge all his life, and for his respect for it and the friendship it represented, he was saying goodbye to it. It would probably no longer be there by the time he would return from Mexico.

Roland thought about his friendship with Rigo. He hoped it would continue, but after having that dream of his having that sneering fiesta with that $20 Roland had sent him, he had a feeling the friendship was in its last days. Actually, he felt like the friendship was closed. Roland could imagine Rigo was laughing behind his back, and he decided to make light of the situation. So, right before leaving to go to Mexico, he typed out a "For Sale" sign for Rigo and his family to hang on their front door. It was written in Spanish, and it read something like:

For Sale: Friendship with the gringo from Tennessee, $5 . . . No, $4 (20% discount). He doesn't drink, doesn't smoke, doesn't dance, doesn't like perfume, nor loud music. He doesn't even have a girlfriend! What do I want him for?!! Inquiries: Zacatón house, Bustamante.

Roland laughed at his own creation. It was a joke sure enough, but if Rigo were to give Roland the cold shoulder, he was going to give him that sign to hang on his front door! No matter what, the sign portrayed Rigo's more recent lack of understanding of who Roland was.

A few days before Christmas, Roland drove on down to Mexico, and he arrived at the border on the afternoon of the second day. He drove across the Colombia Bridge, and Mexican Customs officials were surprisingly very picky! They wouldn't let him in with his things. The Cedar lumber was prohibited. The bicycles were prohibited. The tree seedling was prohibited. The food was prohibited. Good gracious! Everything was prohibited! They brought over a guide book, and the officer was justifying everything, and he was picking a fight by raising his voice. Roland sensed a trap, and he told them he would just drive back over to the Texas side and forget entering Mexico at all! They said okay this time, but if he tried to bring in all that stuff again, they would take his truck and belongings away and leave him on foot!

Roland didn't know what the officer's vendetta was, but he just backed up his truck and drove away. If the officer had been more persistent, Roland was prepared to give him $20 or $40 to appease him and get out of there! Roland had heard a recent horror story. Jaime had a friend who entered at Reynosa three months ago, and the customs officers were abusive and took his truck away from him! The fellow made numerous efforts with lawyers and the police to get his truck back, all to no avail! Everyone was in cahoots with each other, and it was corruption gone wild! And to add, they can be glad they didn't take Roland's truck away from him, because they would have had quite a fight on their hands! Plus, Roland would have been quite a nuisance, reporting the crime to all sectors and levels.

Roland drove back over to the U.S. side. Luckily, they were friendly and didn't inspect Roland's fully loaded truck. They had seen him pay toll and enter Mexico 15 minutes ago. Roland thanked them and drove over to Laredo and parked near Bridge 1. First he crossed on foot and talked to an officer, who said those items would be fine to bring in. Good! Roland walked back across, got in his truck, and drove it across the bridge. They gave him an easy inspection. He paid duty on the extra bicycles, and he entered Mexico.

He took Highway 85 to Sabinas Hidalgo, and he later arrived at Bustamante just before dark. It was wet weather, and there was a constant drizzle.

The first place Roland went was to the Zacatón's house. He felt apprehensive as he knocked on the door. Rigo answered it, and without greeting Roland, he said for him to come inside if he wanted to. He was the only one there, and he told Roland that just an hour ago, his mother and sisters had taken a bus to Zacatecas to visit family in Pinos. They had waited to see if Roland might arrive and take them, and they had N$1,000 ready to pay him for gasoline. Roland likely would have taken them, but he had been delayed at the Colombia Bridge, and for having to cross a different bridge instead, he had arrived later than he would have.

Rigo said he had not gone with them because he had too much homework and finals to study for, coming up in January.

Without telling Rigo, Roland analyzed the scenario in his mind. Something had stepped in and delayed him from arriving to Bustamante in time to take Lavinia and her daughters to Zacatecas, and it was probably for the best. Roland didn't need to go to Zacatecas anyway, and even though he didn't exactly want to go, he probably would have accommodated them and taken them. As it turned out, there was indeed a good reason why he was delayed this afternoon.

Rigo looked okay, and he seemed complacent to some degree. Roland was beginning to feel a positive feeling of friendship.

"Aquí no puedes quedar," Rigo suddenly said, telling Roland he could not stay with them.

"¿Por qué?" Roland asked, wanting to know why.

"No me siento agusto," Rigo replied, saying that he didn't feel comfortable.

They talked a little while. Roland asked Rigo if he had received the second letter. He answered that he did, and he "assured" Roland that he did spend the money for school supplies and not on beer. Rigo said he had been quite bothered by the incident back in August when he and Angelo had stepped down from Roland's truck and walked that 10 kilometer stretch of highway. However, despite everything, he said he could go on being friends, but Roland wouldn't be able to stay with them. He told Roland that Elisa had offered her place for him to come and stay, and that she was expecting him.

Okay, so Roland left and drove over to Elisa's house. He did take notice that Rigo neglected to thank him for that $20. Roland pulled up to her house, which was only one block away and around the corner from the Zacatóns. He entered the swinging iron gate, and he knocked on her door, which was a little bit set back from the sidewalk.

Elisa came forward from the back room where she was. When she saw Roland, a happy smile came across her face, and she greeted him in the most hospitable manner possible. That was kind of her, and he appreciated her welcoming gestures. Though she had never received Roland to stay with her and her family before, she had changed her mind and was glad to receive him now. In fact, she was so interested in having Roland stay with her that she had gone over to Lavinia a few weeks earlier and had informed them of her offer.

Okay, so Roland unloaded his truck and brought his things in. He unloaded his bicycles and placed them by the side of her house. She offered him the bedroom where her two sons sleep. They were away in Monterrey at the moment, along with her older daughter, which meant that Elisa was alone in the house.

After Roland brought all his things in, they visited for a while. A little while later, Roland went back over to Rigo's house to let him know that Elisa had received him well. As it turned out, the movie, "Shindler's List" was showing on TV, and Rigo was watching it. Roland watched it for a while also. It was in Spanish. Roland had earlier seen it in English, but only part of it because the TV networks had purposefully failed to edit out the foul language, and Roland had turned it off in disgust, followed by calling and complaining to the TV station for not editing it for television! Here, being in Spanish, he would not hear all those awful words, and now he could watch it. Later that evening, Roland returned to Elisa's house, and they watched the rest of the movie. The final scene was indeed touching, showing the actors and their real life counterparts side by side placing a stone on Oskar Shindler's grave. Shindler did a grand service for the Jews, buying more than 1,000 of them from the Nazis and therefore saving their lives. He was a rare Nazi, a man with compassion.

The next day, it was still drizzling. Roland went and found the people the bicycles were intended for. They were all grateful to receive them, and they told Roland, "Gracias." One of them also told Roland that if he ever needed help with anything to just let him know and he would be glad to help.

Roland also went to Felipe's carpentry. He found Felipe there, and he delivered the Cedar wood, selling it to him at cost.

While he was there, he also chatted with Sotero, Juan Carlos, Pedro, and with Rigo. They told each other jokes and had some laughs. Then Roland decided to mention to Rigo that he had neglected to thank him for that $20 he had sent him back in early October. Rigo got somewhat irritated, on the defensive actually, and then he said, "Gracias." Roland continued visiting with them, but Rigo wasn't very talkative after that.

Roland knew it wasn't exactly right to mention, in front of the others, the $20 and remind Rigo to thank him for sending it, but then Roland knew how Rigo had actually spent the money, even though he didn't admit it. As a result, Roland was more bothered than usual that it never occurred to Rigo to at least thank him for the money, and he therefore mentioned it in front of the others on purpose!

* * *

Christmas was coming up, and Elisa invited Roland to come with her to Monterrey to spend Christmas Eve with her mother and family. That was kind of her. So, Roland drove her down there in his truck. They stayed overnight where they visited with Elisa's brothers, sisters, and cousins. Her daughter and two sons were there as well, and Roland enjoyed the visit. The next morning, Roland drove Elisa back to Bustamante.

Then he went to Villaldama to see if Leonardo might be home. He was indeed! In fact, the whole family was there. Leonardo was glad to see Roland, and he greeted him by saying, "¿Cómo estás?" They shook hands, and they visited for half an hour, first time in three years that they visited for longer than 10 minutes. Roland enjoyed the visit and showed him his photo album of his stays in Mexico, and they caught each other up on what they had been doing.

Roland returned to Bustamante and stopped by Moises' house. He was actually home! He greeted Roland well and asked him inside. Moises remembered Roland very well from the days back in 1992 when he used to go play with Eliud over at the Quevalos. Moises was now grown, of course, and Roland could tell that he had a very decent personality. He had one more year of mechanics school in Monterrey, after which he would return to Bustamante to be a mechanic.

They talked for a while, and Roland summarized his adventures that he had experienced during his various stays in Bustamante. Moises was intrigued by what all Roland had done, and at some of the strange things that had occurred to him, also. Roland gave him a couple of calendars, for which Moises was grateful, and he showed him his photo album of Mexico. Gazdi was there also, and they talked a while. Roland and Moises enjoyed their visit, and they would become good friends in the years to come.

What a great Christmas day this was! Yes, it was drizzling somewhat, but Roland had succeeded in seeing two friends who he had repeatedly not been able to find at home.

Next, he went over to Rigo's house to visit. Well, Rigo was not nearly so warm mannered. He and his father were there, and while Rigo let Roland inside, he hardly talked. They were watching TV. After a few minutes, Roland could sense that Rigo preferred he not be there. He felt nervous and tense feelings in the house. So, he excused himself, told them Merry Christmas, and he left.

He went over to Elisa's house, and he told her the good news about finding Leonardo and Moises at home, and she was glad for him. He also told her about Rigo's somewhat cold shoulder. Then he pulled his "For Sale" sign out from between some of his calendars, and he went back over to Rigo's house. Rigo answered the door, and Roland told him that since he had been cold shouldered toward him, he had a sign to give him. Roland handed it to Rigo, who looked at it in a somewhat serious way, and Roland sincerely told him to place the sign on the front door, and to inform him of who buys the friendship. In addition to that, Roland also handed Rigo a Xerox copy of the October newspaper article about the Lascassas Bridge closing. Rigo said the "For Sale" sign was not something to joke about.

Roland replied that he wasn't joking. With that said, he rode away on his bicycle and visited friends in town, including Victor and his family, Beto, Fabian, and others.

That afternoon, Roland found out that one of Pegaso's sisters was already *married* and the other one was pregnant by her boyfriend! Both of them were still teenagers. Pegaso, who was extremely protective of his sisters, was so angry that he went looking for the fellow. Out of fear, the boyfriend fled town and went to Texas to work! Nacho and Chela Orolizo, being of good heart, decided they would raise the child once it was born. It would bring joy to the household. That was very reasonable and kind of them, and it was the right thing to do.

Roland was learning that this was a somewhat common occurrence in Mexico. Lots of teenage girls got married, even as young as 15 years in age! Though it didn't happen to Pegaso's sisters, some fellows were known to rob the young girl from her parents and take her to a faraway place to get married and live.

Later that afternoon, Roland returned to Elisa's house. From there, he called his parents to wish them a Merry Christmas. When he picked up the phone to make the call, the dial tone was different. Bustamante had gotten a new telephone exchange, and it had just been switched over in the past few weeks. Candela, Coahuila was cut over a few days later, being the last electro-mechanical phone exchange in the region. Roland also made a local call and discovered that the ringback tone was different. It was softer and not 2 seconds long, like it used to be. The whole world was going digital. Times were moving on.

Roland's parents were doing well, said it was cold and icy back in Tennessee, but things were okay otherwise. They were glad that Roland made it safely to Mexico, and they wished him a good stay and for him to make good progress on his Mexico novel.

That evening, Roland stayed at Elisa's house. Her children were still in Monterrey. They visited and talked about things. She showed him some more interesting books on plants of Mexico and also some books pertaining to culture. They watched TV for a while. Roland could tell that she had an increased liking for him, when compared to previous trips to Bustamante. Outside, the weather was somewhat cold with a wet drizzle. Roland decided to go to sleep somewhat early, since he had been up late last night watching that long movie, "Shindler's List." He went into the bedroom and changed into his shorts.

Just as he was about to climb into bed, Elisa walked to the bedroom entrance and said, "Rolando, quiero decirte algo," telling Roland that she wanted to say something to him. She paused a few seconds and then said, "No, mejor no," changing her mind not to tell him, and she walked away.

Around five minutes later, she returned to the bedroom entrance. Roland got up out of bed and came to her. She repeated the same phrase, hesitated a few seconds, and then walked off again.

By now, this was most strange, and Roland suddenly felt feelings of alarm! So, he walked into the living room where she was, and he asked her if something was wrong. If she was disgusted with him for something . . ."

"No, no es eso," she said, assuring Roland it was nothing like that.

"¿Entonces?" said Roland, asking her to go ahead and tell him.

"Oh, dios mío. Oh, dios mío. ¿Cómo te puedo decir?" said Elisa, commenting the equivalent of: Oh my god. Oh my god. How can I tell you? She went silent for ten seconds, faltered some, and then said, "Quiero hacer amor contigo," telling Roland that she wanted to make love with him.

Oh, law woman! Roland thought to himself. "No, Elisa," Roland told her, as calmly as he could. "Eso yo no hago," telling her that was something he just didn't do. Needless to say, Roland was feeling quite a sense of alarm, danger actually, but he didn't know why! He explained to her that he had never married and that he was therefore a virgin, whether she wanted to believe him or not. He said he had never made love with anybody, that it was just not a concern of his to have sex with people. Premarital sex was something Roland had always been against. Even though he wasn't all that religious, he was when it concerned that aspect!

Elisa was quite surprised at Roland's turning her down. All of her hormones were up, and it was quite a considerable let down for her. Roland said he was sorry to turn her down, but making love was out of the question. A normal friendship was fine, but nothing more intimate. He offered to take his things and leave, if she no longer felt comfortable with his being in the house. She assured him he could continue to stay and told him not to worry about her and her petty wishes.

Okay, so Roland went back to her sons' bedroom where he tried to get to sleep. It took a while. He was feeling quite nervous about the whole thing. That night, he had a nightmare which made him scream out. Elisa heard him, became quite alarmed, and she came to him. She nudged him to wake him up, and he woke up immediately. She asked him what was wrong. Then she began to get in the bed with him, and she asked to sleep with him! Roland immediately got out of the bed, and said No. She asked again, and Roland repeated his answer of No. She then gave up, said she wouldn't pressure him anymore, and she returned to her bedroom.

There she wrote out a small poem in English: The Lost Hug: It would have been tender, my heart surrender, but he was afraid, so I hugged the air.

Roland didn't get much sleep that night. When he got up that morning, Elisa said to him that she wasn't ashamed for any reason that she had asked him to make love with her. She explained that she wanted to offer him the chance to experience what it was like, that is, to teach him the joys of sex. She also said she had enjoyed sexual relations with several other men during her life, and she had done those for the moment, with no conditions attached.

That's also how she had done it with her husband, as well, only she had to marry him because her daughter Carinda was conceived . . . out of wedlock, that is! By him, she had two more children, her sons Carlos and Lalo. Then around 7 years ago, she left him because he was quite abusive to her. Plus, he drank a lot. She had wanted a divorce, but he refused to grant it to her, because they had three children. Even though they were separated, he called her regularly, and he supplied child support at times.

Roland explained that he would be glad to carry on being a friend of hers, but he didn't want any sex, and he asked her to please not ask him again. She accepted it the best she could.

In addition to his religious reasons, there were several more reasons why Roland wouldn't have wanted sex with Elisa. She was short and chubby. Plus, she was 10 years older, and she was prematurely grey! Her mostly grey hair, which was normally supposed to be black, was dyed a reddish-orange color! While Roland was fine with being a friend of hers, the thought of having sexual relations with someone of that type . . . No! Roland was a young fellow. He had no grey hairs, and he would have preferred someone tall, slender, and young, and with her *natural* color of dark brown or black hair.

None of that was nearly as important as the fact that she was married! Separated, yes she was, but since her husband had never granted her their divorce, who knows what he might have done?!

Roland went around town visiting different friends today. He still had one extra bicycle left, a full size girl's bike. He took it over to the Zacatón's house to give to Norma. She wasn't home since she and her sister and mother were in Zacatecas. Alejandro was home, and he was grateful to Roland for giving a bicycle to Norma.

Roland told Alejandro what Elisa had just requested, and he was somewhat surprised, but then he also told Roland, "Pues, dále. ¿No eres hombre?" telling Roland to go ahead and give her some, if he was a man. Roland laughed at Alejandro's comment and explained that he just didn't feel right about it and didn't want to do that.

Roland then asked Alejandro if he could come over and stay with them, like he had done several times before.

"Pues, es que mi hijo Rigo no se siente agusto contigo, Rolando," said Alejandro, telling Roland that his son Rigo didn't feel comfortable with his being in the house. He went on to say that Rigo had already changed, that is, become a man, and he was now a regular drinker and even smoked at the dances. Alejandro didn't approve of his son's actions, but he also realized how rebellious teenagers are and that there wasn't a lot he could do about it.

Roland was sorry to learn that, told him fair enough, and he thanked him anyway.

Then Alejandro told Roland that if he really felt uncomfortable over at Elisa's, then he could come on over and stay, but to not say anything to Rigo.

Roland said thanks, and if things got more shady over at Elisa's place, he would leave her house and come on over.

Alejandro thanked Roland for the bicycle and said he would give it to Norma when they return from Zacatecas.

Roland washed some clothes later that afternoon, and he bought some food and supplies, and that evening, he drove on over to Lucio's ranch to stay several days. There, he strung a clothes line and hung his clothes to dry.

It was cloudy and somewhat cold at the ranch, but at least on this side of the mountain, it was not drizzling, like in Bustamante.

Roland proofread what he had written so far about his adventures in Mexico. One afternoon, several fellows came over from Romulo's ranch to visit Roland. They looked at some of his recent calendars and artwork, which they found intriguing. They went on to say that at times, they have seen strange lights from ovnis and other flying objects in the sky, and since some of Roland's paintings portrayed scenes from alien worlds, they admitted that they believe in life on other worlds, as well.

Roland became friends with several of them. They had names like Juan, Beto, Javier,

Riki, Francisco, Ivan, Chui, Mayo, Kena, Julio, and there were some others whose names Roland didn't know.

The weather became sunny, and on December 30, Roland drove back to Bustamante. Elisa was there and happily greeted Roland, asking him how his stay went at the ranch. They visited for a while, and then Roland went around town on his bicycle visiting more friends.

Lavinia and her daughters were back from Zacatecas already. Norma thanked Roland for the bicycle, and she was glad to receive it. She began to use it regularly around town.

Elisa needed to return to Monterrey for several days, and she was kind enough to let Roland stay in her house. That afternoon, Roland drove Elisa over to Sabinas Hidalgo. They did several errands, visiting Garza Morton and Centro Comercial San José, and they also visited the ferretería to have some keys copied for Roland to use. Also, Roland bought an extra oil lamp for use at the ranch.

Then they returned to Bustamante, and later that evening, Roland carried Elisa over to Villaldama to catch the bus to Monterrey. She would stay there for several days.

He returned to Bustamante, and he went over to the Zacatón's house to visit with them. Lavinia, Norma and Irma were in the kitchen, and they fed Roland some supper. They told him all about their trip to Zacatecas. Their family had asked about Roland, and they sent him their regards.

Lavinia and her daughters were all in happy spirits, and Norma was fun to talk to. She was now grown and between 5' 7" and 5' 8" which was tall for a woman in Mexico. Norma was tall and slender, and her hair was dark brown. Roland had to admit to himself that he admired her features very much. She was even more attractive than the year before.

Rigo was home also, and he was watching TV in the main room. He entered the kitchen to serve himself some supper, and he walked right by Roland to retrieve something out of the refrigerator. As he did so, he showed Roland an angry face, which Lavinia and her daughters noticed. Roland asked Rigo why he didn't talk to him.

"¿Para qué?" he angrily answered, and he returned to the main room to watch more TV.

Roland asked Lavinia what was the matter with Rigo, and she answered that he was continually angry about that 10 kilometer walk on the highway, back when Roland had put them out of his truck. Roland reminded Lavinia that he didn't dismiss Rigo from his truck, only Angelo, and he had told them both 20 times to get back inside, which they hadn't done.

It was so strange that Rigo was so angry! Two years ago, Raul and Beto had stepped down from Roland's car and walked back to Pinos, and they never held any grudges. It never crossed their minds to. Much less, were they angry.

As Roland thought about it, he suddenly realized something. There was a detail that he had overlooked. That 10 kilometer stretch of highway that Rigo and Angelo walked was the exact same stretch of highway where Roland and Rigo, a year and a half earlier, had tossed out all those knick knacks from that green box! Perhaps natural law had punished Roland and Rigo for what they had done, but Roland didn't think so. After all, Isalia and Luke had been so unreasonable about the whole thing, that there had been no other choice. Roland smelled a rat.

(What Roland didn't realize was that in this case the "natural justice" was malignant, the punishment having been designed and administered by none other than Arfifra, Draaktra and their demon friends of Nuevo Wimbisenho!)

Perfume And The Skunk

Roland returned to Elisa's house and stayed there alone that night. He got some sleep, too.

The next day, Roland visited more friends in town. He went over Victor's house and visited for a while. They went over to his grandparents' house where they were having a big family gathering, and they were glad to have Roland visit. They fed him some of the lunch they had prepared in the backyard.

There was a small arcade in town where there were different types of pinball machines and other video games. Some of the younger teenagers went there. Roland happened to see Fabian walking down the street, and they entered the arcade. There were some others Roland recognized, including Ivan, and there was another fellow whose name was Rigo, the same first name as Alejandro and Lavinia's son Rigo. This Rigo was a kind and sincere fellow, and the four of them played some "football" with the table of spinning rods. They had some good laughs and played several games.

Then Roland went over to Hector and Pablo's house and visited a while. Hector suggested that Roland stay in the hotel instead of asking to stay with families. There, he would be paying each day, and all his services would be provided. Plus, staying at Lucio's ranch wasn't a good idea in Hector's viewpoint, because whenever Lucio might want, he could run him off. Roland explained to Hector that he had friends in Bustamante, and anywhere he had friends, he didn't believe in staying in hotels. Plus, he was staying over at Lucio's ranch to have some peace and quiet, which the hotel couldn't offer.

As a result, Roland talked to Jesús Lucio and checked with him about it being all right to stay at the ranch, and he expressed his concern about being run off. Lucio quickly assured Roland that he was welcome at the ranch, and the door was always open for him to stay there. Roland offered him money, and he kindly declined any money. That was kind of him, and Roland felt much more reassured. As far as he was concerned, since there were no hotels on the other side of the mountains, he was staying at "Hotel Lucio" at the ranch.

Roland bicycled over to Felipe's carpentry, and as soon as he arrived, Rigo turned his back to him and turned up the radio! Roland began to talk to him and the others, but the radio was so distracting that he couldn't. So, Roland left. He bicycled over to the Cantu's store to buy some supplies, and then he bicycled back over to Felipe's carpentry. As he approached the building, he heard the radio volume go up. Noticing that, he didn't even stop, and he rode right on by. Once he was around 20 meters beyond the building, the volume suddenly went back down. That irritated Roland. So, he turned around and bicycled in front of that building several more times. Sure enough, Rigo diligently increased the volume of the radio each time he passed by! Rigo was getting good training at how to show his back to certain people and how to give brush offs!

Roland went to visit Beto Enriquez and his wife and in-laws. They were glad to see him, and they visited for a while. Roland decided to imitate some of Rigo's brush-off gestures, all of which gave Beto and his family some good laughs.

While Roland was talking to Beto, a young fellow came over to Roland to talk to him. He had heard about him, and he wanted to see his artwork and calendars. Plus he wanted to see Chiquihuitillos. His name was Ramón Gamboa, and immediately Roland sensed that he was a good fellow. They talked a for while, and Roland went over to his house around the corner and met his family. Ramón was in the same school as Rigo, and he was also training to be a school teacher.

That evening, Roland locked the door at Elisa's house, and he returned to the ranch. It was New Year's Eve, and it was also the end of the millennium. No way was Roland going to remain in town, with all the Y2K paranoia going on. He went to the ranch for several days, where there was no electricity and where nothing would change.

The next morning, he woke up to the year 2000. Everything was fine. Lucio and his helper came over and said quite surprisingly that everything was perfectly normal in town. The electricity had not even gone off, and there were absolutely no mishaps anywhere in the world. Great! People had really taken appropriate measures to prevent any computer failures and other complications.

Roland made some more progress on his novel. The nights were somewhat cold, but the weather was nice and sunny. Some of the evenings had some great sunsets, and the views were excellent on clearer days.

On January 6, he returned to Bustamante. Elisa was back in town and happily greeted Roland, welcoming him inside. He brought his things in. She asked him how things had gone at the ranch, and he said he had gotten a lot of writing done. Elisa's three children were home, and they greeted Roland, as well.

After a while, Roland decided to go to Sabinas Hidalgo to do some errands. Carlos wanted to go with Roland, and he went into his bedroom to get ready. Suddenly, it occurred to Roland that Carlos might put on perfume, as it seemed to be a common occurrence for teenage boys to do that prior to going to Sabinas Hidalgo. Several times, Roland had had to ask people to change shirts or wash their face, because he couldn't tolerate it in his truck. Roland went to the bedroom, and he was only just in time! Carlos had the perfume bottle poised in his hand when Roland made his request.

"Oh, sí," Carlos responded. He set the bottle back down, and Roland told him gracias. The two of them went to Sabinas Hidalgo.

They did several errands there, and Carlos had a couple of his own. Elisa also sent some money with Roland to buy frozen fish and some other hamburger supplies for her customers. He obliged her and bought the stuff at Centro Comercial San José.

Later that afternoon, they returned to Bustamante. Carlos was more of a quiet type, but he was a good fellow, as best as Roland could tell.

That evening, Roland happened to see Gilberto, who had gone camping with him and Julian back a year and a half ago. He was now grown, nearly Roland's height, and they were glad to see each other. They talked about what they had been doing, and they also went over to Gilberto's house, which was a one-room adobe house. Roland talked to his mother and older brother, as well. They were glad to see him and thought it was great that Roland brought bicycles to the people. They could see that Roland was a person who cared for others.

Later that night, Roland visited with Elisa. She seemed concerned about something, as if she was contemplating a decision. She was acting a little strange, actually. Roland asked her what was the matter. So, she talked about her life and told Roland some more stories, including some past relations she had had with previous men. She even went on to talk about some of the joyous relations she had experienced. She asked Roland what he thought of her as a woman, and in a manner as indirect as possible, she hinted at the fact that she still wanted to make love with him.

So, Roland went through his explanation, and this time he leveled with her even more, telling her it was "beyond his skill" and that he felt strangely nervous at her request. Further, he sensed a very strong feeling that danger was eminent if he *did it* with her. He didn't know why, but it was like he saw a line in front of him, and he couldn't cross it. He told her he was sorry, that he hoped she understood, and he wished her the best of luck in finding a good husband.

Elisa wasn't exactly okay with Roland's reasons, but that was the best he could do for her. She then again told Roland not to worry about her petty wishes. She walked off into another room as if she was going to cry. Roland felt bad, but for the above reasons, plus those of Christmas night, he just couldn't do it.

* * *

Nuevo Wimbisenho

"Never, *never* in his life is he going to do it with a woman!" shouted Arce-fera. "Oh!! I'm so angry at that Roland!"

"He sensed us!" Draaktra declared.

"I know," Sasjurech admitted. "I couldn't block the feelings!"

"He's escaping our clutches!" Sojornbloc admitted with alarm.

"And we had such an excellent group of programs poised and ready for exchange at the moment of ecstasy!" Arce-fera stated.

"Can't exchange any of it unless they do it," Arfifra pointed out.

"Maybe we can get them into bed, still," Torxtalo said.

"I don't think so," Arfifra disagreed. "Roland's very stubborn and set in his decisions. I think we'll just have to kill him."

"Already?!" Draaktra reacted with surprise.

"Get him and his alma over here as soon as possible!" Arfifra commanded with a quite a touch of anger in her voice. "Ferúpsula, we have a mission for you. Draaktra, send Rigo some more dreams and false memories, and provoke a problem, immediately!! Arce-fera, I should have known he was going to reject your protectee. Now listen, I want you to . . ."

* * *

Little did they know, Martonción had recently bugged their cave with a telepathic micro-transmitter. Oyamel was listening to their malicious and barbaric plans, and appropriate action would be administered. Igor would be contacted to reinforce his protection of Roland's life.

* * *

The next day, Roland stayed in town all day. He rode around on his bicycle, and he visited friends. He went over to Gilberto's house, and they rounded up two more friends, including Armando and Fabian, and they went to the Ojo del Agua. It was a moderately warm day, and they went swimming in the small pond at the spring. They also ran up and down the small creek, looking at the fish. Some of them were quite large, at half a meter long.

Later that afternoon, Roland also went over to Felipe's carpentry to visit with Sotero, Juan Carlos, and Pedro. Rigo was there and attempted to turn up the radio upon Roland's arrival, but since Felipe was present, he called Rigo down. Plus, Sotero, Juan Carlos, and Pedro told Rigo to let Roland chat with them for a while, which he did. While Rigo remained sullen, Sotero and Juan Carlos told several stories, and they had some good laughs. Felipe returned to the hotel for a while.

Roland talked to Rigo, and he insisted he tell him why he was being so cold shouldered to him. Rigo finally spoke, but only angrily and with scathing remarks, telling Roland he was a *maricón* and an *idiot*! Further, he accused Roland of being *gorroso*, that is, always coming on too strong! Roland denied those accusations, and he called Rigo by his nickname *Molonco*.

"¡Huh! ¿Qué dijiste?!!" Rigo shouted aggressively, angrily asking Roland what he called him.

"Molonco," Roland firmly repeated.

Rigo uttered some foul language in Spanish, and he picked up a wood chisel to strike Roland! Sotero, Juan Carlos, and Pedro were standing there watching. The glare in Rigo's eyes was spell binding and quite frightening, really!

Roland stood his ground and told Rigo not to hit him with that. The police station was two blocks away. If he liked, they could straighten everything out, down there!

Rigo heard what Roland said, and he slowly put his chisel down. He told Roland he had no right to call him *Molonco*. Roland told Rigo he had no right to call him *maricón* and *idiot*!

The others realized that Rigo was hopping mad at Roland, and they thought it was most strange!

Roland left the carpentry, but not before he reminded Rigo that since he was training to be a school teacher, he ought to put forth an example like one, to quit showing his back to people, because a teacher (leader) doesn't show his back to anybody! And how about thinking more positively, as well!

Rigo sneered with laughter!

Needless to say, Roland left quite disgusted and feeling rejected. He knew Rigo Zacatón was no friend, not anymore. He was so changed. The friendship was definitely closed. It remained to be seen if his friendship would last with Rigo's family. Perhaps not. Roland had for several years thought that Norma was the predestined one to be his wife, that is, well in the future, since he had seen those flowers posted on that Fir tree on her date of birth, but then how could he possibly marry into that family and have a hothead brother-in-law like Rigo?! It wouldn't work, and even though Roland was already liking Norma's features very much, he would have to refuse her. Roland's philosophy was that whomever he might marry, her brothers and sisters and her parents would consider Roland like family, welcome him with open arms, and his brothers-in-law would be his *best friends*. They would love him like a brother, and they would defend him at crucial moments. Roland's expectations were very reasonable. Nothing less would suffice, and Rigo had just now miserably failed the requirements!

Roland needed to wash his clothes, and he went over to the Zacatón's house to use the washer he had given them back in 1997. There was just enough time for him to get his clothes washed before Rigo would get home from work. Roland really didn't wish to see him, much less have any confrontation with him! Lavinia and her daughters were home, and they didn't want to let Roland enter, because neither Alejandro nor Rigo were at home, which meant there were no men in the house. What would the neighbors say? That didn't sit well with Roland at all, and he told them he thought they were his friends. After all, he used to stay with them. He expressed his disapproval, and he reminded them that he was the one who had given them that machine in the first place. Of course they knew that very well. No matter what, Roland thanked them for the times they had previously let him come and use it. He also told them what Rigo had just done, and with that said, he walked away.

Roland went around town on his bicycle that evening visiting friends. He happened to see Fernando, and they talked for quite a while. Roland told him what had just happened between him and Rigo.

Fernando shook his head in disapproval. In a straightforward manner, he told Roland he wasn't surprised, and that Rigo wasn't a friend of his anymore either.

Roland looked at Fernando in disbelief. He thought he and Rigo were good friends.

Fernando said Rigo used to be a friend, but he had changed quite a bit during the past year, and he was now only interested in people with money and was basically ungrateful! Fernando went on to explain more to Roland, telling him that Rigo had brushed off all but a few friends. He doesn't know how to greet people anymore, much less converse with them. He has become unreasonable, and he reacts angrily to everything. Because of that, Fernando no longer wanted to talk to him. We have heads on our shoulders and brains to reason with people, but instead Rigo has a head full of rocks!

Roland laughed at Fernando's accurate analysis of Rigo, and he told Fernando he believed Rigo was a German Nazi in a past life. Fernando laughed, and he agreed with him. He went on to tell Roland he did the right thing when he put Rigo and Angelo out on the highway last August. They had provoked the whole problem in the first place and deserved every one of those blisters, especially Rigo, because he and his buddies had been laughing at Roland behind his back for quite some time. Plus, Rigo's subconscious mind was training him very well on how to turn his back to people, how to sneer, deceive, brush people off, and hold grudges.

Fernando explained that there are lots of problems in Rigo's house. His father's an alcoholic, and he's very pressured with all his school and studies, in addition to his work. He feels violated for having to supply his hard earned money to support his family. What was more unfortunate was that Rigo had chosen the same road as his father, as far as drinking and smoking are concerned. Rigo's friends tell him to drink and smoke, and for fear of being accused of being a *maricón*, he won't stand up and say no. Instead, he gathers and drinks with his few friends, putting away one beer after another, not to mention the quantity of cigarettes they smoke! Plus, he goes to the dances every Saturday night with his macho buddies, and they strut around, like they're the hottest dudes this side of the Rio Grande!

Fernando told Roland that if Rigo gives him any more problems, go straight to the police. He also offered to defend Roland, if necessary. That was kind of him. Plus, he advised Roland not to go back to Rigo or their family anymore, because Rigo doesn't deserve Roland's friendship. He had abused it.

Fernando told Roland that one day, well in the future, even though he may never admit it, Rigo will realize that Roland is a good fellow, and he is going to lament his loss, the friendship he tossed aside.

Roland thanked Fernando for the chat. They shook hands and wished each other well.

As Roland left, he realized that Fernando was very tuned in. He understood Rigo 100%. Fernando was also training to be a school teacher, and he was quite upset at Rigo's immature ways. Rigo would need to shape up if he was going to be a school teacher, too. A teacher (leader) doesn't turn his back on anybody!

*   *   *

More than three months after the October 2nd closing, the time had come for the State of Tennessee's highway department crew to begin demolition of the Lascassas Bridge. After all, the state was allotted a certain amount of money in their budget, and they had to spend all of it each fiscal year. Conserving the bridge was out of the question and not even an option! They positioned their jack hammers and wrecking balls into place, and they began the week of hard work, to successfully remove every bit of concrete and road material, leaving the green metal truss standing bare.

*   *   *

Elisa had a washing machine, and she was kind enough to let Roland use it to wash his clothes. It was an EASY brand Mexican made washing machine, and it had a separate spin gyrator. Roland thanked her, filled up the machine with water, and he washed his clothes. Then he hung them on the line to dry.

That afternoon, the phone rang. Elisa happened to be outside at the time. So, Roland answered the phone. It was her husband! He asked to speak to Elisa, and Roland called her to the phone.

She answered, saying hi to her husband, and she listened for a moment.

"Pues, es un amigo," she said, explaining to her husband that Roland was a friend. She paused and listened. "No, no está viviendo conmigo. Va y viene," she said, telling her husband Roland wasn't living with her, that he just comes and goes.

He suddenly hung up on Elisa.

Five minutes later, a call came from her mother, and she accused Elisa of shacking up with Roland. Elisa got very defensive and told her mother she was extremely mistaken! She told her mother that she has few friends, and couldn't they let her enjoy Roland's friendship? She hung up on her mother!

Twenty minutes later, Elisa's husband called again wanting to know who that gringo was that was staying with her!

Elisa got very angry, and she shouted at her husband, telling him he was very mistaken, that she has few friends, to stop meddling in her business, and that it was her right to have Roland stay with her in her house! She quickly hung up!

Roland heard all that, and he offered to leave.

Elisa assured Roland, telling him her husband was all talk and no play. She said not to worry about him, that he was that way about every guest of hers.

That evening, Roland was visiting with Elisa, talking about culture and other things. She told him some more stories of her younger days when she went up the Lion's Head Mountain with her family. Once on the summit, a big lightning storm had come, and things became dangerous! They left immediately and made it back to Bustamante with no casualties. They had been lucky.

Carlos was in his bedroom, preparing to go out visiting with friends this evening. He walked through the living room and left through the front door. Seconds after leaving, Roland caught the awful and putrid smell of his perfume, and he called out, "Carlos."

"Espérate," Elisa said, firmly telling Roland to wait a minute!

Perfume And The Skunk

"Es que tu hijo . . ." Roland began to tell her that her son's perfume was bothersome, and he was going to ask her son if he would be so kind to put it on, once *outside* the house.

"No, Rolando. No tienes ningún derecho para . . ." Elisa immediately answered, quickly telling Roland he had no right to tell her son what to do, not even the right to ask him, because he was in his house. So, Roland asked her to tell him for him, and she explained that she wouldn't do that. Roland had no rights, and he would have to adapt! Roland didn't agree with that. He told her that guests do have some rights, and that hosts need to be more accommodating. Elisa repeated her declaration that he had no right to tell her children what to do!

Well, that was that. She was firm on her decision. Roland felt quite uncomfortable and detected inhospitality from Elisa. Actually, Roland felt squelched and unwelcome. He didn't say any more to her, but there was an unpleasant feeling in his abdomen that wouldn't go away. Even still, he went ahead and spent the night there.

The next morning, Carlos and Lalo started school. Christmas vacation days were over now. Early that morning, they got up and got ready for school, and right before leaving, though Roland was still asleep in their room, Carlos sprayed himself with his putrid perfume! In ten seconds, it went right up Roland's nostrils! He immediately got out of bed and evacuated the bedroom and house as fast as possible! Roland almost vomited, and he waited outside for 20 minutes, even though it was somewhat cold this morning. He wanted to say something to Carlos, but he refrained from doing so. Elisa saw him, and she knew why he was outside, but she said nothing, nor did she show compassion. To her, what was more important was that he *not* tell her children what to do.

Roland packed his truck with his things. He thanked Elisa for having received him, and he returned to Lucio's ranch for another week.

He wasn't sure what to think of Elisa, and he was analyzing in his mind why she had suddenly cooled off. He suspected it had something to do with his having two times turned down her request to make love, but he wasn't totally sure. She had still been friendly when she let him use her washing machine, but she had gone strange as soon as he tried to ask her son not to spray that putrid perfume in the house. Yes, it was true that Roland had no right, in a sense. After all, it was Carlos' house, well, actually Elisa's, but then what's it going to hurt to kindly ask her son to accommodate Roland and respect him as a guest by not bothering him with that putrid perfume! Elisa's declaration bothered Roland a lot, and he was questioning in his mind if he was even welcome with them anymore.

It was a great week at the ranch. The weather was mostly sunny, and the nights were so peaceful and quiet. Roland made some good progress on his Mexico novel.

(Though Roland was oblivious to it, Elisa's husband was quite angry! He was calling her by phone 20 times a day, asking her who in the world that gringo was that was staying with her! Some of those times, when Elisa wasn't in the house, he reached Carlos instead, and he talked to him. Elisa was becoming quite flustered about the whole thing! She had to keep a lid on this somehow.)

On January 14, Roland returned to Bustamante. He arrived at Elisa's house, and she wasn't there. She was in Monterrey for two days, taking care of family matters. Carlos and Lalo were there, and they let Roland stay. He brought his things in.

At mid day, he took Fabian and another teenager named Julio Cesar to Sabinas Hidalgo, and he bought supplies for the next week at the ranch. Fabian and Julio Cesar had a good time. Roland took pictures when they visited the Turbina and Ojo del Agua in Sabinas

Hidalgo. Then they returned to Bustamante.

That afternoon, Roland saw Gilberto in the street. He was on his way to do some work for an older man named José Flores Cázares. He needed some mulch brought to his backyard for his garden. Roland offered to help, using his truck. Gilberto gratefully accepted the offer, and he and Roland got some feed sacks, drove north of town, and collected some good rich mulch from the ditches of several roads. It was a good afternoon, and Roland was glad to help.

Three days ago, while Roland was at the ranch, Isalia and Luke had arrived in town. As Roland and Gilberto returned to town with the truckload of mulch, they happened to see their truck. Roland turned his hat bill down so as not to see their faces, and he passed by their truck going the opposite direction.

There was talk that they were helping poor people by helping them repair their houses. In fact, they were even helping some people build new ones. Luke was a go-getter, and he managed several workers (natives of Bustamante) with the different building projects. Isalia was donating lots of supplies and *Bible* booklets to the schools, not only in Bustamante, but also in the surrounding small towns. Those were noble projects that spoke of good character, but the fact remained that she and Luke had never apologized to Roland and his parents for the major dispute that she had caused two years ago.

Roland decided to make one last attempt to reconcile with Isalia and Luke. Since they were helping people build houses, helping schools with materials, not to mention, handing out *Bible* booklets, perhaps they would now reconcile with Roland. After all, it had been two years since their dispute. Roland wrote them a note praising their noble missions and asking for an apology, and he wrote it on a 12" by 12" piece of tin roofing, so they wouldn't be able to tear it up. He had a friend walk over to their residence and give it to them. Meanwhile, Roland waited in his truck around the corner. His friend came back with a look of terror on his face, telling Roland they said he was loco and that they were on their way to the police right now to report him for bothering them! He got in Roland's truck with him, and immediately they drove straight to the police station to wait for them.

Roland had just enough time to tell the comandante what he had just done . . . when in walked Isalia with the piece of tin roofing in her hand! Her favorite cousin Pancho Quevalo was with her, following her like a piece of candy. What a sight! Isalia glared at Roland with a very angry look on her face! She began to complain, but since Roland was there, she turned and walked out. Pancho stepped in and talked to the comandante for her, and he told him that only psychopaths would hand someone a note on tin roofing. Roland explained why he wrote it on tin roofing, and Roland's friend also spoke and explained what they did. Pancho refused to understand, and he requested that they put Roland in jail, so that Roland wouldn't bother Isalia and Luke anymore. The comandante defended Roland by telling Pancho that was far from necessary. Pancho then dropped some false comments, telling the comandante that Roland had behaved very inappropriately with Raul and Rigo, among other tall tales and monstrosities! He went on and on with his efforts to prosecute Roland, and he stubbornly insisted that they arrest him. The comandante repeatedly told Pancho no. Like a stubborn Nyangshai, Pancho continued persisting and persisting until they finally came to a compromise. They decided to go upstairs to the Presidencia where they would write out a formal agreement, a mandate stating that Roland would never bother Isalia and Luke again. Roland said he would sign it *only* if it also states that Isalia and Luke would never bother Roland again either! They went upstairs where the *Syndico* wrote the mandate in a book that was full of other mandates. Roland and Pancho signed it, and after Roland had vacated the premises, Isalia later entered the room and also signed it.

Golly! How appalling it was that after two years, Isalia still hated Roland so much! Nothing other would describe Isalia's feelings toward Roland than pure hatred! She looked quite a bit older, too. She was very angry, offended actually! She knew good and well why Roland put that note on tin roofing. Never did it occur to her to answer Roland in a positive manner, much less reconcile with him. For the way she and her favorite "pet" Pancho had acted, Roland was glad to have "offended" her with that original piece of tin roofing and its note. As a result, that was the last time Roland ever saw or contacted Isalia and Luke.

Isalia was handing out *Bible* booklets to the schools. Why couldn't she reconcile with Roland? How hypocritical does one get?

As for Pancho Quevalo, what sort of friend was he? None at all! That was the thanks Roland got for all the favors he had previously done for Pancho and his family: bringing a pickup truck, a trailer, and two more trailer cargos full of Luke's knick knacks and a haybaler, plus other gifts! Never did it occur to Pancho to defend Roland, like a real friend would have done, and tell Isalia she was way out of line!

Roland returned to Elisa's house. He was rather shell-shocked after the event down at the comandancia. Carlos and a couple of friends were watching TV. Then they went out for a while. Carlos went to his bedroom, sprayed himself with perfume, and walked through the entire house before going out the front door to leave! Roland became quite annoyed with the nauseating smell, and he evacuated the house for another 20 minutes!

Lalo arrived home, and he and Roland talked for a while. They talked about artwork and also about concepts and speculation from other worlds. Lalo said he believed there was life on other star systems, and they talked about some of the sightings that had taken place there in Nuevo León.

Around an hour after Carlos and his friends had left, they returned to the house. Carlos went into his bedroom, diligently sprayed himself again with his *perfume*, walked through the entire house *again*, and he and his friends left.

That was it! Roland would refrain no longer. He went straight out the back door, walked around the house to the street, and he caught up with Carlos and his friends. He calmly and kindly explained to Carlos that he realized that it was his house, but the fact was that his putrid perfume was very bothersome, and every time he sprayed it, he had to evacuate the house for 20 minutes. Would he be so kind to do his perfuming outside the house upon leaving?

Well, Carlos got extremely angry, and he proceeded to yell at Roland, telling him he was going to do whatever he wanted to do in *his* house, that Roland had NO right to tell him anything, not even to ask him any favors! He went on to rant and rave, making various scathing remarks, including several Spanish cuss words. He told Roland that for his idiosyncrasies, people didn't want his friendship, like Rigo for example! Carlos then even went further to threaten Roland that he better not make love with his mother Elisa, or he would call his father in Monterrey, and he would come straight to Bustamante to bust him up some! He would even search out Roland in Tennessee, if necessary!

Roland was at a loss for words for a few moments, but then he managed to say to Carlos that he had no plans to make love with Elisa. Then he firmly told Carlos that if his father were to come to Bustamante to do him harm, he would report him straight to the police!

Carlos became angrier, and he shouted more insults and threats. He definitely went overboard, and he told Roland he was going to the police with his buddies, right then!

Roland told him that would be fine. He would get his things out of the house, load his truck, and drive straight over there!

In five minutes, Roland had his truck loaded, and for the second time today, he drove to the comandancia. Carlos and his friends were not even there. Roland filed a complaint that Carlos had threatened him and insulted him, and he didn't want any more problems. He told them he had already loaded his truck with his goods, and he was returning to Lucio's ranch to stay for another week.

With all the problems Roland had had today, the comandante said that was a good idea to get out of town for a few days. Then he looked at Roland in a sincere manner, and with a smile, he told him that Pancho comes in there all the time with his outlandish stories and complaints against other people. He was known throughout the town for his tall tales, and no one believed him anymore. Roland laughed, and he assured the comandante he had never made out with anyone. He had always treated Raul and Rigo in a noble, respectful manner. The comandante thankfully believed him. Roland thanked the comandante for his protection. They shook hands, and then Roland drove away.

How dare Carlos get so angry at Roland over so little! What was his problem, anyway? And why did he bring up Rigo as somebody who didn't want Roland's friendship? He had *read* that letter and $20 Roland had sent Rigo back in September!

Half an hour later, Carlos and his egotistical buddies arrived at the comandancia, and they began to file a complaint against Roland. The comandante told them that Roland had already been by, explained everything, and they told Carlos he had no sufficient reason to have gotten angry, nor to have made those insults and threats!

Roland meanwhile went over to Jesús Lucio's house to inform him of what had just happened. Lucio was sorry about all that. He assured Roland the ranch was available anytime. No problem. Roland thanked him, and then he went to talk with his new friend Ramón. They made plans to go see Chiquihuitillos next week.

Roland then drove away, to go back to the ranch. Upon leaving town, he heard his name called. Roland recognized the young fellow's voice as that of Gilberto's. He ran from where he was visiting with other friends and came to the side of Roland's truck to talk.

"Ah, sí, eres tú, Gilberto," said Roland, recognizing him as Gilberto.

"¿Ya te vas al rancho?" asking Roland if he was already going back to the ranch.

"Sí, había un problema con el hijo de Elisa," telling Gilberto there had been a problem with Elisa's son Carlos.

They talked a couple of minutes, and Roland told him he would return next week.

"Que te vaya bien. Cuídate," Gilberto told Roland, wishing him well and to take care. They shook hands, Mexican style.

"Gracias. Tú también," said Roland, thanking him and wishing him well, also.

Gilberto ran back to continue visiting with his friends. Roland drove out of town and returned to the ranch. He suddenly felt better. What a kind and friendly gesture for Gilberto to recognize Roland driving out of town, call out his name, and come over to him to wish him well. The friendly gesture somewhat surprised Roland and made him feel really good. He did indeed have some decent friends in this town. Roland always liked sincere friends who went out of their way for him, and Gilberto certainly passed the test with flying colors.

For bad events, like with Rigo and Carlos, there are good events to compensate.

Roland enjoyed another week at the ranch. He made considerable progress on his novel.

While he was mad at Carlos and Rigo, he realized that he had newer friends like Gilberto and Ramón, who he appreciated.

One morning, Lucio arrived, and to Roland's surprise, Ramón and a friend of his named Joel was with him. On the spur of the moment, they had decided to come over and see Chiquihuitillos. Well, Roland put his camera, some food, and some water in his daypack, and after Lucio fed his cattle he took the three of them over there. It had been more than two years since Lucio had gone himself.

They enjoyed seeing the paintings, speculated about what they represented, and they walked across the top of the mesa afterwards. It was a nice sunny day, and the views were spectacular.

After seeing the paintings, Lucio talked a while with the rancher. He had some new goats, and one of them was very friendly. Roland enjoyed petting the goat as he began to chew on his shoe strings.

In the early afternoon, Lucio took Ramón and Joel back to Bustamante, delivering Roland at the ranch on the way.

Roland stayed several more days and then returned to Bustamante.

He arrived at Elisa's house, almost certain he wouldn't be welcome there anymore. Who knows what Elisa was going to say? With apprehension, he walked up to the door of her house and knocked.

She came forward from the back room, greeted Roland, and told him to enter and have a seat. He entered and took a seat in her front room, and they began to talk.

She was rather irritated at Roland for violating her rules by telling Carlos not to put on perfume in his own house. Roland corrected her choice of words and told her he kindly requested to her son to put on his perfume outside the house, to accommodate and respect his guest. Elisa went on to tell Roland that for his idiosyncrasies, people rejected him, and that he was bad for having asked her son not to put on perfume. Plus, he shouldn't have reported him to the police because that makes her and her family look bad in town.

Roland said it was bad the way Carlos had shouted his abusive insults and scathing remarks the other evening, not to mention his threats! Plus, since Carlos said he was going to the police, he left Roland no other choice than to go to the police and report it!

Roland pointed out a comparison by presenting an analogy to Elisa. How would her son have liked it if he were staying up in Tennessee with Roland, and Roland diligently sprayed himself with skunk odor, three or four times a day, like Carlos did with perfume? Elisa skirted an answer. Roland went on to ask her how Carlos would like it if he sprayed himself with skunk odor early in the morning, in the same room where Carlos was still asleep? Elisa skirted the answer by commenting to Roland that he simply had to adapt and that he was very bad to have asked her son not to use perfume! Elisa had her blinders on! She didn't see the point, did she, nor the absurdity of what her son was doing and how Roland saw it.

Roland said he felt as welcome as a rat running around on the floor, and he also mentioned that he had wanted to wash his clothes, but he had to leave so fast that he didn't even have a chance to do so.

It was right then that Elisa mentioned to Roland that her washing machine had quit working, and she blamed Roland for breaking it by saying that he overfilled it with water! All the oil had spilled out of the machine's transmission. Roland defended himself and told her that the machine was working just fine when he had last used it. Perhaps her son had used it since, and it had broken then.

"¡No vas a echar la culpa a mi hijo!" Elisa shouted, firmly telling Roland not to blame her son.

"Pues, no vas a echar la culpa a mí, tampoco," Roland responded, telling Elisa not to blame him either!

Elisa said it would cost N$500 to repair it, and she asked Roland if he would pay her for it. He said no, but what he could do is come over and attempt to repair it.

No, that wasn't good enough. Besides, she didn't trust Roland's ability to repair it. She wanted the money.

Roland answered that the only way he would pay her for what he knew he didn't break in the first place, would be for her and her son to apologize and make him feel welcome in their house.

Elisa firmed up and shouted NO! She got angry and told Roland that he was more afraid to part with his money than to preserve a friendship, and she made other outlandish and scathing remarks!

What friendship?! Roland thought, and he went on to tell Elisa that she and her son were too proud to apologize.

Elisa told Roland to get out! So, Roland got up and walked out immediately.

He went to a local store and bought N$100 of food, two grocery sackfuls, and he took it over to Elisa, gave it to her, told her thanks for having received him in the past, and that he wasn't a cheat. She accepted the food, and Roland left. Not only was there food in those two sacks, there was also a small box of rat poison, for her future guests!

While Roland was not surprised at Elisa's turning cold, he was quite angry at her for not scolding her son, like a responsible mother, especially a school teacher, would have done. Her son had done very wrong the other night, shouting at and threatening Roland, and she had the audacity to back her son up! Apology was not in their vocabulary!

Elisa was that way. Whenever she had a dispute, she never made any efforts to repair it.

That was the last time Roland ever went to Elisa's house. If one day, she and her son offered an apology, Roland would be their friend again, but without their apology, no friendship. Roland was quite bothered by the unfair manner in which Elisa had treated him, not to mention her son Carlos!

Roland went around town visiting friends. Later that afternoon, he took two of Romulo's grandsons over to Sabinas Hidalgo with him.

Near Villaldama, there happened to be a dead skunk on the roadside. *Hmm . . .* Roland thought to himself as an idea entered his mind, and a mischievous smile came across his face. He pulled his truck over at the next available gravel turnout. His two passengers asked Roland what was the matter, and told them what he was thinking of doing. They looked at him in surprise. No, surely not! *Yes. Yes, indeed!* Roland stepped down from his truck, took three plastic grocery bags he happened to have with his things, and he walked up the road. When he reached the skunk, he carefully collected it into one bag, then bagged it two more times, and he returned to his truck. There, he raised the hood, placed it next to the 6 cylinder motor, and closed the hood.

They went on to Sabinas Hidalgo and did errands, later returning to Bustamante. The skunk surprisingly didn't smell, being in three bags and under the truck's hood.

That night, once it got dark, Roland retrieved the skunk from under his truck's hood, and he opened the three bags. He extracted the innermost bag with the skunk in it, from the other two. Then he carefully walked down the street toward Elisa's house, tossing the two outer bags into a streetside trash can on the way. He reached her house, and making sure no one was looking, he quietly placed the skunk and bag just inside the iron gate of her patio, and he quickly walked away! It was done. Let's see how you and your *precious son* Carlos like that one, Elisa! Serves you right!

Roland got in his truck and returned to Lucio's ranch. When Lucio and his helper arrived the next morning, he told them what he'd done. Lucio told Roland to be careful with his pranks. Elisa might report him to the police.

That afternoon, Roland walked over to Romulo's ranch. Of course, two of his grandsons were witnesses to Roland's having collected the skunk off the roadside. They were quite surprised to learn that Roland had actually gone through with it, and they had the best laugh about it!

Little did Roland know it, Elisa and her two sons smelled a skunk all night long, and they had thought there was one running around in the backyard. It was a strong and putrid smell! Early the next morning on the way to school, Elisa discovered the skunk in the open plastic bag in her front patio. She was madder than a hornet!! Though she strongly suspected it was Roland who had left it there, she had no proof. She even went to the police to report it, but since there was no proof . . . Tough!

Roland made good progress on his Mexico novel. During his stay in Mexico this trip, he managed to write what came out later to be 140 typewritten pages, but that was only part of this long novel, which would take a lot more time to write to completion.

After another week at the ranch, Roland loaded his truck with all his things, closed up the ranch house, leaving it just like he found it, and he returned to Bustamante.

Once in town, he went to Jesús Lucio and thanked him very much. He offered to pay Lucio some money, but he kindly declined and went on to tell Roland that anytime he wanted to stay at the ranch, it was open for him.

Roland couldn't find anyone to go camping with him overnight, so he went up into the mountains by himself, where he enjoyed a peaceful night's sleep in the highland forest.

The next morning, he hiked back down the mountain, said goodbye to various friends in town, and he began his drive back home to Tennessee. It was now early February.

He turned in his permit at the Colombia Bridge, crossed over to the U.S. side, and customs gave Roland and his truck a quick, at-the-booth inspection. They asked him a few questions and then told him he was free to go. That was good. Roland was glad that U.S. Customs had become a little more lenient than in past years.

That was likely true, but the U.S. Border Patrol had become stiffer. One of them pulled Roland over just before reaching San Antonio, and once at a stop, the officer approached the side of Roland's truck, looking through one of the windows of the camper top to check for Mexicans. Then he came to Roland's side and asked him if he had anyone hidden in the back.

"Nope, nobody there," Roland answered.

"You haven't got any drugs or narcotics, do you?" the officer further asked.

"Nothing of the kind," Roland casually answered.

"All right, sir. You have a nice day," and the officer returned to his car.

Roland drove away.

In Salado, he spent the night with Raul and his uncle and family. They were glad to see him, and they went to the flea market and other places.

Then Roland visited his cousins in Dallas and drove on home to Tennessee the next day.

Epilogue: Bridge Goes Down

A few days after Roland arrived home to Tennessee, he drove up to Lascassas to see if the old truss bridge was still standing. When he rounded the gentle curve of the highway, the truss came into view. It was standing, but it was completely bare! All of the concrete and road surface had been jack hammered out. As he approached it and slowly crossed the new bridge, he saw the demolition crew up on the truss, cutting smaller sections out of it with an acetylene torch. One by one, truss pieces crashed into the river or on its rocky banks, way below!

Roland pulled over on the shoulder, and he watched the crew for a few minutes.

"Rigo, our bridge is in its last days, for sure!" Roland quietly commented to himself. He shook his head with sadness, realizing more and more the fact that this bridge's closure and destruction had accurately paralleled his loss of friendship with Rigo.

That night, Roland asked Abraham if he would help him with a project. He wanted to retrieve a piece of the truss as a souvenir, a momento of his past friendship with Rigo. Abraham obliged, and Roland drove them to the bridge. It was the first time he had seen the bridge, and he reacted with surprise when he saw how narrow it was! They crossed the new bridge, and Roland parked on the shoulder. They brought a rope and flashlights with them, and being careful not to be seen, they quickly descended the river bank. Once below the truss, they located a fine 6-foot piece of truss near the bank, and they fished it out of the river. It weighed 120 pounds, but they managed to drag it up the steep and treacherous bank. Once that was done, Roland checked for traffic, and when the highway was clear, they hurriedly carried the piece to Roland's truck and loaded it into the back. Quickly, they drove away!

Two weeks went by. Roland did various carpentry and painting jobs.

In addition to his work, Roland decided to straighten out the piece of truss he had collected. It had become somewhat twisted when it fell nearly 50 feet to the river below. Using floor jacks and other apparatuses, he managed to straighten it. Then he took a chop saw and cut off the ugly cuts that were done with that torch! After that, he sanded it and painted it, and it looked really good. As he looked at it, he realized that it would make a fine bridge on his trail up in the 90-acre woods. It looked like it was just the right size for installing across a crevice, where he presently had an old rickety wooden bridge.

On February 25, Roland found out that the Lascassas Bridge went down. The demolition crew had blown up the main truss skeleton with dynamite. Newspaper reporters were out there to document it, along with camera men and news crews! Surprisingly, it was on the TV news that night!

The next day was the big surprise! Abraham came out to the Jocelyn's farm in Longview that morning to work, and he brought a copy of Murfreesboro's newspaper with him. There on the front page of the February 26 edition was a banner headline and an article about the Lascassas Bridge, plus 3 big photos of the explosion! The banner headline was a sneer, followed by the article which read as follows:

"Lascassas Bridge's Falling Down"

"Era ends for old truss. First London Bridge fell down. Then Friday, it was the old truss bridge along State Route 96 East (Lascassas Highway) that fell - with a little help from some strategically placed explosives. The Lascassas Highway Bridge over the Stones River was blown up Friday morning as part of a project that put a new $1.8 million bridge right next to it . . ."

The article went on with more details. (By the way, London Bridge never fell. It was carefully dismantled, sold in 1967 to a bridge contractor and moved by freighters to Lake Havasu City, Arizona, where it was honored and reconstructed.)

My goodness! Front page! Roland thought to himself. *And right on Rigo Zacatón's birthday! What a coincidence!* Never would Rigo be able to say again that he had never experienced a coincidence. Roland stared at the article with surprise and with his mouth dropped open. He just couldn't believe how much publicity the media had given that bridge. Very unusual indeed! Usually, old bridges get demolished, and hardly anyone bats an eye, but the Lascassas Bridge got full coverage! It must have been very important, more important than people realized.

What more proof did Roland need? That truss bridge was indeed the bridge of friendship between Roland and Rigo. Dangerously narrow, drivers had to use caution when navigating that bridge. It made people nervous to cross it. The same had been true with Roland and Rigo's precarious friendship. Roland had felt nervous at times around Rigo, especially more recently. Roland had to use a lot of caution around Rigo, to avoid angry outbursts from him! Their first year of friendship in 1997 had been great, but since then it had become more complex and had made a steady decline. The friendship had come to an end, and so had their bridge . . . well, not quite all of it.

Roland seeked Abraham's help again. They carted that piece of truss up the trail into the Jocelyn's woods, and they installed that piece across the rock crevice, right on Rigo's birthday. It fit perfectly! Roland fastened a board over the top, and they both walked across it, as if performing a ceremony. A small part of the old Lascassas Bridge was still serving as a bridge, a memorial to Roland and Rigo's past friendship, which had also been very important.

Roland went to Murfreesboro and bought extra copies of the newspaper, and he mailed one to Rigo, and another one to Elisa. To Rigo, Roland also included a short letter declaring the friendship terminated, that their bridge was gone, blown up with dynamite, and since their bridge would no longer resurrect, neither would their friendship.

As for the Zacatón family, they became more distant with Roland. The next time he went to Bustamante, Rigo would hardly talk to him. He thought Roland was loco (crazy) for having compared their friendship to a *bridge*, but Roland knew he wasn't crazy. Elisa believed that Roland was hung up on believing *fantasies*. Well, this was no fantasy. After all, the newspaper's date coincided with Rigo's birthday. One might say it was just a grand coincidence, but with the closure of that bridge occurring right when Rigo and his buddies had that sneering fiesta in the canyon, plus other events, Roland had to admit that it was more than just happen chance. Somebody on a higher level designed that "coincidence" to occur, as an important message for Roland and Rigo.

*　　*　　*

Every bridge represents a friendship. For every bridge built, a friendship is born. While a bridge exists, the friendship exists, and while that friendship exists, its bridge must exist. Some bridges are big and wide, while others are small and short. Some bridges exist on backroads, while others exist on highways. Some bridges are long and narrow and are situated surprisingly on major thoroughfares. Certain bridges serve important missions. At times they exists well beyond their era, until those missions are completed. Other bridges are protected, carrying important codes, messages, and history, and they have missions connected with other level agenda, sometimes beyond human comprehension. Until those missions are completed, it never even occurs to the government to take those bridges down. The narrow Lascassas Bridge lasted surprisingly 20 years beyond the widening of the highway, until it served and completed its important mission, which included the friendship between Roland and Rigo.

*   *   *

Roland and the Zacatón family went their separate ways. However, Roland did make three future efforts to reconcile with Rigo. He put his back to him with indifference every time! (However Angelo, after a two year period, did come around and talk to Roland, and they became friends again.)

As far as the flowers were concerned, they were placed on that Fir tree when Norma was born for genuine reasons from the spirit level, but courses of events change and so does destiny. One fact remained. Those flowers were posted just shy of Deception Pass, and *deception* would be the most appropriate word to describe the friendship Roland had with the Zacatón family. Roland was a person who put forth a good example, but little by little, they had closed the door on him.

Roland never married. He stayed single. However, he did attend Norma's quinciñera (15 year birthday party celebration) in July 2001. The whole family came, except Raul, who stayed in Salado because he was still afraid of a risky return to the United States. Norma's quinciñera was quite a shindig. A beautiful event it was indeed, with a wedding-style ceremony at the main church, followed by a baile with soft music. Fifteen flower girls in red dresses were dancing around Norma and her brother Rigo, who was dancing with her. The baile lasted till 2 AM as usual, but Roland only stayed a little while.

Roland never saw Elisa again. She never came forth to apologize, and neither did her son Carlos. On future trips to Bustamante, Roland sometimes saw her sons on the streets. Lalo was friendly and waved, but Carlos had his usual frown. Elisa and Carlos continued to be angry about that skunk! Months later, Carlos was asking others in town who had placed that skunk in their patio!

Oh, and a fly-by-night business entrepreneur came to town for several months. In a hot flash, he became Elisa's boyfriend, and he satisfied her strongest desires, with *pleasure*. Then they had a dispute, and they broke up. Of course, Elisa made no efforts to fix it. Such is life for some.

*   *   *

Six months after the Lascassas Bridge went down, Martonción landed success in capturing the demons of Nuevo Wimbisenho. Sasjurech and Sojornbloc were caught first, disintegrated, and their remains sent to the same remote, cold, icy dead planet as Sarlo and Malluck. Brutoxlo and Ferúpsula were also caught and given the same treatment.

Arfifra, Draaktra, Torxtalo, Druxtrli, and Arce-fera were a different ball game. They were extremely sly and quick witted, and Martonción thought he had gotten them the first time, only to later discover that he had caught their replicas instead! The judge Oyamel put it on the highest list of all, and he sent an army of spirits commanded by Selím and Igor to their cave. They were armed with the latest demon stealth capturing devices. It was quite a struggle, but with Martonción's brilliantly designed forcefields, they captured them. One by one, over a period of several weeks, they slowly stripped them of their lifeforces and confined them in huge crystalline structures, after which they teleported them straight to Oyamel. Next, a thorough search was done for any replicas to resolve any doubts. They had the originals this time! A verdict was given, after which they were thoroughly disintegrated, except Arfifra, and their remnants were sent to the same remote, cold, icy world, to be buried deep within its confines for an eternity of eons to come.

Arfifra, the ring leader, was given special treatment. Awaiting her was a large blackish colored transparent glass enclosure, somewhat like a large glass encased cabinet, but made of pure glass. With special forcefields, they placed her inside it *alive* for 1,000 years, and then they teleported her and the enclosure to the same remote, cold, icy world, where it was programmed to exist for precisely that period of time, then self destruct!

Martonción, Selím and Igor were given medals of honor for their heroic work. Many human lives would now finally be able to improve.

*   *   *

Roland began to feel physically better and better. Life improved for him.

As the years passed, he continued going to Bustamante, and he furthered his friendship with many of the people. He made plenty of new friends, as well. Some of them camped with him up in the mountains. A year later, Gilberto honored Roland by asking him if he would be his padrino of graduation from the secundaria school. Roland happily obliged, and Gilberto was genuine about it, with no second thoughts either. Roland finally got properly honored. It is interesting to note that Gilberto was born in October 1984, exactly when the highway department was refurbishing and repainting the old Lascassas Bridge. For what Roland had rescued from the river, their friendship continued.

Bustamante remained a town, but it grew, especially in the direction toward the cono. More and more streets were paved, and the town progressed into more modern times. They had recently gotten a new Centro Salud in September 1999, and a digital phone exchange in November 1999. Pemex finally opened their small fuel station in May 2000. The main church in the plaza got a new cross for their hanging statue of Jesus, and it was made of special *Ficus sycomorus* wood and hand crafted by Felipe's carpentry. That was July 2000. A year later, *Internet* service arrived, and in the fall of 2001, Bustamante opened their first Prepa. Now students could go beyond 9th grade, without having to be bussed to Sabinas Hidalgo.

No matter what, some small town aspects remained. The town's people still knew each other. While a bank was installed in July 1998, there were still no law offices, no convenience stores, no fast food restaurants, and no traffic lights. Important and interesting events among the residents still spread all over town like wildfire. Such was the life of small town gossip.

Roland landed success with his artwork. His Mexico novel also became a great success with its unique stories of adventures, friendships, complex family dynamics, misunderstandings, and conflicts. Roland had indeed been walking between worlds.

Over the years, people accepted Roland as if he were one of the town's people. He made a townful of friends, and he felt like Bustamante was his home away from home. He later purchased a ranch north of town where he built a winter home for himself. He continued to enjoy the mountains, and he also explored other parts of the country. For Mexico, there was no substitute. It was a unique country in many ways.

394

Printed in the United States
3504

9 781928 798026